M000028303

POLICE PROCEDURALS RESPECTED BY LAW ENFORCEMENT™

BADGE OF HONOR™

www.CarolynArnold.net

PRAISE FROM LAW ENFORCEMENT
on *Ties That Bind* (Detective Madison Knight series)

"Usually it's hard for me to read cop books without picking them apart but once I started this one I couldn't put it down. *Ties That Bind* was more realistic than anything I've ever read and for the entire book I felt like it was me. The way Carolyn wrote Madison describes me and the way I work and even my personal life to a t. I have never felt more connected to a character. Thank you for creating something so real."
–Rebecca Hendrix, Deputy, Poteau, Oklahoma

"I related to this story immediately. It is truly believable in its writing as it is vivid. I felt a kinship with the main character and that continued throughout the story. Well written and I am looking forward to more in the series. Highly recommended."
–Richard Goodship, Police Officer and Forensic Investigator (retired), Ontario, Canada

continued...

CAROLYN ARNOLD

POWER STRUGGLE

HIBBERT&STILES
PUBLISHING INC.

Hibbert & Stiles Publishing Inc.
www.hspubinc.com

This is a work of fiction. Names, characters, places, and incidents are the products of the author's imagination or are used fictitiously. Any resemblance to actual events, locales, or persons, living or dead, is entirely coincidental.

Publisher's Cataloging-In-Publication Data
(Prepared by The Donohue Group, Inc.)

Names: Arnold, Carolyn.
Title: Power struggle / Carolyn Arnold.
Description: [London, Ontario] : Hibbert & Stiles
    Publishing Inc., [2017] | Series: [Detective Madison
    Knight series]
Identifiers: ISBN 978-1-988353-64-7 (paperback 4.25x7) |
    ISBN 978-1-988353-63-0 (ebook)
Subjects: LCSH: Women detectives--Fiction. | Assassins--
    Fiction. | Mafia--Fiction. | Missing persons--Fiction. |
    Murder--Investigation--Fiction. | LCGFT: Detective and
    mystery fiction.
Classification: LCC PS3601.R66 P68 2017 (print) | LCC
    PS3601.R66 (ebook) | DDC 813/.6--dc23

Additional formats:
ISBN: 978-1-988353-65-4 (paperback 5 x 8)
ISBN: 978-1-988353-66-1 (hardcover)

POWER STRUGGLE

CHAPTER

1

DEATH WAS NOT DISCRIMINATORY, but murder was certainly selective. At least that's what Major Crimes detective Madison Knight had learned in her twelve years with the Stiles PD.

She looked down at the male victim. He was single, fifty-nine, and lying on the king-size mattress in his master bedroom. Silver sheets were covering him to his hips, leaving his upper body bare and exposing multiple stab wounds to his chest and abdomen. Blood was everywhere, staining the bedding and spattered on the walls and ceiling.

Normally, being immersed in such a messy murder scene would make Madison's stomach churn. She'd most certainly feel a burning drive to get justice for the victim. But this time, she was devoid of emotion, flatlined like the man on the bed. If anything, there was lingering bitterness and underlying anger. Because she knew the victim. Jimmy Bates. The man who had killed her grandfather.

Because of Bates, her mother had lost her father as a teenager and her grandmother had to bury the love of her life before Madison was even born. And all this because Bates's father had been the numbers man for the branch of the Russian Mafia that operated out of Stiles, and Madison's grandfather, a police sergeant, had put him away.

Madison pinched her eyes shut briefly. A darker part of her was finding some sort of redemption in the fact that Bates had exited the world not of his own volition. Just as he had snuffed out her grandfather's life, someone had taken Bates's. A working out of Karma as it were...

"Are you all right?" asked her partner of seven years, Terry Grant. He had a light complexion and never had a blond hair out of place, always ran before breakfast, was a loving husband and father to a baby girl named Danielle. He was three years younger than Madison's thirty-six.

She turned to see that he hadn't come into the room alone. Higgins, the first officer on scene and her former training officer, stood next to him. Both men had given her time to be alone with the scene and Bates after learning the vic's identity.

"I'm fine." Her response had come out way too quickly to be believable.

She looked back at the body. Both his arms were over his head and tied to the barred, wooden headboard with zip ties. She let her gaze trail down to his ankles, to see if those were also restrained, but they were still covered. She'd have to wait until the scene was processed to find out.

Given the number of stab wounds he had, though, it was likely that both his arms and legs had been bound, which indicated that the killer knew where to strike to delay death and invoke torture. While the former indicated a professional, the latter suggested the killer may have been after something.

Madison scanned the room. A television was mounted on the wall at the end of the bed, and it was on at a low volume and tuned into a popular crime drama.

Odd how reality can mimic fiction.

"Winston should have sent someone else." Higgins sounded apologetic for the Major Crimes sergeant's decision to include her in the case.

She met his gaze and dismissed his comment with a wave. "He probably didn't even know the ID on the vic when he made the call." She returned her gaze to Bates, analyzing whether he'd paid and suffered enough for his wrongdoings. In life, he'd served a full twenty-five-year sentence, but when he'd gotten released nineteen years ago, it hardly seemed like enough punishment. Was his murder finally enough to satisfy her personal scales of justice?

As her mind relaxed, and she took in the scene, she sensed a familiarity about it. The numerous stab wounds, the bound wrists…

The woman was laid out on the couch, her arms open wide, one resting against the back of the sofa, the other raised in the air, its wrist twisted back at an unnatural angle. Her torso was stained red with blood, which extended to the sofa and the floor. It was as if a can of red paint had been dumped on top of her.

"It looks like she was stabbed dozens of times. The killer must be a professional, too."

At the time, bile had risen in Madison's throat. The odor, the sight—it had been all-encompassing.

The woman's name had been Lillian Norton, and the man who'd killed her had been a Russian Mafia hit man by the name of Constantine Romanov—the same hit man who had almost succeeded in raping and killing Madison ten months prior. Lillian's longtime boyfriend had worked as an attorney for the mob, and she'd been tortured for information.

With Bates's father's involvement with the Russian mob, as well, it didn't seem like it could be a coincidence that Bates's murder resembled Lillian's. And all the stab wounds, the bondage, the time it would have taken, and the seeming lack of concern over getting caught fit with Constantine's personality. But if Madison was going to entertain the idea that Bates was killed by the hit man, that meant—

God, no, please don't tell me he's back.

Madison put a hand to her stomach as her eyes filled with tears. She blinked them away, willing herself to compartmentalize her thoughts. Constantine had escaped police custody and fled the country. Intel indicated that he'd returned to Russia, and he'd be flagged the moment he landed on American soil. Of course, criminals found ways to work around things like that.

She took a deep, steadying breath.

It had to be paranoia that had her dragging the Russian hit man into Bates's murder. After all, the recent loss of her friend and fellow officer, Barry Weir, had the flashbacks surging again periodically. Before his death, they had been starting to ease. Plus, a connection between Bates and the Mafia hadn't even been established.

It was definitely best to keep her suspicion of Mafia involvement to herself for now. "I'd say we're probably looking for a professional," was all she said.

Terry nodded. "Given all the blood, I'd say the vic was alive for most of these stab wounds. That means the killer knew where to strike."

"I agree." Usually the person to find a body was the first under suspicion, and Madison's mind went to the woman she'd seen talking to an officer when they showed up. She was in her twenties and beautiful with long, honey-colored hair. She could have been any number of things to the deceased—a daughter, a lover, a wife, or in this neighborhood, a housekeeper. While she didn't strike Madison as a killer, first impressions could be wrong. Madison turned to Higgins. "Who's the woman who found him? The one talking with Officer Tendum earlier?"

"That's right," Higgins said. "Name's Yasmine Stone. She worked with Bates, as well."

"As well as what?" Madison asked.

Higgins shrugged. "She claims they were sleeping together."

"*Claims?* You don't believe her?" Terry asked.

Higgins's gaze hardened. "I don't take anything at face value."

Terry pointed at Higgins, then said to Madison, "Now I see where you got your skepticism."

"She *claims* she found him just a couple hours ago." Higgins slid his glance to Terry, as if to punctuate his word choice. Maybe Terry was right and she had inherited her doubt of people from her former training officer. But in their line of work, it was better to be wary than gullible.

"She made the call to us at seven," Higgins added.

Terry nodded. "And you said she worked with Bates?"

"That's right. Berger & Stein. It's an accounting firm downtown."

Madison recalled their logo on the top of a high-rise. "Huge company."

"That it is," Higgins replied. "Bates was sort of a bigwig accountant there, according to Yasmine," Higgins began. "She reported to him."

"That could explain how he afforded all this." She was referring to Bates living in Deer Glen, a prestigious gated community, and doing so alone in a two-story house that was large enough for a family of six. Not to mention the grand entry with the curved staircase, marble flooring, high ceilings on the main level that were easily twenty feet, and the chandelier in the foyer that had probably cost thousands of dollars. But Madison couldn't help but wonder if that was the only explanation for his wealth. Was an ex-con that lucky, or was it a matter of a son being like his father? Had Bates taken after his father by cooking the books for the Russians after he got out of prison? By extension, was the accounting firm connected with the mob?

"How long has Bates been working at Berger & Stein?" she asked.

Higgins shook his head. "Don't know. I hadn't gotten that far with her. It's possible that Tendum knows by now."

Madison nodded and made a mental note to find out.

"His old man was an accountant of sorts, too," Terry said.

She met his gaze, and her partner seemed to be prying into her mind through her eyes. Was he thinking the Russians might be involved with Bates's murder? She wasn't convinced yet based on the evidence, and she couldn't allow her past to interfere with her judgment. While she might not care that Bates was murdered, she still had a job to do, and she'd make sure his killer was caught.

"That he was," she said impassively.

"It probably wouldn't hurt to see if Bates had any connections to the Mafia," Terry suggested. "It's not often we see violent murders like this in Stiles." He raised a brow at Madison.

Was he baiting her? She glared at him. She couldn't let herself give into her paranoia; she had to remain objective. "We had that case two Christmases ago—the woman who had her throat slashed in her kitchen."

Terry didn't say anything. He just held eye contact with her. Was he going to bring up Lillian Norton? No, Madison wasn't going to give him the chance.

"We'll look at it from the Mafia angle, of course, but we need to dig into Bates's life," she said, "see who would have had motive to kill him. And we should start by talking with Yasmine."

Higgins touched her shoulder. She flinched, and he pulled his hand back. His brow creased, and his lips pressed downward in a concerned frown. "If you're not comfortable with this case, I'm sure Sergeant Winston would understand."

"He's right, Maddy," Terry chimed in. "As you said, he probably didn't even know the victim's identity when he assigned you. If he did—"

She jutted out her chin defiantly. "I'm staying on the case."

The last few months had mostly passed without an altercation between her and Sergeant Winston. They were working better together than they ever had. After Barry's death, they had moved past their differences and navigated his murder investigation as a team. Even in the cases following that, things had proceeded more smoothly than before. For her to go to him now and request to be pulled from a case would be tantamount to admitting defeat. And all she needed was to resurrect his outdated mentality that law enforcement should be a boys' club. And she knew the request would somehow become about that.

"I'll be fine," she started. "What happened with Bates and my grandfather was a long time ago. I never even knew him." But she had seen pictures and was told that she got her light complexion and blond hair from him. He'd only been blond until he was six, but the rest of her family were brunettes with brown eyes. She'd inherited her dark eyes from them.

Terry tilted his head. "Are you sure? This one *is* personal."

"I'm *fine*." She turned her back to Terry then, not wanting him to see the lie in her eyes. But now she was facing the bloody side of the room, and the situation was starting to sink into her awareness. Even still, she couldn't rouse empathy for Bates.

"Just so you two know, Crime Scene should be here any minute now, and I've made the call to Richards, too," Higgins said.

Cole Richards was the medical examiner, and the sooner he arrived, the sooner they could get some real information.

"Thanks, Chief," Madison said, using her affectionate nickname for him. She smiled at Higgins, plastering on a strong front. Inside, however, her heart was racing and her mind was whirling with thoughts, the foremost of which was that, if Constantine was back in Stiles, it was likely only a matter of time before he'd be coming after her to settle an old score.

CHAPTER

2

MADISON WAS ABOUT TO STEP out the front door of Bates's house when she noticed the security system keypad mounted on the wall. She pointed it out to Terry, who was a couple of steps behind her. "We'll have to get access to his records with the service provider."

"And that may only help us if Bates actually used it," Terry countered with a shrug. "You'd be surprised how many people have security systems but fail to arm them, especially when they're at home."

"Not much point to having one, then." Madison stepped outside, the cold December air forcing her to do up her coat. The medical examiner's vehicle was at the curb, and Cole Richards and his assistant, Milo, were headed toward them.

Richards smiled, showcasing bright-white teeth that stood out in contrast to his dark skin. "Detectives."

Madison smiled in return. Maybe if she just worked to stuff all her thoughts of Constantine deep inside, then no one else would see how truly shaken she was that he could be back in Stiles. Besides, something about Richards always set her at ease, and she respected his work ethic and values. At one point, she might even have had a bit of a crush on him. Of course, the fact that he was married nixed any possibility of a relationship there. "You beat Crime Scene."

"I know. That rarely happens," Richards conceded. "And I don't like it when it does because it holds me up."

Usually investigators made their way around a crime scene, collecting evidence and snapping photos of the deceased and the immediate area around the body, before the ME could get started.

The sound of a vehicle had them turning toward the road where the forensics van was parking.

"Speaking of..." Richards made a move to go inside with Milo, and Madison and Terry stepped back to let them pass.

Cynthia Baxter, the head of the crime lab and Madison's best friend, was a bit ahead of Mark Andrews, who was one of three employees that Cynthia oversaw. Each of them had a specialized skill set. Cynthia was great with technology, documents, prints, and other patterned evidence; Mark excelled with trace evidence; and the other two employees were trained in firearms, ballistics, and forensic serology.

Cynthia's dark hair was swaying in a ponytail, and the pendulum kept going when she stopped in front of Madison and Terry. "He's not going to let us live this down, is he?" She pointed toward the front door, implying Richards and the fact that they'd arrived after he had. Normally her shoulder-length brown hair was down, not that it mattered how she styled her locks. There was something about her—even Cynthia didn't know exactly what—that made men fawn over her. She had played that to her advantage for years until Lou Stanford, another major crime detective, put a ring on her finger. Of course, they still had to officially tie the knot, but the commitment was made.

Madison shook her head. "I don't think so. He doesn't much care for it when it happens."

"That I know." Cynthia moved to the side and turned to Mark. "You go on ahead of me. I'll be in shortly."

Mark acknowledged Madison and Terry with a head bob as he walked inside, but his ponytail didn't sway as much as Cynthia's. He kept his tied low at the back of his neck. In fact, Madison had never seen his hair down.

Madison turned back to face her friend, who locked eyes with her, something Madison would have preferred to avoid because Cynthia had the ability to read minds...or so it seemed. Maybe if Madison pressed on with the case specifics, Cynthia would be distracted enough to drop her focus from Madison. The last thing she wanted was for her friend to see her true feelings, to know that she wouldn't be solving this murder fueled by her regular drive to find justice but rather to quell her suspicions about Constantine's return.

"The victim has a security system," Madison blurted out. "That might provide us with some leads."

"Victim? So either the victim hasn't been ID'd yet or you knew them. Which is it?" Cynthia was scanning her eyes, and Madison knew she'd messed up. Madison always preferred to use names over *victim*.

Madison wet her lips, glanced at her partner, and then turned back to Cynthia. "The latter."

Cynthia's gaze became more penetrating. "Did you know them well? Are you okay?"

When Madison didn't respond, Cynthia eyeballed Terry. "She should probably pull herself off this case," he said.

"Hey, I'm right here," Madison spoke up. There wasn't anything more irritating than being talked about when one was present. "And this victim's identity isn't going to stop me from working this case. No one is."

Cynthia raised an eyebrow. "All right, now I'm curious. Who is it?"

"It's Jimmy Bates." Madison said it in the most detached tone she could muster.

"Jimmy Bates?" Cynthia's voice raised a few octaves. "Isn't that the man who—"

"Killed my grandfather?" Madison finished. "Yes."

"What happened?"

Madison hitched her shoulders. "You'll see for

yourself soon enough."

"He was stabbed multiple times," Terry offered.

Cynthia didn't break her eye contact with Madison. Maybe it was best to just come out with her notion that Constantine might be behind Bates's death, but even her close friend might think she was crazy given how little they had at this point. No, she needed some more evidence first. At least a direct connection between Bates and the Mafia.

"Stabbed multiple times?" Cynthia paused. "We don't see that too often. The last case I remember was that woman… What was her—" Her eyes widened. "Constantine killed her."

That didn't take long…

"Her name was Lillian Norton," Madison replied calmly, proud of her reserve considering the jumbled mess she was inside.

"You don't think…?" Cynthia let her implication go unspoken, but her face paled.

"It's too soon to tell who's behind Bates's murder." Madison sounded steadier in that conclusion than she was in her gut.

"Huh… That doesn't sound like the Maddy I know." Cynthia angled her head. "Lillian's name just popped right into your head when I brought up the stabbed woman? I doubt that. You'd already noted the similarities between the two murders, didn't you?"

Terry turned to face Madison now that she'd been called out. Maybe she should just admit to that much. "I did."

Terry's brow furrowed. "Why didn't you say anything about Lillian upstairs?"

"Why didn't you?" she fired back, and Terry shook his head. "Listen," she said firmly, "we have to look at this murder from all angles, and I'm not going to get stuck on one guess. Now, if you'll excuse us, Cynthia, we need to question the vic's girlfriend and coworker." Madison stepped down the walk toward the driveway, her mind spinning and emotions cresting.

"If you think he's back," Cynthia called out, "you should get protection, just to be safe."

Madison spun to face her friend. "I'll be fine." And there was that word again. She'd been saying *fine* a lot today. When she'd first started seeing a shrink—under mandated orders after her ordeal with Constantine—her doctor had pointed out that she used the adjective often, and that it was a means of deflecting how she truly felt.

"You'll be fine? What if you're not?" Cynthia's shoulders sagged, and her face drained of color. "You need to at least remove yourself from this case. If Constantine's back…"

Madison's body stiffened. Hearing her friend say his name again and seeing her so visibly upset shook Madison to her core, weakening her resolve to just deal with this investigation one step at a time. Her mind was telling her to let go of the idea that Constantine killed Bates, but her heart wasn't buying it. Bates's murder, and what it represented from her perspective, was truly a nightmare she wished she could wake up from, but she wasn't going to cower in a corner. She wouldn't let him win.

"If he's back and he's going to come for me, he'll do it whether I'm working this case or not. Now," she said, "we really do have work to do."

Cynthia waited a few beats. "Just be careful."

"I will. I promise." Madison walked away, and while Cynthia didn't say anything else, Madison could feel her friend's eyes on her back.

"She's right, you know." Terry stepped in line with Madison.

She couldn't bring herself to glance over at her partner. Her body was quaking, a mixture of fear and anger. The latter won out. She met his gaze now. "What? That I should go into hiding? No. He doesn't control how I live my life."

Terry shook his head. "Not hiding, no. But if you really think he's back, you should take precautions."

Madison let out a deep breath. "How about we prove he's back in town and go from there?" she suggested coolly, keeping her strides wide and determined.

She headed toward Tendum, who was in the car with Yasmine Stone, presumably taking her statement. Madison made eye contact with him and gestured to him with a curled finger. Tendum nodded in receipt of her unspoken message to come out and update them, and joined Madison and Terry by the trunk of the car.

"What can I help you with, detectives?" The twentysomething officer's eyes were alert, and his cheeks were flushed with the cold air.

Madison rubbed her hands. "How are you making out with her statement?"

"Almost finished." Tendum's gaze went to the car, and Madison sensed he was eager to get back to Yasmine. "Is there something you need to tell me?"

"We'll be taking her downtown shortly." Madison stepped farther away from the vehicle, and the men followed her. She didn't want Yasmine to overhear them. "I just want to make sure you ask a few specific things so we can see if she replies the same way when we ask the same questions later."

"Understandable," Tendum said. "Shoot."

Shoot? Sometimes the officer's age really didn't do him any favors.

"But first, I want to start with your impressions," Madison said. "How does she seem? Shaken? Distant? Angry? Shocked?"

"I'd say she's scared and shaken."

Madison hadn't expected that. "Have you asked her why she's scared?"

"She said finding him 'like that' was unsettling and that it's scary how we can be here one minute and gone the next."

"So she's analyzing her own mortality. Quite a natural reaction," Terry chimed in.

"I'd say there's more to it," Tendum ventured. "She's shaking and biting her bottom lip quite often and fidgeting with her hands."

Those traits could indicate shock, nervousness, or guilt. After all, she had the attention of Stiles PD and not in a good way. The person to find a dead body always fell under suspicion.

"Did you push her further on why she's so scared and unsettled? Try to break her?" Madison asked.

Tendum nodded. "I did, but I didn't really get anywhere."

Hopefully Madison would be able to apply enough pressure to squeeze something more out of the woman once they got her downtown. "When did she last see him alive?"

"She said she came over last night for a booty call at about eleven and left before midnight."

"And then she came back early this morning? Why didn't she just spend the night? Did you ask her that?" Madison snapped at Tendum without meaning to. She had to be on edge about the prospect of Constantine being in town.

Tendum fumbled with his notepad and thumbed through it. A moment later, he looked up, eyes blank. "I didn't think to…" Tendum seemed embarrassed as he scribbled something down.

"Maybe the guy just preferred to sleep alone," Terry interjected.

Madison glanced at her partner, defender of the newbies. She pointed to Tendum's book. "Make sure you ask her."

Tendum tapped the end of his pen to the page. "I will, Detective. I've written it down."

"And the house has a security system," Madison added. "Did you ask her anything about that? Whether it was armed when she showed up today?

If she has a code and a key for the door?"

Tendum was just staring at her.

"You did see the system, right?" she pressed.

"I...did," Tendum admitted. "But I didn't think to ask her either of those questions."

"Well, add that to your little list, then," she responded.

Tendum winced and scribbled in his notebook again.

Madison took a few staggered breaths to bring her rising impatience under control, and then asked, "And was he all right when she left him last night?"

"Yeah, he was fine."

"So you asked?"

The young officer flushed. "Yes."

"What about how long she's been seeing Bates?" Madison asked, keeping the questions coming.

"For a few months now," Tendum responded without consulting his book. "She couldn't remember exactly when but figured they started seeing each other around October or thereabouts. Before you ask, she's worked with Bates for a year." He squared his shoulders as he regained his confidence.

Good work, Newbie, but it will take more to impress me...

"Have you run her background?" Terry asked before Madison could comment aloud.

"Yeah, of course. Nothing of interest there, though. Like, no criminal record anyway."

Like? Tendum's youth sprouted through the

cracks.

"Is there anything else or should I finish up?" Tendum asked.

"Finish up. Ask her those questions—" she pointed to his notebook "—have her sign off on what she's told you, and then we'll take her downtown."

Tendum nodded and headed back to the cruiser.

A few minutes later, the car doors opened and both Tendum and Yasmine got out. Tendum gestured for her to stay next to the car, but he headed over to Madison and Terry. Yasmine pressed a cheek to her shoulder as she waited.

"I asked about the security system," he said when he approached Madison. "She says she has a code and a key."

"And why did she leave at midnight only to return this morning?" Madison asked.

Tendum glanced at Terry but directed his response at Madison. "It was as Detective Grant said: he likes to sleep alone."

"All right. Tell her to come over," she directed.

Tendum gestured for Yasmine to join them. When she did, he made the introductions. "These are detectives Madison Knight and Terry Grant."

Yasmine tucked a stray hair behind an ear but didn't say anything. Her eyes were wet with unshed tears, and her complexion was blotchy.

"We'd like to take you downtown, ask a few more questions," Madison said gently but without room for negotiation.

Yasmine gave Tendum an uncertain glance

before following Madison. "I'm not sure why I have to speak with you now."

"It's standard procedure," Madison assured her.

"But I didn't do anything." Yasmine stopped walking, her words full of panic as she rubbed her arms.

Madison turned toward the girl. "As I said, it's standard. It shouldn't take too long. We just have a few questions."

A tear fell down Yasmine's cheek, and she wiped it away before continuing to follow Madison.

CHAPTER
3

YASMINE WAS SET UP IN interrogation room one. There was something about questioning a potential murder suspect in this formal setting that gave law enforcement the edge. Even an innocent person could find themselves unravelling under the pressure, and the mind is good at playing games. It can make one feel guilty when they're not, and that's why it was crucial to ask the right questions and be able to read people accurately.

Madison and Terry were about to go in. She had one hand on the doorknob and she was carrying a water bottle for Yasmine in the other when Sergeant Winston called out to her.

"Knight, wait!" Winston sounded winded, and when she turned around, his face was red and his brow was sweaty, and he was panting. "Is it too much to ask for you to come to me? No, I have to go chasing you around the station. What is the update on the Deer Glen homicide?"

"There's not a lot to say yet." Madison slid a

sideways glance to Terry.

Winston glanced at Terry, too, then back at Madison. He drew a pointed finger between them. "I saw that look. What aren't you telling me?"

"The victim was Jimmy Bates," Madison said nonchalantly.

Winston screwed up his brow. "Why does that name sound familiar?"

"He's the man who served twenty-five years for killing my grandfather." There, she'd delivered the facts with cool detachment.

Winston's eyes snapped into alignment with Madison's. "You should probably be taken off the case."

"No." She stood firm, peacocking her stance. "There's no reason for that."

He squared his shoulders. "Last I knew, I was the one to call the shots, Detective."

"Listen, there's no reason to take me off this case. I didn't even know my grandfather."

"He was still your grandfather," the sarge said. "That makes this case personal."

She wanted to counter with the fact that her grandfather had died nine years before she was born, but the defense fell flat even in her head. Instead, she locked her jaw and tilted up her chin. It was probably best that she remain quiet, but the sergeant seemed to be expecting her to say something.

"The man served his time," she said.

Winston turned to Terry. "What are your thoughts

on the matter?"

"If Madison says she has things under control, then she does."

"But she didn't say she has things under control." Winston studied Madison. "Do you?"

She flashed him a cocky grin. "I like to think so."

"I'm sure you do," Winston stated sourly and pointed to the closed door. "Who's in there? A suspect?"

"It's Yasmine Stone, a woman who Bates was sleeping with," Madison began. "She's the one who found his body."

Winston nodded. "Does she look good for the murder?"

Madison's heart pounded. The similarities between Lillian Norton's and Jimmy Bates's murders crashed together in her mind. Her legs began to buckle thinking about Constantine being back in town, but she managed to muster her strength without warranting the men's attention. "It's too early to say."

"Well, don't let me stop you, then. Get in there." Winston waved them along.

"You got it, Boss." Madison turned her back on the sergeant and rolled her eyes.

She entered the interrogation room first, Terry following suit. He walked behind Yasmine and leaned against the wall.

Madison extended the water bottle across the table to Yasmine. "I thought you might be thirsty."

She took it but didn't open it. "Thank you."

Madison sat down across from Yasmine and set a folder on the table. Inside was Yasmine's basic background report and a printed copy of the statement she'd given Tendum. Madison relaxed into her chair. "As I said back at Mr. Bates's house, we have some questions for you."

Yasmine's eyes were glazed over, and she kneaded her purse nervously, which she'd placed on the table in front of her. She was still wearing her coat.

"Let's just start from the beginning, okay?" Madison suggested. Yasmine nodded. "You visited Mr. Bates last night, is that correct?"

"Yes, and he was fine when I left him." Yasmine started trembling.

Was she scared or was she experiencing feelings of guilt or regret? While it was true that she hadn't been found covered in blood, she could have had plenty of time to return home and clean up only to come back and "discover" the body.

"Why are you shaking?" Madison asked.

Yasmine stopped kneading her purse. "I'm… It's just…I've never seen anything like that. What happened to him…"

"It's something most people never will witness, and it would definitely be unsettling." She'd chosen that last word to intentionally downplay the situation to see what sort of reaction she might get.

"It was more than unsettling!" Yasmine fired back.

Madison let silence ride for several seconds after Yasmine's outburst, hoping to draw her into filling the quiet.

"I didn't mean to yell," she said, sniffling. "It's just…horrible."

Madison had no response to that statement. She just felt empty. Yes, it was horrible that someone had been so violently murdered, but that "someone" had also shot and killed her grandfather.

Maybe remaining objective would be more difficult than she'd thought.

Yasmine continued to tremble and began to rub her arms. The fabric of her pants was making noise, too, so she was likely bouncing her legs to self-soothe. The woman was obviously uncomfortable, but Madison couldn't get a strong enough read on her to decide if it was due to a guilty conscience.

"When you left him, was he tied to the bed?" Madison asked, to keep the questioning moving forward.

"No." Yasmine was quick to answer. "We always used cuffs…" She sniffled again.

"When you showed up this morning, was the security system armed?" Madison asked.

"Yeah."

"So you have an access code and a key to his house?"

"That's right. Probably for at least the last month," Yasmine said casually.

Madison plowed forward. "Did he give you a unique code or just let you use his?"

"Uh, I'm not sure." Yasmine shrugged. "Does it matter?"

"It might," Madison responded coolly. They could confirm with the surveillance company how many passcodes were issued and which user armed and disarmed the system in the last twenty-four hours. That could tell them a lot. "What was the code you used?"

"Three-four-seven-one."

"Did you let yourself in last night, too?"

Yasmine shook her head. "No, he let me in."

"And last night when you left, did you arm the security system and lock up behind you?"

"Uh-huh. Jimmy was still in bed when I left."

Madison nodded. "I see... Do you know of anyone who could have wanted Jimmy dead?"

Yasmine's chin began to tremble again, and her eyes went blank.

"If you have any idea, now's the time to tell us," Madison prompted.

Yasmine blinked and timidly avoided eye contact. "I don't know."

"Anyone at work who may have been upset with him?"

"Not that I'm aware of." Yasmine put her palms to her forehead, fingers splayed, as if she was getting a headache.

"What type of accounts did Jimmy handle?" Terry asked, getting involved in the questioning.

Yasmine dropped her hands and turned to face Terry. "Corporate."

"Did any of his customers have an issue with him?" Madison asked, taking another stab at the potential suspect pool.

Yasmine straightened her back in her chair. "No one likes paying taxes, and Jimmy does—*did*—" she touched her left temple "—his best to help people pay as little as possible, but there are always a few clients that still aren't happy. But if your real question is whether Jimmy had enemies or anyone who would've wanted to kill him, I don't think so."

The way Yasmine kept touching her head told Madison she was seeking to comfort herself. Madison also latched on to the *I don't think so.* Combine this with other signs of fear and Madison was pretty sure Yasmine knew a lot more than she was sharing. "Besides having a sexual relationship, did you know Jimmy well?"

"Not really." A splash of pink touched her cheeks. "He was a secretive man," she added.

Given this admission, they couldn't exactly trust her word that he didn't have any enemies. The thought crept in that if he was working with the Mafia like his father had, there was a good reason for him being secretive. And building on the hypothetical, was it just Bates or was the entire firm in cahoots with the mob? The idea had entered her mind at the crime scene, but she pushed it away again. Her personal connection was probably marring her judgment. There could be plenty of other explanations for Bates's secretiveness.

Madison had additional questions about last night and this morning, but she wanted to know more about the nature of Yasmine's relationship with Bates. "How long had you and Jimmy worked together?"

"A year."

"And you were his, what? Secretary? Assistant?" Madison asked.

"I did whatever it was Jimmy needed me to."

"So you were more like his right hand? Privy to some confidential business matters?"

"Yeah, I guess."

"I take it Jimmy did pretty well at the firm," Madison said.

"He's on his— I mean, he *was* on his way to making partner." Yasmine ran a hand down her throat. "Sorry. It's so hard to think of him as being gone."

Madison refused to get sucked into Yasmine's emotional vortex. "Had he worked there for a long time?"

"I guess," Yasmine said, indifferent. "Don't know for how long."

They'd find out from speaking to the accounting firm, so Madison let it go. "Now, going back to your romantic relationship with Jimmy... How long have you been together?"

Yasmine bit her bottom lip. "We've been sleeping together for a few months. It started up some time in October."

That was consistent with what she'd told Tendum. "And why were you at his place this morning?" Madison asked.

"We often had sex before work."

"But you were there last night, too," Madison said.

"That's right." She crossed her arms. "Until midnight."

"Why go home only to come back so early this morning?"

"You know, that cop asked me a lot of these same questions. I'm not sure why I need to go through them again." Yasmine narrowed her eyes, clearly irritated, but her gaze weakened quickly. "I've been through a lot," she said, her chin quivering again. "Finding him like that…"

"Repetitive questioning is common in a murder investigation," Madison assured her.

"Because you think you're going to catch me in a lie," Yvonne snapped. "But *I* didn't kill him. I'd never have hurt him—or anyone else for that matter."

"Why did you leave at midnight?" Madison tried again.

"Because Jimmy likes to sleep alone." Yasmine's gaze flashed with agitation. "There was nothing more to it than that."

"Fair enough." Madison paused, riding the power of silence. "Where were you from midnight until seven this morning?"

"Sleeping." She pinched her nose, blew out a deep breath, and started rocking back and forth. "You really think that I—"

"Can anyone verify that?" Madison interrupted.

"I don't know," she cried out, tears running down her cheeks now. "Maybe my landlord. Actually, yes, my landlord. He opened his door to say good night to me."

The hairs rose on the back of Madison's neck. Had the landlord been obsessed with Yasmine and taken the initiative to get Bates out of her life? "Does he usually say good night to you?"

"Sometimes but not always. It's just who he is. Doesn't have much to keep him busy." Yasmine palmed her cheeks. "It's not like he's not a stalker or anything."

Madison looked past Yasmine to Terry, who was scribbling in his notebook. The MO indicated someone with a lot of rage, and while Madison's gut was screaming that the murder was the work of Constantine, she was determined to follow the evidence in earnest. Rage was fueled by passion, and passion could stem from a very common motive for murder—jealousy.

"Did he know about you and Jimmy?" Madison asked.

"I'm not sure how he would," Yasmine said. "Jimmy never came to my place."

They'd definitely need to confirm Yasmine's alibi. "What's your landlord's name?"

"Oliver Carson."

Terry was writing in his book again, presumably jotting down the name.

"Were you and Jimmy exclusive?" Madison asked Yasmine.

She shook her head. "Not at all. It was very casual."

"And that was your idea or his?"

"Both, I guess." Yasmine shrugged, nonchalant.

Madison leaned forward. "So the idea of him seeing other women never bothered you?"

"No." There was a flicker in Yasmine's eyes that belied her claim, but she was quick to add, "I saw other men."

"We'll need their names and contact information."

"Do you think one of them killed Jimmy?" Yasmine asked, scrunched up her brow as if seeming to view the concept as not worth considering.

"It's far too early to say, but we need to investigate all angles. The men you're seeing are part of that."

"Well, none of the relationships were anything special. They were just about sex."

"Did you ever want the relationship with Jimmy to be more than that?" Madison asked.

Yasmine slipped her bottom lip through her teeth. "I cared about him, but I didn't love him. I'm not the settling-down kind of girl."

"Are you sure about that?" Madison put the question to Yasmine in as friendly a way as possible—woman to woman. "Most women fantasize about their weddings from the time they're little girls."

"Not me." Yasmine crossed her arms and took a deep breath. "Like I said, I know that he slept with other people, and it didn't bother me. I was seeing other men, too."

"Why don't you tell us about them, then?"

Yasmine's gaze drifted across the room, and a single tear fell. But Madison didn't sense sadness coming from her, but rather fear. Her body had sunken farther into the chair, her bottom lip was trembling, and her hands were clenched into fists on the table.

"Who are you thinking about?" Madison pressed.

She shook her head rapidly. "It's…"

"If you think that one of them could have killed Jimmy, talk to us." Madison reached across the table and touched one of Yasmine's fists. She was quick to pull both her hands back and clasp them in her lap.

Madison gave Yasmine a few seconds, then made her request. "Give us some names."

Yasmine remained silent.

"Do you suspect that maybe one of them got jealous of Jimmy and decided to kill him?" Madison asked, flipping Yasmine's earlier question and serving it back to her.

Yasmine jumped to her feet. "No, that can't be what happened."

"The way you're acting right now tells me that you think it's possible, Miss Stone," Madison said.

Yasmine's eyes shot to Madison's. "You're obviously not reading me very well."

Madison pressed her lips together, inclined her head, and said nothing.

Yasmine paced the interrogation room for a few minutes; Terry and Madison remained silent.

"I only see two men other than Jimmy regularly," Yasmine finally said. "There's also this one guy who I hook up with when he's in town."

"We'll need their names," Terry said, heightening the urgency.

Yasmine rubbed her arms quickly. "Lyle Berger

was one I—" She stopped talking.

"One you…what?" Madison prompted. Yasmine dismissed her with a wave, and Madison let it go. For now. "Lyle Berger is a managing partner at the firm?" She assumed so based on the company's name.

"Yes. The firm is run by Sylvester Stein and Lyle Berger."

Lyle would have had a front-row seat to Jimmy and Yasmine's trysts, and maybe it had become too much for him to overlook an employee sleeping with the same woman he was sleeping with. "Did Lyle ever seem jealous that you were sleeping with Jimmy?" Madison asked.

"I don't…think so." Her body stiffened, contradicting her words.

"I'm sensing a *but*," Madison said.

"*But* he would play out like he was. It was just something he did sometimes." Yasmine dropped back into her chair. "One day Jimmy and I had sex in the managers' restroom, and word got out. I don't know how, but Lyle called me into his office not long after. Say, a few hours." Her eyes darkened. "He said he needed to talk to me about some report."

Madison had a sinking feeling in the pit of her stomach, a foreboding of what Yasmine was going to tell them.

Yasmine swallowed roughly. "He didn't want to talk to me about a report…"

"Did he rape you, Miss Stone?" Memories of her own near-rape by Constantine struck Madison hard.

Her stomach churned, and bile soured her throat.

Yasmine nodded and then shook her head. "No, I wanted it."

"Is that what he told you?" Madison asked delicately. "It sounds to me like he raped you…"

Yasmine was rubbing her arms furiously again. "He didn't, all right? I wanted it." She locked eyes with Madison, and Madison dipped her head. Far too often the victim was made to feel like they'd asked for sex and wanted it. It was disgusting and beyond nauseating. Madison couldn't wait to face the bastard.

"When was this?" Terry asked.

Yasmine looked down at her hands. "A month ago… Or something like that."

That was well within the statute of limitations to press charges if Yasmine admitted to being raped. "You had made it sound like you were *seeing* Lyle." Madison monitored her inflection so as not to convey any menace. "Did you have sex with him more than that one time?"

Yasmine nodded.

Madison sat back. "How long had you been getting together?"

"A few times since…" Yasmine rolled her hand. "Since we did it in his office."

There was nothing consensual about what had happened—at least originally. It was written all over this poor woman's expression. But had the creep, Lyle, escalated from rapist to murderer?

"So Lyle was one of the two men besides Jimmy

who you saw regularly?" Madison confirmed.

"Yeah."

"Who were the other men you were seeing? The second regular one and the one you'd hook up with when he was in town?" Madison asked.

Yasmine sank back into her chair. "The other regular guy is married, and I'm not going to risk our affair getting out and ruining his marriage."

Too late for that…

"Then you're interfering with an active investigation, and that's a crime," Madison stated bitterly.

"I'm sorry, but you'll have to arrest me to get his name." Yasmine met Madison's gaze defiantly now.

Although her offer was tempting, there wasn't enough to warrant holding her. "What about the guy from out of town?" Madison diverted.

"His name's Kevin," Yasmine said weakly.

"His last name?" Madison asked. It felt like she was pulling every syllable out of Yasmine.

Yasmine turned away, her gaze flitting about the room. "Jones."

"Do you have a way of reaching Mr. Jones?"

She nodded, still not looking at Madison. "I have his number."

"We'll need that."

"It's on my phone." Yasmine riffled through her purse.

"How long had you been seeing him?" Madison asked.

Yasmine dug for a few more seconds and then

pulled out her phone. Her fingers moved quickly over the screen. "For years. Just whenever he was in town. He travels a lot for business."

Terry stepped forward, coming up next to her. "What does he do?"

She stopped working on her phone and ran a hand through her hair. "We never really talked about it."

"Something tells me you know more than you're letting on," Madison said. "Are you covering for him?"

Yasmine's mouth opened, snapped shut, and then she started chewing on a fingernail.

"Are you afraid of this person?" Leading question or not, she had to gauge Yasmine's reaction.

Yasmine dropped her hand and regarded Madison with a straight face. "He's not even in town. He couldn't have killed Jimmy."

"That you know of, anyway," Madison fired back, intrigued by Yasmine's quick defense of the man and her obvious anxiety at having this conversation.

"Well, why would he kill Jimmy? Because he was jealous?"

"You said it," Madison responded.

"That's ridiculous. As I said, Kevin and I have been seeing each other for years. He knows I sleep with other men. Here you go." Yasmine handed her phone to Madison with a shaky hand. "But I can't be certain he's still using that number."

"He changes it a lot?" Madison asked.

"He's horrible about losing them," Yasmine

explained.

"His phones?"

Yasmine nodded.

"Okay, but if he loses phones, that doesn't explain why his number changes. Unless... Does he use burner phones?"

Yasmine met Madison's gaze and shrugged. "I don't know."

Madison scanned Yasmine's eyes, but they gave away nothing. That only made Madison more suspicious of Kevin Jones. She started writing down his number when notice of a voice mail came up on the screen.

The caller ID showed *S Stein*.

"Looks like Mr. Stein called." Madison raised an eyebrow at Yasmine.

"Oh no. Sylvester's going to be pissed."

Madison guessed that was a yes... "Why?" she asked.

"Jimmy had a meeting this morning and— Oh god. What time is it?"

"Just after ten," Madison said, hardly believing how fast the time was going. It had already been three hours since Bates was found.

"Oh, I can't believe I forgot about—" Yasmine put a hand to her forehead. "What am I talking about?" Tears pooled again. "He's probably wondering where we are."

For Stein to call Yasmine's cell phone, he obviously knew that if he couldn't reach Bates directly, he might be able to do so through Yasmine.

"Let's listen to his message and find out what he wanted." Madison glanced down at the phone, and it hadn't locked her out yet. "What's the passcode for your voice mail?"

"Nine-two-three-eight."

Madison called in on speaker, keyed the code in, and played the message.

"Where are you? Are you with Jimmy? Call me back immediately."

The man was clearly annoyed and frustrated, even angry.

"Whoa, he is pissed," Yasmine said.

"He doesn't normally sound that way?" Madison asked. Sometimes people at the top weren't the easiest to deal with.

"No, he rarely raises his voice." Yasmine was wringing her hands on the table.

"You mentioned a meeting. Who was it with, and what was it for?" Madison pointed to Yasmine's hands. "It must have been important."

"It was with the stuffy uptights."

"Stuffy uptights?" Madison asked for clarification.

Yasmine nodded. "That was Jimmy's nickname for the board of directors."

"It doesn't sound like he had good relationships with them," Madison stated. It was possible one of them had an issue with Bates.

"Not sure if it's that. He just likes to do things his own way. That's what I loved about him. Not that I *loved* him," she clarified.

Yasmine hadn't exactly denied an underlying

conflict with Bates and the directors, though.

"And from what you said earlier, he was secretive." Madison gave Yasmine her phone back. "So he could have had a problem with one of them and maybe you wouldn't have known."

Yasmine bobbed her head. "That's possible."

"Do you know what the meeting was about?"

"He never tells me what's discussed at board of director meetings," Yasmine said.

"One of those things he's secretive about?" Madison asked drily.

"I suppose. It might not be my business to know, either."

"Fair enough."

"Am I good to go now?" Yasmine sounded hopeful.

"We'll still need to confirm your alibi," Madison told her. "Do you have your landlord's number?"

Yasmine got on her phone again and rattled off the number. Madison wrote it down, closed the folder, and got up.

"Please don't leave me here," Yasmine pleaded.

"We won't be long." Madison held the door for Terry, and they stepped out into the hall.

"Did you see the way she kept pressing her palms against her head, running her hand through her hair, and touching her face?" Madison asked. "She's terrified of someone, Terry."

He was nodding. "I agree. It's just afraid *of whom* that we need to find out."

"You call the landlord, and I'm going to try Kevin

Jones."

Terry pulled out his phone and keyed in the digits while she dialed the number for Kevin. She received an out-of-service message and hung up. From her phone, Madison proceeded to e-mail Cynthia Kevin's full name and number and asked her to see if she could track it somehow.

Terry was talking to someone, though. Thank god he was meeting with more success. A few minutes later, he was putting his phone in his pocket.

"Her alibi is confirmed," he said.

Madison didn't love confirming alibis over the phone, but she already had reservations about Yasmine's guilt. And the girl really didn't seem like a flight risk.

Terry gestured toward her. "How did you make out?"

"The number's no longer in service."

"Figures," he said, discouraged.

"Maybe Cynthia can track the number, but if it's a burner, we'll be SOL."

"Here's a question, though," Terry said. "Why would the guy need burner phones?"

"And does he have anything to do with *our* murder?"

CHAPTER

4

YASMINE WAS RELEASED WITH THE direction to go home and not leave town. Madison and Terry's next stop was to notify Bates's next of kin, and that was Rodney Bates, the man who Madison's grandfather had put away.

Madison had never met the man face-to-face before, and she wasn't exactly looking forward to doing so now, but it wasn't because of the news they had to share. Telling people their loved ones died normally churned her gut and filled her with whirling and complex emotions. It was one reason she and Terry liked to keep track of who gave notice and take turns. But with this case, even though hours had passed since she'd first laid eyes on Bates's dead body, she still didn't feel any heartfelt empathy for the man, nor could she conjure any for his father.

She pulled the department car to the curb in front of Rodney's house. It was compact and on the older side—a far cry from the lifestyle his son had been living. But Madison was wiser than to be fooled by first impressions. A man previously locked up for fraud and embezzlement would be wise not to flash his wealth if he'd found it again.

"I'll take this one." Madison stepped up ahead of Terry onto Rodney's front porch before he could argue. She rang the doorbell.

Footsteps came toward the door, and then it opened to a gray-haired man wearing reading glasses and holding a newspaper. He was dressed in trousers and a collared shirt. His brow wrinkled at the sight of them.

"You're cops," he hissed. "I can smell you a mile away." He moved to close the door, but Madison put her hand on it, holding it open.

"We're here about your son, Jimmy Bates, and we'd like to come in," Madison said.

Rodney glared at Madison's hand on his door and put the newspaper under an arm, crossed his arms, and cocked his head. "What about him?"

Was this Karma somehow tempting her to just come out with his son's death right there on his porch? Even now, in front of the the man who had truly started the spiral of events that ended with her grandfather's murder, she felt nothing at all. Surprisingly not even hatred.

She tilted up her chin. "This conversation would be better to have inside."

Rodney eventually stepped to the side to let her and Terry into the house. Rodney closed the door behind them.

"You're inside now, so tell me why you're here."

He was scowling as he curled up his newspaper and tucked into his back pocket.

Madison looked past him into the home. "Do you have someplace we could sit?"

"We can talk here." Rodney crossed his arms again.

"Jimmy is dead." It was always best to come right out with the news, yet normally her emotions would tug at her and she'd share the news more compassionately. Still…she felt nothing.

Rodney retained his rigid posture, disclosing no emotion. "How?"

Did he not care that his son was dead, or was it simply the initial phase of grief—denial?

"He was murdered early this morning," Madison told him.

Rodney's gaze hardened. "How?"

"He was stabbed multiple times." Stating it matter-of-factly, she was more detached than she'd ever been during a notification.

Rodney just stood there silently scrutinizing them. His gaze went from Madison to Terry, Terry to Madison. Usually the family members of a murder victim wanted to know how the investigation was coming, if there had been any arrests, or if there were at least suspects. Rodney hadn't asked about any of this.

"How well did you know your son?" Terry asked, breaking the silence. He must have thought Rodney's reaction was odd, as well.

"I'm not sure how that matters." Rodney arched

his brows. "Do you think I killed him?"

"He's not implying that, but we do need to know how well you knew your son," Madison jumped in, her tone firm.

"I knew him fine enough," he responded curtly.

"I'm not sure what you mean by 'fine enough,'" she retorted.

"I visited him in prison, and we saw each other on occasion after he got out."

She let out a ragged breath, frustration filling every fiber of her being. He was making them drag everything out of him. "How frequent was 'on occasion'?"

"Just that." Rodney turned back toward the door and put a hand on the knob.

"We have more questions, if it's not an inconvenience," she said coolly.

And even if it is, we still have questions…

"Fine. Let's go to the living room." Rodney brushed past them and then turned to the left of the entry. He pulled the paper from his back pocket and slapped it onto a side table next to a recliner. He took a seat there, and Madison and Terry sat on a couch.

"When I was sent to jail—" Rodney said. "I'm sure you're aware of my background and know that my son killed the cop who put me away." A twinkle of something like pride crossed his eyes, and it made Madison want to sock the seventy-five-year-old right in the mouth.

"You think that's something to be proud of?" she

snarled.

Rodney shrugged. "I think it shows the love a son has for his father."

Screw it. She couldn't haul off and hit the guy physically, so she may as well do it verbally. And technically, the old man had brought up the past first. "Was Jimmy involved with the Russian Mafia?"

Terry turned toward her, but she didn't acknowledge him.

Rodney picked up on Terry's glance and slowly said, "I wouldn't know."

"You really expect me to believe that?" she spat.

Terry was staring at the side of her face now. With it, though, she realized how she'd said *me* not *us*. She hadn't included Terry at all. And just when she'd convinced herself this wasn't personal… The hell it wasn't!

Madison continued. "You of all people should know if Jimmy had dealings with the Russians. You were certainly close with them."

"*Were* being the operative word here," Rodney said drily.

At least Terry seemed to have stopped staring at her. But now it was Rodney, and his gaze was doing as much to make her feel self-conscious as it was fueling her rage. His earlier dismissal of her grandfather's murder made her stomach churn and the blood boil in her veins.

Rodney was angling his head now, left and right, right and left. "Why do you look familiar…?" After a few beats, Rodney snapped his fingers. "Aha! I know why."

Her heart began to race. Did he connect her to her grandfather?

"You're the detective who put Dimitre Petrov away." Rodney smiled. "Impressive."

"I don't need you to be impressed." Her jaw was so tight with contempt, she barely got the words out.

Dimitre was the son of *the* Roman Petrov. Roman headed up the Mafia back in Russia, and Dimitre ran things in Stiles. He'd been untouchable up until about eight years ago when Madison was able to tie him to a murder. Dimitre had been given a life sentence and was currently serving it in Mitchell County Prison. But he still had a reach that extended beyond bars.

"You do know, though, that you can't stop a man like that…" Rodney leaned forward, peering into her eyes. "Even behind bars, he has ways to get what he wants done."

"I'm well aware of that." Her body stiffened. She had a feeling Rodney was holding back. Maybe her next question would get him to talk. "Do you think Dimitre's behind your son's death?"

Rodney laughed, but the amusement didn't touch his eyes. Her breathing became shallow. Did that mean Constantine was, in fact, back and possibly acting on Dimitre's orders? It had been on Dimitre's command the first time that Constantine had cleaned house in Stiles, including the assassination of Dimitre's own right-hand men, Sergey and Anatolli.

"Did Dimitre order a hit on your son?" she asked, this time with more conviction.

Rodney's lips set into a scowl. "And why would he want to kill Jimmy?"

"He could be cleaning house again."

"Cleaning house?" Rodney's brow furrowed in supposed confusion, and he glanced at Terry, but Terry didn't say anything.

Rodney had been out of prison for twenty-four years, and Madison found it hard to believe that he hadn't been involved with the Russians in any way. After all, it was difficult to teach an old dog new tricks. But even if he was telling the truth, the murders of Sergey and Anatolli, who had been gunned down on the courthouse steps, had been covered on the news.

"You know exactly what I'm talking about," Madison hissed.

"I'm afraid I don't." Rodney's gaze drifted back and forth between her and Terry.

Madison clenched her jaw. She wasn't going to give him the pleasure of rehashing everything. What mattered at the moment was that Rodney seemed to be avoiding conversation about the Russians and that told her that he had his suspicions about them killing his son. For now, that would have to do. If she kept pushing him on the Russians, he'd show them the door. She wanted to know more about Bates's career and how he'd gotten to where he was. Plus, law enforcement had never found out who had taken over the books after Rodney went to prison.

Maybe she could get Rodney to slip up. Maybe it had even been his son.

"Jimmy did well for himself," she said, managing to tamp down her temper. "He lived in a nice place, had a successful career at an accounting firm." She did her best to hide her judgment and speculation. But as she observed Rodney, she realized he would have left prison a broke man, and given the fact that he was now seventy-five and an ex-con, he wouldn't be at the top of any employer's desirable to-hire list. "Does he take care of you, too?"

"My son caught a break," he growled. "That's all. Nothing more to it." He swiped his hands together the way one would to indicate washing their hands of someone.

"That doesn't really answer her question," Terry said, finally speaking up.

Rodney slid Terry a glance. "He bought me this place and gives me a monthly allowance. Not sure how this helps you find out who killed him."

Madison crossed her arms. "Who gave your son this 'break'?"

Rodney smirked and pointed a finger at her. "I said *caught*, not was given. But you expect me to say the Russians. It's written all over your face and in your body language."

She relaxed her posture, but it wasn't easy. "I *expect* you to tell me the truth."

"Nah—" Rodney shook his head "—you're obsessed with the Mafia. You hold them accountable for your grandfather's murder even more than you blame Jimmy."

She held her breath, frozen. "You know who I am?"

A sinister smile. "From the moment I saw you at my door."

"You son of—" Madison hurled herself off the couch, but Terry caught her by the arm. She shrugged free and turned to glare at him. His expression mirrored her own.

Rodney was chuckling, holding a hand over his mouth. "Temper, temper, Detective."

She was fuming and breathing rapidly, her chest heaving. If the man in front of her hadn't been involved with the Russians, her grandfather might still be alive. Rodney's conviction, his crime, had sealed her grandfather's murder. It took all her self-control not to lay a beating on this man.

"How did Jimmy secure a job at Berger & Stein?" Terry asked the question as if he were just making polite conversation.

Rodney ran a hand over his mouth, literally wiping the smirk off his face. "His employer spotted a natural talent and hired him on."

"A natural talent?" Madison mocked, drawing Rodney's gaze back to her. "Jimmy was an ex-con and a cop killer. In the real world, someone like him is rarely given a second chance and is lucky to get work at a fast-food joint. There's more to this." She was sick of toeing some imaginary line between what was appropriate and what wasn't.

Rodney's pulse tapped in his cheeks. "I might

have put in a word for him."

"At Berger & Stein?" she asked.

Rodney pursed his lips. "Yes, at Berger & Stein."

She tapped a foot on the floor. "With who?"

Rodney looked down, noticing her impatient mannerism. She kept tapping her foot.

"The more cooperative you are with us," Terry told him, "the faster we'll be able to find out what happened to your son and why."

Rodney sat back and clasped his hands on his lap. "Are you telling me that if I don't cooperate, you won't do your job and find my son's killer?"

Terry shook his head adamantly. "I didn't say that."

Rodney fired a glare at Madison. She stopped tapping her foot now.

"And neither did she," Terry snapped. "Let's just talk a minute about Berger & Stein. What's your connection to it?"

Rodney sliced a glare at Madison. "Your grandfather harassed me. He was obsessed with proving my guilt. I wouldn't doubt that he fabricated the evidence."

Heat flared in her cheeks. He was trying to elicit a reaction, and it was a good thing Terry was there. "Don't you dare say another word about my grandfather," she ground out.

"Why? I didn't even think you knew him. How can you defend him?" Rodney's bitter judgment struck her like a bullet to the chest. Searing pain blossomed inside her, rendering her speechless.

Terry glanced at Madison but settled his gaze on Rodney. "We're not here to discuss Detective Knight's grandfather," Terry said firmly. "And she asked you a question awhile ago that still hasn't been answered. Who did you call on at Berger & Stein?"

Rodney gritted his teeth. "Greg Berger. He's retired now, but his son, Lyle, took over as a managing partner."

"Why did he owe you a favor?" Madison asked.

"No one said it was a favor," Rodney replied, nonchalant. "*Caught* a break, remember?"

"Need I remind you again that your son was an *ex-con* and a *murderer*," Madison served back, feeling good about verbally smacking the older man. "It had to be a favor or something even shadier is going on. Now who paid for his schooling?"

"The company."

Madison raised her brows at Terry. "Wow, that's generous."

Rodney patted the arm of his chair but said nothing.

"So Greg owed you a favor?" She reused the word he had hated so much and tossed in a smirk.

"Fine. Whatever," Rodney consented.

"You know, we never found out who took over being the numbers man for the mob. Maybe it was Greg Berger. And then your son went to work for him." She turned to Terry again. "It sounds like a real possibility. Berger & Stein might be laundering money."

Rodney stood up. "It's time for you to go."

Given the man's rigid body language, his statement had in no way been a suggestion. Madison and Terry got up.

At the door, Rodney turned to Madison. "You might want to watch your back."

Madison got to within inches of his face. "Is that a threat?"

Rodney hitched his shoulders. "I'll let you decide."

She'd love to do nothing more than slap a set of cuffs on the old man and bring him downtown, and if she listened to her impulses, she'd have done just that. He had just threatened a police officer! But what good would cuffing him do? It would only prove that he had affected her, and by extension, that this case was more personal than she wanted to admit. And that might get her taken off the investigation. She held eye contact with Rodney as she stepped back. Once they were outside, he slammed the door behind them.

"Oooh!" She balled her fists and walked to the department car. "That son of a bitch!"

She got behind the wheel, and Terry loaded into the passenger seat.

"I'm surprised you didn't take him in," he said.

She turned to him. "Really?"

"He threatened you."

She shook her head and clicked her seat belt into place, her hand shaking as she did so. "It just wouldn't have been worth the trouble."

There was a flicker of knowing that passed over Terry's eyes. "I understand why."

She detected judgment in his tone, and she didn't like it one bit. "What's that supposed to mean?"

Terry's shoulders tensed. "Did you hear yourself in there? You asked him if Jimmy was connected to the Russians, and when Rodney said he didn't know, you said—and I quote—'You really expect me to believe that?' *Me*, Madison, not *we*."

"That didn't mean anything. I was just talking for myself at the time."

"Okay, how do you explain jumping off the couch ready to slug the guy?"

"I didn't, though, did I?"

"Didn't hit him? No, but only because I stopped you. And then your swearing?" He shook his head, a hint of disgust showing on his face. He detested foul language. "No matter what you say, this case is personal."

"Hell yes, it's personal," she fired back. "Is that what you want to hear? That man was pushing my buttons."

"And you gave him what he wanted. A reaction," Terry punched out. "If the Russians are involved in Bates's murder, and Rodney still has connections there, they'll be tipped off that we're looking at them."

"If?" The word slipped out, and there was no backing out now.

Terry shifted his upper body, putting his right shoulder and part of his back to the door. "I know you've suspected them from the start."

"As I said at Bates's, we need to consider all the

possibilities. That includes, but is not limited to, the Russians." There, she'd left out any specific mention of Constantine. Now, maybe if she switched the topic up a little… "I found it interesting how upset Rodney got when I'd alleged that Greg Berger or his company was in cahoots with the mob."

"That makes two of us."

CHAPTER

5

BERGER & STEIN ACCOUNTING TOOK up the top ten floors of a twenty-one-story high-rise in downtown Stiles. Madison and Terry checked in with a man at the desk in the main lobby, and someone from the firm was being sent down to escort them upstairs.

About ten minutes after their arrival, a twentysomething blonde in a black pencil skirt paired with a cream blouse stepped off the elevator and headed straight for them.

Madison and Terry held up their badges.

"No secret that you're the detectives wanting to speak with Lyle Berger and Sylvester Stein," she said pleasantly. "Unfortunately, Mr. Berger isn't in today, but Mr. Stein will speak with you. I'm Anita, Mr. Stein's assistant, and if you'll come with me..." Anita led them to the elevator bank, and within minutes they unloaded on the twenty-first floor. Chrome lettering on the wall opposite the elevator announced the business name. There was a curved reception desk with another twentysomething blonde sitting behind it talking animatedly into a headset.

Berger & Stein sure likes its blondes…

Anita led them to a corner office and gestured for them to enter. "Here you are."

They stepped inside to find walls of windows affording spectacular views of the city. The space was the size of a large studio apartment with a seating area that had a rug, couch, and two sofa chairs. There was a substantial mahogany desk that was more than just practical; it was a piece of art with ornate touches such as the scrollwork that accented the legs. Behind the desk, a man in his fifties sat in a plush leather chair. He had a head of silver hair, piercing gray eyes, and a neatly groomed mustache.

"Mr. Stein, these are Detectives Knight and Grant."

"Detectives." Sylvester dipped his head and smiled cordially.

His friendly reaction was odd given that two detectives from Major Crimes had wanted an audience with him. Most people would have a sense of foreboding from such a request.

"Would any of you care for water or coffee?" Anita offered.

"I'm fine, thanks," Terry responded.

Madison shook her head.

Anita looked to her boss. "Mr. Stein?"

"I'm fine, Anita."

"Very well." She left the office, closing the door behind her.

Sylvester gestured toward two chairs that were set up across from his desk. "Please. Take a seat."

Terry sat while Madison remained standing.

Sylvester's gaze drifted over her. "As you likely know, I'm one of the managing partners of this firm. I understand that you had wanted to speak with Lyle, as well, but he's out of town on business until next week."

"We heard he just wasn't in today," Madison said.

"Was it Anita who told you that? I apologize for any misunderstanding, but he's gone until next Monday on a business trip."

"When did Mr. Berger leave for his business trip?" she asked.

"Last night."

That was convenient timing. "And where did he go?"

"Colorado for a conference on acquisitions and accounting law." The room fell silent, and Sylvester wet his lips and tilted his head to the left. "I'd ask what your purpose here is today, but I heard what happened to Jimmy."

"Word travels fast," Madison said coolly. She wasn't happy that he'd already heard because she'd been robbed of the chance to gauge his reaction to the news. Not to mention her curiosity about the integrity of this firm had been heightened. First, Rodney's reaction to her allegation that the firm was connected to the mob, and second, Bates's murder had already reached his boss.

Sylvester squinted at her. "Yasmine mentioned it."

"Ah, of course." Madison's cheeks heated, and she hated that she'd let her thoughts get carried away. It would make sense that Yasmine told him, as he'd been trying to reach her. She really needed to get her emotions in check. As much as she kept trying to convince herself she was remaining objective, the interaction with Rodney Bates had tilted her scales of logic and reason out of balance. And she hated that errant thoughts of Constantine being back to kill her kept entering her mind. Maybe if she took a seat, she'd be able to concentrate. She sat next to Terry.

Sylvester continued, letting his gaze go back and forth between Madison and Terry. "She said he was murdered?"

She nodded. "Yasmine found Mr. Bates in his home this morning."

Sylvester sank back into his chair, concern etched in his brow. "She told me that much, as well. What happened to him?"

Yasmine apparently left out those details. And while Madison didn't have the chance to see how he responded to the news of Bates's death, she could witness his reaction to how he was killed.

"Mr. Bates was stabbed multiple times," she said, her gaze on him.

His mouth opened and closed shut, and his eyes widened and watered, telling Madison he was shocked by this.

"The exact cause of death is yet to be determined," she added thoughtfully, surprised by his show of emotion.

Sylvester pinched the tip of his nose and shook his head as if demonstrating he thought Bates's murder had been a senseless act.

"Were you close with Jimmy?" This time she intentionally used Bates's first name to establish familiarity and friendliness.

"He was a good employee. Reliable."

Madison nodded, though she hadn't asked about his standing with the company. "Were you close outside the office?"

"We had drinks on occasion."

"Do you know of anyone who might have wanted to hurt him? Someone who he didn't get along with, or butted heads with recently?"

"I've heard detectives ask those types of questions on TV." He paused, reflectively. "But it's quite different in real life, and to be the one faced with them…" He looked her in the eye. "Honestly, I don't know of anyone he didn't get along with."

"He must have been a nice guy." It almost killed her to say that.

Sylvester nodded. "He was."

"We understand that there was a meeting scheduled with the board of directors this morning. What was the purpose of the meeting?" Madison asked.

"It was just a quarterly review." Sylvester tossed out the topic as if it bored him.

If that's all it was, why wouldn't Yasmine have known as Bates's assistant? "And that's all you'd discuss at these meetings?"

"Yeah."

Madison nodded. "And it was imperative that Jimmy be at these meetings?"

Sylvester nodded. "Part of his responsibility was to prepare the financial reports and present them."

"How did the directors react to the news of Jimmy's death?" Terry asked.

"I canceled the meeting when I couldn't reach Jimmy or Yasmine. I didn't get into details with them. Heck, I didn't have any at that point."

"How did the board members react to the cancellation?" Madison asked.

"They weren't impressed."

"Yasmine mentioned that Jimmy called them 'stuffy uptights.' Did he have a beef with any of them?" she asked.

"Not that I'm aware of."

A corporation's board of directors were a matter of public record, and Madison made a note that they should pull the names and backgrounds on all its members.

"What about any clients who might not have been happy with him or his work?" Madison asked.

"Again, not that I'm aware of."

"We'd like to see a list of Jimmy's clients," she said.

"If you have a warrant, I'd be happy to help." Something in Sylvester's eyes belied his claim. Or was she projecting that onto him?

"We'll get a warrant," she assured him.

Sylvester nodded. "At that point, I'll get you the

client list."

Madison's mind turned down another path as she recalled how Sylvester had called Yasmine looking for Jimmy. "You knew about Jimmy and Yasmine's affair, I imagine?"

Sylvester propped an elbow on the arm of the chair and cupped his chin. "I think pretty much everyone did."

"Why's that?" Terry asked.

Sylvester sat back in his chair and swiveled slowly side to side. "Let's just say they weren't too discreet. More than a few employees saw them fraternizing."

Like Lyle Berger.

"And there isn't any company policy against employees dating?" Madison asked.

He shrugged. "It wasn't hurting anyone."

"That wasn't exactly what I asked you." Madison waited a few beats.

"As a general rule," he went on, "we'd prefer that business relationships stay just that, especially between a manager and their staff."

Bates seemed to have had the golden touch. First the company overlooked the fact that he was an ex-con and sinks thousands into his education, and now, it seemed the rules didn't apply to him.

"It seems like Jimmy had it easy here," she summarized.

Sylvester stopped swiveling, leaned forward, and clasped his hands on his desk. "I'm not sure what you mean."

"Jimmy murdered a man. He had a record." She

presented this to Sylvester in a passively judgmental way.

"He went to prison and paid his debt to society." When she didn't respond, he glanced at Terry. "I'm not sure what I'm supposed to say here."

"You don't need to say anything else, Mr. Stein," Madison responded. "It just seems that Jimmy was given a lot of leeway." She laid out her hand, palm up. "Is it common practice for Berger & Stein to pay for the education of its employees?"

Sylvester seemed hesitant and leery about answering. "I wouldn't say that."

"But his was paid for by the company." she pointed out.

"I'm not sure…"

Madison nudged her head forward. "Really?"

"Really," Sylvester shot back. "Lyle's the one who brought him on board."

"Did he say why?" she asked.

Sylvester's posture relaxed. "He doesn't answer to me, so no. And I didn't ask."

"He's the majority owner," Madison reasoned aloud. "His father founded the company."

"That's right." Sylvester adjusted his tie and let his hands fall when he noticed Madison watching him. "What did it matter to me where he got the guy or why? Same thing if he paid for his education: it doesn't affect me."

Madison didn't understand how the latter didn't affect him, given he owed stakes in the company, but she'd let that pass for now. "When did Jimmy come on board?"

"Off the top of my head, I'd say about sixteen years ago."

Bates had gotten out of prison nineteen years ago, so that was swift placement. He must have raced through getting his diploma and licensing. She held eye contact with Sylvester. "And the affair he had going with Yasmine…?"

"Wasn't hurting anyone as I had said. Besides, it probably wasn't going to last much longer." He shrugged.

"Why's that?"

"Because I knew Jimmy, and he wasn't a one-lady kind of man."

"So he had other girlfriends?"

"Girlfriends? No. Women he had sex with? Yes."

She'd thought about it from the standpoint of Yasmine or one of her boy toys getting jealous and knocking off Bates, but maybe one of Bates's other women didn't care much for being one of many, either. Still, Lyle wasn't far from her mind.

"Do you know any of these women's names?" Madison asked.

"Sorry, I don't. It's not like they hung around for long. Not even sure if Jimmy got their names," he added with a smirk.

Madison held eye contact with him, disgusted by the glimmer of male chauvinism, but he seemed to be telling the truth.

"Well…" Sylvester regarded them. "If that will be all?"

"A couple more questions and we'll be on our way," Madison promised. "How did Lyle feel about Jimmy and Yasmine's relationship?"

"Beats me."

If Lyle had actually footed the bill for Bates and brought him on board, he could feel entitled somehow. He obviously thought he could take advantage of Yasmine. "So you never witnessed any hostility between them about Yasmine? Any sexual tension between Yasmine and Lyle?"

Sylvester squared his shoulders, and his body language became guarded. "None. To both your questions."

"So as far as you know, Lyle never raped Yasmine?"

"No," Sylvester ground out, his face reddening.

She gave it a few seconds, then asked. "Where and when did you last see Jimmy?"

"Here. During business hours yesterday."

"And where were you last night from eleven until seven this morning?" They still didn't have a time of death so it was a big window, but she expected most people would be home sleeping during those hours. But if Sylvester was the killer, there'd likely be some tell in his facial expression, body language, or energy.

"Let's see. I worked in the office until about eight and then went home. I watched some TV and nodded off to sleep by midnight." Sylvester rattled off his schedule with boredom.

"Can anyone corroborate your claim?"

"*Claim?*" He mocked. "No. I live alone," he added

bitterly.

"All right. Just one more thing," she said. "We'd like the information on the conference Lyle Berger is attending."

"Sure." Sylvester pressed a button on his phone.

"What can I do for you, Mr. Stein?" Anita answered.

"I need you to print out Lyle's itinerary for the detectives."

"Okay," his assistant said. "I'll bring it to you in a minute."

"No." Sylvester eyed Madison and Terry. "They're leaving now. They'll pick it up on their way out."

"Yes, sir."

Sylvester ended the call and stood. He tugged down on his suit jacket. "I wish you luck in finding Jimmy's killer."

Madison got to her feet and regarded the man, his word choice, and his delivery with scrutiny. *I wish you luck...* Coming from him, that sentiment carried the opposite implication.

"We might have more questions," she said.

"And if you do, I must insist on my legal counsel being present." Sylvester pulled a card from his pants pocket and handed it to her.

She took the card in exchange for one of hers, which he flicked onto the top of his desk.

Pulling her gaze from her card, she met his eyes and turned for the door.

"Anita's office is the room next to mine on the right. First door," Sylvester called out.

Madison was replaying the parts of the conversation that had seemed to be rough for Sylvester. First, there had been the request for the client list, and second, when his innocence was being called into question, he got rather defensive. Third, he clearly hadn't liked it when she'd asked if Lyle had raped Yasmine. Fourth, he had seemed very confident that no one held ill will toward Bates, including Lyle.

Anita was holding out a piece of paper when they stepped into her office, and Terry thanked her and took it. Then he led the way to the exit and out of the building.

Once they were out on the sidewalk, Madison stated her dislike for Sylvester's final wording. "Not really sure what he meant by wishing us luck," she said. "Was there a warning in there? A taunt like we'd need luck on our side to solve this case?"

Terry was shaking his head. "I think you might be reading too much into it."

With this case, she was questioning herself at every turn. Maybe Terry was right. Sylvester could have just meant the words at face value and that he wanted his employee's killer found, but there was a niggling feeling in her gut.

"I was just thinking—" Her phone rang, interrupting her. She glanced at the caller ID before answering. "Cynthia?"

"Listen, you've got to come back to Bates's house. There's something you're going to want to see for yourself."

CHAPTER

6

THE ME'S VAN WASN'T AT Bates's house when Madison and Terry arrived, but the forensics vehicle was, along with four cruisers. There was no sign of the officers who drove them, with the exception of Higgins, who was posted at the front door.

"The others are canvassing?" Madison asked, referring to the officers as she and Terry approached Higgins.

"You got it," he confirmed.

She nodded. Canvassing was a painful but necessary task. A neighbor may have seen or heard something that could aid the investigation, but she wasn't holding out much hope that such a thing would happen in this case. Regardless, she asked, "Anything helpful come back to you yet?"

Higgins shook his head. "It's still early."

Madison put a hand on his shoulder and moved past him into the house. Cynthia was in the entryway, a collection kit on the floor at her feet, and footfalls were padding along the floor upstairs.

Madison walked over to Cynthia. "You said that you have something I need to see?"

Cynthia looked up at her. "That's right. But first, I—"

"Oh, Cyn, you always do this," Madison moaned. She had driven fast enough to break some traffic laws getting there but had justified it given the urgency that had been in her friend's tone. But now Cynthia was going to delay sharing whatever it was that prompted the call.

"What?" Cynthia smiled.

"You hook me and then make me wait."

"It's good for you. Makes you learn patience."

Terry laughed, and Madison punched him in the shoulder.

"Hey!" He rubbed where she'd hit him, playing it up as if she'd hurt him when she'd barely touched him.

"We have Bates's laptop but weren't able to find his phone," Cynthia began.

"There must be something on there the killer wanted or didn't want us to see," Madison reasoned.

"Quite possible," Cynthia began. "Mark was able to find Bates's provider, though, so we'll get his phone records at least."

A sliver of good news…

"Now, we've ruled out a break-in." Cynthia continued. "And there was no sign of an altercation anywhere else in the house. The scene of the crime is limited to the master bedroom."

"So our killer would have needed a key and a

code," Terry interjected. "If the killer came here to confront Bates and he had answered the door, it would be more likely that signs of an altercation would be evident leading to the bedroom."

"Agreed," Cynthia said. "The security company also verified the times when the system was armed and disarmed. I'll forward you the e-mail they sent me, but it was disarmed at ten forty-five, rearmed at twelve fifteen, disarmed again at one, rearmed at six thirty, and disarmed at seven."

"So Yasmine was telling the truth about it being armed when she showed up," Madison stated.

Terry nodded and addressed Cynthia. "You said it was disarmed at one and rearmed at six thirty? The killer was here five and a half hours, then."

"When did Richards place time of death?" Madison inquired.

"He's still reserving final judgment on that," Cynthia began, "but based on his initial findings, TOD was between two and four this morning."

"Two and four?" Madison inclined her head. "But you said the—"

Cynthia was nodding. "Exactly. There's time that's unaccounted for."

"Right," Terry said. "From about four until six thirty. What was the killer doing during that time?" He rubbed the back of his neck the way he often did when the questions outnumbered the answers.

"Well, Richards told me to let you know he hadn't concluded TOD officially yet, so don't get too attached to the time range," Cynthia reminded them.

"Either way, the killer we're looking for won't have an alibi for between one and six thirty," Terry said.

Madison and Cynthia sputtered laughter.

Cynthia jacked at thumb in Terry's direction. "Einstein over here."

"Or King of the Obvious," Madison teased. Her partner glared at her. "Okay, okay. You're right, Terry. That time span should be good enough for us to work with for now." Madison knew better than to ask for cause of death because Richards preferred to have time with the body back at the morgue before drawing any conclusions. Add to that the body having been so mutilated that it would require Richards to conduct an in-depth autopsy. He'd have to map out the injuries, measure the depth of the wounds, and determine what organs had been injured. The body would also be x-rayed to see if any pieces broke off the murder weapon.

"When's the autopsy scheduled for?" she asked.

"In the morning," Cynthia responded, "but Richards recommends that you drop by tomorrow at about two in the afternoon. He should have something for you then."

Madison directed her attention back to the security system. "And what about the code or codes used to get in the house? Were there different ones used at the different times?"

Cynthia shook her head. "Bates only had one code."

"So he must have shared it with Yasmine, but

how did the killer get ahold of it? Through Yasmine somehow?"

Cynthia looked like she was deep in thought.

"Are you all right?" Madison asked.

Cynthia shook her head. "I can't imagine being that girl and finding him like that."

"That *girl* is in her twenties," Madison countered.

"Some days I feel my thirty-five years more than others." Cynthia's voice cracked with exhaustion as if on cue.

Madison smiled knowingly. "You sound tired."

"You have no idea," Cynthia said with a groan.

But Madison did. Cynthia was in the middle of planning her wedding, which was fewer than five months away. On top of that, she was working six twelve-hour days a week lately. Now, if the commitment itself wasn't enough to scare Madison from marriage, all the hoopla certainly should have been, but these days neither was fully doing the trick. After all the years milking her broken heart caused from her breakup with fellow detective Toby Sovereign and swearing off relationships, she'd finally found someone she loved—Troy Matthews, the head of a SWAT team for Stiles PD. And he was a god in man's form—giving lean and mean characterization. But much more than his physical prowess, he was the most caring and attentive man she'd ever been with. And now she was living with him. Well, sort of. She hadn't let her apartment go yet.

Terry cleared his throat, pulling Madison out of

her reverie. "So what is it we need to see?" he asked Cynthia.

She looked at Madison, her face a mask of melancholy and fear. "Looking at Bates is like déjà vu. It takes me right back to what Constantine did to Lillian Norton."

Madison was curious why her friend was bringing that up again, but she sensed there was more to it than Cynthia's concern for Madison. "It could just be a coincidence."

"Coincidence?" Cynthia parroted at a high pitch. She turned to Terry. "Since when does she believe in coincidence?"

"I'm right here, you know," Madison said. "All I meant is that I'm not in a hurry to jump to any conclusions yet." She gestured to Terry. "As he's always saying, we have to follow the evidence."

"Well, I am considering the evidence, and you actually might start chipping away at the 'coincidence' thing when you see what I have for you."

Madison's stomach clenched. "What is it?"

"One thing first," her friend said.

"Cyn, seriously?" Irritation coiled around Madison's heart and constricted her airflow. Patience had never been her strong suit, but with this case, she was tapped out of it from the moment she thought Constantine might be back.

Cynthia held up a hand. "Okay, I see you're not in the mood to fool around." She bent down and pulled out a sealed evidence bag from a collection box. "This was found after I called you." She handed it over to Madison. "It was in Bates's wallet."

The bag contained a receipt from Club Sophisticated and the time stamp showed ten thirty last night. It billed for shots of vodka.

"Not sure if you've ever been, but it's hip and trendy," Cynthia began. "Lou and I have gone a couple times."

"How far is it from there to here?" Terry asked.

Cynthia's brow furrowed in thought. "Ten, maybe fifteen minutes?"

Terry turned to Madison. "Yasmine said she met up with Bates at his house around eleven."

"And the system was disarmed at ten forty-five," Madison added. "I wonder if he was at the club alone or had company."

"Stein said Bates got around. Maybe he was with another woman," Terry suggested.

"Possibly. But whoever it was, was one of the last people to see him alive," Madison concluded.

"Maybe his killer followed him from the club," Terry theorized. "Just keeping an open mind."

"Unless this was a Russian hit." Cynthia drew her gaze to Madison. "They'd know where he lived."

"All right," Madison said, sloughing off the hypotheticals. She refused to give herself over to falling into the rabbit hole that it was Constantine. "What's the discovery we needed to see with our own eyes? The one you called me about?"

"This way." Cynthia led the way upstairs, practically at a jog. "Mark?"

"Yeah?" The investigator peeked his head through an opened doorway into the hall.

"Show them what you found," Cynthia directed him.

"Is it the murder weapon?" Madison ventured.

"Nope, but something good nonetheless," Cynthia said.

For it to be considered "something good" in comparison to a murder weapon, Madison's curiosity was piqued.

"This way." Mark came out of the room and led them down the hall and through the third door on the left. It was Bates's home office. It was bright with a window seat and built-in shelving.

Mark headed to a section that housed tomes on accounting law and pressed his fingers to the top of one of their spines. The width of ten inches, five faux books popped out on an angle, revealing a hidden compartment.

"It's what he found inside that you'll want to see." Cynthia looked at Mark. "Go get the paper."

He ran out of the room.

Madison could barely take the suspense any longer. "What's on the paper?"

"It's not so much what's on it—although, who knows how it ties in—but where it's from is definitely interesting."

Madison was about to scream in frustration at her anticipation.

"You'll see in just a few seconds."

Madison angled her head at Cynthia. "Really?"

Mark came back with a sealed plastic evidence bag and handed it to Madison.

She pretty much snatched it from his hands. It contained a piece of letterhead. "Mitchell County Prison," she said out loud.

Mitchell County Prison was where Dimitre Petrov was serving his sentence. Was this the connection to the Mafia she needed, or did it mean something else? Now the fact that Cynthia had brought up the possible Mafia tie downstairs made sense.

She unfolded the paper and silently read the letter. All that had been written was the number *4734237437*.

"Ten digits." Madison looked up. "A phone number?"

Cynthia shook her head. "We tried that right away."

"What's it mean, then?" Madison countered.

"We don't know yet. A bank account, a passcode? We'll need more time."

"Do we know who wrote it yet?"

Cynthia turned to Mark.

"I did a quick comparison to Bates's handwriting from a legal document I found in there." Mark pointed to a wood-grain, four-drawer filing cabinet. "It's not a match."

"Not Bates's?" Madison's heart was racing, not having expected that answer. She paced a few steps and handed off the evidence bag to Terry.

"The letterhead would only be coming from one place," she started brainstorming aloud, "and that's the administrative offices." She stopped moving, letting her gaze drift over all of them. "Whoever wrote on this letterhead likely works in or has access to the prison offices. Still, why does Bates have this? What was his connection there?"

Cynthia locked eye contact with her. "It's where—"

"I know it's where Dimitre's serving time," Madison countered quickly. "But assuming that Bates *was* in communication with him…why? Is there a connection between that"—she inferred the letterhead—"and his murder?" Her gut told her yes, but she'd have to wait for a satisfactory answer.

"Bates could have been visiting someone else besides Dimitre," Terry suggested.

Madison shot him down with a concentrated stare.

"Or maybe not…" Terry held up the bag and addressed Mark. "The envelope in here…"

"That's what the letterhead was found in," Mark said, answering Terry's unfinished question. "As you'll see, there's no address, name, or stamp on it. It was never sealed."

"So it was handed directly to Bates," Terry concluded.

Mark nodded. "And it's the real deal. It's not forged letterhead—it's embossed. It also has the prison's new logo, and that change was pretty recent, so I'd say it hasn't been in here too long."

"All right, so he had it delivered to him in person by someone who works in the offices at Mitchell

County Prison," Terry summarized. He was rubbing at the back of his neck so hard it sounded like sandpaper.

"We need to find out when Bates got it and what those numbers mean," Madison said. "And the best way to get started with both those things is to go to the prison. We need to check the visitor logs and see if and when we can place Bates there. Either way, someone on the inside was communicating with Bates, and we need to know who and why."

CHAPTER

7

MITCHELL COUNTY PRISON WAS A maximum security facility and located on the outskirts of Stiles. It housed five hundred inmates and some of the most dangerous criminals in the state. Madison and Terry had relinquished their guns at check-in and were waiting to see the warden, a man named Jeremy Schultz. They were at least going in armed with a signed warrant for a copy of the prison's visitor logs as they pertained to Jimmy Bates. Terry had made a good point on the way over, though: why would Bates sign in and let his liaison with Dimitre be known? Assuming there was a liaison between the two of them. But looking into the logs was an avenue worth exploring regardless. Criminals often got cocky, and when they got cocky, they made mistakes.

A buzzer sounded, and a door opened. A man came out into the waiting area. He had shortly cropped light-brown hair, a round face, and wide nose. The receptionist pointed him in Madison and

Terry's direction.

"Detectives," the man said, holding out a hand. "I'm Jeremy Schultz. You wanted to see me?"

Madison made the introductions and added, "We'd like to speak with you in your office."

"Sure." Jeremy's voice sounded strained, hesitant. "Follow me." He turned and headed back to the door he'd come out of just moments ago. He swiped a keycard, and the buzzer sounded again. He opened the door and held it for Madison and Terry, letting them enter ahead of him.

They stepped aside, and once through, Jeremy led the way to his office. He took them to a simplistic space furnished with a metal desk, metal filing cabinets, two metal-framed chairs facing the desk, and a leather chair on the other side. That's where Jeremy took a seat. He gestured for Madison and Terry to sit in the chairs facing him. They did so.

Jeremy leaned back and regarded them with a reserved curiosity. "What is it that I can do for you?"

Madison pulled out a photocopy of the letterhead with the message and extended it across the desk to Jeremy.

He took it. "What's this?"

"That's the prison's letterhead," Madison stated matter-of-factly. "Do you recognize it?"

"Of course, I do." His face scrunched up in confusion. "I'm just not understanding what you're getting at. And where did you get this from?"

"We'll get to that." She pointed to the letterhead. "Is that a recent design for the letterhead?" She wanted him to confirm what Mark had told them.

"Yes," Jeremy said.

Madison nodded. "We'll need to know who has access to this particular letterhead." Madison figured she knew the answer but wanted to hear it from him.

"The office staff."

"No one else?" Madison pressed.

"That's right."

"So office staff… That includes you?"

"Yeah," he said slowly and shifted his gaze briefly to Terry.

Madison pointed to the paper. "Do you know whose handwriting that is?"

"I have no idea." Jeremy went to hand the sheet back to Madison, but Madison didn't reach for it. Jeremy let it drop to his desk.

Madison eyed him as a predator would its prey. "Do you have any idea why this would end up in the hands of a civilian?"

"The prison letterhead? No idea." Jeremy fell quiet. "You said you were going to tell me where you got it…"

"In the home of a murder victim." She tossed it out there nonchalantly, studying him.

Jeremy's reaction was nonexistent. No emotion registered on his face or came through his body language.

"The man's name was Jimmy Bates." She again observed his body language, and this time Jeremy's shoulders tensed. "Do you know him?"

Jeremy shook his head. "Should I?"

"*Should* you? I'm not sure what you mean by that."

Jeremy's brow was glistening with sweat, his gaze ping-ponging between them. "You think I had something to do with his murder?"

"Should *we*?" Madison countered.

Jeremy swallowed roughly. "I didn't."

Given the warden's physical tells, he seemed guilty of something.

Madison leaned forward, putting her elbows on her knees. "Let me put this out there. That letterhead could have only come from someone working in the prison office. You said so yourself." She paused and he nodded. "Then it has to be someone on staff here. But you don't recognize the handwriting?"

"No. As I said." Jeremy shifted his body in his chair, his gaze darting around the room.

"Would you mind giving us a sample of your handwriting?" Madison began. "You know, just so we can rule you out as communicating with Bates." It was time to flip things and play up being his friend and on his side. They didn't have enough to get a warrant signed for this.

"I don't even know this Jimmy person." Jeremy seemed to speak just to fill the brief silence.

"Then it shouldn't be a big deal." Madison tossed in a smile to throw the man off guard, and he returned it.

He proceeded to pull a piece of paper from the tray of a printer on his desk and held his pen over the page. "What should I write?"

"If you would write out your name and the numbers that are on the letterhead I gave you, that would be perfect." She was plastering on the sweetness awfully thick and realized that maybe she wasn't as horrible an actress as she had thought.

"Sure." Jeremy scrawled something down on the page. "Here you go." He handed her the paper, and he had done just as she'd asked of him.

"Wonderful. Thank you, Mr. Schultz," she said, slapping on more charm.

"You can call me Jeremy." He grinned, obviously getting too comfortable.

"Now, there is one other thing we're going to need your assistance with, *Jeremy*," Madison began. "But this one isn't as much of an option." She presented the warrant for the visitor logs.

"What's this?" he asked timidly.

"We're interested in the visitors logbook," she responded.

"What for?" Arched brows and skepticism.

"We're interested specifically in Jimmy Bates. We need to see if and when he came to your prison, as well as who he came to see."

Jeremy wriggled his fingers for Madison to drop the warrant into his hands, but she didn't sense impatience as much as discomfort. She handed the paperwork to him, and Jeremy read down the page for a while. "I'll get a copy of the logs sent over to the station."

"That works," Madison agreed. "When should we expect them?"

"A few hours?"

"All right." Madison got to her feet. "Thank you for your cooperation."

"Yep, don't mention it." Jeremy waved to the door, and Madison got the distinct impression he was rushing them out of there.

GREG BERGER'S HOUSE WAS LOCATED in a gated community in the south end of Stiles. It was eight o'clock by the time Madison and Terry got there, and a woman in a maid's apron answered the door and let them inside. The foyer was grand with a wrapping staircase and wood floors. She left them to announce their arrival to Greg and returned a few moments later to escort Madison and Terry to a sitting area.

An older man was settled in a wingback chair next to a roaring gas fireplace with a closed book on his lap. He lifted his head when Madison and Terry entered the room.

"Mr. Berger, these are Detectives Madison Knight and Terry Grant," the maid announced.

Greg sat there motionless, his face set in a scowl, and given the depth of the wrinkles around his mouth, it was an expression he wore often. His hair was white and his eyes were a faded blue shadowed by sagging brows. His eyebrows were thick and a dark brown but salted with white hairs. Long ones curled at the edges in desperate need of trimming.

"You may take a seat," the maid said, breaking the quiet in the otherwise silent room, which had been haunted only by the ghostly ticking of a clock.

Madison and Terry sat on a couch that faced Greg, and he dismissed the maid with a wave of his hand. He settled his gaze on Madison. "Why are you here?"

"You might have heard that Jimmy Bates was murdered," Madison responded.

"Yes, I've heard. His father, Rodney, is a dear friend of mine, Detective."

"And Jimmy was one of your employees," she added.

"If you have questions about Jimmy or his work life, it might be best that you speak with my son. He runs the company now."

And how she'd love to speak with his son about a couple of things. Yasmine, for one, and Bates, for another. "Yes, but we understand that your son is away on business this week."

"And surely, he'll be back." A slight sardonic grin. "You can talk to him then."

Madison licked her lips, summoning her patience. "As I mentioned, this is a murder investigation, and—"

"I understand it may be an urgent matter," he said dismissively

"It *may* be?" she ground out, trying to hold back the anger rising inside her. Who did this guy think he was?

"I'm not sure how I can help you." Greg slid his gaze to Terry. "I certainly didn't kill him."

"Do you know who did?" she fired back impulsively.

"I'm not going to dignify that with a response."

"Given your friendship with Rodney, you don't seem too shaken by his son's murder," Madison said.

He shrugged. "I hardly knew the boy."

"But you were close to his father?" Madison served back.

"It was a friendship that grew over the years."

"So you weren't always close?" Terry asked.

Greg looked at Terry. "We went to school together, got our accounting degrees. Then he went his way and I went mine. It's common for people to grow apart after graduation."

"But at some point, you became close again," Terry said. "You described Rodney as a dear friend of yours—in the present tense."

The clock on the wall might as well have been thunder in the otherwise silent room.

Greg shifted his book on his lap.

"When did you reunite?" Madison pressed.

"Forty-five years ago, give or take."

Rodney had been arrested and charged forty-four years ago. It seemed all too coincidental and neat. She had a gut feeling that Greg had taken over, at least in some form, for the Mafia's accounting matters after Rodney was imprisoned. And now, given the letterhead from the prison where Dimitre was serving time, it was really getting hard to dismiss the likelihood that Jimmy Bates had been mixed up with the Russians somehow.

"How did you happen to find each other again?" she asked.

"A conference." His response wasn't charged with any energy, and it had come quickly, almost as if he'd prepared for the question.

She cocked her head. "What kind of conference?"

"For accounting," he deadpanned.

"So you hit it off again? I mean, obviously," Madison said, tossing the words out in a lighter manner. "You ended up bringing Rodney's son, an ex-con, on board with your company without any experience."

"The least I could do. But that wasn't actually me. It was my son's decision."

"Ah." Madison smiled. "But you still pull the strings."

Appeal to his pride and ego.

Greg settled back into his chair, his posture relaxing. "I did found the company."

Madison nodded. "And you ended up paying for Jimmy's schooling. That's very generous. It couldn't have been cheap."

Aggression licked the man's features. "What are you getting at, Detective?"

She fought to the urge to gloat. He'd as good as admitted to being involved with the decision to educate and hire Bates. It made her want to come out and ask him directly if he or his company was working for the mob. But if she did, he'd likely have them shown out and she still needed to ask him about his son, Lyle.

Terry beat her to the next question, though. "What certification did Jimmy end up with?"

"His CPA."

"That's a—" Madison started.

"Certified public accountant," Greg finished, interrupting her. His arrogant tone bespoke that everyone should possess this knowledge.

"So he would have known how to prepare and read financial statements?" Madison tossed out.

"Of course."

"Investments and tax returns?" All these avenues would come in handy for hiding and laundering money.

"Absolutely, but I'm not sure those things were his main focuses within the company," Greg replied.

"Which? Investments or—"

"Both."

"But he was responsible for the preparation and presentation of financial reports to the board of directors?" She wanted clarification.

Gregory cleared his throat. "Listen, I don't know all that my son had the man doing, nor do I have a list of his job description and responsibilities handy. You said you were already down at the firm. I assume you spoke to Sylvester Stein?"

"We did," she said.

"Well, then, I have nothing more to tell you on that." He pursed his lips, and his posture tensed.

"Fair enough," Madison said. But she was still curious why Greg had assumed all the financial responsibility in educating and employing Bates. It wasn't unheard of for companies to assist their employees in getting supplemental education directly related to their jobs, but most didn't pay for college.

"You were good friends with Rodney," Madison began, "but I think there's a lot more to why you helped out his son."

Greg angled his head. "Oh, you do, do you?"

Madison's heart was pounding. In her mind, it was getting harder to dance around the feeling that Greg and Rodney were both connected to the Russian Mafia. Rodney may have just passed his position on to Greg, which may have explained why Rodney's son was given special treatment and leniencies. "I think you might have owed Rodney a favor."

"Me?" Greg's nostrils flared, and his face went bright red. "I do not—and *did not*—owe that man a thing!"

Madison held up a hand in an offering of apology, even if it wasn't sincere. Regardless, it seemed to calm Greg somewhat, and she was thankful because they hadn't even gotten around to talking about Lyle yet. She had a feeling this conversation was on borrowed time, though, so she maneuvered things in that direction. "When was your son's business trip planned?"

Greg looked her in the eye. "How would I know?"

"You aren't close?" Terry jumped in.

"We have our differences like any father and son, but we get along fine." Greg crossed his legs and set his hands on his knee. "I just don't keep track of his schedule or his whereabouts."

"What about his love life?" Madison asked, doing her best to erase the images of Yasmine as she told them about how Lyle had abused his power and taken advantage of her.

"What about it?" Greg asked.

It was taking all her willpower not to blurt out that he'd raped a woman. Instead, she gave a casual shrug. "Do you know if Lyle is seeing anyone?"

A shadow crossed over Greg's face, and his mouth set in a straight line. "Why are you asking so many questions about my son? Do you think he killed Jimmy for some reason? Over a girl, no less?"

"We're just following all our leads," Madison responded.

"Well whoever made you think that my boy was involved in Jimmy's murder should be shot." Given the throbbing vein in the older man's head, Greg's words seemed to carry some sort of promise.

Madison glanced at Terry, then back to Greg. If she started to ask about Lyle's relationship with Yasmine specifically, who knows if it would paint a literal target on her back. "I never said anyone named your son."

Greg stood. "I think it's time for you to leave."

Madison got up and closed the distance between them. "Thank you for your cooperation," she said drily.

Greg was all hard lines when he responded, "You are welcome. Now get out of my house."

Back in the car but still in Greg's driveway, Madison turned to Terry. "That man is hiding something."

"They all are," he moaned.

"Are you being serious with me right now or mocking me?" It was hard to tell sometimes, despite how much time she spent with him.

He met her eyes. "One-hundred-percent serious."

"He's obviously a violent man," she said. "When he thought someone put us on to his son and said they should be shot, I could easily imagine him pulling the trigger."

"Me too. And did you notice that he never showed any signs of grief about Bates being murdered?"

She buckled her seat belt. "Wasn't lost on me, either."

"And he played along for a bit about hiring Jimmy, but when it was put to him that he had done so as a favor *owed* to Rodney..." Terry shook his head.

"He lost it," she finished. The image of the older man turning bright red would be stuck in her mind for a while. She didn't understand why he had reacted so strongly, but she sure as hell was going to find out.

CHAPTER

9

IT WAS NINE AT NIGHT when they left Greg Berger's house, making it the ideal time to follow up on another lead—Club Sophisticated, where Bates had been the night before his death.

Trendy music blasted from inside when Terry held the door open for Madison. There was a good-sized crowd spread out at the bar and the tables. It was definitely a classy place, as Cynthia had said it was, decorated with dark wood and accented with classic touches of white.

Behind the counter was a mirrored wall with three tiers of glass shelves mounted to it, showcasing a vast selection of alcohol. Madison was certain some of those bottles were well beyond her pay grade.

Madison wedged between two men at the bar. Both looked at her, but one huffed and left. Oh well, more room for her. She and Terry held up their badges to an approaching bartender, and his smile faded.

"We'd like to speak with someone about a man

who was here last night around ten thirty." Madison had to shout to be heard over the din. "Do you know who would have been working the bar then?" She was banking on the hope that whoever had tended bar that night would be available now, but if not, she and Terry could always visit them at home.

"I was working," he said sourly. "I'm always working."

"And what's your name?"

"Gary."

Madison pulled up a photo on her phone of Bates and extended it to Gary. "Do you recognize this man?"

Gary leaned across the bar and studied the image, but he didn't say anything.

"Gary?" she nudged.

"Never seen him before." His gaze met hers briefly but flicked away. He swallowed roughly, his Adam's apple bobbing.

She snapped her fingers in front of his face to get his attention back on her. "I think you have."

Gary stood back and crossed his arms. With his closed body language, any suspicion that he was hiding something was confirmed. Maybe if she shocked him, she'd jog his memory. She made sure the screen on her phone hadn't gone black and held it up for Gary.

"This man is dead," she said. "Murdered, actually. Not long after he left here."

The man seated beside Madison turned to face her, but she went on as if she never noticed.

"So if you don't want us—" she gestured to Terry "—to take you downtown for interfering with an investigation, I'd suggest you start talking."

Gary ran a hand over his mouth. "If I started talking to the cops about all the customers we get in here, we wouldn't have any."

"Amen." The man on the stool lifted his glass.

Madison shot the man a glare. Directing her attention back to Gary, she said, "At least you've admitted he was a customer."

"I'm outta here." The nosy patron slapped down a twenty and left.

Gary snatched the bill from the counter. "Wow, thanks for that."

Madison wasn't sure if he'd said it because of a bad tip or because their presence had lost him another customer. It was probably both.

Gary leaned over the counter, closing the space between himself and Madison and Terry. He curled his finger for them to lean in, too. "Yes, I recognize him, okay?" He grabbed a towel from the bar and started wiping in a circular pattern. "You said he was dead?"

"Murdered," she said slowly, gauging his reaction.

His movements stopped but he still held onto the towel. Gary paled and took a deep breath.

"Are you afraid of someone?" Terry asked perceptively.

Gary's eyes snapped to Terry, and he nodded subtly as he straightened back up. "I really shouldn't be talking to you."

Madison considered showing him a photo of Bates in his bed, stabbed multiple times, but rather than jolting Gary to talk, it might make him go silent. She couldn't take that risk. "We're just asking some questions. What you say stays with the three of us." She glanced at Terry briefly and shifted her gaze back to Gary.

"With us? You promise?" Gary's timbre fluctuated.

"Hey! Can I get a beer?" a customer called down the counter.

Gary held up a finger to Madison. "I'll be back in one minute."

Gary spoke to another bartender and motioned for Madison and Terry to follow him. He led them to a back office.

"It's probably best we talk back here," he said.

The music was still loud in the office, but not quite as bad as the main area of the bar. At least they wouldn't need to raise their voices now.

"Was he here alone?" Madison asked, getting the conversation started again.

"No."

The skin prickled at the back of her neck. "Do you know who he was with?"

"You mean, have I seen him before?" Gary asked.

So Bates had been here with a man... Madison nodded in response to Gary.

"No, and he's not exactly the type you'd forget."

Her brow furrowed. "Why's that?"

"The man was huge," Gary said. "Think Dwayne 'the Rock' Johnson huge."

Her heart sped up in her chest as flashbacks danced around the edges of her mind of Constantine's hulking frame hanging over her, of him about to… Sweat dripped down her back, and chills ran through her at the same time. In her peripheral vision, she noticed Terry watching her, but she couldn't speak, not right now. It was like her throat was stitched shut.

"What else do you remember about him?" Terry asked. "His hair color?"

"He had blond hair."

Terry pulled out his phone and extended it toward Gary. "Was this the man?"

Madison caught a glimpse of the image on the screen as it went quickly past her toward Gary. Constantine Romanov.

She studied Gary's reaction. He stepped back and twisted the towel he still held onto.

"Gary?" Madison pressed, finally able to command her mouth to speak.

He was looking straight at her, but his eyes were blank. He glanced at Terry and nodded.

"He was here with—" Terry started.

"The dead man? Yeah," Gary rushed out, interrupting.

The hairs rose on the back of Madison's neck, and shivers laced down her spine. First the letterhead was from the prison where Dimitre was incarcerated, and now Bates had been seen having drinks with Constantine, a known Russian hit man who reported to Dimitre.

"How long were they here?" Madison inquired.

"Long enough to order a drink, but not long enough to savor it. At least that big guy—" Gary pointed toward Terry, referring to the image he had pulled up on his phone "—ordered a vodka and shot it back no sooner than it was delivered to the table."

A skilled bartender had a good memory, but Madison sensed Gary's recollection was suspiciously clearer than most people's would be. "You seem to have paid them a lot of attention," Madison said, calling him out. "Why?"

"Like I said, he was huge."

Madison quirked her eyebrows. "And that's all?"

Gary licked his lips and looked away.

If Gary was aware Bates was connected to the Mafia, it could explain his nervousness, but she wasn't going to come out and ask because he might clam up. "Was Bates a regular here?"

Gary hitched his shoulders. "He came often enough."

"Did the two men get along? Do you know what they were talking about?" Madison was determined to get something more out of Gary.

"Well the two of them didn't exactly look chummy, or even like they should be hanging together. The older guy, the one who was…murdered"—he seemed disgusted by the word—"appeared to be nervous around the bigger guy. And I can't blame him."

Madison was doing all she could to suppress the flashbacks, but in doing so, her temperature was rising and her palms were sweating now.

Terry glanced over at her, shooting her a sympathetic look. "Do you know what they were talking about?" he inquired. She knew he was taking the reins while she pulled herself together.

Gary shook his head. "I couldn't hear their conversation." He pointed toward the ceiling, referring to the pumping speaker system. "I know that the older guy handed the big guy something under the table," he continued. "I couldn't see what it was, but they were both leaning forward. It was obvious something was being passed between them."

"And you're sure it was coming from the older man to the larger one, not the other way around?" Terry asked.

The bartender nodded. "Absolutely certain."

"And you have no idea what it was?" Terry confirmed.

"Nope."

"What about its size? Shape?" her partner tried.

"It's pretty dim in here, and they were sitting at one of the most poorly lit tables. It's not exactly easy to make out details, period, let alone at a table where it's really dark."

"Was the object larger than their hands?" Madison asked, finding her voice again.

Gary pinched the bridge of his nose. "I think so, yeah."

Unfortunately, that could describe a lot of things. At least they could conclude it was unlikely drugs.

First of all, most drugs could be palmed, and second, Constantine wasn't exactly a drug dealer. It could have been money, but what for? Was Bates supposed to hand over something to Constantine but crossed him instead? Hence the torture and murder? Did any of this have to do with that letterhead in Bates's office cubbyhole? The questions were coming to her rapid-fire. It would be nice if the answers came just as quickly.

"When did they make the transfer?" Terry asked.

"Just after ordering their drinks...or at least not long after. If I remember right, they talked for a few minutes first."

Terry nodded and kept the questions rolling. "When did the big man leave?"

"Pretty soon after they passed whatever it was between them." Gary paused. "Listen, I really need to get back to work."

Madison plucked her card from her pocket and handed it to Gary. "If you think of anything else, call me."

Gary tucked the card into his shirt pocket and led Madison and Terry out of the office. He scurried behind the bar and didn't even give them so much as a nod goodbye as they left.

Outside, Madison stopped on the sidewalk in front of the club and looked up at the sky, trying to take even breaths.

Terry walked around in front of her. "We should get you into protective custody."

"As I've said before, that man is *not* going to

control my life."

"But he could take it," Terry snarled.

"He might be back, but he hasn't threatened me," she pointed out.

"That's what you're clinging to?" Terry threw his arms up. "God, you're so stubborn."

"I'm determined to stay on the case and remain objective." Even to her own her ears, it sounded like she lacked conviction, especially in regard to the latter part.

"And how's that going for you so far?" he fired back.

The last thing she'd be doing was admitting to the dread lacing through her bones. Confiding her feelings in other people didn't come naturally to her anyhow. And if she made the exception in this situation, she knew it would blow up in her face. Terry would persuade Winston to pull her from the case and justify it as being for her own safety. She wasn't about to take that risk. No, it was much better to keep some things to herself and her fear was one of them. Instead, she referred back to the details of the interview they'd just conducted. "So Constantine met up with Bates here and they exchanged something, but we don't know what or why."

Terry was shaking his head. "Fine. Let's pretend the Mafia hit man who almost killed you isn't back in town."

"We don't know that he *is*. We know that he *was*."

"You really think he's going to leave without

settling with you?" he hurled out, catapulting her to the memory of a past quarrel they'd had when she'd risked her life on a previous case. He had threatened to get a new partner, and for a time, it seemed like he might have gone through with it. Regardless, she wasn't going to back down.

"You're the one who believes we need to remain objective," she said. "That's all I'm doing here."

Terry stepped back, and Madison's chest expanded for a full breath at his surrender.

"They met for a purpose, obviously," Terry said. "Assuming Constantine killed Bates, I'm having a hard time figuring out motive. I mean, it seems like they were in on something together rather than enemies."

When her partner's eyes met hers, tremors ran through her as a possible explanation took root in her mind. Bates was a skilled accountant, and add to that the letterhead in his cubbyhole, a connection to the Mafia, and eyewitness who saw Bates handing something to Constantine… Was Bates paying him for a job?

Nausea slammed into her.

"What is it?" Terry asked.

She explained how her thoughts were jumbling together. "Now this is just a wild-card theory, but what if Bates was inadvertently paying Constantine for the contract on his own head?"

CHAPTER

10

BACK AT THE STATION, Madison pulled a Hershey's bar out of her desk drawer and tore open the wrapper. She bit off a huge mouthful.

"I understand you're hungry, but chocolate's not a good choice for dinner," Terry chided.

Her stomach was growling as the food was going in, and her body was quaking from hunger. "We passed dinnertime hours ago. Are you sure you really want to mess with me?" She glowered at him and bit off another chunk of the candy bar.

"Maybe not." Terry stepped back and laughed. "Speaking of food, though, I'm hitting up the vending machine."

"And how is that better?" she asked, cocking her eyebrows.

"We should have hit a fast-food joint or something on the way back here."

"Again, is that—"

"Yes, it is," he interrupted. "Most of them offer low-cal menu options."

She rolled her eyes at him, but she was actually on board with the whole eating-a-healthy-meal thing as long as she got some chocolate in first.

Terry walked off in search of food, and she continued to devour the rest of the bar. As the snack started to settle, the gnawing pain of hunger subsided a bit and her focus was coming back. Before the chocolate, it had been getting to the point that all she could think about had been food. Of course, thoughts of Constantine were never too far away.

Her mind mulled over the fact that the man who had almost raped and killed her had been in town just days ago and she'd had no idea. She had just carried on with her life as usual. The possibility that he could sneak up on her at any time didn't sit well with her.

And what business did he have with Bates? Hopefully, they'd find out before too long because once they had that answer, she was certain they'd be one step closer to solving this case. At least Cynthia had messaged saying that the visitor logs from the prison had come in and that they'd be working through them in the morning. She'd also sent bad news, even if it had been expected: she'd had no luck tracking Kevin Jones's phone and surmised it must have been a burner.

Madison yawned, envying her friend calling an end to the work day. For her and Terry, though, it was going to be a long night. The first forty-eight hours of a murder investigation always tested human resilience.

With patience being one characteristic that didn't come naturally to her, waiting on answers was painful. Was Bates connected to Dimitre? Madison would say that seemed likely. If Bates wasn't tied up with the Mafia, what reason could he have had to meet with Constantine and exchange whatever it was they had? Another question that begged to be answered was what had made Dimitre order the hit, assuming he had, that was.

Terry returned with a bag of chips and sat at his desk across from her. "I think we should update Winston on what we found out at the club." He popped a few chips into his mouth.

"No. We talked about this in the car." She refused to give over to paranoia. And, yes, the concept of better safe than sorry worked great in theory, but if she jumped the gun, she could be the butt of jokes around the department. They could place Constantine in Stiles last night, not currently.

Terry pressed his lips into a thin line, but he didn't argue.

"We'll start by pulling detailed backgrounds on Rodney Bates and Greg Berger and see how their lives intersected," she said. "Also, if we can confirm that what they're telling us is the truth, we should pull the information on the board members from Berger & Stein Accounting. We don't have enough to get their client list yet, but it's a start."

"Okay. I'll get Rodney's info, you get Greg's?"

"Works for me." She brought up the database

on her computer, but halfway through typing in Greg's name, she stopped. "I'm not sure if I said this out loud, but I really think that Greg took over for Rodney, and then Jimmy was brought onboard when he got out of prison."

"But Jimmy got out five years after his father." Terry scrunched up the empty chip bag and put it in the garbage bin under his desk. "Why didn't Rodney just pick up where he left off?"

"For one, he would have lost his license, and two, we'd be on to him. They needed someone else."

"So they've been grooming Jimmy?" Terry sounded skeptical. "Why not Greg's son, Lyle?"

"Maybe he didn't want to get Lyle involved in that scene."

"But he kept the business involved?" Terry shook his head. "I don't know..." He threw his hands in the air. "The questions in this case just keep on coming."

"Yeah. I just wish the answers would start coming with them." She turned back to her monitor and finished typing in Greg's name. She'd do a simple background search first and expand from there. She'd dig into his life and find out when he started his company. "When was Berger & Stein founded?"

"You're the one pulling Greg's info," Terry responded.

She looked over at him. She hadn't even realized that she'd said the question out loud.

"What are you thinking?" he asked.

"I'm wondering if Greg Berger started the company around the time that Rodney reentered

his life or if he had already been a business owner."
Madison watched as the implication of the question
sank into her partner's eyes.

"Because the company itself could have been set
up as a business front for the mob's accounting…"

She nodded, brought up another search screen,
and got her answer. "Berger & Stein went into
business one year before Rodney went to prison."

"It could be a coincidence."

She cocked her head to the right.

"Fine," he conceded, "it *might* be. The Russians
would have known that Rodney was going down at
that point, too."

"Uh-huh, and they could have set up Greg with
the accounting firm to keep the money moving."
With that, the labor the case required magnified.
Even if this had nothing to do with why Bates was
murdered, Berger & Stein Accounting still needed
to be investigated—or at least checked out—and
that included their board members and investors.
"We're going to need more help."

CHAPTER

11

CONSTANTINE GRABS HER BY THE HAIR, his fingernails digging into her scalp, and he pulls her into the living room.

A cry escapes her throat, and her body arches backward as she tries to keep pace with him. He tosses her onto the couch as if she weighs nothing. For the first time, Madison has a real sense of the man's size and strength. He is a giant among men.

"You stick your nose where it doesn't belong," he says, coming at her with the agility of a linebacker.

"You're not going to get away with this." She lifts her arms to cover her face, and he lowers himself over her. His massive body swallows her, seemingly without effort. She struggles beneath him and feels her power ebb as waves of defeat pulse through her. But she can't give in. This is a fight for her life.

He holds up the gun, pointing it at her. "Do you want it quick, or nice and slow?"

Her head is pounding from the way he pulled on her hair, and it's hard to think clearly. She considers *jerking her knee up swiftly, but it would only send him jutting forward toward her. She'd also be risking him firing the gun in the process.*

"We have time before you go out. You want a goodbye present?" His face lights into a sneer. He runs his tongue from her chin to the side of her eye. "You have never had it so good, bitch." He leans back and places his gun on the coffee table her grandmother gave her.

At this moment, with her life flashing before her yet again, she remembers something her grandmother had told her once. "Madison, we're better than men in three ways. We've got the looks, the brains, and the ability to see things through."

He begins unlatching his belt.

Madison's focus keeps drifting to the table and the gun he had forfeited in a rush to pleasure himself— and violate her—but she can't be caught looking at it.

Maybe if she plays along, he'll lose interest. Willingness often does that to people like him.

"You are a big man," she says.

"Don't worry. It will only hurt a little bit." He laughs, and she feels him hardening against her.

She can't go out like this. She won't. She refuses.

She reaches out and touches his chest.

His head is still angled down as he works on his belt buckle, but he raises his eyes to look at her. He grips her hand and squeezes it so hard it feels like her wrist is going to snap.

"Please, I just want to see all of you." Bile rises in her throat at the words, but she forces herself to

swallow it. "I love a man's chest."

He stops moving. "You are into this now?"

Seconds pass. She wishes she could read his thoughts, but her mind is only on one thing—survival. "Please. Just let me see you."

"You first, sweetheart," he says with a smirk.

He puts his hands on her lower abdomen, and she almost reaches for the gun, but it would be premature. It isn't time. Yet.

He finds the hem of her shirt and rips the material up her torso until she's lying there exposed, her breasts covered by only her bra now.

Her stomach tosses, but she keeps calling on what her grandmother had taught her. She will prevail. She will endure. She will survive.

His hands wrap around her and unclasp her bra. "I should just strangle you with this."

She needs to detach from what is happening, to place herself out-of-body. She closes her eyes briefly. When she opens them, she does her best to act seductive.

"Now show me yours," she purrs.

He sits back and lifts his shirt over his head.

She has a second, at most. She shifts toward the table and grabs the gun. She pulls the trigger, and the bullet burrows into his left shoulder.

Constantine drops his arms. His shirt is left bunched up beneath his armpits, and his crimson blood pulses from the wound, spreading across his chest.

Madison screamed and bolted upright, heaving for oxygen in short, choppy breaths.

"Maddy?" Troy rolled over, reached out for her, and pulled her close. "It was just a bad dream, baby."

But it hadn't just been a dream. No, it had actually happened.

Tears fell down her cheeks, and she wanted to burrow under the blankets, find safety in her own bed, but that security had been robbed from her.

Troy peered into her eyes. "Do you want to talk about it?"

She didn't, not really, but her shrink had told her that the more attention flashbacks were given, the sooner they'd fade into obscurity. And she had thought they mostly had. What she hadn't shared with Troy was that she'd had the odd dream about her brush with death ever since Barry had died. The memories would resurface and images would spark in her mind, but they hadn't struck as a full-fledged flashback like this in a long time. She threaded her fingers in Troy's blond hair.

"I'm on a case right now…" A weak start, but that's all she could get herself to say.

Troy's brow pinched in confusion. She looked away from him at the sound of her chocolate lab, Hershey, padding over. He rested his head on the edge of the mattress, his eyes on her. She petted him, soaking up enough comfort to take a deep breath.

"I think Constantine is back." The words came out without her thinking them through, and she wished she could shove them back in.

"He's what?" Troy sat up. "What do you mean you think he's back?"

Even in the limited light of the room, she could see concern in his knotted brow and the set of his mouth.

"The victim was Jimmy Bates." She put his name out there and watched as his identity sank in.

"The man who killed your grandfather?"

She nodded.

"You really think that Constantine's back, though?" he asked. "He's in the system. If he came back to the United States, we'd know about it."

She didn't say anything, just held eye contact.

Troy sighed. "Right. He's got connections."

They sat there in silence. She couldn't bring herself to tell him what she had learned at Club Sophisticated, how a witness had placed Constantine in town a couple of nights ago. He could, after all, be anywhere in the world by now. If he was coming for her, surely she'd have heard from him already. She took a few steadying breaths.

Troy was still peering into her eyes, and she feared he would be able to read her mind. She could either wither back inside herself, burying herself beneath platitudes that her imagination was overreacting, or she could be honest with the man she loved about everything she knew. But Troy was all about running on facts and logic. If she told him about Constantine being spotted, he'd insist she remove herself from the case.

"Why do you think Constantine killed Bates?" She detected judgment and skepticism, but his laid-back facial expression said that wasn't his intention, telling her those implications were all in her mind.

"He was stabbed multiple times, like a former victim of Constantine's," she started, laying a foundation for him. "And Bates's father was the numbers man for the Russians before he went to prison."

"Yes, I remember that," he replied.

"Well…" Her heart raced as she tried to decide if she should tell him everything. His staring was insistent, waiting for her to go on. She could share *some* things with him and hold back the eyewitness. But given the way he was watching her, she had to say something.

She suddenly became aware of her damp cheeks and how intensely the nightmare had affected her. A great sense of vulnerability washed over her.

"What aren't you telling me?" he asked.

Her brief hesitation communicated the answer—*a lot*.

"I'm here for you. You know that, right?" His eyes were liquid emeralds, piercing hers with intensity.

"I know." She let the two words out on a staggered exhale. The longer she held his gaze, the more her defenses melted away. And as secure as she felt next to him and as soothed as she was by the logical platitudes she kept feeding herself, one truth remained. "I'm afraid," she admitted out loud.

Her confession ran over his features as shadows cast across his face, and his jaw tightened. He reached for her and pulled her closer. He leaned his forehead against hers. "Everything will be all right."

As much as she wanted to surrender to his words, to believe them, he couldn't guarantee anything. She drew away from him. "You don't know that."

"If I have anything to say about it, you will be." Rage danced across his face. "Have you told Winston all this? About your suspicion that Constantine is back in town?"

She shook her head.

Troy's gaze was drilling through her now, and she knew she had to tell him more. But to admit Terry suspected Constantine's involvement in the murder would only amp up Troy's concern, as would telling him about the eyewitness who saw Constantine. She shared the rest with him, though.

"Huh," Troy said when she was done. He got up from the bed, raking a hand through his hair, and started pacing along the foot of the bed.

Was he mad at her? At the situation? Not mad at all? Just worried?

He stopped and stared at her. "When did the flashbacks start up again?"

She bit her bottom lip. "I haven't been doing well ever since we lost Barry."

"So that's when they came back?"

She lifted her shoulders. "More or less. It started out with quick flashes of images. I'm just more aware of my mortality, I guess. And then how close I came to dying…" She swallowed roughly. "I thought the flashbacks were behind me for good. They'd stopped for a while."

"Have you been having other nightmares like the

one you just had?" He was cross now, as if he could have prevented her suffering somehow.

With the intensity of his emotion, she best be forthcoming. "I've had memories come up, images, but nothing as severe as this nightmare. Not in months."

He held her in his steady gaze.

"I'm telling you the truth," she said.

"I want you to go see your shrink lady first thing this morning."

She glanced at the clock on Troy's dresser. *7:05 AM*.

"You mean Dr. Connor."

"Whatever her name is. That isn't important. Talk to her about all that you've been feeling and experiencing. She's helped you so much already."

A part of her hesitated to admit it, but he was right. She'd come to see value in talking about her feelings to an objective thirty party and had kept going to the woman even after the mandated period was over.

And ever since Barry's murder had been solved, she had a standing biweekly appointment. This was supposed to be her week off.

"I want you to see her first thing this morning," he repeated.

"But—"

He walked over, sat on the bed next to her, and pressed a finger to her lips. "No buts. Take care of you first and the job second."

"Sometimes it's hard to distinguish between the

two."

He nodded. "I know, but if you don't take care of yourself, then you're not good for the job." He stared at her, waiting for his point to sink in.

"Fine. I'll be at her office the moment it opens."

"Good girl." Troy smiled, something he rarely did.

"Don't gloat." She shook her head and smirked. "It's not nice."

He laughed, but it was brief. "And after you meet with Dr. Connor, you're going to come clean to Winston about your suspicions about Constantine. We should probably bring Andrea in, too. It might be best if you took yourself off the case."

"No. Not happening." She shook her head adamantly. "And why do we need to bring the police chief in on this?"

"First of all, she's my sister. Second, as chief, she has the right to know if one of her detectives thinks a Russian hit man is back in town, don't you think?"

"Fine." The concession tasted bitter.

"And I'll be there with you. It's nonnegotiable."

"What? Why?" Had she lost all her independence since committing to this relationship? "Isn't it your day off?"

"I'll be there," he replied firmly.

"I'm not going to meet with anyone until I check in with Richards this afternoon at two to see how he made out with the autopsy. I'd rather have more proof about Constantine's involvement before making it a thing." She had the right to make some stipulations of her own.

"So this afternoon?" Troy drew in a deep breath. "God knows, I'm a patient man," he teased, implying that it was hard to put up with her. He'd be right, though. Even she knew she wasn't an easy person to deal with sometimes. She was as stubborn as they came. "I'll give you until three o'clock," he said. "And hey, I know I'm the last person to get worked up about pretty much anything, even less so when there's no concrete proof, but you need to watch your back, Maddy, just in case you're right about Constantine being back."

Her stomach knotted with her lie by omission. Constantine's being back wasn't a case of if she was right; it was a matter of if the man was still in town. Maybe if she shrugged off the serious undertone with deflection…

"*In case* I'm right?" She narrowed her eyes at him.

"I shouldn't even let you out of my sight for the next while. I should just have you removed from the case. I do have some pull, you know."

"Huh, but you know if you did either of those things, I'd—"

"You'd what, Knight? What would you do?" He grabbed her side and started tickling her.

She was laughing and pawing at him to stop, but she had no real desire to turn this man's love and affection away. She leaned toward him and kissed his mouth as he cupped her head, his fingers in her hair. She moaned, and with that, he lowered her back onto the bed and they made love.

CHAPTER

12

"MADISON, PLEASE TAKE A SEAT." Dr. Tabitha Connor gestured to the couch from where she was sitting in an egg-shaped chair, a notepad on her lap, and a pen in her hand, poised over the paper. She was watching Madison, but there was no judgment in her gaze or even a trace of irritation over the fact that Madison had been standing outside her office before it opened.

"Thank you so much for agreeing to see me now." Madison sat down, grabbed one of Dr. Connor's many throw pillows, and hugged it to herself. "I had quite a graphic dream—nightmare, actually—about Constantine last night."

"Why don't you tell me about it?" Dr. Connor extended the invitation in a warm and charming manner that encouraged Madison to talk. For a woman in her midsixties, Madison saw her more as a friend than a mother figure. If she had made Madison view her as the latter, Madison would never have been able to open up. Chalk that up to a troubled relationship with her mother, but that discussion would require another session, if not several.

Madison shared the details of the dream. "It felt so real. It was like I was living it all over again. I haven't had something hit me so hard or so clearly in a while."

"Traumatic memories have a way of resurfacing periodically. The mind, while strong, is also delicate, and a person can only process so much at a time emotionally." Dr. Connor settled back into her chair. "You have made remarkable progress, but you should still expect some flashbacks to occur, as they have been recently."

"Watered-down ones until now, really. Flashes of images. I've been able to pull myself out and stop them before they've become debilitating." When the flashbacks first started, they'd made her react much the same way as she'd woken up this morning—in a heap of sweat, panting for breath, with her vision pinpricked. When they struck during waking hours, they had been impossible to hide from anyone around her.

"Maybe instead of suppressing these images," Dr. Connor began, "let yourself experience and be with them as we've discussed."

Madison nodded. Dr. Connor knew everything that Madison had been through with the Russians and had helped her to get her flashbacks under control through a method called EMDR, or eye movement desensitization and reprocessing. It helped her process the emotional tie to her stressful memories and provided a way for her to break them apart and diminish their effect on her. It involved journaling and "being with" her feelings. But it was one thing to let the thoughts drift in and out, and another—a much more painful thing—to sit with them, to put them on paper. She'd always convinced herself she didn't need to do these things, that it was something other people needed to do to heal and move forward, but not her. She'd justified herself by saying that she didn't have the luxury of wallowing in the haunting memories or sitting around journaling. After all, her job required her full attention and most of her time.

"You have been through a lot lately—the loss of your friend, taking a big step forward with Troy by moving in." Dr. Connor gave her a gentle smile. "Those are huge life changes."

Madison let her gaze drift past Dr. Connor.

"What do you think it was that triggered your nightmare?" Dr. Connor rested her hand on her notepad, and despite Madison having inserted herself into the doctor's day, she was being patient and accommodating. She was as professional as if Madison had booked an actual appointment.

"There's an investigation that started yesterday…"

"Madison?" Dr. Connor prompted gently. "I sense that you're drifting on me a bit."

Madison met the doctor's eyes. "The man who was murdered is the man who killed my grandfather."

Dr. Connor didn't say anything. She was a

specialist at utilizing the power of silence.

Sweat trickled down Madison's back. "When I saw the body, I didn't feel what I normally do. In fact, I felt nothing. No remorse that he was dead, no empathy for him at all." Madison would prefer Dr. Connor's approval, but the doctor was stoic and just perched on her chair, clinging to everything Madison said. "Usually, I struggle with detaching myself from murder victims, but with him…" What she was thinking was almost too harsh to verbalize. But keeping it to herself was slowly eating her alive.

"With him, what, Madison?"

Madison's heart was racing just thinking about verbalizing her feelings in this regard. As if it would somehow confirm she was a bad person. "I…I felt like he got what he deserved."

"It's only natural to feel that way in a situation like this."

"It's natural to be fine with someone being violently murdered?" Madison snapped.

Dr. Connor gave no impression Madison's outburst had even reached her ears. "Did you know your grandfather well?"

Madison shook her head. "He was gone before I was born. Actually, it was because of Bates, the murder victim, that I never met my grandfather."

"I see."

The back of Madison's neck tightened. Two words that said nothing—*I see*. See what exactly? Was there judgment now? Speculation? Was Dr. Connor wondering if Madison was suited to her job anymore?

"I will still find justice for the man." Madison had intended to speak with conviction, but her words fell flat. "Get answers."

"Get answers?" Dr. Connor cocked her head. "About what specifically?"

"Who killed him, of course."

"I sense that you might already have a suspect in mind."

Sometimes the way Dr. Connor would read her mind made Madison think the woman was clairvoyant.

Madison swallowed roughly. "I think Constantine murdered Bates."

Dr. Connor wrote something in her notepad. Madison always found it disconcerting when that happened and tried to figure out what her doctor was thinking. Had Dr. Connor had a revelation as to what prompted the nightmare? Madison couldn't help but analyze what she'd said, and she did so from as detached a perspective as she could manage. Her best guess was that it had something to do with Bates's murder and her suspicions that Constantine was behind it.

Madison cleared her throat and went on. "I thought I was going crazy or being paranoid when I saw his body and thought Constantine was his killer, but the evidence—" She stopped. If she came clean about the eyewitness account, she risked Dr. Connor taking action. Patient confidentiality could be waived when lives were believed to be in danger.

Dr. Connor's expression became one of concern. "Then it is possible he's back?"

"*Possible* as in *hypothetical*, yes." Admitting it out loud caused all Madison's self-talk to wash away. It was as if all the speeches she'd given herself since last night to dispel her fears about Constantine still being in town had never happened. Tremors ran through her, and she closed her eyes for a second.

"You should get protection, Madison."

Madison nodded, suddenly feeling cold. "I'm going to discuss my suspicions with Sergeant Winston today."

"You haven't already?" For the first time today, Dr. Connor revealed an emotion—surprise.

Madison shook her head. "Not yet."

"I see." Dr. Connor was flicking her pen, albeit slowly.

There was that damn *I see* again…

"What?" Madison asked.

"You're censoring and suppressing your gut instincts. Why?"

"I just thought I was dragging Constantine into the murder because of my recent episodes…the images. I thought I was being paranoid and seeing what wasn't there."

"Maybe you were afraid that you were right. And if you're right, that means your power and control are being threatened."

Madison scoffed. "What control?"

"Exactly." Dr. Connor smiled. "Control is, at best, an illusion, and it's a lesson most of us must relearn again and again throughout our lives. Control is something we convince ourselves we need to ease our minds, to assign rationale to things that are not going the way we'd like. With the recent loss of your friend, you've been reminded that sometimes things happen whether you want them to or not."

"Don't I know it," Madison stated sourly.

"You can't fix every situation, just as you can't control everything."

Despite the gentleness of the doctor's words, Madison's eyes snapped to Dr. Connor's. "I know that."

Dr. Connor relaxed her demeanor further, no doubt to prompt Madison to turn inward and gauge how she really felt. She'd told Madison on many occasions that honesty with one's self was also integral to healing and moving forward.

So what if she wanted to fix the situation? Reverse time? Wasn't that a perfectly normal reaction when you lost someone?

"Who wouldn't want to change something like that?" Madison had to stop and breathe as emotion washed over her. "Barry left behind three daughters, a wife who loved him, friends."

"Horrible, for certain. And heartbreaking." Dr. Connor managed a sympathetic stance without sounding condescending.

A tear fell down Madison's cheek, and she let the wet streak sit there. Maybe she held back her emotions too often, embarrassed by them, denying them their existence.

"I think about him and his family most days." The confession ripped from her throat.

"That is completely understandable." Dr. Connor angled her head slightly to the right. "And how do you feel when you think about them?"

"Sad," Madison ground out, but guilt quickly snaked in. What right did she have to grieve when his family had to carry on without him? They had more of a right to feel his loss than she did. Her role was to be strong for them, to be there if they needed anything. "I do remember some good times."

"Of course, you would." Dr. Connor's agreeable tone encouraged Madison to elaborate.

"Troy and I went over for a barbecue this one time and…" Madison's insides were a tangled mess, carrying sadness yet a lightness that came with nostalgia. "Well, Barry had gone on for days about how he was going to cook us this amazing roast chicken on the rotisserie, but it came out so dry." She found that she was smiling. "There wasn't enough water to wash it down. We ended up ordering pizza."

Dr. Connor's smile was sincere, touching her eyes and crinkling the skin around them. "I have been there myself."

Madison's grief rooted deeper down. Her mouth went pasty, her cheeks flushed, and her stomach curdled. "Why is all this coming up today? I didn't come here to talk about Barry. Is it just a matter of me feeling like I've lost control?"

"As we've touched on in recent sessions, you're likely feeling your mortality more these days. It started with Barry's death—"

"Murder," Madison corrected and then looked away from Dr. Connor, sorry that she had interrupted her.

"And," Dr. Connor continued, "now you believe that the man who almost raped and killed you is back in town. Those are more than enough emotional triggers to have flashbacks resurfacing with such intensity." Dr. Connor crossed her legs at the ankles. "I recommend that you take some time off—after you take the necessary precautions in case he *is* back—and just allow yourself to be with your feelings and practice the EMDR method we've discussed. And trust your instincts, Madison. They're there for a reason."

TRUST MY INSTINCTS…

Madison replayed Dr. Connor's advice in her head on the way to her car. It was funny because usually she never had a problem doing just that. If anything, she was driven by instincts more than facts. She had a way of going all-in before she had all the evidence in place, and it had served her well as a cop, even if it occasionally gave Terry heartburn and made him fear being fired.

As these thoughts went through her mind, she mildly chastised herself for doubting what was coming up for her now. And hadn't her instincts been right about Bates having a connection to the Russians? That was almost as good as proven just by him keeping company with Constantine.

As she walked to her car, the air was cold and bitter. Snow was in the forecast, and she hugged her coat to herself. Goose bumps formed on her flesh, but it wasn't from the chill. Something was tucked under one of her wiper blades. It could just be a flyer of some kind, but her instincts were firing off warning signals in rapid succession. As she got closer, she saw it was an envelope. She plucked it off the windshield and read the outside: *Detective Madison Knight*.

Shivers sliced through her body, and her breathing quickened.

Did she really want to open this? What if it somehow confirmed all her paranoia as fact, that Constantine was in town and she had his attention?

Swallowing hard, she slipped a finger under the unsealed lip of the envelope, pulled out a tri-folded piece of paper, and read it:

> *Were you missing me? No need to any longer. I'm back, and I have my eye on you and yours.*
> *C*

She dropped the letter and braced herself against the hood of the car. Her head was spinning and her heart hammering. She felt all the blood drain from her face as dread washed over her, weighing her down to the concrete.

This couldn't be happening. She'd become complacent, lulling herself into a false sense of security by hiding behind words and faulty logic. And for Constantine to have left this here, he would have been here in the last *hour*. That meant he must have been following her. And the parking lot was aboveground with automated gates... He had been brazen enough to expose himself in the light of day.

She spun around, frantically studying her surroundings, but she saw no one. Her gut knotted and breathing was becoming increasingly difficult. It was clear he had every intention of following through with his threat. She looked down at the piece of paper that lay on the ground at her feet and went to pick it up. She found herself hesitating, as if it were a serpent that would bite her hand. Any hope that Constantine was long gone disintegrated, because the truth was, Constantine was still in town and he was coming for her. And, from the sound of it, her loved ones.

CHAPTER

13

THIS WAS REALLY HAPPENING. Constantine was back for her and her family. Her first thought went to Troy but was followed quickly with images of her sister and her nieces. Her parents lived in Florida and should at least be safely out of his reach, but the rest of them? She fumbled as she tried to get her phone out of her coat pocket.

God, who should she call first? She needed to make sure everyone was safe—right now. Maybe if she called Troy and then the station, she could have officers go by her sister's, to her nieces' school and the youngest one's daycare, to her brother-in-law's office, and after that, she could make a call to the local Florida cops to check in on her parents, just in case.

She pressed the speed dial for Troy and let her gaze continue to skitter over the parking lot for any sign of Constantine. She was too exposed and vulnerable standing there, and tremors shot through her. But if he was just going to pull a trigger, why the taunting note? She had a horrible feeling a single bullet wouldn't inflict enough torture for Constantine's liking.

Troy's phone continued ringing in her ear.

"Pick up!" she cried out.

Two women were walking toward her with quizzical expressions on their faces. Madison made eye contact with one of them.

"Are you okay?" the woman asked.

Madison bit down on her bottom lip and ran a hand through her hair. She nodded. "I'll be fine. Thanks."

The one who'd asked how she was shrugged and bugged out her eyes at her friend as if Madison was crazy. They kept walking toward a sedan parked two down from Madison's Mazda and got in.

"You've reached the voice mail of—"

Madison hung up, gripping her phone tightly. Why wasn't he answering?

Troy had the day off. He was planning to go into the station later for her meeting with Winston and the police chief, but otherwise, he could be anywhere. If Constantine knew where to find her this morning, he'd likely tailed her from Troy's house.

She got into her car and tugged on her seat belt.

Maybe Troy was just busy, or his phone was on mute, or...

She tried him again, and it rang to voice mail once more.

This time she left a message. "Troy, it's me. Call

me back the second you get this," she rushed out. "Constantine's back."

She ended the call and thrust the key into the ignition, ready to tear out of the lot, but there was one more number she could try to reach him. It was primarily reserved for his boss in case a call came in requiring Troy's SWAT team since he was on call 24-7, even on his days off.

She tried that number. It went to voice mail, too.

She pressed her phone to her forehead.

Please don't tell me he's...

Madison put the car into gear, and her phone rang. She answered quickly. "Troy?"

"You got the *T* part right, but this is—"

"Terry, something's happened," she blurted out, panic shredding her insides. She pushed the button on the kiosk to lift the barricade at the parking lot's exit.

"What is it?" Terry sounded nauseated, as if he'd already been struck with bad news. "Are you all right? Where are you?"

"I'm fine, but—" She checked her mirrors. Constantine could be watching her right now.

"Maddy?" Terry prompted. "You're scaring me."

She pulled out onto the street. "Constantine's back." She swallowed the mouthful of bile that had risen in her throat. The sour taste hit her tongue, but it was nothing compared to the unsettled and knotted ball in the pit of her stomach, nor the one in her chest. What if he had... No, she couldn't even finish the thought. She just had to get to Troy. She floored it through a yellow light.

"How do you know he's still—"

"He left me a note."

"What? Where are you? I'm coming."

"No, Terry. I need you to get officers to go by my sister's house and check in on her. My nieces' school and daycare, my brother-in-law's office, too. Also my parents in Florida… Please call the locals."

Screw worrying about acting prematurely. She had reasons to take precautions. She added, "He probably has no idea where they are, but…" Ideally, Madison would be able to call her sister first and have her reach out to their parents, but she had to get to Troy right this instant. Then it hit her. If Constantine's threat included those she loved, that could also include Terry and his wife and baby daughter. "You should probably get officers to watch over Annabelle and Danielle, as well."

"What did the note say?" Terry's voice was strained, as if his vocal chords were tight.

Her heart was aching, and her mouth was salivating. It was one thing when it was her life in danger, but what had she done to bring this vendetta on her family?

"Maddy?" Terry prompted.

She merged over to the next lane. "He threatened me and those I love."

"I'll get officers dispatched right away."

"And Cynthia. Make sure she's okay, too. Please." She paused, drawing in a few deep breaths. "I can't reach Troy. I need to make sure he's all right."

"You tried his on-call phone?"

"Yeah, no answer. It just rings to voice mail." Fear and hysteria were churning her insides. She should have listened to her instincts from the beginning. From the moment she first saw Bates lying dead in his bed. But she hadn't thought he'd involve her loved ones. If anything happened to any of them, she'd never forgive herself.

Another driver laid on their horn.

"Are you driving?" Terry asked.

"Yeah. I'm on speaker," she added offhandedly. "It's Troy's day off. I'm going to try the house first."

"I'll get backup to meet you there."

"Please do."

"Be safe."

"I will." She clicked off. The world was passing around her in blurs as she drove. She wished for the lights and sirens of the department car and cursed that she was in her personal vehicle.

Still, she made it in record time. There was no sign of backup, but she wasn't going to wait. Troy's Ford Expedition was in the driveway, so why wasn't he answering his phone?

She parked and ran to the front door. She slipped her key in and realized it was unlocked.

Breathe... He doesn't always lock the door.

The thought did little good to calm her down, though, and she drew her gun. She breezed through the entry and the living room.

"Troy!"

She put her head through the kitchen doorway.

The room was empty.

Shit! Shit! Shit!

"Troy!"

And where was Hershey?

She headed down the hallway to the bedroom. The door was closed.

She put her ear against it and listened, but didn't hear anything coming from inside. There was only one way to find out what was behind the door, and that was to open it. Her hand froze on the doorknob as horrible images conjured by her imagination paraded through her mind.

"You can do this," she told herself.

She turned the knob slowly and pushed on the door. Light filtered into the room from the hall behind her and around the curtains.

Hershey got up from where he had been lying and greeted her with a wagging tail, but her attention quickly went to the bed. Someone was under the blankets.

"Troy!" she cried out.

"What?" he shouted as he bolted upright. His chest and shoulders were heaving. "Maddy? What the hell?"

She jumped onto the bed and threw her arms around him. She kissed his lips and nuzzled into his neck, pecking him there. She pulled back and peered into his eyes. "Thank God, you're okay."

"I *was*, anyway. You almost gave me a heart attack." He put one hand on her arm and cupped her cheek with the other. "What's going on?"

Troy seemed to be trying to read her mind the way he always did, and in that moment, his eyes reflected her own insecurities and vulnerability.

"Why weren't you answering your phones?" she asked.

"I was sleeping, and no work calls today. The other SWAT team's on call."

"But you still have it on just in case of an emergency, don't you?"

"Madison, what is this about?"

"Why are you sleeping?" she fired back, overriding his question.

"It's my day off," he started, sounding annoyed, "and I like to get a few extra hours sometimes." He paused. "Tell me what's going on." His tone was no-nonsense now, but then she remembered the backup Terry had called.

"Just give me a minute." She rushed from the room and looked out the front window. Two cruisers, three officers. Two of them were coming toward the door—Gardener and his trainee. She saved them the trouble of knocking and opened the door. "False alarm."

"Everything's okay, Detective?" Gardener asked, leery and cautious. Madison appreciated why the officer would react that way. It could be that Madison and Troy were being coerced to act a certain way so the cops would leave.

She smiled and nodded. "It will be."

"All right, then." Gardener and his trainee turned around and left.

Madison closed and dead-bolted the front door and spun to head back to the bedroom, but she ran smack into Troy.

"Oh—" She tilted backward but quickly regained her balance. "What the—"

"You really need to start talking to me." His words were rushed and punchier than before.

Hershey was playing referee wedged between them, and when Madison looked down, the dog was looking back up at her and wagging his tail.

Troy tugged on her arm, and she met his gaze. She didn't say anything as she slipped a hand into her coat pocket where she'd shoved the letter and envelope. Her hand wrapped around the former, but she hesitated to pull it out. In the past, she'd handled situations by herself, tamped down her feelings, and managed. But life was supposed to be more than managing or getting by, and it wasn't just her life in danger now. She closed her eyes, took out the letter, and handed it to him.

"What's this?" he asked hesitantly, like a man who hated surprises.

She swallowed hard. "Read it."

He unfolded the paper. She turned her back to him, as if not watching him read it meant it didn't exist.

Hershey got in front of her and sat at her feet. His head was still bent and looking up at her. His tail was wagging—all unconditional love and innocence. What was it like to be a dog with no worries in the world? Cared for and loved just for being cute and cuddly? No Mafia out to—

Constantine is holding Hershey under his right arm. "We've been waiting for you. Why don't you put the gun down?" He places his hands on both sides of the dog's head, staring down into his eyes. "Cute dog you have here. But I've never seen the purpose of dogs. They are so vulnerable. It would only take one twist and your little hush puppy would be in doggie heaven."

"You sick son of a bitch! I'll kill you myself, I swear it."

"Weapon down and out of reach. Now." He pulls a gun and holds it to Hershey's head.

"Maddy?" Her name sounded like it came from far away.

"Maddy?" Louder this time.

She felt a hand touch her shoulder, and she jumped.

"A flashback?" Troy's question was filled with empathy but had been sparked by fire. It was his own inner turmoil she was well familiar with: as much as he loved her, it made him angry to see her hurting. She couldn't bring herself to nod. Her body was paralyzed despite its trembling. She tried to take a long, solid inhale, but she'd have to settle for small, choppy breaths.

"Do you want to tell me about it?" He must have sensed her unspoken answer, obviously benching any curiosity and concern he had about the letter.

Even Hershey isn't safe…

Madison shook her head and licked her lips. "It

doesn't matter. I'll be fine."

"It *does* matter." He waved the letter in the air. "Where did you get this? This is the only time I'm asking."

"It was under my windshield wiper when I came out of my doctor's appointment."

"So he's been following you?" She could see his pulse tapping in his cheek.

"He has to be." She swallowed back the urge to cry, trying to ignore the burning of unshed tears and the lump in her throat. "And he threatened my loved ones. When I couldn't reach you…"

"Come here." Troy opened his arms and drew her to him.

She fell into the embrace, leaning her head on his shoulder, and she soaked in the security that came from being in his arms. She allowed herself to languish there. That was, until Hershey started butting his head against her thigh insistently. She pulled back from Troy and patted Hershey on the head, then got down on her haunches and cupped his face, her fingers rubbing behind his ears. She pressed her forehead to his.

"I want you off this case," Troy said.

She glowered at him. "I told you this morning—"

His jaw clenched, and his body went rigid. His green eyes were now chiseled emeralds. "Things have changed. You need to take yourself off this case and get twenty-four-hour protection. Even take a few days off, or a week, or more."

"I'm not going to hide," she fired back. "That's

what he wants."

"So you'd rather get killed?" he served back with heat, but his words chilled her.

"Of course not," she spat.

"Then I don't see a choice." He took off toward the bedroom.

"Are all my loved ones supposed to hole up, too?"

Troy came back to her. "If that's what it takes? Yeah." He stomped away again.

What was she supposed to say to him? He was right. About all of it. But she just couldn't bring herself to back down, no matter how severe the threats. She had a hard time believing that removing herself from the investigation would really do anything for her welfare.

The sound of slamming dresser drawers came from down the hall, and a couple of minutes later, Troy emerged fully dressed. "We'll drop the letter off to the lab. See if they can pull any prints."

Madison was shaking her head. "He's a professional. He's not going to leave prints."

"He was obviously stupid enough—or cocky enough—to come out in daylight and leave this on your car. Let's hope he was stupid enough to leave behind some prints so we can undisputedly tie the son of a bitch—"

A tremor ran through her, and her knees began to buckle.

Troy came over to her.

"I'm fine," she assured him, while hating the fact that she'd dredged out that word again to describe her feelings.

Troy's stern expression melted away. "Sweetheart, you most certainly are."

Her open mouth clamped shut. She'd been ready to defend herself. Instead, she smiled at him. "I love you."

"And I love you." He pulled her to him again, and this time, she put her head against his chest.

Being held in his arms, listening to the sound of his heart beating, and feeling the heat of his breath on the side of her face, Madison felt so safe. The threat of the Russian Mafia seemed to fade into the background. Here, she was protected; she wasn't alone. In fact, her heart told her that she'd never have to handle anything on her own again. And in this moment, she liked the sound of that.

CHAPTER

14

THE SERGEANT'S AND THE CHIEF'S eyes were on Madison, and she hated the probing curiosity and apprehension that she saw in them. They obviously knew something was horribly wrong, and she found her emotions doing their best to destabilize her. She swallowed them the best she could. At least Troy and Terry were there with her, and they already knew the situation.

Madison jutted out her chin. "There's been a development," she said, setting a basis for everything that would follow.

"There's been a threat on my life and the lives of those I love," she punched out. Maybe it was best to just get it out there and deal with the repercussions that were certain to come.

Andrea turned to look at her brother, then back to Madison.

"A threat?" Winston put an arm on the table and leaned forward. "From whom?"

Madison licked her lips. Constantine being back

was one of her worse nightmares come to life, and as long as she harbored the secret, or it was kept to a knowing few, her mind could downplay the urgency. But being here, her thoughts were betraying her. The words from Constantine's letter slammed against her willpower, and her legs trembled. Maybe sitting down was a good idea. She took a chair at the end of the table.

She took a deep breath as everyone watched. "The threat came from Constantine Romanov." Her statement hung in the air.

"What?" Winston exclaimed, shaking his head. "How? When?"

Andrea's complexion paled. Her mouth kept opening and closing as she drew her gaze from Madison to Troy and back again.

Terry caught Madison's attention, and her partner's resolute expression buoyed her to continue. Still, there was no way that she could bring herself to look at Troy right now or she'd falter. Around him, part of her strength chipped away, as if she didn't need to be strong because he was strong enough for both of them. And she couldn't allow that to happen right now.

"We—" she gestured to Terry "—believe that Bates was connected to the Russian Mafia and it's what got him killed."

"Do you have proof?" Winston spat, seeming to have no problem setting aside the death threat for a moment.

"We have good reason," Madison said. Winston

opened his mouth to speak, but she held up her hand to stop him. "There was a piece of letterhead found in his possession that tied back to Mitchell County Prison where Dimitre Petrov is serving time."

"The head of the Russian mob?" Andrea asked.

Madison nodded. "That's right. Now, we haven't tied Bates directly to Petrov, but it's only a matter of time."

"You sound quite confident for someone without tangible proof," Winston said argumentatively.

A sliver of aggravation wormed through her core. What was wrong with this man? She just told him her life and the lives of her loved ones had been threatened, and he was hammering her about evidence?

She hesitated. She knew she had to tell them the rest of the story, but she also knew how they would all react. She swallowed—hard. "We have an eyewitness who saw Bates with Constantine hours before his death."

Madison's gaze shot straight to Troy, and he met hers. His face was hard lines, and he shook his head. She cleared her throat and went on to disclose that she and Terry had suspicions about the legitimacy of Berger & Stein Accounting.

"That is why you have officers helping you pull backgrounds on their board members." Winston slid Terry a sideways glance and a scowl twisted his lips.

Madison dismissed her observation, not knowing what had warranted that reaction from the sergeant.

But last night, before she and Terry had headed home, they had enlisted the help of a couple of officers to assist. Additionally, the members of the board would have to be scrutinized closer from both personal and professional standpoints.

"The company was founded by a friend of Rodney Bates," she began. She went on to share the related information—how he'd reunited with Greg Berger not long before going to prison and, in that same time frame, started the firm.

Winston bobbed his head. "Highly suspicious," he said to Andrea.

Her weary eyes disclosed that she was torn between focusing on the actual case and the personal facets of the situation at hand. "Get back to the threat on your life," she said. "When did this happen? How? Also, we should probably take you off this investigation." She addressed Winston. "I'd even suggest that she take some time off until this threat is neutralized. Same with Troy."

"Me? I'm fine," Troy said coolly, his eyes locked on Madison's. "I've asked her to take herself off the case, and she refuses."

"We can order her to," Winston put plainly.

"We can order both of them to," Andrea corrected him.

Madison's anger simmered beneath the surface— barely. She hated being spoken about as if she wasn't right there. "It doesn't matter if I'm on the job or not. Same with Troy. If Constantine wants to find me, he will find me either way, and I'd rather be working the case."

"It's not necessarily a matter of what you want." There was a touch of concern in Winston delivery, and it was probably the only reason she didn't snap back with something sharp and defensive.

"Show them the letter," Troy prompted.

She regarded him for a moment, trying to read him, but he was guarded. Probably because he didn't want to be benched, either. And because she'd kept the eyewitness information from him.

"The letter?" Andrea turned to face her brother across the table.

Madison took the letter out of her pocket. She had put it, along with the envelope, into a clear freezer bag before leaving Troy's house. She slid the bag down the table toward Winston, and it came to rest in front of him. He picked it up and held it so both he and Andrea could read it.

Andrea's face blanched as she met Madison's eyes, and Madison didn't care for the chief's unspoken message.

"Please don't," Madison said preemptively, assuming that Andrea was going to make her take time off and put her into protective custody.

Andrea took a breath so deep that her chest visibly expanded and her shoulders heaved. She bit on her bottom lip as if mustering the strength to say something. "We need to get the entire department on this, Sergeant," she told Winston. "Alert them to the threat. And *this* needs to be taken to the lab and analyzed."

"That's my next stop," Madison said.

"Getting back to this sighting of Constantine and Bates," Winston began. "Do we have any idea why they were together hours before Constantine supposedly killed him?"

Madison glanced at Terry. At best they had a theory, but given the way the sergeant was keeping his gaze locked on her, there was no way she could completely sideswipe his inquiry. "We believe that Jimmy Bates may have been a numbers man for the Mafia, and we—" her attention went to Terry "—think it may be possible that he was inadvertently paying Constantine for the contract on his own head."

Andrea's eyes widened, and she slid her gaze to her brother. Madison followed and found Troy seemingly staring into space, his body rigid.

"Do you believe killing…" Andrea's words trailed off.

"Killing me was part of the contract?" Madison finished, assuming she was reading Andrea's mind correctly.

The chief nodded.

"I don't know." Coolness enveloped Madison as if she were drowning in a cold lake of fear. The realization struck again that Constantine had been spotted two nights ago and he'd been following her this morning, and she'd had no idea. If she didn't know about that, how could she begin to assume that she'd have any inkling when he was coming after her?

"We need to get protection on you, Troy."
Winston slid his attention to Terry. "And you and
your family."

Terry winced subtly but Winston's scowl
confirmed he'd seen it.

"Let me guess, it's already in place," Winston
stated sourly.

Terry straightened. "I just found out about the
letter not long before this meeting, but—"

Winston held up his hand, staving off Terry's
defense. "I understand the urgency. What I
don't appreciate—" he drew his gaze from Terry
to Madison "—is the lack of communication.
Although, it's something I suppose I should be used
to with you by now."

"You know what you need to now," Troy said, his
body language rigid.

Madison's heart was racing. She didn't really care
for him stepping in to her defense like that. She'd
handled Winston fine for years on her own.

Winston glowered at Troy. "From this point on, I
must insist that you keep me apprised on this case,"
Winston demanded, his focus on Madison. "Do we
have an understanding?"

The intensity in Winston's expression made it
clear that this wasn't a negotiation. At least he wasn't
insisting that she be removed from the case.

"We do," Madison replied, the haunting thoughts
finally loosening their grip on her.

Winston dipped his head. "Everyone in the
department will be notified of the situation and

briefed on Constantine Romanov. Every cop in this city will be looking for him. One wrong move and we'll have him."

Madison breathed a little easier, surprisingly relieved to have her suspicions about Constantine out in the open.

Winston addressed Madison. "I'll make sure that officers are assigned to watch your family 24-7."

Terry cleared his throat and sunk back into his chair.

"Already done?" Winston asked with a sigh.

"That's a good thing," Andrea said. "This man is a serious threat, and we need to view him as such." The chief had found her strength again and was infusing Madison with renewed confidence. "As you said, Sergeant, I wholeheartedly agree that bringing down this—" Andrea paused.

Madison guessed the words Andrea didn't verbalize were along the lines of *son of a bitch*.

"—Russian hit man," Andrea continued, "needs to become this department's priority."

Winston was sitting with his back firm against his chair, his hands clasped and resting on his stomach. His eyes contained a glimmer of disappointment when they came to rest on Madison, as if she had brought this upon herself. But any time he got that air about him, it usually equated to one thing: the bottom line. The budget and manpower. Pulling officers from the street and their regular duties to babysit one of their own was a predicament that Winston seemed to despise. And now, with the chief's words, it would be necessary to put aside other cases to focus on this one in particular.

But it hadn't been a misstep that garnered the Mafia's attention. It was her doing the job she'd signed up for in the first place that had painted a target on her back and gotten Constantine's attention. And sure, she feared for her own life, but her primary concern was her loved ones. They'd done nothing to deserve being brought into this. It was one thing to mess with her mind, violate her body, and seek her life, but if that's what it took to protect her family, she'd sacrifice all those things.

MADISON WAS THE LAST TO step out of the conference room, and the ache in her chest just wouldn't go away. She needed to call her sister, hear her voice, and be told that they were all right. She had her phone in her hand ready to make the call, but Terry and Troy were waiting outside the door.

"Can we talk?" Troy asked.

Terry slid her a look that said he was out of there and took off down the hall.

"Sure," she dragged out the word, hesitant.

Troy went back into the room and she followed, closing the door behind them. He spun around. "Why didn't you tell me?"

"Tell you what?" Given the fierceness haunting his green eyes, she wasn't going to give him any indication that she knew what he was talking about. It would have been as good as admitting to him that she had withheld the information on purpose.

He scoffed and shook his head. "You want us to be open with each other, but then…" His words trailed off as their eyes locked in a silent battle of wills.

She wondered if his mind went where hers had, to the time shortly after Barry had been murdered and how Troy had shut her out. She had been on him about communicating and relying on her for strength. In effect, now their roles had been reversed.

"I should have told you," she admitted. "It's just that I didn't think it mattered at the time."

"That's a lie, Maddy," he countered, and despite the allegation, managed not to come across as combative. "You told me that you felt Constantine was behind Bates's murder. Why leave out the eyewitness account?"

"Honestly, I discredited its importance." She crossed her arms. "Just because he was in town the other day didn't mean he was still around, and it didn't mean he was coming after me."

"Is that what you truly believed?" His question was direct, as was his eye contact.

She found herself hesitating. After all, there was no way to win by responding to him.

"Just as I thought." He raked a hand through his hair and exhaled. "I thought we were past all this."

"All this, *what*?" Agitation brewed within her.

"You thinking that you have to do everything on your own. I don't know… Maybe you'll never realize that—" He looked away, but before he did, she registered the twinge of pain in the set of his mouth.

Her initial response, like it always was before she had Troy, was to withdraw inside herself, put up a wall, and deny her feelings. But she'd made a vow when in Russian captivity that she would open herself up completely to others, even at the risk of being hurt.

"I know I'm not alone anymore." The admission rubbed her raw emotionally, exposing her weakness and fragility. She reached out and touched his forearm. He lifted his gaze to meet hers. The pain was there in his eyes, even a trace of surrender that things would never change, that he would always want something from her that she could never give. "Please forgive me. It wasn't my intention to hurt you. I'm sorry."

"It's so easy for you to revert to your old ways, to acting like you have to do everything on your own. Sometimes..." He broke eye contact. "Sometimes I wonder if you'll ever fully let me in. Just when I think you are, something like this happens. You hold back just enough to make me question..."

She was afraid to ask for clarification, but she had to. "Question what?"

"Us, Madison." He met her gaze solidly again, and the emptiness she saw in them pierced her heart.

"You don't ever have to question our relationship."

"I don't?"

She didn't know how to respond. Nothing in life was guaranteed. There was a part of her that second-guessed her good fortune with Troy and at least partially expected it to fall apart. Two things she excelled at were solving murders and pushing people away.

"You're not going to say anything?" he pressed and then shook his head. "Of course, what would I expect?"

"Stop," she implored. "Please don't be like that."

"You moved in with me, Maddy. You tell me you love me, and, god, I want to believe it."

Emotion was rising in her throat, and tears were stinging her eyes.

"But there's something that has been bothering me ever since you moved in a few months ago." He stopped talking, as if he expected her to interject. "When are you getting rid of your apartment?"

She frowned at him. "I just haven't had a chance, Troy. You know this job keeps me busy."

"Are you sure that's all it is?" He held her gaze a little while longer before leaving the room.

And she let him. The potency of his question had her doubting herself. Why hadn't she completely moved out of her apartment and passed on her lease to someone else? The answer that immediately came to her was exactly what Troy was ultimately accusing her of: she was holding on to it as a safety net in case their relationship failed.

CHAPTER

15

MADISON SLIPPED OUT OF THE station, watching her breath dissipate in clouds of white, and she was thankful she still had her coat on. The sky was dark, threatening to dump snow on her at any moment.

Her thoughts were even more jumbled than before, as now she had more to worry about than a vengeful Mafia hit man. She had some serious thinking to do when it came to her relationship with Troy. The fact that she loved him was indisputable, but she couldn't deny that feeling in the pit of her stomach when it came to letting go of her apartment. It was almost too much to imagine going through with it. Did she really have such little faith in their relationship? She had let her guard down with Troy, far more than she had with any other man since her cheating fiancé broke her heart over a decade ago. Maybe she hadn't fully opened her heart, yet, but didn't he appreciate how far she had come?

She shook her head, knowing the answer. It wasn't about how far she'd come but how far she was willing to go. Was she willing to surrender all of herself to this relationship by letting go of her backup plan? And if she was, where would she put all her furniture? It's not like Troy's house had room for everything she owned, not that she had much. She'd have to put it in storage, sell it, or sublet the apartment furnished. And the latter wasn't really taking the leap Troy wanted her to take. Except she didn't think he saw it as so much a leap but rather a sure thing. For a man who had been hurt before, he was easily able to let go of the past and move forward. Why couldn't she be like that?

Heck, she still thought of his house as *his*—not hers, not even *theirs*.

She was obviously in the mood to judge herself, but she had to snap out of it because it was doing nothing for her present situation. She'd make things right with Troy, but for right now, she had potentially life-threatening things to take care of.

Madison was still holding her phone in one hand. She pulled up her sister, Chelsea, in her contacts, but her phone rang before she could call. She answered without consulting the caller ID. "Detective Knight."

"Madison?" It was Chelsea. And she sounded irritated...

"Are you all right?"

"Why wouldn't I be?" The words were slathered with sarcasm.

"It was just a question, Chels. You don't call me too often during the day." She was trying to backpedal and doing a terrible job of it. Probably because she knew she needed to tell her sister about Constantine.

Madison cleared her throat. "I was just about to call you actually. There's something I need to talk to you about."

"Does it have anything to do with the police cruiser sitting in front of my house?" she fired back, revealing a trace of dread but also a bit of anger. Probably for being left out of the loop.

"It does. Listen—"

"What's going on?" she interrupted. "And be upfront with me. I might be your younger sister, but I can handle it."

Of that Madison had her doubts, but factoring in Chelsea's tenacity and hardheadedness quelled those concerns somewhat. "I'd rather talk to you about it in person."

"Great. You coming over now? Or I can come to you?"

Madison could imagine her sister on the move through her house to her front door, scooping up her car keys with her phone pressed between her ear and her shoulder.

"I can't right this minute," Madison said.

"Are you safe? Are we? What about your nieces?"

She didn't need a reminder of all that was at stake. "A matter has come up."

"Should I get the girls from school?"

Madison put her free hand to her forehead. If she told her sister that officers had already been dispatched to their school and to the youngest one's daycare, Chelsea would lose her temper. "Let's meet for lunch. Give me an hour."

"Madison, tell me that my girls are safe."

There are no guarantees in life...

The thought assaulted Madison, cinching her gut and churning bile up into her throat. She swallowed roughly, disgusted at the bitter coating in her mouth. "One hour. Meet me at Starbucks downtown." She told her sister which one.

"Fine." Chelsea hung up without saying goodbye.

Madison didn't blame her sister for being pissed off. She'd avoided the question about the girls' safety—twice—but what was she supposed to say? She couldn't assure her they were out of harm's way yet.

She hurried back into the station, and when she reached her desk, Terry stood up from his.

"I've been wondering where you went. I thought we were going to turn in the letter to Cynthia and see if she has any updates."

"I've just been outside talking to my sister."

"You've 'just been outside'?" he mocked. "You have a hit man stalking you, threatening your life, and you're just hanging around outside?" Terry was getting all worked up. His face was turning red, and his eyes were darting all over the place. She could only imagine he'd act similarly years down the road when his daughter, Danielle, reached dating age— overly protective and on the edge of losing his sanity.

Madison tucked her phone into a pocket and put a hand on his shoulder. "I'm fine, Terry. Let's go," she said as she walked past him and headed toward the crime lab.

CHAPTER

16

MADISON LOADED ONTO THE ELEVATOR with Terry to head up to the lab on the third floor. There was an awkwardness brewing in the silence between them, and she remembered the looks Winston had given him in the meeting. "What was up with you and Winston before?"

"What are you talking about?" he asked nonchalantly.

"The glares he was giving you during our meeting, for starters. Usually he's doling them out to me."

He shook his head. "It doesn't really matter."

"Come on, Terry."

"When you didn't come in this morning, I was wondering where you were," he started, still ignoring her question. "Speaking of, if you could let me know when you're going to be late, I'd appreciate it."

"I would have, but—"

"I'm your partner, Maddy. I need to know where you are, especially when we're in the middle of a case."

"I had an appointment," she said, as if it was justification for not filling him in. She really didn't feel inclined to tell him about the nightmare she'd had.

"A two-second phone call next time, okay?"

"Sure." She gave it a moment. "So why the looks?" she tried again.

"I couldn't reach you and went to ask Winston if he'd heard from you, but everything from last night came out. Well, how we enrolled the help of other officers, anyway. He was just feeling sidestepped again, I guess." He wasn't making eye contact. It was clear he was feeling that way, too.

The elevator chimed their arrival at the third floor, and they got off.

Cynthia was at her desk when they walked into the lab, but when she turned and saw that it was Madison and Terry, she got to her feet and hurried over. She threw her arms around Madison.

"I take it you told her when you checked on her?" Madison asked Terry.

"Yeah, it came up."

Cynthia pulled back. "Why wouldn't he have told me? You were threatened by a Mafia hit man." There was a touch of chastisement in Cynthia's tone, and she raised a single eyebrow at Madison.

She didn't have the energy to correct her right now or to point out that, technically, Constantine had also threatened her loved ones, which included Cynthia. Maybe her friend had a little denial going on.

"Life goes on." Madison handed Cynthia the letter from Constantine and walked toward Cynthia's computer.

"How can she be so indifferent?" Cynthia retorted, following Madison. She caught up with Madison and hooked her arm at the elbow.

"You should be taking time off," Cynthia said.

Madison spun and met her friend's eyes. "That's not happening, as I keep telling everyone. It wouldn't matter if I'm on the case or off. If he wants to find me—"

"*Kill* you," Cynthia punched out. "He wants to *kill* you. And you're acting like you forget how close he came the last time."

A shiver raced through Madison as her mind conjured up an image of Constantine's face looming over her, but she managed to shake it before it became a full-blown flashback.

She touched Cynthia's arm. "That's right. He came *close*."

Cynthia threw her hands in the air. "Next time you might not be so lucky."

"Same goes for him." Madison notched up her chin and pointed to the computer. "Have you gone through the prison logs for Bates yet?"

"I just don't understand how you can be so dismissive."

Madison gritted her teeth. Cynthia was going to continue to push and pester until she gave her the response she was after, but Madison had the feeling that her friend wanted something she couldn't provide: surrender.

"I've got the entire Stiles PD behind me, protecting me. Winston and the chief will be briefing everyone on the situation and finding Constantine has become a priority. We will find him. And I believe solving Bates's murder might help us." She sounded so calm to her own ears, it surprised her. It was as if she'd resigned herself—at least for the moment— that life went on, even when a storm was on the horizon.

Cynthia's eyes were rimmed with unshed tears, but a flicker of resolve lit them. "Okay." She took a deep, heaving breath and fanned a hand over her heart.

"We'll get to him first," Madison assured her friend, drawing from a place deep inside her that was beyond giving in to doubts.

"So the logs…?" Terry stepped up to the table, regarded the women, and pressed his lips together.

"Well," Cynthia dragged the word out, "it looks like Bates signed in the morning before his murder, but that's all."

"That's all?" Madison had expected to find a history of visits. "Who was he there to see?"

"Dimitre."

Madison faced Terry. "Dimitre has to have the warden in his pocket. I doubt that yesterday was the first time Bates went to see Dimitre, and the only way he doesn't show up on record is if the warden let him bypass the system." She paused. Government identification was required to visit an inmate at

Mitchell County Prison, but in addition to scanning that information, visitors had to sign their names. "Did you compare Bates's signature to the one on the prison log?"

"I didn't because the scanned ID was legitimate," Cynthia countered.

"I find it strange that Bates is on record as visiting the prison the day before his murder," Terry said, "but doesn't show up on record any other time. Why?"

"Good question," Madison conceded, letting her gaze go to Cynthia.

"I'll make sure Bates is the one who signed in," Cynthia said.

Madison nodded. "I think that would be a good idea." She glanced at Terry. "I'd say it seems that Bates was serving as Dimitre's link to the outside world. At least for the document Bates had in his possession. But maybe yesterday was Bates's first time visiting him at the prison."

Terry angled his head in disbelief.

"Yeah, I don't think so, either," she agreed.

"Regardless, Bates didn't get a chance to pass on the message before he was murdered," Terry added, stating the obvious.

Madison shook her head. "But he had time to meet with Constantine at the club," she countered. "If he had an urgent message, why not pass it on right away? Why hold on to it?"

"Maybe Bates was supposed to bring it to their meeting at Club Sophisticated but didn't," Terry suggested.

Madison regarded her partner, her gaze going through him. Her mind was spinning with hypotheticals. She addressed Cynthia. "You confirmed that about two and a half hours passed after the time-of-death window and Bates's security system being rearmed, right?"

"That's correct," Cynthia confirmed.

"And we already believe that Bates was tortured…" Madison paced a few steps. "So I have to wonder if Constantine was after the document." Now that it had been confirmed that Constantine was back in town, her mind was closed to the possibility that anyone else had killed Bates. "Then, when it seemed obvious that Bates wasn't giving up its location, he killed him and searched his home."

"Sounds plausible," Terry said.

Madison went on. "The house wasn't ransacked or left in disarray. There was no obvious sign that Constantine had searched the house." Thoughts streamed through her mind, but she couldn't quite connect them just yet. She kept talking, hoping they would come together. "But he could've cleaned up afterward or just been careful."

"Why would he do that, though?" Terry asked.

"Because he didn't want us to know about it," Madison responded.

"But even so, Terry's question still applies." Cynthia adjusted her glasses. "Why hide the fact that he was after something? As you said, the torture alone was indicative of Constantine trying to extract something from Bates."

"Yeah. *Something* that could lead us to believe Bates had information that Constantine was after. It didn't necessarily mean something tangible, and it wouldn't tell us that what he was searching for had been in the house." Madison's thoughts were finally starting to take form as a real theory. "Constantine doesn't give up. He's ruthless."

The look in Cynthia's eyes became tender, but Madison wasn't going to let this become about his threat right now. Instead, she desperately clung to making sense of her thoughts, hoping they'd take her to a conclusion.

"I think that Constantine might have known that Bates had what he was looking for in his home. And I strongly believe that was the message on the prison letterhead. Constantine just didn't know where Bates had put it." Madison paced a few more steps.

"Constantine looking for a tangible item—the letter—could explain what he did with his time after killing Bates and before rearming the system," Terry interjected. "But why would Constantine be after the letter at all? It's just a bunch of numbers."

"Yeah, numbers that mean something," Madison pointed out. "We need to figure out what."

"We're doing all we can, Maddy," Cynthia said. "But context also helps. A ten-digit number could be a lot of things."

"We just need to find the one that pertains to our situation," Madison shot back. "So why would it matter to Constantine?" She spun back to Cynthia and Terry, and walked in their direction.

"Would you just stay still?" Terry shot out. "You're making me dizzy."

"Pacing helps me think," Madison replied, more irritated that her thoughts weren't completely gelling than at Terry.

Think, think, think.

"All right, going back to the search for the document… Constantine isn't one who gives up, but he did. Why?" Madison stared starkly at her colleagues. "Why did he leave at six thirty, pretty close to when Yasmine showed up?"

"Maybe he knew she was coming," Terry suggested.

Madison pointed her finger at her partner. "Could be. Then we'd need to question how he'd know that."

Terry shrugged. "Yasmine said she went to Bates's place most mornings before work. It could just simply be a matter of Constantine knowing his target and his schedule."

The spark that had ignited in Madison's chest dampened. Maybe there was nothing more to it than what Terry had said. But there was still a niggling in her gut that told her there was something they were missing. In fact, a lot of somethings.

"Okay, let's put a pin in that question for now," Madison began, "and go back to Constantine's seeming drive to find what Bates had."

"And we're only running with the theory it was the note on the prison letterhead. There might have been something else Constantine was after," Terry said, playing devil's advocate.

Madison nodded. "Whatever it was, Constantine believed it was in Bates's house."

"And you're also assuming he didn't get what he was after," Cynthia said.

"The time that passed between Bates's murder and the security system being rearmed tells us that much. Constantine would have left just after killing Bates if he had gotten what he was after."

"Maybe I'm the only one thinking this," Cynthia said, "but if Constantine didn't get what he was after, he's going to do all he can to secure it." Her face paled. "Threatening you and your loved ones could serve a dual purpose for him. In addition to retaliating for the past, if he calls you out, he could demand the letter in exchange for your family's safety."

Madison took a few steps. "But how would he know we have the letter?"

No one spoke. She had posed the question, but Cynthia and Terry seemed to be waiting for her to answer it.

"Unless he was watching..." Madison's thoughts were coming together as she talked them out.

"You think he had cameras in Bates's house?" Terry asked incredulously.

"That's exactly what I'm suggesting."

"They make some of them pretty small these days," Cynthia contributed.

Madison nodded. "And you'd have had no reason to look for them. If Constantine was as intent on acquiring the note as we've theorized he was, then he'd stop at nothing to get ahold of it."

"I'll get Mark, and we'll both head back to Bates's," Cynthia said, already on the move. "And if you're right about this, Constantine would have been accessing the cameras through the Internet. And that could lead us straight to him."

CHAPTER

17

MADISON HAD LEFT THE LAB with light steps and hope in her heart. She finally had a good feeling about this case and that brought some relief. But until they had Constantine in custody, the threat against her and her family was still a very real one. It took a bit of convincing for Terry to let her leave his sight to go meet her sister at Starbucks.

The fact that the case potentially had a solid lead helped Madison set aside her hunger for other updates from Cynthia for the time being. If the camera thing panned out, the rest of the evidence would be a beautiful surplus.

She parked her Mazda at the curb out front of the coffee shop and looked inside. Chelsea was at a table by the window, and it made Madison cringe. Scanning the area, she saw no sign of a patrol car, and fear began to rise in her chest. Why had she chosen a public place? She originally had thought the crowds would protect them, but now she wasn't sure.

She hurried out of her vehicle, locking her car with the key fob on the move. She heard the reassuring honk that came after pressing the button twice before pulling on the door to Starbucks.

Madison stepped inside and enjoyed the blast of heat that rushed over her and caused her cool cheeks to tingle. She was instantly searching for another place to sit. She caught a break and spotted two available chairs next to the fireplace. There was a coffee table between them and two other identical but occupied seats across from them, but the location took them away from the windows and into the heart of the coffee shop.

She went over to her sister. "Do you mind if we sit there?" She tilted her head in the direction of the seats.

Chelsea's eyes were a storm of irritation and inconvenience when they met Madison's. She wasn't sure if it was just because Chelsea had her purse set out on the table, her phone next to it, and a coffee cup already in hand or if its source was the surveillance that had been outside her house.

Speaking of surveillance, where were the officers now?

"Fine." Madison took a seat across from her sister, her senses at high alert as she searched Starbucks and outside the window to the city streets for any sign of Constantine.

"What's going on?" Chelsea asked. Her serious tone left no room for avoidance, but that was all right because Madison had come here to lay everything out. But now that she was face-to-face with her sister, admitting that she'd brought the attention of a Mafia hit man upon them wasn't going to be an easy task.

Madison eyed the counter and considered delaying the inevitable by placing a drink order, but the thought of a cappuccino or a coffee sitting in her empty stomach soured it.

"Madison?" Chelsea prompted.

"Where are the officers who were watching over you?"

"Don't sidestep my question with one of your own." Chelsea's gaze was intent and ablaze.

"It's important, Chels."

"What can I say? I don't like being followed and watched even if it is by Stiles's finest." The last part came out sounding sardonic, but Madison sensed it had more to do with her sister feeling her privacy was being violated than disrespect for the force.

"You gave them the slip?" Madison asked.

"I might have."

Madison felt a deep sense of pride toward her sister at this moment and struggled to keep a straight face. Madison had essentially done the same thing by not bringing backup with her, but she had a feeling Terry was out there somewhere anyway.

"What is so funny?"

Obviously, she wasn't hiding her amusement very well.

"What's wrong with you?" Chelsea's seriousness sobered Madison back to reality.

"It's just…I don't blame you." Madison bit her bottom lip. "You remember the Russian Mafia hit man?" Madison asked quietly as a man and woman walked by their table.

"The one who almost killed you?" Her breathing became small, choppy breaths. "It's kind of hard to forget him."

"Well—" Madison swallowed "—he's back."

Chelsea's face dropped, her shoulders sagged, and her complexion paled. "You've got to get into protection! I can't lose you. What are you even doing here? We should have met somewhere private." She was in full-blown panic mode now.

Madison was going to admit to thinking the same thing, but it was too late. Maybe she didn't choose a public place for the crowds, but rather to make a statement that she wasn't going to let Constantine control her life.

She eyed the seats that were still available next to the fireplace. In fact, the people that had been seated across from them had left. She pointed toward them. "Can we please move over there?"

Chelsea followed the direction of Madison's finger. "Fine." Chelsea started collecting her things but knocked over her cup in the process. The lid came off, and her drink spilled across the table.

"Crap!" Chelsea picked up her phone, sparing it from the hot liquid headed its way, and then set the cup upright.

People were looking over at them.

"Here, don't worry about it." Madison put her

hand on her sister's, staying her from reaching for the napkins. Chelsea's hand was quaking beneath hers, and it instantly suffused Madison with grief. If she'd just left the Mafia alone months ago—maybe even from the beginning—her family wouldn't be in danger.

"Ooh." Chelsea was wiping her phone on her jeans, even though Madison didn't think it had gotten any coffee on it. "I can't have something happen to my phone. If the girls or Jim ever need to reach me…"

"I know, and I've got this," Madison said, inferring the mess from the spilled drink. "You go over there."

Chelsea nodded, her body visibly trembling.

"Everything will be all right." Normally it was a blanket reassurance, but seeing the state her sister was in, Madison intended to ensure its fulfillment.

She watched her sister walk across the shop and then quickly soaked up the drink with a wad of napkins. She tossed them into a garbage container on her way to join Chelsea. Madison extended the cup and what was left of the drink to her sister.

"I don't want it anymore," Chelsea said coolly.

Madison sat beside her sister and reached out for her arm. Chelsea withdrew and turned to face her.

"He's going to kill you this time." A lone tear fell down her cheek, and she swiped it away. "I have a horrible feeling."

"Nothing's going to happen," Madison said.

"Nothing's going to—" Chelsea charged out but stopped talking when a bunch of people looked over at her. She continued, speaking more quietly. "How do you know that? You can't predict the future."

"Neither can you." The response came quickly.

Chelsea was shaking her head and rubbing her arms. "You still haven't told me why the police are watching my house."

Madison leaned in close to her sister, and as she did so, she chastised herself again for picking a public place. There were too many ears around, even if they were just passing by. She hated that she was second-guessing herself. Not having a grasp on her emotions from one minute to the next was frustrating. She'd have a sense of complete control— an illusion, of course, but she was convinced she had a hold on it, nonetheless—and then she'd feel like a helpless victim.

She spoke only loud enough for Chelsea to hear. "I received a note from him that threatened me and the people I love."

"The girls…" Chelsea's eyes pooled with tears, and she snapped a hand over her mouth.

"I've got officers watching them. And posted outside Jim's work. In fact, the whole department is focused on finding Constantine."

"You should have killed that bastard when you had the chance." Chelsea's unshed tears had turned into icy resolve. "He's not going to tell me how I live *my* life."

Madison nodded, an unexpected sense of understanding blossoming between them. "I feel the same way."

Chelsea met Madison's gaze. "But the girls... You... Jim..."

"We're doing all we can to keep them safe," Madison said. "I promise."

"What about Mom and Dad? Are they safe?"

"I think so, yes."

"You *think* so?" Chelsea exclaimed.

"I don't know how Constantine would even know they are in Florida. And he's here in Stiles, not there."

Stiles was in the northeast, and it would take a few days' drive or a short flight to reach them. And what would be his motivation? Madison was here. Many of her loved ones were here already, too.

"You have to get surveillance on them, though, just to be sure."

Madison nodded. "That's already in place."

"What did Mom say when you called her and told her all this?"

Madison glanced away to the fire on the hearth and wished to escape into a trance in the blue lick of the flames.

"You haven't called them, have you." A statement, not an inquiry. "I can't believe what I'm hearing."

"Come on, Chels," she appealed. "You know what my relationship is like with her."

"You're going to let that stand in the way of *this*?"

Madison shook her head. Her mother's biggest issue with her was her choice of career. "That *is* this. Don't you see that? If I weren't a cop, I wouldn't be in this position. None of you would be."

"She still deserves to know what's going on."

As Madison dipped into her sister's gaze and absorbed her words, she had to admit that Chelsea was right. And it was probably best that her mother find out why the cops were hanging outside their house from Madison and not the local police. "Can you call—"

"Nope. No way." Chelsea was shaking her head.

"Just explain—"

"I'm not doing that. This is your responsibility." Her sister crossed her arms, her body language rigid.

Madison bit her bottom lip, wishing all of this were a bad dream.

"Just be honest with her," Chelsea began. "Tell her why the cops are watching over her and Dad. She was the daughter of a cop. She understands that sometimes the hazards of the job hits home."

All too well...

But Madison couldn't bring herself to speak.

"She loves you and knows you're making a difference. Much more than you give her credit for." Chelsea watched her, irritation not far from the surface of her expression.

"Sure." Madison hitched her shoulders. All she could envision was a fight of epic proportions. Every time she talked to her mother, the woman steered the conversation back to Madison's career as the source of Madison's downfall. It was why she wasn't married to the perfect man with two-point-five kids and living in a house with a picket fence.

"She'll want to hear this from you," Chelsea

pressed.

Madison's heart hammered. "So she can say, 'I told you so.' You know what she's like. She hates that I'm a cop, and now her daughters are being threatened, her granddaughters…"

"Not your fault," Chelsea punched out.

Madison wished that she could believe her sister's words, but they fell on deaf ears. She was responsible. If only she'd left the Mafia alone… She stood and pulled out her phone.

Her sister looked up at her. "Who are you calling?"

"I'm getting an officer to follow you home."

Chelsea held eye contact with her and must have read Madison's stance on this: negotiating wasn't an option.

CHAPTER

18

MADISON LEFT STARBUCKS AND STEPPED out onto the sidewalk. She had the feeling someone was watching her, and it was making her skin crawl. She glanced over her right shoulder, then her left. No one seemed to be paying her any attention, except for the man she had backed into when she had spun around.

The man scowled and held up a hand. "Watch where you're going!"

"You're the one who ran into me," she called after him.

Even that slight altercation had her heart beating faster. It could have just as easily been Constantine. If she thought about that too long, though, she'd go mad. No doubt that was exactly what Constantine wanted. He wanted her to question every move and live life a hairbreadth away from insanity—and it was working to an extent. She shook her head and her arms, letting the tension flow out through her fingertips and into the air. Then she got in her car.

The next thing she needed to do was call her mother, but it was the last thing she wanted to do. How exactly does a woman tell her parents she's being hunted by a Russian hit man? Again. Not that she had to tell her mother the first time, but it had come out when Madison had almost died at his hands. Chelsea had basically made Madison tell them. And that was not an easy conversation on the back end. Madison figured this one would be worse.

She turned the key in her ignition, and her phone beeped with a text message. She pulled it out to read it. It was from Cynthia: *Found three cameras. Will be tracing.*

Madison celebrated this minute victory. Would this be the break they needed? A way to actually find Constantine and end his tyranny over her mind and lift the threat on her and her family?

She sent back a quick text—*Let me know ASAP*—and went to set her phone in the console, but her hand wasn't letting go. She'd hit her head against the steering wheel if it would do any good, but the phone call to her parents was one that needed to be made. Maybe she could somehow get her father on the line and explain everything to him. He'd always been far more reasonable than her mom. Of course, he wasn't living to stir up conflict. Even if she got him on the phone, though, when the message got back to her mother, it would be worse than if she'd just told her directly.

Madison took a deep breath, brought up her contacts, and called her parents' house. As the phone rang, her gaze went across the street to a parked car. The male occupant was wearing a baseball cap, and when he saw her looking his way, he turned and sank down in his seat. But it was too late because she already recognized him. She smiled.

Good ole Terry.

"Madison? Why are you calling? It's the middle of the day." Her mother said it as if Madison had interrupted something important.

"Everything's all—"

"Were you going to say all right?" she asked, interrupting Madison.

"Maybe if you gave me a chance to finish." The words flew out without much thought.

"Humph."

Madison could imagine her mother jutting out her chin and pursing her lips.

"I didn't mean…" Madison let the sentence go, not knowing how to finish. "There's something I need to tell you."

"I figured that, given you're calling me," she retorted.

Her mother could never wonder why they didn't have a warm and fuzzy relationship when Madison wasn't just allowed to call for no particular reason.

"What is it?" her mother pushed.

"You might have noticed a police presence outside your house. A squad car sitting there or one driving by often?"

"What have you done, Maddy?"

Madison clenched her free hand into a fist. With

her mother, it was always about placing blame, and it always came to rest on Madison's shoulders. But given the circumstances this time, she didn't need her mother applying any more pressure because it was obvious all this was her fault. She really should have killed the guy when she'd had the chance…

"Are you there? Hello?" Her mother knocked the receiver against something hard.

"I'm here!" Madison called out.

The receiver hit the object again.

"Mom!"

"Hello?"

Madison rolled her eyes. "I'm just going to come out and say it. There's a situation that's come up—"

"And there always will be as long as you're a cop, Maddy."

"Mom, please. This is serious."

"Very well," she said primly. "I'll zip my lips."

I'll believe that when I see it…

Guilt snaked through Madison for thinking that so quickly.

"I've been threatened and so have my loved ones," she said directly. "This person is highly dangerous and more than capable of following through."

"What do you mean *threatened*? Threatened how?" Her mother's voice seemed stretched thin and took on a note of seriousness.

Madison had to consider her next words carefully. The last thing she wanted to disclose was that the threat involved the Russian Mafia. She was certain her mother held them just as responsible for the death of Madison's grandfather as Madison did. Bringing them up would only escalate the matter and fray emotions.

"Our lives, Mom," Madison said, letting the words carry on a breath. "Our lives have been threatened."

"Well, we're coming up there, then."

Her mother continued talking, but Madison had stopped listening. The thought that her parents would want to come to Stiles hadn't even occurred to her.

"My girls are in danger and—"

"Mom," she interrupted, "I need you and Dad to stay put. A call's been made to the local PD and they're watching over you both."

"You can't expect me to just do nothing while some animal comes after my girls."

Her mother's tenacity and the words *my girls* had Madison's heart swelling. But the moment was short-lived.

"If you'd just walked away years ago…" Now Madison pictured her mother's face going red from her rising blood pressure. "Did your father and I not provide a good enough example for you on how to live a happy life?"

A grinding ache formed in Madison's chest. It was a common side effect of trying to communicate with her mother, and it was also a signal that it was time to put an end to the discussion. "You and Dad just stay where you are. You'll be safer there."

"And you've never been a mother," her mom growled. "How can I expect you to know how I'm feeling right now?"

Tears stung Madison's eyes. The woman could be so vindictive. "Please, just stay where you are."

"You'd like that, wouldn't you?" Hysteria licked every word.

Madison's hands were shaking. "I've got to go."

"Yeah, of course, you do."

One final attempt at piling on a guilt trip, and the line went dead.

CHAPTER

19

MAYBE A BULLET TO THE head wouldn't be such a bad thing. Her mother was certainly reliable, at least at making her feel like a failure. Once she got the flashbacks sorted out, the next topic she really needed to discuss with Dr. Connor was her relationship with her mother. Although, Madison didn't really hold any hope that the shrink could salvage the charred remains of their mother-daughter relationship. She and her mother butted heads as far back as Madison could remember. There were only pockets of time when she seemed to have her mother's approval, but they were always ripped apart just as quickly as they'd been stitched together. And usually any sort of grace bestowed upon Madison was because she'd done something her mother wanted her to do; it was never a result of living life her way.

But that conversation had ended fifteen minutes ago. Her hands were still shaking as she walked through the station to her desk to meet up with

Terry before heading to get the autopsy findings from Richards. She wondered if she had driven slowly enough for Terry to beat her back here. It turned out she had.

Terry jumped up from his chair when he saw her. "Where have you been?" He was out of breath, though, and had probably just sat down.

"I told you I was going to see my sister," she said, playing along for now so he didn't know he was spotted tailing her. "Why are you so excited?

"Cynthia and Mark found cameras in Bates's house and—"

Madison held up a hand. "She texted me. They're going to trace them."

"Yeah." The one word came out like air from a deflating balloon.

"You were worried about me." She smiled. "You seem happy to see me."

"Of course, I was," he said, gesturing emphatically. "You're out there running around without protection—"

She tapped her waist above her gun holster.

He sneered. "You know what I mean."

She gripped his shoulder. "I do. But everything is just fine."

"Thank God. I never should have agreed to let you out of my sight."

Madison consulted the clock on the wall. It was nearing two, and Richards was a stickler for punctuality.

"We should go." She ushered Terry along by

making a brushing motion with her hands.

Terry stepped in line with her. "Troy came over looking for you, by the way. So did Winston. I was surprised that the chief didn't stop by, too."

He could have been watching her part of the time, but she didn't think so. She'd wager the moment she left the lot, so had Terry. For now, she'd continue to play along… "What did you tell them?"

They reached the elevator, and she pushed the "down" button. The doors opened right away, and they got on.

"That you must have slipped into the bathroom or something."

Now she was convinced his story about Troy and Winston coming by was fiction. Either man would have just waited at her desk for her return.

"And they bought that?" she challenged. "I was gone for almost an hour."

Terry bobbed his head side to side. "It worked out."

"It did."

"I'm still mad at myself for letting you go alone," he lamented.

Withholding the fact that he'd tailed her must have been eating away at him for him to say what he had. Madison scanned his eyes, though, and they didn't give any indication he was going to fess up to following her. "I know you were there. Watching me at Starbucks."

Terry shook his head. "No, I just told you that I'm mad at myself for—"

"Save it, Terry. I saw you. Black Nissan Sentra?" She moved in front of him, trying to force eye contact. "And everything you just told me happened with Troy and Winston? That didn't happen, did it?"

"Fine." He lifted his head. "I followed you from the moment you left the lot. But did you really expect me to let you go on your own right now?"

She hugged him.

He stepped back. "What was that for?"

"For caring about me."

"Don't let that get out of this elevator." He smiled, uneasy. "You can be one confusing person sometimes."

She grinned. "It's a special skill of mine."

The elevator dinged, and the doors opened.

"I'd say," Terry replied, stepping off first and leading the way to the morgue.

Richards was at his computer in the corner and turned around when they entered.

"Right on time." Richards stood and came toward them and Bates's body, which looked worse on the metal slab than it had at the crime scene. The blood was gone, but the autopsy had left its marks and the stab wounds were more noticeable. Even seeing Bates like this, Madison experienced no empathy for him. There was just a twinge of anger and a sliver of aggravation that he seemed to what brought Constantine back to Stiles. But why? And would she ever get the answer to that? Or would she die trying?

"The victim was stabbed twenty-seven times," Richards said as he moved around the body and pressed his fingers next to some of the wounds. "The killer took his time, knowing where to inflict injury and how deep to go without immediately killing the victim."

"He put up one hell of a fight," Terry said.

"As best he could anyhow. You'll recall how he was bound to his bed? The jagged edges on some of the wounds, as well as the cuts on his wrists from the zip ties, indicate the victim was bucking at his constraints." Richards spoke with his eyes on the body.

"What was the cause of death?" Madison asked.

"The killer struck the left renal artery, and it caused extensive hemorrhaging. He bled out internally."

Madison nodded. "What about the type of blade that was used?"

"It was straight-edged." Richards smacked his lips. "This case reminded me of a woman I had through here about ten months ago, so I did some research." Richards slid his gaze from the body to Madison. "Her name was Lillian Norton. Do you remember her?" The way the ME was looking at her told Madison that he figured she did, and he continued without waiting for a response. "Norton had been stabbed the same number of times, even though the killer took more time with her."

Madison gestured to Terry. "We were considering the possibility that the killer knew Bates would be expecting company at seven in the morning. He could have moved things along for that reason."

"The *killer*? You don't have a suspect in mind?" Richards regarded her skeptically.

Her chest became heavy and her head light. "You don't like it when we hypothesize."

Richards tightened his jaw.

"Fine, I have someone in mind," she confessed. "And, yes, I remember Lillian, and I am very well aware of who her killer was."

"You of all people should be," Richards served back. He passed a look to Terry.

"Has someone told you that we suspect Constantine Romanov as Bates's killer?" Madison asked. She needed to make sure the medical examiner's opinion hadn't been swayed.

Richards shook his head. "You referred to the killer as a man a minute ago, and as for Constantine Romanov, I drew that conclusion myself. The stabbings in both Norton's and Bates's murders were inflicted in a similar pattern, and in both cases, it was apparent that the killer knew where to strike."

Madison's cell started ringing. "I have to take this. One minute."

"Knight," she answered.

"It's Gardener." His grave tone shot a sliver of pain through her. "There's been a murder—"

Madison's eyes widened, the phone nearly dropping from her hand. She stood there, unable to respond as the shock and the fear drained her blood from her veins.

"Madison? You there?" Gardener asked.

She swallowed, trying to wet her dry throat.

"Yeah," she said. "Who's the vic?"

"Yasmine Stone."

Relief whooshed through Madison's body, and she tried to temper it outwardly. It might not have been one of her loved ones, but a twentysomething woman had just been killed.

She looked at Terry. "We'll be there in ten."

CHAPTER

20

MADISON AND TERRY WERE STANDING in Yasmine Stone's apartment with Officer Gardener. His trainee was in the hall guarding the scene.

"The landlord called us in when she didn't answer her door," Gardener began. "He lives directly across the hall and said that he hadn't seen her leave since she came home yesterday afternoon."

Yasmine's lifeless eyes were staring at the ceiling. She was laid out on her back on her bed, over the sheets, and dressed in silk pajamas. She was on a bit of an incline with her head supported by pillows against her wood headboard. Her arms were at her sides, and her mouth rested in a smile giving her a peaceful appearance. The comforter was bunched up at the end of the bed. Blood had poured from a bullet hole in her forehead down the side of her face and had seeped into the sheets. It was dry now, though, meaning the death had happened hours ago.

Gardener continued. "There are no signs of a

break-in."

Madison nodded at Gardener. "So she likely knew her killer."

Terry jingled the change in his pocket, something he normally reserved for interrogation rooms and throwing suspects off guard, but this time he must have been anxious. "What about company? Did the landlord see anyone come over?"

Gardener shook his head. "No, he didn't, but he couldn't have been watching 24-7. I told him to go back to his apartment and wait there for the detectives to come over to talk to him. I also got ahold of building management, and they're going to get us the surveillance videos from the front lobby and the stairs. We might be able to tell who came to 'visit.'"

"Any cameras in the hall?" Terry asked.

"No, just the lobby and stairs. I also called in to Crime Scene and left a message for Richards." Gardener stepped toward the door. "Well, I'll leave you guys to it. I'll be in the hall if you need me."

"Thanks," Madison said and turned her attention back to Yasmine. Only twenty-three years old— what a waste. Feelings of empathy and sadness for a life cut short washed over her, and she welcomed both after her stone-cold detachment to Bates's murder.

Thinking of Bates, they'd pegged—not proved— Constantine as the killer, and now he'd taken out Yasmine? She was having a hard time accepting that her murder wasn't committed by the same hand, despite the difference in MO. It just meant Constantine was versatile in his killing methods, which they already knew from previous experience.

"I'd say it was a nine-mil bullet," Terry surmised.

Madison nodded. "Yeah, I agree." Of course, the crime lab would confirm the caliber. She searched around the bed, on the floor next to it, and got down on her haunches to peer beneath it. "No sign of the murder weapon or bullet casings. The killer cleaned up after himself."

"Himself, or more specifically Constantine?" Terry raised his eyebrows.

"It's too coincidental not to be him. We know that he doesn't have a preference for any particular weapon. He's killed with a sniper rifle before, so what's a handgun?" Not that handguns were the only weapon that fired 9mm bullets.

Terry pulled out his notebook and pen. He pointed the tip of the pen at Yasmine. "What's his motive for this, though?"

"At this point, it beats me. Maybe he thought she had the note he'd been searching Bates's place for?" She observed Yasmine again and how she came across so serene, even in death. Madison would wager she was asleep and hadn't seen it coming. Then Madison recalled how shaken and scared Yasmine had been when they'd talked with her. Almost as if she had an idea who had killed Bates. What if Yasmine *had* known Bates's killer? And what if they knew she knew?

"Do you remember how afraid she was when we

questioned her?" Madison asked Terry. "I think she may have known who killed Bates. But why not tell us who it was? We could have protected her."

"She was more afraid of snitching than dying," Terry said drily.

"And who do we know that can put that sort of fear into someone?" Madison asked rhetorically. "Maybe she knew Bates was involved with the Russians."

Terry's gaze went to Yasmine. "If she did, that secret died with her."

"Well, let's go talk to the landlord and see if he has something useful to tell us." She took the lead out of the bedroom.

Madison stepped into the hallway and nearly smacked right into Cynthia.

"That came close to hurting," Cynthia said.

"You can say that again." Madison acknowledged Mark behind Cynthia with a bob of her head.

Cynthia put a hand on Madison's arm. "You all right?"

"I'm fine. You?"

"I'll live." Cynthia's comment was meant to be lighthearted, but it fell heavy with the weight of irony.

"Have you gotten anywhere with tracing the cameras?" Madison asked, sliding her arm away from her friend's touch.

Cynthia shook her head. "A third party is working on it. And before you get on me, he knows what he's doing and has worked with us before. There's nothing definitive for us to go on yet, though. He was smart about it and used an IP scrambler. So…" She winced.

"It might not lead us anywhere," Madison stamped out. "Unbelievable." She bit back the urge to cry out in defeat. Constantine was always one step ahead; it made her feel so powerless. And here she was at Constantine's mercy, on his timetable, waiting on him to strike again.

"I know it sucks, but it's still early," Cynthia added with a tight smile. But Madison wasn't going to latch on to her friend's optimism. An awkward silence followed, and Cynthia added, "If you guys could just step to the side and let us in, we'll get to work."

Madison and Terry moved out of their way. She watched Cynthia and Mark as they moved into the apartment.

She took a deep breath and rubbed her temples. A headache was setting in, and it was going to be one pounding son of a bitch.

Terry's hand was braced to knock on the landlord's door, but it opened before he got that far.

The man on the other side was easily in his sixties with gray hair and gray eyes. "She's dead, isn't she?"

"You're Oliver Carson?" Terry ignored the man's question.

"I am."

"I'm Detective Terry Grant. We spoke on the phone yesterday."

Oliver's face fell. "Yes, well, nothing personal, but I wish I'd never heard of you."

"None taken." Terry paused and gestured toward Madison. "This is my partner, Madison Knight. Can we come in?"

"Certainly." Oliver opened the door wider to let them enter. "Just take a seat wherever you'd like." He gestured to the living room on the immediate left.

Madison and Terry sat on a couch, and Oliver settled into a ratty reclining chair and put the leg rest up.

"Is she dead?" Oliver asked, timid this time, his gaze on Terry.

"I'm afraid she is," Terry replied.

He reached for a glass of dark liquid from a table next to him, and ice cubes chinked when he lifted it to his mouth. Madison couldn't smell it, but she guessed it was a whiskey and cola. And who could blame the man if it was? He'd just found out one of his tenants was murdered.

"I had a horrible feeling when she didn't answer." Oliver swallowed a mouthful of his drink and licked his lips. "What happened?"

"We can't disclose the details at this time," Madison said.

Oliver sniffled. His hand was shaking as he went to replace his glass on the side table. "Which is police-talk for murder."

"Officer Gardener mentioned that you hadn't seen Yasmine leave her apartment since she came home yesterday," Madison said, pressing past his comment.

"That's right."

"And what time was that?"

His brow furrowed in thought. "Say, one or two in the afternoon."

"Did you notice if she had any visitors?" she asked, repeating the question Gardener had already asked.

"No, and I would have seen them, too," he said. He seemed completely unashamed of the creepy habit he had of keeping tabs on Yasmine.

They didn't have a time of death yet, but Madison's mind went to the dry blood. "Is it possible that you missed someone going into her place? Maybe during the night?"

Oliver shook his head. "I would have heard someone knocking. The walls are paper-thin, and I'm a light sleeper."

But he didn't hear a gunshot?

Even if a silencer had been used, the sound could be mistaken as something else to the unwitting listener. Also, Madison wasn't going to verbalize it, but it was possible Yasmine's visitor—aka killer—hadn't knocked at all. They could have picked the lock or had a key, especially since it seemed Yasmine had known her killer. There was no way to know how well.

Madison froze.

Yasmine had said she had a boyfriend from out of town. A boyfriend she had seemed afraid of. And if that boyfriend had a key…

Were Constantine and Kevin Jones the same man?

Oliver was squinting at her.

Madison took a second, then asked, "Could you hear it when she unlocked her door and opened it?"

"Yes. That too." Oliver picked up his glass again and took a long pull from it.

"Maybe you stepped out and missed her guest arriving? Say earlier in the day? Are you always home?" Madison peppered him with questions.

Oliver tucked his chin into a shoulder. "I am most of the time."

"What about in the last twenty-four hours? Did you leave your apartment for any reason?" Terry asked.

"Oh!" Oliver tapped the arm of his chair. "I went down to get my mail."

"At what time?" Madison inquired.

"Around three, three thirty."

"And that was?" Madison pressed.

"Yesterday. Soon after Yasmine got home."

Terry leaned forward. "Did you see anyone in the lobby? Pass anyone on the stairs?"

"I'm too old for the stairs. I always take the elevator."

That would leave room for the killer to use the stairs without Oliver's knowledge. It might be a secured building, but that was easy to bypass. If bypassing had even been necessary. Yasmine could have buzzed him in. For that matter, he could have tagged along when someone else unlocked the door.

Madison looked at Oliver, who was worrying his lip. "You never answered my partner's question about the lobby. Did you see anyone?"

Oliver shook his head. "It doesn't matter."

"It certainly does," Madison said firmly.

Oliver swallowed roughly, his Adam's apple heaving. "No. I'm not saying anything."

Madison narrowed her eyes, letting the seconds tick off and utilizing the power of silence.

"You don't know if that man had anything to do with her death." Oliver's declaration sounded definitive, but his shifting gaze said otherwise.

Madison straightened her back and squared her shoulders. "So it was a man."

Oliver flushed at his slipup.

Madison glanced at Terry, then back at Oliver, and pulled out her phone. She brought up a picture of Constantine, angled her screen so Terry could see it, and held it steady for Oliver. "Is this the man you saw?"

Oliver didn't say anything, and the room filled with a tangible silence.

"Has this person been to this building before?" She was trying to gauge why Oliver was withholding the man's identity. "You know him?"

Oliver pointed at her screen. "I recognize *him*."

He was avoiding her question about the man in the lobby, and Madison's neck and shoulders tensed. She cradled the phone, rocking it left and right. "Was Yasmine seeing this man?"

"I think so," Oliver said. "He'd spend a night here and there with her."

"When was the last time he was here?" Madison

asked.

Oliver screwed up his face. "Haven't seen him in a while."

"Do you remember his name?" Terry inquired.

Oliver pointed to the phone. "Kevin…something. I can't recall his last name."

Madison's entire body pulsated. "Jones?"

The man nodded. "Yeah, that's it."

Madison's suspicion had been confirmed: Kevin Jones and Constantine Romanov were one and the same. It still left unanswered questions, of course, like how much had Yasmine known? Was she in the dark about what Constantine did, as she had claimed? Did any of this result in her murder?

But according to the landlord, Constantine wasn't the man from the lobby. Maybe she'd get something out of him going about things another way.

"Let's talk about the man you saw downstairs yesterday," Madison began. "Would he come to visit with Yasmine, too?"

Oliver finished off his drink and ran the back of his hand over his mouth. He still wasn't meeting her gaze, and his eyes were darting about the room.

"Oliver?" Madison prompted.

"I don't know."

Madison remembered Yasmine had mentioned a married man, one whose identity she'd refused to disclose. Was that, by chance, the person Oliver was protecting?

"What did he look like, Oliver?" Maybe if she used his name enough, it would encourage him to speak up.

Nothing.

"Can you tell us anything else about the man?" She tried not to show her exasperation, but it was becoming a struggle.

Still nothing.

Fine, he wants to play this way? We'll play.

"We understand that Yasmine was seeing a few men," she said. "Did any of them have a key to her place?"

"I never saw any use a key."

The more he refused to discuss the man in the lobby, the surer she was that this man was involved. Who had he been to make the landlord so intent on keeping quiet? It was obvious he knew the man. Maybe he felt the man was above reproach. Or maybe he really didn't think that he'd had anything to do with Yasmine. Whatever it was keeping him quiet, she didn't sense fear coming from him.

"You realize you're interfering with an open *murder* investigation," Madison fired off.

Oliver crossed his arms and looked away.

She sighed. Whoever he was would remain a secret for now.

She got to her feet, plucked a card from her pocket, and handed it to him. "Call if you decide to tell us who you saw in the lobby yesterday."

"I wouldn't be waiting by your phone, Detective."

Madison and Terry left Oliver's apartment, and he shut the door behind them. Madison leaned up against the wall next to the landlord's door. "So

Kevin Jones is Constantine." It was easy to see in hindsight. Too bad she hadn't been gifted with a crystal ball.

"Yeah, that surprised me," Terry admitted.

"I know we have no idea who this man in the lobby was, but I still think Constantine killed her."

Terry scoffed. "Of course you do."

"Terry, are you—"

"Let's consider everything before we jump to any conclusions," he interrupted.

"You don't think—"

Terry held up his hand. "I'm not saying this doesn't feel like Constantine, or even that Yasmine being murdered within days of her boyfriend being murdered is too much of a coincidence for me to accept, but first we need to find out if the man Oliver saw in the lobby matters to our case."

She understood what he was saying, and she tried to tamp down her bias. "I agree." She paused. "It's possible Constantine got in without Oliver knowing, though, despite his claim of seeing and hearing everything. He did say that Kevin, or Constantine, would sleep over with Yasmine from time to time."

"The same thing she told us when we spoke with her yesterday," Terry added.

"I wonder if she didn't know more about him than she let on." Madison had thought it a possibility when they'd first interviewed Yasmine, but now she was even more sure of it.

"It wouldn't surprise me," Terry concurred.

"And I wonder if that's exactly what got her killed."

CHAPTER

21

MARK WAS PROCESSING YASMINE'S KITCHEN and didn't pay Madison and Terry much attention when they walked into the apartment. He had the contents of a garbage bin spread out on the floor and was digging through the pile with latex-gloved hands. They found Cynthia in the bedroom.

Cynthia was taking a picture but lowered the camera when they shadowed the doorway.

"How's it coming along?" Madison asked.

"I found condom wrappers in the bathroom," Cynthia said. "No sign of the used condoms, yet, but they could have been flushed."

A chill blanketed Madison, and her stomach tossed. Yasmine could have had sex with her killer just hours before her death.

"Otherwise, we're ready for Richards to take over. I was just getting a few more pictures. One can never have enough."

Madison loved that her friend was thorough and dedicated to her job. And since technology had taken them from the days of processing photos in a dark room to the digital age, pictures were a lot more cost-effective.

Madison looked at Yasmine again, and her thoughts began to bounce around in her head. How had she gotten involved with Constantine? Speaking of Constantine, he might be a professional hit man, but Madison didn't think he was in it just for the money. She had no doubt he enjoyed killing, but he was hired to take specific lives. With that, she wondered about the value on her own head or if Constantine was making an exception for her. Madison knew what she'd done to make him hungry enough to kill her, but what had Yasmine done? What had gotten her a bullet to the head?

From there, Madison's thoughts only got darker. She'd likely get more than a bullet...

Her stomach churned some more, and tremors ran through her body. Her gaze fixed on Yasmine's body, on the eyes that would never see again. Would that be how Madison would look when—

Her legs buckled. Terry rushed to buoy her, but she dismissed him with a wave of a hand.

Cynthia's brows pinched together. "Are you all right?"

Madison took a deep breath. She had to stop letting Constantine get to her. She had to be strong, do her job, and stop him once and for all. "I'm fine."

"I understand the body is in here?" Cole Richards stepped into the room, his assistant, Milo, behind him.

Of course, the medical examiner's question had been rhetorical. Yasmine's body was on full display.

"And she's all yours." Cynthia shot Madison a worried look as she walked past.

"All right, let's see what we have here." Richards moved toward Yasmine and set his case down on the floor next to the bed. He snapped on a pair of gloves and took a few minutes to study Yasmine. "Gunshot to the head," he said, stating the obvious. "There isn't any stippling or gunpowder burn. I'd say the shot was made at an intermediate range, from eighteen to twenty inches away. Based on blood loss, as well, it would appear the GSW is the cause of death." He touched the blood on the side of her face. "Dry to the touch. She's been here awhile."

"Any idea how long?" Madison asked.

"I'll let you know shortly." Richards's tone advised her to be patient. He held up Yasmine's hand and lifted her arm. "Rigor has fully set in, so it's been at least twelve hours. That's a *rough* estimate."

"That would put her time of death around three in the morning or so," Terry said.

Richards turned a hardened gaze on Terry, and that said it all: he hadn't concluded that yet.

The ME bent over the bed and rolled Yasmine onto her side so that she faced away from him. "There's a shored exit," Richards commented. "The bullet traveled through her skull and met with her solid wood headboard on its exit. It's mostly intact from what I see here."

"Good, so Samantha should have something to

work with," Madison said. Samantha was their in-house ballistics expert, and given enough bullet, she could pick up the striations left from the gun that fired it. From there, she could determine the manufacturer and, in some cases, the model of the gun.

He lifted her pajama top and pulled out on the top of her shorts and looked inside. "Lividity in her lower back and buttocks confirms that she died in the supine position."

Richards returned Yasmine face up, took out a thermometer, and pierced it into her abdomen. A few seconds later, he pulled it out and rhymed off her liver temperature to Milo. "Let me know what the apartment is set at," Richards directed, and his assistant left the room to check the thermostat.

He returned and had everyone's attention. "I've already done the calculation."

"What was the tempature?" Richards asked.

Milo told him, and Richards looked contemplative for a few seconds. "And, what did you come up with?" Richards queried.

"The victim would have died between two and five this morning," Milo concluded.

"I'd agree with that assessment." Richards slid his gaze to Terry. "*That* is why I don't base TOD on one factor alone."

Terry clenched his jaw.

At that time of day, Oliver easily could have been fast asleep and wouldn't have heard anything happening in the hallway, let alone in Yasmine's apartment, no matter how much of a light sleeper he claimed to be.

"Given the way she was found, I'd surmise that she was lying down, likely sleeping, at the time of the shooting," Richards went on.

Madison's eyes went to Yasmine again and quakes tore through her. She stared at the hole in the young woman's forehead, letting her vision blur out of focus and her mind drift. Yasmine could have been in the middle of a good dream, the imaginary trip cut short, her life along with it. She hadn't had any idea that she wasn't going to wake up when she'd fallen asleep. Would Constantine do the same to her? She doubted she'd get off that easy. He'd want to toy with her mentally and then torture her physically before he took her life. Well, he was already succeeding in the former.

"Detective Knight?"

Her name struck her out of nowhere, but everyone's eyes were on her, including Officer Gardener's. He was the one who had called her name.

"The landlord wants to talk to you again," Gardener went on. "He's in the hall."

She was on the move immediately, and not long later, she was standing in front of Oliver.

"I've decided to tell you who I saw." Oliver's eyes went to Gardener's trainee, who was posted next to Yasmine's door, and the older man's facial tic told Madison he wasn't comfortable with the officer hearing what he had to say.

Madison guided Oliver down the hall a few doors. "Who was it?"

"You know the man running for mayor?" Oliver paused. "He used to be the police chief. You know him, don't you?"

Her heartbeat was thumping in her ears. "Patrick McAlexandar?"

Oliver pointed a finger at her. "That's him."

McAlexandar had been more than just a shady cop. He had been a corrupt one. He'd been in bed with Dimitre Petrov, at least in the past, but as the saying goes, a leopard doesn't change its spots.

"You saw him in the lobby?" She didn't want to leave any room for misinterpretation.

"Yes. I know it was him," Oliver confirmed.

"And did you ever see him here before, or ever see him with Yasmine?" As she asked the question, the assumed answer sank in her gut. Yasmine had been seeing a married man.

"First time seeing him here," Oliver said.

Madison's anxiety ebbed slightly. It was possible McAlexandar had come to see someone else in the building. But her gut wasn't convinced. He had ties to the Russians and so had Bates, and it seemed Yasmine had, too. And while Madison had never pegged McAlexandar as one to do the dirty work, it was his violation of confidential information that had led to the assassination of Sergey and Anatolli, Dimitre's former right-hand men. Of course, none of that could be proven so McAlexandar walked about a free man, flaunting his worldly success in

Madison's face any chance he got.

Madison snapped out of her moment of reflection to find Oliver staring blankly at her. "Did you see when he left?" she asked.

Oliver looked down the hall and didn't say anything.

"Did you?" she repeated firmly. A moment later, she pressed him again. "You didn't see when, did you?"

Oliver met her gaze and shook his head.

So much for seeing everyone's comings and goings…

"Well, thanks for letting me know who you saw." She left Oliver standing there and met up with Terry, who was stepping out of Yasmine's apartment.

"We're going to see Patrick McAlexandar," she said, grabbing his arm and guiding him down the hall. "I'll explain on the way."

CHAPTER

22

THE FRAME OF THE DEPARTMENT-ISSUED vehicle rolled with each turn as Madison raced through the city. But Terry, who was normally a nervous passenger, wasn't saying a word about her driving or even gripping the dash. Instead he was shaking his head, and Madison guessed he was preoccupied with the fact that the former police chief had even been in Yasmine's building.

"I can't believe it," Terry said. "He had to be there to see someone else."

"I'm not so sure."

"I thought you were convinced Constantine was behind Yasmine's murder."

"Oh, I'm not abandoning that idea, but we both know that McAlexandar isn't a saint. He's communicated with Dimitre in the past; we have the warden from Dimitre's previous prison who has already confirmed that much." Except he wouldn't go on record saying that.

"I don't know if I can see McAlexandar taking a

life with his own hands, though."

Madison wasn't going to admit to having the same doubts earlier, in case she came to regret them. "He's a proud man. I think he might go a long way to protect his way of life."

"You think Yasmine had something on him?"

Madison glanced over at Terry. "Yasmine had admitted to sleeping with a married man—one she refused to name. McAlexandar is high profile—the former police chief and now running for mayor. He had a lot to lose if they were sleeping together. And if Yasmine was going to expose him to his wife…"

Terry blew out a breath. "That could be reason enough. People have killed for less."

"We just have to keep an open mind," she said, channeling Terry's earlier comments. "Hopefully we can at least confirm if he was having an affair with Yasmine."

She breezed through the tail end of a yellow light.

"And you expect him to confess to that?" Terry asked skeptically.

"Oh, I'll get him to talk."

"Um, how do I say this?" Terry pursed his lips. "He doesn't like you."

"The feeling is mutual." She certainly wasn't going to lose any sleep over the fact that McAlexandar didn't like her.

Her mind spun with hypotheticals now as to how McAlexandar fit into all this. If Bates was passing along messages from Dimitre, were they going to McAlexandar and then on from there?

She made the final turn into McAlexandar's driveway.

The house was an ostentatious display, not that it surprised her given how much importance the man placed on material things.

Guess that's what blood money gets you.

Being an inside man at the police department wouldn't have come cheap even if Dimitre could easily intimidate McAlexandar. And with McAlexandar set on becoming the next mayor, if he was appointed, he could provide Dimitre an ally in political power. McAlexandar could potentially have even more pull than he'd had as police chief.

Madison parked the car, and she and Terry headed to the front door. She rang the bell and knocked immediately afterward.

Footfalls came toward them, and the door cracked open. It was McAlexandar's wife. Madison recognized her from a charity gala for fallen officers months ago, but McAlexandar had never made a proper introduction. Although, with McAlexandar's secrets, he did a pretty good job of keeping his personal life private, even with a media spotlight on him.

"Detective…" The woman squinted in thought. "Knight, isn't it?"

"That's right. Madison. And this is my partner, Terry Grant. I'm not sure I ever caught your name."

"Holly," she stated.

"We need to talk to Patrick. Is he home?"

Holly stepped aside to let them in. "He's in the

den having his afternoon tea and reading the paper. It's this way, let me show you." She led them through the home to a lavish office with mahogany walls and built-in bookcases. There was a large wood-burning fireplace, and flames were raging on the hearth. The mantel showcased an antique clock, and a painted portrait of the McAlexandars was mounted on the wall.

Patrick McAlexandar was sitting in a plush leather chair next to the fire, his legs crossed, with a paper in his hand and a cup of tea on a side table.

"Darling, you have company," Holly said.

He slowly pried his eyes from what he was reading, but when he saw Madison and Terry, he did a double-take and got to his feet.

"Thank you, Holly." McAlexandar pretty much backed his wife out of the room and then closed the door. He turned and came to within a few inches of Madison. "What the hell are you doing here?"

"Nice to see you, too." Every word dripped with sarcasm.

"Why are you here?" McAlexandar's nostrils were already flaring, and they hadn't even started questioning him yet.

Madison bypassed him and sat down on the leather couch. She put her feet up on the table in front of it.

"If you don't mind, that table costs more than your yearly salary," McAlexandar snapped.

I don't mind, but you're an idiot for paying that much for a coffee table!

McAlexandar waved his hands for her to put her legs down, and she smirked as she complied.

His jaw clenched. "Why are you getting comfortable anyhow?"

"I figured we might be here awhile." She tossed out a sardonic grin just to provoke him, if for nothing more than the fun of it.

"I asked you what you're doing here," he repeated firmly. He glanced at Terry, obviously thinking he might have more luck getting an answer by redirecting his question.

Terry gestured to Madison, directing McAlexandar's gaze back on her. Questioning him would bring her more pleasure than it would Terry, and her partner knew it. Not only did she despise him for his lack of ethics but he'd treated her horribly when he was chief and had always been pursuing her badge.

The former police chief puffed out his cheeks and wagged a finger at her. That was his signature move, and while she hadn't been on the receiving end of it in some time, she hadn't missed it.

"Get talking," he ground out.

She relaxed back into the couch and crossed her legs at the ankles. "Do you know Yasmine Stone?"

"No," he answered quickly.

"So you've never heard of her?"

"That's right." He jutted out his chin, and his body stiffened.

"Why were you in her apartment building yesterday afternoon, then?"

McAlexandar sat back down on the leather chair. "Who said I was?"

Madison managed not to gloat—somehow—but she'd trapped him already. If he didn't know Yasmine, he would have responded with an inquiry on where the building was, not with concern over who had seen him. He'd as well as admitted to being there and knowing Yasmine. He must have been getting slower since he retired from the police force.

"Who saw you doesn't matter right now," she said nonchalantly. "Because Yasmine Stone was murdered this morning."

His face fell, and he put a hand to his forehead.

If there was any doubt that he'd known Yasmine before, there certainly wasn't any now.

For Madison, this clinched the idea that McAlexandar was the married man Yasmine had refused to identify. "How long were you lovers?" she asked, going for the jugular and daring him to deny his acquaintance with Yasmine again.

He began rubbing his jaw. His eyes were glassy, and Madison was surprised by the emotion he was showing. The man had always struck her as disconnected from everyone else. Then again, he was probably more worried about how the media would spin this than Yasmine's death.

"My wife doesn't know anything about her," he confessed.

"They usually never do," Madison said drily.

McAlexandar fixed his beady eyes on her. "I know you think I'm a piece of shit, but if you're here because you think I killed her, you're knocking on the wrong door."

Madison put on an air of indifference and leaned forward. "You sure about that?"

"Yes, I'm sure," he spat. "I think I'd remember killing someone."

She shrugged. "Where were you between two and five this morning?"

"I was here with my wife," he hissed.

"So if we asked her…?"

"She'd tell you I was here." He clenched his jaw and glared at her. "But I'd prefer you don't say anything to her."

She scoffed. "Of course you would."

McAlexandar didn't touch her comeback.

"Where were you yesterday afternoon around three, three thirty?" she asked next.

A pulse tapped in his jaw.

"You know what?" Madison waved a hand. "We know where you were."

McAlexandar's gaze chilled and glazed over. She'd push him more, see if she could bait him. "Yasmine had other lovers besides you, you know."

"I'd expect she would have," McAlexandar said.

"Two days ago, one of those men was murdered. His name was Jimmy Bates."

He pursed his lips and reached for the arm of his chair, nearly upending his tea in the process. He eased himself farther back in his chair, staring off into space.

Minutes passed, and then she asked, "Why does

hearing about his murder bother you so much?"

He remained in his own world.

She decided to take a leap. "Is it because Bates served as a liaison between you and Dimitre Petrov?"

McAlexandar met Madison's eyes, and his were aflame.

"I wonder," she continued, "how the fine citizens of Stiles would feel if they found out a candidate for mayor is in bed with murderers."

"You've always been a good storyteller." McAlexandar turned to Terry. "I see nothing's changed."

"That's right," Terry said, and McAlexandar's bitter expression began to sweeten. "She's still a damned good detective."

Attaboy, partner!

Her former superior's face twisted back into a scowl.

"We know that you were in direct communication with Dimitre Petrov at one time," she told him. "You tipped him off as to where Sergey and Anatolli would be—and when—so he could arrange for their assassinations."

McAlexandar gave a brief belly laugh. "If you had any proof of that, we wouldn't be talking."

"I still wonder how people would take the accusation, though. Your poll numbers would no doubt plummet." He was already working the circuit, trying to rouse up voters, flinging crap at his opponent, Leo Blackwell. "I'm sure Blackwell would love to know what I know."

He ground his teeth and crossed his arms. "I should ask you to leave my house."

"Maybe," she said dismissively. "But you're not going to. And you know why?"

He splayed out his hands. "Amuse me."

She hadn't let him intimidate her in the past, and she wasn't going to start now. "I have something on you, starting with your affair with Yasmine."

"I'll deny it."

"A rumor is enough to destroy your political aspirations," she pointed out. "People love scandals, but scandals don't garner votes."

He was seething now. "You bitch."

"And not only were you cheating on your wife, but your mistress ended up dead," she goaded. "The media sure would be interested in hearing that."

"But I didn't kill her!"

"Again, all it takes is a rumor." She held eye contact with him. "Give us something, Patrick, or we're leaving, and our next stop will be the *Stiles Times*."

"What do you want from me?" Sickening desperation leeched into his inquiry.

"You were shocked and upset by Bates's murder," she said. "Why?"

"No, no, no." He was shaking his head so fast that his otherwise unnoticeable jowls jiggled. "I'm not commenting on that at all."

"Suit yourself." She moved to get up.

"Listen, I can't say anything," he rushed out. He

swallowed a few times and licked his lips.

She was getting the distinct impression that he was afraid of something or someone.

"We know that Constantine is back in town." Even though she strove to separate this investigation from the threats on her and her family, shivers ran through her.

McAlexandar's eyes widened. "Do you think he killed Bates?"

"You know we're not at liberty to discuss an open investigation with a civilian."

"I'm the former police chief," he roared.

"As you said, *former*," she retorted.

Scowling, he said, "I should have both your badges for coming into my home and accusing me of murder and conspiracy with the Russians."

"And *I* should tell your wife about your affair with Yasmine."

"I don't know if Constantine killed Bates," he mumbled.

She didn't know what had prompted him to say this, but there was something more that McAlexandar *wasn't* communicating. Factoring in his upset over Bates's murder and McAlexandar's ties to Dimitre, Madison suddenly had a feeling that Dimitre hadn't ordered Bates's death. But if that was the case, what were they looking at? Had Constantine gone rogue?

"Did Bates work closely with Dimitre?" she asked.

Silence.

She'd take his lack of response as confirmation.

"That's why the news shocked you," she said. "That also means you're still in touch with the Russian Mafia czar."

McAlexandar stood, moved to the door, and opened it. "It's time for you to leave."

Madison rose to her feet, pleased. She'd touched a nerve. "Stay in town."

Once Madison and Terry got into the department car, she leaned her head back on the headrest. "I don't know what's going on here, but it can't be good," she started. "It seems like the people being murdered have been targeted as part of a bigger picture. I'm also wondering if Constantine is acting on his own."

Saying it out loud made it feel even more terrifying. The Russian Mafia was deadly, but they killed purposefully and selectively. They adhered to a standard of sorts. A rogue hit man would have no rules to follow but his own.

Terry clicked his seat belt into place. "McAlexandar was shocked to hear Bates was murdered, but even more shocked by your suggestion that Constantine killed him." Terry's face became serious. "If you're right about Constantine working on his own, you really should lie low."

She wanted to argue, to push back, but she was starting to think he just might be right.

CHAPTER

23

MADISON PARKED THE DEPARTMENT CAR back at the station. There were too many unanswered questions about what the hell was going on in her city. If she went by McAlexandar's reaction, Bates's murder was definitely not a sanctioned hit ordered by Dimitre. And that actually left two possibilities, not just one.

She turned to Terry, who was reaching for his door handle. "If Constantine hasn't gone rogue, he could be acting on someone else's orders, and that means someone is trying to overturn Dimitre."

"Another Russian powerhouse in Stiles?" Terry lowered his head, regarding her skeptically. "We're barely big enough for one."

"Stranger things have happened. I'm just saying how it *could* be."

"Let's say you're right, just for a minute…" Terry shifted his body to face her. "Why would someone come up against Dimitre, and who would be brave enough?"

"I don't know, but we need to find out."

Terry was shaking his head. "This case has a lot of tentacles. Just when I think we're getting somewhere, boom!" He clapped his hands. "Denied."

Madison wasn't even going to touch her partner's choice of words.

"We need to look into who the power people are down the Mafia chain," she said. "We've never been able to identify who took over as Dimitre's right-hand men after Anatolli and Sergey were taken out."

"All right. I see your point, but our first priority is finding out who killed Bates and Yasmine." He paused. "And you can't just say it was Constantine. We need proof."

"You're forgetting the other priority." Her stomach soured thinking about Constantine being out there stalking her and her family.

"No, I'm not. We've got Stiles PD behind us looking for Constantine."

"I know…" It still left her feeling powerless and at Constantine's mercy, though.

He was watching her with a somber expression as if he'd read her mind. But his earlier word, *tentacles*, began to sink in. It had struck her as funny when he'd first said it, and maybe it was her quest to find some levity, but she snickered.

"And this is about my word choice." Terry waved a dismissive hand toward her, and then pulled on the handle and opened the door.

One of his legs was already out when Madison said, "Sor…ry." The word was fragmented by laughter.

"Uh-huh. You sound it." He got out.

She joined him and locked the car. They both headed inside, and her phone rang. The caller ID said it was Troy.

"You go on ahead," she told Terry. "I'll catch up." She waited until he was down the hall a ways before she answered. "Hello?"

"Where are you?" Troy asked, concerned.

Hearing his voice made her long for his touch, for his embrace. She just wanted to soak up the familiar comfort that she found in his arms. But given their last interaction, she wasn't sure how things would be between them.

"I just got back to the station," she said. "There was another murder."

"Yeah, I heard. There's certainly enough to keep everyone busy for a while."

"No luck on tracking down Constantine, I take it." It was a throwaway comment because if anyone had, he would be the first to notify her.

"No," he said bitterly. "We're making headway with the board members of Berger & Stein, though. I can fill you in. Meet me in the planning room."

"See you in two minutes." She hung up and hurried through the corridors of the station. She went by her and Terry's desks to get Terry, and he was coming back from the bullpen with a cup of coffee. She wasn't even sure why he drank the stuff. She'd been desperate enough before, but she wasn't there now.

"Come with me," she said to him and kept moving.

Terry fell in line. "Where are we going?"

"The planning room. I think Troy has some updates."

"Let's hope he has something." Terry slurped his coffee, struggling to do so at the pace they were moving.

Madison went into the room first, and Troy looked up at her from the head of the table where he was standing. He'd been reading something he held in his hand. Madison guessed it was a report of some sort. His face fell when he saw Terry, and she wondered if she should have come alone. But this was an investigation, and Terry was her partner.

"You said you were making headway with the board members?" She'd keep things business despite the overwhelming urge to close the distance between them and hug Troy.

"Yeah. All backgrounds have been pulled and will be examined closely to see if any of them have ties back to the Russian Mafia." He gestured to a two-inch-high stack of paperwork on the table. "These are some of them."

"Anything of interest yet?"

"I wish I could say yes." Troy pressed his lips together. "As for some good news, though, the warrant's been signed and served for Berger & Stein's client list."

Hope flared inside her. "We have it already?"

"We've been assured it will be here tomorrow morning."

The door opened, and Marc and Nick came into

the room. Both reported to Troy for SWAT and were close friends of his. Of the two men, Nick and Troy were the tightest, and Troy had told Madison he thought of him as a brother.

"Hey, Madison," Marc said, then passed a glance to Terry and nodded to him in greeting.

Nick came over to Madison and touched her shoulder. "How are you holding up?"

"I'm fine." She pasted on a smile, and her eyes caught Troy's across the room. They were a cool green, but the shape of his brow and the intent gaze he had fixed on her told Madison that he wasn't buying it. Of course he had the innate ability to see right through whatever wall she wanted to project to the outside world.

"Well, you're braver than I would be if..." Nick didn't bother to finish his sentence, but Madison knew it would have been along the lines of *a Mafia hit man was after me.*

Madison gestured to Troy. "You're keeping this guy safe, I see."

"Of course." Nick smiled. "Not that this guy needs our help."

"You know I need you guys," Troy said.

Nick leaned into Madison. "Don't believe that for a second. He gets his hands on Constantine, and—"

The door swung open, and Winston swept into the room. His eyes went straight to Madison. "I heard you were back." He bobbed his head to Troy, Nick, and Marc. "I take it these guys are filling you in?"

"They were about to," she replied.

"Do you know about the warrant for the client list yet?" Winston asked.

Madison nodded.

Winston stood with his back ramrod straight, the posture making his protruding gut that much more pronounced. "I understand that the woman who found Bates was murdered in her apartment."

"That's right." She kept her answer brief, despite Winston's grievance over her lack of communication. Things had worked like this from the beginning between the two of them, so why change now?

"Do we think Constantine is behind her murder?" Winston held her gaze.

With the way he was watching her, she briefly questioned if McAlexandar had called him, but there would be no advantage for the man to do so.

"We have a suspect," she said.

Winston let his gaze drift around the room, a subtle smile on his lips. "Do you care to elaborate?"

"Not right now."

"Not right now?" Winston huffed and walked a few steps toward her. "I have the entire department hunting down Constantine."

"As you should," Troy interjected, stepping away from the front of the room and joining everyone closer to the door.

Winston jutted out his chin and put his hands on his hips.

"She received a death threat." Troy squared his shoulders as he stood beside Madison.

"There is also a lot of manpower being dedicated to this accounting firm…" He rolled his hands, seeming to have forgotten the company name.

"Berger & Stein," Terry offered and hitched his shoulders when she looked at him.

Winston leveled his attention on Madison again. "Everyone is searching for a connection between them and the Mafia because of your hunch that he killed Bates."

"I still believe he did." She wasn't going to back down to this man. She never had before, even when he had McAlexandar pulling his strings. "Don't forget that the firm's founder and a former numbers man for the mob have a friendship that goes back years."

"Bates's father," Winston said. "What's Bates's connection to Dimitre, though?" Winston arched a brow. "An assumption based on him meeting with Constantine?"

Madison shook her head.

"Of course," the sergeant grumbled. "I should have known. There's something else you haven't told me about."

"The prison logs showed that Bates went to see Dimitre the day before his murder," she told him.

Winston's face became a mask of shadows. "Why wasn't I informed of this?"

"Because I just found out." A small lie, as she'd found out at about noon or so. She glanced at the wall clock. It was going on nine at night now.

"Just found out? Why don't I believe that? We've

got to start communicating, Knight." His face rested in a scowl, and he was by no way including himself when he said *we've*. His attitude made it clear that, in this case, *we* referred to *her*.

She felt her cheeks flush at being reprimanded in front of three colleagues and Troy. She jutted out her chin. "I've been a little busy."

Winston didn't say anything but just held steady eye contact.

"None of the board members are standing out so far," Nick said, slicing through the growing tension in the room.

The sergeant kept his eyes on Madison. "Well, we keep digging."

"Has anyone started looking into known associates of the Mafia?" Madison asked.

"Officers have started surveillance on known business fronts, but so far no sign of Constantine," Winston responded.

Madison nodded. "Good." And it was. But while it was worth a shot, she had a feeling that Constantine wouldn't be gracing any of them with his presence. It wouldn't exactly be a wise choice because he'd have to know they'd be watching. And if he wasn't working for Dimitre or was going rogue, who knew where he could be.

"Why did you ask about known associates?" Nick inquired.

Madison glanced at Nick, then at Winston. If her sergeant wanted communication… "We," she began, inferring Terry, "have reason to believe that

Constantine might be acting either on his own or under the orders of someone other than Dimitre."

Winston glared at her. "Anything else you want to share?" When she didn't speak, he added, "You said someone else. Who? I thought Dimitre was the boss in town."

She pressed her lips together and shook her head. "That might be a matter of past tense."

Winston frowned. "What makes you think this hit man is following another man's orders? And please don't tell me it's a hunch."

Madison glanced at Terry. It was far too early to mention their visit to McAlexandar. Until everything shook out, she didn't want to bring him up if she didn't have to. Winston was familiar with the fact that she and McAlexandar had never seen eye to eye, and he'd probably resort to questioning her ability to remain objective.

"It's an angle we feel is worth exploring," Terry interjected.

She turned to her partner and mouthed, *Thank you.*

Terry nodded subtly.

"It's why it's worth exploring I'd like to know about." Winston cocked his head to the side.

"With Yasmine's murder," Terry continued, "we followed a lead and—"

"We followed a lead, and it's too early to concern you with it at this point," Madison finished.

"It's too early to update your boss?" Winston fired back.

"I don't want to waste your valuable time if it doesn't pan out."

If all else fails, resort to flattery.

Winston regarded her skeptically. "But you want manpower assigned to researching known associates?"

"It's something we should be doing anyhow. We find them and we might find Constantine," Troy reasoned.

Winston regarded him for a few beats. "Fine. For now, though, you guys should wrap this up for the day."

Madison glanced at Troy and his men, then her partner. "Terry and I just picked up a homicide this afternoon," she said to justify them staying around.

"And from what I understand, it also might be connected to Constantine. But might not."

"Yes, but I'm not sure what that—"

"It has everything to do with it," the sarge interrupted. "Forensics will have collected everything from the crime scene, and as you said, you already have a lead."

"A lead we have yet to follow all the way through," she said.

"Then I suggest you follow it all the way through," Winston snarled. "But for right now, all of you guys should go home, get some sleep, and start again early tomorrow."

Troy, Nick, and Marc didn't report to Winston and were looking at one another as if they were confused.

Winston seemed to pick up on the underlying communication. "I realize I'm not your boss, but it's a suggestion. Besides, weren't all of you supposed to be off today?"

"Yeah, but there's nowhere else we'd be given the circumstances. One of our own—" Nick glanced at Troy "—possibly more than one of our own, has been threatened."

"And I appreciate that. But there are a whole lot of other officers who are fresh to their shift and haven't been here all day." Winston paused a moment. "Make sense?"

Marc bobbed his head side to side. "I *am* tired." He regarded Troy with a look that spoke of an apology.

"Go on." Winston opened the door for everyone to leave. "I'll get the nightshift officers on known Mafia associates, and I'll make sure surveillance is on your place all night," he said to Troy, who nodded.

Madison balled her fists, angry and frustrated by the sergeant's directive.

CHAPTER

24

"I CAN'T BELIEVE HE SENT us home." Madison slipped off her shoes in the front entry of Troy's house, still fuming over Winston making them call an end to the work day.

"Me either, really." Troy walked past her and dropped onto the couch. Hershey came over to him, and Troy rubbed his ears and put his forehead to the dog's.

"Yasmine was murdered, and it's the first twenty-four for crying out loud." She was pacing the living room and ran a hand through her hair. She cringed and wished she hadn't. She needed a shower—bad. But how was she supposed to function normally when a hit man was out there knocking people off? *And* threatening her family?

Still, as much as she disliked McAlexandar, she questioned his ability to actually pull a trigger and take a life directly. Somehow Yasmine's death had to tie back to Constantine. Hopefully the footage from the apartment would come in the next day and they could get some answers. Even if Constantine managed to slip in without the landlord knowing, it would show on the recording.

Madison looked over at Troy. He was still petting Hershey, and the dog's tail was wagging wildly.

"Aren't you going to say anything?" she asked.

He drew his gaze from Hershey, but he seemed to do so reluctantly. When he met her eyes, their conversation from earlier in the day hurtled back to her. The hurt coming from him was tangible.

"What do you want me to say?" he asked indifferently.

"I don't know... Something. Anything."

"That's a big help." He turned back to Hershey.

Pain knotted in her chest as she kept her gaze on Troy. "I do love you, Troy," she said, trying to reassure him.

"I know you do." He didn't bother to take his eyes off the dog.

She frowned. "But you don't believe me."

"If I know you do, I believe you."

"Troy, will you please look at me?" She stopped in front of him, close enough to Hershey to have the dog spinning and nudging her for attention.

Troy complied and sank back into the couch. "I said all I had to say this morning. I'm not sure what you want from me. An apology?"

"Why would I—" She took a few deep breaths. She hated the disappointment in his eyes, the reserved and resigned body language. "I did move in with you."

He remained silent.

"That's the biggest commitment I've made in years. To anyone." Defensiveness was building up within her.

Troy held the eye contact, his gaze probing hers.

"Now I don't know what you want me to say," she added.

He scoffed. "Guess now you know what it feels like."

"Like what feels like?"

"Not knowing where you stand, not knowing if there's even anything you can do or say to just make peace." He looked away.

She dropped onto the couch beside him, resisting the urge to run, to go take a shower and put space between them, to shelter her heart. She took his hand and moved her body to face him. "If it means that much to you, I'll sublet my apartment."

Troy shook his head. "No. I don't want you to."

She drew her hand back. "I thought that's what you wanted."

"I want you to do it because *you're* ready, because *you* want to."

"Do you really think I'm not committed to this relationship?" she slapped back.

Silence fell between them.

"Troy?" she pressed.

He briefly met her eyes with a blank stare. "I don't know what to think anymore."

"All this got stirred up because I didn't tell you that an eyewitness spotted Constantine the night before Bates's murder?" She was grasping, trying to make sense of his strong reaction.

"If you were listening to me earlier today, I told you what this is about." His jaw clenched. "But yes, that's part of it."

"You know me better than anyone else," she began, her heart fracturing with speaking the truth. "You see me for who I am."

Troy's body relaxed; her words were working to melt his tough exterior.

"I appreciate you so much," she went on. "For believing in me, for being by my side, for being committed to us. For being you…"

He turned to meet her gaze.

"For taking your day off and working anyway. Who does that?" She grimaced. She received a partially formed smile, and she hated to risk removing it, but she had something else to say. "Just give me some more time, okay? With the apartment stuff."

"How much time?" He came across uncertain and still hurt.

"I don't know." She took a deep breath. "Just let me get through these two cases and get Constantine behind bars."

He let a moment pass in silence and then said, "We don't know how long that will take."

She pinched her eyes shut for a second and steadied herself. "You're right, but I need to know that he's no longer a threat."

Troy touched her arm. "Just know that I'm here

for you through all of this. I'll do whatever I can to get this guy… And I'm just as pissed about being sent home as you are, by the way."

Madison grinned. "Oh yeah?"

"Yeah. And the guy's not even my boss."

"It was a *suggestion* for you. You could have stayed."

"Nah. It was supposed to be my day off. Besides, as much as I hate to admit it, Winston had a point."

"*You* hate to admit it? How do you think I feel?" she grumbled.

"You would have fought him on it if you truly wanted to stay."

Called out, she turned away and smiled.

He tucked a strand of her hair behind an ear. "You do look whipped."

"I can't deny that." She went on to tell him how she'd met Chelsea for lunch and was quick to mention that Terry had followed her. She left out the part about intending to go solo. "She's scared but hardheaded."

He raised an eyebrow at Madison. "Must run in the family."

She glowered and hit him in the shoulder. He grabbed her hand, and when she went to pull it back, he took one of her fingers and kissed the tip. Her heart fluttered, and her breath quickened. Before Troy, she had never thought of her fingertips as erogenous zones. But he had a way of remapping her body and making her experience pleasure all over.

Focus, Maddy…

"I called Mom and told her what was going on, too," she told him.

"Oh." Troy winced. "How did that go?"

"I've told you enough about her, so you should know that it didn't go well at all. She threatened to come up here with Dad."

"Threatened? You make it sound almost as bad as the situation with Constantine."

"It pretty much is," she said it seriously but laughed when he smirked at her, another finger almost to his lips. Less than a second later, he had put the tip in his mouth, and the magic he worked with his tongue had her whispering, "Sweet Jesus." He took her hand, put it on his thigh, and then leaned across the couch toward her. He took her mouth with abandon, and it didn't matter how tired she was, she let herself go.

CHAPTER

25

MADISON MET TERRY BACK AT the station the next morning at seven. Officers had worked all night combing through databases for people who were suspected to be affiliated with the Russian Mafia in Stiles. She suggested that they were searching for someone with enough power and backing that could justify their standing up to Dimitre and defying his authority.

She stuffed the last bit of a chocolate muffin into her mouth and washed it down with a swig of coffee.

"Sometimes I wonder if you only know two food groups: coffee and chocolate," Terry chided her from his desk.

"The world would be a glorious place if they were included in the food guide," she tossed back with a smile and a show of licking her lips. "Mmm. Though, I suppose chocolate could be considered a vegetable."

"A *vegetable*?" Terry quirked his eyebrows.

"Hey, look it up online. Cacao comes from a bean."

"I think you're reaching here."

Madison shrugged. "Just saying." She got up and motioned for Terry to come with her. "Let's go see what they have for us in the lab."

Cynthia was sucking back coffee from a giant takeout cup when Madison and Terry walked into the lab. She was standing in front of the table, and there were pieces of evidence scattered on the surface. Madison's eyes went right to the letter that Constantine had left on her windshield. It was in a proper evidence bag now.

Madison pointed to the letter. "Did you find any prints?"

Cynthia lowered the cup, revealing the bags under her eyes. "That was my second cup of coffee. It's just not working this morning. And I'm sure this is going to be another hell of a day. The letter from Constantine showed prints all over it. Yours and his." She set her cup on the table.

"The bastard's not even afraid of getting caught," Madison said, seething.

"No, it doesn't seem that way. But that shouldn't surprise you."

"He did sign it *C*," Terry pointed out.

Madison glanced at Terry but didn't say anything.

"What?" Cynthia narrowed her eyes, splitting her attention between the two of them, skeptical.

"We have reason to believe that Constantine is either acting rogue or carrying out someone else's orders other than Dimitre's," Madison said.

"What?" Cynthia spat. "Who? You think there's a

shift in power going on?"

"Too early to say for sure, but *something* is going on." Madison considered telling her friend about their conversation with McAlexandar. Maybe she'd leave his name out of it, though. "Another lead made us realize that Dimitre wouldn't have taken out Bates."

"What lead?" Cynthia looked from Madison to Terry.

He shook his head. "We don't want to say yet."

Cynthia rubbed her hands together. "Ah, this is good, then."

"It could be, yeah," Madison conceded. "So what do you have for us? Bates's case? Yasmine's? I'm not fussy."

"All right, so you know that we got Bates's laptop but weren't able to locate his phone. Nothing stands out on the laptop, and I put in a request to get his call history from his provider." Cynthia went to the corner of the table, picked up a packet of paper that was stapled together, and handed it to Madison. "That is the report. Now, I compared it with Yasmine's phone. There were a couple numbers that were the same between them—Sylvester Stein and Lyle Berger. Makes sense seeing as they both worked for the company. In fact, Stein called Bates several times the morning we worked his crime scene."

"He was trying to reach him for a meeting," Madison said.

"Okay, but there was another number... Go to page two. I've highlighted it."

Madison flipped to the appropriate page and immediately recognized the number that called Bates the afternoon before his murder. And less than a day later, it was out of service. "That's the number Yasmine gave us for Kevin Jones."

"Uh-huh."

"And now we know that Kevin Jones and Constantine are the same person," Madison said, thinking out loud.

Cynthia's jaw dropped. "We do? When did you find that out?"

"Yasmine's landlord ID'd a picture of Constantine as Kevin Jones," Madison told her.

"Okay, that makes sense in hindsight. Do you think Constantine killed Yasmine?" Cynthia asked.

Madison glanced at Terry and shook her head.

"It's too early to say," she offered.

"Ah," Cynthia said. "And you're not going to tell me any more."

"I'm sorry, but not yet."

"Fine, then, maybe I should zip my lips." Cynthia twisted them and pretended to throw away the key.

"What about the prison visitor records? And, speaking of *zip*, anything useful come from the zip ties that bound Bates?" Madison pressed on. She wasn't going to let her friend's jest at keeping quiet deter her.

Cynthia's face turned serious. "Well, we've worked through both. The bad news is that nothing forensic came back on the ties."

"Can't say I'm surprised. Constantine is a

professional hit man," Terry interjected. "It's one thing to leave trace on a threat, another at a murder scene."

"He has before," Madison corrected him. "We had him, and he slipped away."

"Unfortunately, in *this* case, there's nothing that forensically ties Constantine to Bates's murder. The cameras we found were free of fingerprints. The out-of-house tech guy was S-O-L when it came to tracking down a location."

"Because of the IP scrambler?" Terry surmised.

"That's right." Cynthia paused a moment. "But I do have some news for you. Bates wasn't the one who signed himself in. As I told you before, the ID was Bates's but we hadn't checked the signature made to come into the prison. Now that we have, I can confirm that whoever signed in for Bates wasn't Bates."

"Someone forged his signature," Terry said.

"And had access to his ID," Madison added.

Cynthia nodded. "Seems so."

"The warden," Madison spat. "He's the link in all this. He has to be. He'd have direct access to Dimitre, and he could get messages to Bates. He must have gotten a hold of Bates's ID at some point in the past to be able to use it."

"So he let Bates into the prison or got messages to him without him signing in before, but signs him in the day before his murder," Terry ruminated.

Cynthia's mouth opened to speak, but Madison rushed out, "They wanted Bates to appear guilty.

But why? It would only fall back on the warden. His involvement with Dimitre and the Russians would stand out. Why would he risk that?"

"At this point, he's already got our attention, and he knows it," Terry said.

"Uh, guys," Cynthia spoke up, breaking into the conversation again. "I compared the warden's signature to the one used to sign Bates in, and they weren't a match."

"Of course not." Madison sighed. "He could have bribed someone else to do it. Keep digging into Bates's phone records, though. See if you can find any communication between him and the warden." She handed the phone report back to Cynthia.

"I don't have to," Cynthia said. "There isn't."

Madison tried to cool her frustration at the lack of evidence. "What about the ten-digit code? Any luck figuring that out?" Madison knew she was being relentless, but she needed answers.

"Not yet," Cynthia stamped out.

Terry turned to Madison. "Do you think that we should pay a little visit to the warden again?"

"Not yet," she responded. "We dig into him first, find out for sure if Dimitre has him on his payroll, and determine what can be held over him."

"All right. Sounds like a plan," Terry said.

Madison addressed Cynthia. "Did Richards say when Yasmine's autopsy is scheduled?"

"This afternoon at three o'clock."

Madison looked at her watch.

CHAPTER

26

MADISON WAS ANALYZING THE BACKGROUND on the prison warden. "Jeremy Schultz has a wife and two young girls," she told Terry.

"Maybe he's got a secret he wants to keep from his wife. Dimitre's people could have found out and are using that against him," Terry suggested.

"Possible. Or he could just be threatening to hurt his family."

"Either way, the family could tie into how Dimitre gained power over Jeremy." Terry tapped the bottom of his mug against the corner of her desk.

Madison nodded. "I'd like to look into his financials to see what sort of a picture they give us."

"Where's his house?"

"It's in a good area of town." Madison rattled off the address.

"That it is, and it doesn't come cheap."

"More than a man could afford on a warden's salary."

"What about the wife? Does she work?" Terry

swiveled his chair.

"What is wrong with you? You can't sit still."

He jumped up. "I'm having a hard time, yeah."

"What's going on?"

"It's just…" He growled. "It's Annabelle. All this with Constantine has her pretty upset. She's usually supportive of my job, and maybe it wouldn't bother her so much if—"

"If it wasn't for Danielle?" Madison guessed at what Terry was going to say.

"Yeah." He paced in a circle. "And I understand where she's coming from. You know I do." He paused, and she remembered that time in his life clearly. They had been on a case, and he'd pretty much left Madison to work a lot of it on her own. As far as she had known, their marriage had righted itself from the moment they were expecting, which also happened not long after that case had been solved.

Madison nodded. "What are you going to do?"

"You mean am I going to turn in my shield? No way." Terry's jaw tightened. "Being a cop is in my blood. Heck, I don't know what else I'd do at this point in my life."

Now wasn't the time to point out that he was only thirty-three and still had a lot of life ahead of him and plenty of years to change his vocation if he so chose.

"We'll get Constantine, Terry, and all this will be over soon." It was said to reassure him, but she couldn't help but feel like she was trying to convince herself just as much.

He let out a deep breath. "Let's hope it's before my marriage falls apart. She hates having cops outside the house all the time, following her wherever she goes. She said that she feels like a criminal the way she's being monitored. And I can't blame her."

"I'm sure it will all work out. She knows that you love your job."

"I *love* it?" He laughed. "It's who I am, but no one said anything about loving it."

Madison held up her hands.

Terry dismissed her with a wave. "Never mind all this. You're probably right and everything will be fine." His complexion paled, though. "You don't think that Constantine will be coming after me or them do you?"

"I have no reason to think he would. Not that you're not a loved one," she hurried to add.

"Good catch."

"I think quick." She smiled.

"Well, Miss Think Quick, let's get this guy so I can get back to my normal life."

"Hallelujah to that!"

Terry sat back down. "So, the wife?"

"Right." Madison recalled Terry's question about her occupation. "Let's see." She went to her computer and brought up a simple background on Melissa Schultz. "From the looks of it, she doesn't have a day job."

"All right, so the good warden supplements his income with dirty funds," Terry suggested.

"Seems possible. I wonder when he started at Mitchell County…" She referred to the printouts she had on Jeremy. "He's been there for ten years, so pretty much nine of them were before Dimitre got transferred there."

"And when did he buy the fancy house in the fancy neighborhood?"

Madison skimmed the page. "Eight months ago."

"Interesting," Terry began. "And Dimitre was moved to Mitchell County Prison around ten months ago."

"Uh-huh."

"All right, but playing devil's advocate here, he could have come into an inheritance of some sort."

"Leave it to you to come up with something that will take longer to figure out."

"What can I say? It's a gift." He smiled at her.

"I really want to nail his ass to the wall, but my hands are tied. *Our* hands are tied. If we go to the warden before we have everything in place, we could upset something far worse," she reasoned.

"In regard to…?" Terry queried.

"Well we're already leaning toward the possibility there may be a shift in power. We don't know what direction that's coming from yet," she said.

"Yes, but—" Terry stopped with a gasp. "Oh, I can't believe you didn't think of this."

"What?"

"Bates signed in the day before his death, and we assumed that he got the letterhead that day. Of course, there's no way of knowing for sure."

"All right…" She had no idea where he was headed with this.

"And McAlexandar and Dimitre must still be communicating or he wouldn't have been so shaken by Bates's murder. He knew that Dimitre didn't order the hit." Terry paused. "Now we figure the warden was bought by Dimitre, but it was the last message given to Bates that got him killed. Or so it would seem," he added quickly as she opened her mouth to speak. "The warden could have reported to someone other than Dimitre. He could have passed on the contents of the message to this person, and maybe they weren't too happy. This person could have simply wanted to intercept the message and Bates was the collateral. Of course, we're still left with the question of who and why."

Madison nodded. "We really need to get access to Jeremy's financials, even his cell phone activity."

"Yeah, but we don't have anything concrete on him. The signature for Bates in the visitor log isn't a match to the warden's handwriting," Terry said. "And he could have kept in touch with Bates through the prison landline, so his cell records might not matter."

"But they could tell us who else he *is* in touch with on his cell."

"We still don't have enough for a warrant yet," Terry said again.

"He's responsible for what goes on in his prison," she snapped, exasperated.

"Hey"—Terry held his hands up as if in

surrender—"I agree, but I'm not sure if a judge would sign off…"

Madison sat up straighter. "We don't need a judge."

"Uh, to get a signed warrant we do."

Madison was shaking her head. "We can go about it another way."

"Is it a legal way?"

She pressed her lips together. "We use the one thing against him that we can."

"Which is?"

"His family," she said. "Dimitre's not the only one who can play that game."

"I don't know. We should be armed with more intel before we talk to him," Terry cautioned.

"If we're assuming the warden's working for this other power figure in the mob, he could lead us to whoever is giving the orders now, and possibly even to Constantine himself."

"Yeah." Terry was bobbing his head. "But if we show our hand too soon, we'll lose Constantine altogether."

She chewed on that for a moment. He was right: it was too high a risk to ignore.

"Fine, then. We take what we have to the DA's office, see if we can persuade them to sign a warrant."

Terry shrugged his shoulders. "I guess it doesn't hurt to ask."

"Nope. And I'd still like to know why the visitor log was falsified at all. Why did they want to place Bates there the day before his murder? Everything these people do is for a reason."

"And the reason for this?"

She met Terry's gaze and locked on. "Maybe it's just to let us know that someone else is in charge of the Russian Mafia now."

CHAPTER

27

MADISON MASSAGED THE BACK OF her neck. She and Terry had been pouring over the client list that came in from Berger & Stein Accounting and looking into the various backgrounds for hours. They'd also filled out warrant requests for the warden's cell activity and his financials. It had yet to be approved.

"My back is killing me," she groaned.

"Tell me about it."

"I would, but we don't have time." She pointed to the clock. It was ten minutes to three.

They both jumped up, ran to the morgue, and were pushing the door open with barely a minute to spare.

Richards's gaze went straight to the clock on the morgue wall. "I was just about to lock the door."

"Well, we're here so you'll have to save that fun for next time." She smiled at him, and the medical examiner returned it.

Yasmine's body was under a sheet on the slab in front of Richards. He took a gloved finger and pointed to the bullet wound. "The bullet was a nine-millimeter, and I've passed it along to Sam for analysis." He paused. "It's safe to rule the cause of death as being the GSW to the head," Richards said, confirming what he'd initially deduced. "Now, there's no sign that she was bound or any indication she fought back."

"So she *was* asleep when she was shot, after all." Madison's stomach soured.

"I'd say it's quite likely."

Madison's gaze went down to Yasmine's lifeless form, and her mind skipped to Constantine, aka Kevin Jones. It also went to McAlexandar. "There were condom wrappers found in her bathroom, but is there any physical evidence that she had sex not long before she died?"

"I already took a swab from her, and there wasn't any sperm present. If she had intercourse, it would appear that it was consensual and not rough."

Madison nodded. "Do you have anything else for us?"

"Not yet."

"Okay," Madison said. "Let us know if anything else comes up. You know how to reach me."

Richards nodded. "That I do."

Madison's phone rang just as she and Terry were stepping out of the morgue. She answered after looking at the caller's identity and took a deep breath when she noticed it was her parents' number. "Mom?"

"Madison, it's your mother."

"Yes, that's why I said *Mom*," Madison couldn't help but say. "Are you okay?"

"I…uh, I received a strange e-mail." Her mother sounded confused and a little scared.

She obviously wasn't calling about spam. "What was it?"

"There wasn't a message, only an attachment. Maddy, it was a picture of Chelsea, the girls, and Jim. I don't know the sender."

Tingles ran over her entire body and turned her insides to jelly. "Forward me the e-mail."

"I'm worried. You called the other day, told me that someone threatened you." Her mother fell silent for a moment. "Did they do something to my girls?" She sniffled. "Should I be worried?"

Hell yeah, you should be worried! But she couldn't say that to her mother. Somehow she had to respond calmly.

"I'll look into this right away, Mom. We will figure it out."

"Check on Chelsea, will you? I couldn't reach her. I only get her voice mail."

Chelsea's comment from the day before echoed in Madison's mind: *I can't have something happen to my phone. If the girls or Jim ever need to reach me…* She swallowed. "I want you and Dad to pack some things and head to a hotel."

"You still haven't answered my question."

"Just get you and Dad into a hotel. Let me know where," Madison said forcibly. "I'll call the local police and update them on the situation."

Terry was studying her, and she could tell he was trying to get a read on her face, her body language, and the conversation. Based on his intent gaze, he had figured out the call wasn't to relay good news.

"I'll tell you what we're going to do," her mother started. "Your father and I are coming up there. I should have bought tickets yesterday. We could be there now."

"No, Mom." Madison paled, hating the thought of her entire family being in Stiles when Constantine was. "Don't."

"Why, Madison?" she asked at a high pitch. "My girls are in danger! Why else would I get this picture? And there's a circle around Chelsea's head."

The feeling of dread became suffocating at the new piece of information. What if the e-mail was sent to lure her parents to Stiles, to get them all in one place? Even the fact that Constantine had gotten her mother's e-mail address was disturbing. It wasn't like she was on Facebook. It would likely have been more difficult to get her e-mail than it would be to get her parents' physical address. Constantine was showing Madison that he had no bounds.

"I'll call the locals. Just send me the picture," Madison repeated.

"I already have."

Madison held out her phone and saw the envelope in the top left-hand corner. "If you don't want to go to a hotel, just stay put, though, okay? Please?"

"No!" her mother spat. "We're coming."

Before Madison could argue again, her mother

hung up.

"Just great…"

"What is it?" Terry asked.

As it sank in that her parents were coming to Stiles, she tried to convince herself it might not be a bad thing, after all. She could make sure they were all safe. But right now, her primary concern was Chelsea and her family.

"Talk to me," Terry pressed.

"I think Constantine has my sister or maybe my nieces… I'm not sure."

His eyes widened. "Why do you think that?"

"My mom received an e-mail with a photo attachment of my sister and her family." Madison was working to open the forwarded e-mail, the panic and fear rising and making her hands uncooperative. Eventually she scrolled down within the message to see the address associated with its sender. It was a free account anyone could have set up, and the e-mail had been sent at 8:03 AM. It had taken her mother pretty much all day to see this.

She opened the attachment, and it was a photograph of a family portrait. It showed Chelsea, Jim, and the three girls. And just as her mother had said, there was a circle around Chelsea's head. What was worse was that Madison recognized the picture. It sat in a frame on a table in Chelsea's living room. The bastard had been in her sister's place!

She dialed Chelsea's phone, and it went straight to voice mail, just like her mom had said.

"No." Madison's insides turned cold.

"Maybe her phone is dead," Terry suggested, "or she doesn't have it on or with her."

Madison shook her head.

"She's under surveillance," Terry went on. "So are your nieces and your brother-in-law."

"Chelsea lost her tail yesterday. And her phone is her lifeline to Jim and the girls. She keeps it with her and charged at all times."

Silence fell between them.

She might as well have been free-falling from thousands of feet in the air. She met her partner's eyes. "Constantine was in my sister's house."

"Let's just take this one step at a—"

"I'm not in the mood for some bullshit, Terry. This is my sister. I can't reach her, my mom can't reach her, and Constantine *was in her house.*" She held her phone up for him to see the picture. "That is in a frame in her living room."

"Let's move." Terry sped down the hall. "We'll go over there right now."

She kept up with him. "I'm going to kill him." Ice-cold fear mingled with resolve, gripping her tightly.

They made it all the way to the parking lot when she realized she needed to tell Troy what was going on.

She called his on-call cell, and he answered on the first ring.

"Something's wrong," she blurted out.

"Where are you? I'll be right there."

"I think Constantine might have Chelsea. Maybe the girls, also." She told him about her mom's call, the e-mail, the attachment, not being able to reach her sister. "He had to have been in their house."

"Where are you?" he pushed again, disclosing stress and urgency.

"At the station, just about to go over to her place."

"Where specifically? I'm here, too."

"We're getting in a department car now," she said. "I'm sorry. We can't wait."

"We? Who's with—"

"Terry."

"Fine, but I'm meeting you over there," he said. "Be careful, Maddy. This could be a trap."

She couldn't bring herself to argue with him.

MADISON MADE A CALL FOR backup from the passenger seat of the department car while Terry drove. The closest cruiser would be sent to Chelsea's place immediately. She also contacted the officers watching her nieces and brother-in-law and confirmed they were all safe and accounted for. Brie, the youngest, was at daycare. Lacey had left school with a friend and her family, and the officer who was assigned to watch her had followed behind. Marissa was still at the school. Jim was at work.

"Who was assigned to watch the residence?" she asked Dispatch.

"Officer Tendum."

Madison clenched her fists so tightly, her nails dug into her palms. Tendum was a rookie in Madison's mind, even though he'd be driving without a training officer by this point. She'd just recently forgiven him for an incident from earlier this year, but God help him if something happened to her sister because of his negligence.

"Did he leave his post at any time?" she asked.

"Let me see…" The dispatcher's voice trailed off. "At seven fifty this morning he called in that he was stepping away and was given the approval to do so."

Madison clenched her teeth. "He didn't wait for a replacement?"

The dispatcher was quiet on the other end of the line, and Madison drew her own conclusion. The surveillance was in place, but it wasn't around the clock.

"Thanks," Madison hissed and ended the call. "Officers are being routed to Chelsea's as a Code Three," she told Terry.

Lights and sirens…

"Good." He kept his eyes on the road. "Why did I sense a darkness come over the car, though?"

"Don't even get me started." Her skin was probably hot enough to fry bacon.

He flicked a glance at her. "Come on. Tell me what's going on."

"Tendum was assigned to watch her," she said. "He called in this morning that he was stepping away."

"And it was cleared?"

She was seething and too angry to respond with more than a jerk of her head.

"You've got to be kidding me," Terry said.

"I wish I were."

Terry turned down Chelsea's street, and a cruiser was already out front. Madison spotted Higgins behind the wheel.

Seeing Higgins brought her some comfort because around him, she didn't need to keep up the tough front. But a part of her still feared letting it down. She had to keep a level head, try to detach. After all, she didn't know for sure that her sister was abducted. She hoped she'd be laughing with Chelsea over a cell phone mishap in just a minute or two. But Madison had this horrible feeling...

Higgins got out of his cruiser while Terry parked.

A quick assessment of the house didn't show that anything had happened here, but she was going to reserve optimism until she got inside.

"Do you have a key?" Higgins asked her, keeping to the business of the matter. She appreciated him refraining from emotional inquires.

She pulled out her key ring. "I do." She looked over her shoulder at the sound of more cars pulling up in front of the house. One was a cruiser, but it wasn't Tendum behind the wheel, and the other was Troy in a police-issued SUV.

The officer stayed in his car, but Troy came rushing toward them.

"Have you gone in yet?" he asked her.

"Getting ready to." She led the way down the front walkway. After studying the lock, she wouldn't say it had been tampered with, and for a moment, she imagined her sister opening the door to Constantine and him concocting a ruse to get inside. Her hand froze with the key in the lock. What if she found her sister—

She couldn't even finish the thought. She

swallowed roughly and unlocked the door. Before she opened it, though, she drew her gun. Troy and Terry did the same.

"I'll stay posted here," Higgins said, and Madison nodded.

She took the first step inside, and dread buffeted her, chilling her to the core but also urging her forward. Madison went straight to the garage-access door. She opened it—no car. Nausea gripped her gut. And sure, maybe her sister was out, but her phone being off and the mysterious e-mail... Constantine's threat...

"He's got her." Her mouth was dry with fear, and her skin was clammy.

"Let's clear the rest of the place," Troy said.

The three of them spread out and searched the house. Troy went up, Terry went down, and she stayed on the main level. She headed to the living room first and went directly to where she knew her sister displayed the picture Constantine had sent her mother. Once she reached it, she found the photograph still in its frame. So he must have just taken a picture of it. She'd still make sure that Cynthia dusted the frame for prints, though. Next, she looked over at the computer on the desk in the corner and noticed the CPU light was on. She put on gloves, and walked over to turn on the monitor. The computer was already logged on, and in the bottom of the screen, Madison noticed an e-mail program. This could explain how Constantine found her mother's e-mail address. She should probably have the keyboard, mouse, and monitor dusted for prints, too.

Troy came back downstairs once he'd checked the second floor. "It's all clear, and there's no sign of your sister."

Where the hell was she?

She pulled off her gloves. "We have to call Jim," Madison said, already dialing her brother-in-law. She really hoped that he could take personal calls on the job. If not, they'd have to show up in person. The phone rang about six times, and when Jim answered, he sounded so robotic that she wasn't sure if it was him or a voice mail greeting.

"Madison?"

"Thank God, I reached you," she blurted out. Then she realized maybe she was still jumping to a conclusion here. No matter how the coincidences were stacking up, she still didn't know anything. Maybe instead of scaring Jim, she'd approach it from another angle. "I'm trying to reach Chels," she said, trying to sound as casual as possible.

"You've tried her phone?"

She mustered all the strength and positivity she could. "She's not answering her phone, and she's not home."

"She's helping out at the school today," Jim said, still responding normally. "Marissa is in the Christmas play, but her phone is always on and with her... Wait a minute. Don't tell me something's happened to her." His tone turned sharp and bitter. "She told me about your conversation yesterday. I don't want to say about what out loud."

Madison could imagine Jim hunching down and cupping the receiver to avoid eavesdroppers.

"What's going on?" he asked. "What made you go looking for her in the first place?"

She told him about the e-mailed photo and what she thought the picture frame meant.

Seconds passed in silence. She could only surmise what he was thinking.

"You're telling me that someone who works with the Mafia was in our house?" His voice was a cocktail of shock, anger, and fear.

She wasn't going to disclose that it wasn't just *someone*, but likely a specific hit man who had a grudge against Madison and had a job to finish. "What was her schedule today?" she asked.

"As I said, she should be at the school now."

Madison took a few deep breaths, trying to calm her nerves. Who knew when Constantine had gotten ahold of Chelsea? It had to be after dropping the girls off at school and daycare. But maybe her sister was just fine, and the photo had been nothing more than a warning from Constantine that he could get to Chelsea and the rest of Madison's family anytime he wanted.

The message from his letter came back with the subtlety of a jackhammer. No one she cared about was safe, and even her own mind was playing games with her.

"What about the girls? Should I pick them up?" The tension was thick over the line, and she could tell he was starting to unravel.

"I understand Lacey's at a friend's house?"

"Yeah." He didn't even question how she knew. "And Marissa should still be at the school and Brie's at daycare."

"The girls are fine, Jim."

A huge exhale came across the line.

"I'll have the officers surveilling Lacey and Brie pick them up," she said, "and I'll get Marissa myself."

"And what about me? Should I go home?"

"I'd actually suggest you go to Troy's house." Madison glanced at Troy, and he nodded. "There should be an officer outside your office. Let them know what's going on. I'll make sure Troy's at his house to meet you, and I'm going to the school to get Marissa and see if Chelsea's there."

She was grasping here, but maybe Chelsea was just late getting to the school and that's why the officer who confirmed Marissa was there never said anything about Chelsea.

"Call me the second you know anything." Jim sounded like he was going to be sick.

"Will do." She hung up, feeling heartbroken for him, for the girls, for her parents, for herself. What if she couldn't save Chelsea?

"Good idea sending Jim to our place," Troy said, cutting through her thoughts.

She wasn't about to correct him that it was *his* place, especially after their conversation yesterday.

"All right. I'll call the station," Troy began, "and let them know what's going on, get Crime Scene here, and hurry home so I'm there in time for Jim."

"You better call in and have uniforms watch over you," she fired back.

"I will."

She bit her lip and nodded. Troy gave her a quick hug, and he pointed a finger at Terry. "Watch her back."

"Always," Terry assured him.

"And, you—" Troy locked eyes with Madison and jacked a thumb toward Terry "—let him drive."

"I don't need to be chauffeured around." It was bad enough it had happened on the way here.

"Not a request," Troy said firmly. "You're not in any shape to drive, and you know once Winston and my sister catch wind of this, they're going to want you to take leave."

She ground her fists into her hips. "We've been through this."

Troy didn't say anything but still managed to cool her temper.

"Fine," she said. "Terry will drive. But I'm not backing down."

He moved closer to her, and she inhaled his scent. Something about it made her feel safer just because he was within reach. "I wouldn't expect you to, Bulldog. We'll find her and get her home safe."

With his confidence fueling her, she tilted up her chin. "We will."

Troy cupped her cheek, tapped a kiss on her lips, and was gone.

CHAPTER

29

TERRY PULLED INTO THE SCHOOL'S parking lot next to a patrol car. There were about fifteen other cars there, likely belonging to straggling teachers and parents who might be helping with the play. Madison didn't see Chelsea's Ford Fusion.

"She's not here," she blurted out and tried her sister's number again. It went straight to voice mail. She lowered her phone. What if she never got to see her sister again? She fought back the tears threatening to fall down her cheeks.

Madison looked over at the officer in the patrol car, at least feeling somewhat reassured by his presence.

Her mind never strayed too far from thoughts of her sister, but they were also on Constantine. His hatred was directed at Madison, and he'd want to see her suffer. But could she hinge her faith on believing he'd just use Chelsea as bait and not harm her? And if he had her, why hadn't he reached out to Madison in some way?

Terry turned to her. "Want me to go in with you?"

She thought about her ten-year-old niece and didn't want to overwhelm her. The officer who'd checked on her had done so discreetly without Marissa's knowledge, but she'd wonder who Terry was if he went with Madison. She would explain that when she had to and not a moment before. "I'll go alone," she said.

Terry dipped his head, and Madison exited the car and entered the school. The main office was to the right of the front door, and a woman was behind the desk. She was bent over reaching for something on the floor. She came up and slapped a hand to her chest as she gasped. "I didn't hear you come in." The fortysomething secretary paused to catch her breath. "How can I help you?"

Madison held up her badge. "I'm looking for Chelsea and Marissa Carlson. Chelsea is Marissa's mother, and I'm Marissa's aunt."

The secretary's brow scrunched up in confusion. "I'm not sure why Mrs. Carlson would be here."

"She's helping out with the Christmas play," Madison said. "Maybe they're in the gymnasium?"

"Ah, yes." The woman smiled. "They are."

Madison's heart lit with hope. "They're both here, then?"

"I didn't say that. I don't actually know, but if they are working on the Christmas play, that's where you'll find them."

"And where's the gym?"

"Just go out the door here, take the first hall on

the left, and the gym entrance is down a ways, also on the left."

"Thanks."

"Hey, is everything all right?" the secretary called out.

Madison was already at the office door, but she spoke over her shoulder to the woman. "I hope so."

She bolted out of the office.

Please be here...

A woman's voice carried from inside the gym to the hallway. The speaking stopped when Madison opened the door, and the woman turned to see who had interrupted her. The people in the gym were all facing the loud woman, so she must be the teacher in charge of the play.

And she was scowling. "Can I help you?"

Madison scanned the room. There were easily twenty kids under the age of thirteen in the gym, and about as many women—probably other mothers. But there was no sign of her sister or her niece. How was that possible?

Madison held up her badge. "I'm looking for Chelsea Carlson."

The woman's eyes drifted over the room. The mothers' gazes were all on Madison now, no doubt wondering why Chelsea was of interest to the police.

Madison tucked her badge away. "She's my sister."

The teacher's face softened—somewhat. She addressed the kids and their mothers. "Let's take five." She came toward Madison and escorted her out into the hall.

"Your sister never showed up. It's not like her to bail when she volunteers." The teacher scanned Madison's face.

Despair gripped her, making her dizzy. "And Marissa?" Madison managed to say.

"She's here."

Madison could barely breathe. "I didn't see her in there."

The teacher's energy became somewhat subdued, no doubt sensing Madison's anxiety. "She just excused herself to use the restroom before you got here." The woman continued in a kind tone. "She was embarrassed that her mother never showed up and took it hard. I tried reaching Chelsea but just got her voice mail."

"When was that?"

"About half an hour ago."

Madison had been trying to reach her before that. How long ago had Constantine taken Chelsea?

The teacher continued. "I got ahold of Marissa's father. He said her aunt Madison would be picking her up. That's you?"

Madison nodded. "When was Chelsea supposed to be here?"

"Three thirty." The teacher opened her mouth to speak, shut it, then opened it again. "Her phone battery could have just died. Or she could have hit bad traffic…"

Madison appreciated the teacher's efforts to offer other possibilities, but they fell flat.

The teacher's neck and cheeks were splotchy—a

sure sign of anxiety. "You think something might have happened to her?" the woman asked.

Madison swallowed. "It's too soon to know for sure, but I'm going to need to take Marissa with me."

"Of course."

"Aunt Maddy?" Marissa came running down the hall toward her but stopped about five feet away. "Where's Mom? Why are you here?"

How was she supposed to answer that? For one, she had no idea where Chelsea was, and two, if she said that, Marissa's instincts that something bad had happened would kick in. "I thought she was going to be here," Madison said delicately so as not to upset her niece.

"She was supposed to be." Marissa crossed her arms in a huff, but the stance was short-lived. She grinned at Madison. "Hey, did she send you in her place?"

Madison's heart clenched. *I wish she did, honey.*

Madison coaxed her mind to slow down to process everything, to take the time to have this interaction with her niece, but she couldn't very well let herself get worked up in front of her. At least she had one of her three nieces safely in hand.

Marissa was staring at her blankly, seeking an explanation. The thought occurred to lie to her niece, tell her that her father had asked Madison to pick her up, and while that wasn't entirely a lie, kids had a knack for seeing through bullshit. There was only one way forward and that was to—

"Marissa," the teacher said.

Marissa turned around to the face her.

"Maybe you should go home with your aunt." The teacher's gaze met Madison's.

Marissa put her hands on her hips. "But what about the play?"

"It will be all right for today." The teacher pressed her lips into a smile that was intended to be reassuring, but with Madison's skill at reading people, it wasn't convincing.

"Okay…" Disappointment creased Marissa's face. "I'll just grab my stuff."

Marissa entered the gym, and Madison watched after her.

"I hope you find Chelsea and everything turns out all right," the teacher offered sympathetically.

"Thanks… Me too."

The door swung back open, and Marissa came out in her coat with a small backpack flung over one shoulder. Madison's heart swelled, and she put her arm around her niece. But while Marissa walked out of the building standing tall and confident, Madison was falling apart inside.

CHAPTER
30

MARISSA STOPPED WALKING ABOUT FOUR feet from the department sedan where Terry was sitting behind the wheel.

"Where's Mom?" she asked.

Madison bit her lower lip to keep it from trembling. "I don't know, sweetheart."

Her niece was scowling, and her arms were crossed.

"I'm sorry, honey." Madison wasn't even sure what she was apologizing for specifically. It could have been for at least a couple of reasons: one, because she didn't know where Chelsea was, or two, because it was her fault that a Russian hit man was targeting her family in the first place. Or it could be both.

"Why?" Marissa asked. "It's not your fault Mom didn't show up."

"She would have—" Madison stopped speaking.

If she could...

"Why don't you get in the car, and we'll go to Uncle Troy's, okay?"

Marissa's face screwed up and contorted in such a way that Madison wasn't sure if the girl was going to cry or scream. "Is Mom okay?"

Madison crouched down and put her hands on Marissa's shoulders. Facing her niece's blue eyes, she knew saying what she had to say wasn't going to be easy, but she'd held off as long as she could. "I'm sure she is fine." Madison hoped to God that was the truth, but the possibility that it wasn't soured her gut.

"What do you mean? Why did you show up and not Mom? Why are we going to Troy's?" Her niece peppered her with questions.

"The truth is I don't know where your mom is right now," Madison said, moving gingerly. "But we're going to find out."

Her niece's face fell. "Is she hurt?"

There would be no avoiding the question anymore. "We don't know."

Marissa's chin quivered, and she began to cry.

"Hey now…" Madison wiped away some tears with the pad of her thumbs. "We're going to do all we can to find her, all right?"

"Okay." The young girl's demeanor told Madison that she was anything but okay. Marissa pointed to the front seat of the car. "Who's in there?"

"That's my friend and partner from work, Terry."

"Ah." Marissa hitched her shoulders and got into the backseat.

Madison closed the door behind her and then pulled out her phone to call Winston. "We need to get a BOLO out on my sister's car *now*."

"I'll do it immediately." The words had poured out of him, and then he fell quiet. She figured he wasn't sure what else to say and took his silence to mean that he felt for her predicament.

"Thanks, Sarge."

"Of course." He hung up without saying another word, and it left Madison with mixed feelings. She had to believe he was worried for her sister, but she also knew he'd rather she removed herself from this one.

She had one more call to make. She dialed Troy, and he answered before the second ring.

"How did it go?" he rushed out.

Madison's chest balled into a knot and she could easily have a good cry, but her niece was watching her through the car window. Madison held up a finger to tell her just a minute.

"Chelsea never got to the school," she said into the phone.

She was officially living a nightmare.

Troy was quiet for a few seconds, and then said, "I was hoping you'd have better news."

"That makes two of us." She paused to take a deep breath. "Winston's getting a BOLO out on her car."

"I don't even know what to say, Madison."

She could tell he was devastated for her, and really, there was nothing that could be said to make the situation better. "We're heading to our place now."

There was a slight pause on his end. "Okay, see you soon. Jim's left work and is on his way, and your two other nieces have been picked up. I'll fill Jim in once he gets here."

"Thank you."

"Don't mention it."

She ended the call and suddenly realized that she'd called Troy's place *our place*. And it had come out so naturally...

Madison went around to the passenger side and got in the front seat. Terry put the car into gear, and after about twenty minutes, they were pulling up in front of Troy's—their?—house. She'd figure all that out later.

Marissa hadn't said anything during the drive, and Madison could only imagine what was going through her niece's mind.

Jim's truck wasn't there yet, but by the time Terry parked, Jim was rolling up and so was a cruiser. Her other nieces' heads were barely visible in the back above the height of the front seat.

Madison got out and went around to Marissa's door, but she was already out of the vehicle. With her backpack slung over a sagging shoulder, she was running toward her father.

Terry came up next to Madison. "You want me to stick around for a bit, or do you think it's best I get back to Chelsea's and meet up with Crime Scene?"

"Stay for a bit. Then we'll go back together."

Terry didn't say anything, and his eyes were full of conflict. She had a feeling he thought it best that she recuse herself from the case.

"She's my sister, Terry. I can't—"

He nodded. "I know."

"Aunt Maddy!" Chelsea's youngest daughter, Brie, came running toward Madison.

"Hey, honey." She got down to receive the hug coming her way. As her niece threw her arms around her, Madison sank into the embrace, soaking up the comfort and love Brie offered so unknowingly, but it also awakened Madison's instincts, her need to protect her own.

"Daddy hasn't told us why we're here. Is it a party? I love cupcakes. Do you have cupcakes?" Brie was clapping and practically jumping up and down, but she stopped when she saw Terry. "Who's he?"

Madison smiled and rose to her full height, placing a loving hand on Brie's head. "He's my friend, and I work with him. His name is Terry."

Brie smiled at Terry and held out a hand.

Terry smiled back and let the expression carry to Madison. Brie wasn't anything if not a little lady. Her manners had always belied her age—an old spirit in a young girl.

Terry took the girl's small hand with his fingers. "Nice to meet you, Brie."

"You too, Mr. Terry." Brie pulled her hand back, her gaze scrutinizing him for a few moments before she ran toward the front door.

Madison watched her niece leave and noticed that Troy was standing just inside the open front door. She pulled her gaze from him and briefly locked eyes with Jim before looking away, trying to find Lacey. She must have already gone inside the house.

Jim's brow wrinkled. The stress was already making him look ten years older than he was. "Did you find her?"

She shook her head.

"What are we going to do? We have to find her."

"We—" she gestured to Terry but inferred the whole of the Stiles PD "—will do everything we can." Madison paused. All of this was her fault... If it hadn't been for her, Constantine wouldn't be coming after them. And it all went back to that damned cold case she just *had* to solve, even though it had meant poking the Russian Mafia. Part of her almost wished she'd left that case cold. Then at least her family would be safe. But even as that selfish thought hit her, she knew that young defense attorney had deserved justice.

Jim pinched his eyes shut, turned his face heavenward, and exhaled deeply. His warm breath created a white fog in the cold air. "I keep hoping this is a nightmare and that I'll wake up any second. Or that she'll just show up or call and tell me her phone died."

Madison swallowed, trying to force down the lump of terror in her throat. "Me too."

"Why would they want her, though? It's you they're mad at." Jim sucked in air after his last words, and his gaze was full of apology when he tilted his head back down. "I didn't mean it that way."

Madison bit her bottom lip to quell her emotion and shook her head.

"They're trying to get to you," Jim summarized matter-of-factly.

"It's likely."

"Likely? Or is that the case, Maddy?" Jim used a form of her name, which at any other time would indicate a kinship and friendliness between them. Now it came out sounding painful and pleading.

"I'm not sure..." She watched as the uncertainty cast his face in shadow.

"Are they going to kill her? They are, aren't they?" His voice was rising in volume. "And it's all some sort of sick game just to upset you." The accusation pierced her heart.

"It's possible they just want to draw Madison out," Terry said, clearly stepping in to help ease the tension.

Jim kept his gaze on Madison, and when she moved to touch his arm, he moved out of her reach and held up his hands.

"Please, don't." He was breathing through his mouth, his facial features hardening. "They're using her as bait. And bait..."

Madison didn't need him to finish. Tangible desperation rained down over him.

"A CSU team will be going through your house to see if they can find anything to help locate Chelsea. And we have issued a Be On the Lookout bulletin on her car," she told him, breaking down the acronym.

"I know what a BOLO is," Jim snapped. "What are we supposed to do in the meantime?" He gestured toward the house, toward the girls.

"Just stay here for a few days."

"What about clothes? And I work tomorrow, and the girls have school and daycare." Jim was going through the motions, trying to give the impression that he was just being responsible, but stress was etched on his face. Madison knew he didn't care so much about the inconvenience of changing their schedules around as he did Chelsea's welfare.

"I can get whatever you need from the house. As for the rest, it's best you stay here under police protection."

"And just put our lives on hold?" He clung to what normalcy he could, even as it was slipping through his fingers.

"For a bit, yeah." Madison felt like a hypocrite for dispensing the very advice she was refusing to heed. "Let's go inside," she suggested. The chill was making her hands ache.

He flailed his hands in the air. "Sure."

She didn't need her brother-in-law to say any more. That single word carried defeat. Tears were threatening to fall, but she refused to let them. She had to be strong for all of them—even when weakness crept in and threatened her sanity.

Constantine had chosen the wrong woman's family to come after.

CHAPTER

31

MADISON STEPPED INTO THE HOUSE, and Troy hugged her and pecked a kiss on her lips.

"Auntie and Unkie sitting in a tree," Marissa started singing. *Unkie* was what she'd been calling Troy ever since she'd slipped up one day and Troy had teased her about it.

Madison smiled at her niece's lightheartedness despite the circumstances. Marissa was old enough to know something was wrong—she'd even cried at the school, wondering about her mother—but she was being brave for her younger sisters.

"You're going to find Mom, Aunt Maddy. I know it," Marissa said.

As much as Madison wanted to soak in her niece's confidence, her experience as a cop clashed with what her heart longed for. There weren't always happy endings.

"We will do our best, sweetie," Madison said gently.

Marissa walked off toward Hershey, where her

other nieces were playing. Lacey had yet to say anything to Madison, but the girl was watching her now. She smiled, and Lacey came over.

"Hi." Lacey stood in front of Madison.

"Hey, sweetie." She pulled her niece in for a hug, and the girl didn't fight the display of affection.

After a few seconds, Lacey drew back. "Mom's going to be okay, right?"

Madison froze. Words wouldn't form on her tongue. What if she wasn't going to be okay?

"Your aunt's going to bring her home," Troy interjected, coming to Madison's aid and resting a hand on the small of her back.

She should have been touched by Troy's confidence, but it struck her another way. Maybe they shouldn't make promises they didn't know they could keep.

Madison addressed Troy. "Terry and I are going back to the house."

Lacey walked away, probably sensing adult talk was coming. Once her niece was out of hearing range, Madison continued. "We'll see how Crime Scene is making out, get clothes for the girls and Jim." Her phone rang then, and everyone in the room fell silent.

"That could be him now." Jim paled, but anger flashed in his eyes.

Madison pulled her phone out and answered. "Madison Knight."

"How are you holding up?" It was Cynthia, and the couple of seconds that passed before she spoke had Madison's heart rate spiking.

"Is there anything I can do?" Cynthia sounded desperate to remedy the situation, as if wishing she could snap her fingers and bring Chelsea back.

"There's a silver picture frame in the living room on the table behind the couch. It has a photo of Chelsea and her family in it. Dust it for prints, as well as the computer monitor, keyboard, and mouse."

"Will do, but I meant anything of a personal nature."

"We just need to find her, Cyn."

"I could track her phone."

"It's off," Madison fired back, instantly regretting the bitter edge. "Sorry, I—"

"No apology necessary. I get it." Cynthia let the line fall silent for a moment. "There could still be a way to track her phone."

"How?" As far as Madison knew, a cell phone had to be on to be traceable.

"I don't want to get your hopes up, but there are different ways to track a phone's location. One way is based on Internet access."

"I'm not sure I understand." A tension headache burrowed into her brow.

"Does your sister have an iPhone or Android?"

She thought back to lunch with her sister, how she'd had her phone on the table. "An Android."

"Okay, did she register her phone with Android Device Manager?"

"I don't know. Jim," Madison called out to her brother-in-law, who had walked over to his girls.

He came back, and Madison asked him what Cynthia needed to know.

"Knowing how important her phone is, probably," he replied.

"Ask him if she opted to turn on Location History or Timeline for her Google account," Cynthia said, obviously having heard Jim's answer to her other question.

Madison relayed what Cynthia had said to Jim.

"Again, probably," Jim began. "Why? Can this help—"

"He's not sure," Madison told Cynthia.

"Well, we'll find out soon enough. I'm going to need her log-in information."

"I'll get it," Madison said. "Just explain what you're going to do."

"Google could have saved the location where her cell phone last had an Internet connection."

Madison's chest expanded with the first good breath she'd taken in a while. "Thank you."

"Don't thank me yet," her friend cautioned. "Let's just check it out and go from there."

Cynthia's words dampened Madison's spark of hope.

"Do you have her account info?" Cynthia asked.

"We'll need the username and password that Chelsea would have used for Google on her phone," she said to Jim.

"You got it." Jim started rattling it off.

"Did you catch that?" Madison asked Cynthia.

"I did. I'll call you the second I have something."

"Thanks."

"Please. Whatever I can do to help." Cynthia hung up, but she had left Madison feeling optimistic despite her friend's advice to temper her expectations.

Besides, even if they found out where Chelsea's phone had last logged its location, she could be a long way from there now. However, it would give them a start and a possible timeline for when Chelsea was taken.

"What did she say?" Jim's eyes softened, and he seemed to be teetering on the brink of hope.

She filled in Jim, Troy, and Terry, and added, "Let's just take this one step at a time, though. Not get too attached to this working."

"She's my wife," Jim blurted out, causing the girls to look at him. "I—we—have to cling to whatever hope we're offered."

Madison pressed her lips together and nodded. "Run us through what her schedule was for today."

"You already know about the play." Jim's gaze took in all the adults. "But she gets up at about six and gets the girls off to school and daycare. She leaves the house around eight."

That was around the same time that Tendum had left his post unattended.

"Obviously that much happened." Jim said. "You're trying to figure out when and where she was taken?"

"Yeah. What were her plans after she dropped off the girls?" Madison asked.

"I'm not the best listener sometimes." Jim's face fell, and his shoulders sagged. "Your sister has a lot to say— But if she was here right now, I'd let her talk all night."

"It's all right," Madison consoled him. "She does talk a lot." She found herself smiling, no doubt her soul's attempt to buoy her spirits and his.

"Anyway, I don't catch everything she says," he went on.

"You're only human."

"Right now I wish I was more."

I know how you feel.

"Do you know of anything else on her agenda today besides the play?"

"She probably hit the grocery store. She goes pretty much every day for something." He gave her the name of the store Chelsea frequented. "I don't know what time she'd have gone. She could have gone after the gym or planned to go after the play rehearsal."

Terry eyed her skeptically. "*Your* sister has a gym membership?"

Just because her partner knew she thought running was the Devil's pastime…

She glanced over at him, and he was smiling. She appreciated his attempt to lighten things, even if for a moment. "Ha-ha." She aligned her gaze with Jim's again. "So she would have gone to the gym at some point today?"

"Probably." He seemed disappointed with himself that he didn't know for sure.

"It's all right, Jim," she said gently. "It's hard to think clearly with all this going on."

"As long as you are."

Again, the burden of being held responsible should she not find and rescue her sister sat roiling in the pit of her stomach.

"Lately, she's been going after she drops the girls off at school," Jim offered.

"Okay, good. We can check there and see." Madison turned toward Terry. "Let's go." She couldn't just sit around here doing nothing, waiting on a hope and a prayer that Cynthia would find something or there'd be a hit on the BOLO.

Madison had her hand on the doorknob when her phone rang. "Madison Knight," she answered.

"I have something for you." It was Cynthia. "Her phone was last connected to the Internet in Stiles this morning at eight thirty-five."

Oh god. She had been abducted this *morning*…

Madison's stomach somersaulted. "Please tell me you have more than that."

"Oh, I do. I have an intersection."

"That's great." Madison's gaze slid to Jim, who was watching her eagerly. "Which one?"

Cynthia told her.

Madison's mind went blank. "What's there again?"

"A gas station, a coffee shop, a grocery store, and a McDonald's."

"Get the video footage from the city," Madison told her. "We can see if her car shows up, and if so, what direction it was headed."

"I've run it by Winston already, and he's got an officer working on the warrant."

"You're the best."

"Anything for you, Maddy."

Madison hung up and announced, "We have a lead." With the spark of optimism in Jim's eyes, she couldn't bring herself to share the time of day Chelsea's phone had last been active. She turned to Terry. "Ready to go?"

Jim stepped toward her. "What's the lead?"

Madison glanced at Troy, who was watching her with those piercing green eyes of his.

"Her phone was last online at..." Should she just disclose everything to her brother-in-law? She was feeling lost and sick, not understanding why Constantine would have taken Chelsea so early in the day and not have contacted her. Was it just a matter of him wanting to batter Madison's emotions and show her that he was in control?

"What is it?" Troy asked tenderly. Obviously her internal anguish had not gone unnoticed.

She nodded and told the men about the intersection.

"She uses that gas station. It's on the way to the school," Jim said. "Or back from. And the grocery store on that corner is the one I told you about."

With his words, Madison was hit with an idea. "Jim," she punched out.

"What?"

"Check your online banking. It should show any transactions from earlier today."

"Good thinking," Troy praised her.

She was busy chastising herself for not thinking of it earlier. But then again, it wasn't like everything could hit at once.

"Is there a computer I can use?" Jim asked.

"Yeah, but you can log into your banking on your phone." Madison pointed to his waist where his cell was clipped into a holder.

"Not this guy. I prefer to take precautions," Jim started. "It's surprising I even have an online log-in."

Madison never knew her brother-in-law was so behind when it came to his acceptance of technology. She put a hand on Jim's shoulder. "Come with me." She led him to Troy's desktop computer, which was set up in an alcove off the kitchen. The computer was on, as it often was for whatever reason, though Troy barely used it. But right now, she was happy it was warmed up and ready to go.

She flicked on the monitor and opened the Internet browser. "There you go."

Jim sat down and looked at her as if silently requesting his privacy.

She held up her hands and backed up. "I'll be in the living room."

She stepped away and listened to Jim's keystrokes and mouse-clicking. When both stopped, she asked, "What have you got?"

Jim came into the doorway. "She made a purchase at the gas station on that corner."

"Great." Madison was on her way to the door.

"Wait. The amount she spent would have easily

filled the tank, though, and she rarely fills it. She likes to play the gas-pump price war, as she calls it. Could she be being forced to drive somewhere?"

Trepidation wormed through Madison as she turned around and saw the fear in Jim's eyes. "Stay strong, all right?" She held eye contact with him until he nodded ever so slightly. She glanced over at her nieces, who were still preoccupied with Hershey. She turned her attention to Troy. "Take care of my family."

"You know I will." Troy pulled her close and held her tightly. She gave him a quick kiss and then flew out the front door with Terry right behind her.

CHAPTER

32

MADISON STOPPED SHORT OF THE department car. Her body felt heavy, weighed down and grounded to the pavement.

"Maddy?" Terry asked, seeming to have sensed her predicament.

The flick of the curtain moving in Troy's front window caught her eye. Troy and Jim were looking out.

"Let me drive," she said.

"I don't think you should," Terry began. "You're under a lot of stress."

She couldn't argue with him, but she felt like she would be more in control if she could just be behind the wheel. "Please." She held out an open hand.

"Fine, but be careful." He passed over the keys.

They both got in and buckled up.

Terry turned to her. "We'll find her and get her back safe."

"Everyone has to stop saying that," she barked. "We don't know that she will be." She hated how she was bouncing back and forth between hope and defeat. She met her partner's gaze. "I wish I had your confidence…Marissa's confidence. But what if we don't—"

"No," he said firmly. "We're not going to think about that. Nothing good will come of it."

She loved his conviction and just hated feeling so damn weak and vulnerable. Part of her had always lived in a world of hesitation, wondering when the ground would fall out from beneath her. Everything had been going great in her life… So was it time for the ground to drop?

She put the car into gear and took off.

The gas station was about twenty minutes from Troy's, but she'd make it in record time. She flicked on the lights and sirens.

As she raced across the city, thoughts of Chelsea haunted her. She was likely alone and terrified. And who knew what the hell that monster had done to her or was doing to her now.

Madison's pulse sped up as images layered on top of one another… Constantine above her on the couch about to—

It will only hurt a little.

"Madison!" Terry grabbed the wheel and cranked it to the right. She slammed on the brakes.

She blinked, tears seeping from the corners of her eyes. As her vision came into focus, she realized that she was in the middle of an intersection. The light facing her was red. The hood of another car was mere feet from her driver's-side door.

Terry turned off the lights and sirens. "Clear the intersection," he directed her. "Pull over there." He pointed to a free parking spot at the curb.

She eased onto the gas pedal and did as he'd told her to. Once she had parked, he reached over, turned off the car, and pulled the keys from the ignition.

Terry's face was bright red. "You could have killed us."

She pinched her eyes shut and counted to ten in her head.

"Madison? Do you hear me?" Terry touched her shoulder, and she flinched.

A few tears fell, but she shook her head, sniffled, and looked over at him. "If Constantine lays a fucking hand on her—"

"He'll wish he hadn't," Terry finished.

"That's damn right." She was nothing but an ice-cold, dark, empty shell. She wiped her cheeks. "I'm sorry, Terry."

"For swearing?" He waved her off. "That's understandable right now."

"Not for that. For almost killing us."

"Oh, that little thing…" He was doing his best to make light of what had happened but wasn't convincing. "Come on, let's switch places and get going."

They got out, and the driver of the car that had almost hit them had parked on a side street and was yelling at her. Madison had to admit their swearing was understandable, too. Lights and sirens aside, she still should have checked all directions before entering the intersection, but she'd just blown through.

With both of them back in the car, and Terry behind the wheel, they got moving again.

"If Constantine doesn't plan to hurt her, and he's using her as bait to get to me, why hasn't he contacted me yet?" Her heart was fracturing.

Terry glanced over at her. "Because he wants to shake you."

She hated to admit that it was working. The silence was unsettling.

"He's not going to kill her," Terry said.

His words sounded good, but that's all they were. There was no guarantee. "And how do you...know that?" She swallowed the harsh reality that life could be unpredictable and heartless, but that didn't mean it settled well in her stomach.

"He's all about mind games, and I bet he's simply using your sister to play with you."

"But so much time has already passed."

"Every step he's made since he left that note on your windshield has been to taunt you. Sending that e-mail to your mother? He just wants you to suffer for a while."

"Well, enough already."

Terry pulled into the gas station and parked near the storefront. There was only one car filling up at one of the four pumps.

Madison and Terry both got out of the car and headed toward the entrance. She dismissed the negative thoughts creeping in telling her that coming here was a futile exercise. For one, the people who had been working this morning might have already finished their shifts, and two, even if they could get the surveillance video, it might not provide them with anything to go on. After all, this was the intersection where Chelsea was this morning at eight thirty. That was hours ago. It was going on five in the afternoon now.

She was reaching for the door when her phone chimed with a new text message. She let her hand drop and stepped to the side, staying outside. Terry followed suit.

"Who is it?" he asked before she even had her phone out.

Bile rose in her throat as she pulled her phone from her pocket. What if it was a message from Constantine? A picture of her sister...

"It's my parents." She read the message: *Plane will be in about midnight. Need to be picked up.*

She gripped her phone. Maybe she should have regretted not calling them about Chelsea, but she didn't. Was it so wrong that she wanted to be armed with something before letting them know Chelsea was abducted by a Mafia hit man?

"What is it?"

"It's official. My parents are on their way."

"It's probably not a bad thing that they are," he said.

"It's probably worse." She could imagine the conversation with her mother already. How she'd back Madison into a corner and force her to defend herself. But, really, wasn't that where she was already? She couldn't feel any more responsible.

Terry cocked his head. "Come on."

"Listen, you might think I'm exaggerating, but trust me, I'm not. My mother as good as hates me."

"She doesn't hate you."

"She disapproves of me, and this isn't a new conversation for us."

"You're, what? Thirty-six. You don't need her approval. Besides, you'll always be her daughter."

"Are you trying to make me feel better or worse?"

"Which effect is it having?"

She scowled and rolled her eyes.

He held up his hands. "Hey, don't say I didn't try."

Nope, I won't say that… Sarcasm all the way.

She sent a quick text to her mother to let her know she'd be there to pick them up and then fired one to Troy as a heads-up. "All right, I'm ready." She put her phone away, and Terry grabbed the door.

"Go ahead," he said.

There was a gangly twentysomething male behind the counter, who saw them and quickly diverted his gaze. He was either shy or figured them for cops and was hiding something.

She thought she'd get right to it. She pulled out her badge. "Detectives Knight and"—she gestured to her partner—"Grant."

The guy slowly drew his eyes up to meet hers. Definitely shy.

"Were you working this morning?" she asked, starting with the basics.

"Y-yes," he stuttered nervously.

"In that case, we have a few questions for you." She took out her phone again and brought up a photo of Chelsea. She extended the screen toward the clerk so he could see. "Do you recognize this woman?"

The guy leaned forward, really studying the photo. "Yeah. She comes here sometimes."

Madison did her best to tamp down the bit of excitement his acknowledgment brought her. "Do you remember her from *this* morning?"

"Hmm." He tapped his chin with an index finger a few times. "I think so."

"What time?"

"Don't know exactly. Around eight thirty?"

"Was she alone?" she asked.

"No," he said. "There was a guy in the front passenger seat. I remember him because he was big. Like tall and solid, not fat. His head was almost hitting the ceiling of the car."

She drew back her phone, pulled up a picture of Constantine, and held it out for him to see.

He nodded. "Yes, that's him."

Her breathing quickened, and she stepped away, turning her back to Terry and the clerk.

"When she pulled in, was he already in the car?" Terry asked, taking over the questioning.

"Yeah."

So where had Constantine hijacked Chelsea? Given the time of day, it seemed likely that Chelsea had dropped the girls off and had come right here.

So Constantine had either abducted her at the school after the girls had left the car or…

Madison's skin went clammy as another possibility struck. He could have been waiting in the trunk. He had been in the house to take the picture, after all. And he'd sent the e-mail at 8:03 this morning. It could have been when Chelsea was leaving with the girls. Doing so, though, he'd risked her mother seeing the e-mail earlier in the day. But Constantine would know that no matter how quickly her mother got the message, it would be too late. It had to be another ploy to further upset Madison. A matter of being close but just out of reach.

He could have waited it out in the garage, then the trunk. Typically, Chelsea would have no reason to go in there, not that Madison could imagine anyhow. Even if she brought her gym bag along when she had the girls, they'd be in the backseat and she'd have plenty of room in the front. Maybe she wasn't going to work out until later that day. Either way, Constantine risked being spotted with the girls around. Her blood ran cold at the thought of that man taking all four of them.

Madison turned around. "Did you happen to see which direction they went in when they left?" It might be a reach, but it could be faster than waiting on access to video footage from the gas station or the city.

He nodded. "They used the west exit and went south."

That would take them to a rural area that went on

for miles. Add to that, they could have turned onto the interstate and gone who knows where.

"Wish I could help more than that," the clerk said genuinely.

"Do you have surveillance cameras?" she asked.

"Yeah. Inside and out."

"We'll need the footage from this morning." She presented it as if he didn't have an option.

The clerk winced. "I'm sorry, but I can't give it to you. My manager will be—"

"Someone from the Stiles PD will be in touch with a warrant." She left for the door.

Outside, she turned to Terry. "I think Constantine was waiting on Chelsea in the trunk of her car. It would be easy enough to get from there into the backseat. Most cars have seat release pulls in the trunk, and I'm sure Chelsea's Fusion has them."

Maybe she was jumping to a conclusion, but right now, that theory was probably the most logical. If he'd intercepted her at the school, it was likely someone else would have seen it, including the officer posted there. Of course, he could have pulled it off in such a way that wouldn't arouse suspicion.

"Okay, here's the thing," Terry began. "Assuming Constantine got into your sister's house while the family was asleep—so either sometime during the night, or in the wee hours this morning—I'd like to know how. Surveillance was in place."

Her insides churned as the answer sank in the pit of her stomach. "They were posted out front, but their backyard butts against a neighboring one."

"Oh."

"Yeah. We need to get to Chelsea's and get clothes for everyone, but I also want to see if the bastard left any clues there."

Terry nodded. "Let's do it."

"I'll call Cyn to tell her what we're thinking, and then I'm calling Winston to arrange for a meeting." As much as Madison would love to go it alone sometimes, handle situations solo, there were benefits to having others by her side. And she couldn't be everywhere at once. If she wanted her sister back alive—and sooner rather than later—the best course of action would be to assemble everyone. Sometimes more heads were better than one.

CHAPTER

33

HIGGINS WAS STILL OUT FRONT of Chelsea's house. The forensics van was there, too, and that didn't surprise Madison. If there was something to link Constantine to Chelsea's home, her friend or her team would find it.

Higgins got out of his cruiser and headed toward Madison and Terry, as they also approached him.

"How are you holding up?" Higgins asked with the tenderness of a loving father.

"As good as can be expected," she responded.

Terry put a hand on her shoulder, and for a second, she thought she'd fall apart.

She glanced toward the house to break eye contact and distance herself. "We know it's Constantine now," she began. "A witness saw him with Chelsea this morning."

Higgins was shaking his head. "That SOB should have stayed out of the country."

"You're damn right about that." She found her gaze going to the front door. "We're going to see how Cynthia is making out."

Higgins dipped his head, and Madison and Terry went into the house.

They found Cynthia in the garage with Mark. Her friend stopped what she was doing and hurried over. Cynthia wrapped her arms around Madison and hugged her so tightly that she thought her back might go out of alignment. But there was no way she was letting go. She'd soak in as much support as she could. When she'd successfully blinked back the tears, she stepped back.

"Any luck tying Constantine to here?" Madison asked.

Cynthia shook her head. "No sign of forced entry, but we've got lots of prints…"

"Which could belong to anyone in the family," Madison replied. "Same for the frame and computer accessories?"

Her friend frowned. "I wish I had more for you, and I hate to pile on bad news," Cynthia continued, "but that e-mail he sent isn't going to get us anywhere, either."

"Why am I not surprised," Madison stated sourly.

"Hey, something's got to turn around soon." Cynthia's upbeat response didn't begin to make Madison feel better, but she appreciated the attempt.

"And…" Cynthia glanced at Mark, who was coming over. "We're done here, Maddy, as much as I hate to say it."

"I understand." She balled her fists, and given the shift in Cynthia's gaze, she'd noticed.

"Hang in there."

"All I can do." Madison expelled a lungful of air in a whoosh. "Well, I've got to get some clothes for Jim and the girls."

Cynthia squeezed Madison again. "I understand there's a meeting in about two hours to discuss where the search for Constantine stands."

"Yeah." This was all so surreal, as if they were discussing any case, not her sister's abduction. But there were moments when the nightmarish reality set in with a heavy weight.

"Come on." Cynthia waved for Mark to follow her. "We're going to do all we can before the meeting."

As optimistic as her friend was, a couple of hours wasn't a lot of time, even if it sometimes stretched on for an eternity.

Madison followed them from the garage back into the house, Terry behind her.

Cynthia and Mark packed up their things and left while Madison headed upstairs. She stopped on the third step and turned around to face Terry.

"I think they keep their luggage in the furnace room. Would you mind?"

"Not at all." Terry set off in the direction of the basement.

Looking back up the stairs, she closed her eyes briefly, remembering the last time she saw her sister from this stairwell. It had been a few months ago when the investigation into Barry's death was starting to take its toll on Madison. Chelsea had woken up to find Madison sleeping in her car in their driveway and had insisted that she come in to spend the night—or what had been left of it.

Madison gripped the railing and resumed walking up the stairs. It was as if touching the wood brought her closer to her sister somehow. What was she going to tell their mother when she got there? There was no doubt she'd think all of this was Madison's fault. After all, she's the one who worked in law enforcement and garnered the attention of psychopaths.

She reached the top landing and stepped into the master bedroom. It appeared to have just been cleaned, but that was her sister. Three kids, a perfect marriage, and she still managed to keep her house tidy. Even the bed was made. How were they even related?

Madison smirked at that thought. There were many ways they were alike, but they were so different in others. Madison had never come to appreciate the importance of making the bed, and now in her thirties, she likely never would.

Madison scanned her sister's dresser and its spread of makeup and hair products. She walked over, picked up a perfume bottle, and sniffed it while closing her eyes. It smelled like Chelsea, and Madison let herself imagine that her sister was there with her.

"I found the luggage. One suitcase should be enough, I would think, right?"

She turned to see Terry in the doorway holding up a large, hardside suitcase. The truth was, she didn't know how to answer him. How long would they be staying with her and Troy? Probably not long, she supposed. Jim was cooperating for the time being, but he was strong-willed and likely wouldn't want to turn his life or the girls' lives upside down forever.

"Should be fine," she said, thinking they could always come back for more.

"Point me in the direction you want me to go."

She looked across the room at Jim's dresser and was thankful Terry was with her. She didn't exactly want to be elbow-deep in her brother-in-law's underwear drawer. She jerked her head in the direction of his dresser. "Why don't you pack some stuff for Jim?"

Terry didn't say anything, just went and did what she'd asked.

They moved from Chelsea and Jim's room to the girls' rooms, finished up packing, and headed out.

Madison was staring at the house from the sidewalk, noting how dark and empty it was now. It hammered home the nightmare they were all living.

"You all right?" Terry asked.

"Not really."

"Come on, you're not going to let a Russian Mafia hit man call the shots, are you?" Terry rallied around her. "Since when has Detective Madison Knight ever backed down?"

She met his eyes, fire burning in her belly. "You're right."

"Of course, I'm right. You beat the asshole once. What's a second time?"

She couldn't help but give a brief smile. "We figure out where he's holed up, we rescue Chelsea, and we take the bastard down."

"That's my partner!" Terry whooped, wrapped an arm around Madison's shoulder and guided her back to the car.

CHAPTER

34

SERGEANT WINSTON WAS COMING DOWN the hall toward her. "How are you holding up?"

She understood people's need to ask, but she couldn't give any real thought to the answer or she'd crumble. "I'm fine."

"Any leads as to where she might be?" he asked.

She shook her head.

"How's Bates's murder investigation going? Do you need me to assign it to someone else?"

"No." She'd blurted it out rather fast, and the sergeant's eyes flashed with skepticism before he held up his hands in acquiescence.

"All right, then. As long as you think you can handle that on top of your missing sister."

"She isn't *missing*," Madison bit out. "She's been abducted."

Winston's face flushed, and he remained quiet for a few beats. "And what about that girl, Yasmine Stone? I'm thinking I should put Stanford and Sovereign on it."

"No. She's connected to Bates and Constantine."

"Why is this the first time I'm hearing about this?" Winston let his gaze trail to Terry.

"There's been a lot going—"

Winston held up a hand to silence Terry. "I've never been a fan of excuses." He left them there and entered the conference room.

"I can't believe that man sometimes," Madison grumbled.

"Just let it go. You know how he gets when he's not kept up to speed."

"I know how he gets all right." She balled her fists and squeezed them to release some tension and then joined everyone else in the room.

Detective-grade officers were in there, including the men from Troy's SWAT team, along with sergeants from other divisions. Troy wasn't here, though, because she'd begged him to stay home with her family. Officers were also posted in front of Troy's house and on the block behind it, just to ensure that there was no way for Constantine to gain access.

"Sorry to hear about your sister," Nick said.

"Yeah, sorry," another detective added.

She nodded in acknowledgment to everyone there. In doing so, she noticed that her ex, Toby Sovereign, and his partner, Lou Stanford, Cynthia's fiancé, weren't in the room. They must have been called to a case.

"If you would all take your seats," Winston began. The door opened, and Andrea came in. She beelined for Madison and stopped short of hugging her, though Madison sensed she wanted to. But this was a professional setting and Andrea was nothing if not a professional—and immaculate. Even now at eight at night, she was dressed in a black business suit with a white blouse. The suit appeared to be freshly pressed as if it hadn't already been through a workday. Her hair was pulled back, not a strand out of place.

"I've been in meetings and just heard. How are you?" Andrea asked.

"Fine."

Andrea was peering into Madison's eyes, reading them with a skill her brother had down all too well. It obviously ran in their family.

Madison could feel everyone watching them. "We'll talk later." She barely brushed the chief's elbow as she walked to the table. She took a seat next to Terry near the front. Andrea sat on Madison's other side.

"All right, now that everyone is here," Winston began, "let's get started. We know that Constantine Romanov, a known hit man for the Russian Mafia, has returned to Stiles and has threatened one of our own."

While everyone's attention had shifted from Madison to Winston, who was pacing in front of a whiteboard, it returned to her with Winston's introductory words.

"Most of us in this room have been diligently working to find his whereabouts, and so far, haven't had any luck. But we need to push ourselves even more." Winston paused. "Detective Knight's sister has gone missing, and it's believed that Romanov has taken her."

"It's more than a belief," Madison snapped back and shrunk under Winston's glare. She composed herself and continued. "We have an eyewitness who saw him with my sister."

"When and where was this?" Nick asked.

She named the gas station and the intersection. "Warrants will be processed for their surveillance footage." Madison cleared her throat. "We know that when they left the gas station, they headed south."

"That leads to the rural area surrounding Stiles," Nick said, even though everyone in the room already knew that.

"That's right," Madison confirmed. "And all this happened at eight thirty this morning, which is also when her phone went offline."

"We need to dig deeper, harder, longer," Winston said, taking charge again. "There's something that we're obviously missing. I want teams in place outside residences of known Mafia members and associates, as well as their business fronts."

"And you should know by now that it's believed that Constantine is either acting under the direction of a power player other than Dimitre Petrov or—" her stomach clenched and breathing became difficult "—or he's gone rogue."

Questions filled the room.

"Gone rogue? What are we supposed to do in that

case?"

"How are we supposed to find him without any leads?"

They drove home the dire possibility that they wouldn't find Constantine unless he wanted to be found.

"Quiet!" Winston roared.

The room hushed instantly.

"We will find him and get Madison's sister back. It doesn't matter if this guy is working on his own or backed by an army, we're Stiles PD." He went quiet for a few seconds. "Did everyone hear me?"

"Hell yes!" Nick cried out, and he was joined by several others expressing the same sentiment.

"Now get out of here and get to work. And remember, no one acts without running it past their superior, and we need to carry out our surveillance as discreetly as possible. There's a civilian's life at risk here, and we don't need to encourage anyone's trigger finger."

People started getting up, and chair legs scraped along the floor. Andrea turned to Madison with wet eyes.

"What is it?" Madison asked.

Andrea addressed the people who were still in the room. "Could you all excuse us, please?"

Terry remained in his seat, and Andrea gestured over Madison's shoulder at him.

"You too, please."

"Oh, okay." Terry got up and said to Madison, "I'll be at our desks. Want a coffee?"

"Sure," she said without thinking it through. Bullpen coffee was deadly. But maybe tonight, it was just a matter of it being caffeine.

"You got it." Terry left.

Winston was the last out of the room. The second the door closed behind him, Andrea flung her arms around Madison.

"I'm so sorry this is happening to you," she said, drawing back. "This is the sort of reward you get for being good at your job, I guess. A madman with an obsession with revenge."

"Any way of sending it back?" Madison teased, but any attempt at joviality fell short.

Andrea fidgeted with her fingers, and the silence that was mounting between them brought a chasm of uncertainty. There was something the chief clearly didn't want to say, and Madison could only think of one thing that could be right now.

"You don't want me investigating this." When Andrea remained quiet, Madison's suspicion knotted her gut. "You're benching me?"

Andrea licked her lips and let the silence ride out for what felt like forever. "Only from this aspect," she eventually said.

"*Only* this aspect?" Madison exclaimed. "She's my sister, Andrea. My flesh and blood." Her plea didn't seem to be making any sort of impact if Andrea's resolved expression was any indication. "What if it was Troy?" she spat.

"No," Andrea said. "Don't do that."

"Would you just sit back and do nothing?"

Madison continued pressing. "I bet no one could tell you to lie low, to stay out of it."

"Madison, please." While the words alone could come across as a loving plea, it was in their delivery that Madison knew there would be no swaying the chief on this matter.

"Are you taking me off the murder investigations, too? Bates's and Yasmine's?"

"Not at this time."

Madison gritted her teeth. "What's that supposed to mean?"

"Just that, Madison. I'm giving you more leeway here than I would anyone else." Andrea stood up and braced herself on the back of the chair. "Don't you realize that?" It was obvious she never intended it as a real question. "I just don't want you to wind up hurt."

"Fine." Madison got up and left the room.

How could Andrea expect her to just stay off the investigation into her sister's whereabouts when the only key to getting Chelsea back would likely involve her direct violation of that directive? As much as she respected Andrea and loved her like a sister, she'd go behind her back if she had to.

CHAPTER

35

MADISON STORMED OUT OF THE conference room and met up with Terry. Coffee was in a mug on her desk. He was holding one to his mouth. He lowered it when he saw her.

"What's wrong?" he asked.

"I've been removed from investigating my sister's abduction."

"You've what?" Terry jolted as he got up, spilling coffee over the edge of his cup. "The chief?"

"Yeah… I can't believe this." She punched one hand into the palm of the other. "I can't imagine her standing on the sidelines if something happened to Troy."

"But she ordered you to—"

"Yes, Terry, and she wasn't changing her mind about it."

"What about the murder cases?"

"I'm still fine to work those." She scoffed.

"Well, then you work those. Maybe something there will provide a clue to Constantine's whereabouts."

She angled her head. "If so, it should have turned up by now."

"You know that's not true. Berger & Stein has fifty board members alone. We have their client list, too."

"Which is already being combed through."

"Right. The emphasis on *being*. There's still something we could uncover."

"We?" She eyed him skeptically. "You weren't taken off my sister's case. I want you all over it."

Terry opened his mouth, then closed it.

"What?" she pressed.

"Others have the surveillance of the known Mafia members and associates covered. Let's see what we can find with the murder cases."

She held eye contact with her partner. "All right," she said, but the moment she was out of there, she'd be calling Troy and getting him to work on changing his sister's mind.

For the next two and a half hours, they read background reports and analyzed them. Nothing was sticking out on its own or even when tidbits of curiosity had them detouring. She bowed out at eleven thirty and headed to the airport to get her parents.

Another joyous moment…

She called Troy from her Mazda, and he answered before the first ring died.

"How did it go?" he blurted out.

"Not good."

"What do you mean?"

"*Your* sister took me off *my* sister's abduction case," she ground out. "I need you to talk to her and make her see how—" She stopped talking, getting the feeling he wasn't listening. "Troy?"

"I know what you're going to say."

"Then you'll do it? You'll call her and talk her out of this? I need to—"

"I won't."

"You won't?" she spat. Her earlobes heated and her chest burned with anger.

The line stayed silent for a few beats.

"Troy," she pressed.

"This guy is set on killing you, Madison," Troy said, striking her with the brutal truth. "If you're out there looking for your sister, he'll get you in his sights."

"It might be the only way to get her back," she pleaded hysterically. "Why doesn't anyone understand this? Everyone knows he's after *me*!"

"If there comes a time when it's you for your sister's life—"

"She better let me do my job, Troy." Heat saturated every word.

Troy remained silent for a moment. "Do you not realize how much you mean to me?" he asked. He was clearly trying to tread carefully, but it enraged her.

"You can't compare my life to Chelsea's. She's a wife, a mother, she's—" Emotion balled in her throat.

"It doesn't make her life more valuable than

yours."

"It—"

"You're both important, and you're both loved by the people in your lives," Troy said, attempting to smooth things over. And on a small scale, it worked.

She let her eyes drift to the clock on the dash. It was eleven forty-five. "I've gotta go. Mom and Dad will be deplaning soon."

"I love you, Madison," he said.

"I know you do." She hung up and gripped the phone. She hadn't said the words back, and she regretted it instantly. She considered dialing him right away for that express purpose, but she didn't. Instead, she got out of her car and went inside the small Stiles airport. As she entered, she heard the rumble of a jet and figured it was likely her parents' flight.

She paced the baggage claim area, her mind racing as she tried to figure out how she was going to tell them about Chelsea. The conversation she'd had with Troy shook her, but it was more in regard to what she believed about herself than anything— how she devalued her life because she wasn't married with kids. But that thinking and measure of self-worth had been encouraged by her mother. Most times she spoke with the woman there was some mention of Madison's love life or job. And right now, Madison wouldn't blame her mother for verbally attacking her. It was because of her job, her obsession with finding justice, that they were in this mess in the first place.

People started filtering into baggage claim, and her mom and dad were near the front of the crowd. Her mom saw her and elbowed her husband. He smiled at Madison, but her mom didn't. Of course, Madison had given up expecting any fanfare upon her mother seeing her a long time ago. She couldn't ever remember receiving a big overhead wave and exuberant grin. The best she'd usually get was a wave and a scowl indicating, *I'm over here. Hurry up.*

Madison approached them and offered to take a bag from her mother, who had a large carry-on slung over one shoulder and her purse on the other. She was also pushing a wheeled suitcase, and her dad had one, too.

"I've got it, Madison." Her mother stepped back.

Madison held her hands up in surrender and turned her attention to her father. "Hey, Dad," she said, hugging him.

"Glad to see you're okay, honey," he said pleasantly and patted her on the back.

The hug was brief but sincere, and between that and his kind words, it had tears springing to her eyes. She turned away hoping that her mother wouldn't notice.

"What's wrong?"

Too late...

The sooner she told them about Chelsea, the better. She couldn't very well wait until they got to Troy's. Maybe it was best to handle this how she did when giving notice to next of kin—directly and succinctly. "Why don't we sit down..."

"Oh no. What is it?" Her mother's face paled. "I can read you, and I see it all over your face that something is wrong."

How Madison wished she could assure her that everything was fine. "Let's just sit down. We could get a coffee."

"It's just after midnight. If I drink one now, I'll be up all night," her dad said.

Once they heard what Madison had to say, sleep probably wouldn't be coming anyhow.

"Madison," her mother said in her demanding tone.

A man was trying to get by, and Madison had to guide her mother to step aside and let him pass.

"Follow me." Madison turned and walked toward a grouping of chairs. She got to a bench and took a seat. "Here, Mom. You sit beside me." She looked past her mom to her dad. "And you sit beside her."

Her father sat down, but her mother was stubbornly refusing to.

"I don't like this one bit. What's happened? Is it Chelsea? The girls?" Her mother pushed out the questions as if it was hard labor, her cheeks starting to flame, her blood pressure seemingly rising.

"Please, Mom, sit."

"Tell me," she barked, but her fear was disclosed in the trembling of her bottom lip.

If Madison could make the woman sit, she would, but she made Madison seem compliant by comparison. Her mother's face was resting in a scowl, but her eyes were full of tears. Madison didn't doubt her when she'd said she could read her and knew that something was wrong.

"Fine. You want to remain standing—"

"I do." Her mother jutted out her chin stubbornly.

Madison took a deep breath and blew it out. Suddenly it was as if the entire airport had fallen into silence, and there was no one else around but her parents. She took a few seconds to compose herself, and her mother put a hand over her mouth.

Time to come out with it. "Chelsea's been abducted. We're—"

"Oh!" her mother gasped, dropping her now-trembling hand.

"We're doing everything we can to find her."

"My god, Noah! A psychopath has my daughter!" her mother cried out, and her legs buckled. Her bag and purse fell to the floor, and Madison moved quickly to buoy her mother before she joined them. Her mom let her guide her by the elbow to the bench.

Once she had her mother safely seated, Madison looked over at her father. His eyes were full of tears now, too. Her mother was staring into space.

"When did this happen?" he asked.

"We believe she was taken this—" How could she possibly tell him this morning and explain why she hadn't called them. She didn't find out until this afternoon, but still… Her mother had reached out to her first.

"When?" Her mother had a bunched-up tissue in her hand, which she must have taken out of her coat pocket.

There would be no easy way to say this and no way around it. "This morning."

"This morning!" Anger swept over her mother's features. "She was taken *this morning* and you didn't tell us? Did you plan on telling us?"

Emotion welled up in Madison's throat and tears burned her eyes, but she willed herself to remain strong. She had to provide a beacon of hope for her family and instill confidence in them that she would get Chelsea back. And with that thought, she replayed her conversation with Andrea, how she'd officially been removed from actively taking part in the search. Surely, Andrea had just meant she didn't want her showing up at Russian business fronts. Maybe she should have clarified. Maybe it wasn't as black-and-white as Andrea had made it seem.

"Madison?" her father prompted. "When did *you* find out?"

She swallowed roughly. "Just this afternoon."

Her mother burst out in a fit of crying, her hands cupping her mouth as tears flowed. She was starting to draw the attention of people walking by, many of whom offered solemn, sympathetic faces. Her father put an arm around his wife.

"We're doing all we can to find her and get her back," Madison said, though fear and doubt snaked through her.

Her mother sniffled and pressed the well-used tissue to her nose. "Was it the Mafia?"

Madison's mouth gaped open at her mother's

conclusion. "The Maf—"

"I know you've been after them because of your grandfather's murder. Did you stir them up?"

Madison swallowed roughly. "We have reason to believe—"

"Be straight with us, Madison."

Madison bit her lip and nodded. "Yes," she said simply.

Her mother started crying in earnest again but managed to get out, "What have you done, Madison?"

Madison's chest splintered with the attack. Her breath hitched, and she bit down on her bottom lip, hoping to hold back the tears. But a few fell anyway.

Her father was rubbing her mother's arms. "This isn't Madison's fault."

Her mother said nothing, and by doing so, said it all: she held Madison responsible, and Madison alone.

CHAPTER

36

MADISON GOT HER PARENTS SETTLED into the spare room at Troy's house. Jim and the girls were set up in the living room, and he'd done his best to sell the experience as a slumber party, but none of the girls were buying it. They wanted their mother, and none of the adults could blame them.

Madison and Troy were in the master bedroom with Hershey, who wasn't his normal self, either. He pawed at his bed in the corner of the room, spun enough times to make Madison dizzy, and finally dropped with a sigh.

"Why hasn't he called?" She drew her legs to her chest, her back against the wall.

Troy didn't say anything, but what did she expect him to say? She glanced over at him and found him watching her with evident concern.

"We know that Constantine has an ego, is a narcissist, and loves the power of being in control."

"Which is an illusion," she said slowly as her shrink's words struck her. She hopped from the bed.

"We need to destroy his illusion," she ruminated. "But how?"

"Good question. But when we do, he's going to lash out."

"And that means…" Oh, she hated where her thinking was headed. "I need to give him evidence that his calling the shots is getting to me." It was the opposite of how she'd been thinking up until this point. Her pride would have shot down the notion of showing him that he was affecting her.

Troy shifted on the bed, sitting up straighter. "You might be on to something with this. You let Constantine know he's got power over you, and—"

"Well, let him believe that anyway," she corrected him. The truth was, Constantine *was* affecting her.

"He's going to feel in control, like he's won this little game of his."

"And that should keep Chelsea safe. But how do I make it clear to him that he's getting to me?"

"That part is tricky," Troy conceded. "At least until he makes contact with you."

She nodded and looked at the clock. *2:05 AM.*

"At this point, I'd guess he's holding out until morning." She shuttered as she thought about her sister. She must be terrified.

Madison's thoughts turned darker still, and her heart started beating faster as the images of Constantine assaulting her piled on, terrorizing her and threatening to consume her alive. She could feel herself slipping, the flashbacks tugging her into the past.

Troy rushed to her and kept her standing. "I've got you."

She peered into his eyes, and all she saw was love. This was all it took for the dam holding back her emotions to break. Her body shook, and she cried in heaving sobs.

Hershey lifted his head and came over. Troy patted Hershey on the head and directed him to go back to his bed. Troy then got up and guided Madison back to bed, too.

She palmed her cheeks. "I need her to be okay." She couldn't look at him now, as if by doing so she'd be more overcome with emotion than she already was.

"I know, baby." He gently brushed the hair away from her forehead. The action was so sweet and soothing that her tears started to dry up, but it didn't make the ache in her chest go away. But it had set in when she knew Constantine had her sister and it likely wouldn't ease up until Chelsea was safely back at home.

"If only I knew where she was." She braved looking at him, and the feeling of desperation sank in her gut. She was so used to having the answers, or at least the strength to find them. "How am I supposed to—"

"Shh," he cooed.

She leaned forward, putting her ear over his heartbeat.

Troy let her stay there for some time before he pulled back. "Get some rest."

She blinked as she nodded, and the last of the tears trailed down her cheeks.

CHAPTER

37

MADISON'S SLEEP WAS RESTLESS AND she saw most hours on the clock, but when she was out, she had strange dreams that were more a series of images than anything that made sense. But then again, how often were dreams logical?

Mental snapshots from Yasmine's murder scene had paraded through her mind: her dead body, how young and beautiful she was, and how tragic it was that her life had been cut short. But it was the motivation for it that was still missing. Madison had a confirmed connection to Constantine as Kevin Jones, but had she been telling the truth when she'd said that she didn't know what he did for work or had she been covering it up? And how did her affair with McAlexandar tie in? Had he actually been pushed to pull the trigger for some reason? To protect his lifestyle? To keep the affair from his wife? The questions piled up higher and higher. She just couldn't accept that Bates's and Yasmine's murders, which took place within days of each other, were coincidence.

Yasmine's face had morphed into Bates's and brought with it the bloody murder scene with scarlet everywhere. How devoid of emotion she still was when it came to his death. She hadn't been able to get past the feeling of Karma being repaid.

As images of Bates faded, those of Constantine looming above her became vivid—his smirk, his energy, his intention to defile her before murdering her.

She jolted awake with a racing heart. She read the alarm clock on Troy's dresser. *6:00 AM.*

She reached out to Troy's side of the bed and looked over when her hand met with nothing. He must have already gotten up for the day. She glanced over at Hershey's bed, and he was gone, too. She wondered when the two of them had slipped out. The last time she remembered being up was four o'clock.

As her mind cleared and she shook off her grogginess, chatter filtered in from the other room. She could hear her mother's voice above everyone else's.

Madison got out of bed, slipped a robe over her pajamas, grabbed her phone, and left the room. She padded down the hall in bare feet and found her nieces in the living room playing with Hershey. He let out a bark and pranced around in front of them while Marissa dangled a rope toy from her hand.

"Morning, guys," Madison said to her nieces, still moving in the direction of the adults.

Her mom and dad and Jim were all at the kitchen table cradling cups of coffee while Troy was at the counter holding a mug in one hand and the pot in the other.

Troy put the mug down, stopping short of pouring a cup, and came over to her. He stopped in front of her, wrapped his arms around her, and hugged her. "Good morning, sweetheart." He dropped a kiss on her earlobe and then on her lips.

She appreciated his love and affection, but was having a hard time swallowing the *good* part of his greeting. She was numb while everyone carried on around her.

"Hi." She touched Troy's cheek and held his gaze for a few seconds. He left to return to the coffee machine. "Hello," she said to her family.

"Hi, honey," her father said.

Her mother now appeared almost comatose, and Madison had to wonder if it was her presence, as she seemed to have been talking a lot before Madison had come into the room. But maybe she'd said everything she had to say. Unlikely, though. This was her mother, and she had something to say about everything.

Troy held the pot toward her. "Want some?"

"Do you have to ask?"

A subtle smirk touched his lips, and he poured the cup he had been going to take for himself and proceeded to make it how she liked it. He extended it to her. "Here you go."

"Thanks." She kissed him on the cheek and

wandered over to the table. She sat down at the end between her brother-in-law and her father.

Her mother only glimpsed at her when Troy sat down across from Madison.

"Why hasn't the man called yet?" her mother asked Troy.

"We believe that he's trying to—"

"Sometimes there is no explaining a psychopath." Madison was quick to cut Troy short. The last thing she needed was for him to say that Constantine was using Chelsea to get to Madison. Her mother already laid blame on Madison's shoulders and didn't need any more fuel to justify doing so.

"That's ludicrous!" her mother exclaimed. "That's what you're supposed to do, isn't it? That's your job as a cop. It's called profiling."

"Mrs. Knight—" Troy put a hand on her mother's forearm "—we can only best-guess situations, but we have good reason to believe that we'll get her back safely." His gaze kept flicking to Madison while he spoke, as if silently seeking her approval of what he was saying.

"Why?" her mother snapped. "Is there a guarantee?"

"There's never a guarantee, Mom. That's life," Madison blurted out. Screw it. Maybe she should just come out and tell her mom, make it clear what a failure she was and how she'd brought all of this on them. "I'm the one he's after, and he's using Chelsea to get to me."

Jim rubbed his jaw. Her father was staring across

the table. Her mother's mouth rested in a scowl, and her gaze was blank. Troy was the only one meeting Madison's eyes.

"Did you hear me? All of this is my fault," she burst out.

The girls in the other room fell silent. Layer on the guilt. Layer on the things to feel sorry for.

Anxiety bloomed in Madison's chest. "I am doing everything I can to bring her back. The Stiles police department is, too. But he wants me."

"He is using Chels as bait," Jim stated on an exhale.

Her mother shot him a glare that could freeze the Caribbean. "To get to my other daughter!" Her mother cried out, and the girls came into the kitchen and gathered around their grandmother.

Brie was crying, and Jim scooped her into his arms and set her on his lap.

Madison heard a subdued ringing sound, and it was coming from the pocket of her robe. She stood up and fumbled with getting to it fast enough. "Knight," she answered and took off down the hall toward the bedroom for privacy.

"Maddy, help me!" Chelsea begged.

Her sister was crying and hysterical, but she was alive.

Fear gripped Madison's chest. "Where are you?"

Sniffles and crying.

Madison closed the bedroom door. "Chels, stay with me. Are you okay? Has he hurt you?"

"He's…he's going to—"

"Chels! I'm going to find you. Do you hear me?"

"I don't have long. Please, Mad—" Her sister shrieked as her words were cut off.

"Chels?" Madison's heart was pounding, her blood pressure rising by the second.

"Ticktock." A man's voice and one she recognized.

Her stomach dropped. It was Constantine, the man who'd haunted her mind for the better part of the last ten months. She could hear the muffled cries of her sister in the background. "I'm going to kill you with my bare hands, you son of—"

"Now, now. You have such passion for me. When we meet again, we can carry on from where we left off before you shot me." His tone was psychotic, flavored with the sweet overtures of a fallen angel.

Troy stepped into the bedroom and locked the door behind him.

"If you lay one finger on her—"

"Mere words, Detective," Constantine interrupted. "And you and I both know it."

Suddenly a calm came over Madison, a cool blanket of clarity. If anything, her outburst and promise to kill him would have been enough to disclose her turmoil, but it could also be construed as her fighting against him, of refusing to be controlled. She had to make him believe she was bowing to his power and letting him call the shots. If that's what was necessary to save her sister's life, then it was certainly worth the blow to her ego.

"I'll do whatever you want." Being submissive to him was gripping her gut mercilessly. "Just tell me."

"Huh." He sounded amused, like he was smiling

into the phone. "You'll meet us at eight thirty tonight."

"Just tell me where."

"Now, now. That would be kind of stupid of me to give you time to do your research, have that SWAT boyfriend of yours plan out his approach to take me down."

Madison spun to look at Troy. Constantine did know about him.

"And when you come," he continued, "bring what is mine."

What is his?

"I don't know what you're talking about," she said.

He didn't respond.

"When will you tell me where to meet you?"

Constantine laughed, and then the line went dead.

She pitched her phone across the room with such force, it made a hole in the drywall before falling to the carpet.

"She was… Chels was…" The sound of her sister crying stabbed at her.

Troy moved in front of her and placed his hands on her forearms. "Just breathe."

She bucked against him. "I don't have time to—"

He tightened his hold on her. "You keep this up, and he'll be the one winning."

Anger festered within her as she met his gaze. "I did everything we talked about last night. I let him call the shots. But your sister, she wants me off this. How can I—"

His hold on her arms remained firm, but he didn't say anything.

"You think she's right about this? You thought the same last night." She shrugged free of him.

"I think you need to step back."

She scanned his eyes, partially not believing what she was hearing. "My sister is in the hands of a psychopath." She realized she'd used her mother's terminology again—not that it was far off the mark—and couldn't care less.

"I know that, Madison," Troy said gently yet decisively. "But if you're going to beat this asshole at his game, you're going to have to detach."

"Detach?" She was on verge of complete hysteria. She heard it, she felt it, but Troy's energy remained calm. "She's my sister," she added.

God, if only there were a way to sink into a fantasy world that would let her believe that her sister's abduction had been nothing but a bad dream. Then maybe she could detach.

"What happened to letting him have the power, letting him see my agony?" she punched out.

"I've slept on it. It could go both ways." He paused when she cocked her head and narrowed her eyes.

"Maddy?" It was her mother on the other side of the door. "What is going on?"

"I'll be out in a minute," she called past Troy and shortened her gaze to meet his.

"You have to be convincing to fool Constantine," he said.

"Given how I'm feeling, it's not hard for him to

see my agony. As you can clearly see, I'm losing it." She flailed her arms toward the hole in the wall.

He was shaking his head. "It not just a matter of letting him witness your agony, as you put it, or knowing he's getting to you. It's how he perceives—"

"How can—"

Troy held up a hand to silence her. "You can't control how he's viewing your reaction, but you need to do what you can so that he sees your compliance as sincere. Because if he even gets the inkling that you're leading him on…" He let his words trail off, but the message was clear.

"He'll kill her."

CHAPTER

38

MADISON THREW ON SOME CLOTHES, caring little about what she was wearing. She had to find a way to hunt Constantine down, get the jump on him somehow, so she could swoop in and save her sister. How was she supposed to wait until eight thirty tonight? She was bound to go mad before then if she didn't do *something*.

She picked up the phone from where it had landed on the floor after she'd sent it flying across the room.

"What are you doing?" Troy asked her.

"I'm going downtown. We need to get her, Troy. You...You didn't hear her. She was crying. She was..." She swallowed roughly. "She was terrified."

"Of course she was. Did you expect her to be otherwise?"

"He said to bring something that belongs to him..." She had a niggling feeling that she should know what that was, but it was as if the answer was obscured by a fog. "I need to get down to the station.

I have to find out what's happening and get the status on hunting him down, how the surveillance teams are making out." She brushed past him toward the bedroom door.

"I'll come with you." He was quick to step in line with her.

She spun. "No, please stay here."

"I can help more if I'm down at the station," he said, making his case. And she agreed. His sister hadn't taken him off the search for Chelsea so maybe she could finagle her way in through Troy.

"I want to hurry." She pulled the door handle, at first having forgotten Troy had locked it. She opened it to her mom, dad, and Jim standing in the hall. Her mother stepped back quickly, and Madison imagined that she'd had her ear pressed to the door. "We heard from the man who has Chelsea."

"Is she okay?" her mother asked.

"I talked to her very briefly." She wasn't about to disclose the upset, the tears, the desperation that licked each of her sister's words.

"Oh, thank god!" her mother exclaimed and slapped her father on the shoulder.

The two of them hugged, blocking the hallway. Madison's gaze went to Jim, and he was crying. He must have sensed her watching him, and he caught her eye.

"Go get her," he said.

Madison nodded and made an attempt to move down the hall. Her mother put a hand on her arm to stall her.

"Please be careful." Her mother yanked Madison back to her and threw her arms around her. The action had been so unexpected and carried such love and warmth that fresh tears filled Madison's eyes. She pulled back.

"I will be." Emotions made it difficult to get the words out. She cleared her throat. "Troy's going to come with me."

Madison had made it a couple of steps down the hall when her mother called out to her. "Where are you going?"

She turned around to three sets of eyes on her, all of them desperate to find their missing loved one and afraid for Chelsea. She wasn't going to tell them that Constantine didn't want the meet until eight thirty that night, but she owed them that much. Look at the torture Constantine had already inflicted by making them wait until the light of a new day. Her parents, Jim, and the girls would just be sitting around the house all day awaiting word.

She came back to them. "This might be hard to hear, but I have to tell you this."

Madison caught Troy's eye, and she could tell he was wondering what she was about to say.

She continued. "A meet has been arranged."

Her mother cried out in joy.

"But—" Madison began, recoiling inwardly as she thought about what she had to say next.

"Madison?" her mother prompted.

"The meet is tonight at eight thirty."

"Eight thirty!" Jim roared. "What kind of a fu—"

"The girls," her mother stepped in to stop him from swearing.

Jim continued, speaking just above a whisper. "What kind of a prick is this guy? What's he doing with her all this time?"

Images assaulted the edge of Madison's mind, threatening to seep in and bring her down, but she fought hard to will them from taking hold. "She's going to be okay. All right? We have to believe that."

Troy nodded, followed by her father, then Jim. Her mother remained motionless, and her eyes were like a storm—not one during its stage of ravaging but in the aftermath. She appeared lost and devastated.

"I'll be back," she assured them, taking some comfort in the words herself. "If you need to reach Troy or me, we have our cell phones."

And hopefully mine still works.

She pulled it out and touched a button, and the screen lit up. She slipped it back into the pocket she'd taken it from and then proceeded toward the door with Troy right behind her. The other three followed him.

Madison put her coat on and so did Troy. She had her hand on the doorknob when her mother nudged Troy's arm with her hand. He turned to face her.

"Make sure both my girls come home alive."

CHAPTER

39

MADISON JOGGED INTO THE STATION with Troy, and they headed to the conference room where she knew several officers from different divisions were working on tracking down Constantine.

Outside the door, Troy turned to her. "Go update Winston on your call."

"If you think that I'm not going in that room because of your sister possibly finding out, you're dead wrong." She stared at him defiantly and went in.

She'd follow Andrea's rules when it came to the stakeouts and surveillance, but surely she was entitled to be informed the moment they found out anything.

Troy came in behind her, but he didn't say anything or make a move to stop her. Probably because he knew better.

She beelined for Nick. "Do we have any leads on Constantine's whereabouts yet?" she came out with the question quickly.

Nick's gaze went past her toward the door.

"You'll be the first to know once everything's in place." It was Winston, and she turned to see that he'd come up behind her.

"This is my sister we're talking about."

"And the chief has made it clear that you're to leave the search for Constantine to the rest of us."

"I don't understand why I can't be kept apprised," she shot back.

"Because you'll go off half-cocked and mess everything up. Maybe get your sister killed in the process. At the very least, we'd probably end up with two hostages instead of one."

Her core temperature was rising at the way he was talking to her. "He called me this morning."

Winston tucked his chin in. "Who?"

"Santa Claus," she retorted drily. "Who do you think? Constantine. And my sister is still alive."

"Is this true?" Winston looked past her to Troy, and she resented that. She reported to him, not Troy.

"That's why we're here," Madison said. "I've already called ahead, and Cynthia is tracing the call."

"So everyone knew before me."

Madison rolled her eyes, caring little about the man's wounded pride and left the room. Now the plan was to pick up Terry and get to the lab. She'd stand by Cynthia as she traced the call if she had to.

MADISON'S PHONE RANG AS SOON as she stepped off the elevator with Terry. She answered it as quickly as possible. "Knight," she said as she pushed on the lab door.

No one said anything on the other end of the line.

"Hello?" Her heart sped up, and she pulled her phone and read the caller ID. It was Cynthia. She looked across the lab, and Cynthia was at her desk and lowering her phone.

"I was just calling, but seeing as you're here…"

Madison put her phone away, but her breathing was still ratcheted from the scare that the call was from Constantine. Even though she kept trying to convince herself that Constantine would hold on to her sister until he had Madison instead, doubts remained. What if he killed Chelsea just to satisfy his sick lust for murder? It would be just the psychotic thing to do—give Madison hope that she could get her sister back, let her talk to her, and then, at just the moment when it would cause Madison the most pain, take Chelsea's life.

Sweat beaded on Madison's forehead, and she blinked, willing herself to remain strong. But doing so was becoming a constant struggle.

"Did you…" Madison took a heaving breath, and Terry stepped closer to her, his hands extended as if to brace her from falling. "I'm fine."

He didn't say anything but moved back. Cynthia rushed over.

"Were you able to trace the call?" Madison asked, finally feeling some strength return.

Cynthia winced. "I couldn't. The phone is off."

"Try what you did with Chelsea's."

"I can't," her friend said. "I'm sorry. I need a number and log-in information for that."

Madison nodded. Some moments she felt so adrift in hopelessness.

"I will continue to monitor the phone, and if it comes back on, we'll be in luck." A consolation offering that did little to please.

"What about the e-mail?"

"As I told you before, there's nothing more we can do there, Madison. I have some findings on Yasmine's murder you'll want to know about, though. Sam conducted ballistics tests on the bullet."

"That was fast," Terry said.

"These two cases are a priority," Cynthia said curtly. "Came straight from the chief."

Madison's heart warmed a bit for the woman she'd been angry with since last night. "What did she find?"

"The bullet was mostly intact so she had a lot to work with."

"Enough to narrow down a gun type?" Madison asked.

"Even better." Cynthia paused. "We know the exact gun used."

"The *exact* gun?" she asked. Rarely did they get that lucky.

"That's right. A Ruger nine-millimeter with the serial number scratched off." Cynthia's gaze drifted to Terry, and she went silent.

"What is it, Cyn?" Madison could tell by Cynthia's hesitation that her message was going to be upsetting.

Cynthia met Madison's gaze. "It was the one used to shoot your grandfather."

Madison lost her balance and reached for the table. "It…what?"

"You heard me right. But here's where it gets interesting," Cynthia went on.

Terry was squinting like he had a headache. "More interesting than that?"

"Uh-huh," she said. "The gun is missing from the evidence locker."

"Who signed it out?" Madison asked eagerly.

"McAlexandar. Years ago. But it was signed back in."

Terry rubbed the back of his neck. "So you're telling us that, for all intents and purposes, the gun *should* be in evidence, but it's not?"

Cynthia nodded.

"Where is it, then?" He was rubbing his neck so furiously now that his flesh sounded like two pieces of sandpaper scraping together.

"That's the question of the day," Cynthia said quickly, catching Madison's eye. "Well, maybe not *the* question."

The system wasn't foolproof, but it was damn near close. And Madison found it hard to believe evidence from a cop killing just went missing, even after the case had long been tried and prosecuted.

Cynthia moved toward her computer. "I've also got something you'll want to see." She brought up a video on her computer, then clicked some buttons, and the image from her monitor showed on the large TV screen mounted on the wall.

"What are we looking at?" Madison asked.

"That is the lobby of Yasmine's building at the time the landlord said that he saw McAlexandar." Cynthia hit "play."

Oliver came off the elevator and McAlexandar entered the front lobby. The men offered basic greetings to each other and kept moving—McAlexandar to the elevator and Oliver to his mailbox.

Madison turned to her friend, irritated. This told them nothing new. "Okay, so we have it on tape that McAlexandar was there. We already had an eyewitness who said that."

"Well, this video also tells us when he left." Cynthia forwarded to five the next morning as per the time stamp in the bottom corner of the screen.

The elevator doors opened, and McAlexandar came out, straightening his tie.

"That's after…" Madison's throat felt stitched together.

"After the time-of-death window," Cynthia finished.

The truth sank in her gut, and it was there on the screen in black-and-white. At the very least, the circumstances seemed to be mounting against McAlexandar. "Is there any sign of Constantine on the feed at any time of day?"

"No."

"Even in the stairwell?" Madison was grasping

here.

"No sign of him in that building."

Madison spun to face her partner. "Maybe we were naive to think McAlexandar was incapable of pulling the trigger."

"Maybe." The one word weighed heavily with Terry's skepticism. "But this is more than enough to bring him in, even get a warrant to search his residence."

Madison didn't move, though. Something about all this seemed too easy, too perfect. She'd been wanting to nail McAlexandar for a long time, and it seemed like he was being handed to her on a silver platter. But why? How did he fit in with everything else? Had McAlexandar refused to work with the new man who was assuming Dimitre's role and so he was being eliminated? Framing him for murder would draw less attention to the Mafia than murdering him would. And maybe they were premature to assume, based on McAlexandar's reaction, that Dimitre would be upset by Bates's murder.

But it was hard to say if McAlexandar was in the loop of what was going on or out of it. It seemed like such a stretch that he was at Yasmine's at her time of death—on video, no less—arriving and leaving her building. No sign of Constantine, either. He'd have to have been a ghost, but that was still within the realm of possibility as far as Madison was concerned. What he did for a living dictated that he'd be good at being invisible. But she was still having a hard time accepting the former chief as Yasmine's killer.

"We have to find the man who is trying to usurp Dimitre's position in the hierarchy," she blurted out.

Terry raised his eyebrows. "Are you forgetting that a bunch of officers are already assigned to this task?"

"I think we need to go to the source," Madison continued. "Dimitre is a smart man, and he probably knows who would do this to him."

"You're thinking of talking to him?" Cynthia exclaimed.

"Do you really think he's going to tell you?" Terry asked.

"What does he have to lose? He's already being stripped of his power, cut off from the outside world."

"You're assuming he's already aware of it," Terry countered.

"You don't think he is?" Madison let the question sit there. No one touched it. "The warden passed on a message to Bates, and it seems that it came from Dimitre. And while Bates may have received the message, he didn't get a chance to do anything with it."

"Or at least it would seem," Cynthia interjected.

"Right. So you don't think Dimitre would find it odd that he never received confirmation that whatever it was he wanted taken care of hadn't been completed?" Madison posed.

"Who knows what he was or was not told," Terry said grimly. "We don't even know what the message was. It was just a number."

Both Madison and Terry turned to Cynthia, but a thought struck Madison. Constantine wanted something that belonged to him brought to him. He'd tortured Bates, set up cameras...

Cynthia snapped her fingers. "Maddy?"

"Constantine told me to bring what was his along with me tonight when I meet him." She paused and split glances between Cynthia and Terry. Her mind must have been a mess not to figure it out before now. "It has to be the note on the letterhead." With her focus fully on Cynthia, she continued. "He's using my family to get his hands on it. We really need to figure out what is so important about it and why he wants it so much."

"I've personally stared it at it until I've almost gone blind," Cynthia said.

"Well, I need you to keep trying. Bring your entire team in on this. Put your heads together."

Cynthia was expressionless, and it didn't instill much confidence. "I'll call them here and see what we can do, but I'm not making any promises."

"And I wouldn't expect you to."

CHAPTER

40

MADISON SPEED-WALKED OUT OF THE LAB. Her mind was on one thing, and that was getting the jump on Constantine and getting her sister back. Screw playing by his rules.

She pressed the "down" button for the elevator, but the doors didn't open right away. She didn't have time to wait, so she bypassed the elevator for the stairwell. Sometimes it was just faster to use the stairs, and today was one of those days.

"I have a sinking feeling I know what you think you're going to do," Terry said, hustling behind her.

She didn't respond to him and entered the stairwell. It was far more than a thought; it was going to happen.

"You think if you go to the prison to talk with Dimitre that he'll open up to you?" Terry was breathing heavily, and it wasn't because of poor cardiovascular health because he ran every morning.

She stopped moving and spun around.

"If we go to the prison, you do realize that the

warden will be tipped off?" Terry quirked his eyebrows. "The same warden who we believe is double-dipping, or at least being coerced to work for Dimitre and this other power player at the same time. Again, assuming this is the case…"

"I need to rescue my sister," she said with heat. "Dimitre just might give us a lead as to where Constantine could be holed up. We can use Dimitre. Lord knows no one else seems to be getting anywhere." Patience had never been her strong suit, and tack on her sister being in the hands of Constantine and it was even less so.

"Are you forgetting that the chief doesn't want you directly involved in hunting down Constantine? Don't you think talking to Dimitre would qualify?" Terry tightened his jaw and stared in her eyes. "She's going to bench you altogether if you disregard a direct order. She's not going to give you a pass just because you're practically family."

Madison wished she could argue that point, but she knew he was right. One quality that she loved about Andrea was the fact that she was unbiased and professional, and when she made up her mind, there was no changing it. Like sister like brother.

Madison kept hustling.

"Come on, don't throw your career away. Don't let Constantine win like that."

Something between the words, the way Terry said them, and the way he was looking at her, made her relax a bit. It was one thing to play along with the man, let him believe he had control over her;

it was another if he demanded she sacrifice the life she loved.

"And do you really want a murder on your hands?" Terry continued.

"What do you mean?"

"The warden. Ever think that if our running theory is correct and word gets back to the power player, it might cost Dimitre or the warden his life?"

She shook her head abruptly. She wasn't going to say so out loud, but the world would be a better place without Dimitre.

"Really? You're willing to risking two men's lives?"

"Yeah. You know what? That's a chance I'm willing to take if it gets me closer to saving my sister." Maybe more Dimitre's than the warden's, but still. She resumed walking, and Terry grabbed her arm on a backswing. She turned around and shrugged free of his grasp.

"And the warden?" Terry pressed on the sore spot. "What about his wife and kids?"

Maybe he'd been coerced into working with the mob, but he had to have known what he was getting himself and family into.

"Come on, Maddy. Think this through. One, you're not a killer, and two, your career means everything to you."

"Not as much as my sister."

Terry held up his hands. "I get that."

"Don't say *but*."

"*But*," he said purposefully, "we're going to get her back, and if you do what you're thinking of doing…

Well…" His shoulders sagged, and he glanced away. "I can't help you. Troy can't help you. The sergeant—"

"He won't hesitate to take my badge." The sober realization sank into her bones and had her grounding the heels of her shoes into the floor.

And Constantine will have won… Terry's earlier words came to her mind as an assault.

"Then what am I supposed to do?" she lamented. "Constantine doesn't want to meet me until eight thirty. How can I think about anything else?"

"You focus on what you can investigate, and maybe we'll stumble across a clue that will lead us to him," Terry suggested. "And if we do, great. You wouldn't have technically broken the chief's directive. You'll hand it off, and a team will swoop in and save your sister."

She'd love to believe the fairy tale he was dishing out, but she wasn't buying it. Constantine would not let Chelsea go without an exchange. It would come down to Madison's life for her sister's. Not if Madison could help it, though.

"And if we don't find a lead to Constantine," Terry continued, "we'll at least be getting more answers to the two other murder investigations."

"Like, if McAlexandar killed Yasmine," she said.

"We have him on tape leaving after the time-of-death window, and that's enough for a search warrant and an arrest warrant probably, too. That ought to keep us busy for a while."

"That's for sure." She got along with paperwork about as well as she did with running. "We should let Winston know about McAlexandar now."

"You think?" Terry said sarcastically.

She narrowed her eyes at him and resumed walking. Somehow, she was feeling a little calmer. The answers were going to come, and as much as she hated that they weren't coming fast enough, her hands were tied. And Terry was right: she had to focus on what she could. Maybe, if luck was on her side at all, they'd stumble across something that pointed them to Constantine's whereabouts.

They found Winston in his office. He was scowling, as he seemed to be doing a lot these days.

"Come in." He waved them forward. Just as was always the case, there were stacks of paper on his desk, including one directly in front of him.

Terry took a seat in one of the two chairs across from him, and Madison got the door before sitting down.

The sergeant leaned back in his chair and clasped his hands across his stomach. "Am I going to want to hear what you have to say?"

"Probably not." In most cases, honesty was the best policy, and this was no exception. In fact, it was likely best not to dance around the message, either. "We need to have two warrants issued. One to search Patrick McAlexandar's home, and another for his arrest."

Winston just sat there, his gaze moving between the two of them for a few moments. "The former chief?"

Madison nodded. "Uh-huh."

"Whatever for?"

"We have an eyewitness who placed him at Yasmine's apartment building, and now we have even better," she began. "We have him on video leaving after the time-of-death window."

Winston guffawed. "He could have been there visiting anyone."

"And leaving at five in the morning?" Madison served back. She shook her head. "He already confirmed he was having an affair with her."

Winston's posture stiffened, and he stretched his neck from side to side like a boxer getting ready for a fight. "And how would you know that?"

This was the part she wasn't going to savor. "We spoke with him."

"You what?" he spat. He pressed a fingertip into his desk. "You spoke to the former chief and accused him of murder?"

"Not exactly." Maybe she could dance around the meat of it a little.

"But you questioned him about this murder without my knowledge." Winston turned to Terry. "And no one bothered to say a thing to me."

"We followed a lead in an investigation, and now, well, it's shown to have merit." Madison relaxed her body into the chair, but she was still ready to pounce given the right provocation.

Winston clenched his jaw, and his gaze was going through the both of them. "We've had the conversation about communication more times than I can count." He drew his gaze back to her.

"What seems to be so hard to understand about keeping your superior informed?"

"You know that I don't like to give you anything unless it plays out."

"But that's not what I ask for, is it, Knight? I ask for *updates*. I don't ask for the case to be solved by the time I hear anything."

Madison held up a hand in acceptance.

Winston shook his head. "I should just write up the both of you. This is not the first time you haven't shown respect for authority, Knight. And Grant—" he turned on Terry "—I'd expect more from you."

Madison ground her teeth, but there was no point in firing back at him with a snappy comeback. He'd think she was too emotional to remain objective. Now was a good time to swallow her pride and keep quiet.

When Terry didn't say anything, either, Winston continued. "I'm surprised McAlexandar didn't call me after you saw him."

"And that right there should tell you something," Madison said. It earned her a glare from the sergeant, but it was true.

Winston tapped his chin and clicked his teeth repeatedly. It was an odd mannerism that showed itself at times when he was feeling conflicted. "You're sure that you have enough to go after him? The man is running for mayor."

She nodded. "Ballistics from Yasmine's murder tied back to a gun that should be in evidence lockup."

"Should be?"

"That's right." She wasn't going to tell him it was the one used to kill her grandfather.

"And you think you'll find it in McAlexandar's possession?" Winston cocked an eyebrow. "You think he'd be stupid enough to hold on to it all this time and bring it out to murder that girl?"

Madison hitched her shoulders. "People have done crazier things."

Winston seemed to be looking through her again but eventually nodded. "Very well. Do what you have to do, and let's hope this doesn't bite us in the ass."

CHAPTER

41

MADISON HAD EXPECTED A LOT more resistance at the DA's office getting the warrants signed, but it had been an in-and-out affair. It somehow seemed like a letdown on top of the hours of paperwork they'd had to do. Strange thoughts to be running through her mind, really, considering she wanted everything to go on without a hitch—and quickly. Any other time, the ability to execute a search warrant on the corrupt former chief would have made her beyond happy, but the circumstances dampened her joy. Namely the niggling feeling in her gut that told her all of this was moving along too easily. She said as much to Terry when they were on their way to McAlexandar's house, warrants in hand.

"It's *too* clean? *Too* easy? You don't have a fight, and you want to make one." He smirked. "I don't get it. You must be a conflict junkie."

"What I don't get is…" She paused, chewing on Terry's accusation and dismissing it, her mind turning fully back to the case. It was clear that

McAlexandar adhered to his own code of ethics, so why was she questioning his innocence in this murder? And she'd been wanting to pin him since the beginning of the year when his connection with Dimitre had become apparent. Maybe she should just take what was given to her.

"He's brought this on himself," Terry said, as if reading her mind. "Even if he's not guilty—though the video footage sure appears damning to me, plus the gun from your grandfather's murder—he was the lead investigator on that case. He'd easily be able to get the gun in and out of evidence."

"Yeah, and the records show that he did just that," she drove home. "We have no way of knowing where the gun is now without the record being kept properly."

"There could be something else going on here." Terry pursed his lips.

"I know..." The unspoken possibility being that there were people on the mob's payroll within the police department. It wasn't a new concept to her.

She pulled into McAlexandar's driveway, and the officers who had been sent as backup followed in two patrol cars.

"We check his place out, see what we see, and go from there," Terry said. "That's all."

"Go from there," she mumbled.

"What's the problem now?"

"Nothing. It's just..."

"Your sister?"

She turned the car off. "This delay is killing me."

"You're doing well. Probably better than I would be in your place," he admitted. "In a few more hours, you'll be meeting up with Constantine and getting your sister back."

She glanced at the clock. *3:25 PM.*

A few more hours?

Madison took a deep breath and reached for the handle. "You ready?"

"Absolutely." Terry was out of the car before she'd even opened her door.

It was like her body was partially frozen in place. She'd dreamed of taking McAlexandar down, and now that the time had come, she was hesitating? It certainly wasn't the moment to entertain doubts as to his innocence, either, because McAlexandar would pick up on them and use them to his advantage. She got out of the car.

"McAlexandar might even know where Constantine is," Terry said.

His words prompted her adrenaline to start surging through her bloodstream. After all these years as a cop, she rarely noticed it anymore, just appreciated what it made possible: the ability to detach to the point that she could handle a crime scene or compartmentalize her emotions. Two things she still struggled with from time to time. But what Terry had said had fueled her drive to get in there and talk with McAlexandar.

She hurried past him to the front door and banged on it as if trying to rouse the residents from sleep to let them know the house was on fire. She waited only two to three seconds before banging again.

"What the—" McAlexandar swung the door open. His gaze swept over her and Terry, as well as the officers who were standing about ten feet behind them, but landed back on Madison. She held up the search warrant and stepped toward him to enter the house.

McAlexandar held up a hand. "Hold on a minute here."

"Watch him while we search the premises," Madison told the officers. As one of them worked to wrestle him to the side so Madison and Terry could enter, she addressed McAlexandar. "Is your wife home?"

McAlexandar bucked. "Do you have any idea what you're doing? You get off me. I'm the former chief."

Madison leaned in close to McAlexandar's ear. "You're right, and we went through this last time. You are the *former* chief." She glanced at the officer holding on to McAlexandar and hoped that he'd received her silent recommendation that he hold on tightly. "Now, I asked you a question. Is your wife home?"

"No, thank god!"

Madison entered the house with Terry. They both put on latex gloves, pressing down between the fingers because the darn things never fit right.

"Madison," McAlexandar yelled out, but she ignored him and kept walking.

"Huge place." Terry gestured to their

surroundings—from the coffered ceiling, easily twenty feet above their heads, to the heavy drapes that adorned the floor-to-ceiling windows. "We should have brought more backup."

For any other suspect, at any other time, she would have, but she wanted to have some time alone with McAlexandar before she dragged him down to the station. She wanted to pressure him and see what she could find out about this mystery power player she was certain was out there, but even more importantly, she wanted to see if he had any idea where Constantine might be holding her sister. It would be difficult to do with eyes and ears on her downtown.

"I say we start with his office and branch out from there," Madison suggested.

The warrant included the mention of the Ruger 9mm used to kill her grandfather and was extended to cover anything that could be used as proof that McAlexandar had been involved with Yasmine's murder. While the video footage had been enough to get arrest and search warrants signed, as was the case with any investigation, the more evidence, the better chance of a conviction.

They entered the office, and even as Madison stepped inside, she felt overwhelmed by its sheer size. She'd noted how large the place was yesterday, but being here for the express purpose of working through it all seemed an impossible feat. At least the task should help distract her somewhat, though thoughts of Chelsea were never far off. Not that she expected them to entirely go away until they had her back.

"You take that side, and I'll work over here," Terry suggested, pointing to the right side of the room for her.

"Works for me." She went straight to McAlexandar's desk.

She started with the top of the desk and then went on to riffle through the drawers, emptying the contents onto the desk's surface as she saw fit. She'd glance up periodically at Terry to see how he was making out, and so far he was having about as much luck as she was—which wasn't much.

She'd just moved on to a filing cabinet when Terry said, "Ah, Maddy."

"What is—" Her eyes went to an exposed wall safe. She hurried over to him.

Terry pulled on the door. "It's locked."

She ran out of the room and went to McAlexandar, who was being held at the front door.

"What's the combination for the safe in your office?"

An arrogant smirk lifted the left corner of his mouth.

"May I remind you that I have a search warrant."

McAlexandar tightened his jaw and glared at her.

"The combination," she demanded. "Now!"

He rattled it off for her, and she ran back into the office and joined Terry.

"Try this," she began and gave him the combination.

Terry punched in the number, and the tumblers gave way. He pulled on the handle. "Moment of truth…"

She moved in closer to Terry, practically hanging over his shoulder. Inside the safe, there were stacks of cash. "There must be sixty to a hundred grand in here."

Terry went to reach inside.

"Let me," Madison said.

"Okay." Terry stepped aside.

She slipped her gloved hand into the safe and passed the cash to Terry, one bundle at a time. When all the money was out, the safe was empty except for one thing: a Ruger 9mm with an attached silencer.

CHAPTER

42

THE WEAPON WAS HEAVY IN Madison's hands. Emotion crashed over her as she looked down at it. The serial number had been scratched off. This could be the gun that had taken her grandfather's life…

"Madison?" Terry prompted. "Are you okay?"

She let the shiver run through her and nodded. "I'm good."

Madison proceeded with a visual check of the gun and confirmed that the magazine was loaded. She released it, observed what rounds remained, and handed the mag to Terry. She went on to clear the chamber. She angled the gun toward the floor and drew the slider back before doing a physical inspection. She saw a bullet and placed the gun upside down, still conscious of where the barrel was pointing, and the round dropped into the palm of her hand. She inspected the gun one more time just to ensure it was clear, and it was.

"We've got to get all this into evidence bags and back to the lab for prints and a comparison to the bullet that killed Yasmine," she summarized.

Terry slipped the magazine into an evidence bag and then held it open for her so she could put the gun and single bullet inside.

"He did it, Terry." She was struck with sadness and grief, and she wasn't entirely sure if it was just because of Yasmine's murder or if the loss of her grandfather was mingling there, as well.

"Hopefully we'll find out."

"No. We *will* find out." She jutted out her chin and left the house with the evidence bag.

She headed straight for McAlexandar and held up the gun. "*This* was in your safe."

His eyes fixed on the weapon as if it was an apparition. His face blanched, and his jaw dropped. He snapped it shut.

"Really?" she asked. "That's how you're going to play this? That you've never seen it before?"

"Where did you—" He shook his head, seeming dazed.

"In your safe," she repeated. "You murdered a twenty-three-year-old woman."

"I told you, I didn't do it. Someone must be framing me."

"Yeah, because I've never heard that one before." She rolled her eyes. "Did Dimitre order you to kill her?"

"What?" he spat. "No!"

"So you are in communication with Dimitre?"

"No."

She wasn't accepting his answer. "I said, are you—"

"No! Not since you moved him to Mitchell County," he said.

There would normally be a sense of satisfaction that would come with believing she'd limited Dimitre's connection to the outside world, but she wasn't buying it. "Bullshit."

"Someone's got to be setting me up."

She cocked her head.

"No, I swear to God."

"And you expect me to believe you're on speaking terms with God?"

"That's a little harsh, Detective."

"Is it? You killed Yasmine Stone while she was sleeping in her bed." Her entire being was full of contempt for this man. All the wrongdoings and slights from their past were hitting her progressively.

"I'm telling you the truth. You're just not listening to me."

Rage was boiling over within her and making her lightheaded. Thoughts of her sister being held by Constantine weren't helping. "Tell me where he took her."

"What?" McAlexandar eyes widened. "I don't—"

"Constantine Romanov abducted my sister." She stared at him as she spoke the words, scrutinizing him for any tell that he had known.

"I don't know anything about that."

She moved toward him, her face mere inches from his. "Tell me where she is," she said through gritted teeth.

"I don't know!" Spittle flew from his mouth, and

she moved away and wiped her face in disgust.

"Turn around," she barked out and spun her finger. "You are under arrest for the murder of Yasmine Stone."

He jerked away from her, but she gripped his shoulder.

"I didn't kill that girl!"

"I said, *turn around*."

"Oh, this must bring you a lot of pleasure."

"Turn around," she ground out.

McAlexandar puffed out his cheeks and they shot bright red, but he complied. She pulled out her cuffs and slapped them on him. "Anything you say or do—"

"I told you I'm innocent," McAlexandar pleaded, anguish setting into his features.

Madison finished reading his Miranda rights and addressed the officer who had been standing with McAlexandar. "Get him out of my sight."

"You got it." The officer hauled him off and loaded him into the back of a patrol car.

The second officer stayed behind. He'd leave once they'd cleared the place.

Terry was watching her but didn't say a word.

"We're leaving," she said to him.

"What about the rest of the place?"

She was shaking her head. "We'll make a call, have others take over. Or you can stay if you want. But I'm going back to drill McAlexandar. I'll take the evidence we've collected so far with me."

"I'll go with you." Terry stepped in line with her.

"I don't need a babysitter," she fired back.

"I know that," he hissed. "I'm just… We're partners, and we stick together."

She blinked and nodded.

CHAPTER

43

McALEXANDAR WAS IN INTERVIEW ROOM ONE, and Madison and Terry were observing him through the two-way mirror. She wanted to get in there and start into him, but that's what he'd expect. So she'd let him simmer a bit first.

They'd already dropped off the gun, magazine, and bullets to the lab where Cynthia and her three employees were racking their brains still trying to figure out the mystery of the ten digits.

"Are you waiting on his lawyer?" Winston came into the observation room.

"He hasn't asked for one," Madison stated drily, keeping her gaze on McAlexandar.

"That surprises me."

The man who represents himself has a fool for a client.

She shrugged. "It is what it is."

Winston came up close to the two-way mirror beside her. "And what's that supposed to mean?"

"Nothing." She tapped the file folder she held in

one hand in the palm of her other hand.

"I'm not buying it."

"What do you want me to say, Sarge?" She'd blurted it out and had to stop herself before she added something else that didn't have any immediate bearing on what she and Terry were about to do. But she'd been especially on edge ever since handling the gun that had likely killed her grandfather. It was the right type of gun anyhow, and its serial number was scratched off—just like the one used in her grandfather's murder. And it was more than coincidental to Madison that it was locked in a hidden safe behind a pile of money. When Sam had laid her eyes on the bullets, she was certain that they were the same brand as the one extracted from Yasmine's body. She was excused from brainstorming on the letterhead digits to run her tests, and Cynthia was focused on seeing what she could get in the way of fingerprints.

"There's nothing to say, apparently." He stepped back and gestured toward McAlexandar. "When do you plan on going in there?"

"Right now." She left the observation room with Terry, and they went to join McAlexandar.

"I've been cooperative," McAlexandar said as she sat across from him.

She didn't say anything and neither did Terry as he made his way to the far wall and leaned against it.

"Is this where you play the silent game?" McAlexandar's brows knitted together. "You've left me sitting in here for hours."

Madison dropped the folder onto the table in front of her and pulled out a video still. It showed McAlexandar in the lobby of Yasmine's building after the time-of-death window. She slid it across the table in front of him.

"What's that supposed to be?" he asked.

Madison pursed her lips and nudged her head toward it.

He picked it up. A few seconds later, he said, "Yeah, that's me. So? I told you I was at her apartment two days ago."

"That's yesterday." Madison pointed at the time stamp.

"Yesterday at five in the morning? No." McAlexandar rapidly shook his head. "I wasn't there then. Someone is setting me up."

"And let me guess, that gun magically appeared inside your *locked* safe?"

"I don't know how that got in there. I have a gun safe, but it's in another part of my house."

While she was stalling coming in here to talk to McAlexandar, one of the officers who was continuing the search on McAlexandar's house had texted that highlight, and the finding of a rifle and two handguns.

"And all the money," Madison began. "It was just in there for a rainy day?"

"I hadn't made it to the bank yet," he said snidely.

She held his eye contact and said nothing.

"I don't like how you're looking at me."

"Where did you get all that money? Did the

Mafia pay you to kill Yasmine? Did Constantine?" She thought she'd just toss that out there and see if it stuck.

"No. I told you I haven't been in contact with Dimitre since—"

"Since he changed prisons. Fine, fine. But I didn't mention him."

The silence rode out for about a minute.

McAlexandar's gaze kept going to the picture of him in Yasmine's lobby.

Maybe it was time to switch things up a bit. "Did she threaten to tell your wife about the affair?"

"Yasmine?" A rhetorical response, really. The former police chief didn't seem to be thinking clearly. He shook his head. "No, she didn't."

"A man like you has money," Madison pointed out, "but maybe you were tired of paying for her silence."

"That's not the case at all." He sat back in his chair and shook the picture in his hand. "I was at her building, but the afternoon before."

"So you said."

"But you don't believe me."

"I've never trusted you," she said frankly. "Why should I start now?"

"Maybe I could offer you something…" He spoke low, in contrast to his usually loud and brash nature. What he was probably going to say next would be probably good, but she couldn't let her guard down.

"I guess that would depend on what it was," she said coolly.

"Constantine is back in town."

She guffawed in derision. "We know that much."

"What you *don't know* is that he visited me last night after you came by."

The skin at the back of her neck tightened. "Why was he there?"

"The truth?"

"Always a lovely notion."

"I don't know."

Madison leaned back in her chair, and she regarded the man. Sweat was beaded on his forehead.

"What did he say or do?" she asked, only half-interested but certainly curious.

"We drank some brandy in my office, and I passed out. Or at least that's what my wife told me."

"Your wife factors into this how?"

"Constantine saw himself out, she told me later. I woke up with a migraine and a foggy head."

"Do you remember what you talked about?" Madison ventured but wasn't hopeful. If he was drugged, often these types of pills didn't grace the user with a strong memory of events.

"Only bits and pieces, but none of it really meant anything. Just idle chitchat."

Madison shook her head. "You really expect me to believe—"

"I'm telling you the truth. I have no idea why he came by. But I think it's starting to come together."

If he was going to claim Constantine had set him up, she might laugh out loud. What would be his motivation? Then it struck her. McAlexandar had a relationship with Dimitre, not necessarily this new guy in power, and maybe that guy didn't want Dimitre's hand-me-downs and wanted McAlexandar out of the picture. As she'd thought previously, pinning a murder on McAlexandar would be a surefire way to go and wouldn't draw as much attention as murdering him would.

"Why do you think he came by?" Madison asked, humoring McAlexandar.

"I think he drugged me and planted that gun in my safe!" he roared.

Madison didn't let him see that his baritone and rage had shaken her. "The video—"

"Had to have been messed with!" McAlexandar took a few heaving breaths, his chest contracting and expanding swiftly, but then it slowed down. He looked her in the eye. "Did you even wonder why I haven't asked for a lawyer yet?"

"I can say it's crossed my mind."

"Well, I didn't ask for one because I know how you work, Madison."

Her hatred toward him thawed—just a fraction—despite wanting to deny that fact. The man had never called her by her first name once in their entire working relationship.

"And how's that?" she asked, bracing herself for his response, not sure what he was going to say.

"You find the truth, and you don't stop until you get it." He opened his arms, palms out, and pressed his lips together. "I trust you to get to the truth, no matter how damning the evidence against me might be."

His words struck her with such sincerity that they stole her breath. What she would have given to hear that when she'd reported to him as her first sergeant or when he went on to become police chief. But she couldn't allow herself to become a victim of his manipulations. She had to remember all the times he'd come after her badge and did everything in his power to derail her career. Saying all this could just be his way of bringing down her guard. But what if that wasn't the case?

MADISON'S HANDS WERE BALLED INTO FISTS, and she was pacing the hall outside the interrogation room. Terry stood in front of her and stopped her with two hands on her shoulders.

"We'll figure all this out," he said.

She summoned her patience, which was a shallow well on the best of days. But if she heard one more person tell her that everything would be all right, she might literally scream. It was taking all her resolve just to remain calm and objective enough to do her job, and sometimes she even wondered if she was pulling that off.

"Listen, we have enough on him," he said, meaning McAlexandar.

"Yeah, and I should be happy about that," she sprang back.

"But you're not. And why is that?"

She stared at him. "Who are you, my shrink?"

"I'm just trying to figure you out."

"Well you can stop."

Terry dropped his arms. "We have him on video, the gun in his possession, the bullets…"

"All of which still needs to be compared and confirmed a match to the murder weapon." She stopped talking, but when Terry didn't say anything, she added, "He claims not to have put the gun there, not to even have known about it."

"And if that's the case, it won't show his prints," Terry finished her line of thought.

"But if he is being framed as he claims…"

"They'll be all over everything."

And if they were, Madison was more willing to accept that McAlexandar was telling the truth about being framed. Rarely did everything fall together perfectly in a murder case, if ever. But try stringing together that fraying thread for a jury to accept. All they'd see was what was in front of them: the damning evidence.

She walked toward her and Terry's desks, haunted by McAlexandar's faith in her morality: *I trust you to get to the truth.*

"We should get him tested, see if any drugs show in his system," she said.

"It couldn't hurt," Terry agreed. "You wanting to question him more, though?" He was trailing a few steps behind her.

She stopped and shook her head. "I really don't see the point. Not right now. Let's have him taken down to holding."

"Your sister's location? I thought—"

"I don't think McAlexandar has a clue," she

interrupted. "I really don't."

"And what makes you think that? Just because he hasn't opened up about his relationship with the Mafia?"

"Actually, Terry, just the opposite."

His brow furrowed. "Huh?"

"He hasn't denied his connection to them. Not once," she pointed out. "He detours, sideswipes, but he's never come out and said that he's never been in contact with Dimitre."

Terry turned contemplative. "So for that, you're willing to believe he didn't kill Yasmine? Because from what I see—"

"I know what you see, and if I just look at it squarely, yeah, I'd say it doesn't look good for the man."

"Do you believe that Constantine went to see him last night and drugged him?"

"I guess we'll find out once the results come back," she said. She resumed heading toward their desks. Her eye caught the clock on the wall. One thing investigating McAlexandar had done was pass the time. It was seven o'clock now. Her heart cinched in her chest as she realized that Constantine still hadn't called with the location. What was he waiting for?

She took out her phone and checked it for missed calls and messages, even though her ringer was on. No updates from Cynthia and no missed calls from anyone else.

Sitting down at her desk, her intention was to examine everything from the cases one more time.

Everyone else would think she was doing so to solve the murders, but her true motive was to see if she could find out where Constantine was holding her sister.

"I'm just going to grab a cup of coffee," Terry said. "Want one?"

She'd need to be awake for tonight, and she figured the only reason she was even moving now was because of anxiety. "Why not? Thanks."

He nodded. "Be right back."

Madison pulled out a copy of the case file for Bates. There was still some mystery surrounding him, but the answers might only ever come as creative narrative—a cog in the Russian Mafia that was no longer needed.

Her mind drifted to McAlexandar, the thought of him being put in a cell, arrested for murder. There would have been a time she would have greatly relished his downfall, and she cursed that his words must have been having an impact on her. But then again, maybe they weren't. She hadn't been completely convinced he had pulled the trigger from the start. If he was framed, however, the question of why begged to be answered. But there was one more thing she needed to remember: while McAlexandar may not have killed Yasmine, he was far from innocent.

"Here you go." Terry handed her a mug of sludge.

She took it from him, trying not to gag thinking about that first nasty sip. "Thanks."

"Course. So what are you working on?" Terry

pointed to the open file on her desk.

"Bates's murder."

"Thought we pretty much know who did that."

"We do, but I was also thinking about McAlexandar."

"Madison, you should let it go. The evidence will prove his guilt or innocence one way or another."

"But he knows I'm not the type to just run with the seemingly glaring proof."

"You're referring to all the buttering up he did in there?" Terry pulled his chair around so it was at the side of her desk. "He's a man facing murder charges. He's desperate."

"I know, but—"

Terry pursed his lips and shook his head. "No buts. Did he ever compliment you in the past?"

"No."

"Then…?" He bugged his eyes out for emphasis. "It's seems clear to me he's trying to play you and the system. All this, 'I haven't even demanded a lawyer.' That's his stupidity." Terry slurped back some coffee.

Madison studied her partner. He'd always been just as set in his opinions as she was, and it was common for them to view several aspects from cases from opposite perspectives. It was probably one of the reasons their partnership and their close rate was so successful: they opened each other's minds, even though they'd initially resist. If she was going to make Terry drop his hardened attitude toward McAlexandar, she was going to have to provide some sound reasoning.

"Let's just talk something out for a moment," she began, hoping to hook his curiosity. "It seems clear that Constantine was hired to take out Bates. And we figure this was because there's a new power player who wanted to cut off Dimitre's tie to the outside world. Maybe Bates didn't want to switch his loyalties." She hitched her shoulders. "Or wasn't given the opportunity."

Terry bobbed his head.

"Then there's Yasmine," she continued. "We know that Kevin Jones, a man she told us she was sleeping with, was really Constantine. So if we take out McAlexandar," she spat out preemptively, "what are we left with for motive?"

"She could have known more than she should have," Terry suggested.

Madison nodded. "She was terrified when we interviewed her. She knew something. Like we said before, maybe even Bates's killer, which we now know she did, whether she realized it or not. But we're still left with the question of why *she* had to die."

"If she did know—or even had proof of some sort—that Constantine was behind the murder, she could have threatened to come forward with it. Even if she didn't, he might not have wanted to take the risk that she would."

"Right," Madison said. "Let's consider McAlexandar now. We've discussed his possible motives for wanting Yasmine dead, but once a cheater, always a cheater." With that statement, something clicked into place. "Wait... He's never been a faithful husband, but I don't think any of his other mistresses ended up murdered."

"That we know of."

She gave him a coy smile. "This has to be connected to the Mafia, Terry. The question we should be asking is, why would they want him framed for Yasmine's murder?" Her mind had formulated the answer by the time she finished speaking. "They must be cleaning house from Dimitre's 'administration,' for lack of a better word." She leaned forward, excited. "They took out Bates because he no longer fit into their picture, and Yasmine because she was a threat to them, or at least had a relationship with their hit man. And then they frame McAlexandar because it gets him out of the way without killing him."

"Except he's as good as dead if he goes to prison since he's had a hand in putting so many people away."

Terry was right. Her stomach soured, and she was surprised by the empathy she felt for a man she had up until now despised. Even if former cops weren't typically placed in general population, they weren't unreachable.

Terry didn't say anything, and silence fell between them.

"You're forgetting the video, though," he said eventually. "It shows McAlexandar clearly leaving her place after the time-of-death window, remember?"

She shook her head. She wasn't forgetting the

video at all; it was one of the puzzle pieces she had yet to figure out. There was no doubt the Mafia had inroads into all sorts of places, and they also had a lot of holdings. "Constantine had a relationship with Yasmine, and he's cocky but doesn't usually take chances when he doesn't have a shot of getting away. He'd want to keep an eye on Yasmine even when he wasn't there, just to make sure nothing slipped that could hurt him."

Terry raised an eyebrow. "You're telling me he's in charge of the security footage somehow?"

"Not exactly, but what if the Mafia owns Yasmine's apartment build—" Madison's ringing phone interrupted her, and they both fell silent. Madison's chest froze on an inhale, and it hurt to force the air out. All this and the first ring hadn't even finished by the time she answered. Time was going in slow motion. "Knight."

"Ah, how nice to hear your voice again," Constantine cooed.

She dug her fingers into the phone, her anger coursing through her veins like a speeding freight train.

Come on, Karma. Give me another chance to shoot him, and I'll put the bullet right between his eyes.

He gave her directions to a rural property and told her there would be a farmhouse, but she was to go into the barn. "And you come alone," he demanded.

"Let me talk to my sister," she said. "I want to know that she's still…"

"Can't bring yourself to say it, eh? *Dead.*" He

laughed, and as he let his merriment taint the line, she imagined squeezing the trigger, the bullet exploding his brain…

Something made noise on his end, and Madison sat up straighter.

"Maddy?" It was Chelsea.

"Are you okay? Has he—"

Chelsea sniffled. "He hasn't touched—"

"That's enough," Constantine barked. "The reunion will start at eight thirty, Knight. Don't be late."

He disconnected.

Madison blinked tears from her eyes, but there was a shift that had happened within her. The tears were no longer tinged with fear or uncertainty; they had turned bitter and vengeful. When she'd talked to Constantine the first time, she had a brief sense of calm come over her, but this sensation was different. For the first time since she'd learned her sister had been abducted, she was centered and focused.

"Did he tell you where to meet them?" Terry asked.

She told him where she'd been directed to go.

"What were you about to say before your phone rang?" Terry asked. "Something about the Mafia owning—"

"Right. McAlexandar says he's being set up, and videos can be modified, clipped, and edited. But the only ones who could do that would be those who owned the videos in the first place." She logged on to her computer and brought up the file on Yasmine

Stone. She scribbled down her address and did a quick property-owner search. The answer came back in seconds. "Vytek Holdings," she said out loud.

"One second." Terry clicked some buttons on his keyboard. "Vytek is a client of Berger & Stein Accounting."

"That can't be a coincidence."

"I'll check who owns the property where you're heading to meet Constantine." Terry did the search. "It's owned by Vytek, as well."

She got up and walked around his desk. "And who owns the company?"

"That could take a little while."

"It's a corporation. How hard can it be? All of this should be public knowledge," she said.

"Yes, it should be, and it is, but…" Terry clicked keys. "Nothing at a quick glance tells me anything useful. More sets of eyes would speed up the process, though."

Madison nodded. "I'll update Winston and Troy about the meet and Vytek Holdings." SWAT would also want to plan an approach strategy. "Also, about your suspicion with Yasmine knowing something she shouldn't, you and I should go to the lab and see if they've found anything on Yasmine's laptop or cell phone that incriminates Constantine for Bates's murder. Maybe have them look to recover any deleted files."

"Do you have time for that right now? Shouldn't you be getting ready?"

"There's plenty of time," she countered, determined to keep herself busy up until the very last second at the risk of losing her mind. Her thoughts fired back to Yasmine and her connection to Constantine and how she might have tied into Bates's murder. She had an access code to his house, but she'd also need a— "Terry," she exclaimed.

"I'm right here," he said as if she startled him. "What?"

"Constantine would have needed to have a code and a key if he killed Bates. Yasmine told us she had one to let herself in. I wonder if Cynthia or Mark found the key for Bates's house among Yasmine's things."

"Hey, good thought. We'll have to ask them."

CHAPTER

45

ALL MADISON WANTED TO DO was run out the door and throw caution to the wind. The justification was simple: she had to save her sister. But something was holding her back from being impulsive. It probably had to do with Terry's comments about not letting Constantine win and knowing that Troy would never forgive her if she didn't go about this the right way.

"I'm going to go see Troy and then Winston," she told Terry.

"I'll come with you," he said.

"Actually, you update Winston. I want to talk to Troy."

"What happened to 'there's plenty of time'?"

She glowered at him.

"Sure, send me in there," he groaned. "Alone."

She angled her head as if to say she wasn't asking a lot of him.

He held up his hands. "Fine. I'll see him."

"We'll meet up in the lab in a bit," she said over a

shoulder.

A few minutes later, she was going into the conference room. Troy stood when she entered and came over.

"He called," she told him and let him know the address.

Troy let his gaze take in everyone in the room. "Get everything you can on that property." He guided Madison to the hall.

Once out of the room, she said, "He told me to go alone."

"Not happening." His green eyes took on a cool intensity.

She glared right back at him. "If you don't let me handle this alone, he will kill her."

"There's no way I'm going to agree with you running in there—"

"And what? She's my sister, and her life is at stake. I'm not just going to stand around here and do noth—"

"And you're my friend and my lover," he countered.

"I've been a detective for years, Troy, and I've put away I don't know how many murderers." The truth was she knew the exact number. "My point is, I'm going to do just as he told me. I'm going in alone. And if you or your sister or the sergeant, or anyone else for that matter, has a problem with that, tough."

Troy clenched his jaw. "We don't put an innocent civilian in the line of fire to secure another hostage." He sounded like he was clinging to a police procedure manual.

"I'm not a civilian," she barked. "I'm a trained law enforcement officer."

"We don't negotiate with terrorists. Why would we negotiate with a Mafia hit man?"

Her shoulders lowered. "Because he has my sister."

Troy raked a hand through his hair, and she could see his pulse tapping in his forehead. "I'll talk to Andrea, but no promises. And you'll be wearing a wire, do you hear me?" He pointed at her. "Several, actually, because if he finds one, he'll likely stop there and not search for any others. And that, my dear, is nonnegotiable."

She left him and headed for the lab, torn between running in for her sister guns blazing or doing this with backup. But maybe she should have considered the options before letting everyone know where she was meeting Constantine. Her urge to go in solo dissipated thinking about the love in Troy's eyes when he'd told her she was his friend and his lover. Madison took a deep breath.

Surely, Constantine would anticipate that she'd bring company. That still didn't mean the idea of having SWAT backing her up settled fully into her stomach just yet. She could only trust that Troy would make sure they kept their distance and were discreet.

She took out her phone and brought up the meet address in Google as she got on the elevator. Just as she'd figured, there were fields surrounding the property, and the neighboring houses were a long way down the road. As she stared at her screen, she wondered what Constantine's play was going to be. Was he going to let Chelsea go or kill them both? And how did he really think he could get away with this? He had to have an escape plan.

She entered the lab and found Terry already there with Cynthia, Mark, and Jennifer, another CSI who reported to Cynthia. Everyone was seated at the table, except Samantha. There was no sign of her, but that was likely because she was still running ballistics tests and comparisons on the gun recovered from McAlexandar's house.

"Did they find the key?" Madison asked Terry.

"Nope," he responded. "There were only two keys on her ring. The one for her apartment and one for her mailbox in the lobby."

"So Yasmine had to know that Constantine killed Bates." Madison let out a deep breath.

"He could have taken the key without her knowledge," he surmised.

"What about the code, though?" Madison served back. "She probably handed over both. No wonder she was so afraid when she actually found Bates and had to be questioned by us."

"She would have known her usefulness was over, too."

Switching to the next topic at hand, Madison addressed Cynthia. "What about Yasmine's laptop and cell phone? Anything useful on those?"

Cynthia frowned but said nothing.

"Cyn?" Madison prompted.

Cynthia licked her lips, then bit on the bottom one. "It's almost time."

"It is," she said, resigned to getting this over with and ending it once and for all. "And I've got to be ready to go."

"You?" Cynthia stepped forward and was studying Terry. "She's going? I thought the chief benched her from this?"

"If she thinks that I'm going to sit back while SWAT storms in for Chelsea, she doesn't know me at all," Madison ground out. She loved having her inner strength back. Ever since it had been confirmed that Constantine was in town, it had been shaky.

Cynthia's face paled further, and she addressed Terry. "Please tell me she's kidding."

"I don't think she is."

"I'll be wired up, and SWAT is planning an approach. But they'll need to be discreet, because Constantine had wanted me to come alone."

"And you know why he wants you to come alone, right?" Cynthia hardened her jaw. "He's going to kill you."

"He plans to, yes," Madison said calmly.

"How are you okay with that?" Cynthia was shaking her head.

"I'll need the letterhead," she said, sticking with business. It was best if she didn't get drawn in by Cynthia's emotions.

Mark set a clear bag on the table. "It's a color

copy."

Madison retrieved the letterhead. "Have you guys had any epiphanies on the ten-digit code yet?"

Cynthia stared at her, and Madison sensed she was shutting her out because she wasn't happy about Madison going in—period.

"I'm going to take precautions," Madison assured her. "Despite what everyone might think, I don't have a death wish."

Cynthia studied her as if hunting for even a hint of doubt in Madison's voice. She must have passed because Cynthia glanced at Terry, then back to Madison. "The team's been working on the numbers. We've spent actual time staring at it, even. You know, hoping something pops... But nothing." Cynthia gestured to the mounted TV, where they had a photograph of the number on the screen. "We couldn't just stare at it, though, as other things needed attention, but it's never been far from our minds."

Madison focused on the ten digits: *4734237437*. They'd originally thought it was a phone number and that hadn't worked out, but what if they hadn't been too far from a clue with that? Her thoughts were filling in slowly. Viewed as a phone number, it would have been organized as 473 423 7437.

"Maddy?" Cynthia prompted.

"I'm just looking at the numbers." She didn't take her eyes off them when she responded.

"And are you seeing something?"

Madison glanced at Cynthia. "We thought it

might have been a phone number."

"Yes, but it wasn't."

"Right. But what if we've been complicating things?" Madison hurried over to Mark. "Piece of paper."

He handed her one.

"Pen?" She held out her hand, and he put one in it. She scribbled down the numbers, arranging them as they would be as a phone number.

Cynthia came up behind her. "What are you—"

Madison held up a hand to quiet her. "Tell me the letters associated with each number on a telephone keypad," she requested of Mark.

"Oh, this could be something," Terry said.

She was just following the flow of her thoughts and had no idea exactly where they were leading her yet. It might not even end up being anywhere. The number could be any number of things.

Mark rattled off the letters associated with each number, and Madison wrote them under the number in a column and worked her way through. When she was finished, she had ten columns of letters underneath the numbers and no clue. She stepped back.

"I can't make anything out of this," she said.

Mark wrote the numbers and letters down on another sheet, but he did it in such a way that the numbers were together as they were on the letterhead. "The number four repeats three times and same with the number three and seven…"

Madison wasn't sure what he was getting at. "I'm

not sure what that means, if anything."

"I don't know if it means anything yet," Mark began. "I was just making an observation. But what if we still ran with your theory of the numbers as letters and played with the arrangement..." He scribbled the numbers and letters down again. The first time making it four digits, then a space, four more digits, another space, and the final two digits.

Madison was starting to notice a bit of a pattern. Viewing the first four digits—4734—as a word, it could start or end with a *G*, *H*, or *I*. Building on the concept of this being a word, she'd first consider words that began with *G* and then move on to the next digit. It could be a *P*, *Q*, *R*, or *S*.

GP didn't gel for her and neither did *GQ*—unless one was talking about the men's fashion magazine. With *GR* she could be onto something. She continued, searching her brain for any words that started with *GS*, but none came to mind.

Think...

She stepped back, taking in the ten digits as a whole. The last number was seven and could be *R*. The second last number could be an *E*. She went back to the beginning and let her mind fill in blanks, just like the puzzles she used to be so good at. Her heart started racing as a name came to mind.

She took a deep breath. "Greg Berger."

"Greg Berger?" Terry asked incredulously. "Why would his name be in code on a piece of paper?"

"I don't know." Madison didn't claim to have *all* the answers.

"And why would Constantine want this?" Cynthia asked.

"Well, if we figure that Constantine was after this, and that's why he tortured Bates and set up the cameras," Madison started, "I can only think of one reason for Greg's name to be encoded on a piece of paper. Dimitre was calling a hit on Greg Berger."

Terry stepped forward. "And maybe Berger found out—"

"From the prison warden," Madison finished. They'd discussed the possibility of the warden being on the payroll of Dimitre and a mystery third party. "Who must have known what the message was and passed it on to Greg."

"Berger could have sent Constantine to kill Bates, retrieve the message, and stop it from reaching its intended target," Terry surmised. "Aka whoever was going to be tasked with the hit. But if Constantine was on Dimitre's payroll in the past—"

"Berger must have sweetened the pot," she finished.

Terry nodded. "But that doesn't explain why Dimitre would want Berger dead."

She opened her palms. "I don't know. Maybe he figured out that Greg was up to something."

"Up to what, though?" Terry asked. "Is *he* trying to take over as head of the Mafia here in Stiles?"

"I don't know, but I think we've underestimated Greg Berger," Madison concluded.

"That seems like an understatement now," Terry said drily. "He obviously had Dimitre's attention."

"And Greg would only carry all this out, stripping Dimitre of his power—"

"If he was suicidal," Terry said.

She shook her head. "I was going to say if he had power behind him." She paused, thinking her next statement through before saying it aloud. It was a leap, but a possibility nonetheless. "What if Greg Berger and Roman Petrov were close?"

Terry cocked his head. "Dimitre's father is working with Greg to bring down his own son?"

"It could explain why Dimitre hasn't been killed."

"Punishment." Terry's eyes sparked. "For the mess from ten months ago, maybe?"

When she'd dug into her cold case and poked into the Mafia's affairs, she'd unleashed secrets they'd preferred remain such. And to contain them, the body count had piled up.

"We need to take another look at Greg Berger, and see if we can connect him to Roman Petrov," Terry said. "In the meantime, I'll have officers bring him in immediately."

"Well good luck with that." Madison's eyes darted to the clock on the wall. Her stomach twisted. It was game time. "I've got to get wired up." Madison went to leave the room, and Cynthia pulled back on her and gave her a strong hug.

"You better come back to us." Cynthia pecked a kiss on her cheek.

"I intend to." Madison hurried from the room and didn't look back.

It was time to save her sister.

CHAPTER

46

Troy handed Madison a small mic to insert in her shoe. "The wires and bugs stay in place unless he finds them and takes them off." He paused a moment. "I told you I'm not crazy about you going in there."

Thankfully, they'd been able to persuade Andrea to let Madison do this, but as Troy had said, not being wired wasn't negotiable. Madison would be going in unarmed, though. Bringing in a gun could do more to incite Constantine to violence than it would to protect her or Chelsea.

"I'm not risking my sister's life or mine." Madison hugged him.

He put his arms around her, but it was a hard for them to get too close as he was suited up for war. His heavy-duty vest alone added at least thirty pounds to his frame.

It didn't matter that they were in the mobile SWAT command center and that his men were watching them. If something went sideways with

Constantine, they might never see each other again. She shook the sliver of doubt before it could cripple her confidence.

"I've got to go." It was said with a desire to get on with saving her sister, but she was also hesitant to leave Troy. She took his mouth in a brief but deep kiss and pulled back. "I'll see you soon."

"You better." Troy touched her cheek and blinked slowly.

She left and got into her Mazda. SWAT was positioned about a mile down the road from the meet-up spot and were concealed by brush that lined the edge of a field.

As she drove, images started to enter her mind, but she was able to squeeze them out. She'd save her sister and put this nightmare behind her.

She took the turn down the drive, her hands gripping the wheel so tightly that her knuckles were turning white. She parked the car about twenty feet from the barn and got out. A chill ran through her, but she wasn't sure if it was the wind or her nerves.

She approached the barn and opened the door slowly. The wood moaned on the hinges. She peeked inside, and for the most part, it was dark, but in one corner, there was light coming out around the edges of what must have been another door.

She took the first step inside, still cautious about her surroundings and preparing to be ambushed, but nothing came. Constantine was still playing his game.

In fact, it was almost too quiet in here. She heard

her own breath but not much else. A moment later, there was scuffling from behind her and the *thwack* of the barn door slamming shut.

She spun around and reached for a gun but remembered she wasn't armed. It was too dark now to make out much of anything.

More silence and then a switch was flipped, and the barn was bathed in light. She stubbornly refused to close her eyes, even as they watered profusely. Through them, she made out a hazy silhouette— large and foreboding. It was Constantine, and he was holding a gun on her. There was no sign of her sister.

"Where's my sister?"

"Did you come unarmed?"

"Yes." She held up her arms, showing her hands.

"But you didn't come alone, did you?" It wasn't really a question. "You have a hard time following directions, Detective."

"Call it a gift," she retorted snidely, surprised at how she was standing her ground with him.

"Ha, you Americans think you're so funny," he continued through clenched teeth. "If you ever wanted to see your sister alive again, you should have come alone."

"Please! They tracked the phone call," she pleaded, hoping he would buy it. "I'll do whatever you want."

A flashback of him on top of her struck like a lightning bolt, and bile rose into her mouth. She swallowed it with disgust, cringing at its flavor. "Where's my sister?"

"Oh, we'll get to that."

"Just let her go," she begged. "Take me in her place."

"And what? Have Stiles PD storming in here?"

"Please, I never wanted them to come."

"But they did," he roared.

Her heart was racing, and she could hardly breathe.

"Nonetheless, I am nothing if not prepared. And I'm sure they're listening. But that's all right because your boyfriend will get to hear everything but be powerless to stop me." A sinister grin curved his lips. He still held the gun on her but reached into his pocket. He pulled out a cell phone. "One call and this barn, your sister, us, and everyone who moves in on us is dead."

She was staring at his phone as if it held the secret of life and death, because it sort of did. "Just let her go. Let them—"

"You're not in charge here." He stepped toward her and leaned in, sniffing her hair, and ran his hand down her arm. Instinctively, she stiffened.

"Where's my sister?" she asked again. If she just focused on getting to Chelsea, maybe she could tune out his touch.

"I told you we'd get to that."

He circled her, sticking close to her body, mere inches between them. She sensed his raw strength and knew that, physically, she was no match for him. Even hopped up on adrenaline, it would be like an ant fighting a rat. But maybe if she could keep him talking, he'd somehow let his guard down long enough for her to get the jump on him.

"I brought the letterhead." She held up her hands. "I'm just going to reach for it—"

He gripped her wrist tight enough, splotches of white light pinpricked her vision. "Where is it?"

"In my left back pants pocket."

His hand touched her ass, and she strived to put herself out of body and distance herself from this nightmarish reality. But her mind was scheming ways to get her and her sister out of this mess.

She took in the barn, the rafters overhead, the few bales of hay on the floor in the corner, and the walls that held an assortment of tools. Of the ones she recognized by name: saws, picks, shovels, and hand cultivators. Some of them appeared old enough to have been left here a hundred years ago. But one thing they all held in common was they'd make good weapons—that was if she could get to them. But they were all mounted and at least fifteen feet away from her.

Constantine walked around in front of her, the letterhead in his hand. "Have you figured everything out yet?"

She stared through him, even as she felt his breath on her face.

He snatched the paper, crumpled it up, and tossed it to the floor. "I asked you a question," he hissed.

"I figure there's a power shift happening, and those numbers are a code that spells out *Greg Berger*."

"Ah." He smiled. "You have some of it right."

"Is Greg the new head?" she wagered.

"As I said, you had some of it right."

Her mind was spinning. Why did he want them to know about Greg Berger? What was it they had missed? Bates had been killed—something that would anger Dimitre. And then there was Yasmine's murder, but Madison wasn't entirely sure who benefited most from her death. Taking down McAlexandar would be another blow to Dimitre, though. All of this indicated someone working against Dimitre…

"Nothing, Detective? Has your mind gone blank?" He circled her, then moved in and nibbled her ear, and the pain from his teeth sinking into her flesh sent waves through her. But she wasn't going to show him.

Instead, she remembered how he didn't like it when she had seemed to cooperate with his advances. But there was no way she could bring herself to role-play—not again and not with Troy listening.

"Does your SWAT toy pleasure you?"

You sick bastard, she screamed in her head.

"Are you working for Roman Petrov?" she asked, bringing up her earlier theory about father teaching son a lesson.

"Now, you're very hot." He kissed her neck aggressively.

I'm going to kill you the first chance I get!

She pretended to like his attention, and she lolled her head farther to the side. He stopped and scowled at her. He took the barrel of the gun and put the tip to her lips, watching for a reaction. She refused to look at him and, instead, honed in on a pick on the wall and imagined drilling it into his head. But she couldn't rush things. She had get him talking.

"What am I missing?" she asked, despite the placement of the gun.

He groaned and lowered the gun. "Why must we talk business?"

"Who do you work for? Dimitre or Roman?"

"What makes you think they're on opposing sides?"

"You killed Bates, Dimitre's link to the outside world."

"I only kill under orders."

"So why? And why Yas—"

He cupped her chin with one hand and squeezed with a viselike grip. She cried out, pain shooting through her jaw.

"I like it when you're hurting," Constantine snarled, his nose practically touching hers.

She could still see the pick to the side of his head, but it was so far away. She let her body fall limp, and with her resignation, Constantine again lost interest. He let go of her and put about six inches between them. Her jaw was throbbing so hard he may as well have been gripping it still.

Obviously, Constantine had actually cared for Yasmine. And what he had said about Dimitre and his father not being on opposing sides was starting to sink in, too, along with the fact Greg wasn't the new power player. But why did he want their attention drawn to Greg? And why frame McAlexandar, assuming that was what had happened?

She opened her mouth to speak but quickly snapped it shut. The pain was almost unbearable. But she'd be strong—for Chelsea. "Take me to my sister," she demanded, tiring of his games.

"You want to see your sister?" He yanked her hair, pulling it so hard and close to the scalp that her vision was again reduced to pinpricks of white.

"You want to see your sister, fine." He spun her around and jerked her toward the lit room.

Her heart dropped when she saw a plane in front of the barn's back doors.

That was his escape plan. It was also probably how he'd gotten into the country.

He hauled her into the room, and in the corner was a large built-in kennel. Chelsea was tucked away in the corner of it.

"Madison!" her sister screamed at the same time Madison called out to Chelsea.

Tears were falling down her sister's face, but Madison was too angry to cry. Constantine holstered his gun and put his back to her as he unlocked the kennel.

Stupid, stupid mistake.

She scanned the room quickly. If only she could find some way to take him down. She spotted a shovel hanging on a hook seven feet away. Madison made eye contact with her sister, but that was a mistake because Constantine caught it and spun around. She darted to the hook, and her fingers had just grazed the handle of the shovel when it fell to the floor. Constantine was pulling her backward, his thick arms wrapping around her torso like she was a twig he could easily snap. She struggled against him, attempting to move forward, but she was making no headway. In fact, she was losing ground, and he was dragging her back toward the kennel.

She lifted up her right leg and kicked backward, slamming the heel of her boot into the shin of his right leg. He stopped for a second but then tightened his grip, resuming as if nothing had happened. She did it again, this time putting even more strength behind it.

Constantine let go of her, and she dashed toward the shovel again.

"I wouldn't do that if I were you," he said.

She turned around, and he had his gun aimed on her.

"No!" Chelsea screamed.

Madison tightened her jaw and jutted out her chin. "Let her go."

"You're not in any position to barter." He took the gun and turned it on Chelsea.

Tears were streaming down her sister's cheeks. But it was the dire resignation in her eyes that had Madison going cold inside. There was nothing stopping Constantine from killing Chelsea except for her, and she was at a loss of what to do right now.

"Please, I'll do whatever you want me to."

Seconds passed.

"Get in the kennel," he directed.

Madison didn't move.

"Now!"

Shudders shook through her and she stepped slowly toward the cage.

"You unlatch it and get in."

Madison held up her hands and proceeded to do exactly as he'd directed. She crawled to her sister, who had stopped crying but was quivering.

"I'll get us out of this," Madison whispered to her.

Constantine smacked the side of the steel kennel, startling both of them. "I wouldn't bet on that." He latched the kennel and clicked the padlock shut and stood straight. "Don't miss me while I'm gone." He then left the room, a slight limp to his right leg, laughing.

"He's going to kill us." Chelsea was trembling.

Madison rubbed her sister's arms. "Not if I can help it."

"What are you going to do?" Chelsea's eyes were pools of fear, but Madison dare not take a dip. If she did she'd lose all thinking ability and it would be game over for both of them.

CHAPTER

47

MADISON SQUEEZED CHELSEA'S TREMBLING HANDS. "SWAT's listening to everything." She let go of her sister just long enough to point at her chest with one hand.

"Save us," Chelsea cried out.

Madison's eyes flicked right to her sister's and enclosed the warning to keep quiet. They didn't need Constantine storming back in here.

Chelsea took a few deep breaths.

"We're going to be all right." Madison spoke calmly for her sister's sake, but she meant it. Come hell or high water, she'd figure a way out of this with both of them surviving.

"He's going to… He's…"

Madison caressed her sister's face, hoping the touch would soothe her. She watched as her sister's breathing evened out and the storm in her sister's eyes began to clear and her hands stopped shaking.

"He's got a plane in the barn," Madison said for the benefit of the wires, and she wished she was rigged for two-way communication. She could only trust that they were hearing everything. "And he's got a bomb in place rigged to—" She stopped talking when she heard something. A groan and creaking. A draft gust into the room, and she was certain what it must have been. Constantine had opened the barn's back doors. "I think he's preparing the plane to leave," she said, again speaking to SWAT.

"That's what I've been trying to tell you." Chelsea gulped air. "He's going to take you with him."

Madison's lungs were expanded in an exhale. "What do you mean he's going—"

"He told me what his plan is." Chelsea took Madison's hand. "He's going to…" Her chin quivered. "Blow me up and take you with him."

Her insides wrenched as her sister's words sank in. "He told you that?"

"Yeah." Chelsea paused. "I tried to tell you on the phone, but he snatched it from me before I could."

Madison's mind propelled her back to the call. "He's…he's going to—"

Why would Constantine tell Chelsea his plans, and then put them together to talk? He'd have to know Chelsea would tell her his intentions.

God, she wished she could get confirmation SWAT was hearing all this!

"What are we going to do?" Chelsea gaze traced over Madison's face. Her sister's words might have included herself, but she was looking to her for help, and it only strengthened her resolve.

"We're not going to cooperate." She slipped her

hand free of Chelsea's and turned to the door of the kennel.

"He's padlocked it."

"If I can figure out some way to bust the lock." She put her hand through a square of the metal kennel and gripped the padlock. Turning it to an angle so she could see the bottom, she confirmed it required a key. When he'd unlocked it the first time, she couldn't tell for certain. She scanned the small room and came up empty for a solution. Where were bolt cutters when you needed them?

"Can you shoot it?" Chelsea asked.

"If I had a gun."

"You came in unarm— Or he took it from you?"

Madison spoke over her shoulder. "I came in unarmed."

"On purpose?" Chelsea screeched.

Madison held a finger to her lips.

Chelsea's gaze ignited and she clenched her jaw. "Why?"

"Because he would have found it and things could be a lot worse." In light of their current predicament, she wasn't sure how that was exactly possible, but that had been the reasoning.

"A lot worse? Than this?" Chelsea pulled from her thoughts.

The door swung open and Constantine's hulking frame stood in the doorway. "Ready?" He took huge strides toward the kennel, eating up the space between them like twenty feet was four.

He pulled out a key from his left jacket pocket

and unlocked the padlock, but left it inserted in the overlapping latch. He backed up and held his gun on them. "You get out."

Madison couldn't get herself to move. How was she just supposed to leave Chelsea here?

"I said, get out!" Constantine roared.

Instead of making Madison jump, his rage, his directive, pumped through her veins, infusing her with resolve. She met her sister's gaze. She hoped that her sister could read the promise in her eyes. She would be back for her.

Constantine kicked the kennel and Madison noticed that it was with his left leg. And he had walked favoring his right. Her kicks to his shin had done more damage than she'd originally thought.

"Now!"

"Fine." She held up her hands. "I'm coming." She gave one more look to Chelsea, hoping her sister was getting her message.

Madison turned and took the lock off the latch and let it fall. The thud of the metal hitting the barn floor marked in her brain as a sliver of doubt weaseled in. Would it be forever associated with the day she lost her sister?

She crawled out of the kennel and was working to get upright when Constantine pressed his gun to the back of her skull.

"Relock the kennel."

She took a deep breath, hesitating.

"You do everything I say or I'll pull the trigger."

"Why should I if you're going to kill us anyway,"

she spat out.

"Yes," he said with a smile, "but timing is everything. Now lock it!"

His bellow shuddered through her body and she did as he said. Snapping the padlock shut, the guilt of all of this threatened to suffocate her.

"Get up."

She did as he said, making eye contact with her sister, blinking deliberately, doing her best to send her sister strength.

He nudged Madison in the shoulder blade. "Move."

"Where are you taking me?"

"You'll find out soon enough."

She needed to get him to say something for the wires, but he wasn't going to be that stupid. As it was, his cockiness let her remain wired.

He shuffled her out of the room. The entire time, the muzzle of the gun rarely broke contact with the back of her head.

They entered into the main part of the barn. As she'd suspected, the plane had been pushed outside and the back doors were open. The winter wind was howling and gusting into the space carrying with it small snowflakes. She gripped her coat tighter.

"Just let my sister go," she stopped walking about seven feet from the doors. "She didn't do anything to you."

"But she's family and must pay for the sins of her sister."

Was he quoting scripture to her? Madison

recalled Sunday school as a little girl and talk about sins being repaid on generation after generation. She questioned now why so much fear was instilled in children, but it had to be about control.

"She's innocent. Let her go," Madison pleaded. "Do whatever you want with me."

"Oh, I will do that. Now move." He shoved her again, but this time hard enough that she almost lost her balance and fell forward.

As they continued to walk toward the plane, maybe falling wasn't a bad idea. If nothing else, it could buy her some time. She pretended to misstep a few seconds later. This time, letting herself crumble to the ground; her knees meeting barn wood flooring and shooting slivers of pain through her legs.

"Get up!" he barked.

He was towering above her and another Bible story came to her mind. In this scenario she was like David, tiny and seemingly nonthreatening, pitted against a man of Constantine's size—her Goliath. She hadn't been to church in many years, but the recollection buoyed her. It only took one small stone to bring the giant down.

So what is my stone?

She was farther away from the mounted tools than she had been before, and there was nothing she could see within attainable reach that she could get to fast enough. Hope began to fade as the rest of the account filled in. Supposedly David had been backed by God.

Constantine gripped onto her coat and pulled her to her feet, easily as if he were just doing arm curls at the gym. "Move it." This time he emphasized his point by jabbing the gun forward into her head with enough force it had her crying out and reaching back instinctively.

The gun had bit into her flesh and she was bleeding. But her fingers came into contact with something else—the barrel of the gun. Without thinking it through, she wrapped her hands around it, ducked, and spun.

A shot fired over her head, deafening her.

She rose up, struggling to get control of the weapon. But he wasn't relinquishing it easily. And there they stood playing a tug of war with a loaded gun. Each yanking and shifting their bodies to the side.

But she was still at the losing end. The gun fired again, but only fractions of a second before she juked out of the way.

She heard it then: the screams of Chelsea in the other room, but they were dulled to Madison's ears due to the close-range gunfire.

Constantine wrenched back on the gun, nearly tearing her shoulder from its socket. Her hand opened and the weapon slipped out of her reach.

He was heaving for breath, as was she. "Maybe I'll just put a bullet in her head for fun."

He turned, heading back toward the room, and she sprung after him, jumping onto his back and clinging to him.

"You stupid bitch!" He shook her off and this time when she hit the ground, she fell back and her head hit the floor. She lay there, winded, and momentarily unable to move. Her arms and legs weren't responding to her commands. Her gaze went across the barn floor and landed on a short length of chain nestled in a corner between a jut out and a bale of hay. It was only a few feet away.

And Constantine had already resumed walking toward the room.

Come on... She coaxed her body to move, and now it responded.

She got to her knees and crawled across the floor. She grabbed the chain—it was about four feet long but the links were half an inch thick and a couple inches long—and stood to her feet. She closed the distance between her and Constantine—doing so with lightly placed steps. Once she got within striking distance, she pulled the chain back and pitched it forward without letting go.

The metal hit him in the back of the head and he crumbled to the ground.

His gun fell from his hand and skittered across the floor.

For a second, she hesitated, breathing, taking in that she'd actually brought him down. But the daze broke and she snapped to, let go of the chain, and hurried to secure his weapon. Once she had it in hand, she stood there looking down on his unconscious form.

One bullet... That's all it would take.

She aimed the gun on his forehead and moved her finger from the guard, placing it on the trigger.

"Madison!" Her sister's high-pitched yell hit her ears.

She was torn between running to Chelsea and finishing this once and for all. Her finger stayed on the trigger, time coming almost to a standstill as she debated whether to pull back on it and bury him in the past. But he was unconscious and unarmed and the shot wouldn't be made in self-defense. She'd be no better than the cold-blooded murderers she hunted. Still, she found herself struggling to side with ethics. This man had taken so much from her—her sanity, her freedom, and her and her family's security.

"Madison!" her sister cried out again.

This time, she broke Madison's concentration, and she lowered the gun. "I'm coming." She rummaged through Constantine's coat pocket for the key, fearing that he'd come to and kill her, but he was out cold. She found the key and got up, heading to free her sister.

She practically slid across the floor on her knees to the kennel and stuck the key in the padlock, setting the gun down for only a second while she did so. Chelsea was right at the door and sprung out the second Madison tossed the padlock across the room.

"You came for me." Chelsea was sobbing, and Madison's eyes filled with tears. She threw her arms around her younger sister, kissed her forehead, and squeezed her as tight as she could. She didn't ever want to let her out of her sight again.

"All's clear," Madison said for the benefit of SWAT.

"You didn't think this through, Detective." Constantine stood behind them, holding up his phone.

The bomb...

She lifted his gun and shot him right between the eyes. It was an instant kill shot. No hesitation, no thought. Just as she'd promised herself she would.

The phone clattered to the ground as the giant fell again, and this time he wouldn't be getting up. Blood seeped from the wound, trailing a path of red down the sides of his face.

She helped her sister walk past him and out the door, her gaze fixed on his lifeless form, peace washing over her. The threat was off her head, off her family.

"Timing *is* everything, you son of a bitch," she mumbled as she stepped over him.

CHAPTER

48

PARAMEDICS ENTERED THE BARN, and Madison swatted them away from her and directed them to Chelsea. They helped her onto a gurney, but Madison noticed her sister's unsteady legs before they did.

"Is she all right?" she asked the medical staff, but her attention was on her sister.

"She's fine. She's just weak," one of the two responded.

"Did he feed you? Give you water?" Madison asked.

"Some, yes," Chelsea responded.

"And he let you go to the bathroom?"

"Yes."

"She's been in there—" the paramedic pointed to the kennel "—for almost two days. She's bound to have weak legs."

Madison's insides ached as her mind went to what that must have been like for her sister. Hunched down, not able to stand, likely unable to sleep, wondering if she was going to die…

Troy came rushing into the barn and scooped Madison into his arms. Her feet came off the floor as she sank against him and whispered into his ear. "I love you."

He put her down, cupped her face, and captured her mouth with his.

Better than words…

When they parted, they were smiling at each other.

"You pulled it off, Bulldog," he said. "Now, can you go the rest of your life without attracting a killing maniac?"

"What fun would that be?" She smiled, then laughed. So did he.

She savored this period of light at the end of a nightmare she'd been living for so long. But it wasn't to last long as her mind turned to the name on the prison letterhead.

"Did officers bring in Greg Berger?" she asked.

Troy's face grew serious. He blinked slowly and shook his head. "No sign of him. His place was emptied out. No trace of Lyle, either."

"What about Sylvester Stein?"

"He's in the wind, too. So far we haven't turned up anything criminal on the board members at Berger & Stein Accounting, but Greg's connection with the Mafia was enough reason to call in the Feds to look closer at the company."

"Greg's connection?"

"Yep. Nick found a picture of Greg with Roman Petrov."

"What?" she spat. "From when?"

"It was taken in Stiles, and he figures it dates back forty-five, fifty years. Greg was standing next to a pregnant woman. Greg's sister," he punched out. "She's dead. Died years ago in a car accident. The records show that she had a son, but the father was marked as unknown. The kid's name was Sergey."

"As in Dimitre's right-hand man? The one that he had taken out?"

"The same one."

"How did we not find this before now?" she asked, exasperated, and not really expecting an answer to this question. She did, however, seem to have a roundabout motive for Bates's murder. "Greg was getting revenge for Dimitre taking out his nephew."

Troy nodded. "Seems so. And we don't believe Greg was acting on Roman's blessing. We believe that Constantine was sent back by Roman to kill you, to finish what he'd started months ago, but was intercepted by Greg and given additional orders."

"Did Greg know about the hit out on him?" she asked.

"Terry's brought in the prison warden, and he confessed to working for Dimitre and Greg. He was told to relay any messages from Dimitre to Greg. And the writing on the letterhead was Dimitre's. Now, we've figured out that Greg was one of the owners of Vytek Holdings and the warden's financials confirmed he'd been receiving deposits from that company for the better part of ten months."

"Basically from the time Dimitre was transferred

to Mitchell County," Madison began, "And from the time of Sergey's murder."

"Uh-huh."

Her mind was on the warden, on the tight timing between Bates getting the message and Constantine coming to Stiles. The timeframe wasn't impossible, but likely a coincidence. And if that was the case, Dimitre would have had someone keeping an eye on Greg for any signs of revolt. That someone had probably been Bates. But why frame McAlexandar?

"Did the results come back on the gun recovered from McAlexandar's?" she asked.

Troy nodded. "His prints were all over the gun, the bullets, and the magazine."

Guess Karma had a way of working itself out one way or another.

"And the drug test?"

He shook his head. "It was done, but the results aren't back yet."

"And how much do you want to bet that when they do come back nothing will show up?"

"There's a good chance. There are a lot of drugs out there that Constantine could have used that wouldn't show up." Troy paused. "We got a hold of McAlexandar's phone records and confirmed that he was in regular contact with Jimmy Bates. On Bates's side, the number was blocked."

McAlexandar was probably set up to serve the same purpose as Bates: to cut off Dimitre's connection to the outside world. But why Yasmine? Was she just collateral damage?

"Do we know why Yasmine was killed?" Madison asked.

Troy's face paled. "On the record, motive is still being established for McAlexandar. Off the record, she knew too much. Cynthia took a closer look at the video from Yasmine's building, and she found a small glitch. She concludes that it could have been modified. Yasmine's role must have been to provide access to Bates's house. Whether she did that intentionally or not, who knows."

Madison's heart sank, and she preferred to believe that Yasmine had been duped.

"There she is!" Terry rushed into the barn, and he hugged Madison. "Happy you're okay."

Madison smiled at him.

"Guess we know how Constantine got into the country." Terry pointed to the privately owned plane.

"It seems likely."

"So you heard about Greg Berger? His sister? His nephew?"

"I did." She glanced at Troy, and he put an arm around her. Terry smiled at them, and she shot him a snide look in jest. She had a feeling that her partner was probably thinking about the two of them taking the next step. And maybe…

She leaned toward Troy, and he rested his head against hers. Constantine was no longer a threat, and she *had* promised to do some real thinking about her apartment and their living arrangement.

"What about Vytek Holdings?" Terry asked. "Did

he update you on them?"

"Yep," Troy interjected.

"Humph."

Troy held up his hands. "If you had been here sooner, you could have told her."

Terry simpered. "What about the fact that everything Greg and Rodney told us was a lie?" He paused for a few beats. "No? Well, Greg's been involved all along, right in front of us. He probably was the one who recruited Rodney way back. He was just really good at covering his tracks. Greg also did a good job of keeping himself separate from Rodney because there's no mention of him in your grandfather's files."

"That would explain why Greg got so angry when we implied that he did Rodney a favor by hiring Jimmy Bates," Madison surmised.

"Uh-huh. And it could explain why he wanted Bates bad enough to pay for his education, et cetera. Keep it in the family, so to speak."

"That's still a bold move hiring another Bates for his accounting company," Madison said.

Terry nodded. "I think he just wanted to ensure that he had control over the Bates family."

"Just in case Rodney decided to expose him," Madison guessed. "Though we both know that would have been a deadly mistake."

"That's for sure, but we figure the Russians are probably going to move their affairs out of Stiles now. A certain detective wouldn't leave them alone to conduct their illegal business." Terry laughed.

Madison drew her gaze to the paramedics who were wheeling Chelsea toward the door.

Madison stepped in front of them, and they stopped. "Where are you taking her?"

"We're going to get her hooked up to some fluids and take her to the hospital to be checked over," one of them said, and they started moving again.

"I'm coming with her." There was no way Madison was letting Chelsea out of her sight. Madison beseeched Troy with a glance.

"Go." He waved her off with a smile.

Madison watched the paramedics load Chelsea into the ambulance, and she got in the back with her. Chelsea was already hooked up to an IV.

"Did he rape you?" Madison could barely scrape the question from her throat.

"No," she replied weakly. "But I'm going to have nightmares for months."

"At least you'll be alive to have them," Madison countered, and in that moment, holding her sister's hand while she was lying in the ambulance, any guilt that she had tormented herself with melted away. It wasn't her fault that Constantine was a psychopath. She smiled, thinking about their mother's label for him. And really, in a simplistic state, that's exactly what he had been.

"What are you smiling about?" Chelsea raised a brow. "Maybe I should be worried about you."

Madison chuckled. "Oh, I was just thinking about something Mom said."

"You've been talking with Mom?"

"Ah, yeah. There have been extenuating circumstances," Madison teased. "Actually, Mom and Dad flew in last night and stayed with Troy and me."

"Can you pinch me just so I know I'm— Ouch!" Chelsea rubbed her hand. "You weren't really supposed to pinch me, you brat." Chelsea started laughing.

Madison joined her but stopped abruptly when searing pain shot through her jaw. She cupped her cheek and winced.

Chelsea struggled to get up, but the paramedic held her down. "You all right?"

The paramedic glanced at Madison.

"I'll be fine," she assured both of them. It was just the damn adrenaline wearing off. Come to think of it, the back of her head and wrist hurt, too. She looked down at it and saw the colorful shades of early bruising. Maybe she'd get it tended to, but her sister was the priority.

And while she knew that she and Chelsea would be fine, there would be tough days ahead for them. Her sister, for being held captive and seeing what she had seen, and Madison, for doing what she'd had to do. Even though a chapter of her life had ended, it wasn't exactly a fairy tale. It would leave residual emotional wounds, no matter how much she wished to deny it. But in this moment, she would continue to ride the high that came with facing death and coming out the other end alive.

Madison called Jim to let him know she had

Chelsea and that she should be fine, and to tell everyone to meet them at the hospital.

When she hung up, Chelsea said, "Let me guess, Jim's freaking out?"

Madison smiled and pinched her fingers together. "Just a little."

"I should be happy. The man's crazy about me." Chelsea actually appeared wistful for a few moments and closed her eyes. Madison noticed then how dark her eye sockets were from lack of sleep.

Chelsea opened her eyes again. "Speaking of men being crazy…" One corner of her mouth lifted. "I saw you and Troy. The way he literally swept you off your feet."

"*Lifted* me off my feet," Madison corrected with a smile.

"Mince words if you wish, but he really loves you, Maddy."

"And how do you know that?" Madison asked, raising an eyebrow.

"The way he looks at you, the way he stands beside you."

"Uh, the way he stands beside me?"

"Yeah." Chelsea paused. "You know, shoulders relaxed but he's at the ready if he needs to defend you. He's proud to have you by his side."

As Madison listened to her sister, tears formed in her eyes.

"Oh, I struck on the truth," her sister teased. "And you know it. You might have to make an honest man out of him."

"Marriage?" Madison blurted out, almost choking on the word.

"Why not?"

"Why?" Madison countered. "There are a lot of couples who live together without being married. I just moved in with him two months ago!"

Two months ago...

And he loves me, and I love him...

And I've known him for years...

She swallowed as she realized what she had to do, but it would be taking another step in the vulnerability arena and losing the safety net that her furnished apartment represented. Madison looked over at her sister, who had gone quiet. Chelsea's eyes were closed, and she was snoring softly.

CHAPTER

49

THE DOCTORS THOUGHT IT BEST that Chelsea spend the night in the hospital just to get her fluid levels up and some much-needed rest. They had just moved her into a room and gotten her settled when the curtain was pulled back and Jim came through.

Madison watched as her sister and brother-in-law openly cried upon seeing each other, but they were also smiling amid the tears. Jim went over and hugged his wife. Madison was grinning as she watched, thinking about what Chelsea had said to her in the ambulance. She looked over at Troy, who had somehow managed to beat the rest of the family here, and smiled at him. He had his arm around her, his hand resting on her lower back.

"Can we talk for a moment?" Madison asked him.

"Ah, sure."

She led him outside the curtain and nearly bumped right into her mother.

"Mom? What are you—"

Her mother starting sobbing and hugged

Madison. Her father appeared to be in his own world at the moment, and next to him, her three nieces were all wide-eyed and teary.

"Chelsea's all right, Mom." Madison held her tighter when it seemed obvious her mother wasn't going to let her go.

"She wanted to give Jim some time alone with your sister before we went in," her father offered by way of an explanation. He never liked it when any of them cried, and he still got awkward, even after all these years being around women.

Her mother pulled back slightly but continued to hold on to Madison. She looked her in the eye.

"I know I come across gruff sometimes, but don't think I don't care…about you." Her mother sniffled, and Madison blinked away tears. "You do know that I do, don't you?"

"Yeah, of course, I do…"

"How could you? I give you such a hard time about everything. Every decision you make or don't make."

As her mother spoke, an ache formed in Madison's chest. It wasn't one of pain but rather of healing.

Her mother cupped Madison's face, and Madison winced. The doctors had told her the cut on the back of her head was superficial and there was no permanent damage caused to her jaw or wrist. They had prescribed some pain meds, but she had yet to take any.

"Oh, sorry, sweetheart." Her mother dropped her hands but brought her forehead down to meet

Madison's.

She hiccupped a sob, soaking up more love in this moment than she'd felt from her mother in years. In fact, she couldn't remember ever feeling this loved, this accepted by her.

Her mother pulled back again, glanced at Troy, but then settled her gaze on Madison. "Don't mess this one up." Her mother's lips twitched as she spoke.

Madison rolled her eyes. "Oh, here we go…"

Her mother laughed, and so did Madison.

After a few seconds, her mother tapped the back of Madison's hand and said, "I'm going to see my other daughter now. Thanks to you."

Madison wiped her cheeks with the palms of her hands and watched as her mother went in to see Chelsea. Her father stopped and hugged Madison. Her three nieces followed suit.

Once they were all gone, Troy said, "See, I told you that you were loved. And you didn't want to believe me. Do you now?" He rubbed the pad of his thumb beneath her eye, wiping away a tear that had just fallen.

"I'm going to get rid of my apartment," she said it quickly before she could give it any more thought.

Troy's face brightened, but he seemed reserved. "You don't have to do that."

"I know I don't. I want to." She smiled at him. "But I don't want to live in your house, either." Her heart bumped off rhythm just from knowing what she was about to propose.

"I don't understand," he said, sounding weary.

"I want us to find a home that's ours. I mean, if we're in this thing," she said, playfully dismissing the depth of their relationship, "I say we might as well get bold about it." She paused, but he didn't say anything. He was peering into her eyes, and she wished she had magic mind-reading abilities. "Well, you're not going anywhere. I'm not going any—"

He planted a tender kiss on her lips.

"Auntie and Unkie sitting in a—"

"Why, you little—" Troy set out like he was going to chase Marissa, and she squealed as she tried to stay out of his reach. She failed, and Troy scooped her up and swung her in the air so her legs swayed side to side. Marissa started laughing hysterically.

"Put…me…down…"

Troy did as she asked, and Marissa turned around and put her thumb to her nose, wriggled her fingers, and stuck out her tongue. Then she went back into the room with the others.

Troy was smiling, but it faded, his face taking on a serious edge. He met Madison's gaze. "What are your thoughts on kids?"

"What are my—" Her chest felt heavy. She couldn't breathe.

"I'm just kidding, Maddy. Breathe before all of you turns blue."

She narrowed her eyes at him, and then she followed her niece's lead, going in to see her sister and the rest of her family. Troy joined her, but she headed straight to her mother and put her arm around her. Her mother wrapped hers around

Madison and smiled.

"Mom," Madison said, "tell us about Grandpa again."

Read on for an exciting preview of
Carolyn Arnold's FBI thriller
featuring Brandon Fisher

REMNANTS

PROLOGUE

THE TIME HAD COME TO select his next victim. He had to choose carefully and perfectly—he wouldn't get a second chance. The mall was teeming with life, and that made for a lot of eyeballs, a lot of potential witnesses. But he supposed it also helped him be more inconspicuous. People were hustling through the shopping center, interested solely in their own agendas. They wouldn't be paying him—or what he was doing—much attention.

He was standing at the edge of the food court next to the hallway leading to the restrooms eating a gyro. The lidded and oversized garbage bin on wheels that was behind him would ensure that anyone who did notice him would just think he was a mall janitor on his lunch break.

The pitchy voice of a girl about eight hit his ears. "Daddy, I want ice cream."

Trailing not far behind her were a man and woman holding hands. The woman was fit and blond, but his attention was on the man beside her. He was in his twenties, easily six feet tall with a solid, athletic build. He'd be strong and put up a fight. Yes, this was the one. And talk about ideal placement—he was across from the Dairy Queen.

He wiped his palms on his coveralls and took a few deep breaths. What he was about to do wasn't because of who he was, but rather, because he had to do it.

And he had to hurry. The family was coming toward him.

"It's almost lunchtime," the woman said, letting go of the man's hand.

"Daaaaaaddyyyyy." A whiny petition.

The man looked to the woman with a smile that showcased his white teeth. "We could have ice cream for lunch?"

The little girl began to bounce. "Yeah!"

"Really, Eric?" The woman wasn't as impressed as the girl, but under the man's gaze she caved and smiled. "All right, but just today…"

"Thank you, Mommy!" The girl wrapped her arms around the woman's legs but quickly let go, prancing ahead of her parents and toward the DQ counter.

"Brianna, we wash our hands first." The woman glanced at him as she walked by and offered a reserved smile. Had she detected his interest in them?

Breathe. She thinks you work here, remember?
Smile back.

Remain calm.

Look away and act uninterested.

"Oooh," the girl moaned but returned to her mother anyway.

"We'll just be a minute," the woman said.

"Hey, doesn't Daddy have to wash his hands?" the girl asked.

Sometimes things just work out...

The woman smiled at the man. "Eric?"

"Yes, he does," he playfully answered in the third person.

Mother and daughter headed to the restroom, the man not far behind.

It was time to get to work.

He took the last bite of his sandwich, crumpled the wrapper, and tossed it into the bin. He casually moved behind it and pushed it down the hall into the men's room.

He put up a sign that said it was closed for cleaning and entered, positioning himself next to the door. From there, he could see his target at one of the urinals and another man washing his hands at the sink. Otherwise, it was quiet.

Just as if it was meant to be...

The stranger left the restroom without a passing glance. This left him alone with his target.

He twisted the lock on the door and then moved behind the man, who paid him no mind. He took the needle out of his pocket and plunged it into the man's neck.

The man snapped a hand over where he'd been

poked. "Hey!"

It would take a few seconds for the drug to fully kick in. He just had to stay out of the man's way and block the exit in the meantime.

"What did you..." The man was away from the urinal now, coming toward him on unsteady legs. Both his hands went to his forehead and then it was lights-out. He collapsed on the floor.

He hurried to the bin, wheeled it over to the man's body, and lifted him just enough to dump him inside. Once the man was in there, he lowered the lid, unlocked the restroom, collected his sign, and left.

His heart was thumping in his ears as he wheeled the bin out a back service door. Some people were milling around, but they didn't seem curious about him. He went to his van and opened the back door. He put the ramp in place and simply wheeled the bin inside.

When he was finished, he closed the doors and headed for the driver's seat. He wanted to hit the gas and tear out of the lot. The adrenaline surging through his system was screaming, *You got away with it again*, but he didn't like to get too cocky.

Still, he did take some pride in the fact that he'd gotten what he'd come for—and it had been so, so easy.

CHAPTER

1

VALENTINE'S DAY WOULD HAVE TO wait until next year, and I couldn't say I was disappointed—or surprised. Working as an agent in the FBI's Behavioral Analysis Unit makes planning anything impossible. This time, being swept out of town for an investigation was saving me from a day that was otherwise full of expectations and pressures. And even though my relationship with Becky was casual, it had been going on for several months now and she would be expecting a romantic evening.

But all that was hundreds of miles behind me now...

When I stepped off the government jet, the warm Savannah air welcomed me and made me think of my childhood in Sarasota, Florida. No cold winters there, either, unlike Virginia, where it could dip below zero this time of year, occasionally bringing that white stuff along with it.

My boss, Supervisory Special Agent Jack Harper, walked in front of me. This was his first time heading into the field after an unsub had almost killed him this past summer. He'd barely scraped by, but he was far too stubborn of a bastard to die. Having come so close to death, though, he had to be looking at life differently. I knew when I had just *thought* I was going to die during a previous investigation, it had taken me a long time to shake it.

He had more gray hairs than I'd remembered, and the lines on his face were cut deeper. His eyes seemed darker these days, too. More contemplative. He had been cleared for field work, but I still questioned how he could have fully bounced back in six short months.

I looked over my shoulder at the other two members of our team, Zach Miles and Paige Dawson. Zach was a certifiable genius, and although he was older than my thirty-one years, he had the sense of humor and maturity level of a college student. He'd found endless amusement in calling me "Pending" for the entire two years of my probationary period. Another reason I was happy to be a full-fledged agent now.

Paige was another story. She and I had a rather complicated history, and whether I wanted to admit to it or not, I loved her. But we had to make a choice—our jobs or our relationship. Since we'd both worked far too hard to throw our careers away, the decision to remain friends was, in effect, made for us.

We silently weaved through the airport and picked up a couple of rental SUVs. Jack and I took one, as we usually did, and Paige and Zach were paired together. We were going straight to meet with Lieutenant Charlie Pike, who commanded the homicide unit of Savannah PD, and his detective Rodney Hawkins, at Blue Heron Plantation where human remains had been found in the Little Ogeechee River. According to our debriefing, an arm and a leg were found there a week ago, and yesterday, another arm showed up. Savannah PD had already run tests confirming that we were looking at three different victims, and that was why we'd been called in.

The drive went quickly, and when the plantation's iron gates swung open, I spotted a female officer guarding the entrance. She lifted her sunglasses to the top of her head as Jack rolled to a stop next to her and opened his window.

Jack pulled out his credentials. "Supervisory Special Agent Jack Harper of the FBI. I'm here with my team."

The officer's hazelnut eyes took in Jack's badge, then she looked behind us to Paige and Zach in the other SUV. She lowered her sunglasses. "Lieutenant Pike is expecting you. He's just down there." She pointed to a path that came off a parking lot and seemed to disappear amid cattails.

We parked the vehicles and wasted no time getting to where she had directed us. The echoing calls of red-winged blackbirds and the whistling cries of blue herons carried on a gentle breeze, but the presence of investigators wearing white Tyvek suits drove home our purpose here and it had nothing to do with relaxing in nature.

As we approached, a black man of about fifty was talking animatedly into a phone. He was easily six foot four, thin and fit, and he had a commanding presence, even from a distance.

A younger male officer in a navy-blue uniform stood in front of him and gestured in our direction.

The black man turned to face us, his phone still to his ear. "Gotta go." He tucked his cell into his shirt pocket and came over to us while the officer went in the opposite direction. "I take it you're the FBI."

"SSA Jack Harper, and this is my team." Jack gestured to each of us.

The lieutenant took turns shaking our hands and getting our names. He finished with me, and I was surprised by how firm his grip was.

"Brandon Fisher," I said. "Good to meet you."

There was a loud rustling in the tall grass then, followed by a splash.

"Probably just an alligator," Pike said.

Yeah, just *an alligator…*

As if on cue, twenty feet down the bank, someone began wrangling one of the reptiles, the animal's tail and head swiping through the air as it tried to regain its freedom. No such luck, though, as its captor worked to get it away from the investigators. I took a few steps back. There was no harm in being extra cautious.

"I'm glad all of you could make it as quickly as you did. I'm Lieutenant Pike, but most people call me Charlie."

Maybe it was his age or his rank, but I knew I'd continue to think of him as Pike.

"Unfortunately," he went on, "Detective Hawkins won't be joining us today or for the remainder of the case. He's dealing with a family matter."

"I hope everything will be all right," Paige said, showing her trademark compassion.

Pike shook his head. "They were expecting and just found out that they lost the baby."

His words had my past sweeping over me. I knew exactly how that devastation felt. My ex-wife, Deb, had gotten pregnant once, but her body had rejected the fetus. She'd never really been the same after that, truth be told. And by the time she had seemed to return to a version of her normal self, she'd asked for a divorce.

Jack's body was rigid. "Where was the arm found yesterday?" As always, his focus was solely on the case. While he was a person who sheltered his emotions quite well, he usually could muster some empathy.

"Ah, yes, right out there." Pike pointed toward a boat in the water, about halfway out from the riverbank. A diver surfaced next to it. "The arm was lodged in some mud and sticking out above the surface."

To be out that far, either the limb had been dumped from a boat, had come down the river and settled here, or our unsub had a good throwing arm. If we could determine which, it would give us some helpful insight into our unsub.

The investigation by Savannah PD had dismissed the idea of the murders taking place on plantation property, though. But if our unsub had chosen here as the dump site, it would tell us how organized he was, whether he assumed risk or preferred isolation.

"Are the gates normally left open for the public?" I asked. "It seems rather remote back here, but is there much traffic?"

Pike wasn't wearing sunglasses, and he squinted in the bright sunshine. "It's not an overly busy place, and they close at night."

"But could a person come down the river to the plantation on a boat at night after hours?" I asked.

Pike curled his lips and bobbed his head. "Yeah, I suppose that's possible."

"I want the parts of the river going through the property under surveillance. Twenty-four seven," Jack directed, drawing Pike's gaze to him.

"I'll make sure that happens."

"And make sure the officers are hidden so if our unsub is brazen enough to return—"

Pike nodded. "Not our first rodeo."

"And make sure the search for more remains continues during daylight hours."

"Those are already their orders." Pike put his hands on his hips. "The community has gotten wind of yesterday's finding, and on top of last week's discovery, let's just say people are panicking.

Somehow a local news station found out that the FBI was being brought in. Don't ask me how."

While I probably should have, I didn't really care. My senses were too busy taking in the crime scene: marshland, relative seclusion, an arm and leg discovered last week, an arm yesterday. Aside from the human remains that had been found here, the property had a serene feeling to it, a sense of peace. There was a tangible quality to the air, though—or maybe it was the presence of law enforcement and crime scene investigators—that made it impossible to deny that death had touched the place.

"What else can you tell us about the limbs that were recovered?" Paige asked.

The lieutenant cleared his throat. "Well, both arms didn't have hands, and the leg didn't have a foot. We found incision marks indicating the hands and foot had been intentionally cut off."

"Our killer could have taken them for trophies or to make identification impossible," I suggested.

Pike gave a small nod and continued. "And while we know the hands and foot were removed, it's not as clear how the appendages separated from the torso. It would be something we'd need the medical examiner to clarify."

Jack's brow furrowed, and I could tell his mind was racing through the possibilities.

"But," Pike continued, "all the limbs have one thing in common: muscle tissue remained, even though the skin had been removed."

"It is possible that the skin was also taken as a

trophy," Zach speculated.

"We could be looking for a hunter or a sexual sadist," Jack said.

Hunters were typically identified by the type of weapon they used—a hunting knife, rifle, or crossbow, for example—and they tended to dispose of their victims' bodies in remote, isolated areas. A sexual sadist, on the other hand, got off on the torture and pain. But we'd need to gather more facts before we could build any sort of profile on our unsub. Even knowing more about the victims themselves would help. Was the killer choosing people he or she was acquainted with? Were the victims of a certain gender, age group, occupation? The list went on and on. From there, we could more easily speculate on our killer's motive and what they had to gain.

"Any IDs on the victims yet?" I asked.

Pike shook his head. "Not yet, but they're working on it. I'm not sure when we'll know."

I looked at Jack. I didn't know all the steps involved with processing DNA, but it could take weeks, if not months, to go through the system. Things could be sped up if the government was willing to foot the bill for a private laboratory, which was costly and would still take days. Oftentimes this was approved for cases involving serial murder, but primarily when we had seemingly solid evidence that we believed would lead us to the killer.

Jack gave a small shake of his head, as if he'd read my mind and dismissed the private laboratory.

"Anyone reported missing from the area recently?" Zach asked.

"No." Pike's single word was heavy with discouragement.

"It could be that the victims aren't being missed by anyone." Zach's realistic yet sad summation was also a possibility.

"The ones from last week were all Caucasian males in their mid- to late twenties," Pike offered next.

"What about the arm from yesterday?" Jack asked.

"It was male. I called in a friend and colleague to get us more information. She's an anthropologist, and she'll take a look at it as she had the other remains, but she won't get to it until much later today."

"She?" Paige queried.

"Shirley Moody. She's one of the best in the field but from out of town."

Jack nodded his acknowledgment. "What can you tell us about the guy who found the arm yesterday?"

"Name's Jonathan Tucker. He works at the plantation, and we took his statement, of course," Pike began. "His record is clean, and he seems like a down-to-earth guy. He's got two young girls and his wife died a couple years back. He seemed really shaken up by all this."

"What about Wesley Graham?" Jack asked.

"The man who found the remains last week? Nice guy. He's single and proud of it. Never been married.

No record, either. But he didn't seem too upset by the whole situation."

So far we weren't getting much more out of Pike than we had his detective's reports. Graham didn't work for the plantation, and the file noted that his reason for coming to the plantation was to de-stress.

"This site attracts tourists and locals," Pike said. "People like to surround themselves in nature. Personally, I could live without mosquitoes." He swatted near his face as if to emphasize his point. "I know you'll probably want to pay Tucker and Graham visits yourselves, but—" Pike made a show of extending his arm and bending it to consult his watch "—right now, I've got you an appointment with the owner of the plantation. We should probably get moving toward the main house."

"Lieutenant!" A female investigator shouted as she waded through the water toward the riverbank in a hurry. She was holding a clear plastic evidence bag.

"We found a cell phone," she called out as she reached us.

Pike looked at the investigator skeptically. "Where?"

Her eyes dipped to the ground, but she regrouped herself quickly. "It was near where the arm was found."

"And it took a day to find it?" Pike raised his eyebrows.

She squared her shoulders but shrank somewhat under the lieutenant's gaze. "It was in a tangle of weeds, but it could have just come to rest there in recent currents."

It seemed Pike was a hard one to please, and he reminded me of the way I used to view Jack—an unforgiving perfectionist. And while Pike might not be impressed, I was pleased. That phone could lead us to a killer.

Also available from
International Bestselling Author
Carolyn Arnold

REMNANTS

Book 6 in the Brandon Fisher FBI series

All that remains are whispers of the past…

When multiple body parts are recovered from the Little Ogeechee River in Savannah, Georgia, local law enforcement calls in FBI agent and profiler Brandon Fisher and his team to investigate. But with the remains pointing to three separate victims, this isn't proving to be an open-and-shut case.

With no quick means of identifying the deceased, building a profile of this serial killer is more challenging than usual. How are these targets being selected? Why are their limbs being severed and their bodies mutilated? And what is it about them that is triggering this person to murder?

The questions compound as the body count continues to rise, and when a torso painted blue and missing its heart is found, the case takes an even darker turn. But this is only the beginning, and these new leads draw the FBI into a creepy psychological nightmare. One thing is clear, though: The killing isn't going to stop until they figure it all out. And they are running out of time…

**Available from popular book retailers or
at CarolynArnold.net**

CAROLYN ARNOLD is an international bestselling and award-winning author, as well as a speaker, teacher, and inspirational mentor. She has four continuing fiction series—Detective Madison Knight, Brandon Fisher FBI, McKinley Mysteries, and Matthew Connor Adventures—and has written nearly thirty books. Her genre diversity offers her readers everything from cozy to hard-boiled mysteries, and thrillers to action adventures.

Both her female detective and FBI profiler series have been praised by those in law enforcement as being accurate and entertaining, leading her to adopt the trademark: POLICE PROCEDURALS RESPECTED BY LAW ENFORCEMENT™.

Carolyn was born in a small town and enjoys spending time outdoors, but she also loves the lights of a big city. Grounded by her roots and lifted by her dreams, her overactive imagination insists that she tell her stories. Her intention is to touch the hearts of millions with her books, to entertain, inspire, and empower.

She currently lives just west of Toronto with her husband and beagle and is a member of Crime Writers of Canada and Sisters in Crime.

CONNECT ONLINE
Carolynarnold.net
Facebook.com/AuthorCarolynArnold
Twitter.com/Carolyn_Arnold

And don't forget to sign up for her newsletter for up-to-date information on release and special offers at CarolynArnold.net/Newsletters.

CPSIA information can be obtained
at www.ICGtesting.com
Printed in the USA
LVHW092154110721
692439LV00015B/250

9 781988 353647

"I've Spent My Whole Life Avoiding Women Like You."

There was humor along with desire in Adam's voice. "You never think of the consequences of your actions."

"After you kiss me, you can start avoiding me again. I promise." Lorna wanted to be devoured. Right now. In this parking lot. It was naughty and it was irresponsible, but she wasn't herself. Not her *old* self, anyway.

Adam's lips hovered a fraction above hers. "Women like you never keep their promises."

"Maybe I'm different than other women like me."

"Tell me another one."

"But it's the truth...."

"Shh."

"Really, Adam. I'm telling the—"

Lorna's protests were cut off, since at that moment Adam Gantry's self-control lost the battle with his senses....

Dear Reader:

Welcome to the world of Silhouette Desire. Join me as we travel to a land of incredible passion and tantalizing romance—a place where dreams can, and do, come true.

When I read a Silhouette Desire, I sometimes feel as if I'm going on a little vacation. I can relax, put my feet up, and become transported to a new world...a world that has, naturally, a perfect hero just waiting to whisk me away! These are stories to remember, containing moments to treasure.

Silhouette Desire novels are romantic love stories—sensuous yet emotional. As a reader, you not only see the hero and heroine fall in love, you also feel what they're feeling.

In upcoming months look for books by some of your favorite Silhouette Desire authors: Joan Hohl, Ann Major, Elizabeth Lowell and Linda Lael Miller.

So enjoy!

Lucia Macro
Senior Editor

CHRISTINE RIMMER
TEMPORARY TEMPTRESS

SILHOUETTE *Desire*®

Published by Silhouette Books New York

America's Publisher of Contemporary Romance

SILHOUETTE BOOKS
300 East 42nd St., New York, N.Y. 10017

ISBN: 0-373-05602-8

First Silhouette Books printing November 1990

Printed in the U.S.A.

CHRISTINE RIMMER's

favorite pastimes include playing double-deck pi-
nochle, driving long distances late at night, swim-
ming in cold mountain rivers and eating anything with
chocolate in it. She's also a voracious reader and an
inveterate romantic daydreamer who's thrilled to have
at last found a job that suits her perfectly: writing
about the magical and exciting things that happen
when two people fall in love. Christine lives in California with her young son, Jesse.

Prologue

Adam Gantry shifted the car into park and switched off the engine and lights. He peered through the late-night darkness at the house he had sought and found by taking the address from Astrid's address file and consulting a map bought at an all-night liquor store.

The house was one of those low, flat-roofed structures, without any distinguishing features. Adam thought it a surprisingly average-looking place for an ex-lover of Astrid's to live in.

Wondering ruefully if he'd ever see a good night's sleep again, Adam rubbed the stiff muscles at the back of his neck. He had a problem with insomnia and hadn't been able to sleep last night. And tonight, of course, would end up a total loss. His eyes felt grainy, his tie too tight. He pinched the bridge of his nose between thumb and forefinger in a futile effort to massage away the tiredness, then loosened his tie.

Guilt, dread and anger had carried him this far. But now he hesitated. Was he doing the right thing? He spent several seconds debating, staring rather blankly at his watch. The time was 3:00 a.m. He really hated to disturb the house's occupants at this ungodly hour.

If he had any sense at all he'd give it up. Return to L.A. and get on with his life.

But he couldn't. He was too worried about Astrid. Growing up with her for a mother hadn't been his idea of the perfect upbringing. But still, she had done her best. He loved her, and he owed her. And the note she'd left behind for her stunned fiancé when she ran out on her own engagement party had rung a shrill warning in Adam's mind and heart.

Max,
My secret sister needs me in Palm Springs, so I must go to her at her hotel there.

And I want to be honest with you, my darling. I must see Arthur Utulo before I can marry you. I was in love with him once, long ago. And he lives there now. I must have some time to be sure. Please understand.

Yours,
Astrid

Max had handed Adam the note without saying a word, and then told Adam very quietly that he wanted to be alone. Just thinking of the stunned, despairing expression on the older man's face made Adam's stomach twist with guilt.

Maxwell Hollander was the senior partner in Adam's law firm, Adam's mentor and the father he'd never had. Max never would have met Astrid Gantry if Adam hadn't introduced them two years before.

But worse than Adam's guilt, even worse than his fury at his mother for pulling such a cruel stunt, was his dread.

"My secret sister needs me..." she had written. What the hell was a *secret sister*? Adam was afraid he already knew. He was all too aware of his mother's fatal weakness for odd societies and fringe groups.

Adam was terrified that if he didn't get to her soon, she'd sign over everything she owned to this mysterious secret sister. He was afraid she was throwing away both her chance for happiness *and* her solvency. As her only child, he just couldn't sit by and let her ruin her life.

Positive that he was in the right, Adam left the car. He strode purposefully up the cement walk, past the crouching shadows of spiky-leaved century plants and a pair of runty yuccas. There was a wooden plaque beneath the porch light that read The Utulos.

Adam rang the doorbell. When there was no immediate answer, he waited a respectable ninety seconds and rang again. A light went on in a side window. He waited some more, and then the door, held by a chain, opened a crack.

A matronly middle-aged woman, her head covered by pink foam rollers and a flowered hair net, peeked around the door.

Adam's quick mind drew the logical conclusions. This had to be the ex-boyfriend's wife. The likelihood that he'd find Astrid wrapped in Arthur Utulo's arms had just greatly diminished.

"Yes?" Through bleary eyes, the woman peered at him warily. He knew that his clothes and manner spoke well for him, and he was careful not to present a threatening stance. He gave her a moment to look him over before he spoke.

"Excuse me, I'm sorry to bother you...." Adam began.

"It's very late," the woman murmured, looking a bit less wary.

"I know, but I'm trying to find someone and I was afraid if I waited until a more respectable hour, the—" he paused significantly, hoping he was taking the right tack on this "—trail would be cold."

The woman narrowed her squinting eyes even further. "Are you with the police?"

"No." He cleared his throat officiously, and then dropped his voice to a confidential whisper. "This is a private matter." He whipped out a picture of Astrid standing in front of Stellar Attractions, the hairdressing salon that Max's money had bought.

The woman gave the picture one quick look and then swore in a distinctly unmatronly manner. "I should have known."

"Then you've seen her?"

"What's she done?"

"I'm not at liberty to say. I hope you understand."

"I certainly do." She glanced over her shoulder, no doubt eager to get Astrid in as much hot water as possible before her husband could interrupt. "All I can tell you is, about seven tonight, she came into Icy Delights, the frozen-yogurt store that Artie and I own. She just strolled in bold as you please and pranced right up to the counter where Artie was ringing up a sale. 'Hello, Art,' she says in this low, sexy voice. Then she grabs him around the neck, kisses him right on the mouth in a way that left no doubt they'd once been, well, you know. Then she steps back, shakes her head, and prances on out. Artie swears he hasn't seen her in forty years, but I—"

"Enid, what the hell is going on out there!" The man's voice came from somewhere in the back of the house.

"Nothing, Artie!" She grinned at Adam, rather slyly. "He's sleeping in the back room tonight." She turned as footsteps approached behind her.

Then Artie, older than Enid and totally bald, was squinting around the door. "What's this? Man can't get no sleep in his own damn house."

"I'm sorry to bother you—"

"Then don't."

Adam stuck his foot in the door before Artie could slam it. "Please, Mr. Utulo. Just one question."

"Make it snappy."

"Do you happen to know where Astrid Gantry might have gone?"

Artie cackled. "Nope." He shook his head, and a gleam came into his watery eyes. "What a woman."

"Artie!" Enid screeched from behind him.

"She didn't happen to mention anything to you about a *secret sister*, did she?"

Artie shook his head. "Get your foot out of the door now, sonny. As you can hear, I got me a little domestic problem to take care of."

"Thanks." Adam removed his foot and Artie shut the door.

Adam stood on the cement walk for a moment, hearing the arguing voices behind the door and wondering what to do next. Then he returned to his car.

The problem was that he had no lead at all on this mysterious secret sister. A call to Rafael Potts, Astrid's assistant at her salon, had revealed only that Rafael "thought it was something to do with some women's group," which told Adam hardly anything. Calls to two or three of Astrid's closer friends had gotten him no more information. They all said they had no idea what he was talking about, but that Astrid always had been one to get involved with "interesting" people.

Intent on finding some kind of clue, no matter how minimal, Adam took the crumpled note from the glove compartment and, by the dim interior light, read it again.

My secret sister needs me in Palm Springs, so I must go to her at her hotel there....

Adam switched off the light and sat in the darkness, staring at the shadows of the surrounding mountains against the night sky.

How many hotels could there be in a resort town like Palm Springs?

"Too many," he answered his own question aloud with a weary sigh.

But what else did he have to go on? Zero.

He pictured Palm Canyon Drive in his mind. Several miles of main street, packed with exclusive shops, restaurants—and countless hotels.

Grimly, he slid the key in the ignition and started up the car again. If he intended to visit every hotel in Palm Springs in hopes that his mother had registered in one of them using her own name, he'd better get started. Somehow, he had to find Astrid before her "secret sister" took her for everything she was worth.

One

Lorna Smith was lazing abed in her honeymoon suite when a timid knock, barely audible in the bedroom, came at the sitting room door.

Lorna snuggled deeper beneath the satin sheets, feeling deliciously self-indulgent. Then she languidly rolled over. Her skin felt like silk, the result of a long, luxurious soak in a tub full of foaming bath salts. The bath salts had smelled like fresh strawberries and so had the special soap Astrid had bought for her to use.

Half-asleep, Lorna smiled, thinking of Astrid. Whatever else had gone wrong in Lorna's life, she'd certainly hooked the gold ring when she drew Astrid for her secret sister.

With her leather cosmetic kit under one arm, Astrid had driven all the way to Palm Springs to come to Lorna's aid. She had arrived at Lorna's hotel at eight the night before, wearing a man's tweed sport coat tossed rakishly across her shoulders and waving a bottle of expensive champagne.

"I'll have you know I stopped in the bar to get us this champagne," were the first words out of Astrid's mouth. Then the older woman had shivered. Trailing a cloud of musk, her signature scent, Astrid waltzed into the room, shedding the tweed jacket. "It was *freezing* in the bar. Why is it they always keep the temperature subzero in desert hotels?" She'd tossed her makeup kit on the sitting-room couch. "But, as luck would have it, I met the sweetest little redheaded man who loaned me his jacket. Chivalry, whatever they say, is far from dead. Now, call room service and order us up some champagne flutes and let's have a toast to sisterhood—and to your new freedom that you're going to thoroughly *enjoy*!"

Now, the morning after, Lorna indulged in a contented yawn. With her eyes still closed, she went on smiling. As Astrid had so wisely pointed out, life was all in how you looked at it. Lorna could think of herself as jilted at the altar—or as set miraculously free. When you saw it that way, the choice was a simple one to make.

Lorna sighed, happily. It was going to be a beautiful day, because *she* was going to make it that way. After a while, she would get up and take a long, hot shower. Then she'd pamper herself with a leisurely breakfast in the hotel's best restaurant—not the coffee shop today. Oh, no. She'd eat slowly and pleasurably on good china in elegant surroundings. And then she was going to hit every boutique in Palm Springs, buy herself a whole new wardrobe—and not one single item in it would be her usual beige.

Lorna Smith might in actuality be nothing more than an ordinary, practical lady who owned a bookstore in Westwood. But that didn't mean she couldn't start dressing in bright colors. "If you want to be different, you have to be willing to change," Astrid had said the night before. And

Lorna intended to take her secret sister's advice completely to heart.

Out in the other room, the knock came again, slightly louder and more insistent.

"All right, I'm coming!" Lorna sat up among the acres of bed linens and reveled in a long, lazy stretch. Then she allowed herself to gaze on her own reflection in the wall of mirrors on the other side of the room.

Her plain brown hair now cascaded down around her bare shoulders. Astrid had trimmed it in layers, so the natural curl became apparent, and she had frosted the ends, so it glowed with bronze highlights. Her makeup, which looked so good last night that she hadn't wanted to wash it off, had a smudgy look now, but it didn't matter to Lorna. Beneath the smoked teal eyeshadow, her blue eyes shone back at her, full of mischief and promise. She looked golden and decadent, she decided, in her apricot silk teddy and absolutely nothing else.

The tapping on the door came again. Lorna tossed back the covers and entered the suite's huge bathroom. A fluffy terry-cloth robe, provided by the hotel, hung on a peg behind the door. She snared it and stuck her arms in the sleeves, belting it haphazardly as she went to answer the knock.

When she flung the door wide, the response of the man waiting on the other side was extremely gratifying. He gulped and stared.

Lorna granted him a dazzling smile. "Yes?"

He stuttered out a nervous explanation. "I, uh...last night I loaned my jacket to the lady in the room across the hall. But when I asked about her at the front desk just now, they said she'd checked out already. I wonder if you..." His voice trailed off as Lorna casually rebelted her robe. It was obvious that he found Lorna quite attractive. He seemed to be mesmerized by the bit of apricot silk that rebelting her robe had revealed.

"I'd trade my Mercedes to be like you," Lorna had moaned to Astrid the night before.

Astrid had gazed measuringly back at her for a moment, and then replied, "No, be yourself. Always." A mysterious smile had crossed her full mouth. "Besides, you're going to be surprised at what a knockout you are once I'm through with you."

As the redheaded man stared at her with his mouth open, Lorna felt naughty—and wonderful. Her new look was having its intended effect. The poor man's face flamed as red as his hair.

"There's a siren inside of every one of us," Astrid had told her the night before. "It's only a matter of bringing her out."

Of course, Lorna had no intention of indulging the siren within herself full-time, but it couldn't hurt to flirt just a little every now and then. She upped the wattage on her smile, feeling like a completely new and beautiful woman, like someone just a little wild on the brink of a grand adventure.

She heard Astrid's voice again in her mind. "So what if your fiancé jilted you? Let him go. Someone better will always come along—take it from a sister with a wealth of experience in games of the heart. Now. To go ahead with the honeymoon anyway was a stroke of genius. But you ruin the whole idea if you just sit here in your room and mope." Green eyes flashing, Astrid had waved her expensive shears, which glittered brightly in the light of a nearby ginger jar lamp. "What you need is adventure, something different and utterly wild. First, though, we get rid of the Marian Librarian hair and brighten up the makeup. We're talking makeover here, darlin'. We're going to totally change your self-image, starting with what you see when you look in the mirror...."

The redheaded man, still waiting for his coat, cleared his throat uncomfortably. Lorna went on smiling.

What a wonder Astrid was, Lorna thought with fondness. Astrid was the sister she wished she'd had, the mother she should have had, a true friend for life. Astrid was— She paused in her mental testimonial as the young man's first words to her suddenly sunk in. "Excuse me, I wasn't listening," Lorna said. "Did you say Astrid had already checked out?"

"That's what they told me at the desk."

Lorna frowned. She'd thought perhaps she and Astrid would hit the stores together today. For a moment she felt cheated. But then that sense of promise and excitement, Astrid's gift to her, overrode the rest.

Of course. How like Astrid to do what needed to be done and then be on her way. Like a modern fairy godmother, Astrid had waved her magic wand. And like a fairy godmother, she'd disappeared before the dawn. And, of course, they would meet again in L.A. soon enough.

Lorna's admirer made a questioning noise in his throat. Lorna realized she'd kept him standing there waiting for several minutes while she privately rhapsodized about Astrid.

"I'm sorry. Your jacket, you're looking for your jacket?"

He nodded, smiling bashfully, and she noticed a gap between his two front teeth. She thought it charming because it suited him, with his shyness and his ready blush.

"Yes, I think I can help you there." She asked him his name and he said, "Teddy." She stepped aside and gestured him into the suite.

The jacket was draped over one arm of the couch. She picked it up and gave it to him.

"Thanks," he said. He was looking at the champagne bottle, upended in the bucket of melted ice, at the two champagne flutes on the glass coffee table. "I hope I didn't disturb you."

Lorna grinned and took his arm to lead him back to the door. "Well, I *am* on my honeymoon."

"Oh, I'm sorry. I really am." He was blushing furiously. "I hope your husband——"

They had reached the door, which stood wide open. Lorna went on tiptoe and kissed him on the cheek. "Don't you worry about him," she said. "He's a very sound sleeper. In fact," she lowered her voice to a confidential whisper, "until you brought him up, I'd forgotten all about him."

Teddy blinked and his blush spread, until even his ears turned red. He looked nervously at the half-open door to the bedroom. "Er, ma'am . . ."

"Lorna," she said.

"I really have to go now."

Lorna shrugged, and tried to keep from giggling out loud. "And ma'am . . ."

"Yes, Teddy?"

"You really shouldn't talk like that." He was already backing down the hall.

Lorna leaned against the doorjamb and crossed her arms beneath her breasts. "I just have no idea what's gotten into me."

Teddy, visions of a large and jealous husband presumably flashing through his brain, had reached the elevator. He barely pushed the button when the doors slid wide. He disappeared inside, not glancing in Lorna's direction again.

Remaining propped against the jamb, Lorna stuck both fists in the pockets of the robe, looked down at her bare feet, which had been so beautifully manicured by Astrid, and realized she'd probably carried the joke a bit too far. She'd liked Teddy. And teasing him about her nonexistent husband had been rather mean. In her own mind, of course, the joke had been on herself. But Teddy hadn't known that.

Mentally chastising herself, Lorna pushed a strand of bronze-tipped hair behind her ear and then captured her index finger lightly between her teeth. The new Lorna might be wild, she decided, but in the future she was going to stop short of being mean.

Softly, behind her, someone coughed. Lorna turned her head toward the sound.

A man stood, behind and across from her, in the open doorway to the suite that had been Astrid's. Over six feet tall and expensively dressed in a pin-striped suit over a white shirt, he wore cordovan shoes and a nubby silk tie of a deep maroon that was echoed in his precisely folded pocket handkerchief. Thick, dark blond hair was neatly trimmed around his squarish oval face. His jade-green eyes assessed her coolly.

Though he appeared a little tired, and his tie was slightly askew, everything about him shouted success—and the absolute assurance that things would always go the way he made them go. He was precisely the sort of man the old Lorna would have thought too exemplary to be true. She would have been intimidated by him. But the new, slightly naughty Lorna, decided he was smug and superior and not her type at all.

Having defined him as of absolutely no interest to her, she didn't have to be mortified that he had probably just observed her kissing a strange man goodbye in the hallway while wearing little more beneath her robe than a wisp of silk and the lingering scent of strawberry bath salts.

"Sorry to interrupt your thoughts," he said in a quiet, well-modulated voice. His hesitation before the word "thoughts," told her clearly that he'd already assumed her most strenuous mental activities revolved around such quandaries as what to do about a broken nail and how to get rid of one boyfriend before the next arrived.

Lorna decided she loathed him. If he wanted to think of her as wild and naughty, well, fine, let him think it. She lounged more obviously against the door. "Exactly how long have you been standing there?" Though she didn't care in the least what he thought, she couldn't help asking how much he'd seen.

"Long enough," he replied. Lorna felt the flush creeping up from between the fluffy facings of her robe and ordered it back down. At the end of the hall, the elevator doors slid open again. The man glanced toward the sound. There was something in the movement, in the way he tipped his head, that Lorna found obscurely familiar. The doors glided shut again, no one getting on or off. Green eyes focused on Lorna once more, and the moment of familiarity ended.

The interruption had served a useful purpose, though, in giving her time to realize that this standoff in the hall with an arrogant stranger was not one bit wiser than teasing the bashful Teddy had been. The new Lorna needed a lesson in discretion from the old. She reached for the door handle.

"Wait a minute, Ms.—?" He managed a reasonably polite smile. "I didn't catch your name."

"I didn't throw it," she snapped tartly, then relented enough to tell him. "Lorna Smith."

He gave her a disbelieving frown, as if to say, *Naturally, all women like you have the last name Smith.* Lorna set her shoulders and glared right back.

"Just one question, Ms. Smith," he went on after a moment.

"All right."

"The woman who was staying in this room—do you happen to know where she went?"

"What woman?" Lorna asked without missing a beat, feeling a strong protectiveness toward Astrid well up within her. She had no idea what this man wanted Astrid for; maybe Astrid didn't want him to find her. And besides, she also had no idea where Astrid had gone.

"Blond, sixty but looks younger." The man rattled off a shopping list of Astrid's physical attributes in a deep, businesslike voice. "Green eyes. About five foot seven. I have a picture." He reached into his inside jacket pocket.

"No," Lorna shook her head. "I'm terribly sorry, but I can't help you at all." She shut the door in his handsome, overbearing face.

Adam stared at the closed door and debated whether or not to knock. The woman knew something; he was sure of it. As a lawyer, he was trained to notice every nuance of voice and gesture for clues to the truth beneath an artful lie. He'd seen the flash of indecision cross that gorgeous face when he'd mentioned his mother. The little temptress was hiding something. Adam raised a determined fist and rapped sharply on the door.

"Go away," the infuriating creature on the other side called after a moment.

He knocked again.

"I'm going to call Security," she threatened in a sweet little singsong, still not opening up.

Adam waited. He was betting she wouldn't be able to resist checking to see if he'd truly gone. Beautiful, provocative women like this one were like cats—too curious for their own good.

But Ms. Lorna Smith did the unexpected. Minutes passed, and she didn't reappear. Since she was all he had that even remotely resembled a lead, he knew he was going to have to wait her out.

Disgusted and annoyed, he went back across the hall to the suite he'd rented when the desk clerk had told him Astrid was already gone. He took the small vanity chair from the dressing area and, with the door open just a crack, positioned himself to be ready when his quarry ventured out of her lair.

The time seemed to creep by. Adam spent it studying the pattern in the Navaho rug underfoot, staring at the prints on the walls, and listening to his stomach, which hadn't been fed since the afternoon before, complain.

Precisely forty-seven minutes later, his patience was rewarded. She emerged, humming and smiling to herself. All that wild chestnut-and-gold hair was piled every which way on her head, so that little strands of it corkscrewed down her neck as she turned to lock the door of her room. Surprisingly, she was wearing a perfectly modest pair of tan Bermuda shorts and a simple white shirt.

He considered following her surreptitiously, and then felt like a fool. This was hardly international intrigue, after all. He wanted an honest answer as to what she knew about Astrid, and nothing more. Therefore, sneaking around behind her while she cut a swath through the Desert Fashion Plaza would be a ridiculous exercise in overkill. If she knew anything about his mother, or the "secret sister" sect, Adam would find out soon enough—by demanding the truth.

In fact, watching this bronze-haired seductress, obviously fresh from an invigorating shower—he, of course, hadn't dared leave his post for a shower, though his fastidious nature cried out for one—and ready to while away her day prowling Palm Springs for new diversions, he began to feel more than a little provoked. And then it occurred to him that feeling provoked was irrational. He didn't even know this woman; what she did with her time was no business of his. Realizing he was responding irrationally provoked him even more.

Disgusted with himself, furious with Astrid and fed up with this woman whom he didn't even know, he quietly rose to his feet, stepped silently into the hall and inquired in a voice so level and controlled it would have sent the paralegals at Engalls, Hollander and Gantry running for cover, "Ready for breakfast?"

Lorna spun around.

So he hadn't left after all, she thought. It appeared he'd been lurking in Astrid's suite, waiting for the chance to pounce. He strode toward her, looking so calm and determined that she had to admire his composure, at least. She noted with a wayward stab of satisfaction, though, that his tie was even more askew than it had been when she'd shut her door in his face. Mr. Impeccable, as she'd begun secretly to think of him, was becoming more peccable by the moment.

"Not with you," she replied in dulcet tones.

But he'd already taken her arm. Surprised by the warmth of his touch, she fell in step with him.

"I thought I said no," she told him without much conviction as they waited for the elevator.

"A lady always has the right to change her mind," he countered pleasantly. His stress on the word lady was so faint that she wisely decided to let it pass.

Two

In the hotel's best restaurant, Georgia O'Keeffe prints of calla lilies and hibiscus flowers graced the walls. The colors were soothing ones of turquoise sky and golden sand.

Mr. Impeccable ordered eggs Benedict, tomato juice, buttermilk, an extra English muffin, a side of pancakes and cantaloupe. "I haven't eaten since yesterday," he explained somewhat defensively on observing her awed expression.

Lorna ordered coffee, melon and a poached egg.

"You should give up coffee," he remarked imperiously when the waiter had left them. "And it wouldn't hurt you to have toast. Grains are a mainstay of any balanced diet."

She stifled a groan. Not only impeccable, but an expert on nutrition. The old Lorna would have been licking his cordovan shoes. "I'm watching my weight."

"Why?" He drank from the glass of tomato juice that appeared at his elbow. "There's nothing wrong with your weight."

"My Lord. That was almost a compliment."

He lifted an eyebrow at her. "You're beautiful. You know it. I know it. It's reasonable to assume that all the men you know know it. Is it something you also need to have talked about all the time?"

The acid smile she tossed him would have eaten through lead. "I'm insecure." He snorted disbelievingly in reply.

A few minutes of weighted silence ensued, while Lorna wondered what had possessed her to ruin her morning by having breakfast with—"What is your name, anyway?"

"Adam Gantry."

Luckily, Lorna was not in the middle of a sip of coffee, because she surely would have choked on it.

Of course, she thought grimly, schooling her features to reveal none of her surprise. Mr. Impeccable was Astrid's son.

In her memory's clear vision, she could see Astrid, sitting cross-legged in a straight-back chair at the June Street library where they met every week.

"I love my son very much," Astrid had said. "And I'm proud of him. He's only thirty-six and already a partner in his corporate law firm. He works hard and he's extremely responsible. But he's, well, stuffy and bossy, and he's never approved of the way I live my life. His father died before he was born. In Korea, sad to say. And unfortunately, I hadn't gotten around to marrying the dear man before he stepped on a land mine and went to his reward. I don't think Adam's ever really forgiven me for making a baby without a ring on my finger. Adam's so proper and perfect, you see. He finds it extremely imperfect that I never provided him with a daddy."

Across from her, Adam spoke with gruff accusation. "You know who I am."

Lorna made herself sigh airily. "Oh, do I?"

"Give me the truth, Ms. Smith. Who are you and what do you know about Astrid?"

Not until you're honest with me, Mr. Impeccable, she answered silently. She asked, all innocence, "Is your name supposed to mean something to me?"

"Does it?"

She pretended to consider, then answered, "Well, there is the fact that it's perfect."

"That's all?" he demanded. She merely smiled. After a moment's pause he went on suspiciously, "What do you mean, perfect?"

She started on the melon, quite pleased with herself to have regained her equilibrium so quickly after learning who he was. "It fits you, that's all. Adam. Number one and unflappable. Your last name's somewhat out of character, though. It's a little, well, dashing. But don't worry. Looking at you, I can see that you've utterly squashed any dashingness that might be lurking deep down inside."

"That takes a load off my mind," he muttered drily.

"I'm sure it does."

"Is there anything else you've discerned about me merely by learning my name?"

"Only that you have some sort of really distinguished and enviable profession, am I right? One at which you just naturally excel. I have it." She batted her eyes at him, provokingly. "A lawyer. Corporate law, probably."

He straightened his tie. "Admit it. You know who I am."

"I'm admitting nothing."

"You look uncomfortable."

"Do I? I'm not."

"Would you like me to change the subject? Stop pressing you for how you know what kind of work I do?"

"That would be lovely," she said. The waiter slid her poached egg in front of her. She poked her spoon at it.

"What shall we talk about instead?" he prodded.

Lorna shrugged and swallowed a bite of egg. "Why don't you tell me?"

"All right. Let's get back to Astrid."

Well, she thought, I walked right into that one. "Who?" she asked, feigning ignorance.

He precisely spread butter on his stack of pancakes. "Come on, Ms. Smith. I know you've at least talked to her. I saw it in your eyes when I first mentioned her to you. Even the type of woman you are can't hide the truth all the time."

"Have I just been insulted?" Lorna queried lightly.

"Not unless you find honesty insulting."

Lorna could almost have dumped her empty melon rind in his lap. Honesty, indeed. The man certainly had nerve, to sit across from her and talk about truth when he wasn't even admitting his own identity. Deciding self-righteously that her own deception was totally justified, she said in a sexy little purr, "Hmm. The *type* of woman I am...and just what type is that?"

He looked up from his meal, scanning her casually pinned hair and the smoky shadows above her eyes that Astrid had taught her to apply so artfully. His glance lingered on her full, lushly tinted lips. "Wild. Footloose. A woman who never worries about who'll pay the bill, because there's always some man falling all over himself to grab it."

She looked back at him levelly. "You can't be sure I'm like that."

"Can't I?"

"You don't know me at all."

"Yes, I do, Lorna Smith. I know you all too well." His quiet, polished voice was suddenly like velvet, his jade eyes shadowed.

In an arrested moment of crystal-clear perception, Lorna understood that this too perfect, arrogant man did indeed find her beautiful.

And bad.

And probably dangerous to know.

He was drawn to her, just as surely as the shy Teddy had been, because she represented the power and magic that all sirens promised, as well as the imminent risk of destruction at their hands.

Such a realization was intensely exciting. Her heart beat a little faster, and she felt a delicious surging in her blood. A hectic flush rose to her cheeks.

"Stop it," he ordered, as if she'd done something overtly sensual. He very carefully wiped his mouth with his napkin, and then slipped the soft linen beneath the lip of his plate.

As she had in the hallway when Teddy had disappeared in the elevator, Lorna felt chastened. What in the world was happening to her, anyway?

One part of her wanted to look straight into Adam's eyes and tell him the whole truth and nothing but the truth: that she was really just an ordinary, everyday kind of person. That she owned her own business and paid her own way. That she kept the figure he admired through watching her diet and exercising three times a week without fail. That she was going through a crisis due to being stood up at the altar. That therefore she needed to kick up her heels and behave a little recklessly to get over the natural reactions of hurt and insecurity.

It was the truth. You could never go wrong by telling the truth....

Adam was watching her guardedly, that shadow of suppressed desire in his eyes.

That shadow would disappear, of course, once he learned who the *real* Lorna Smith was. It shouldn't matter that it would; she was never going to see him again, anyway. Not to mention the fact that any desire he might be denying was for someone who didn't really even exist.

But then, if she did reveal her true self, how would she explain her overnight transformation without admitting that she *did* know Astrid, after all?

And then, coming right down to it, what in heaven's name was he after Astrid for, anyway? And if Astrid didn't want to see her son right now, what kind of a secret sister would Lorna be if she gave him any clues that might tell him where to find her?

"Just tell me what she said to you," he prompted, reading her silence, correctly, as a weakening in her stance.

Stalling, Lorna made an elaborate show of pulling her compact from her purse, applying lipstick and powdering her nose. "Why in the world are you after this poor woman, anyway?" she asked at last.

"Then you admit that you talked to her?"

"Did I say that?"

"Did she tell you anything about—"

Lorna cut him off, not wanting to hear more and be drawn in. "Slow down, Counselor. You're leading the witness."

He shifted in his chair, no doubt planning his next interrogatory attack. The light from a nearby window fell across his face, casting his strong features into sharp relief. He looked stern enough to be one of the faces on Mount Rushmore.

"Are you going to answer any of my questions?" he demanded when the silence had stretched to the breaking point.

Lorna considered this query, and then demanded more firmly than she had asked before, "If you want me to answer your questions, I have a right to know why you're chasing this woman."

"It's a private matter."

"That tells me nothing. Did she do something illegal?"

"Well . . ."

"Something illegal. Yes or no."

"Who sounds like a lawyer now?" he asked.

"You're stalling."

"All right. No, not precisely illegal."

"*Sort* of illegal?"

"No," he glared at her. "Not illegal, but unethical. She broke a promise to someone she loves. Now, will you let me ask a few of the questions?"

Lorna evaluated. Was what he'd grudgingly disclosed enough to make her betray Astrid? After all, she owed Astrid a lot for rushing to her side when her whole world seemed to have fallen apart and for showing her how to turn things around.

"No." Lorna reached for her purse. "No more questions." She pulled out her wallet.

"What do you think you're doing?"

Extracting several bills, she dropped them in the middle of the table. "Paying for my breakfast. Whatever you may think, no man pays my way."

"I didn't say—"

"You didn't have to say. You saw me kissing a man in the hall and you naturally assumed I make my living that way."

"I said you were wild. That doesn't mean I think you're a—"

"Please." She stopped him before he could say the ugly word. "There's no need to put too fine a point on it."

"Then pick up your money and sit down. I offered you breakfast, I'll pay for it."

"I'm finished eating, and I have things to do."

"Sit back down, we're not through here."

"Have a nice life, Adam Gantry."

Not looking back, Lorna wove her way between the linen-covered tables and through the reception area with its sky-lights and sun-speckled potted palms. Once out of the res-taurant, she went straight to the bank of elevators in the main lobby.

She'd pushed the Down button for the parking levels when Adam caught up with her.

"That was childish and rude," he told her condescend-ingly.

She shoved the button again.

"Please be reasonable," he said.

"How many ways can I say it? I have nothing whatso-ever to tell you, so our brief association is terminated."

"Lorna—"

The doors to one of the elevator cars opened, and Lorna found herself face-to-face with Teddy, who was wearing jogging shorts and shoes and a sweatband around his fore-head, obviously fresh from the hotel gym. At the sight of Lorna, his blush seemed to start at his bare knees.

She decided to brazen it out. "Hi, there," she said cheer-ily. "Did you have a good workout?"

He gulped, and stared over her shoulder. Lorna realized that the bashful redhead assumed Adam Gantry was her big, jealous husband.

"Damn it, Lorna." Adam grasped her elbow. Lorna shook him off and stepped over the threshold as poor Teddy dwindled to the back of the car.

Persistent as a bloodhound on the scent, Adam fol-lowed. Before the doors closed, several others, including a blue-haired lady clutching a French poodle, and three teen-aged girls laden with shopping bags, piled on behind them.

By the time her mind finally registered that the car was going up, Lorna found herself wedged between the back wall and the lady with the poodle, flanked by the furiously blushing Teddy on one side and the relentless Adam on the other. The teenaged girls giggled among themselves. The poodle sniffed disdainfully.

At the third floor, the teenaged girls got off, but two couples took their places. The lady with the poodle backed up until she'd squeezed herself between Teddy and Lorna. This left Lorna closer than ever to Adam, who obligingly moved into the corner and pulled Lorna back with him.

"Hands off," Lorna whispered.

They were fitted together like spoons in a drawer, Adam's large and warm hands resting firmly at her waist.

"Stop squirming," he ordered quietly. "Things are tight enough in here as it is." Lorna subsided as the car began its upward journey again.

In the seconds before they stopped at the next floor, she became all too intimately aware of him, pressed so close against her. The matte fabric of his slacks tickled the tender skin behind her knees, and his chest was hard and firm at her back.

Lorna stared miserably at the wet nose of the poodle, who seemed by now to radiate canine disapproval.

"What's the matter?" Adam's breath teased her ear, and she actually thought she detected a note of humor in his soft whisper. "Are you afraid he'll be hurt that you've found someone else so soon?"

"Who?" She tried to sound utterly guileless.

"The one with the knobby knees and the red face to match his hair." He kept his voice low enough that only she could hear.

The elevator stopped. One of the couples got off. Teddy saw his chance, and slid around the blue-haired lady and out just before the doors closed.

"Another day, another broken heart," Adam murmured, and rather sanctimoniously, too, Lorna thought.

"You really don't need to hold me so tightly anymore," she shot back sweetly. "There's plenty of room now...unless you're *enjoying* it."

His hands immediately dropped to his sides. She shifted a little closer to the scornful poodle.

The digital display above the door went right past her floor. "By the way, where are we going, anyway?" Adam asked with exaggerated nonchalance.

"I don't know about you. I'm going to my car."

"Where is it? On the roof?"

"No, actually." The car stopped at the top floor. The doors slid open. "I got on this car because I was trying to get away from you." She granted him a sugary smile.

"Didn't do you much good, did it, honey?" the blue-haired lady tossed over her shoulder as she and her poodle finally got off.

The ride back down to the parking level seemed to take longer than going up had, but both Lorna and Adam kept their mouths shut.

When the elevator finally discharged them, Lorna turned to him and arranged her face into its most stubborn lines. "Are you planning to follow me around all day?"

One corner of his mouth curled in a half grin. "Just until you tell me what I want to know. Unfortunately for both of us, you're the only lead I happen to have." The charm and humor in his face at that moment took her by surprise.

She dropped her obstinate stance, unable to maintain it while she was thinking how very attractive he was. She turned and marched resolutely toward her car.

Adam's steps fell in behind hers—and halted at almost the same time. "I'll be damned," he said quietly.

Lorna felt a sick dropping in the pit of her stomach, as she wished fervently that her eyes were deceiving her.

But they weren't, and in her heart she knew it. There, where her beautiful new Mercedes should have been, sat Astrid's car, a decade-old pink Cadillac.

Three

There was an envelope on the dashboard. Scrawled across it were the words *Lorna, the key's in your purse.*

"So you never in your life heard of anyone named Astrid," Adam accused from behind her.

Lorna opened her purse and felt for her ring of keys. "I never said that. Not specifically anyway."

"Where is she?"

"I have no idea. But she's taken my car, and if you don't mind, I'd like to find out what's in that envelope." She withdrew her key ring. Two strange keys were on it; her own car keys were not. Sometime during the evening before, Astrid had managed the switch.

Adam waited, not interfering, as Lorna unlocked the car door, reached in and took the envelope from the dashboard and slit it open. The paper was hotel stationery, but it smelled faintly of Astrid's perfume.

Lorna,

Remember you did say you'd trade your Mercedes, even if you weren't entirely serious.

The truth is, darling, that a little makeup and a haircut is not enough to accomplish your total transformation. You need ADVENTURE, as I mentioned last night. I'm going to see that you get it.

Your adventure should be an open-ended kind of thing—one you invent as it's happening. I think trying to get your beautiful car back will at least get you going in the right direction. But the whole point is that you remain open to whatever comes along.

Also, I have a few things to straighten out in my own life, and I need a dependable car to do it. Yours will fill the bill just fine.

The Caddy's been overheating lately, but it should get you as far as Prescott, Arizona, where I need to see an old flame. Pay a visit to Bucky O'Neill at ten tonight, and I'll be in touch with you there.

Yours,
Astrid

Very carefully, Lorna folded the scented paper and placed it back in its envelope. She put the envelope in her purse.

"Well?" Adam asked.

Lorna said nothing.

"Is it a valuable car?" Adam prompted grimly.

"My pride and joy. A Mercedes 450 SL."

His mouth formed a bleak line. "New?"

She nodded.

"I suppose you'll want to call the police."

Lorna considered.

"Lorna, are you all right?"

"Yes, fine," she mumbled distractedly. She leaned against the old Cadillac, and looked at the cement floor, folding her arms beneath her breasts.

In a puddle that had dribbled out from under the car, she could see the bright reflection of her carelessly pinned hair, like spun bronze in the halogen lights from above. Her face itself, though, was in shadow. In shadow like the real me, Lorna thought, and like Astrid's true intentions.

In a strange way, it all came down to belief. Did she *believe* in Astrid?

If she believed in Astrid, Lorna would need to forget about the car for the time being—as well as the substantial financial investment it represented. Lorna would need to have faith that her car, as well as her own immediate future, was in trustworthy hands.

On the other hand, if she didn't believe, then there was a flaky sixty-year-old woman out there somewhere driving her Mercedes.

Twenty-four hours earlier, there would have been no decision to make. The old Lorna would have raced to a phone booth and dialed the authorities.

"You know what?" she asked, half to her shadowed reflection and half to the man beside her.

"What?"

"It was beige."

Adam put his hands on her shoulders and turned her around until he could look into her eyes. "Lorna, I know you're upset. If you're telling the truth, you've just lost a very valuable piece of machinery. But I hope you'll try to understand. I have reason to suspect that Astrid is being manipulated by a fringe group of dissatisfied women who don't have her best interests at heart."

Lorna hardly heard what Adam was saying. She felt her lower lip quivering, and it wasn't with tears. "Adam. You poor man. You don't understand at all, do you? My car. It was *beige*." She tossed back her head and let the laughter ring toward the steel-and-concrete ceiling overhead.

A marvelous sense of excitement and anticipation swept through her. If she was deluded, so be it. She was going to follow Astrid's lure. It was going to be wild.

"Listen to me." Adam gave her shoulders a gentle shake. "Do you want to call the police?"

Her decision made, she became aware of Adam once more. His golden eyebrows were drawn together in a grim, resigned expression.

Lorna felt sympathy for him. He was worried about Astrid. Suddenly, Lorna wanted the deceptions cleared up—both his and hers. But she didn't quite know how to start, so she asked noncommittally, "Wouldn't you call the police, if you were in my position?"

He dropped his arms from her shoulders and glanced away. "I imagine so."

"But you don't want me to do it, do you?"

"Stealing a car is grand theft," he muttered, perhaps more to himself than to Lorna. "She'll have to deal with the consequences, that's all."

She touched his sleeve. "Adam?"

He turned, and in the tilt of his head, the green eyes with a sadness in their depths, she saw Astrid. And she couldn't let him worry anymore. "I'm not calling the police. Astrid and I traded cars, that's all."

He looked grimmer than ever, standing there so stiffly in his expensive suit. "You're sure?"

"Of course."

His expression left grimness behind and became completely impassive. "That's not what you said a few minutes ago."

"I was surprised, that's all. Trading cars was sort of an, er, open-ended kind of thing. I mean, it was something we talked about, but never really firmed up. You know?" Lorna cringed inwardly at how forced her explanation sounded. If she were listening, she wouldn't believe herself for a moment.

Apparently, neither did Adam. "Who are you, and more importantly, *what* are you to my mother?" The voice was one of steely command.

Lorna decided she could no longer afford to take a defensive position in this conversation; she was just too culpable. But Adam Gantry had a few things to answer for, too. "Oh, so now you're ready to admit that Astrid's your mother?"

"Since you obviously knew it all along," he countered without a pause, "why didn't you say so?"

"I was waiting to see what you were up to. I care about Astrid. And I want to respect her wishes. It's logical to assume that if she hasn't let you know where she is, it's because she doesn't want to see you right now."

Her argument was reasonable. Adam wisely decided to go back to his other point. "Who are you, Lorna Smith? And how do you know my mother?"

A station wagon pulled in a few spaces over. A harried-looking young couple and three rambunctious children climbed out of it. Lorna waited until the parents had herded the kids to the elevator before giving him an answer to the second half of his question.

"We're in a support group together. She's my secret sister."

"I should have known," he said softly.

"We're committed to *being there* for each other in difficult times. It's a way of extending and intensifying the

benefits of our weekly meetings, to have one other woman
you can count on no matter what.''

"And, in this situation, who's *being there* for whom?''

She scrunched up her nose at his sarcasm, but did her best
to make her reply reasonable. "Astrid came to Palm Springs
to help me out of a . . . negative frame of mind.'' Inwardly,
Lorna shook a finger at herself. She knew she should make
a clean breast of it, tell him the plain truth: she'd been jilted
and she was nursing a broken heart. But it just wouldn't
come out.

Adam Gantry had no idea who she really was: plain,
practical Lorna, an unremarkable woman with about as
much sex appeal as a profit-and-loss statement.

"You're a wonderful woman, Lorna,'' her fiancé had told
her. "But I've fallen in love with someone else. I just can't
see myself spending the rest of my life with a woman whose
spice rack is always in alphabetical order. You're perfect,
and I just couldn't live with that day after day.''

Adam Gantry, on the other hand, didn't think she was
perfect. Far from it. To him, she was exciting—a forbidden
siren who tempted every man in sight. It was wonderful to
be the seductress in a man's eyes for a change, even at the
cost of complete honesty.

But lying was wrong. She shouldn't go on doing it.

As Lorna waffled, Adam continued his attack. "Where
is Astrid now?''

"I don't know, Adam. She came to my room last night,
and she was gone when I woke up this morning.''

"Gone where?''

"She didn't say.'' It was another half truth, since the note
in her purse told more. But Lorna couldn't show Adam the
note, because that might be betraying Astrid's trust.

"Let me see that letter,'' he said, as if he'd read her
thoughts.

Lorna shook her head. "The letter was meant for me, not you."

He held out his hand. "The letter," he reiterated. "Now." He took a step toward her, no doubt trying to intimidate her with his masculine size and presence.

Irritation replaced indecision, as she backed toward the acres of chrome on the grille of the Cadillac. Adam Gantry had no right to demand to read her mail. "I can just see you in the courtroom," she taunted, "turning every hostile witness in sight to a mass of quivering jelly."

He made a grab for her purse, she whipped it behind her back. "Damn it, Lorna..."

With elaborate provocativeness, she leaned toward him and walked her fingers up his shirt front. "Tell me why you're following her." She gave a tug to his tie.

He wrapped his fingers around hers. The touch was electric. That smoky, hungry look moved in his eyes again as it had during breakfast. The fascination of the new Lorna was working its magic. It took an effort of will, she could see, for him to hold to the subject. But he managed.

"What is this *support* group?"

His hand was warm over hers, sending tingling sensations down her raised arm. "Nothing mysterious," she said. "A group of women. We meet once a week. We share our feelings, our hopes and disappointments, what goes right and what goes wrong in our lives. We listen and talk and try to help each other." Her voice, she realized vaguely, was like the purring of a petted cat.

"That's all?" The prodding question held an unmistakably husky undertone.

There was a war going on inside him, Lorna observed. His mind didn't trust her, but the rest of him was captivated by her allure. His little finger moved, slightly, a feather-light caress against the skin of her wrist. Lorna,

mesmerized by how wonderful it felt just to have his little
finger doing that, drew a breath deep into her lungs and
licked her lower lip.

"Yes, Adam. That's all."

His grip became infinitesimally tighter. "It would be nice
if I could believe a word you say."

Lorna's whole body seemed to be warm and shivery-cold
at the same time. The sensation centered in the hand Adam
grasped, and was sent out and down through her body by
the tiny action of his stroking little finger. Jeffrey, her two-
timing fiancé, had certainly never made her feel this way.
She was having trouble thinking about anything but how to
keep Adam making her feel this way.

"Whether you believe me or not, I have Astrid's wishes
to consider," she told him, still sounding like a well-stroked
cat. "She'll find you when she wants to see you."

"By then we both know it could be too late." Could eyes
devour? Adam looked at her as if his could do just that.

"Too late for what?" Lord, Lorna decided, she really did
want to be devoured. Right now. In this parking lot. No
matter how many families in station wagons drove up. It was
naughty and it was irresponsible, but she wasn't herself. Not
her *old* self, anyway.

"I think you know what," he said. And then he was suddenly speaking aloud what they were both thinking. "You'd
better tell me not to kiss you. You'd better do it now."

She smiled, and she knew the smile was full of forbidden
promises. "I think you should kiss me first. Then I'll make
up my mind whether I should have let you or not."

"You're so bad," he said, and there was humor in his
voice, along with the roughness of desire. "I've spent my
whole life avoiding women like you. Women like my
mother. You never think of the consequences of your actions."

"Um. Yes. Very smart, to avoid women like me." She lifted her mouth in brazen invitation. "After you kiss me, you can start avoiding me again. I promise."

His lips hovered a fraction above hers. "Women like you never keep their promises."

"Maybe I'm different than other women like me."

"Tell me another one."

"I *always* keep my promises."

"Liar."

"But it's the truth...."

"Shut up." The command was infinitely tender.

"Really, Adam. I'm telling the—"

Her protests were cut off, since at that moment Adam Gantry's self-control lost the battle with his senses. His lips touched hers. Lorna sighed in delight. Adam released her hand and clasped her waist, bringing her closer. He nudged her lower lip, and she opened her mouth just a little. His tongue traced the inner surface of her lips, in a warm caress.

Lorna smiled against the kiss. Her arms found their way up his firm, broad chest until they encircled his neck, letting her purse dangle behind him by its leather strap.

"I wasn't going to do this," he breathed against her mouth.

"Oh, I know," she murmured back. "But I'm so glad you did."

He made a low, hungry noise then, and his lips went from teasing exploration to command as they closed over hers. His tongue slid inside, tasting deeper secrets, and she pressed herself against him, feeling marvelously beautiful and desired. She let her tousled head fall back. He cupped it with his hand, holding her in place so he could kiss her some more.

Then she lost his mouth, and a small sigh escaped her. But he was only laying a warm trail of tiny kisses down her neck to the collar of her white shirt, and then back up again. Then his lips were on hers once more, slanting the other way, staking once again their erotic claim.

Lorna heard the sound of leather soles on pavement and the drone of oncoming voices at the same time as Adam did. Three men in business suits were approaching. Lazily, Lorna opened her eyes enough to watch Adam lift his head at the intrusion. His stern face was somewhat flushed, but a gleam of challenge sparked in his heavy-lidded eyes. The men very scrupulously pretended not to see what he and Lorna were doing. He gathered Lorna closer against his chest.

As the footsteps of the men receded, Lorna realized the thrill of the moment had passed with the interruption. The beautiful, erotic kiss was over. And she was left with the warmth of strong arms around her and the most inappropriate wish that those arms would never let her go.

Just as she was wishing he might hold her forever, he released her. He put his hands on her waist and pushed her away, frowning slightly at the way she clutched her bag to her side, protecting it from any more sudden grabs he might attempt.

She studied his face, which was still slightly flushed. She decided he looked tired, beneath the flush and the powerful aura of self-control he possessed. She wanted to reach out, stroke his face, tell him—

Lorna stopped herself in midthought. She had nothing to tell him, she reminded herself firmly. She hardly knew him. And what he knew of her was a lie from start to finish.

Not a lie, she told herself a bit defensively. Not a lie, a fantasy. And there's nothing wrong with a little fantasy now and then. Nothing wrong at all.

"Give me the letter," he said.

Lorna took a fortifying breath and met his eyes. "Tell me why you're chasing her."

"All right," he muttered, "though I'm sure you already know. But I'll go through it step by step, and then you'll let me read that note."

"Correction. Then I'll decide whether to let you read the note."

Adam turned and leaned against the driver's door of the Cadillac, though he was clearly not the kind of man who ordinarily leaned on things. "She ran out on the best man she's ever known. His name's Maxwell Hollander and he's the senior partner of my law firm. They've been happy and they're totally in love, so it makes no sense at all. Max has locked himself in his room and won't see anybody, and none of Astrid's friends have a clue as to where she's gone. She left a note that her *secret sister* needed her and that she had to see an old boyfriend before she could marry Max."

"You found me through the note?"

He nodded. "It said you were in a hotel in Palm Springs."

"Whew." Lorna shook her head. "You went from—"

"—hotel to hotel until I found the one she was registered in. I ran into you, and I was sure you knew something and that's all. I was right."

"What about the old boyfriend?" Lorna wondered, thinking of the note in her purse. Astrid had mentioned a boyfriend in Prescott, too.

"I arrived here about 3:00 a.m.," Adam said, "and I found the boyfriend first. He was just as much in the dark about the whole thing as I am. His wife's story, though, was that Astrid appeared at their frozen yogurt franchise early yesterday evening, kissed him on the mouth in front of several customers and left."

Lorna considered this tidbit of information. "*Kissed* him. But why?"

Adam's shrug spoke volumes. "That's what I'm trying to find out. Now give me that letter."

Lorna hoisted herself up on the Cadillac's hood and crossed her legs at the knees like a teenager without a care in the world. Adam watched her with evident disapproval. She was positive the women he dated never sat on the hoods of cars. "Is this Max person threatening to sue her for breach of promise or something?"

"Of course not." Adam's voice was curt. "Right now, Max is too broken up to think of getting even. And that's not his style anyway."

Lorna put her hands behind her on the hood and leaned on them. "Then let Max chase her down." She recrossed her legs and added with finality, "Astrid deserves to be in charge of her own life and affairs, Adam."

She could tell by the rocklike hardness of his jaw that he was losing patience. "She's my mother. I introduced them. And she owns a successful hairdressing salon that was started with Maxwell's money." He impaled her on a lowering glare. "She's not going to lose that salon, Lorna. It's her future, and her security."

Puzzled by the determination in his voice, she said, "I don't see what you're so concerned about. If the business is thriving, I'm sure it can run itself for a while."

Adam spoke with iron firmness, each word clear and cold. "Understand me. I'm not allowing her to lose everything this time. No matter what tricks you and your *support group* have up your collective sleeves."

"What in the world are you talking about?"

"You're very good at playing the innocent. Too bad you haven't done or said one thing so far that I can trust, or I just might be tempted to believe you."

"Adam. Just explain what you're talking about, okay?"

"Weird groups," he said coldly. "Like yours. Like the hundred other causes and cults my mother's been involved in. Like the ashram in Oregon where they made her go barefoot in January and she ended up with no savings account and chronic bronchitis. Like the Save-The-Bluenecked-Grackle association in Santa Monica to which she donated five thousand dollars before learning there is no such thing as a blue-necked grackle to save in the first place. Or the crystal channelers in Vermont who charged her five figures for a bunch of rocks and an instruction sheet on how to connect up to her inner forces. Or the greasy-haired gigolo she invited to stay in her house because he swore he'd been her father in their last life. When he disappeared, it was with her collection of Lladro figurines and her compact disc player. The list is endless. Do I have to go on?"

Lorna sighed, thinking how tired he looked. "No, I guess not. And I'm sorry that Astrid's been used, Adam. But it hasn't really damaged her. You have to see that. She's the most alive person I've ever met. And she's not bitter at all. So I'd have to say that, whatever she's done or is doing, it's probably the right thing for her. And she should be let alone to do it."

Adam took her hand and very deliberately pulled her off the hood of the car. "That's easy for you to say, especially if you're the next in line to take her for all she's worth."

Lorna gaped up at him. "You think I'm after your mother's money."

His eyes were hard as emeralds. "You. Or that strange group you belong to. Or maybe you just don't want her to marry Max, to be happy. There are a lot of dissatisfied people in the world today who'll go out of their way to see that others don't find what really counts."

"Let me get this straight." Lorna spoke as slowly and deliberately as Adam had. "You believe I'm a member of an anticommitment fringe group out to break up your mother's engagement and steal her hairdressing salon?"

"Naturally it sounds ridiculous when you put it that way. Now give me that letter." His hand shot out and closed on her purse.

She whipped it out of his grasp. "No."

"I could wring your neck." Adam spoke through clenched teeth. "I'd get off with a reprimand, once the judge heard the circumstances."

"If Astrid wanted to see you—" Lorna clutched her purse and restated her position "—she would have told you where she was going. It's clear to me that she needs to be left alone right now."

"I have been inordinately patient, Lorna," he said in that so calm voice that Lorna was beginning to realize meant he was seething with tightly leashed fury. "I've let you tease and flirt and bat your eyelashes all through breakfast. I've played Sardines in the elevator, going up and going down. I've stood in this parking garage for—" he glanced at his gold watch "—twenty minutes while you broke down because your car was stolen and then decided it wasn't stolen and then seduced me into making a display of myself kissing you—"

"Just a minute there." She glared at him. "You weren't fighting it too hard, and we both know it."

"I'm not finished. And then, after you proved I couldn't resist you, you demanded to know why I was following my own mother as a condition of telling me where she was going. Well, I kept my end of the bargain. You know why I'm after her. Now tell me where she's gone."

"I can't. It wouldn't be right. She's—" Lorna sought the right words "—very special to me. And when she wants to see you, she'll contact you herself, I'm sure." She hooked her bag over her shoulder and brazenly stepped toward him. "I have to go now. Please get out of the way so I can open the door."

"Give me the letter."

"Get out of my way." She reached for the door handle.

He calmly leaned against it, so she was forced to pull back her hand. "I intensely dislike what you're forcing me to do," he said.

"Please step aside." She did her best to look formidable.

For a moment they just watched each other, sizing each other up, like all adversaries have done since the dawn of time. And then Adam moved.

With a lightning swiftness that made Lorna gasp, he grabbed for her purse. And he got it, too. Lorna felt the strap slipping down her arm. In a split second, he would have it free.

With clutching fingers, she caught the strap before it escaped her completely. And, digging in her heels, she yanked—and fell backward, when the strap snapped in two.

"Ooof!" She landed on her backside in the puddle of dirty water from the Cadillac's damaged radiator. "You overbearing—" she sought a suitably crushing adjective "—stuffed shirt. Give me back my purse!"

"As soon as I see what she wrote," he replied. He'd already slipped the clasp and retrieved the envelope.

Lorna knew she had to think fast. "That purse is my property!" She pretended to try scrambling upright, and then let out a strangled cry. She clutched at her lower back. "Oh! Oh, no..."

Adam, who had just smoothed the note open, paused to look at her.

She went on clutching her back and contorting her face into a grimace of pain. She groaned tightly, convincingly.

He set her purse on the roof of the car and knelt down next to her, wary but concerned. "Where does it hurt?" His voice was careful, but gentle, too. She could see that he was the kind of man who would watch over the victim at the sight of an accident, whether he had anything to do with the situation or not. Lorna felt like the sneaky troublemaker he believed her to be and almost dropped her ruse of injury and let him read the note. But then she thought of Astrid, to whom her first allegiance was sworn.

"I . . . don't know. I tried to get up and . . ."

"Don't move. You might just make it worse." He put a soothing hand on her shoulder. It was the hand holding the note.

She gazed up at him, right into his eyes. "Oh, Adam. I'm scared."

"Don't be. I'm sure you just twisted something. In a minute, the spasm will pass and you'll be fine."

"You really think so?"

"Certainly."

"Oh, Adam." She touched his face, as if doing so could reassure her in her fear and pain. He blinked, and just as he did that, she moved her hand the fraction necessary to whip the note from his grasp.

He gazed at her in a kind of numb disbelief for a moment, just the time she needed to stick the wad of paper in her mouth and reduce it to a soggy mass.

His light brows drew together, like the clouds before a storm. "You little witch."

She chewed diligently, watching his face as he considered forcing her jaws apart and extracting what was left of his mother's note. He apparently decided against such a useless maneuver, since he did no such thing.

She swallowed.

He stood up. "I'd offer you my hand, but I'm sure you never needed it anyway."

With no difficulty, but some regret at having had to deceive him once again, she scrambled upright herself. "Adam, I had to do it."

Coldly, he took her purse from the roof of the car and held it out to her. "Tell me where Astrid has gone."

"I can't."

"You think you're going to just drive out of here in her car?"

"That's exactly what I'm going to do."

"I could have you picked up. I could say you stole it."

"Come on, Adam. Then I'd just say we traded cars. When they found Astrid, they'd learn I was telling the truth."

"Maybe, but you'd have to tell them where to find her, wouldn't you?"

She gazed at him levelly. "No. I wouldn't tell them a thing. I'd say just what I'm saying to you. That I don't know where she went and she'll turn up when she's ready. You see, I'm on a kind of open-ended vacation, Adam. And if I have to spend it in a Palm Springs jail, well, that's just how it's meant to be as far as I'm concerned."

He shook his head, and there was a musing expression on his stern, handsome face. "This isn't the end of it, Lorna."

"After that kiss," she said with the frankness that being a temporary siren allowed her, "I almost wish you were right."

His smile was no less attractive for being somewhat unwilling. "I am right. Count on it."

"No, Adam." She let herself go, let herself be the enchantress he saw when he looked in her eyes. "I've learned not to count on anything. It's a part of my nature, remember? I'm wild and I'm free and I live for the moment."

"There's a lot more to life, Lorna Smith," he answered quietly. "You'll miss the best part by always being on the run."

"And just what will I miss, Adam Gantry?"

"Commitment, steadiness, a firm hand in yours. Someone to turn to in the darkest hours of the night...."

"Shh." She put a finger against his full mouth. "No more. You might tempt me. And *I'm* the one who does the tempting around here, remember?"

His lips moved against her touch, but before he could form words, she shook her head and dropped her hand, turning to the car. She pulled open the door and slid in behind the wheel.

To distract herself from thoughts of the man who stood watching her through the side window, she set the practical side of her mind to ticking off the exigencies of the adventure ahead.

She needed a map to find her way to Prescott, Arizona. And somehow she needed to reach a man named Bucky O'Neill. She also had to get her suitcases and check out of the suite, but she couldn't do that until she'd safely shaken Adam. He'd be naturally suspicious if he had any hint of a sudden change of plans.

The pink leather upholstery held the scent of Astrid's perfume, and Lorna smiled to herself as she started the engine. Adam knocked on the window, and she rolled it down.

"You could save yourself a lot of trouble, just by being honest."

"Ah." She batted her eyelashes. "But what fun would that be?" She backed out of the space and headed for the exit ramp, sparing only a single regretful glance for the handsome, well-dressed man who watched her go. By the time he reached his own vehicle and tried to follow, she'd be long out of sight.

An hour later, she had her route mapped out, her suitcases in the trunk, and she was roaring down Interstate 10, on her way to the state highway that would lead her to Prescott.

The gently rolling desert that sped past on either side was dotted with the proud sentinels of saguaro cactus and the spiny, red-tipped blooms of ocotillo. The trip to Prescott, according to her map, would take around five hours. If all went well, she would be there by six o'clock. That should leave her enough time to find the mysterious Mr. O'Neill.

Lorna kept her eye on the temperature gauge, but so far it had stayed safely in the medium range. She went without the air conditioner, just to be on the safe side. Instead, she rolled the front windows down and turned on the radio and sang along to country and western songs while the hot desert wind whipped her hair around her face.

She'd crossed the border to Arizona and was almost to the State 60 turnoff when she realized that the burgundy Chrysler in her rearview mirror had been there for a long time. She slowed down and switched to a slower lane. The Chrysler did the same. She speeded up, and the Chrysler followed suit.

Utterly disgusted, she stuck her arm out the window and signaled the other car alongside the Cadillac. It slid smoothly into place and Adam rolled down the window and waved at her.

"I did see the words Prescott, Arizona, in that letter before you ate it," he shouted jauntily.

Lorna put her foot on the gas and left him behind. She turned the radio up full blast and sang at the top of her lungs and refused to decide whether she was ecstatic or upset that he hadn't given up.

Unfortunately, she forgot to watch the temperature gauge, and by the time she remembered to check it, she was barreling down State Highway 60 with nothing in sight for miles but cactus and sagebrush and the burgundy Chrysler that she couldn't seem to shake.

Four

Muttering an unladylike expletive under her breath, Lorna pulled over onto the shoulder. She was afraid to turn off the engine, having heard somewhere that overheated cars should be allowed to cool down a bit before being shut off.

She had either heard wrong or it was just too late for letting the car idle to matter, because she could now see steam escaping from under the hood.

As she considered her next move, the Chrysler slid in behind her. Adam jumped out, sped to her driver's door, and reaching in the open window, yanked the keys from the ignition.

"I was just thinking I should do that myself." With elaborate nonchalance, she studied a fingernail that had been chipped in the tussle back at the hotel garage. In the desert silence, the car wheezed and groaned like a winded moose. "Maybe we should look under the hood," she suggested after a moment.

"Maybe you want a few third-degree burns." He gave her a look so patronizing that she wished she had a large blunt object to hit him with. "You've got to let it cool down first, and then I'd have to predict that it won't be capable of taking you anywhere near where you want to go."

"I do adore your positive attitude."

He gave her one of those smiles that men give women when they have them where they want them. "It's still about a hundred miles to Prescott, and I imagine it's desert most of the way. This car won't get you there, I'm afraid."

"You don't sound very regretful."

"I suppose you'll have to ride with me."

She blew on her chipped fingernail. "I could just sit tight. Somebody else will come along."

"If you're lucky." Very neatly, he slid out of his suit jacket, slung it over his shoulders and proceeded to roll up his shirt cuffs. His tanned forearms had gold hairs on them. They looked very strong. Lorna decided he probably played tennis or squash at some exclusive L.A. club at least three times a week. "Whew," he said, really rubbing it in, "sure is hot out here."

He was putting it mildly. Without the whipping wind created by the speeding car, it was ninety degrees at least. Lorna's hair, which had slipped out of its loose confines completely, lay damp against her neck. She casually began stroking the tangled mass upward, repinning it as haphazardly as before. "I've always loved the heat," she purred. "It's so . . . sensual."

"Say that in an hour or two when your lips start cracking and your eyeballs go dry." Still behaving in an infuriatingly jaunty manner, he unknotted his tie and slid it from around his neck. Then he tossed the keys in the air and caught them. "Are your suitcases in the trunk?"

She said nothing. There was no need to. She was going to be stuck riding with him. He knew it, and she knew it. He strolled to the trunk of the car and transferred her bags to the Chrysler. Then he cheerfully tossed his coat and tie in the back seat and returned to where she sweltered behind the wheel of the wheezing Cadillac.

"Let's be on our way." He swung open her door.

"Could you please stop being so jovial? It's really getting on my nerves."

He reached for her hand and gently, but firmly, pulled her from the car. "Might as well make the best of an unpleasant situation."

"Might as well gloat a little, is what you mean."

He merely grinned in response. Then, pausing only to slip the Cadillac's keys beneath the floor mat, he led her to the Chrysler.

The interior of his car was marvelously cool. She settled into the leather seat with an internal sigh of contentment. Adam got in on his side and turned the engine over. The air conditioner hummed. Already, Lorna felt her clammy skin cooling.

"Please fasten your seat belt," a masculine voice issued from somewhere in the dashboard.

Lorna groaned. "Even your car likes giving orders." Adam granted her a forbearing glance. "All right, all right," she said, and did as the car had instructed.

They glided back out onto the sun-shimmered highway. In the rearview mirror, Lorna watched the Cadillac until it was only a speck of gleaming silver and pink. Then it disappeared.

Adam saw her watching the old car fade from sight. "I'll call for a tow truck," he said, picking up his car phone.

Lorna said nothing as Adam arranged to have the Cadillac towed back to Los Angeles where Astrid could reclaim it later. When he hung up, he made no more attempts at small talk. Apparently he felt complaisant now that he had the situation—and Lorna—firmly in hand. They drove on through the desert heat, enclosed in their little cocoon of cool air and mutual silence.

More than once, she glanced at his profile, so strong and determined-looking as he stared out through the tinted windshield at the flat road ahead. He must be tired. Chasing the elusive Astrid, he'd had no time for sleep in at least the past twenty-four hours. Still, he appeared utterly alert.

"Do you want me to drive for a while?" she suggested, her voice hesitant in the stillness between them. "You could take a nap."

He shot her a glance. "No, thanks. I'm fine."

"You mean you don't trust me."

"Partly."

"At least you're honest."

"Somebody around here has to be."

"I'm not even going to dignify that remark with a response."

"Glad to hear it." He spared her another jade-green glance. "Take a nap yourself if you want. It's still over an hour to Prescott."

"Maybe I will."

Lorna leaned her head back against the smooth leather and closed her eyes. The wheels whirred beneath her and the air conditioner hummed. After a while, she was vaguely aware that they were climbing, and that the road had more turns than before. She let her body roll with the movement of the car, not quite awake and not quite asleep.

When she opened her eyes again, they were surrounded by ponderosa pines. They had left the desert for national forest. Adam was resetting the clock as he drove.

"We lost an hour back there at the Arizona border," he explained. The digital display now read six-thirty.

Just then they passed the Prescott city limits sign. Adam pulled into the first gas station they came to and fueled up in the full service lane.

As the attendant took Adam's credit card, Lorna pushed open her door.

"Where do you think you're going?" Adam demanded.

"Even femme fatales have to visit the rest room occasionally," she replied sweetly. "Do you mind?"

"Just don't get any ideas. I'm right with you until we get to Astrid."

Lorna quietly closed the door in his face. She had to go into the station's convenience store to get the key from the gray-haired lady clerk. Adam actually got out of the car and stood right outside the glass door where he could see her. Then he stayed there while she went in the ladies' room a few feet away.

Lorna used the facilities, reapplied her lipstick and wondered how in the world she was going to ditch him again and also track down the mysterious Mr. O'Neill by ten o'clock. Still in the dark as to what to do next, she returned the key to the clerk, who looked at her rather oddly, she thought.

And why not? Excluding captured fugitives from justice, few grown women required an escort to go to the bathroom. Adam appeared oblivious to her disgusted grimace as she strode right past him. He followed close behind her back to the car.

"What now?" he asked, when they were both inside once more.

Good question, she answered silently. "Let's, um, just drive around town for a while, all right?"

"Where and what time are you meeting Astrid?"

"You are relentless."

"Where and when?"

Tossing him a quelling frown, Lorna did her best to re-member the wording of Astrid's note, not easy since she hadn't exactly had time to study it in depth before being forced to eat it. It had said something like *visit Bucky O'Neill at ten tonight*, but there'd been absolutely no ex-planation as to how to find the man.

Could he be well known in Prescott? Perhaps some sort of local celebrity? Lorna stared blindly out her side win-dow, thinking.

Just then, the clerk who'd watched her so suspiciously came out of the convenience store with the rest room key in her hand. Seeing her chance to question someone presum-ably from Prescott without her unswerving inquisitor lis-tening in, Lorna just about leaped from the car.

"Where the hell are you going?" Adam was right behind her.

"Left my lipstick in the ladies' room," she tossed over her shoulder. She slipped around the white-painted metal door just as the clerk tried to shut it.

As the door closed and locked automatically, Lorna leaned against it. She found herself facing the single sink, and the wary clerk who'd backed against the wall between the towel dispenser and the gray plastic wastebasket.

"Don't be afraid. I just want to ask you a question," Lorna tried gamely.

The woman watched her, narrow-eyed over the rims of her bifocals. "You just step aside, miss, and let me out of here," she said.

Lorna tried a congenial smile. "It's not what you think. Really."

Adam rapped sharply on the door. "Lorna, this is point-less. You can't get out without going through me." His voice came through slightly muffled, but quite understandable.

"Out in a minute," she called back amiably, then she focused on the clerk again. "It's nothing illegal, I mean, I didn't *do* anything. He's just looking for his mother, and he thinks I know where she is."

The steel door handle rattled. "Lorna! Open this door."

"Why don't you tell him, then?" asked the clerk.

"She doesn't want to be found."

"Lorna!"

"Settle down, young man!" the clerk piped up. "She'll be out in a minute!"

The door handle immediately stopped rattling. Silence came from outside the door.

Lorna and the clerk regarded each other. "Thanks," Lorna said, then grinned again, sheepishly. "He's now mortified. Your voice reminded him that he's made a fool of himself in public. Adam Gantry never makes a fool of himself."

The clerk grinned back. "Know him that well, do you?"

"We met this morning."

"Love at first sight?"

"No. He's not my type at all."

The clerk made a humphing sound in response to that. Then she asked, "Now what's your question?"

"Oh, right." Lorna lowered her voice, to make sure it wouldn't travel to listening ears outside. "Have you ever heard of a man named Bucky O'Neill?""

The woman grunted. "Maybe I didn't go to college, but I do know my history."

"History?"

"Captain William Bucky O'Neill. Of the Rough Riders. Fought in the war with Spain."

Lorna gulped. "The Spanish-American War?"

"You bet."

"But that was back at the turn of the century. That would make Bucky O'Neill—"

"Dead," the woman said with finality. "He died in the war. He was a hero."

Lorna let out a long breath. Now what? she thought. Visit Bucky O'Neill indeed. Was Astrid playing some kind of joke on her? If so, Lorna didn't get it.

The woman went on. "We've even got a statue dedicated to him. Over in the town square on Gurley."

Lorna had let herself slump against the door. Now she snapped to attention. "A statue? Of Bucky O'Neill." The joke was starting to make sense.

The woman shifted from one foot to the other. "You bet. Now, is that all you wanted to know?"

"The statue. Where is it?"

"Just keep going on the road you're on, to the center of town. Courthouse Square at Gurley and Marina. Can't miss it." The clerk was beginning to look uncomfortable. "Now, if you don't mind . . ."

"Oh. Oh, yes. Sorry." Lorna pulled the door open, then paused to look back at the clerk one last time. "Thank you."

"No problem." She winked. "And good luck with that man who isn't your type at all."

The door closed behind her and Lorna found herself face-to-face with a little over six feet worth of annoyed male. Adam immediately captured her arm and began herding her toward his car. "That was a ridiculous thing to do, Lorna. I'm running out of patience."

Lorna dug in her heels. "So am I. Let go of my arm." Surprisingly, he did. She took that small victory over his recent dominance of her and ran with it. "I appreciate your giving me a lift here. But now I can fend for myself. I want my things out of your trunk now, please."

"Lorna, don't be childish."

"I am not being childish, Adam Gantry. I'm an adult who has a perfect right to go where she wants when she wants with whomever she wants. And I don't want to go anywhere else with you. Is that clear enough? Now please get my things from your trunk."

"I'm not going to go away," he said grimly.

"We'll see. Now, open your trunk."

Short of using physical force, there wasn't much more he could do. He opened the trunk for her and set the suitcases near the phone kiosk where she instructed him to. Then he got in the car and started it up. Lorna couldn't believe he was giving in so easily, and she was right. He wasn't. He was only moving the car out of the fill-up lane. He pulled in right beside her suitcases and sat there, glowering, while she called a taxi.

The Ace City cab arrived in minutes. After she and her suitcases were safely inside, she asked for a hotel near Courthouse Square.

"Ma'am, do you know there's a guy following us?" the cabby asked as they jockeyed through the light early-evening traffic.

Lorna turned and glanced at Adam's car. "Unfortunately, yes. Ignore him."

"Oh, it's like that," the cabby said knowingly.

Lorna shrugged and looked out the window. Within minutes, she was deposited at the Hassayampa Inn, a splendid modified Spanish structure of ruffled brick in shades of deep red and blue. Copper cornices gleamed in the fading sunlight, and the trim was white, with plaster medallions set at intervals near the tile roof.

Lorna admired the architecture and ignored the Chrysler that slid in right behind the cab. "What a lovely old hotel," she said to the driver.

A uniformed bellman appeared and loaded her bags onto a cart.

"You're lucky it's May," the cabdriver said. "In June and July it's hard to find a last-minute vacancy in this town." He pointed across the street. "And there's the square. In walking distance, like you wanted."

Lorna handed him the metered amount plus a generous tip. Then she entered the doors the hotel. She checked into a small but beautifully appointed room on the second floor and went back to the lobby after getting rid of her suitcases. Adam dogged her every step.

She strolled unconcernedly out onto Marina Street. She would have to find a way to lose him, but right now he had no way of knowing she was on a foray to scout out the location where Astrid would contact her.

Courthouse Square was a place of maple trees and thick green grass. The statue of Bucky O'Neill on a spirited horse reared up at the toe-end of a horseshoe-shaped walk into which was set a time line of important events in Prescott history. Aware every moment of the man who dogged her steps, Lorna made a great show of reading the tiles set into the walk.

At the statue itself, she stopped and slowly let her gaze travel upward. The plaque at the base declared it one of the finest equestrian monuments in the world, and Lorna did find it beautiful, the powerful rearing horse and its Rough Rider, all action and excitement cast forever in rich bronze.

She studied her immediate surroundings. Trees. Grass. The horseshoe-shaped walk. Benches. A gazebo not far away. The big stone courthouse loomed behind the statue. To her right lay Gurley Street and a mailbox and a set of phone kiosks. Behind her was Marina Street and the Hassayampa Inn.

She fervently hoped this was the place.

Well, she told herself, if it wasn't she'd find out at ten o'clock.

Now to get rid of Adam....

He'd taken a seat on a nearby bench. She decided, rather regretfully, that the best way to shake him would be to deceive him again, to let him think she'd given in to his refusal to leave her alone and then, later, nearer the appointed time, to slip away when he least suspected it.

She turned and, very slowly, strolled toward him. He watched her, his green gaze wary.

"You're not going to give up, are you?" she asked when she stood looking down at him.

"No." He was facing the sun, which hung heavy in the western sky above the pine-blanketed hills. He shaded his eyes with his arm. "Just tell me when and where."

"I'm starving," she said, and held out her hand. "Let's eat."

Shaking his head, smiling in spite of himself, he grasped her outstretched palm. Once again, she felt that curling warmth at his touch, and she let her mouth curve into a come-hither smile. It felt so good, to be utterly free for the first time in her life and to be touching someone who made her feel as reckless as a Rough Rider on a powerful stallion.

Adam was squinting at her, against the red ball of the sun. "You won't tempt me off my guard again," he said. His voice had that delicious roughness that made her want to rub herself against it.

"The lady in the hotel lobby said that's Whiskey Row over there." She pointed toward Gurley Street. "After dark, all those bars open and every one of them has a band. I'm going to eat, Adam. And then I'm going dancing. Want to come?"

He grunted. She laughed, pulled him to his feet and led him back to the hotel.

The boutique in the lobby was open, so she made him wait while she bought some of the bright new clothes she'd promised herself, including a pair of white cowboy boots and a bag to match, some tight red jeans, a silky camisole top and a rawhide jacket with plenty of fringe. She modeled the clothes for him, twirling between the blue velvet chair where he sat and a long dressing mirror.

"It's exactly your style," he gave out grudgingly after a moment. His voice tried to be condescending, but she saw the heat in his eyes as his gaze unwillingly traveled up the formfitting line of the crimson jeans.

She turned to the clerk. "I think I'll wear this outfit now," she said. The clerk agreed to have the other new clothes, as well as the ones she'd been wearing, returned to her room.

After a quick trip to Adam's car where he once again donned his coat, they ate in the hotel dining room which lay beyond Peacock Alley, a hallway tiled in peacock blue, of which the hotel was justly proud.

Lorna ordered a nice big bottle of Chardonnay, but Adam refused to touch it. Adam watched her chatter happily through the meal, while he chewed the excellent food stolidly, looking as if he couldn't afford to relax his guard for a split second.

It was near nine o'clock when they finished eating. "Now, we go dancing," she announced, once they stood beneath the plaster medallions in front of the old hotel.

She pranced off down the street toward the music that could already be heard on nearby Gurley. Out of the corner of her eye, she noted the rearing shadow of Bucky O'Neill in the night-lighted square. Somehow, she had to get rid of Adam and be waiting beneath the bronze horse's hoofs within the hour.

When they reached Whiskey Row, Lorna's hopes of leaving her escort behind rose considerably. Though it had seemed just an ordinary commercial street in the daylight, on Saturday night the place clearly came alive. Already, good-natured partiers jostled each other as they went from club to club. If luck was with her, within the hour the crowds would really thicken. It would be easy to lose Adam in the crush and sneak across the street.

Dragging Adam behind her, she followed a group of revelers dressed in shiny boots and spotless hats into the Palace, the first saloon that struck her fancy.

Beyond the long, crowded bar the big room inside opened up to a pine-paneled dance hall. The band at the far wall played fast country music while couples two-stepped and a few adventurous souls practiced the intricate footwork of a line dance across the wooden floor.

High tables and a few stools along the wall provided a place to watch the action. Lorna quickly claimed a rare clear space and hoisted herself up on the stool. Adam, looking completely out of place in his expensive suit, stood right beside her. His expression defined the word stoic.

A waitress in jeans and a tank top asked what they'd have.

Adam shook his head. Lorna ordered a strawberry daiquiri and heard Adam's knowing snort.

The waitress left them. "What was that supposed to mean?" Lorna demanded.

He moved in a little closer, so they could talk while the band played. "What?"

"That *noise* you made when I ordered my drink."

He shrugged. "Nothing. I just knew you were going to order something pink with an umbrella in it."

She slipped out of her fringed jacket and tossed it across the little table in front of her. More than one set of masculine eyes took a slow walk over her bare, gleaming shoulders in the skimpy camisole.

"Put that jacket back on," Adam said impassively.

"Why?"

He snared the soft leather and draped it over her shoulders. "Let's just say there's a draft in here."

Her pink drink arrived. She took a quick sip and then slid off the stool. "I want to dance, Adam. And with you standing there looking like my keeper, no one's going to dare ask me." Defiantly, she slipped the jacket from her shoulders once again and tossed it on the table. "So it looks like you'll have to do for a partner—or would you rather I pulled a Sadie Hawkins and did the asking myself?"

Apparently, he preferred taking her in his arms to letting her two-step out of his reach with some obliging cowboy. He led her out on the wooden floor.

The band played a slow song. Around them, the other couples shifted into a slower, more intimate rhythm, their bodies moving close to one another. Adam, true to form, assumed a rigid ballroom stance. You could have wedged a beach ball between his cordovan belt and Lorna's denim waistband.

As always seemed to happen when she touched him, Lorna felt her pulse pick up. And she felt that naughtiness, that wildness that was so unlike her real self, come all the more to the fore. Something about all the control Adam exhibited inspired her to give her all to break it down.

In a smooth, slithery movement, she circled his neck with both hands and brought her body up against his.

"Lorna," he said. It was supposed to be a reprimand, but the huskiness in his voice betrayed him.

His body was so nice and solid. Pressing against him made her feel secure, and yet excited. She lifted her head and tipped her face up to his. "I've changed my mind, about your name," she said.

He looked down at her, saying nothing, his golden brows drawn together in a questioning expression.

"Maybe the Gantry does fit after all. Maybe there's some dashingness way down inside you that you haven't quite been able to extinguish, like an ember that just won't die. A sleeping spark."

"Next you'll be telling me it's your mission to fan that ember to a flame." His voice was rueful, bordering dangerously on tender.

She traced little figure eights on the back of his neck with one oval fingernail. "I wish..."

"Go on."

That just once in my life a man would look at the *real* me the way you're looking at me now. Her mind whispered the words, but of course she didn't say them.

"Hey, why so sad suddenly?" He was tipping her chin up so she looked in his eyes once again.

"Oh, Adam..."

His fingers slid backward, cupping her neck beneath the wild spill of her hair, cradling her face in a grip that was at once achingly sensual and full of gentle understanding. "You can tell me."

"No." A single traitorous tear welled over and trailed down her cheek. He brushed at it, in a stunningly compassionate caress, with the pad of his thumb. "I'm sorry, Adam. I just can't."

Miraculously, he seemed to accept her refusal to confide in him. He pulled her head against his broad chest and held it there, saying no more. She listened to the steady, reassuring beat of his heart, her sadness fading as the dance came to its inevitable conclusion.

As a fast number began again, he led the way for once, pulling her back to the little table. He scooped up her jacket, draped it on her shoulders, and headed for the door, still firmly holding her hand.

"Where are we going?" she asked, struggling to get the jacket on, as they passed the long bar and went out into the brightly lit, crowded street.

"Somewhere quiet," he tossed the words back over his shoulder as he pulled her along.

He plowed through the crowds. "No, wait, I want to dance some more." He ignored her protests, and Lorna knew why. She sounded totally unconvincing. The emotions that had surfaced in the Palace had somewhat dampened her party spirits.

"We'll go across the street," he said, not pausing in his purposeful stride. "There are a few benches by that statue."

Lorna had to restrain herself from groaning aloud. Without knowing it, he was planning to drag her right to the place where Astrid would be contacting her in—she darted a glance at her watch—twenty-five minutes.

"No, Adam!" She stopped stock-still just before they reached the corner, and jerked her hand from his grasp. She shoved the hand into the other arm of the fringed jacket, which she'd been only half wearing as he towed her down the street.

He turned to her. "What's the matter now?"

"I, um, came here to dance, and I'm going to have a good time."

People milled around them, but Adam ignored them completely. "Lorna, be honest with yourself for once. You were upset in there. You need to deal with it. The time comes when the party has to end, and you have to face the things that are really bothering you."

Saying nothing in response, Lorna turned and walked away, around the corner, down the darkened side street in the opposite direction from the park and the hotel. Behind the corner building, there was a small parking lot rimmed by a low brick retaining wall. Lorna sat on the low wall and stared down at her new white boots.

Slowly, Adam came after her. He sat beside her.

For a time, neither spoke. Muted on the night air came the cacophony of sounds from the bands and milling throngs around the corner.

Lorna debated with herself. She was tired of running, tired of trying to keep one step ahead of the relentless man beside her. He'd been so tender, so understanding in those few moments on the dance floor, that she was having second thoughts about keeping him from Astrid.

When you came right down to it, she found herself reasoning, Astrid had never said a word about her own problems when she'd appeared at Lorna's hotel room last night. It wasn't as if Astrid had actually asked Lorna to keep her whereabouts a secret. Last night, Astrid hadn't even *mentioned* her son—let alone the man she'd left waiting at their engagement party.

And it wasn't as if Adam were some kind of monster, after all. He was truly concerned about his mother, about her welfare and her future, and that was why he was being so overbearingly persistent about finding her.

Why not, Lorna wondered, let mother and son settle this problem between themselves? Why not step aside and let them handle their family matters without her interference?

She cast him an oblique glance. He looked calm and unruffled as always, sitting beside her on the low brick wall.

"Ready to talk about it?" he asked.

"Do you realize you haven't asked me where or when I'm meeting your mother in at least two hours?"

A smile played on his lips. "Asking you hasn't been terribly successful up to this point. And besides, I think if you start being honest with me, you might be honest about everything, including where I can find Astrid."

Not everything, she thought, her emotions equal parts defiance and sadness. Because I can't help it, Adam. I love the way you look at me. It's just what I need right now, to know a man sees me as everything sexy and feminine and dangerous that there is in the world. I want to go on feeling like that, for a little bit longer, just a little bit more....

"All right." Lorna stood up. "Let's go."

"Where to?"

"You want a chance to talk to Astrid, don't you?"

He stood up beside her. "Lead the way."

Five

—

"Astrid said she would contact you here at ten, and that's all?" Adam asked.

"The letter said to visit Bucky O'Neill and she'd contact me there. Since the man's been dead for almost a century, this statue was the closest I could come."

They were sitting on a bench a few feet from the statue in question. It was five minutes to ten.

"I still don't get it, Lorna. Can you tell me now what the hell is going on?"

She looked at him levelly. "Adam, I really don't know."

It was the truth, when she came right down to it. She had no idea what was driving Astrid. As for her own actions, it was as if another, totally different woman had come alive inside her. And the old Lorna often had no inkling what the new Lorna would do next.

"It's something to do with that group you two belong to, isn't it? They're manipulating you both and you've taken a vow of secrecy."

"Adam, for a solid citizen, you certainly have a vivid imagination."

"I'm concerned about my mother." He captured her glance. "And heaven help me, I'm starting to feel the same way about you."

"Concerned, you mean?"

"Yes."

She assumed a pose of bad-girl bravado. "Don't be. I can take care of myself."

He shook his head. "Your life's a mess. Look at you. It's obvious you don't even know day to day where you'll lay your head at night. What about your job—do you have a job?"

"Yes."

"Is your boss holding it for you until you decide to come to work again?"

"I'm on vacation, Adam. And I own my own business, anyway."

"What kind of business?"

She thought of her bookstore, of the neat rows of shelves labeled Fiction and Nonfiction, History and Psychology, Gardening and Art. He'd never for a moment believe her if she told him that bad Lorna Smith owned a bookstore in Westwood, usually wore her hair in a bun, and preferred PBS to commercial television.

"I'm in communications," she said.

"Lorna—"

She didn't let him continue. "Look. You wanted to talk to Astrid. That's what we're here for. If you want to be concerned about something, why don't you worry if this is the right place at all, and if she'll even show her face once she sees that you're here?''

''All right, Lorna. If that's how you want it.'' He sounded so infinitely patient and sympathetic that she once again felt the wild Lorna taking over.

If it was Adam Gantry's mission to save bad Lorna Smith, she thought, then maybe it was naughty Lorna's calling to let the air out of his stuffed shirt.

She nimbly scrambled to her knees on the bench and put her mouth against his ear. ''If I told you how I *really* want it, would you give it to me just that way?''

She heard his sharp indrawn breath as he turned his head toward her, pulling back at the same time, like a man scenting danger, facing it, but claiming distance.

And then he smiled. ''You *are* bad.'' Wisely, he didn't answer her question. ''And, all right, we'll change the subject.''

She resumed a more decorous position on the bench. ''Thank you.''

They waited in silence as the minutes crawled past.

''It's ten after ten,'' he said.

Lorna shrugged, wondering wistfully how her Mercedes was holding up. ''As I said before, I'm not even sure this is the right place.''

Just then, the phone in one of the kiosks across the lawn by the sidewalk rang. For a split second, their gazes locked. And then Adam was up and sprinting across the grass.

Since she was too late to get there before he did anyway, Lorna followed at a more sedate pace.

''Just what the hell is going on?'' she heard Adam demanding into the mouthpiece in an intense, low voice as she came up beside him on the sidewalk. ''Tell me where you are.''

Lorna stepped back, turning away, to let Adam have some privacy as he spoke with his mother.

His voice rose. "Astrid, be reasonable. I'm concerned about you. Listen, whatever it is, tell me. Let me help you—" Suddenly, he stopped arguing. For a moment, he said nothing. Then, "If you'll just—all right. Don't hang up. All right." His tone held total resignation.

"She wants to talk to you," he said.

Lorna took the receiver.

"Hello, Sister," a low, throaty voice said in her ear. "Better let me do the talking, okay?"

Lorna made a small noise of agreement.

"My goodness, darlin'," Astrid went on, "I'm sorry about this. Believe me, I would have told you my own situation if I'd thought Adam would have any way to track me down. I'm just a little stunned, to tell the truth. I need some time to rethink this thing—your Mercedes is fine, by the way. Is the Caddy holding up okay?"

"It died in the desert," Lorna said flatly.

"Oh, no. But you managed anyway."

"Adam was there."

"Well." An airy sigh came from the other end of the line. "Whatever works."

Lorna cupped her hand over the receiver and whispered, so the nearby and glowering Adam couldn't make out what she said. "What now, Astrid?" Her low tone was as grim as the words.

"I need to think."

"Would you mind thinking fast?"

"Okay. Look. I'll be in touch again tomorrow morning, say seven o'clock. The Boca Grande Café in Winslow. I know you could probably strangle me by now, but if you would just . . ."

Astrid's voice trailed off, as if she couldn't quite bring herself to ask so much. Lorna realized that it was Astrid's turn to need reassurance.

"Anything," Lorna said firmly. "Just tell me."

"Keep Adam with you until I decide what I should do, but don't let him come with you to the café in the morning." Lorna was silent. "I know, he's persistent," Astrid went on.

"That's putting it mildly," Lorna remarked.

"Do you think you can handle it?"

A few feet away, Adam was eyeing her suspiciously. "Mission accepted," she said into the receiver.

"Thanks, pal," said the husky voice in her ear. "Tomorrow, then." The line went dead.

"Where is she?" Adam asked the question in a monotone, as if he felt obliged to do so, though he knew he'd get no satisfactory answer.

"She didn't say." Lorna almost hated herself for having no more to tell him than what he expected. She added after a wordless moment, "I have to go."

"Where?"

"I—"

"I know. You can't tell me."

She let her answer be found in her silence.

"I'll have to rent a car," she said, as if talking to herself.

"No you won't," he said, as she'd known he would. "I'll take you."

She shook her head, knowing she mustn't go along too easily. She thought, deception upon deception, and wondered where and how it would end. She was going to have to ditch him briefly in the morning, and it was important that he have no clue of when or where she might do that. Keeping him totally in the dark as to what she was up to seemed the only way she'd have a chance of getting him to let down his guard at the appropriate time.

Unfortunately, everything she *didn't* say was bound to make him more sure that she and his mother were being manipulated by some mysterious cult of man-hating women.

"It's late to try to get a car," he argued reasonably.

She pretended to consider. "I really couldn't tell you anything, Adam. You'd just have to go where I asked you to take me."

"Fine," he said.

"Does that mean you'll stop the unending questions?"

"That means I'll take you wherever you want to go. I'm *not* going to give up trying to find out what the hell's going on. Promising I will would be a lie." He gave her a chiding frown and added, "I've always detested lies."

His dig hit her where it hurt. The real Lorna Smith prided herself on her scrupulous honesty. But somehow the naughty Lorna seemed to spend all her time rearranging the truth to suit her own needs.

Across the street, the bands played on. Lorna tapped her foot to a drumbeat that pounded louder than the rest.

"You detest lies," she tossed at him, her hostility a product of her guilt. "So you're saying you detest me, right? Because you think I'm lying."

"I know you're lying. But no, I don't detest you, Lorna."

His tone of extreme forbearance set her teeth on edge. Not even for Astrid's sake, she thought, could she put up with this.

"Forget it." She spun on her heel. "I'll get my own transportation."

He was beside her within three steps, catching her arm, and whirling her around to face him. "All right. I promise I'll *try* to stop asking questions."

She pulled her arm from his grip. "It won't work. You know it, I know it. You're not going to give up until I lead you to Astrid."

He grunted. And then he smiled. "You still need a ride tonight. And I'm still available."

Enchanted once again by the charm and humor that lurked beneath his facade of puritanical self-control, she replied, "Let me get my things."

There were two roads that would take them to Interstate 40 and eventually to Winslow. Lorna chose Highway 89, which seemed the most direct. The road wove through the mountains and down into the desert again.

As they left the trees behind and the land opened up before them, Lorna stared silently out the window, mesmerized by the austere beauty of the desert world that fled by on either side. By the silvering light of the waning moon, the dry earth seemed to roll on forever, dotted here and there with clumps of sagebrush, proud saguaros and the tortured shadows of joshua trees. She did her best to simply appreciate the stark scenery and not to even try to figure out how she was going to evade the man beside her when morning came.

They began climbing again, up into the gray-green stands of ponderosa pines. By midnight, they reached the interstate and sped on to Flagstaff. There, she made Adam stop at a phone booth where she pretended to place a call.

"I have to be in New Mexico by noon tomorrow," she said when she rejoined Adam at the car. It was a total fabrication, meant to throw him off guard.

"Where in New Mexico?" he asked, taken in.

She shook her head. "You know I can't say."

He took the map from the floor of the car and spread it out on the hood. "It's less than two hundred miles to the

New Mexico border," he said. "Why don't we call it a night here in Flagstaff and try for a few hours' sleep? We can get an early start and—"

She shook her head again. "Let's go a little farther, okay? We're still too far away for me to feel comfortable stopping."

He shrugged. "You know where you're going." She pretended not to notice the irony in his words as she settled back into the passenger seat.

They drove on through the deepening night, past towns named Winona and Two Guns, right by the turnoff that could have taken them to Meteor Crater. In spite of the lateness of the hour, Lorna felt her imagination stirring.

On the road ahead, there would be hundreds of turnoffs to choose from. And each one would bring its own special kind of adventure. And that, in the end, was what she was after. Adventure. A change in her perspective, a new way of looking at the world. And if she thought of recent events in that light, well, she was getting just what she wanted. Just because Adam insisted too often on being a harbinger of gloom didn't mean she had to be gloomy right along with him.

She was flushed with a new resolve to keep things light and upbeat when they reached Winslow.

Lorna stretched, elaborately, and said, "All right. Let's find someplace to sleep."

Winslow's two main streets, called Second and Third, were each one-way, so Adam ended up navigating a circle while Lorna pretended to look for a suitable place. In actuality, she was watching for the Boca Grande Café, which they passed not too far from the freeway on Second Street.

She waited until they were parallel the café on Third Street, before settling on the Super Duper Motel. One block over and two blocks up and she'd be at the café in the morning. It would be a nominal distance, even on foot.

Though the Super Duper Motel itself was distinctly *un*-distinctive, boasting forty rooms on two floors, each opening on the parking lot, Lorna found its upbeat name appealing.

When they pulled up to the office, Adam turned to her. "One room, all right?"

No way, she thought. One room would be too dangerously intimate, let alone making it all the harder to get away in the morning.

But then she reconsidered. The naughty Lorna would never quibble about anything so trivial as sharing a room with a man she was attracted to. Saying no would be out of character. He'd become doubly suspicious. His guard would be up and she'd never escape him in the morning.

She smiled at him—tauntingly, she hoped. "Hm. One room. Is that a proposition?"

"Don't worry." His voice was flat. "I'll get separate beds."

She tried a teasing smile, wishing vainly for one in return. "But do you snore?"

"No," he said. His face remained impassive.

Sighing, Lorna put her hand on his arm. "Adam. Let's lighten it up a little, okay? I mean, we're in this situation together and we might as well make the best of it."

"Right," he said, and went in to the motel office to register for their room.

The room had two double beds with worn red chenille bedspreads. The television was bolted to its stand and water could be heard dripping in the bathroom sink.

"Charming," Lorna said. "I especially like the drapes. They look like modern art from the brush of a crazed orangutan."

"You chose it," Adam muttered.

"All right if I use the bathroom first?" she asked, insolently cheerful.

"Go ahead."

Lorna closed the door behind her, engaging the privacy lock.

As Adam heard the sound of water running in the sink, he smiled grimly to himself. The opportunity to uncover a little of the mystery of Lorna Smith was now at hand. She'd taken one full-size suitcase and her overnight case into the bathroom with her. But the white shoulder bag that she'd bought to match her new boots sat waiting on the vanity counter by the bathroom door.

Adam avoided meeting his own eyes in the mirror as he unzipped the little purse. Pawing through another's belongings offended his moral sense of right and wrong. However, in this case, he didn't see what else he could do. So he ignored the nagging of his conscience as he spread out a hand towel to muffle the sound and dumped the purse's contents on the counter.

He discovered immediately that she was carrying a substantial sum of traveller's checks and several major credit cards.

Her driver's license said she was almost thirty and just who she claimed to be. The picture of her, though, made him stop and stare for precious seconds. It was a plain, unadorned version of the Lorna he knew. As if she'd scrubbed her face clean and raked her hair back to take her driver's test. He couldn't help smiling at it. She looked so wary and vulnerable that way.

In an accordion strip of photo windows, she carried studio portraits of three babies and a little girl in pigtails. She also had three snapshots, one of a gray-haired couple and the others of two very pretty women. By the obvious physical resemblances, he assumed that the older couple were Lorna's parents and the two women either cousins or sisters. They were all very wholesome-looking, with their attractive faces and friendly smiles. He imagined Lorna must be the black sheep.

He stood for a few moments, staring at the pictures, wondering about her childhood and about how she'd grown up. But then the water stopped running in the other room, and he realized he should get on with it.

He opened her business-card case. On ivory parchment stock, her cards announced that she was the proprietress of The Book Nook, used and hard-to-find books being her specialty.

I own my own business, she'd told him. Was that actually the truth, then? Or was she just outrageous enough to have business cards printed for a make-believe concern?

Now, he decided, was no time to ponder that question.

Swiftly, Adam pocketed one business card and jotted down her home address from her driver's license. Then he shoveled the contents back into her purse and set it just where Lorna had left it. He shook out the towel and hung it back on the rack.

He considered chancing a phone call, but decided against it. She'd be through in the bathroom any minute. Besides, the detective he needed to contact would be hard to reach at one in the morning on Saturday night, and this was hardly a situation where Adam could leave a number to call back.

Intrigued with the information he'd uncovered, Adam stretched out on one of the beds and tried to make himself relax. He knew, however, that relaxation was unlikely, in spite of the deep-breathing exercises his fitness trainer had taught him.

Plagued as he was by insomnia, it was often difficult for him to get a full night's sleep even under ideal conditions. Tonight, in a strange and lumpy bed, worried about Astrid, and wondering what wild thing Lorna Smith would do next, sleep was not even an option.

Not that he wanted it to be. No, he was better off wide-awake and ready for action. Around Lorna Smith, that was the only way to keep up.

In the bathroom, Lorna donned one of the more modest gowns from her wedding trousseau, a slinky ivory silk that covered her from low neckline to ankles, but clung a little more provocatively than might be appropriate. The peignoir that went with it disguised a few more of her curves, but made what didn't show all the more enticing.

She shook her head at herself in the cracked mirror. No, poor Adam would expire of grimness if she emerged from the bathroom dressed like this. He'd be sure she was out to ravish him.

She dropped the slinky silk to the floor and foraged around in her opened suitcase, finally coming up with a huge white T-shirt with a pink unicorn printed on the front that had been a gift from her eight-year-old niece.

The T-shirt would have to do. She slipped it over her head and the hem fell halfway to her knees.

"Done?" Adam asked absently when she rejoined him in the main room. He was stretched out on one of the red-covered beds, reading a brochure that had been left on the nightstand.

"Your turn."

Still not looking at her, he swung his feet off the bed, and reached for the little overnight kit he'd taken from his trunk. "I'm going to shower," he announced. "A long, hot shower."

"Good idea," she said.

He disappeared in the bathroom, significantly taking his car keys from the top of the television as he went by. After a few minutes, she heard the shower running.

Lorna set her travel clock for 5:00 a.m., thinking that would give her two hours to get away from Adam. Then she slid beneath the covers of the other bed, and switched out the lamp on her side. She plumped her two flat pillows and thought vaguely of turning on the television, seeing what the late-night viewing was like in Winslow. But there was no remote, and she would have had to get up to do it. She was just tired enough that the bed seemed almost comfortable, and before she was even aware she was sleepy, her eyes were drooping closed.

Lorna had no idea what woke her in the deepest part of the night. A glance at her travel clock told her it was 3:00 a.m. Fitfully, she turned over to face Adam's side of the room.

He'd turned off his light. The room lay in deep shadow, the only illumination was that which bled through the ugly drapes from the garish motel sign out front, but she could make out his shape. He was sitting up against the headboard. His chest was bare and the covers were pulled up to his waist.

"Adam?"

"Go back to sleep."

"Adam, what is it?"

"There's nothing wrong. Go back to sleep."

"Did you sleep at all?"

"I'm fine."

She sat up and turned on her light, squinting against the sudden glare. Then she rubbed her eyes and turned to him. He still sat against the headboard, his expression grim, his bare, well-muscled chest covered with a light dusting of hairs the same golden color as his eyebrows.

"Turn off the light. Go back to sleep," he said.

"Adam, I know you didn't sleep last night. You need some rest."

"I'm fine."

"You keep saying that, through clenched teeth. It's not very convincing. Aren't you tired?"

"I want to keep an eye on you."

"Eventually, you have to sleep."

"That's what you think." He uttered the words so bleakly that she had a sudden urge to throw back her covers and go to him.

She stopped herself. "What do you mean?" she asked cautiously.

"I mean I have trouble sleeping, that's all. No big mystery."

"You mean like insomnia?"

"Yes."

"But don't they have treatments for that. Sleep clinics, that sort of thing?"

He spoke defensively. "I saw a therapist about it."

"And?"

"He said that in my case it appeared to be a problem of control. When I sleep, I have to relinquish control. And I'm not good at that."

Something welled up inside her—a soft little ache. Lorna recognized the emotion: tenderness. Here was this big, strong, domineering man, and he was scared to death to let himself be vulnerable enough to get a good night's sleep.

"How long has it been, since you slept?"

"I've slept," he said, sounding like a recalcitrant little boy.

"Just answer the question, Adam."

"I slept for five hours Wednesday night."

"You haven't slept the past two nights?" she murmured disbelievingly. "Not at all?"

"I've gone longer. Believe me."

"But it's *bad* for you, not to have your rest."

"Lorna, no one ever died from insomnia. Think about it. When you finally get tired enough, you go to sleep."

"But how long does that take?"

"I went for over a week once."

"That's awful." It suddenly occurred to her that his grim behavior since they had checked into the motel was probably directly related to his inability to sleep. He knew bedtime was coming, and he knew he was going to spend the night staring at the wall.

"Turn off your light and go back to sleep. It's nothing to be upset about," he said after a moment.

Lorna tossed back the red spread and stood up. "Turn over," she said. "And lie on your stomach."

His glance flicked over her bare legs and the huge shirt and settled on her sleep-flushed face. "Get back in that bed."

She folded her arms and frowned obdurately. "Turn over. I'm going to give you a massage."

"I'm not in the mood for games, Lorna."

"Neither am I. You need to relax, whether you think you can go to sleep or not. A massage will relax you." He stared at her, warily. She showed him her hands, palms up. "Adam, please. I'm just trying to help."

"You mean that," he said after a pregnant silence. It was a statement, not a question.

"Yes. Please let me help you."

"I'll never fall asleep, so you'll be wasting your time. Especially if you're thinking you'll sneak out while I'm unconscious."

"Come on. I'm not your prisoner, and we both know it. I can walk out that door any time I want, whether you're asleep or not."

"But if I'm asleep, I can't follow you."

"Look. How about if I promise not to run out on you?" Or if I do, it'll only be for a little while, she added silently.

He was regarding her skeptically from under lowered brows.

"I would never break a promise, Adam," she said quietly, "no matter what you may think of me." She strode purposefully to the vanity counter, feeling Adam's gaze boring through her back the whole time. She took a tube of lotion from her overnight case.

When she turned to him again, he was still sitting against the headboard, frowning. She walked toward him, trying to look brisk and no-nonsense, like a nurse with a difficult patient.

He looked up at her. "You only want to help me, do you?" That husky undertone had come into his voice.

Standing there, her bare feet chilled on the threadbare motel carpet, Lorna Smith clutched her tube of lotion and examined her motives. Silently, she admitted that her motives were mixed. She shifted her gaze to the velvet painting of a big-eyed child on the wall above the headboard.

Yes, I want to help you, she thought. And I also want you to be sound asleep when I go to meet Astrid in the morning. And, beyond that ... She caught her lower lip between her teeth as she admitted to herself, I want to touch you....

"You can answer any time," he prompted.

She forced herself to look at him, and as soon as she did it, she realized she never wanted to look away. He was so beautiful. His chest was strong and deep, the cords of muscles in his arms powerfully defined. The gold hairs on his skin looked crisp and inviting to the touch. Her fingers itched to trail down his flat belly, where the hairs disappeared beneath the red bedspread. She realized that a man in his thirties with a sedentary job didn't keep a body like that without a great amount of hard work and self-discipline. And, of course, if there was one thing Adam Gantry had in excess, it was discipline.

His discipline was part of what attracted her so strongly. The Lorna she had been until the night before admired it. And the new, naughty Lorna longed to make him lose it completely, at least for the night.

Lorna gulped. "You're right." She saluted him with the tube of lotion. "Bad idea. I'll just get back in my own bed." She started to turn.

His hand shot out and closed on her wrist. The warm, firm touch sent a hot little shiver clear down to her chilled toes. She looked into his eyes.

"You never did answer my question," he said.

"No, and I'm not going to now."

For some inexplicable reason, that seemed to satisfy him. He released her and rolled onto his stomach, keeping the red spread up at his trim waist. "I'd appreciate a massage," he said in a neutral tone. "You're right. It'll make me less tense, if nothing else."

Six

Lorna gulped again, wishing the lump that kept rising in her throat would stay down. She stared at the golden-brown expanse of Adam's muscled back and shoulders. Where to begin?

She considered perching on the edge of the bed, but that would have her rubbing from the side, not nearly as effective as a more direct angle would be.

Holding onto the tube of lotion as if it were a lifeline, she hoisted a bare knee up onto the side of his bed, and then swung the other leg over him, so she came to rest astraddle his waist and the hard curve of his masculine buttocks.

"Am I too heavy?" she asked, hoping he didn't notice the breathy break in her voice.

"You're fine." He tossed the pillows to the floor and slid his sculpted arms up and out, bent at the elbow, so that his hands were parallel with his head. She assumed that was to give her easier access to the various muscle groups.

The knot in her throat was still there. She forced it down once again and squeezed some lotion into her palm. She rubbed her hands together, preparatory to beginning work on his shoulders.

That's just how I'm going to think of this, she told herself determinedly, as work. Purposeful activity to help poor Adam relax.

Staunchly, she laid a cream-slicked hand on either side of his powerful neck. He gave a low, satisfied groan as she began to knead the hard knots of muscle that moved out to his shoulders.

Slowly, deeply, she rubbed, pummeled and punched at each of his shoulders and out to his arms. She kept her concentration on easing the muscles beneath her hands, and was pleased to feel them gradually relaxing. As she worked over him, his big body perceptibly loosened beneath her soothing touch.

After she'd pulled and stroked his hands right down to his fingers, she worked her way back up to his shoulders and began slow, deep long strokes on either side of his backbone.

He sighed contentedly beneath her hands.

Lorna smiled, realizing that the knot in her throat had disappeared. Somehow, by putting her attention on the action of the massage, it had become an end in itself. She'd stopped thinking of what might happen between them *if*. There was only his smooth skin and the muscles beneath.

Lorna closed her eyes, reveling in the feel of him under her hands. She took her thumbs and set them by the nubby bones of his spine, rubbing in an outward circle, working her way down until she had to lift her hips from the saddle of his buttocks to go farther.

Then she realized that perhaps she'd gone far enough. Gently, she lowered her hips to his again and lightly slid her hands back up to a less dangerous location.

"You continue to amaze me, Lorna Smith."

His voice, when he'd said nothing for so long a time, surprised her slightly. The tone of it surprised her even more. She'd never heard him sound like that. Lazy, content...*relaxed*. A soft smile curved her lips. However mixed her motives might have been, she'd succeeded in her objective. Under her soothing hands, Adam Gantry had managed to loosen up a little.

She put her hands on his shoulders again and bent her head down to his. "Feel better, don't you?"

"Much." His warm breath stirred her hair, which had fallen across his face when she leaned down to him.

Not questioning her action, only feeling *close* to him at that moment, intimate with him in the way she'd never really been with any man, she pulled her head back enough that the fall of hair stroked across his cheek and down his neck.

He groaned softly, and she thought he breathed her name as she went on teasing him with the cascade of tumbled curls. His muscles, which she'd worked so hard to relax, tightened again beneath her. But it was a good kind of tightness, a luxuriant awakening of desire and physical need.

Lorna forgot all about her resolve not to ravish the man. She felt herself, suddenly, as a flame of pure feminine sensation, her only desire to feed the fire of her man's need.

And Adam Gantry was definitely her man. Now, tonight, in all his masculine strength and beauty, he was everything the old, inhibited Lorna might have dreamed of in her most secret fantasies. And for the new Lorna, he was power and steadiness and the promise of wild fulfillment beneath a steely mask of self-control.

She put her lips where her hair had been. His skin was smooth and scented faintly of her lotion. She kissed him, first with just her soft lips, feeling him, learning him. And then she opened her mouth and tasted the firm skin with her tongue.

"Lorna." He said her name again, almost pleadingly.

She went on kissing him.

"Lorna..." His body moved, beneath her hips.

In an instinctive answer to the call of flesh to flesh, she began to stroke herself against him, in a rhythm as old as time.

And she went on kissing him, sliding her lips and tongue upward until she found his neck, and his mouth that kept murmuring her name.

He strained his head to meet her hungry kiss and when their lips met, as she lay almost full-length against him, he deftly turned over beneath her, catching her as she slid off him, and settling her back on top of him, but this time front-to-front.

His powerful arms, freed now to have their own way, wrapped around her, and then slid over her shoulders until his hands cupped and held her face. He lifted his head, hungry for her as she was for him, and he kissed her, deep and aggressively, his fingers thrust deep in the bronze spill of her hair.

Unashamed, Lorna opened her mouth to him. His sweet tongue learned all the secret, moist places beyond her eager lips.

The kiss went on and on forever, and as their tongues sparred and stroked and teased, Lorna let herself be aware of all the places she was touching him. At that moment, touching him seemed the most important thing in the world.

She sat atop him, her knees on either side of his waist, and her stomach and chest against his, with only the barrier of her T-shirt between them. Below her gently rocking hips, she could feel the hardness of him, the readiness, and everything that was woman in her responded with a sensation of opening, of sultry invitation.

He'd kicked the blanket down, so as her hands made questing forays across his skin, she felt the elastic band of his briefs and realized he was wearing nothing else.

As he playfully bit her lower lip, and then licked it, she decided she wanted to be closer to him. Closer even than she was while half lying on top of him.

She wanted to be rid of the barrier of her T-shirt, to feel her soft, full breasts against his hard chest. With a last nipping kiss that promised much, she placed her palms on his shoulders and levered herself to a full sitting position astride him. He groaned, luxuriously, as her hips made even closer contact with his.

She looked down at him, at his hard body and his handsome, squarish face and his green eyes that were now luminous with wanting, with sensual need.

Very slowly, she crossed her hands in front of her and grasped the hem of her shirt. She pulled it up and over her head, losing the hold of his shimmering gaze for only seconds.

She felt the cool air on her bare skin, as she dropped the shirt beside her on the tousled red spread. Naked but for a wisp of silk on her hips, she captured his gaze again.

He was shaking his head. The shimmer was still in his eyes, but dampened a little.

"Uh-uh," he said. He gazed on her bare breasts, and she saw the fire leap again in his eyes, just as she saw him quell it. "We need to stop this now."

She began to register just exactly what was happening. She was as nearly nude as it was possible to be, straddling

Astrid Gantry's son in an ugly motel room in Winslow, Arizona.

He felt around near her thigh, and came up with her discarded shirt. Numbly, still reorienting herself to the reality of the situation, she clutched it against her chest.

With stunning sensitivity, he stroked a strand of hair behind her ear. "You are beautiful," he said gruffly. "And I'd like nothing better than to let nature take its course."

"But?"

"I don't think I'm ready to be another notch on your garter belt."

The lump was back in her throat. "Oh, I see." Slowly, she slid off of him to the worn carpet at the far side of his bed. Turned away from him, she pulled the shirt over her head and felt it mercifully drop around her thighs, covering her flushed nakedness from his sight.

She slid him an over-the-shoulder glance, since he was so deathly silent behind her. Caught off guard, his gaze burned into hers, smoldering with the heat of unsatisfied desire. He instantly averted his eyes.

"Give me just a minute," he growled. Then he was off the bed and headed for the bathroom. She didn't miss the way he scooped up his car keys again before leaving her alone.

He needn't have bothered, she thought with as much irony as she could muster in her state of frozen embarrassment. At the moment, she was too stunned by her own actions and by his rejection of her, to move. She stood rooted to the spot until he returned and slipped again beneath the covers of his bed.

"Lorna."

She refused to answer him, but realized she couldn't stand there staring at the far wall forever. She began to edge around the foot of his bed back to her side of the room. Never in her life had she felt so empty and deflated, so utterly alone and undesirable. Even Jeffrey's leaving her hadn't made her feel this bad. Some siren she'd turned out to be.

"Lorna, come back here."

She marched resolutely to her own empty bed. And she almost made it. But then, six-foot-one of nearly naked male stopped her by grabbing her arm.

"Please let me go."

"Not until you look at me." He pulled on her arm.

She slumped to the bed beside him. His hand, as usual, felt good—warm and secure. She squeezed it, her sense of humor slyly beginning to poke its head through the heavy veil of her mortification.

Then she turned her head slightly and dared to meet his steady look. He was sitting up against the headboard again, the spread once more tucked around his waist. He grinned, crookedly, and she felt her own lips curving upward in response.

"So much for helping you relax," she said wryly.

"The massage did help." He looked completely sincere.

"May I go back to my own bed now? My feet are freezing."

He tipped his head to the side, considering, and she was reminded of Astrid. And then he was sliding down under the covers, guiding her by the shoulders to stretch out beside him, with the blankets between them.

"I like the way you feel against me," he said simply in her ear. "It'll help me relax if you sleep here."

"You mean it will help you relax if I can't even move without you knowing it."

"Um. Whatever." He wrapped an arm around her waist and tucked her closer against him. His big, solid body felt wonderful wrapped around her back.

"But my feet are still freezing," she gave out, sounding sulkier than she meant to, like a child who hadn't got her way and now hungered for pampering to make up for being thwarted.

Adam reached up and flicked the wall switch, turning off her lamp and his simultaneously. Then he flipped the chenille spread off of himself and over her, keeping the blankets and sheet underneath for himself. He carefully tucked the spread around her and then gathered her close again. "Better?"

"As a matter of fact, yes." She pressed her feet against the warmth he was generating from under the blankets and felt marvelously cozy.

"Now go to sleep," he instructed softly in her ear.

But that was easier said than done.

Outside, some late-night customer slammed a car door and shortly thereafter a trunk lid. A diesel truck rumbled by on the street. From the bathroom, she could hear the steady dripping of that leaky faucet in the sink. The drip, to her ears, seemed to make a chiding noise. It sounded like her conscience, clicking its tongue in disapproval at her multiplying deceptions.

Lorna was feeling guilty again for misleading the poor man whose warmth and strong arms felt so good around her. He was a good man, a *real* man, one who cared for those he loved and always put right behavior above his own fleeting desires.

And he *had* wanted her. Now that her first humiliation had faded, she could see that clearly. But he'd felt it wouldn't be right to make love with her, given who he thought she was, and given the short time they had known each other. So he'd called a halt—later than he should have, perhaps, but at least before it was *too* late.

Now, with the heat of his body dispelling the predawn chill, she felt so *close* to him. And it was a closeness far deeper than the warmth their bodies shared in the darkness. She felt just as close, though in a totally different way, as she had felt when she'd thrown wisdom to the winds and started making love to him.

But, no matter how close she felt to him, in a few hours, she was going to be called upon to deceive him again. And that made her feel as guilty as a naughty child.

She wished, fervently, that she didn't have to do it. But she couldn't let Astrid down, not now when she'd given her word to meet the older woman alone.

However, her conscience scolded, *there's also the matter of your real identity. Nothing's stopping you from telling him that. You could manage to explain it without betraying Astrid at all, if you tried.*

But then he won't look at me like I'm the most wild and wonderful creature in the world anymore....

Real closeness always begins with honesty, her conscience reminded her.

Tucked against Adam's broad chest, Lorna sighed. And then she spoke.

"Adam? There's something I haven't told you. Something I want you to know...."

She let her voice trail off and waited for his questioning response.

None came.

"Adam?"

His chest moved in and out, even and slow against her back.

Lorna squirmed under his arm enough to roll faceup, so she could see him. He made a protesting noise and snuggled up closer to her, tucking his head into the curve of her shoulder.

He was sound asleep.

Lorna smiled, and allowed herself to trace the bridge of his nose with her index finger. "Never mind," she whispered. "We can talk about it some other time."

Still smiling, she rolled to her side again and settled cozily back into the curve of Adam's body. Then she closed her eyes.

Lorna woke to the insistent beeping of her travel alarm. She instinctively reached out toward the sound, before it occurred to her sleep-drugged mind that the clock was way over on the far side of the other bed. Groaning, she struggled out of the masculine arms that held her and scrambled across the other bed, managing to silence the irritating sound at last.

In the resounding quiet that followed, she sank to a crouch on the empty bed, clutching the alarm between her hands. She stared at the face of the clock for a time, then she slithered off the far side of the bed and peeked through the drapes.

It was still dark. The blinding motel sign out front went on blinking Vacancy. Lorna dropped the edge of the curtain and sat down on the bed again, putting the alarm back on the nightstand.

Finally actually waking up, she looked over her shoulder at the man on the other bed. He was snoring very softly.

"Adam?" she tried.

He went on snoring. Lorna thought it a nice kind of sound, even and soft, like a big cat purring with contentment. She longed to crawl back in beside him and let him purr in her ear until at least noon.

But there was her promise to Astrid to think of. If Adam was really as sound asleep as he seemed, now would be the time to get out of here. She could find some way to while away the time until seven, though what specifically, she wasn't sure.

She glanced out the window again. Besides looking dark, it all looked quiet as a tomb. Not a soul in sight. She'd be lucky to find somewhere to wait until the Boca Grande Café opened at, she assumed, some time before seven.

Lorna straightened her shoulders and ordered herself into action. As stealthily as she could, she darted about the room, tugging on a pair of trim jeans and a white embroidered shirt from her suitcase, giving the ordinary clothes dash and flare by pairing them with her new white boots and fringed jacket.

Then she scribbled a brief note and propped it up with the keys he had guarded so carefully, right on his nightstand, where he would see it first thing should he wake before she returned. Adam was still snoring happily when she tiptoed out the door.

As the door clicked shut, Adam opened his eyes. The enchanting little witch had made good her escape, just as he'd intended.

Tossing back the tangle of blankets, he jumped out of bed and began rapidly pulling on his clothes. As he buttoned his cuffs, he quickly scanned the note on the nightstand.

Starving for donuts. Be back soon.

L.

"Donuts, hah!" he muttered, as he slid on his shoes and reached for his jacket.

Her leaving the keys told him much. Chances were she was meeting his mother, and that the meeting was going to take place somewhere nearby.

All he had to do was keep up with her, and he'd get to the bottom of this whole mess at last. He felt rejuvenated; he'd actually slept for over an hour with Lorna's delectable body tucked up against his own. It had been a deep, satisfying kind of sleep, too. The type of sleep he rarely experienced. So that the length of it had mattered little; it had renewed him. He felt ready to tackle anything: even his mother and her tempting little bronze-haired secret sister.

He pocketed both his car keys and the room key and let himself out the door. He strode purposefully past the silent row of rooms and the darkened office until he reached the street. There he hesitated, sticking his head around the side of the building to peer down both sides of the street.

Lorna Smith was nowhere in sight. In the time it had taken him to pull on his clothes, she'd ducked into a side street, evading him though she didn't even know he was on her tail.

Her temporary escape didn't faze him in the least. She couldn't have gone that far on foot anyway. He'd methodically cover all the nearby streets on foot himself, until he found her, and then he'd hang back until he discovered exactly what she was up to.

Caught up in the chase, Adam didn't stop to analyze the smile that played on his lips or the lightness of his step as he stalked Winslow's predawn streets. Adam Gantry hadn't allowed himself enough fun in his life to recognize when he was having it.

Lorna briskly strolled the few blocks to the café and learned that it would open at six. She had a little over half an hour to kill.

She spent the time walking, aimlessly exploring the quiet streets of the desert town as the sun pinkened the expanse of sky in the east. At last it was six o'clock and she returned to the café.

The solitary waitress poured her coffee—and left her alone. Lorna watched the waitress for a while as the tall, thin woman flirted with the only customer at the counter, a man who wore his cigarettes rolled up in the sleeve of his white T-shirt and had a tattoo on his bulging bicep that said THELMA FOREVER. So much for forever, Lorna thought wryly, remembering that the waitress's name tag had said VONDA RAE.

There was an old-fashioned jukebox selector on her table, so Lorna thumbed through it. She chose a few love songs which she played in honor of Vonda Rae and her new love, Thelma's ex. In the middle of a K. T. Oslin song, Vonda Rae returned with the coffeepot.

Just then the pay phone on the wall rang. Vonda sauntered over to it.

"Boca Grande. Just a minute, I'll check." She put her hand over the mouthpiece and held it out toward Lorna. "You Lorna Smith?"

Lorna nodded and took the phone. Vonda Rae went back to flirt with Thelma's ex.

"Did you manage to get away from Adam?" Astrid asked without preamble.

"He's sleeping like a baby back at the motel."

"Wonderful."

"Astrid, what is going on? Adam says you ran out on your own engagement party. He says your fiancé has locked himself in his room and won't come out."

Astrid made a disbelieving noise in her throat. "Maxwell will be fine. I wouldn't be in love with him if he weren't a survivor."

"Then you *are* in love with him?"

Astrid sighed. "Totally and completely, I'm afraid."

"Then *why* did you run out on him?"

There was a silence on the line then Astrid said, "Marriage is a big step for me. I've never been married. I must be absolutely sure."

"But what are you *doing*?"

There was no answer. Astrid, her voice suddenly sly, asked a question of her own. "Tell me, what do you think of my son?"

Lorna groaned. "He's an overbearing stuffed shirt who wants to control everything and everyone in sight."

"He's perfect for you," Astrid declared smugly. "I've thought it over, and I've decided that you two are meant for each other."

Lorna made her voice slow and patience. "Astrid, the makeover was great, but this is going too far."

"Tell me you're not attracted to Adam."

"Astrid—"

"Just say it, and I'll drop the whole plan."

"What plan?"

"You *are* attracted."

Lorna didn't speak for a moment. Unbidden images of the night before had risen in her unruly imagination. She saw herself sitting on Adam Gantry, felt his hands in her hair and his lips against her own....

"All right, Astrid. I'm attracted."

"Ha. I knew it."

"But it's all one big mess. He thinks I'm some wild and free mantrap on the make who's out to keep you from being happy with your fiancé and maybe steal your hairdressing salon besides. He thinks our support group is an anticommitment cult."

"I'm sure you'll work it out eventually. In the meantime, are you having a great vacation, or what?"

"Astrid, you're not listening."

"Darlin', I have a few more old boyfriends to look up in the next couple of days."

"But *why*?"

"I told you. I have to be sure."

"Adam said you kissed some guy right in front of his wife in their frozen yogurt franchise in Palm Springs."

"That was Artie," Astrid's voice went musing. "Such a sweetheart. And I know I loved him, once. But when I kissed him, all I felt was longing—for Maxwell."

"You're traveling around the country, kissing your old boyfriends?"

"More or less. I've got to be sure. If the flame still burns with any of them, then I'll have to tell Max I'm simply not the marrying kind."

"But where are you going?"

"Back to where I started, eventually. Hot Springs, Arkansas, where I was born and raised. Meet you there in, say, six days. Saturday, the twentieth. Just don't tell Adam until then where I'm going."

"Astrid, you're asking the impossible."

The sultry voice dripped reproach. "Well, I suppose you'll do what you have to do."

"I'll have to keep lying to him."

"Not lying exactly. Just not revealing all the truth."

"Astrid, it's wrong."

"Do you know he's never had a vacation that I can remember? He was a driven little boy and he's a driven man. When he was ten, he got his first paper route. He was working at a fast-food franchise as soon as he was legally old enough. He held down two jobs while he put himself through UCLA. For relaxation, he has a fitness trainer who comes to his house and tortures him with push-ups and sit-ups until he's so exhausted he can finally sleep a few hours—did I mention he's insomniac?"

"You didn't have to. I found that out myself."

"Darlin', this is all unfolding just as it should."

"Astrid, I hate it when you go mystical on me."

"Admit it. When you drew my name as your secret sister, you thought, 'What in the world will I ever have in common with a woman like that?'"

"There's nothing to admit. We both know that's how I felt. You felt that way about me."

"But we were wrong. We were meant to be sisters, so I could follow you to Palm Springs and realize at the same time that I must reexamine my own engagement. I have to do what I'm doing so I'll know if Max is right for me, and you lost Jeffrey because it is your destiny to discover other dimensions to yourself. It all fits together because Adam followed me, and as you discover your other selves you will also aid my son in learning that there's more to life than work and rigid self-control. Isn't it marvelous?"

"It's a mess," Lorna reiterated.

"It's life," Astrid declared. "And it's mad and marvelous!"

At that moment, Lorna spotted the blond-haired man who was pushing through the glass doors at the other end of the café.

"Uh-oh," she said.

Seven

"**W**hat is it?" Astrid asked in her ear.

"Adam. He's found me."

"Then I must go. Meet you at noon Saturday in front of the main post office, Reserve Avenue at Central in Hot Springs." And then Astrid hung up.

Looking resignedly grim, Adam strode toward her. He took the receiver from her hands. He held it to his ear, heard the silence on the other end, and very gently put it back in its cradle.

Then he took her by the arm. "Where are you sitting?" He sounded very reasonable.

She pointed at her coffee cup and he guided her back to the table. He signaled to Vonda Rae, who tore herself away from her boyfriend long enough to take Adam's order. Lorna didn't even object when he presumed to order eggs, toast, bacon and hash browns for her as well as for himself.

"I was feeling pretty cheerful," he said after Vonda Rae had placed a large tomato juice on the table and left them alone. "Until I walked in here and saw you were already on the phone." He sipped from his juice. "That was Astrid, wasn't it?"

Lorna nodded. "You weren't asleep at all," she accused.

"Not after your alarm went off. But I lost you, getting dressed. I passed this place once already, but it was closed."

"I went for a walk until it opened."

He eyed her warily from across the table, silently sipping again and again from his glass. Lorna knew he was trying to devise a new approach, trying to come up with a way to pry Astrid's whereabouts from her.

Vonda Rae appeared, slid their breakfasts in front of them, and then strolled away again.

Lorna discovered she was hungry. She spread jam on her toast and mixed her eggs with her hash browns and dug into the hearty fare.

While she ate, she watched Adam, just as he was watching her. He watched her like a duelist, looking for an opening. She, on the other hand, was studying him.

He'd been in such a hurry to follow her, that he'd left his tie behind. The top button of his shirt was undone, his collar flying. His hair was still mussed from sleep. Lorna thought he looked wonderful, a bit rumpled and windblown. Comparing him now with the image of tense perfection he'd presented yesterday in the hotel hallway, she decided she much preferred him delightfully mussed.

Made uneasy by her steady regard, Adam smoothed his hair back with his fingers. "What are you staring at?"

She swallowed a bite of toast and tried to keep from grinning. "You forgot your tie."

"I was in a hurry." He sounded deliciously defensive.

Naughty Lorna took over. "You should forget your tie more often. You look like a rumpled bed. It's very sexy."

He gulped down the bite of egg he was chewing and pointed his fork at her. "I want you to behave yourself."

She looked at him from under her lashes. "Do you, Adam? Do you *really* want that from me?" She shook her head. "I don't think so." He glared at her. She tipped her head, still studying him, and then she heard herself say,

"Adam, the...situation's been reevaluated. It's been decided that you're welcome to come along with me if you want to."

He was looking at her through narrowed eyes. "Reevaluated? By whom?"

"Who doesn't matter." Lorna could hardly believe she was doing this. But, the more she thought about Astrid's convoluted reasoning, the more that reasoning made sense. Adam Gantry needed a crash course in lightening up. Lorna Smith was making progress with him. In six more days, she just knew she could work wonders. He'd come so far already.

"Lorna, this is insane. Come along with you *where*?" he was demanding.

She let the silence stretch out before answering. "On my vacation, of course."

"Tell me the truth."

"I can only say that it'll all be over within a week."

"A week?" He uttered the word as if she'd asked for a lifetime. "I can't afford a week. I have clients who depend on me, responsibilities that I can't possibly put off."

She knew the grin on her face was a cunning one. "You mean maybe Max would have to stop sulking in his room and go back to work if you don't go home?"

"Maxwell Hollander is not sulking. He's devastated."

"So, he could use a little extra work to make him forget his personal problems."

"You have absolutely no comprehension of Maxwell's feelings or my professional circumstances, Lorna. I'll thank you to refrain from making light of them."

She popped the final piece of bacon in her mouth, and pushed her plate away, sighing airily. "Of course it's up to you. I certainly can't force you to come with me."

"Just tell me here and now where I can find Astrid."

"But, Adam, I have no idea." And it was true. At least until Saturday.

He ran his hand again through his adorably mussed hair. "I'm tired, Lorna, very tired."

"I know. Because you never sleep." She looked up from under her lashes. "But you slept with me, didn't you? If I hadn't been foolish enough to set that alarm, you'd still be sleeping."

"I'm not talking about *that* kind of tired," he insisted.

"But what other kind of tired is there?"

"There are a hundred other kinds of tired." His voice, usually so low and controlled, was getting louder. "Tired of being led across the country by two loony women. Tired of being made a fool of. Tired of being *lied* to. Tired of being totally and completely in the dark as to what the hell is going on!" He was on his feet, pounding his fist on the table, before he caught himself. "I have had it, Lorna! Up to here!"

From the counter, Vonda Rae stared. Her boyfriend applauded.

"That's tellin' her, man!" The boyfriend cheered.

"Earl, you hush up," hissed Vonda Rae.

Adam glanced over his shoulder at Earl, who stuck a hammy fist in the air in a gesture of encouragement.

"Thank you," Adam said gravely.

Earl nodded and lit up a cigarette.

Adam sat down. He pushed his half-finished breakfast away. "My appetite has disappeared."

Lorna wanted to reach across the table and touch him— a soothing touch. But she held herself back, because she knew the last thing he wanted right then was to be touched by her.

After he'd been staring morosely at his congealing eggs for several seconds, Lorna realized some kind of action was called for. She stood up.

Immediately, his gaze pinned her. "Where are you going?"

She tossed some money on the table, including a generous tip for Vonda Rae. "Back to the motel." She restrained herself from asking if he was coming, betting that he wasn't ready to let his only clue to Astrid escape, no matter how fed up he was with the situation.

Adam watched her go. Then he asked the waitress for more tomato juice and carried the glass over to the phone on the wall.

He reached Manny McGill at home, still in bed. Manny and Adam had attended high school together. Adam had used Manny's detective agency more than once in the process of preparing a case.

"Anything you can come up with, Manny," he said after he'd given him the information from the business card as well as Lorna's home address. "This one's personal, and I need it soon. I'll call you. Tomorrow, or as soon as I get the chance."

"I'll do what I can," Manny promised.

Lorna was sitting beneath the tasseled swag lamp at the little round table in the corner, poring over her map, when she heard Adam's key in the lock.

He closed the door quietly and came up behind her.

"Where are we going next?" he asked. He didn't sound too happy, but the words were the ones she'd been longing to hear.

Relief—and excitement—flooded through her. She didn't bother to restrain herself anymore. She jumped up and threw her arms around him. "Oh, Adam. We're going to have such a good time. Just you wait and see."

Reflexively, his arms went around her and he hugged her in return, but only for a moment. Then his hands were at her waist, setting her back so he could look at her. "You really do behave as if this is nothing more than a crazy, impromptu vacation." He was eyeing her with obvious suspicion.

"But that's exactly what it is," she answered, utterly ingenuous.

He grunted in disbelief and dropped his hands from her waist. Then he snared up his tie and went to the vanity mirror to put it on. "I'm going to need to stop and buy a few things." He watched her watching him in the mirror as he efficiently looped and knotted the tie. "This shirt is a disgrace and my suit needs cleaning. And here at the Super Duper Motel, they've never heard of a concierge."

"Mr. Impeccable," she mused fondly.

"What did you say?" He was brushing his hair with a brush from the little emergency overnight case he'd brought in from his car.

"Er, I said that's do-able."

"Do we still have to be in New Mexico by noon?"

Quickly, Lorna calculated. The distance chart on the map said they were a little over a thousand miles from their Saturday destination, if they were to take Highway 40 straight through. But, of course, she planned on several detours.

Random detours. Into delightfully off-the-beaten-path locations.

"Plans have changed. We need to be near Albuquerque by evening," she improvised.

"Plans are always changing," he muttered dryly. "As if you were making them up as you go along."

"You've found me out," she replied with mock remorse. Then she bent over the map spread out on the table. They were two hundred and fifty miles from Albuquerque. They had plenty of time to reach there by evening, and enjoy the sights along the way.

Done making himself as impeccable as possible under the circumstances, Adam said, "I'll call my office from the car. Let's go."

Adam drove in silence as they left Winslow behind. To her few attempts at conversation, he grunted or gave terse answers. Lorna quickly decided she wasn't going to let him get away with this for the whole drive. Her assignment, as both she and Astrid saw it, was to get him to lighten up. So she soon began casting about for ways to accomplish her objective.

At Holbrook, when they'd been on the road for about half an hour, Lorna had him pull off at a roadside dairy stand. Adam declined to follow her inside, apparently reasoning that she wouldn't be ditching him in the middle of the desert when she could have so easily escaped him in Winslow.

She bought two Fudgie Bars—a decadent concoction of vanilla ice cream, fudge syrup and fudge topping speckled with nuts, all stuck on a stick and guaranteed to elevate the blood sugar and expand the waistline. Remaining obstinately cheerful, she bounced back out to the car, slid into her seat and held one out for Adam, who was already turning the key in the ignition.

"What is *that*?" He looked at the ice cream bar as if she planned to poison him with it.

"Fudgie Bar." She bit into hers, sighing voluptuously.

"No, thank you," he said, as she continued to hold his out for him. He started to shift the car into reverse.

"Suit yourself." She shrugged, and laid his bar, still wrapped, on the little pull-out cup holder beneath the dashboard.

"It'll melt there," he said.

"I'll take care of it in a minute," she said between slurps.

Lorna realized with an internal smirk of satisfaction that he seemed momentarily to have forgotten all about what a hurry he was in to get back on the road where he could go on driving he knew not where in ominous silence. Instead, he watched her with a kind of grim fascination as she continued nibbling at the nutty semisweet fudge crust that encased the layer of snow-white ice cream, and the thick ooze of more fudge beneath that.

"It's not even nine in the morning." The words were disapproving, but the tone was mesmerized.

"But it's so *good*." With her tongue, she licked at the creamy vanilla where she'd revealed it by nibbling off the chocolate.

"But it's not good *for* you." He sounded like he was trying to convince himself, even more than her.

She looked at him, steadily, as she continued to lick the melting confection. She was thinking how sexy green eyes could be, and how the person she'd been two days ago would never have indulged in anything so debauched as a Fudgie Bar.

"Adam." She stroked her tongue up the stick, where a dribble of vanilla had almost escaped. "Life is all about balance."

He blinked, then tried to assume a superior air, though the huskiness of his voice betrayed him a little. "What do *you* know about balance?"

"I'm learning. Every day." She picked up his Fudgie Bar again and waved it tantalizingly at him. "Have you ever even eaten a Fudgie Bar?"

"No, and I never will." He didn't sound terribly convincing.

"How sad for you. You're missing one of the premiere experiences of life." She took her attention from her own bar and peeled back the wrapper on his very delicately, with her teeth.

He shook his head, slowly, like a man spellbound by a sinuous snake. "I'm not going to eat that."

Her lips curled upward and she leaned across the console toward him. "Say that like you mean it."

He looked down at her, and the hunger in his eyes had nothing to do with a craving for ice cream. "I'm not going to kiss you, either," he said, the words seeming to drop from his lips of their own volition.

"Um. Just like you weren't going to kiss me back in the parking garage in Palm Springs."

"That thing is melting."

"Then lick it."

He did. "You have to start learning to consider the consequences of your actions," he said as soon as the ice cream no longer endangered his slacks.

"Oh, but I have. I am. Come on, Adam. Another bite." He did as instructed, while she polished off the last of her own bar. "Your mother tells me you're obsessed with physical fitness," she said as she continued to feed him.

"My mother's entitled to her opinion." The engine was still running, so he fumbled for the power window switch.

"What are you doing?" she asked.

He took her stick and the remains of his ice cream bar and tossed them neatly out his open window into a waste can by the car door. "There," he said, turning back to her. "That takes care of that."

"Oh, well," she gave in gracefully and began pulling back to her side of the car. "At least I got you to take a little taste."

"Wait." He held on to her elbow.

"What?"

"You've got chocolate..." He took his handkerchief from his pocket and dabbed at the corner of her lip. "There."

Lord, she wanted to stretch just the little distance it would take for her lips to meet his. But in the moment it had taken him to dispose of the sweet treats, she'd decided she wasn't going to throw herself at the poor man again. He'd begin to think her insatiable. For this magical week, she might be wild and free. But she was stopping short of insatiable or heaven knew what might transpire.

Adam seemed to have forgotten that there was no need to keep holding on to her arm, now that he'd so considerately dabbed the bit of chocolate from her mouth.

"Thank you," she said and tugged lightly, to remind him that he could let her go now.

He held on, gently. She could have broken his grasp if she'd wanted.

But she didn't. "Adam—"

"I'm not going to kiss you," he said, each word slow, husky, and deliberate.

"I think you told me that already."

"We're going to be in close proximity for a week."

"That's right."

"Boundaries have to be set. Limits maintained."

She tried a little smile. "Okay. No more Fudgie Bars, I promise."

"I'm not talking about ice cream."

"Fine. I get the message. You can let go of my arm now."

He held on, and spoke firmly. "I want you to stop teasing me. I don't want to take advantage of you." His expression softened. "I have a feeling you've been taken advantage of too much in your life."

"Don't bet on it," she said, without thinking.

"Go ahead." His voice was tender. "Treat your pain as if it's all a joke. But I know you've been hurt, Lorna. And hurt badly. No woman lives on the run like you are without a reason."

"Well, now," she said. "I won't argue with that."

With the hand that wasn't holding her arm, he smoothed her wild hair back away from her face. Lorna felt her breath stick in her throat. He'd done the very same thing the night before when she'd been sitting on top of him, nude to the waist.

"So beautiful, and so confused," he said, his voice soft as melting ice cream. "I want to help you, Lorna. If you'll let me."

It occurred to Lorna that she'd very much like to be helped by him. Especially if he'd go on stroking her hair in that tender, wonderful way. "Adam, I think . . ." But her voice trailed off as she realized she had no idea at all what she thought.

"Were you mistreated as a child?" he prompted.

She shook her head, and told the truth. "My father sells insurance and my mother's a teacher. I have two sisters, one older, one younger. Both prettier and more popular than I ever was."

He blinked, as if she'd surprised him. "Two sisters," he mused. "Is that so?"

"Yes. We lived in Long Beach, California."

"I see." His tone made her suspicious, though she couldn't quite put her finger on why. It was as if he were correlating information, though how he could do that when he had no information but what she'd given him was beyond her. "Tell me more," he coaxed.

Shrugging off her suspicions, she continued, "My parents still live there. I have a degree in library science from Cal State Long Beach. And I own a bookstore, in Westwood."

His eyes gleamed, briefly. "A bookstore. In Westwood."

"It's the truth," she said, feeling noble.

"I'm sure." The words were bland.

"Is there anything else you'd like to know?" she asked in saccharine tones after a moment.

He didn't miss a beat. "Tell me about the *support group*."

"I told you. It's a group of women who get together every week to share—"

He cut her off. "How did you become involved in it?"

"There was an ad. In the *L.A. Weekly*. I felt there was something missing in my life, a closeness with other women that I'd never found with my mother or my sisters. My mother's kind of undemonstrative, you see. And I never had much in common with my sisters. We weren't close at all. They were both so outgoing and gorgeous. But I was the bookworm—the mousy one."

"The mousy one." He repeated her description softly.

Lorna sighed. "You don't believe a word of this, do you?" He just went on looking at her, measuringly, not even stroking her hair any longer. "I suppose it would fit in better with your idea of me if I said my mother ran a bordello in New Orleans and I went to work there myself at a very tender age. Or if I told you I'm the runaway daughter of one of the Beverly Hills One Hundred, spoiled and indulged until I have no other purpose in my life but where to find the next good time."

"Is that closer to the truth?"

She pulled away from him, then, sharply. "I've told you the truth," she said, staring out the window at the redwood fence that separated the dairy-stand lot from a gas station.

"I guess I just can't see it through all the lies," he said.

Sitting back in her own seat, she turned to him. "By the end of this, you'll know everything. I promise."

"Do you have convincing evidence as to why I should believe your promises?"

Lorna shrugged. "You might as well believe me as not, since you've decided to go with me either way."

"The logic in that argument escapes me completely."

"Because it's not logical. It's just good sense. Why brood and pout all the way across the country, when you could just as well relax and have a good time?"

"I never pout. Is that where we're going? Across the country?"

"Right now let's take that road there." She pointed. "It leads to the Petrified Forest National Park. Or so the sign on the highway said."

Without another word, Adam shifted into reverse and backed out of the dairy stand onto the road she'd indicated. Lorna turned on the radio and punched the digital channel selector, looking for a program to fill the testy silence between herself and Adam. She found a country station that kept fading in and out, but still the wavering signal was better than listening to nothing and feeling the emanating disapproval from the driver's side of the car.

In twenty minutes, they reached the park. Lorna turned off the radio then and exclaimed over the brilliantly colored remains of ancient coniferous trees. Adam grunted occasionally and piloted the car with a kind of dogged determination that cast a dreary pall on all her efforts to have a good time. He followed her through the Rainbow Forest Museum with his hands in his pockets, not saying a word. He refused to even let out one "ooh" or the slightest "ah" over Agate Bridge, a huge petrified log that spanned a forty foot ravine. And though he accompanied her to Newspaper Rock on a 120-step trail down the face of a cliff, he glared at the Indian petroglyphs there as if they, too, were keeping secrets they had no right to conceal.

Lorna tuned back into her country and western station when they merged back onto the main highway at a little past noon.

"Go on straight through to Gallup," she instructed Adam blithely. It was becoming like a contest between them. He refused to crack a smile; she absolutely would not relinquish her good humor. "We can stop and buy you the things you need there." She tossed him a broad, friendly smile. "If that's okay with you, of course."

"Wonderful," he said flatly.

Lorna began tapping rhythm to the music on her bluejeaned thigh, and humming along. She stared out the window at the big, pale sky and the occasional cotton-puff clouds and the red desert that seemed to go on beyond forever, broken only by scrub-brushed hills and high mesas. The flat tablelands fascinated her, thrusting as they did straight up from the desert floor, their sheer sides almost purple where they were shadowed from the bright midday glare.

Adam stopped for gas just before they crossed the New Mexico state line and they reached Gallup before two o'clock. They ate mouthwatering chili at a place called the Ranch Kitchen where the waitresses wore bright gathered skirts and Lorna exclaimed over the beauty of the authentic Navaho rugs hanging on the walls. Adam ate in silence, giving her little more than a nod and a grunt now and then.

He chose an ordinary department store in which to buy his clothes, but Lorna did find it gratifying when he emerged from the dressing room. He was wearing tan jeans, boots and a plaid shirt and carrying several more shirts and jeans in various colors.

"Don't give me that smug look," he muttered, as he added a sheepskin jacket to his pile of new clothes. "If you're going to be dragging me up and down cliff faces to stare at Indian rock paintings, a business suit is totally inappropriate."

"I couldn't agree with you more," she said, knowing full well that she sounded every bit as smug as she looked. Even though he was still scowling, he had to be considerably more comfortable in the casual clothes—and comfortable was good. Comfortable was a plus in the direction of lightening up.

The sales clerk agreeably hung and bagged Adam's much-abused suit. "Tonight," Adam told her as he paid for his new vacation wardrobe, "we stay at a decent hotel where I can get this suit cleaned and pressed."

Some adventure, Lorna thought wryly. Driving around with a stuffed shirt whose major concern is getting his suit cleaned.

They were returning through the store to the car, laden with purchases, when she spotted the sleeping bags on sale in the sporting goods section.

She stopped and set down the bags she was carrying. "Adam, I see something we need."

He followed the direction of her gaze. "No," he said. "Oh, no."

"Oh, Adam. I've always wanted to camp out."

"You said Albuquerque tonight," he accused darkly. "There are plenty of good hotels in Albuquerque."

"I said *near* Albuquerque."

"So? There's no problem. You can go where you have to go and do whatever you have to do and then we can find decent lodgings and get a good night's sleep on actual beds."

"You know you won't sleep anyway," she chided. "So what does it matter whether you don't sleep in some boring hotel room or out beneath a blanket of stars?"

"This is rattlesnake country," he threatened. "And at night it gets cold up in the mountains around Albuquerque. Snakes are attracted to warm, close places. Like a sleeping bag."

"How do you know?" she quizzed suspiciously.

"Astrid's my mother, remember? When I was a kid, she dragged me all over this country. She went through a back-to-nature phase when I was not quite in my teens. We slept out under a *blanket of stars*," he stressed the words ironically, "enough times to last me the rest of my life."

"Good," Lorna enthused. "Then that means you're an expert. We won't have any problems."

"Lorna, why do you always insist on taking what I tell you and twisting it to fit your next harebrained scheme?"

"We have to sleep out, Adam," she told him solemnly.

"Why?"

"Because I'm receiving my next set of instructions sort of out in the middle of nowhere. In the middle of the night."

"*Sort of* out in the middle of nowhere? Where exactly is that?"

"You know I can't tell you," she said. She thought, mainly because I don't know yet.... "Now, watch these bags, will you?"

"Lorna..."

"Be right back."

Eight

"The weather report said a forty percent chance of rain."

"Adam, don't be such a pessimist. There's not a cloud in sight."

"Desert storms can strike almost without warning."

"We're not in the desert anymore, or didn't you notice?"

"In spite of the occasional piñon pine, this is still semi-arid territory. Storms can come and go in a flash."

"Fine. When it starts to rain, we'll get in the car."

"Do you realize how far we drove on unpaved road to get here? We'll be driving back through a quagmire if it rains. My car is hardly an all-terrain vehicle."

"So, it'll be a challenge getting back. Now, I don't want to hear one more word about the weather. Please?"

"Don't ever say I didn't warn you."

"Never. I'll never say that."

"And beyond the threat of thundershowers, this whole escapade has no logic to it whatsoever."

"How so, Adam?"

"Do you actually expect me to believe that someone's meeting you out here in the middle of nowhere?"

"Believe what you like. I'm waiting for . . . a message."

To that, the man on the sleeping bag across the camp fire gave a disbelieving grunt and fell blessedly silent for a time.

Lorna, lying on top of her sleeping bag but under a blanket from the car, sighed in gratitude for the moment of peace and laced her hands behind her head. She stared up at the stars that seemed like holes of light in the black fabric of the sky.

They were camped up against a large rock near the base of a brush-dotted mountain at the end of a nameless road somewhere northwest of Albuquerque. Their fire had burned low between their bedrolls and now Lorna felt the heat from the coals as a lovely warmth on one side of her face.

The fire, like just about any other subject one might care to name, had been a bone of contention between them.

"We don't have a permit," Adam had argued.

"But we haven't seen a soul for miles. We probably don't even *need* a permit," Lorna reasoned back.

"This is the end of the twentieth century, Lorna. You need a fire permit almost everywhere now. And where do you think we're going to get the wood anyway?"

"There was that dead tree by the road aways back."

"You want me to go back there and throw it in the trunk on top of your designer luggage?"

She'd refused to be drawn. "I'll be glad to help you."

So, against Adam's better judgment, they'd had a fire. She'd admired his expertise in building it, using the pieces of wood they gathered from the fallen pine and a few broken-up tumbleweeds for kindling.

"At least the wood isn't wet," he had grumbled when the logs caught and the blaze was crackling away.

As night crept across the mountains and the thin air acquired a bite that soon became a true chill, they'd eaten sandwiches bought before they left the main highway and shared a thermos of steaming tea.

"What kind of message?" Adam prodded from the other sleeping bag, putting an end to Lorna's musing on the hours just past.

Lorna shifted her position a little to avoid a few rocks that were poking her in the back. "Isn't it beautiful out here?"

"What I'm asking is, are we expecting someone?" Adam pressed on.

"Expect . . . the unexpected," Lorna advised.

Adam, who'd been stretched out on top of his sleeping bag, now sat up and wrapped his arms around his knees. Aware of his movements, Lorna rolled to her side, propping her head up on her hand and grinning at him across the red coals of their fire.

"Come on," she said. "This isn't so awful, is it?"

He utterly surprised her by giving her that charming smile that had been so depressingly absent through most of the day. "No, it isn't so awful," he confessed. He tipped his head, thinking.

"You know, I can see Astrid in you when you do that." The words were out before she considered if the mention of his mother would snap him back into surly silence.

But he took no offense. "When I do what?"

"Tip your head like that. Even if you'd never told me your name, I would have figured out you were related eventually because of the similarity when you make that gesture."

"But you knew me the minute I said my name."

"Yes."

"Because Astrid had told you all about me, right?"

"Yes."

"In your *support* group, I suppose."

"Yes. In our *support* group."

"What did she say?"

"Adam, I can't tell you that. What gets said in the group has to be completely confidential, otherwise no one would speak freely."

"I see."

Of course he didn't see. Not at all. And Lorna knew that was mostly her own fault. She looked away for a moment, off to the southeast and the slight glow on the horizon that must be the lights of Albuquerque. When she looked back at him, he was staring into the fire, a funny half smile on his face.

"When I was ten, Astrid took me on my first camping trip."

"Where to?" she prompted softly, pleased by his change to a reflective mood.

"Near L.A. In the Los Padres Forest. It was just as her beatnik phase was coming to an end."

"Astrid had a beatnik phase?" Lorna could hardly picture the bright, bubbly Astrid as having had a beatnik phase.

"You name a phase," Adam said, "and Astrid's had it."

For a moment he said no more, so Lorna asked, "What was it like—your first camping trip?"

"A nightmare."

"Oh, Adam. It couldn't have been that bad."

"No?" He looked up from his contemplation of the fire long enough to meet her eyes. "Do you really want me to tell you what it was like?"

She nodded. "In detail."

"Why?"

"Oh, honestly, Adam. I like you and I like your mother. I'm always interested to learn about people I like."

He granted her another dubious glance, but then he gazed into the red embers of the fire again and began to speak.

"I remember the two of us driving to the edge of the Dick Smith Wilderness. Night was coming. The sky was orange and purple to the west. At twilight, Astrid parked the car by the side of the road and handed me my roll of blankets while she tucked her own up under her arm."

Adam chuckled wryly. "Those blankets were straight off the beds at our apartment," he explained. "I, at least, was wearing tennis shoes and jeans. My mother had on a black minidress, black heels and black tights. You see, she'd decided to go camping more or less on the spur of the moment, as she did just about everything."

One of the logs, burned through, collapsed in the red bed of coals, sending sparks arcing in the air between them. A section of smoldering log rolled beyond the ring of coals. Adam took the stick he'd been using as a poker and pushed it back in among the glowing embers.

"As I said, it was already almost dark by the time we parked the car," he went on. "And she just marched right out into the bushes on the edge of a dry wash. I followed. She walked for over an hour in high heels, her dress and tights getting torn to shreds, but she didn't even mind. She was singing the whole way. Bob Dylan songs. 'Blowin' in the Wind' and 'One Too Many Mornings.' When she finally got too tired to take another step, she just stopped and laid out her blankets on the rocky ground. I stood there beside her. I was so *angry* at her."

"For dragging you out there like that out of nowhere?" Lorna asked.

He grunted. "For that, yes. And for a thousand other reasons. For being different than other guys' moms, for never having meals at regular times, for falling in love with a new man every other day, for creating an aura of excitement around herself where I could never relax from one minute to the next because I was always wondering, *what next?* Where will she drag me off to, what will she say that will embarrass me in front of my friends?—not that I had many friends. We were always moving, always going someplace better that never turned out to be any different than the place before—" He caught himself up short, and his eyes, which had been focused on the past, fixed again on Lorna's face across the fire. "Anyway, when she stopped and laid her blankets on the ground, I was mad."

"And then?"

"She looked at me. And she knew I was furious. She gave this little half shrug and she said, 'Adam, I wish I could be the kind of mother you want. But what I am is the only mother you've got. I'm doing my best, baby. But I'm looking for something. And until I find it, things are always going to be just a little bit up in the air in the Gantry household.'"

"So you came to an understanding?" Lorna asked quietly.

"Not at all," Adam said. "I was still furious. But, as the years went by, I did realize that she always did her best for me. It wasn't easy, especially in those days, for a woman to raise a child on her own. But I was one responsibility that she never tried to shirk." He laughed again, dryly. "Until I was old enough to be on my own, whatever trouble she got into, she took me right along. And yet she never tried to hold on to me, either. I was allowed to stay home alone from sixteen on. And as soon as I turned eighteen, I moved out on my own with her blessing."

"So the point is," Lorna concluded, "that even if Astrid wasn't exactly the mother you might have chosen, she was an excellent one on the whole."

"The point is," Adam amended with an irritatingly superior glance, "that I never forgot what she said on that camping trip. A month ago, when she told me she was going to marry Maxwell, she showed me her ring and she smiled at me in that mysterious little way she does at times—you know the way I mean?"

"I do," Lorna said.

"She said, 'Baby, I think I've found it at last.' And she meant it, Lorna. I know she did. After years of searching, she's found someone she could be happy with for the rest of her life." He stared at Lorna challengingly across the remains of their fire. "And now she's throwing it away."

Lorna gazed back at him, that dangerous ache of tenderness moving within her again. Tenderness mixed with the familiar longing to give him the truth. It would ease his concern for Astrid if he knew she was only making sure that her marriage to Maxwell was the right step. And if he knew the truth about Lorna herself, well, he'd drop her off in Albuquerque in the morning and return to his well-ordered, well-pressed life.

"I suppose—" she sat up and wrapped the blanket around her against the increasing chill in the air "—that this whole thing with me just reminds you unpleasantly of when you were a little boy. Being dragged all over the place without really knowing why."

"It has occurred to me that there are certain similarities," Adam replied.

"How old are you, Adam?"

"Thirty-six." He narrowed his eyes at her suspiciously. "Why?"

"And for the first sixteen years of your life you were at the mercy of Astrid's urge to find herself."

"Yes, that's about right. What are you getting at?"

"That leaves the last twenty years where you've done exactly what you want when you wanted. Where you've had nothing but order and predictability."

"I wouldn't go that far," he cut in, too quickly. "Life is never entirely predictable."

"But in so much as you could make it that way, it *has* been for you?"

"I don't like the direction of this conversation."

"Because you know my conclusion already."

"Then there's no need for you to draw it." He was giving her that jade-eyed glare, hard and impenetrable as rock.

"Balance, Adam," she drawled amiably, once again feeling justified in keeping her secrets for a while longer. "Life is all about balance. And you've been too long in too much control."

For his part, Adam was finding the tenor of this discussion increasingly uncomfortable. "No one can be in too much control of his life." He loathed the defensive tone of his own voice.

"He can if he finds it's turned dry as dust in his hands." Lorna was talking about her own life as much as Adam's.

But Adam had no way of knowing that, and now, with that remark, he realized she'd hit something inside him that recoiled at being touched.

My life is not dry as dust, he said firmly to himself. My life is well ordered. My life is already balanced.

But, for some absurd reason, he kept seeing his closet at home with his rows of shining shoes, arranged by color and wearability on wooden shoe trees—business and dress shoes in front, casual wear behind. He saw the rows of hangers with his suits on them, every hanger hooked over the bar front to back. His shirts were all folded precisely, and his sweaters the same.

"You're so perfect, Adam," a woman he'd dated seriously had told him the year before. *"Too perfect. And completely self-contained. You're a wonderful lover, so I must admit I'll miss that part of our relationship. But, still, there's always been a part of yourself that you've held back. If there's ever going to be someone to break through your reserve, it's not me or I would have succeeded by now...."*

Adam shut out the memory of his ex-lover's words and came back to the present to find himself staring at the fire-flushed face of his mother's secret sister.

Lorna was wrapped in the lap blanket from the car, her hands hugging her knees, so he could see nothing but her naughtily grinning face, the tips of her white boots and all that glorious hair. He thought of how that hair felt, trickling like liquid silk through his hands. He thought of the milky globes of her breasts the night before, when she'd tossed her shirt over her head and driven him almost insane with longing to let go of every shred of reserve and control he'd ever possessed. He'd wanted her to take him inside her, to take him to that place of total abandonment that her every sultry glance had promised since the moment they had met.

Damn you, Lorna Smith, he thought, glaring at her as she grinned back at him. Why, with all of the suitable women that there are in the world, did it have to be a footloose temptress like you who would make me want to lose control?

Lorna stared back at him, wondering what on earth was going through his mind. His glare was hard and hot, sending conflicting messages of both anger and desire. Her nerves tingled in what might have been warning or anticipation. She lost her grin as she gathered the blanket closer about her, suddenly feeling uncertain and vulnerable. Images of the night before flashed through her mind—of Adam's hands in her hair, his lips on hers, of his body so beautiful and strong beneath her as she sat astride his hips.

He'd wanted her, a lot. Only his much-vaunted self-control had kept him from having her. And he could have her any time he wanted, Lorna admitted to herself as she watched him watching her. And if he did ever decide to make love with her all the way, *then* where would she be?

The fantasy Lorna might take such intimate activities in stride. But not the real Lorna Smith. The real Lorna Smith would be bound to him, and she had a sinking feeling the bonds would be much harder to let go of than dealing with Jeffrey's desertion had been.

A shiver skittered up her spine and Lorna drew the blanket even closer about her. Maybe, she thought, she should be grateful that Adam Gantry was such a demon for self-control.

At that moment, Adam tore his gaze from hers and began pulling off his boots and shrugging out of the sheepskin jacket he'd bought during their afternoon's shopping spree.

"I take it this conversation is terminated," Lorna said, trying for lightness, though it came out a little strained.

"I'm turning in," Adam said. "Maybe you'll get lucky and I'll actually fall asleep. Then when your *message* arrives, you won't have to try to keep me from intercepting it."

Lorna decided that the wisest course would be to withhold further comment and follow his lead. She took off her boots and jacket and crawled into her sleeping bag. After a few minutes of fitful wriggling, she managed to arrange herself for a minimum of discomfort around the various pebbles and rocks that kept trying to poke her. Far off, she heard a howling sound—a wild dog or a coyote barking at the sliver of moon. After that, sleep fell upon her like a curtain of night.

In the distance, someone pounded a massive drum. The pounding was intermittent and without any discernible rhythm. In her dreams, Lorna beheld a giant Apache warrior looming over the land, resplendent in war paint and feathers, beating a tom-tom with a huge mallet.

Someone shook her and urged, "Lorna, come on. Wake up. We have to get out of the open."

Lorna grumbled and snuggled farther under the covers, trying again to get comfortable in spite of the rocks in her bed.

"Lorna, come on. It's going to rain."

As if to punctuate those words, the Apache in her dreams hit the tom-tom with all his might.

Lorna groaned, rolled to her back and opened one eye. "Whazzat?" she said.

Adam was looking down at her. "Thunder."

Lorna sat up. It was still dark. Overhead, the stars were being swallowed up as thunderclouds devoured the sky. Billowing and rolling they came, with the speed of a rushing train, obscuring the thin slice of moon until it could barely be seen. Straight bolts of lightning cracked out of the sky to the northwest, followed by the crashing of thunder that Lorna recognized from her dreams. For a moment, as the cobwebs of sleep cleared, Lorna just stared up at the sky. Then she threw her arms out, as if she could embrace all of nature's magnificence in her two slender arms.

"Oh, Adam," she cried. "Isn't it spectacular!"

"Hurry up," Adam ordered. He had his rolled sleeping bag under his arm and was headed toward the car. "We've got five minutes tops and then it'll be pouring rain." He tossed the words over his shoulder at her as he rushed to the car.

Lorna began pulling on her boots, but apparently she wasn't moving fast enough for Adam. After throwing his sleeping bag in the trunk, he charged back to her side.

"Get up."

She did as instructed, jumping on one foot to get the other boot on. With unbelievable speed, he rolled her bag and trotted to the car with it while she stuck her arms in the sleeves of her fringed jacket.

"Adam, a little rain isn't going to kill us," she called out good-naturedly, flipping her tangled hair out from under the collar of the jacket and tipping her face up to the wild, roiling sky.

At that moment, the sky cracked open and a wall of cold water fell on her face. And kept falling. Lorna couldn't believe it. It was as if there were firemen up there with a hose trained on her. She was so stunned by the suddenness and force of the deluge that for several seconds she stood and let it soak her to the skin.

Then Adam grabbed her arm. "Come on." He started running for the car and since he had a firm grip on her elbow, she was dragged right along behind him.

When he reached the vehicle, he yanked open the passenger door and shoved her in. Then he ran around and got in on the driver's side.

Lorna sat in a puddle made by her dripping hair and clothes and stared out the windshield at a wall of water punctuated fitfully by javelins of lightning. Adam started up the engine and turned on the heater.

Then he began taking off his clothes.

He dropped one boot and then the other behind his seat, followed by his tan Levi's and then his plaid shirt. His socks stayed on, apparently because the practical boots he'd bought had kept them dry. Lorna gaped at him, amazed partly at his dexterity in getting out of his clothes in the confined space and partly struck once again by the masculine perfection of his body.

"Get those clothes off," he commanded. "You're soaked to the skin." He'd apparently managed to grab a few things from the trunk, because he reached into the back seat and came up with one pair of his new blue jeans and a new shirt. He then slithered into the jeans by sliding around to face her on the seat and shoving one beautifully formed, rock-hard hairy leg and then the other down inside. He shimmied them up over his briefs and buttoned them quickly. Then he stuck his arms in the shirt, not bothering to button it. He laid an arm across the back of the seat and turned to her.

Lorna, who had pressed herself against the door to give him room to maneuver, realized she was staring at his deep, broad chest framed by his open shirt—and that the chattering sound she kept hearing was her own teeth knocking together.

"I said, get out of those things." He levered himself up, tossing the order over his shoulder as he reached in the back seat. "I got one of your suitcases from the trunk. I hope there's something warm in here," he said.

Teeth still chattering, Lorna cast a glance to the back seat, only to see a froth of lace and satin spilling out of the suitcase in question. He'd chosen the one with her honeymoon lingerie in it.

"What is this?" Adam demanded, disgusted. "A whole suitcase full of underwear?"

"Nightwear," Lorna corrected through clenched teeth. She'd discovered that clenching them kept them from knocking together.

"I'll refrain from comment," he said, shaking his head.

"Do that," she shot back. "There should be a T-shirt or two at the bottom."

He dug around and came up with one. "You can use the blanket, too." As he grasped the blanket she'd been wrapped in earlier, she silently applauded his foresight. He'd remembered to throw it in the cab while stowing her sleeping bag in the trunk.

Blanket and T-shirt in hand, Adam slid back over the seat to the front. "You're still dressed," he accused when he was facing her again. "And you're shaking like a leaf. Strip. Now."

Lorna began peeling off the ruined jacket and then the soaked white shirt. She was down to her lacy bra on top when Adam said gruffly, "Never mind the bra. There's not enough of it to worry about anyway."

He shoved the T-shirt at her, and she pulled it over her head. "Now, give me your feet," he ordered. "One at a time." Numbly, she did as instructed. He took off the soggy white boots and threw them in the back with his, likewise her thin socks. "Your feet are like ice cubes," he muttered. "But we'll deal with them in a minute. First, the pants."

She wriggled out of them, with much less grace, she thought, than he had. With the wet clothes gone and the heater blasting away, she found that her teeth no longer needed to be locked together to keep from chattering.

She giggled, softly, as he reached toward her, engulfing her in the big, warm blanket, draping it over her head for a minute and using it as a towel on her hair.

"You find this all hysterically funny, I take it," he grumbled, scrubbing at her hair with the towel.

"I was just thinking how much better you are at taking off your clothes in a confined space than I am."

"And that's funny?" His golden brows drew together. They were still wet from the rain, as was his hair. He smelled wonderful, she thought. A cool, wet smell of wood smoke and rain and man.

Lorna reached out from the cocoon of blanket. "Your eyebrows are crooked." With her fingers, very lightly, she smoothed them into even wings.

He caught his breath, and she let her hand stroke down over the chiseled planes of his face and neck to the crisp mat of damp hair on his chest. His skin was so warm and resilient beneath the corkscrews of hair, just as she remembered from the night before.

"You're still a little wet here." She let her fingers curl in the whorls of hair. Her voice had that purr in it. She didn't really know how the purr had gotten there, because she wasn't doing it on purpose.

Adam caught her hand. He held it motionless between them and his expression was very still. Very controlled. Then he released her and slowly backed to his side of the car.

Lorna realized at the same time as he did that neither of them was breathing. To the droning of the rain on the car was added the sound of a mutual indrawn breath.

"Give me your foot," he said.

"Adam, I..." she heard herself say. And then she couldn't go on. There were so many ways to go on. *Adam, I want you. Adam, I'm not who you think. Adam, the real me is frightened. Adam, would you... Adam, could you still want me if you knew...*

He interrupted the words she didn't have the courage to utter. "Let me rub your feet. You have to get warm, Lorna," he said with calm logic. "We can't leave here until dawn. Even though the rain will probably stop soon, those dirt roads we have to drive on are going to be a disaster. In daylight, I'll at least be able to see what's coming. And I can't leave the engine on all night. We'll run out of gas."

Hesitantly, she slid around in the seat and lifted her bare feet, swinging them into his lap. His hard thighs beneath the blue jeans were warm as toast.

"You're warm." She said it simply, with no coquetry at all.

A smile, all the more welcome to her because she knew it came unbidden, curled his mouth. "How do you do it?" he mused. He began stroking her feet with his big, strong hands, bringing the blood and the heat back into them.

"Do what?" She was thinking about how lovely it felt as he rubbed her arch and massaged each of her toes, and about how there was a rightness to it. Last night, she'd massaged him. Tonight it was his turn to do the work.

"Sometimes, it's as if you're someone else altogether," he explained.

Lorna swallowed, and almost pulled her foot away. But he held on and continued with that delicious rubbing. "Someone else?" she dared to ask.

"Yes, someone kind of shy. Someone utterly unsure of herself as a woman."

Lorna stared at him. Inside her, a war raged.

Tell him now, one part of her mind commanded.

It'll all be over if you do, another voice inside her head shot back.

His hand felt so wonderful, caressing her foot. The time they'd had together had been so short. And parts of it had been utterly magical. Only a few more days, a time apart. To be the woman she could never be in real life. But the price was continued deception; if she told the truth, most likely the next few days would be ended before they even began.

Lorna quickly shifted her gaze out the window. "Look. You were right. The rain's stopping."

He kneaded the ball of her foot, and she knew he was staring at her quizzically. She said nothing, but kept her gaze out the window. She could feel his shrug through the hands that caressed her foot as he decided not to pursue the mystery of her shier self. She tried to disguise her sigh of relief.

Outside, as quickly as it had come, the storm left them. The rolling clouds rolled on toward Albuquerque, and the sliver of moon shone its bright sideways grin once again.

"Better?" Adam asked as he left off stroking her foot.

Lorna sat up again while Adam buttoned his shirt. "Much." She wrapped the blanket down around her bare feet. "What now?"

"Adjust your seat back all the way, and then I'll turn off the engine. You can try to sleep until dawn."

Lorna pushed the little button and the seat slid to a nearly prone position. She settled herself in, and was aware that Adam, next to her, did the same.

For a time, she lay there, looking through the beads of water on the windshield at the stars and the humpbacked shadows of the mountains that surrounded them.

"Lorna?" Adam's voice in the silence startled her.

"What?"

"What about your message?"

She rolled her head to look at him, and saw in the darkness the gleam of his eyes and the upward curve of his mouth.

She grinned back at him. "It's not morning yet."

He grunted. "Shall I tell you what I think?"

"Why not?"

"I think this whole trip out here was designed to throw me off the scent."

"You do?"

"I think you'll be making a simple phone call when we get to Albuquerque tomorrow and that's where you'll find out where to go next."

Lorna turned her head and stared out the windshield again, saying nothing.

Adam assumed her silence meant he'd guessed right. "Lorna, I want you to tell me something," he said after a moment.

She turned to him again. "Adam, I can't—"

He lifted a hand. "Let me finish." It was his turn to glance away. "Look. I've thought about what you said tonight. And maybe you're right. Maybe there *is* something missing in my life. And maybe it wouldn't hurt me to follow someone else's lead for a few days."

Lorna sat very still, hardly daring to believe what she was hearing.

"There are just three points that would have to be clarified," he went on, turning back to face her at last.

"Yes?" The single word that she tried to make sound neutral came out thick with suppressed hope and excitement. Five more days, she was thinking, of Adam and me and a whole big country to explore!

"One," he said grimly. "I have to know." He pinned her with a look, his eyes boring through her, seeking the unvarnished truth. "Is there anything illegal about this group you and my mother are involved in? Any nefarious activities *whatsoever*—from tax evasion to fraud to... drug running. Whatever. I want the truth, Lorna. And if you lie, I may not know what you're holding back, but I'll be able to sense you're not being honest."

For once she was able to look him right in the eye and not worry if he'd guess all that she wasn't telling. "Nothing, Adam. Nothing illegal at all. I swear to you."

He sighed, and she realized it was a sigh of relief. "I can see you really believe that. So whatever negative activities are going on, you, at least, aren't involved in them purposely."

Lorna made a concerted effort to quell her exasperation. "Adam, I don't only *believe* it, I *know* it."

He waved his hand at her. "All right. We've been going in circles on the subject for two days now, so let's put it to rest for a while. We won't bring it up again until this *vacation*, as you insist on calling it, has come to an end. Agreed?"

"Absolutely." In her mind's eye she was picturing the magical week stretching ahead of them.

"Point number two," he said.

Lorna sat up a little straighter in the laid-back seat. "I'm listening."

"We'll be traveling companions," he explained. "You'll tell me where we're going and I'll get us there without argument. I'll even do my best to be cheerful about it—"

"Wonderful," she couldn't help interjecting.

"But," he said.

"I'm listening."

"Point number three is that we *won't* be lovers."

Lorna felt her face flaming at the directness of his demand. She was glad that the darkness hid her reaction from his sight. "You mean I have to stop trying to seduce you, is that right?"

"There are too many things you're keeping secret from me, Lorna. I could never feel right about myself if I made love with a woman I didn't even know. And it wouldn't be fair to you, either. I hope you can understand that."

"Well." Lorna cleared her throat. A part of her was grateful, because she knew that physical intimacy between them would be terribly dangerous for her. The naughty Lorna, however, was already wondering just how long he could hold to his resolve in the face of sharing every moment with her for the next several days. "Yes, all right," she said at last. "I do understand."

"Bluntly," he reiterated, "I mean no sex."

"No sex. I heard you," she said levelly. "But I want you well rested if you're going to be doing the driving."

"Don't worry, I'll be fine."

"Fine isn't good enough. You have to sleep."

"What are you getting at?" He eyed her warily.

"Turn on the engine and lever these seats out of the way." She tossed back the blanket and bounced over the headrest to the back seat. Then she began tossing all the soggy clothing to the front.

"Lorna, I asked you—"

She hoisted her suitcase of lingerie into her own empty seat. "Put the seats up," she ordered. "And get back here."

He'd turned around and was glaring at her warningly. "Lorna, we just agreed—"

"Oh, stop it. I'm not going to entice you, for heaven's sake. I'm just going to make sure you go to sleep."

"How?"

"We'll sleep together."

"What kind of a solution is that?" He looked at her as if she'd finally gone over the edge.

Disgusted, she planted her hands on her hips as she sat scrunched between the two laid-back seats. "Adam, you fell asleep with me beside you last night. I'm betting you can do it again tonight. I think you *like* sleeping with me."

He shook his head, his eyes accusing.

"Oh, Adam. Why can't you stop thinking everything that isn't logical is immediate cause for suspicion? So you like sleeping with me next to you, so what? Don't analyze it. Just be grateful that for tonight at least you can get some rest."

He tipped his head and she knew she was swaying him.

"Put up the seats, Adam. And get back here with me."

He did as instructed, not saying another word.

Fifteen minutes later, as she lay against his chest listening to the steady beating of his heart and the gentle rhythm of his breathing, she found herself unable to quit thinking of the promise she'd made that they wouldn't be lovers during the days to come.

After all, it's for the best, the real Lorna reassured herself.

But the naughty Lorna wasn't nearly so resigned.

You'll be mine within twenty-four hours, the wayward temptress promised silently, laying her hand possessively over his heart.

Lorna and Adam slogged into Albuquerque at a little past noon the next day. Lorna raised not the slightest objection when Adam checked them into a high-rise luxury hotel. They shared a suite of two bedrooms and a sitting room.

He left her to luxuriate in strawberry bath salts while he found a garage to investigate the strange creaking that had been issuing from the undercarriage of his car ever since they'd hit a particularly deep mud hole on the way back to civilization. While the car was being serviced, Adam placed his call to Manny McGill.

"Sorry, Adam, no dirt," Manny announced. "What we've got here is a nice, straight lady who pays her bills before they're due. The bookstore exists and Lorna Smith owns it. She's got two sisters, three little nephews and one niece. Her parents are Mr. and Mrs. Suburban America. She *is* in a support group with your mother, but it's just that, a bunch of women kibitzing over their problems.

"The only semihot tidbit I could find is that this Lorna just got dumped by her fiancé. But she took her honeymoon anyway. In Palm Springs. Her employees expect her back in a week or so."

"Manny," Adam said, "this woman isn't the marrying kind in the first place. And if she were, you can bet *she'd* be the one to do the dumping." But even as he spoke, he was putting things together, remembering Lorna's suitcase full of honeymoon-style lingerie, her scrubbed-clean face in her driver's license photo, and, when they'd been outside the dairy stand in Arizona, she'd given him her own half-serious description of herself as "mousy."

"So," Manny suggested, "maybe you're dealing with an impostor."

"No," Adam said, thinking of Astrid's skill with make-up and a blow dryer. "I think I've got the real thing here. What I have to figure out now is what I'm going to do about it."

Lorna was all dressed for a night on the town when Adam returned before five. He told her she looked beautiful, said the car was as good as new and then he disappeared for a half an hour into the bathroom on his side of the suite.

He emerged scrubbed and shaved and, best of all, smiling. As he asked, "Where to, now?" Lorna realized he really did intend to uphold his end of the bargain. He'd go where she instructed—and without complaint.

She decided they would explore Old Town, the Spanish heart of thriving, modern Albuquerque. Adam was marvelously agreeable, so they toured the beautiful San Felipe de Neri Church and wandered the shops and galleries of Old Town Plaza. As dark drew on, they ate arroz con pollo in a lovely Mexican restaurant.

"Tired?" she asked him when they emerged from the restaurant.

He smiled at her. "No. Why?"

"I don't know. You seem kind of far away."

"Just thinking." He took her hand, with none of the wariness he usually displayed when he touched her. Enchanted as always by the pleasure just his touch brought her, she curled her fingers in his.

"I suppose you'll want to go dancing," he said.

But she didn't want to go dancing. She just wanted to be alone with him, though she knew such a wish was again tempting fate.

She said, "I don't think so. No dancing. Not tonight."

"The hotel then?"

She nodded. On the way to the car he continued to hold her hand. They drove in silence through the brightly lighted streets, sharing few words during the time Adam parked, or in the elevator, or even after they entered their suite.

The fully stocked wet bar in the sitting room included a complimentary bottle of good champagne, which was chilling in the half icebox beneath the marble counter.

Adam offered her a glass. She nodded, and watched as he expertly popped the cork and poured the fizzy beverage into a pair of crystal flutes. When he handed her her glass, she suddenly thought of Astrid, just three nights ago, proposing a toast to "the new Lorna Smith."

Adam raised his glass. "To you, Lorna Smith," he said in an eerie echo of Astrid's words. "Whoever you are."

He was smiling warmly. There was absolutely no taunt in the salute at all. Yet Lorna felt like crying.

She downed one obligatory swallow of champagne and set her glass down. "I think I'll turn in."

He arched a brow at her. "Alone?"

Lorna cleared her throat. "Well, yes, I mean..." She drew in a breath and ordered herself to stop stammering like a schoolgirl. "You're the one who asked for two bedrooms, remember?"

He waved his hand as if that had been a momentary aberration on his part. "You know I can't sleep without you. And I imagine you'll have me driving all over the country tomorrow. I need to be well rested. For the sake of highway safety." He took a step toward her. She stared at the open collar of his shirt, and the skin of his strong neck. She was thinking how smooth his skin was. And how wonderful to touch.

"I'll help with the driving," she heard herself say.

"But I like to drive." His beautiful, sensual mouth moved softly, tauntingly.

Lorna realized she was leaning toward him. She caught herself, stepping abruptly back. "I'm going to bed, Adam," she said firmly.

He only smiled. "Sleep well, Lorna."

But sleep wouldn't come. Instead, Lorna lay in her bed and wondered what in the world had happened.

Since he'd left her to fix the car in the afternoon, Adam had been behaving strangely. He'd been so sweet and gentle, and so unbelievably agreeable, going along affably with her every whim. And he'd actually seemed to be enjoying himself. She didn't think he was pretending to have a good time at all.

Lorna shivered, though the room wasn't cold.

It was as if, without her knowing exactly when or how, the scales of their relationship had tipped. Something had happened, and now, though she was in complete control of where they went and what they did, she wasn't really in control at all.

There was just something about Adam since this afternoon. Something different. A lack of frustration. As if he were actually letting himself relax—which was just what Lorna was after, so she couldn't see why it made her so nervous.

She sat up in bed.

On edge, and not understanding why, she straightened the silk pajama top that had rucked itself up around her waist. The slinky fabric slid over her skin caressingly, and she felt edgier still.

Lorna switched on the lamp. The room the light revealed was beautifully appointed. The walls were papered in the palest yellow and ecru stripes. The furniture was rich mahogany. The bed linens, of that same ecru and yellow as the walls, enfolded her in the softest, sweetest-smelling cotton and lace. On the polished table that stood before the doors to the small balcony sat a crystal vase of fresh-cut flowers. Lorna had left the glass door open a crack and a slight breeze ruffled the filmy curtains.

It was a room to calm the senses. Yet Lorna was not soothed. She turned off the light, deciding she preferred the soft glow of the city lights beyond the gauze curtains to the brightness of the lamp.

She lay in semidarkness for a moment, and then found herself pushing back the covers and swinging one foot to the carpet.

She was spared deciding what to do next, because the door to the sitting room opened.

Lorna gulped. "Adam?"

"I've changed my mind," he said, his face in shadow, his powerful arms and shoulders outlined in the golden light beyond the open door behind him. He wore the bottoms to a pair of striped pajamas she'd watched him buy the day before.

"About what?" Her voice was low, and seemed to come from outside herself.

"Our agreement." He left the doorway and approached her, his bare feet whispering across the expanse of eggshell-white carpet.

"Oh," she murmured, inadequately. Then, not knowing what else to do, she swung her feet back beneath the covers, making room for him to sit on the edge of the bed. She waited for him to start asking questions again, to demand to know who she was and where Astrid was and what, exactly, was going on.

Lorna let her head drop backward onto the curving headboard of the graceful sleigh bed. She stared up at the shadowed ceiling. She decided that she was going to tell him everything. Get it all out in the open, just as soon as he asked.

But he said nothing. And then he reached out and she felt the sweet caress of his fingers down the slender length of her neck.

Lorna gasped, softly, and lifted her head to look at him. He held her gaze, as his fingers deftly began unbuttoning her pajama top.

It was then that she understood exactly which part of their agreement he was referring to.

She also realized that she wasn't going to do anything to endanger the magic of this moment. In the end, the truth would catch up with her. But not now, not tonight. . . .

"Are you going to make love with me, Adam?" she heard herself asking as the buttons continued to slip from their holes.

"Yes."

Nine

———

Adam peeled open the front panels of her silky top and Lorna felt the night air on her bare breasts.

"Do you know how beautiful you are?" he said.

"I am?" She looked down at her breasts. They shone like alabaster in the dim light, the nipples hardening with growing arousal.

He chuckled. "You are." She glanced up, and met his eyes again. His gaze was sleepy, full of promise and sweet desire.

He bent his golden head toward her, and he kissed her, at the top swell of one breast.

Her heart, which had been beating very fast, suddenly decelerated in rhythm, as though her blood had thickened, and now flowed through her body with the slow sweetness of honey.

She took his head in her hands, guiding him, reveling in the silky feel of his hair against her palms and through her fingers. His mouth moved slowly downward and then closed on her nipple.

The honey in her veins turned molten and she groaned as he suckled her, first gently and then more insistently, until she felt she had been turned inside out by the hot, increasing demand of his mouth.

Then his lips stopped their magic torment. She clutched his golden head closer, unwilling to let him go. In answer to her sensual plea, his mouth closed on her other breast, and he gave it the same stunningly erotic attention as he had the first.

Her senses reeling in a dance of escalating delight, Lorna moaned aloud. Adam lifted his mouth again from her breast. Stroking his hair, Lorna looked down into his face. His lips were full and moist with pleasuring her.

"You like that," he said, his voice like rough velvet.

"I love it," she purred with total frankness, her hands trailing down to caress his shoulders. Never in her life had she felt this free, this able to respond just as her body and heart commanded. And it was all because she was someone completely different. A magical, new self who was utterly at ease with her own sensuality, a woman who knew how to give and receive pleasure without hesitation or guilt.

Sighing, the pleasure like a voluptuous heaviness swelling every nerve, Lorna let her hands drift down his muscled arms to rest on the yellow coverlet. Then she slid to a prone position among the pillows, arching her back like a cat seeking strokes. "Kiss me there again, Adam," she said.

He chuckled. "You're greedy."

"Yes. I'm greedy for you."

He shifted beside her, lifting his weight enough that he could toss away the pile of sheets and blankets. Boldly staring into his eyes, Lorna toyed with her own hair as it spread and coiled in wayward tendrils on the pillows that cradled her head.

"Please kiss me there again, Adam," she coaxed.

"I will. Soon."

"Promise?"

"I swear it. But first . . ." The way his voice trailed off insinuated much.

Lorna reveled in such insinuations. "Yes. Name it, Adam. Whatever you want."

His glance licked along the entire length of her, from her fanned hair to her bare toes. "Those pajamas are very pretty."

"But?"

"But the top's covering your arms and shoulders. . . ."

"And?"

"The bottom's covering your legs."

Brazenly, she lifted her hips off the bed. "Then take them off of me."

His white teeth flashed as he put both hands on her waist, just above the elastic waistband of the silky pajama bottoms. Lorna gasped, loving the warmth and firmness of his palms against her bare skin.

His thumbs slid beneath the elastic, and then his hands were under there. She lifted herself to help him as the silk whispered down her legs and off the ends of her pointed toes.

"Better?" she asked.

"Much." He was looking at her legs, his gaze caressing them as surely as if he were actually touching her. The skin of her thighs prickled in a wholly hedonistic sensation.

"Now, the top," he said.

Obligingly, she sat up again. He took the collar of the shirt in either hand, and began peeling it back from her shoulders. But he had to get close to do that, his face near hers, his breath warm against her neck.

Brushing her hair out of his way, Lorna turned her head toward him. What happened next stunned her with its beauty.

A kiss. Just a meeting of the lips, but a meeting so achingly sweet that Lorna wondered if she'd ever know its likeness again.

He breathed her name against her mouth, she took the breath inside herself. He went on nibbling at her, kissing her, sharing his breath with her as he guided the nightshirt down her arms, and dropped it on the floor.

Then he drew her close, deepening the kiss, and rubbing himself against her in a thoroughly delightful way, so that the crisp hairs on his chest chafed her soft breasts in a delectable torment.

She dropped her head back, breaking the lovely kiss, but losing nothing when his mouth immediately found her neck, the delicate perfection of her collarbone and at last her full breasts once more. She moaned and offered herself up to his lips, writhing with pleasure in his arms.

Soon, her roving hands discovered the elastic that held up his pajama bottoms. With little wordless, hungry urgings, losing the feel of his mouth on her breasts but intent on claiming new ground, she coaxed him to his knees on the bed beside her.

In the shadowed room, there was the sound of a woman's and a man's husky laughter, as she worked his pajamas down over his hard hips and consigned them to the floor next to her own. He had nothing on beneath.

Lorna looked down at him, thinking that every single part of him was just about as perfect as could be.

He was chuckling again. ''What?''

She looked into his slumberous eyes. "Everything. You're perfect." She touched him. It was a totally natural thing to do. "All of you." Her hand closed around him.

Adam groaned, and threw his head back, muttering a short oath under his breath.

Lorna went on exploring him. "You like that?" she asked.

He didn't answer. He didn't have to. By the way he moved to her touch, he was telling her that he was hers to command.

"Adam?"

He growled in his throat in reply.

"Remember the motel room, in Winslow?"

He growled again.

"Remember how I was on top? Do you think we could do that again?"

For a moment, she stopped touching him to look into his face. He took advantage of the moment to carry her backward on top of him, giving her an answer without saying a word. And then he was sliding the little triangle of silk that covered her hips down over her bottom and off to the floor.

She reached for him again, but he stopped her. His eyes had that absolutely still, deep look that she remembered so well from the night before in the mountains, when he had taken her hands in the rain-pelted car and stopped her from touching him.

Only now, everything was changed. He *was* stopping her from touching him—but only because he wanted to touch her.

Which he did. Holding her gaze, he caressed her as she sat astride him, doing to her just what she'd been doing to him. She twisted and bucked above him, lost in the sensual glory of what he did to her, finally throwing her head back and giving in completely to the magic of pure sensation.

Beyond the filmy curtains, the city of Albuquerque glittered like a cache of jewels in a desperado's pocket. But inside the darkened room, there was only a woman and a man.

When at last he felt her complete openness to him, he guided her above him. She sank down upon him, taking him fully into her, and the sound he made at their joining was an echo of hers.

She rose up as he moved wildly beneath her, and she followed the rhythm he set. And he said things—crazy things—into her mouth when she claimed him with a kiss, and into her hair which fell in wild tangles onto his heaving chest.

Wild, it was. For both of them. An emancipation each had sought a lifetime to find. And now, locked in the most ancient dance of all, they approached freedom. The dance had a thousand different cadences. It melted and changed without prelude, so that, at last, neither knew who led and who followed.

While at first she rode him, the time came when he rose up above her and drove into her, hard and fast. And she took every inch of him, crying out rashly for more, holding him to her as his heart beat, reckless and untamed, against her breasts.

The culmination, though, came on a slow build, as they rolled to face each other. There, the rhythm established itself, like slow-rolling thunder, tumbling down from high mountains over a thirsty, waiting land.

Lorna couldn't stop crying his name, over and over, as her release came to her. She clung to him then, tightly, wondering inchoately how she had ever survived without Adam Gantry's arms to hold her and his touch to set her free.

At last, they lay against each other, heart to heart. And Lorna smiled into the darkness. Adam's breath was slow and even. He was fast asleep.

* * *

From then on, they didn't bother with the pretense of separate bedrooms. They would hang out the Do Not Disturb sign wherever they stayed and then immediately proceed to set each other free. Then later, when their passions were thoroughly spent, Lorna would sleep curled against him.

More than once, just before dawn bleached the sky, she would wake, warm in the heat of his body.

This, she would think, is what happiness is. This is love, and thank heaven I've found it at last.

And then she would remember the thousand ways she had deceived him, and long only to have the truth revealed once and for all.

"Adam?" she would whisper, hesitant but determined.

"Go back to sleep." And he would settle her more comfortably against his heart, pressing his lips in the tangled cloud of her hair.

Coward, her conscience would scold. But his arms felt so sheltering around her, and nothing was so wonderful as the feel of his breath against her hair. So she'd surrender to the moment, snuggling closer to him, closing her eyes against the coming dawn.

And then somehow, with daylight, adventure would beckon in the form of the long, leading strip of the highway. They'd snatch a quick breakfast and be on their way.

On Tuesday, just outside of Amarillo, she made Adam stop the car on the shoulder of the highway and then she dragged him across a huge grain field. In the distance, several cows bovinely observed their progress.

Adam argued the whole way that they were probably trespassing, but he too stood in awe when they finally reached their destination: ten upended Cadillacs half-buried nose-down in the rich ploughed-up earth.

Later, they would learn that the nose-down machines were millionaire Stanley Marsh III's pop-art homage to the fifties. But right then, to Lorna, the magical absurdity of the half-submerged cars charmed her utterly. She wasn't sure exactly why. She supposed it was partly the twenty rear wheels hanging in the air, as if the row of old luxury cars had dived from the sky in tandem only to land nose-down in the mud. But mostly, the sight made her think of Astrid, who had set her off on this grand adventure, and whose own Caddy had bit the dust in the desert between Palm Springs and Prescott.

"Oh, Adam, isn't it great?" Lorna breathed reverently.

Adam shook his head. "Only in America," he said. And then he pulled her into his arms, told her she was crazy and kissed her right there for all the cows to see.

"Why, Adam," she said with a sigh when he was finished. "What's happened to you?"

He gazed down at her ruefully. "Something wonderful," he said. "Something absolutely wild."

They spent that night in Amarillo. The next morning, Lorna placed another of her mysterious phone calls and then informed Adam that they were detouring down into Texas.

Wednesday and Thursday, they rode through wide open spaces and wandered the streets of Lubbock and Abilene, cutting across the center of the state to Dallas–Fort Worth and then back up through Wichita Falls. They spent the night there Thursday.

And it was as she lay against Adam in the wee hours, experiencing those nagging pangs of guilt, that it suddenly struck her: six days was a very short time. Though it seemed as if they'd barely begun, their time together was coming to an end.

After a leisurely brunch the next morning, they crossed the Red River and entered Oklahoma, reaching Oklahoma city late Friday afternoon.

"Let's just keep driving," Lorna suggested, her voice sounding too light, almost brittle to her ears. Since the night before, when she had at last admitted that the moment of truth was approaching, she'd had to make a concentrated effort to keep from bursting into tears every time she looked at the map and realized how close they were getting to Hot Springs, Arkansas.

Adam cast her a quick sideways glance, and a warm smile. "Where to?" His window was down, his dark gold hair blown slightly by the wind. He looked tan and relaxed. Fit as ever, but not one bit tense. If her goal had been to get him to lighten up, then she could give herself a big hand for a job well done.

For some reason, though, she didn't feel much like clapping.

"Lorna?" Adam's glance this time was tinged with the beginnings of concern. "Something wrong?"

"No. No, nothing." She looked down rather blindly at the map, and forced her eyes to focus on their route. "Henryetta," she said.

"Who?"

"Oklahoma. Henryetta, Oklahoma. That's where we have to be tonight."

"I've learned never to ask why." Adam smiled at her again, an open, good-humored smile, the kind of smile he had for her all the time since their magic night in Albuquerque. The kind of smile she'd probably never see again after they met up with Astrid and the full truth was revealed.

Our last night, she thought. Tonight.

Suddenly, this moment and every moment of the too-brief hours ahead seemed infinitely precious. Lorna wanted to memorize every second, to imprint each fleeting heart-beat of time on her senses for all the years to come.

She turned to look out her open window. Oklahoma farmlands rolled by, great expanses of new corn and still-green wheat. The air that swirled in to tease her hair and caress her face held the moisture of a land crisscrossed with rivers, so much different than the thin, dry air of the south-western deserts that they'd left behind when they reached the Texas panhandle three days before.

"Beautiful, isn't it?" Adam said, sensing her apprecia-tion.

"I wish it would never end," she said.

Adam said nothing. Lorna dared a sideways glance at him, but the glance told her nothing. He drove with easy concentration, one elbow resting in the open window.

"But it is going to end," she added, though she knew she shouldn't.

He glanced at her, and then took his gaze back to the road. "Did you imagine it wouldn't?"

"I didn't let myself think about it."

"I know."

She felt irritated with him, though she knew it was un-fair. "What's happened to you, anyway?" she heard her-self demanding waspishly. "You're certainly taking this all in stride."

"Isn't that what you wanted?" His tone was infuriat-ingly mild.

"You could at least pretend that you're going to miss me when it's over," she said, sounding like a petulant child and hating herself for it.

"Don't be a brat, Lorna. And stop trying to pick a fight."

"I'm not—"

He glanced at her again, and that was all it took. She admitted to herself that she *was* indeed being a brat and subsided into silence in her seat.

After a time, she said, "We're going out tonight, Adam."

He chuckled. "For a wild night on the town in Henryetta, Oklahoma?"

"Exactly. I'm getting a major message in Henryetta's hottest night spot."

"I see." He sounded very tolerant. Very patient. And why shouldn't he? He'd waited almost a week, and now the truth he'd bargained for would finally be his. He could wait a little longer with ease and grace.

A frantic recklessness assailed her. "It's going to be our last night together, Adam."

"Oh, is it?"

"Yes. And I'm going to do my very best to make sure that you never forget it."

The night spot that Lorna chose was only a few miles from their motel. She'd found it by asking their waitress at Ken's Pizza about Henryetta nightlife when Adam had gone to the rest room.

"You mean like a club?" the waitress had quizzed in that soft friendly twang of the native Oklahoman.

When Lorna had assured her that a club was exactly what she meant, the waitress had given her directions.

The Clubhouse, as the sign out front proclaimed, was surrounded by a parking lot bursting with cars. The building itself looked like nothing so much as a huge gray barn, complete with rounded roof and clapboard walls.

"This isn't bad at all," Adam murmured after paying the cover charge and leading her to one of the tables against the wall. Lorna said nothing in response to that, but his implication didn't escape her. Since he'd known her mood was rash, he'd probably expected some sort of honky-tonk dive.

He glanced approvingly at the two burly uniformed security guards near the door. Lorna knew what he was thinking: if there was going to be trouble in Henryetta, Oklahoma tonight, it wasn't likely to happen at The Clubhouse.

A cocktail waitress came by and Adam looked at Lorna. She shrugged. "A beer." He asked for one, too. The cool, long-necked bottles came and Lorna and Adam sat just sipping for a while, listening to the fiddle player in the band at the end of the dance floor. Lorna took in the layout of the place, thinking without much enthusiasm of how she was going to have to lose him for a while to receive her latest— and final—"message."

The big room was arranged in a horseshoe shape, with the bar at the toe end, the dance floor in the center, and the band in the heel. She and Adam sat on one side of the "shoe." Across the way were rows of pool tables.

Though she tried to concentrate on her surroundings, Lorna's gaze kept returning to Adam. He was wearing the dressy Western clothes she'd made him buy when she'd dragged him through Luskey's Western Store in Fort Worth. His yoked dress shirt had mother-of-pearl snaps. His smooth weave cowboy hat bore a Mansfield Cutter crease. A silly lump formed in her throat as she thought of the two of them, poring over the hats together, arguing over styles and colors. In the end, he'd bought the hat she liked.

He caught her looking at him.

"Love that hat," she got out over the noise from the band.

He took it off and set it on her hair, winking at her when she had to tip her head up to see him.

The wink almost did her in. It took all the will she possessed not to burst into tears. She realized she had to escape him for a few minutes, to get her emotions back in line.

She slid out of her chair, setting his hat on the table as she went. "Be right back."

"Lorna?" he asked, his voice tinged with apprehension. But she kept moving, leaving the elevated seating area behind and losing herself among the couples on the dance floor.

Not looking back, she ploughed through the dancers, murmuring "excuse me's" right and left as she went.

Lorna emerged from the dance floor and rushed up the few steps to the other side of the room, her eyes brimming with the tears she was determined not to shed. The tears, unfortunately, blurred her vision. That was why she rammed right into two hundred and fifty pounds of pool player just bending over to drop his winning shot.

Unaware of the sudden deathly silence in the immediate vicinity, Lorna tossed off another "excuse me" and tried to forge on. But the pool player grabbed her arm.

"Just a minute there, little lady," he said.

Lorna furiously blinked back the tears and stared up into a narrowed pair of small ice-blue eyes. "I—I'm sorry," she stammered. "I wasn't paying attention."

"You just blew my game." The big man's breath was ninety proof. Lorna realized that though he spoke with deadly clarity, the man was far from sober. He pointed to the felt. "You see that ball there, little lady?"

"You mean the eight ball?"

"That's right." He chose each word very carefully, as if he was talking to someone of minimal IQ. "I was just about to drop that ball, and now, see that man over there?" He pointed to a rangy character across the table, who was leaning against his cue stick and grinning.

Lorna nodded.

"That's Lester. And now Lester is going to get a turn. Lester ain't as good as me, but he's good enough."

"Look, I am really sorry—"

"Let her go." Adam's calm, quiet voice seemed to cut through the air behind her.

The big pool player was looking over her head. "This yours?" he asked, as if Lorna were something that had dropped out of Adam's pocket. "She's real nice to look at, but she needs to learn to pay attention to where she's going."

"I said, let her go."

Lorna whipped her head around to see Adam moving in. His face was utterly, terrifyingly composed. Frantically, she scanned the room for the security guards. One was across the room near the door and looking in the wrong direction. The other was nowhere in sight.

Adam had reached her side. She was sandwiched between the two men. Though the band played on and the dancers on the floor two-stepped merrily along, everyone in the immediate vicinity seemed to be watching with bated breath.

The pool player and Adam stared at each other. Lorna glanced from one hard face to the other.

"Look," she said. "I was in the wrong. Isn't there some friendly way we could settle this?"

The pool player peered down at her. And then back up at Adam. Then his broad face split in a challenging grin.

"Sure," he said. "Let's dance."

"Forget it," Adam said. "Let go of her arm."

"No," Lorna cut in quickly. "Adam, it's all right." She shook off the pool player, who released her since she'd agreed to his terms.

Placatingly, she laid a hand on the front placket of Adam's shirt. "It's okay." She stared up into his expressionless face, willing him to let her handle this herself.

After a moment, he backed away. She felt the collective exhaled breath as everyone nearby realized a fight wasn't in the offing after all.

"All right," she said to the pool player. "Let's dance." She walked ahead of him out to the floor, thinking it wouldn't be so bad to stand a foot away from him and gyrate to the music the way most of the other dancers were doing.

Unfortunately, a slow number started up the minute they reached the floor. Lorna was immediately hauled against a barrel chest by a pair of beefy arms.

"By the way, I'm Del Dearborn."

She craned her neck to look up at his heavy face—the action was also an attempt to keep a reasonable space between his body and hers.

"You mean Del as in Delbert?" she asked sweetly.

His wiry brows furrowed. "I'll let it pass this time, pretty lady, for you. But I'm warning you now. Nobody—but *nobody* calls this old boy Delbert." He yanked her close again and exhaled the threat against her ear. She was once again reminded that he wasn't entirely sober. "What's a gorgeous thing like you doing with a weekend cowboy like that?"

Lorna had the urge to stick two fingers in Delbert's beady little eyes and stomp on his arches. Instead, she murmured sweetly, "He's not what you think at all. Actually, I'm his prisoner."

"His *what*?" Delbert blessedly pulled back for a moment, long enough to scowl down at her disbelievingly.

"I'm his prisoner. He's on the trail of Astrid Gantry. And I'm his only lead."

"Who's Astrid Gantry?"

Lorna scoffed. "You never heard of Astrid Gantry?"

"Sure, I heard of him," Delbert muttered defensively. "I got a TV, you know." He yanked Lorna back against his chest. "But I don't believe you for a second, little lady. You're just havin' you some fun at this old boy's expense."

His huge hand was rubbing her back through her thin camisole top. Lorna tried to bear with that, but when his hands slipped to the pocket stitching on her skin-tight black jeans, she drawled, "One inch lower, and you'll be shooting pool one-handed, Del."

Mercifully, his hand roamed back to where it belonged. "How 'bout you and me, we ditch that guy you came with and have us some fun?" he whispered suggestively in her ear.

The dance ended. "No, thanks," she said. She whirled neatly out of his arms—and into Adam's, who had been waiting on the edge of the floor.

They danced in silence for a while and Lorna clung to him, aware from the stiffness of his body that he wasn't entirely happy with her, but grateful for his clean scent and the firm strength in his arms.

Once or twice she tipped her head to glance up at his face, appealingly, she hoped. But beneath the shadow of his hat brim his expression remained stoic. She was just about to suggest that they depart The Clubhouse and return to the motel when a beefy hand tapped Adam on the shoulder.

Del Dearborn had not surrendered the field. "Mind if I cut in?" he said, in a pushy mockery of courtliness.

"Yes," was all Adam said. He went on dancing.

"I asked real polite-like." Del's hand closed over Adam's shoulder.

"I suggest you remove your hand," Adam said. He'd stopped dancing, and so had most of the couples nearby.

"Where you from?" sneered the pool player. "Yale? And where'd you get this fancy hat?" He whipped the hat that Lorna loved off of Adam's gold head.

"Delbert!" Lorna cried, unable to contain herself. "You give that back!"

"What'd you call me?" Delbert turned on Lorna.

"Stay out of it, Lorna," Adam ordered.

"I will not. He's a bully. And he's not going to get away with it!"

"I warned you not to call me that, little lady." The music played on, but most of the dancers were still.

Lorna planted her hands on her hips. "Delbert," she said, "Give that hat back this minute!"

"Better do it, Del," one of the unmoving dancers advised. "That lady sounds serious."

Delbert dropped the hat on the floor and stomped on it.

Lorna saw red. With an exclamation of total frustration, she leaped at the big pool player. She never made it, though, because Adam stepped in front of her and neatly decked the giant with a hook to the jaw.

The rest was total confusion. When Delbert dropped among the dancers, he didn't go down alone. He was like a massive tree falling in a forest, taking everything in his way down with him. Suddenly, in the tight press, everybody had a punch to throw. All the men jumped to the defense of their ladies and everyone thought the next guy was out to get him.

It was a brawl, pure and simple. A free-for-all that the two security guards could no more quell immediately than Noah could stop the flood. As fists flew and bodies reeled around her, Lorna had only one thought: the hat that they'd chosen together. That precious hat that he'd bought to please her. Adam wasn't going to lose his hat!

She kept her eyes on it, through the milling press of bodies, as boots and high heels unheedingly kicked and pummeled it toward the edge of the dance floor.

Adam had a hold of her arm. "Damn it, Lorna, let's get out of here...." He was trying to pull her in the wrong direction.

She shrugged him off and dived for the hat. Her hand closed around the brim as Adam caught her again, yanked her up just before an alligator boot came down on her arm, and hauled her backward through the throng.

Ducking flying chairs and dodging wild punches, he dragged her behind him up to the raised level by the bar and into the hall beneath the sign that said Rest Rooms. She dared one last glance at the room as they left it. Delbert Dearborn, sporting a bloody nose and the beginnings of a black eye, was being held firmly between the two burly guards. Gratifyingly, he looked as if he'd had enough of picking fights for the night.

Adam tugged her right past the rest rooms to the end of the hall and the emergency exit there. He shoved at the red bar, cursing under his breath when the alarm went off.

Together, they ran into the cool, moist night air, pounding through the rows of cars to the waiting Chrysler. Adam unlocked her door, shoved her inside and leaped the hood to his side.

She reached across and had his door open for him before he got there. He started up the engine and backed out.

Miraculously, Adam got them out of the parking lot without incident. Lorna held her breath the whole time, because the other drivers who'd somehow also managed to escape the fracas were zipping out of spaces with no awareness of what might be behind them. To Lorna, for that heart-stopping few minutes, the parking lot seemed like a giant game of bumper cars played for real.

But soon they were back on the short strip of highway that led to their motel, and shortly after that, the Chrysler was sliding into the parking space near their room.

The car seemed eerily silent when Adam turned off the engine.

"We're lucky we weren't invited to spend the night in the local jail," Adam said after a moment.

"I know." Lorna looked down at the cowboy hat, still clutched in her hands. It was smashed flat and covered with dirty boot prints. The unwelcome tears rose in her throat again, pushing for release.

"I suppose you're going to tell me you received your next set of instructions during the scuffle," Adam suggested blandly.

She forced herself to look at him, feeling the tears pooling in her eyes and willing them not to well over and disgrace her completely.

"No, Adam. I'm not going to tell you that."

"So you've got to make a phone call?"

"No."

For a moment, he just looked at her. Then he asked, "Are you trying to tell me something, at last?"

Lorna kept her chin defiantly high. "Yes. There were no instructions to get in the first place."

There was another silence, an awful one. Then he asked carefully, "What do you mean?"

Lorna dragged in a painful breath and told the truth. "I made them up. All of them. Since Astrid's phone call at the Boca Grande Café in Winslow last Sunday morning."

Ten

———

Saying nothing, Adam got out of the car and took her into their room. Lorna sat in a chair at the foot of the bed and told him everything, from the humiliation of Jeffrey's desertion, through her transformation at Astrid's hands, to the misunderstanding about the man she'd kissed in the hallway, and on and on. The deceptions, as she revealed them, seemed never-ending.

Adam sat, unspeaking, in the chair at the small table. Lorna found it impossible to really look at him as deceit upon deceit came to light. She stared instead at a watercolor print over the bed. It was a winter scene of leafless, skeletal trees reaching toward a pewter sky. In the frozen stream beneath the trees, a white-tailed doe attempted to drink.

In its stark way, the picture was lovely, Lorna thought. Not bad at all for a modest motel room in Henryetta, Oklahoma. But though she couldn't stop staring at the picture, she knew that she hated it. The doe looked so cold and lost in its frozen winter world. Like Lorna's own heart, which had basked for a while in the warmth of spring, only to find, too soon, that the winter of cold truth was upon her.

When she was finished, Lorna forced herself to look at Adam.

"That's all of it?" he asked.

Lorna nodded.

The lamp over the table was on, shedding a halo of light on Adam's hair, but shadowing his eyes so it was impossible for her to tell what he was thinking. Lorna realized she was shredding the tissue she held clutched in her hands, so she set it on the low dresser beside her, next to her open suitcase.

"We're meeting my mother tomorrow, then?" he said.

"Yes. Noon. In front of the post office. In Hot Springs—"

"It's okay. I heard you the first time."

"It's true." She looked straight at him, earnestly, and then down at her empty hands. "But I guess I haven't given you much reason to believe anything I say."

"But I do believe you," he said.

"You do?" She knew she should feel relief, but all she could think of was that he'd never forgive her now that he knew how she'd duped him.

He was nodding. "It makes perfect sense when I put it all together."

"Oh," she said in a small voice, vaguely bewildered because he wasn't responding at all the way she'd expected him to. He didn't seem all that angry, for one thing. And he was having no problem accepting the idea that wild Lorna Smith was, in reality, a jilted little mouse who peddled books for a living.

"When you put *what* all together?" she asked, after watching him apprehensively for a moment.

He looked away and cleared his throat. "All right," he said. "You're not the only one with confessing to do. The truth is that I went through your purse in Winslow. And I called a detective I know and had him check you out. When I went to fix the car in Albuquerque, I checked in with him and he told me all about you."

Unbidden, a vivid image flashed through Lorna's mind. She saw herself, writhing on soft cotton sheets in their Albuquerque hotel room, begging Adam to kiss her breasts once more. She had felt then, as all the nights since, like some erotic enchantress.

"You knew?" Her voice came out a weak whisper. Her magical dream of herself as a sensual siren was evaporating in the harsh light of reality. "You knew since Albuquerque who I really was? But you let me go on thinking you just couldn't resist me?"

"Lorna..." His eyes, she could see now, were gentle. Kind. Of course he wasn't angry with her. He felt sorry for her. He probably had felt that way the whole time. "You were enjoying yourself so much. And as soon as I was sure that there was nothing sinister going on with that support group, I didn't see any harm in playing along with your game."

"Even to the extent of making love with me under false pretenses?" Lorna could barely get the question out.

"My pretenses," he reminded her gently, "were no more false than yours."

She had to admit he was right. He, at least, hadn't been pretending to be someone he wasn't. And then there was the fact that she'd so relentlessly thrown herself at him. Once he'd seen through the glitter to the gray mouse beneath, he'd no doubt felt the most graceful way to behave under the circumstances would be to go ahead and indulge her fantasies.

"Lorna, you *did* want to make love with me," he said, echoing her own thoughts. "And when I finally knew who you really were, I didn't see any reason why I had to go on turning you down."

Lorna stood up. She went to the window and looked out through the miniblinds at the night-lighted pool. "I see. It was like a kindness," she said, her back to him. "A kindness to a lady who needed to feel desired."

"It most certainly was not," he said. She heard him approaching behind her.

She turned, quickly, and put up a warding-off hand. He stopped in his tracks, showing her his palms.

"Okay," he said. "I won't touch you. But I can't allow you to believe I made love to you for any other reason than that I wanted to. Very much."

Lorna thought of all the times he had loved her. Of all the crazy things he'd whispered in her ear through all the wonderful nights of their magical week. Surely he was telling the truth now. No man could pretend to be as aroused by a woman as he had seemed to be by her.

But what, on the other hand, did Lorna Smith really know about men and what they were capable of pretending to feel? There hadn't been many in her life, and she'd always said she didn't understand them one bit.

Witness Jeffrey. She'd been so sure he was the ideal man for her. And he'd seemed to feel the same way—right up until he'd dumped her. And if she couldn't hold a rather shy, unassuming accountant, what had possessed her to imagine she could keep a man like Adam Gantry?

Adam was so handsome. So intelligent. So perfect. So totally beyond what a woman like herself could ever dream of holding. The fantasy Lorna might have wanted him and enchanted him and claimed him for her own. But the fantasy was over; reality had to be faced.

There was absolutely no point, Lorna decided then, in pursuing this subject any further. She'd deceived him; he'd misled her. Their time together would end tomorrow at noon, and that was all there was to it.

"I'm tired, Adam," she said. "And we should start early in the morning."

He looked at her sympathetically. "I understand. We can hash out the rest of this later, after we've met up with Astrid and wrapped up that whole mess."

"There really isn't much more to say," Lorna told him.

"We'll talk about it later," he insisted quietly. "I realize I invaded your privacy in going through your belongings. And I apologize."

"We were both in the wrong," she said quickly. "Let's just let it go, okay?"

"All right, for now."

There ensued another of those awful silences where he kept looking at her so understandingly that she wanted to scream.

At last she said hesitantly, "I guess I'll go brush my teeth, then."

"Good idea," he replied, and she thought he sounded relieved that this embarrassing conversation was coming to an end. "We should try to get some sleep." But then he just stood there, blocking her way to the other room, looking at her as if he was waiting for her to say something more.

"Excuse me," she murmured.

"Oh, sorry," he said, like a stranger who had accidentally blocked her way on a public street.

He stepped aside. She edged around him and made a beeline for the bathroom door.

Once in there, Lorna brushed her teeth and cleaned her face as fast as she could. It was so unpleasant, after all, having to look at her own lackluster reflection in the mirror. She kept thinking, miserably, that it was all just like the old fairy tale. Midnight had come, and Cinderella was a dreary little nothing once again.

When she emerged from the bathroom, Adam took his turn. Lorna climbed into one of the two double beds. She turned over and buried her head in the blankets when she heard him come back out, praying he'd just climb into the other bed and not decide that anything at all needed to be said about the sudden change in their sleeping arrangements.

But he didn't make it easy on her. She heard the brushing of his bare feet on the carpet as he came to the side of her bed.

"I take it you're trying to tell me something, wrapped in those blankets as if they were armor." His voice was flat.

She tried to go on pretending she was asleep, but it was no use. It was emotional agony, lying there while he stood behind her and waited for her to get up the nerve to reply to his question.

She pushed the covers away from her face and turned her head to look at him. "I'm really tired."

"Are you saying you prefer to sleep alone?"

"Yes." How a single syllable could crack in the middle, she didn't know, but it did.

For a moment she thought he would argue with her and a tiny flame of hope flared in her heart. But then he shrugged, and the weak flame went out.

"All right," he said in that same bland voice. Then he turned away and she heard him pulling down the covers on the other bed.

* * *

The next morning they were on the road by seven. The five-hour drive to Hot Springs seemed never-ending. Confined in a limited space yet with an emotional chasm yawning between them, both Lorna and Adam tacitly retreated behind a painful mutual courtesy.

The green and rolling farmlands of Oklahoma slowly turned to dense Arkansas woods. Lorna commented on the beauty of the hillsides of ferny sumac. Adam agreed; the scenery was lovely.

They left the main highway at Russellville, taking a two-lane road that wove in and out of close-growing trees until they reached Hot Springs, a resort city which wrapped itself around the national park of the same name. The highway they traveled became Park Avenue and then they were passing the famous Tussaud Wax Museum, Park Avenue having flowed into Central.

They came then to Bathhouse Row, where for more than a century travelers had come to take the healing waters of the mineral springs that welled up from deep underground.

"Astrid says my grandmother worked as a masseuse at the Fordyce," Adam said, as they passed a bathhouse of that name.

"Really?" Lorna responded, too brightly. "How interesting."

In no time at all they reached Reserve Avenue. Adam turned left and there was the imposing brick post office. Lorna spotted Astrid immediately. She was standing by Lorna's shining Mercedes, wearing a jewel-green cotton dress, her blond hair gleaming in the noonday sun.

She'd seen Adam's car and was waving blithely with her free hand. Her other hand was twined most companionably with the hand of the tall, distinguished-looking man at her side.

"Is that who I hope it is?" Lorna asked.

"Yes," Adam said. "Maxwell Hollander." He smiled, looking rather abashed. "It appears they managed to work it out between themselves without my help." He cast Lorna a wry glance. "Just as you said they would."

Lorna looked back at him, sure all her love and longing were written plain as day on her scrubbed-clean face. Then she remembered how she must look to him, now she'd finally been honest and admitted who she truly was. She'd scraped her hair back and anchored it with a rubber band, and she hadn't even allowed herself the luxury of lipstick.

"Lorna," he said softly.

She knew he was about to start being kind again. She tore her gaze from his beloved face and pointed out the window.

"There's a parking space. Right there," she said.

As soon as he stopped the car, Lorna jumped out of it. Astrid ran toward her, laughing, pulling Maxwell Hollander along behind. When Lorna and Astrid were face-to-face at last, Astrid froze for a moment, like a beautiful, exotic bird hovering in midair. Her bright emerald glance darted from her son to Lorna and then back again.

"Well," she said, her soft Arkansas drawl more pronounced than ever. "We're all here at last." She turned to Maxwell and smiled, a smile of love and belonging. "Together," she said. "Just as we were meant to be."

Maxwell Hollander looked down at her like he'd like to hustle her off somewhere and prove to her just exactly how together they were. Astrid's smile widened.

Then Astrid was looking at Lorna again, and holding out her arms. Lorna went into them, hugging Astrid and breathing in the exotic, haunting scent of her friend's perfume.

"What's this," the husky voice whispered in her ear. "A little sackcloth and ashes?"

Lorna blinked and pulled back. "Excuse me?" she said, pretending she didn't know what Astrid meant. But of course, she did. She thought huffily, How dare she insinuate that I'm punishing myself?

"Never mind." Astrid's voice was mild. She pressed the keys to the Mercedes into Lorna's palm. Then she turned to her son and hugged him as she had Lorna. "Baby, you look terrific," she said when she let him go. "All rested and tan."

"Thank you, Mother," Adam said good-naturedly.

"I think it's time we had a short family conference." Astrid took Adam's arm. "We'll just take a little walk. Maxwell, keep Lorna company?"

Maxwell gave Lorna a friendly wink. "I'll do my best."

Astrid and Adam strolled off together toward Central Avenue. Lorna tried her best to make polite conversation with Astrid's fiancé as she waited for the other two to return. But in the corner of her eye, she kept seeing her car and thinking of one word: escape.

She needed to get away, off to herself. But she knew she couldn't do it without telling Adam she was going. It was only fair, after all they'd shared, no matter how illusory, that she tell him goodbye at the end. Otherwise, she'd be running away. And Lorna Smith was a straightforward sort of person who never cut and ran.

But that's exactly what you'll be doing, a voice suspiciously like her nagging conscience whispered in her ear, *if you leave without telling him how you really feel for him. If you run out of his life without saying that you love him.*

Say she loved him, out loud? Lorna cringed at the thought. Hadn't she already made a big enough fool of herself, pretending to be someone she wasn't and never would be? It would only serve to compound their mutual embarrassment if she threw herself at him again, this time with protestations of undying love.

"Are you all right?" Maxwell Hollander was asking. "You look a little pale."

Lorna forced a smile. "We got an early start this morning," she excused lamely. "And I didn't get much sleep."

Astrid and Adam came strolling back. "That was quick," Maxwell said.

Adam put on a chastened expression. "There wasn't much to say except, 'I'm sorry, Mother, and I promise to let you run your own life from here on out.'"

"A mother could do worse than to have a son who cares so much," Maxwell pointed out.

"That's what I said," Astrid beamed. "Now what about lunch? There's a great little restaurant called Dad's Place over at the hotel we're staying in."

Lorna could bear it no longer. She *had* to get away. She spoke quickly, without stopping to think how very gauche she was going to sound. "I, um, really need to be on my way."

There was a deadly silence.

Adam said, "What?"

"Back to L.A." Lorna's voice sounded ridiculously weak to her own ears. "It's a long drive."

Adam was looking at her through eyes like green ice. "You're leaving? Just like that?"

Astrid said tactfully, "We'll just leave you two alone for a few minutes."

"No," Adam said. "If Lorna wants to go I would never try to stop her. I've learned my lesson about interfering in other people's lives."

Eleven

Once behind the wheel of her car, Lorna drove with single-minded determination. She did her best to keep her mind a blank, concentrating only on the road before her and on what she could see in her side and rearview mirrors. She tried to completely disengage her emotions, to imagine herself as a machine that knew one thing only: how to drive a car. Cutting off her emotions was imperative, because she knew that as soon as she let herself start to feel again, what she'd be feeling would be pain.

But in spite of all her efforts, she couldn't completely keep the unwelcome images at bay. They rose up tauntingly between herself and the black ribbon of the highway. She'd see again the rocklike set to Adam's jaw as he'd tossed her suitcases into the trunk of her car and slammed the lid. She'd hear his voice. *"That should do it. You've got everything that's yours."*

All except my heart, she'd think, and her throat would close up dangerously. Then she'd swallow and blink and force her traitorous mind back to the job at hand: driving the car.

The Arkansas hills melted into Oklahoma farmlands and then the stands of wheat and corn became the rolling, rich grasslands of the Texas panhandle. Lorna hardly noticed the changing of the land as she raced back the way they had come.

She drove until midnight. Then she realized that her eyes were burning and her hands were stiff from clutching the steering wheel. To push herself farther would have been to endanger herself and other travelers.

Amarillo lay before her, and she stopped there, checking into the first motel she found. She went straight to bed.

And she realized after an hour of punching her pillow and staring at a faint watermark on the ceiling that bed was the worst place in the world for her to be. Somehow, in the space of a week, she'd become like a woman married for fifty years, who'd never slept a night away from her husband.

She couldn't relax without Adam beside her. She missed his warmth against her back, his breath in her hair. She decided, with the first stirring of humor since the truth had been revealed, that Adam Gantry had stolen her heart and in return left her with a bad case of insomnia.

Just before dawn tinted the sky, Lorna gave up on chasing sleep. She rose and took to the road once again. But she didn't get far. Just west of the city, as the sun rose behind her, she came to the ten nose-down Cadillacs in the middle of the field.

And suddenly, all unbidden, she was seeing herself and Adam racing across the ploughed, dark earth. She could hear her own carefree laughter as she towed the balking

Adam along behind, until they stood at the foot of the half-buried cars.

She felt again his arms going round her, and his lips on hers, stealing her breath.

Why Adam, she'd asked him, *what's happened to you?*

Something wonderful, he'd told her, *something absolutely wild....*

Now, alone behind the wheel of her car, Lorna's eyes were brimming. There was no way to stop it. She could barely see the road. Giving in at last to all the emotions she'd been fleeing, Lorna pulled over to the shoulder and burst into tears.

She sat there, sobbing, until a highway patrol car pulled in behind her.

She dried her eyes and blew her nose as a patrolwoman got out of the car and came around to Lorna's side window. At the officer's discreet tap, Lorna rolled the window down.

"Driver's license and registration, please," said the patrolwoman.

Lorna silently handed them over. The woman studied them and passed them back. Then she took off her military-style dark glasses to reveal eyes as blue as Texas skies. "Is there a problem here?"

"Just a minor breakdown, Officer," Lorna managed to say ruefully.

For a moment, the blue eyes studied Lorna keenly. Then she said, "Will you be all right, then?"

"I'll be fine." Lorna forced a tremulous smile.

"You'll have to pull out. No stopping on the shoulder except for emergencies."

"I'll pull out right after you," Lorna said, her gaze wandering once again to the row of half-buried luxury cars.

"Procedure is that you pull out first," the officer instructed.

"Oh. Okay."

The woman intercepted Lorna's glance and laughed. "They're something, aren't they? I drive past them maybe ten times a day sometimes, and they still make me smile."

"Only in America," Lorna said, thinking with a tender pang of Adam.

"Texas, to be specific," drawled the patrolwoman. "Now get that fancy foreign car out on the road where it belongs."

Lorna did as instructed and once she was safely rolling toward Los Angeles again, it occurred to her that the car was too quiet. She turned on the radio and punched buttons until she found a country and western station. She sang along, switching stations when the signal got weak, all the way to Albuquerque, which she reached in the early afternoon.

She pulled into a gas station just east of the city to fuel up and visit the rest room.

"Yuck," she said trenchantly to her bedraggled reflection in the metal mirror over the basin. It was then that she decided to stop in Albuquerque for the night.

And, of course, she knew just the hotel to stay in. And just the suite she wanted.

"That's a two-bedroom suite," the desk clerk reminded her.

"I know," Lorna replied. "But it's my favorite." She granted him a mischievous grin.

"Well, then," he said. "As the lady desires."

"My sentiments exactly," Lorna remarked, reaching for the key.

She went to the pool first, for an invigorating swim. And then she made use of the sauna and steam room. She had a massage, luxuriating in every moment of pounding and pummeling at the hands of an expert.

Then she showered, and fixed her hair and makeup. Finally she donned a fuchsia-pink bustier sundress and matching bolero jacket.

A final twirl before the dressing room mirror told her just what she'd begun to perceive outside of Amarillo. The beautiful woman who smiled naughtily at her in the mirror was as much herself as the serious gray mouse who'd studied library science in college and owned The Book Nook.

There's a siren inside every one of us, Astrid had said. *It's just a matter of bringing her out.*

"And, once she's out, believing she's real," Lorna added to the mirror.

It had never been, as Lorna had assumed, a question of believing in Astrid. The challenge had always been to believe in herself and in all she could be.

Such insights made Lorna realize she was starving. She considered room service and then decided she would enjoy the sounds of other diners talking and laughing around her.

She descended to the restaurant and ordered a cocktail before deciding on what to eat. The drink was something called a Triple Enchantment. Frothy and yellow, it had two paper sombreros on toothpicks sticking out of it, not to mention a pink swizzle stick bearing chunks of maraschino cherries and pineapple.

Lorna savored the foot-high drink slowly, winking once at the man at the next table who promptly dropped his fork. She was considering the wisdom of ordering a second drink when she saw the tall, blond-haired man striding in her direction.

Lorna slurped up the last of her drink, hoping the alcohol content would slow down her heart, which suddenly seemed to be doing calisthenics beneath her bustier dress. And as Adam stalked so resolutely toward her, she decided that a very nice day in Albuquerque had just become perfect.

Because he looked wonderful. His tie was slightly askew and his shirt just a little wrinkled. His eyes were a little red. Of course, he hadn't slept for two nights. But he looked better than a Fudgie Bar, and more intoxicating than a Triple Enchantment.

"My mother called me a damn fool," he said when he reached her side. His gaze devoured her, and Lorna felt her skin tingling. She was remembering how very pleasurable it was to be devoured by Adam Gantry.

"Astrid is so succinct," Lorna said, then added, "I imagine she had a few things to say about me, as well."

Adam snorted. "One or two. But I'll let her tell you herself when you meet in your support group back in L.A."

Lorna took a miniature sombrero from her drink and twirled it between her fingers. "How did you know where to find me?"

"I didn't. It was purely a hunch. The same way Maxwell found my mother."

Lorna stopped twirling the sombrero. "You mean he went to Hot Springs on a hunch?"

Adam nodded. "He knew she was born there, and that she still owns her mother's house out by Lake Ouachita. That's where he found her."

"In her mother's house?"

"Yes."

"How beautiful," Lorna said, twirling her sombrero again and pondering the mysteries of love. Then she asked, "And you're telling me that you had a hunch I'd be here?"

"Yes." Adam looked around and realized that the waiter was hovering nearby, waiting discreetly to learn whether Adam intended to eat or move on. "Let's go to your room."

Lorna considered this suggestion. "If I go with you—"

"It's not a question of if."

"I thought you said you were through interfering in other people's lives."

"I am. Except for your life. I'm going to keep on interfering in your life until—"

"Yes?"

"Until we get it right. If you go with me, what?"

Over the twirling sombrero, she memorized his handsome face. "Never mind. I forgot." And she had, too. Because all she could think of was that Adam was here, again, in Albuquerque with her and that all was at last right with the world.

For endless moments, they stared at each other. Then the waiter said in a thoroughly incongruous east coast accent, "Go with him, already. You can eat anytime."

In spite of the fact that he'd served her no more than one Triple Enchantment, Lorna left that waiter a generous tip.

Outside beyond the balcony, the sun still hovered, hot and orange, above the Rio Grande. The glass door had been left slightly ajar, so the filmy curtains moved in the early-evening breeze.

"We need to talk," Adam said.

"Yes, Adam." Lorna slowly peeled off her bolero jacket and then tossed it onto a side chair.

For a moment, Adam seemed to forget what he was saying as he stared at the gleaming skin of Lorna's shoulders. Then he recollected himself. "There are a thousand things that need to be settled between us. There'll be no more running away from this thing until we've hashed it all out."

"You are so right," Lorna replied, easing off her high-heeled shoes.

"The problem was that I didn't expect you to take my knowing who you really were so hard," Adam said. "In hindsight, of course, I can see just what happened. Since you were insecure after what happened with your ex-fiancé, you assumed that no man would really want you if he knew your real self."

"That's true," Lorna said.

"But you had it all wrong," Adam told her. "I wanted you even more, when I learned about the other aspects of you."

"You did?"

"Yes. The woman I knew first was enchanting and beautiful and exciting to be around. But it's the part of you that you call mousy who gives you depth and gentleness and those haunting secrets behind your eyes. I made love with you because, once I knew all of you, there was no way I could have stopped myself."

"You mean I completely broke down your famous self-control?"

He nodded, looking grim. "Broke it down and stomped on it and hung it out to dry. And then, when you confessed everything in Oklahoma, I realized I was going to have to come clean, too. And the minute I did, I could see the mistake I had made by not telling you sooner. You cut yourself off from me completely. I told myself you needed some time to digest everything. Then in Hot Springs, out of the blue, you announced you were leaving. I couldn't decide whether to strangle you or beg you to stay, so I let you go."

"Poor Adam," she said softly.

"Poor Adam?" he repeated. "Is that all you have to say?"

In answer, she padded over to him on nylon-clad feet and offered him her back, gently sweeping aside the veil of her hair. It was extremely gratifying to hear his sharp intake of breath.

"Would you help me with this zipper?" she asked.

The question hung in the air for a moment. Then the zipper skittered down. She felt the evening breeze on the small of her back and it was her turn to gasp as his index finger skimmed her exposed flesh, starting at her nape and caressing down the length of her spine. "We're getting off the subject," he murmured huskily.

"I disagree," she purred. "I think we're really starting to communicate now."

His finger trailed back up to toy with the short wisps of hair on her neck. "You do, do you?"

"Absolutely. Kiss me there, Adam," she said. And felt the velvety touch of his lips at her nape and then traveling deliciously downward and back up again.

"I love when you do that," she said.

He grasped her waist and pulled her back against him. He breathed into her ear, "You *are* bad."

"Umm." She took his hands and helped them to peel the dress to her waist. And then she laid his palms against the swelling curves beneath her lacy strapless bra. "But only with you."

"Exactly," he said, his voice rough and low, a sound that stroked each of her nerve endings in turn. "That's what drives me crazy."

She slithered around and danced out away from him, laughing with pleasure. Then she unhooked the bit of lace and let the bra fall to the floor.

"You mean like out of control?" she asked.

"I mean like absolutely wild," he said, as he came to her. His hands found her, pushing the dress off her hips and making short work of her panty hose, as well.

And as soon as he had her completely revealed to his sight, she began tugging at his tie. Slowly, sensuously, she snaked it from around his neck and tossed it across the room. Then she unbuttoned his slightly wrinkled shirt, and pushed it off his shoulders. And after that, lingering long about it, she gathered the soft cotton of his undershirt up from beneath his belt, guided it over his muscled rib cage and smoothly pulled it off over his head.

"You're so beautiful, Adam," she said with a sigh as she stepped back to admire the sculpted perfection of his torso and arms. "I guess there's something to be said for discipline, after all."

His appreciative gaze licked over her, showing her her own beauty more clearly than words ever could. "Come back here," he said.

She sighed, opening her arms to him as he brought her close, chest to breast. When his mouth closed over hers, she opened herself without hesitation to the questing entry of his tongue, meeting it with her own, and reveling in the pure eroticism of his tongue stroking hers, and hers stroking back.

The passionate kiss went on and on, as she unbuckled his cordovan belt and slid it through its loops, unhooked his slacks and unzipped his zipper.

In no time at all, they stood nude before each other in the shadowed early evening light.

"No more secrets, Lorna?" he breathed, as he looked at all of her again, from wild, curling hair to slim, fuchsia-tipped toes.

She faced him proudly, glorious in her nakedness and set free by the desire she could see in his eyes. "None, Adam. You know everything now."

He brought her close once more. She moaned as they slid to the thick, soft carpet at the foot of the bed.

He kissed her everywhere. And she, being wild and unashamed, kissed him everywhere right back. Until there was nothing in the darkening room but soft cries of pleasure and husky encouragements, the thrill of an intimate touch and the answering gasp of delight.

Lorna rose up above him, at last, as she loved to do, and poised herself to take him within her. But he stopped her, and he held her with his jade-green gaze and his strong hands at her waist.

"Say it first," he said, his voice deep with his need of her.

She wanted him; her body strained blindly toward his. But still his arms held her slightly away. "Say it, Lorna. Tell me. Now. As you take me inside you. We'll say it together, what we should have said then."

She smiled, with the pleasure and the wonder of it. Slowly, she claimed him and as she did, she said, "I love you, Adam."

And he said, "I love you, Lorna."

And they said it together as their bodies met and mated. Over and over, as true lovers have always done. In mutual surrender to something bigger and grander than either ever is alone.

And then words became impossible as once more they found their freedom, locked tight in the tender bondage of each other's arms.

"Marry me?" he asked simply, when they could both talk again.

"Um, yes, I think I'll do that." She sighed, toying with the crisp hairs on his broad chest.

"You only think?" He lifted his head from the carpet and attempted to glare at her.

She slid up his chest and kissed his chin. "Absolutely, my darling. I'll marry you. Yes."

"That's better." He relaxed again.

She rested her tousled head on his chest and listened with drowsy pleasure to the sound of his heart. "I suppose with Maxwell in Arkansas, you're going to need to go back to that exemplary law firm of yours right away."

"For at least a week or two," he told her. "But then Max has promised to return and I could manage some more time."

Lazily, he reached for the pale yellow comforter on the bed and settled it over the two of them. A pillow conveniently dropped to the carpet with the blanket, and Lorna arranged it under his head.

"How about Palm Springs?" he asked, when they were cozy and warm in their nest on the floor. "You could end up having your honeymoon there, after all."

She shook her head. "We've been there."

"Well, then?"

"I'd like to see the Great Lakes. And meet an Eskimo. And wrestle an alligator in the Florida Keys. And then there's Europe, and China and Australia and—"

"Whoa," he said, laughing. "One country at a time."

"You're right." She planted a light, dewy kiss on his neck. "And it doesn't really matter where we go anyway. As long as we're together." She nibbled on the place she'd kissed, and felt him stirring again beneath the yellow blanket.

"Why, Adam," she murmured, "what's happening to you?"

"Something wonderful," he told her. "Something absolutely wild."

* * * * *

PASSPORT TO ROMANCE
SWEEPSTAKES RULES

1. **HOW TO ENTER:** To enter, you must be the age of majority and complete the official entry form, or print your name, address, telephone number and age on a plain piece of paper and mail to: Passport to Romance, P.O. Box 9056, Buffalo, NY 14269-9056. No mechanically reproduced entries accepted.
2. All entries must be received by the CONTEST CLOSING DATE, DECEMBER 31, 1990 TO BE ELIGIBLE.
3. **THE PRIZES:** There will be ten (10) Grand Prizes awarded, each consisting of a choice of a trip for two people from the following list:
   i) London, England (approximate retail value $5,050 U.S.)
   ii) England, Wales and Scotland (approximate retail value $6,400 U.S.)
   iii) Carribean Cruise (approximate retail value $7,300 U.S.)
   iv) Hawaii (approximate retail value $9,550 U.S.)
   v) Greek Island Cruise in the Mediterranean (approximate retail value $12,250 U.S.)
   vi) France (approximate retail value $7,300 U.S.)
4. Any winner may choose to receive any trip or a cash alternative prize of $5,000.00 U.S. in lieu of the trip.
5. **GENERAL RULES:** Odds of winning depend on number of entries received.
6. A random draw will be made by Nielsen Promotion Services, an independent judging organization, on January 29, 1991, in Buffalo, NY, at 11:30 a.m. from all eligible entries received on or before the Contest Closing Date.
7. Any Canadian entrants who are selected must correctly answer a time-limited, mathematical skill-testing question in order to win.
8. Full contest rules may be obtained by sending a stamped, self-addressed envelope to: "Passport to Romance Rules Request", P.O. Box 9998, Saint John, New Brunswick, Canada E2L 4N4.
9. Quebec residents may submit any litigation respecting the conduct and awarding of a prize in this contest to the Régie des loteries et courses du Québec.
10. Payment of taxes other than air and hotel taxes is the sole responsibility of the winner.
11. Void where prohibited by law.

COUPON BOOKLET OFFER TERMS

To receive your Free travel-savings coupon booklets, complete the mail-in Offer Certificate on the preceeding page, including the necessary number of proofs-of-purchase, and mail to: Passport to Romance, P.O. Box 9057, Buffalo, NY 14269-9057. The coupon booklets include savings on travel-related products such as car rentals, hotels, cruises, flowers and restaurants. Some restrictions apply. The offer is available in the United States and Canada. Requests must be postmarked by January 25, 1991. Only proofs-of-purchase from specially marked "Passport to Romance" Harlequin® or Silhouette® books will be accepted. The offer certificate must accompany your request and may not be reproduced in any manner. Offer void where prohibited or restricted by law. LIMIT FOUR COUPON BOOKLETS PER NAME, FAMILY, GROUP, ORGANIZATION OR ADDRESS. Please allow up to 8 weeks after receipt of order for shipment. Enter quickly as quantities are limited. Unfulfilled mail-in offer requests will receive free Harlequin® or Silhouette® books (not previously available in retail stores), in quantities equal to the number of proofs-of-purchase required for Levels One to Four, as applicable.

OFFICIAL SWEEPSTAKES
ENTRY FORM

Complete and return this Entry Form immediately—the more Entry Forms you submit, the better your chances of winning!
- Entry Forms must be received by **December 31, 1990**
- A random draw will take place on **January 29, 1991**
- Trip must be taken by **December 31, 1991**

3-SD-3-SW

YES, I want to win a PASSPORT TO ROMANCE vacation for two! I understand the prize includes round-trip air fare, accommodation and a daily spending allowance.

Name_____

Address_____

City_____ State_____ Zip_____

Telephone Number_____ Age_____

Return entries to: **PASSPORT TO ROMANCE**, P.O. Box 9056, Buffalo, NY 14269-9056

COUPON BOOKLET/OFFER CERTIFICATE

Item	LEVEL ONE Booklet 1	LEVEL TWO Booklet 1 & 2	LEVEL THREE Booklet 1, 2 & 3	LEVEL FOUR Booklet 1, 2, 3 & 4
Booklet 1 = $100+	$100+	$100+	$100+	$100+
Booklet 2 = $200+		$200+	$200+	$200+
Booklet 3 = $300+			$300+	$300+
Booklet 4 = $400+				$400+
Approximate Total Value of Savings	$100+	$300+	$600+	$1,000+
# of Proofs of Purchase Required	4	6	12	18
Check One				

Name_____

Address_____

City_____ State_____ Zip_____

Return Offer Certificates to: **PASSPORT TO ROMANCE**, P.O. Box 9057, Buffalo, NY 14269-9057

Requests must be postmarked by **January 25, 1991**

ONE PROOF OF PURCHASE

3-SD-3

To collect your free coupon booklet you must include the necessary number of proofs-of-purchase with a properly completed Offer Certificate

See previous page for details

He'd bro...being a cop—he'd replaced discipline with emotion, and gotten involved.

Each day the subtle nuance of her every movement branded itself in his brain. He had a picture frozen in his mind—A.J. with her head bent over her work, dark, thick hair draping her breasts, molding her curves with intimate detail.

He watched her. He wanted her.

"Damn!" Michael scrubbed a hand across his face while the thought of those curves sent heat arrowing straight to his loins.

Why couldn't he relegate her to some dark part of his subconscious and get on with business? Why the hell did her obvious desire to avoid all but essential interaction with him only fuel his need to demolish the wall she'd built?

The wall intended to keep him out.

Because you're crazy about her....

Dear Reader,

Any month with a new Nora Roberts book *has* to be special, and this month is *extra* special, because this book is the first of a wonderful new trilogy. *Hidden Star* begins THE STARS OF MITHRA, three stories about strong heroines, wonderful heroes—and three gems destined to bring them together. The adventure begins for Bailey James with the loss of her memory—and the entrance of coolheaded (well, until he sees *her*) private eye Cade Parris into her life. He wants to believe in her—not to mention love her—but what is she doing with a sackful of cash and a diamond the size of a baby's fist?

It's a month for miniseries, with Marilyn Pappano revisiting her popular SOUTHERN KNIGHTS with *Convincing Jamey*, and Alicia Scott continuing MAXIMILLIAN'S CHILDREN with *MacNamara's Woman*. Not to mention the final installment of Beverly Bird's THE WEDDING RING, *Saving Susannah*, and the second book of Marilyn Tracy's ALMOST, TEXAS miniseries, *Almost a Family*.

Finally, welcome Intimate Moments' newest author, Maggie Price. She's part of our WOMEN TO WATCH cross-line promotion, with each line introducing a brand-new author to you. In *Prime Suspect*, Maggie spins an irresistible tale about a by-the-book detective falling for a suspect, a beautiful criminal profiler who just may be in over her head. As an aside, you might like to know that Maggie herself once worked as a crime analyst for the Oklahoma City police department.

So enjoy all these novels—and then be sure to come back next month for more of the best romance reading around, right here in Silhouette Intimate Moments.

Yours,

[signature]

Senior Editor and Editorial Coordinator

Please address questions and book requests to:
Silhouette Reader Service
U.S.: 3010 Walden Ave., P.O. Box 1325, Buffalo, NY 14269
Canadian: P.O. Box 609, Fort Erie, Ont. L2A 5X3

PRIME
SUSPECT

MAGGIE
PRICE

Published by Silhouette Books
America's Publisher of Contemporary Romance

To Bill Price, for his unwavering support. You opened
your arms and swept me into a life filled with love and
laughter…and even a measure of intrigue. Thank you,
husband, for all that and so much more.

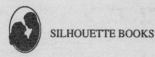 SILHOUETTE BOOKS

ISBN 0-373-07816-1

PRIME SUSPECT

Copyright © 1997 by Margaret Price

MAGGIE PRICE

turned to crime at the age of twenty-two. That's when she went to work at the Oklahoma City Police Department. As a civilian crime analyst, she evaluated suspects' methods of operation during the commission of robberies and sex crimes, and developed profiles on those suspects. During her tenure at OCPD, Maggie stood in lineups, worked on homicide task forces, established procedures for evidence submittal, even posed as the wife of an undercover officer in the investigation of a fortune-teller.

While at OCPD, Maggie stored up enough tales of intrigue, murder and mayhem to keep her at the keyboard for years. This book, the first of those tales, won the Romance Writers of America's prestigious Golden Heart Award for Romantic Suspense.

Maggie invites her readers to contact her at 5208 W. Reno, Suite 350, Oklahoma City, OK 73127-6317.

The Silhouette Spotlight
"Where Passion Lives"

MEET WOMAN TO WATCH Maggie Price

What was your inspiration for *Prime Suspect*?

MP: "As a civilian crime analyst at the Oklahoma City Police Department (OCPD), I often received, prepared and disseminated confidential information. What would happen, I asked myself, if sensitive information disappeared while on my watch? What if it not only disappeared but wound up in the wrong hands? How would I defend myself? When A. J. Duncan sprang from my sub-conscious, proving herself innocent under similar circumstances was one problem she faced. Steely-eyed, by-the-book Lieutenant Michael Ryan was another."

What is it about the Intimate Moments line that appeals to you as a reader and as a writer?

MP: "I want a holdup or a chase...a secret, perhaps. When I settle back with an Intimate Moments, I know I'll find that intriguing thread that weaves its way to a celebration of the fundamental relationship between a man and a woman."

Why is *Prime Suspect* special to you?

MP: "In *Prime Suspect*, my hero and heroine walk the same corridors I walked for two years. And, in a blending of reality and fiction, it was at the OCPD that I also met my own tall, handsome lieutenant."

Any additional information about yourself or your book?

MP: "*Prime Suspect* won a coveted Romance Writers of America Golden Heart award as Best Romantic Suspense for 1996."

Chapter 1

A.J. Duncan drove through the icy November dusk, the apprehension holding her in its grip deepening with every mile. Ten days ago the grim-faced police chaplain had broken the devastating news of her brother's line-of-duty death. Since then, the outer world had appeared unfocused and unreal, like something viewed through a pool of water.

The needles of dread that now pricked her skin were all too real.

Tightening her gloved hands around the steering wheel, she took a deep breath, then exhaled slowly. She had only a few more minutes to get her emotions under control. A glance at the department memo on the seat beside her heightened the sick feeling in her stomach. A uniformed officer had delivered the summons as she locked the door to the Crime Analysis Unit after her first day back at work. *Report to Internal Affairs.* Below the computer-generated sentence, Sgt. Michael Ryan had signed his name in precise, angular letters.

Internal Affairs. Cops investigating cops. The feeling of dread settled into a hard knot in her chest. God, there was no avoiding what lay ahead, no getting around the awesome power that Ryan's unit yielded.

The sprawling brick structure housing the Oklahoma City police department's training, personnel and internal affairs divisions came into view just as the clock on the dash glowed 5:30. A.J. nosed her red Miata into the ice-glazed parking lot. The reserved spaces were empty, except the one marked Commander—IAD. In it sat a black Bronco, its antennae encrusted in ice. Across the lot a few cars huddled in the gloom near the door that led to the gym where the department's recruits and officers trained. A.J. bit her lip against an instinctive sureness that told her Ryan had timed their meeting so they'd have the building essentially to themselves.

She shoved open the car door and stepped into the frigid wind, wincing against tiny pellets of sleet.

Clenching her teeth against the constant age-old ache in her right thigh, she paused in the building's dim foyer, her stomach churning. She had never met Michael Ryan, yet a disgruntled cop whose career had barely survived an IAD investigation once told her Ryan was the worst of the lot— because he was the best.

He would ask her about Ken. What would she say? What the hell *could* she say about her brother?

IAD's outer office was dark. Like a moth pulled to a scorching flame, A.J. made her way through a shadowy labyrinth of desks and chairs toward the wedge of light that jutted from a back office. A low voice drifted on the still air; A.J. paused outside the door, her spine stiff as wire.

Inside, Michael Ryan stood beside his desk, telephone receiver trapped between his shoulder and cheek. Even after a full workday, his starched white shirt appeared unwrinkled, its collar a crisp fold over a knotted paisley tie. He had one hand clamped at his waist, holding back the flap of his navy suit coat. Light glinted off the gold badge clipped to his belt.

A.J. pulled off her gloves then slipped out of her coat. The hand she used to smooth the skirt of her gray suit trembled. Inching back into the shadows, she used the time to look Ryan over.

He was in his midthirties, she judged, tall and lean with the build of an athlete, his thick hair as dark as a starless night. His face was high boned, his mouth firmly molded, his eyes ice blue. Under Ryan's command, Internal Affairs operated with spit and polish, and he had the same look about him—sharp and controlled.

"We agreed Megan would spend Christmas with me," Ryan said into the phone. "That was the deal." A.J. picked up an undertone of steel in his voice.

Folding her coat across her arm, she pulled her gaze from his intense profile. Ryan's office was cool black metal and white walls. No clutter. Except for the telephone, an overstuffed file folder was the only item on his desk. The credenza spanning the back wall displayed a lone brass frame holding the picture of a preteen girl with an impish, lopsided smile. Her dark good looks and piercing blue eyes gave silent testimony of a blood lineage with the man who stood scowling inches away.

"One weekend in three months." Ryan's hand curled into a fist as he spoke. "That's not too much to ask." He paused to listen, his shoulders stiffening. "Have Megan call me. Collect," he added, then settled the receiver onto its base with a thud.

"Dammit!" he muttered. He shoved his fingers through his dark hair. A muscle flinched in his jaw. He stepped to the credenza, swiped up the photograph and stared down at the picture. Regret, raw and dark, settled in his eyes.

Breath hitching, A.J. stood outside the doorway, still as death. She knew what it was like to gaze at a photograph and feel the ache of remorse.

As if suddenly sensing her presence, Ryan's chin came up and he turned. The small clench of empathy that had tugged at A.J. died when his expression sharpened.

"A.J." He returned the photograph to the credenza; his unwavering gaze locked with hers while he walked the few steps to the door. "I'm Michael Ryan. I don't think we've ever met," he added, extending his hand.

"We haven't," she confirmed. Heart pounding, she slid her hand into his, hoping direct contact wouldn't betray her uneasiness.

"I appreciate you meeting me here."

She forced a thin smile and pulled her hand from his firm, warm grip. "I wasn't aware I had a choice, Sergeant. When someone needs information from my unit, they usually just call."

He raised a dark brow. "I'd have done that if I needed the services of a crime analyst." He stepped aside and motioned toward the chairs at the front of his desk. "Have a seat."

She left her coat and purse in one chair, then settled into another, feeling his blue stare following her every move.

"This concerns Ken," Ryan said as he leaned a hip against the front edge of the desk. A.J. waited, feeling time inch its way forward as his gaze slid from her eyes, to her mouth, then down her body. He was sizing her up, assessing her—looking for what, she didn't know. With tension knotting her throat, she shifted in her chair and waited.

"I apologize if this is painful," he continued after a moment. "But it's waited too long as it is."

"What about my brother?" she asked, forcing an evenness into her voice.

"Are you aware of any problems Ken was having—personal or with the job?"

For a mindless instant, the threatening voice of the anonymous caller who'd startled her from a sound sleep swirled in her brain. *"Your brother's gone bad. Tell him to cooperate with his new partners...or else."* She'd tracked Ken down after anxious hours of searching and told him about the call. He'd cursed, rage darkening his face. "I'll kill the bastard for involving you in this, A.J. So help me God, I'll kill him."

"Involving me in what?" she'd demanded, more frightened than she'd ever been in her life, and not sure why.

But her question and the ones that followed drew only Ken's unnerving, thin-lipped silence. Without saying another word, he had stalked out, his oath to kill some unnamed person her final memory of him.

It was the last time she'd seen her brother alive.

A.J. took a deep breath against the familiar swell of grief that settled around her heart. Ken had always been there to fix her troubles. They'd had a parentless childhood; he'd helped their aunt raise her, been her adviser, protector and a million other things. Now he was dead, and she was left with a black void of questions.

"Was Ken having problems?"

The hard edge that had settled in Ryan's voice snapped her gaze up. "My brother died while investigating a burglary. Shouldn't you be looking for the bastard who murdered him?"

"No," Ryan answered bluntly. "That's Homicide's job. But you've spent your fair share of time working with that unit, so I'm not telling you anything you don't know."

She shifted her attention to a metal bookcase filled with precise rows of binders and departmental manuals. Ryan had done his homework. He knew that beside her duties as civilian supervisor over Crime Analysis, her training as a profiler drew her special assignments to homicide task forces. Dread tightened her jaw. OCPD had hundreds of employees—this man, with whom she'd never before exchanged words, wouldn't know her work history unless he'd made the effort to find out.

"Was Ken having problems?" Ryan persisted.

"If he was, he didn't confide in me." Whatever his secrets, Ken had taken them to the grave. A.J. intended they stay there.

"I know you and your brother were close," Ryan commented, his gaze unyielding. "I understand loyalty. But Ken's dead now, and things will go easier for you if you tell me what you know."

A.J. stared at him, her spine going rigid. She'd heard cops interrogating suspects before, and that was how Ryan sounded now. As if *she* were a suspect. "I have no idea what you're getting at, Sergeant."

"Then I'll make my point. Ken had a checking account at Savings National." As he spoke, Ryan reached behind him and lifted the thick file folder off the desk. "During the last week of Ken's life, separate cash deposits totaling over ten thousand dollars were made into his account."

"I... There's some mistake," A.J. said with disbelief. *She* was the one with a head for finance, not Ken. Her brother had no talent for managing money; he lived from paycheck to paycheck.

"No mistake," Ryan answered. "I have copies of the deposit slips. The records show you're a cosigner on the account."

A.J. blinked and gave a wary nod. "Ken opened it after his divorce. He wanted my name on the account in case something happened."

Ryan pushed away from the desk, straightening to his full height. "Something *did* happen. Ken died. And he left a lot of questions."

"That I don't have the answers to." Ten thousand dollars, she thought weakly. Where the hell had the money come from?

Mouth set in a thin line, Ryan pulled a computer printout from the file folder and handed it to her. "This came out of Ken's locker."

Sweat slicked A.J.'s palms as she stared at the printout, its top page smudged with black fingerprint powder. She knew the exact day the printout had disappeared from her office. Moved by an instinct she didn't understand, her search for it had turned frantic after she'd received the anonymous call.

"The data on those pages is classified, is it not?" Ryan asked.

She met his gaze. "Yes."

"From it, your unit sends Patrol reports of the districts hit hardest. Those areas are assigned the highest number of black-and-whites. Right?"

A.J. gritted her teeth and nodded. Why was Ryan even bothering to ask? The sureness in his eyes made it clear he already knew the answers to his questions.

"You also recommend the times and locations for plain-clothes stakeouts," he continued. "Say, for instance, some-one running a burglary ring knew those assignments in advance, he'd move his operation to the districts with the fewest patrols. Tell his people to avoid the stakeouts. Wouldn't be hard to find a buyer on the street for that kind of information."

A.J. rose slowly; the thick ream of paper slipped from her fingers, waterfalling into a heap at her feet as she glared up at Ryan through a haze of anger. "Maybe the printout wound up in Ken's locker, but you can't prove *he* put it there."

He nodded, his expression unreadable. "True."

Turning her back on his piercing gaze, she willed her knees not to tremble as she walked the few steps to the room's only window and stared out at the frozen parking lot. *Think,* she commanded herself, her hand rising to her throat. *Think.*

A car backed out of a space near the gym door, its head-lights licking across the lot's blacktopped surface.

Think.

"You said the deposits to Ken's account were in cash," she said, watching the car make a cautious turn into the street.

"That's right."

"Anyone could have made them. All they'd need to know was the name of Ken's bank and the account number."

"Possible."

She turned back to face Ryan, refusing to allow the doubt she'd heard in his voice to further unsettle her. "Ken got his paycheck by automatic deposit. Most of us do."

Ryan shrugged. "What's your point?"

"Ken had to fill out an authorization card for that. It has the bank's name and his account number, and it's kept on file in payroll. Any enterprising cop with a lock pick and a talent for computers has access to the files.''

Ryan cupped his hand to his chin and tapped a finger against his firm-set lips. ''You have an explanation for everything.''

''I'm guessing, Sergeant, but so are you. In themselves, your allegations mean nothing.''

''They suggest quite a lot.''

''So does your timing.'' She shoved a tumble of dark hair behind one shoulder. ''If you had proof Ken and I were selling information, you wouldn't have waited until now to pull me in.''

''You're right, I don't have proof,'' Ryan agreed quietly. ''Not yet.''

''You'll never get it,'' she countered, her voice shaking. ''Because I didn't give that printout to anyone, and I resent your implying I did. I know right from wrong—because of Ken. When I was little, he'd read me the riot act if I lied about brushing my teeth. Ken taught me honesty. That's how he was. Honest.''

Ryan gave her a dubious, narrow-eyed look. ''You're talking about a cop who not too long ago came off administrative suspension.''

''IAD's entire case was based on circumstantial evidence,'' A.J. said through her teeth.

''We had enough to prove Ken violated department policy. Enough to bust him from detective to patrolman.''

A.J. gestured toward the floor. ''And because of that, you think he took this printout.''

''No. I think he took it because his fingerprints are all over it.''

''I can explain that.''

Ryan cocked his head. ''I'm listening.''

Courage seeping out of her, A.J. retraced her steps and lowered herself onto the chair. Inside, she was falling apart. Her right thigh ached, her pulse hammered in her ears. The idea that Ken had involved himself—and her—in something illegal was like slow paralysis.

"The printout disappeared from my desk the day before Ken died," she said in a wooden voice.

"Had he been in your office that day?"

"Yes," she said, and raised her gaze to meet Ryan's. "He and his partner came by."

"Greg Lawson?"

A.J. nodded. "They wanted a computer run done on robberies that had gone down in their district. Greg met with one of the analysts—Tim Ford, I think it was. While Greg did that, Ken came in my office to talk."

"What about?"

A.J. narrowed her eyes. "A personal matter."

"I need to know."

"Our aunt's ill," she answered after a moment. "I'd taken her to the doctor that morning. Ken wanted to know how it went."

Ryan nodded. "Go on."

A.J. gestured toward the floor. "I had the printout spread across my desk, using it to compile a report." Her throat tightened against the image of her tall, wide-shouldered brother striding into her office in his sharply pressed uniform. His dark, solemn-eyed handsomeness habitually pulled women's gazes like radar, and taking into account the wistful looks A.J. had seen coming from the two female analysts in the outer office, Ken's appeal on that day was as devastating as ever.

"Ken gathered up the printout and held it so he'd have room to sit on the desk while we talked." A.J.'s voice hitched. God, the memories hurt. Tears welled and she blinked them furiously away. She hadn't cried since Ken's death, and she'd be damned if Michael Ryan could make her start now.

"I can get you some water," he offered in a soft voice.

"The only thing I want is to leave."

"When we're done."

She took a deep breath, thinking about the grimness she'd seen in Ken's eyes that last afternoon. When she'd asked him what was wrong, his gaze shifted for a split second out the door of her office, then settled back on her face. "I'm worried about Aunt Emily," was all he'd said.

A.J. had sensed there was more bothering Ken than just their aunt's health, but she hadn't pressed. Ken had taken his suspension and resulting demotion hard—if his current assignment to the Patrol Division had put the bleak look in his eyes, she hadn't wanted to bring it up.

"How long did Ken stay in your office that day?"

"Maybe fifteen minutes," she answered, meeting Ryan's gaze. "Then Greg came to get him."

"Did Lawson come in?"

A.J. frowned. "I don't think so," she said after a moment. "I barely knew Greg...then. He and Ken hadn't ridden together long. I seem to remember that Greg poked his head in to tell Ken he had what they needed. Ken handed me the printout and left."

Ryan leaned toward her until his face came even with hers. "You're sure?" he asked, his voice a soft presence on the still air. "One hundred percent sure Ken didn't walk out with that printout?"

"Positive." The warm, spicy scent of Ryan's aftershave filled her lungs as A.J. kept her gaze locked with his.

"What makes you so sure?"

"I started back to work on my report after Ken left. Tim and I went to a meeting about an hour later."

The room had suddenly become uncomfortably warm. A.J. felt her flesh heat beneath her gray wool suit. She ran a hand across the back of her neck before continuing.

"The meeting ran long, so Tim and I didn't go back to the office. The next morning, the printout wasn't in the desk drawer where I'd left it. I asked the two other analysts if they'd seen anyone in my office while I was at the meeting. They'd been at the computers with their backs to the door. They hadn't seen anyone."

Ryan shifted his gaze to the floor where the crumpled printout lay, the lines in his forehead deepening. "Confidential information came up missing from your unit, and you didn't make a report. Why?"

"I intended to. Captain Harris had taken a day of leave, so I made an appointment to see him the following day. But Ken died that night." A.J. bit back the anger that surged inside her. This was what Ken had gone through before his demotion, she realized. Facing an accuser with no evidence to back him up.

She rose, feeling as though she'd spent a lifetime in Ryan's disconcerting presence. "If you're finished grilling me, Sergeant, I have a question for you."

The ghost of a smile played at his lips. "I'm not quite finished with the...grilling, but go ahead."

"Why don't you quit wasting time looking for dirt on Ken, and find out who set him up?"

Ryan took a step toward her, his eyes intense. "All right, A.J., let's suppose for a minute Ken was set up. Whoever's behind it implicated you, too. Think about it. Just because Ken's dead doesn't mean whatever's going on is over." Something in Ryan's expression softened before he added, "If that's the case, you'd best watch your back."

"I don't know anything." She dragged an unsteady palm across her forehead. "I don't stand in anyone's way to anything."

"Someone may think you do," he countered. "You're grieving for your brother. People with their defenses down make perfect targets."

"I told you, I don't know anything."

A headache pounded behind her eyes; her throat was bone-dry. She needed to think, needed to remove herself from Ryan's unsettling presence, was desperate to get out of range of those see-through-you blue eyes.

She snatched her coat and purse off the chair, then turned to face him. "I'm late for an appointment. I'll be in my office tomorrow if you feel the need to continue this... interrogation."

As she spun toward the door, a sudden wave of nausea lurched in her stomach. A.J. grabbed for the back of the chair; her coat and purse tumbled into a heap at her feet.

"Sweet Jesus!" Ryan caught her by the shoulders as dizziness swirled up from the ground.

"I'm...fine." She made a weak attempt to escape his iron grip. "Fine," she repeated a split second before her knees buckled.

"Fine, hell," he muttered and eased her onto the chair. "The last time I saw someone as pale as you was at the morgue."

"Just need...a minute..." She shut her eyes against the blinding white spots spinning before them.

Ryan's hand settled against her spine and nudged her gently forward. "Lean down and take deep breaths."

Please, God, don't let me heave on his shoes, A.J. prayed as she dragged a series of shaky breaths into her lungs. Her hands shook; clammy perspiration covered her heated skin.

Ryan crouched beside her chair, his hand sliding down to rest at the bend of her waist. Despite her dazed senses, she felt the pressure of each of his fingers through the fabric of her skirt, was aware of the latent strength in his touch.

"Will you be all right if I leave for a second?" His voice held a softness that had not been there before.

His touch, his closeness made A.J.'s pulse quaver. She wanted desperately to leave, but she could barely stand, much less walk.

"I'll...be fine," she mumbled, keeping her eyes on the blurred toes of her shoes. Ryan was right, she thought miserably. At this instant her defenses were down and she was about as helpless as a newborn.

"I'll be right back." He rose and disappeared from her line of sight, his footsteps hollow echoes as he stepped around his desk. She heard a drawer slide open, then close.

He returned in less than a minute, carrying a bottle of apple juice and a paper cup. "I keep a stash," he explained, using a foot to maneuver the other chair inches from hers before he sat down. "When was the last time you ate?"

She eased herself upright and inhaled a tentative breath. The room had stopped spinning. "Lunch."

Eyeing her with quiet skepticism, Ryan filled the cup,

then handed it to her. The graze of his fingertips against hers jolted her already raw nerves. "Lunch, what day?"

She sipped the juice, letting the revitalizing liquid slide down her throat. His question made her suddenly aware that she hadn't eaten a full meal in the ten days since Ken's death.

A.J. forced down another swallow. If she got some sugar into her system, maybe her knees would function again and she could get out of this place. Get away from this man, whose touch had become so disturbingly personal.

"Yesterday," she answered. "Lunch, yesterday."

He leaned back in his chair, looking concerned and intense. "No wonder you're about to faint."

She cast him a sideways glance. "I was fine until I got here."

He gave her a long, considering stare, as if conducting some internal assessment of her. Finally he said, "I was out of town when your brother died. When I got home, I had a message from him on my answering machine."

A.J.'s eyes widened. "What did Ken say?"

"Nothing specific, just that he'd gotten into something that had to do with a dealer named Snowman and needed help getting out. He said he had evidence to turn over."

"What evidence?"

"I have no idea. I didn't hear the message until two days after Ken called. I phoned here, thinking he might have heard I was out of town and contacted someone else. That's when I found out he was dead."

A.J. swallowed around the lump in her throat. "Did he talk to anyone here?"

"No. Ken's locker was the most obvious place to start looking for the evidence he mentioned. That's where I found the bank-deposit slips and the printout from your unit. I added two and two and got four. That's why I called you in."

"To accuse me."

"To find out what you know."

"And what are your findings?"

He cocked his head. "At this point, I'm inclined to believe you're in the dark about what's going on."

"What about Ken?"

Ryan narrowed his eyes. "I don't share your convictions about his innocence."

A.J. stared at the remaining juice in her glass. "He was a good man," she insisted softly. "He wouldn't have come to you for help if he'd crossed the line."

"Maybe he'd gotten too deep into something and wanted to work a deal," Ryan countered.

"Do you always look for the worst in a situation, Sergeant?"

"What I do is look at both sides," Ryan answered in an even voice that betrayed no emotion. "Facts are facts, A.J. Classified information from your unit wound up in your brother's locker, with his prints all over it. There's an extra ten grand in a bank account to which you have access. Put it all together, how do you think it looks?"

Like Ken went bad, A.J. thought, as she forced down the last swallow of juice. *And maybe myself, as well.*

Ryan leaned in, resting his elbows on his knees. "Talk to me, A.J. If you believe Ken's innocent, telling me what you know may help clear him."

I'll kill the bastard for involving you in this, A.J. So help me, I'll kill him.

The memory of Ken's words put a knot of panic in her chest. What if he'd done it? What if the brother she'd idolized had gone bad, then committed murder to hide his sins?

She stared into Ryan's waiting face and for an instant considered telling him about the anonymous phone call and Ken's reaction. Her jaw clenched. She couldn't do it. Couldn't initiate steps the heart-wrenching consequences of which she and her ill aunt might have to deal with the rest of their lives.

"There's nothing to tell, Sergeant. I didn't know until a few minutes ago that Ken called you."

She set the cup on the floor. "Are we done?"

"Two more things. Your brother had a reputation as a

ladies' man. I'm sure you're aware of that. I can't get a line on any special woman in his life. Do you know of someone he'd confide in?''

A.J. raked back damp tendrils of hair from her face. ''No. After his divorce last year, Ken dated a succession of women. If there was someone special, I don't know about her.''

Ryan nodded. ''I went by Ken's apartment the day of his funeral. The place was empty. Cleaned out. What happened to his belongings?''

A.J. frowned, not sure where this was leading. ''Did you intend to go through his things?''

''Yes.''

''You'd have needed a search warrant for that.''

''I had one. Help me out on this, A.J. I need to know what happened to Ken's belongings.''

She blinked. God, was there no end to Ryan's probing? ''The furniture went back to the company he'd leased it from. Greg Lawson took care of everything else.''

Ryan stared back at her in silence. The unrelenting watchfulness in his eyes increased her tenseness.

''Greg closed Ken's apartment as a favor to me and my aunt,'' she explained. ''Ken's landlord read in the paper that he'd died. The man called the house that same day, saying Ken's rent was past due and if we didn't clear his things out he'd toss them in the street. Thank God, Greg took the call, and not Aunt Emily.''

''Or you,'' Ryan added.

''Or me,'' A.J. agreed. Her chin rose. ''It just hit me. Ken let his rent get behind. That doesn't sound like a man who knew he had an extra ten grand in his checking account.''

''It sounds like a man who needed money in a bad way,'' Ryan countered. ''When did Lawson pack Ken's things?''

''The same day the landlord called. I wasn't thinking too clearly. I remember Aunt Emily telling Greg to give Ken's clothes to charity.'' A.J. rubbed her temple, trying without success to remember details of those grief-numbing days following Ken's death. "I have no idea where the rest of his things are. I haven't even thought to ask."

"I realize it's a long shot, but Ken might have hidden the evidence he mentioned somewhere in his apartment. I need you to ask Lawson where he put your brother's property."

"Why don't you ask…" A.J.'s voice drifted off in sudden realization. "My God, do you suspect Greg of something?"

"He was Ken's partner."

"And I'm his sister, but that doesn't make me guilty."

"You're right. But until I get some answers, I have to wonder about most everyone. And you should, too."

A.J. dropped her gaze. What was going on? What the hell was going on?

"You can use my phone to call Lawson."

She shook her head and rose. "He's visiting his parents in Colorado. He'll be back in a couple of days."

Ryan retrieved her coat and purse as he stood. "What about your aunt? She might know where Ken's things wound up."

"She might," A.J. said between her teeth. She turned to face him, her spine as rigid as cold steel. "I told you, Aunt Emily is ill. She has leukemia. She's in the hospital, undergoing experimental treatment. She has enough to deal with, without me asking about her dead nephew's belongings."

Ryan expelled a slow breath. "You'll let me know what Lawson has to say when you talk to him?"

Hands clenched into a tight, white grip on her purse, A.J. stared at him, saying nothing.

He took a step toward her. "Whatever the evidence Ken had, he wanted me to have it. Remember that."

"I'm not likely to forget."

Ryan looked steadily back at her. "I don't imagine you will." He raised his hand with slow precision and brushed a loose curl away from her temple. A wayward fingertip grazed her cheek, soft and light. "Get something to eat," he added softly.

The awareness that arrowed through A.J. jarred her into momentary immobility.

This time, it wasn't a lack of food that weakened her knees. Michael Ryan's touch was the culprit. A gentle, beckoning touch that kicked her heartbeat into a thrumming rhythm she hadn't felt in years.

Saying nothing, A.J. turned and limped out the door.

He shouldn't have touched her, Michael thought while concentrating on the uneven staccato of A.J.'s retreating footsteps. What the hell had gotten into him? He was conducting an investigation. A.J. Duncan was a suspect, and that meant hands off.

Had been a suspect, he corrected. Although he doubted she'd told him all she knew, he was almost sure what she'd told him had been the truth.

Back to square one.

Sudden movement in the dark outer office stiffened Michael's spine. "Who's there?"

"It's me, Mike."

Tony DiMaiti stepped from the shadows, hands in the pockets of his wrinkled corduroy jacket, mouth set in a grim line. "Thanks for paging me. I got here in time to hear it all."

Michael expelled a tension-filled breath and watched the drug enforcement agent drop into the chair A.J. had abandoned moments before. The man had the build of a fireplug, all round and solid with a full head of dark, curly hair that lapped across a thick neck.

Crossing a scuffed brogan over one knee, Tony gestured at the printout heaped on the floor. "You believe her? That she doesn't know how that wound up in her brother's locker?"

"If she lied, she's one hell of an actress," Michael said, scooping up the printout. He tossed the bundled paper onto his desk and settled into his chair, brows knitted. "And if she's innocent, I hate that I was so rough on her."

"I don't see you had much choice. The message her brother left on your machine, combined with what you found in his locker, has 'dirty cop' written all over it."

"I was damn well convinced of that before A.J. got here," Michael said, rubbing at the tension knotted in the back of his neck.

Tony arched an eyebrow. "You thinking now that Duncan was set up?"

"It's possible." Michael's thoughts veered to the brown eyes that had steadily matched his gaze moments before, to the masses of dark hair that shadowed her high-boned cheeks. A.J. had defended her brother with an unswerving, to-hell-with-the-evidence loyalty. In his years with Internal Affairs, Michael had seen iron-nerved cops break down in the face of lesser evidence. Not A.J. Duncan. *Determined* was a tag he'd give her. A woman of courage and smoldering intensity—and probably hell to live with when hot under the collar.

"Mike, you want to tell me what planet you suddenly decided to visit?"

Michael blinked. "Sorry. I've got a lot on my mind."

"I can see that."

Tony's presence helped ease the gnawing frustration that held Michael in its grip. They'd been friends since childhood; Anthony DiMaiti was one of the few people Michael trusted implicitly.

Michael held up the printout. "Finding this and the deposit slips in Ken's locker was convenient. Could be too convenient. Maybe instead of Ken doing something illegal, he caught another cop in the act."

Tony raised a broad shoulder. "Wouldn't be the first time one cop got the goods on another."

Frowning, Michael shoved the printout into its folder. "If that's the case, where the hell does A.J. fit into all this?"

"Good question. Do you think she came clean with you?"

"Hell, no." A grim smile curved Michael's mouth. "I

think she held something back to protect Ken. And I suspect she'd have cut her arm off before she told me.''

A.J.'s fortitude hadn't surprised Michael. After all, she'd had the grit to sit stone-faced through her brother's funeral, eyes fixed, lips tight. She had unblinkingly watched the cold ground swallow up Ken's casket, all the while comforting her frail aunt. A.J. hadn't shed a tear. Not one. Michael knew, because he'd kept his eyes on her the entire time.

Yet, here in his office, she'd been on the brink of tears. Because of him.

Dammit, he'd had a job to do and he'd done it, but that didn't stop him from feeling like a jerk. To make matters worse, he'd almost made her faint.

He remembered the feel of her, so small and fragile, as if she might come apart in his hands. So vulnerable...and so damn pale.

He scrubbed a hand across his face. His eyes felt gritty. A headache had worked its way up from the base of his skull.

Shifting his gaze back to Tony he said, ''Any word on Snowman?''

''Nothing. The DEA's been trying to get a lead on whoever he is for months, then Ken Duncan all of a sudden drops his name.''

I'm into something...need help getting out. Has to do with a dealer named Snowman. I've got evidence to turn over.

Damn Ken Duncan and his cryptic phone message, Michael thought. There was no deciphering the meaning, no interpreting the officer's intention.

Michael clenched his jaw against the nerve-aching frustration that had been building in him since the Duncan case landed in his lap. ''Meanwhile, word on the street is that there's a pair of dirty cops dealing drugs,'' he stated. ''Snowman could be their supplier. And just maybe, Ken Duncan got the goods on them.''

''Or, he could have been one of them.''

"If he was, there's still one left. And it's my bet he's wondering if Ken told A.J. anything."

"Yeah," Tony agreed. "You got any better idea which way the wind blows where Greg Lawson's concerned?"

"Right now, he looks squeaky clean. And I've got no reason to think otherwise."

Tony nodded and glanced toward the dark outer office. "She was watching you," he said almost absently.

Michael frowned. "A.J.?"

"Yeah. I drove up after her and followed her in." Tony grinned and pointed at his scuffed boots. "Rubber soles. Great for sneaking up on do-wrongs. Anyway, A.J. waited outside your door while you were on the phone. She was checking you out."

"Sizing up the adversary, I imagine."

"Probably so." Tony dropped his gaze to examine his watch with suspicious concentration. "You know, Mike, all the time we've talked about this case you never mentioned A.J.'s looks."

Michael lifted his chin. "Her looks make no difference."

"Right," Tony scoffed. "All you said was she lived with her spinster aunt and was married to her job. I figured A.J. was some office drone who'd have to sneak up on ugly." Tony swept a hand toward the outer office. "I'm creeping up behind her. She does a half turn and the light hits her face. Knock out are the two words that come to mind."

"*Knockout* is one word," Michael said levelly.

"Whatever," Tony countered with a flick of his wrist. "Now that I've seen her, I'm wondering if you've gone blind since your divorce."

Michael propped a forearm on his desk. "I'd be dealing with the same mess if A.J. had three eyes and weeping sores. Whatever the hell the mess is."

"Well, you don't have to deal with it much longer," Tony commented. "Chief McMillan's announcing your promotion tomorrow. *Lieutenant Ryan—Homicide.* You'll forget about IAD when dead bodies start piling up."

"Wrong," Michael said, pulling the thick file across the

desk. "For whatever reason, Ken Duncan called me. He could have brought what he had to any of this unit's officers, but he chose me. That makes it personal." Michael crammed the file into his briefcase. "Besides, somebody pumped two slugs into a cop's chest. Duncan's death was a homicide, and as of tomorrow, homicide is my business."

"I can't argue that."

"Just like the DEA's business is drugs," Michael observed. "So don't take forever to get the goods on Snowman. He has something to do with the Duncan case, and I need to know what the hell it is."

"We'll do our best." Tony rose, stood for a quiet moment then said, "A.J. limped like hell when she left here. I didn't notice her walking like that when I followed her in."

The limp had been more pronounced at Ken's funeral, Michael thought. She'd leaned on Greg Lawson's arm while her faltering gait distanced her from her brother's grave. Clad in black, with her dark hair pulled off her face, she'd appeared as breakable as glass. About the same way she'd looked moments ago when her knees gave out and it had been all she could do not to faint.

And all he could do to keep from pulling her into his arms.

He'd wanted to touch her, needed to make contact, *had* to trace a finger along that hypnotic curve of her cheek.

"Car wreck," Michael said, his throat tightening with the memory of the personal tragedy the background check had revealed. "A.J. was in a car wreck when she was in college. She and her fiancé went to a party. He had a few too many, so she drove home. It was dark. Raining. A dog ran in front of the car and they skidded into a tree. A.J.'s leg was broken in three places."

"What happened to the fiancé?"

"Went through the windshield. Dead at the scene."

Tony gave a thoughtful nod. "You sure as hell got all the details—"

"I'm investigating her," Michael said and rose. "It's my

job to know her background." He saw no need to admit the intense curiosity that had driven him to discover what lay beneath the outer shell of the woman.

"Yeah," Tony agreed as he delivered an affable slap on Michael's back. "Listen, why don't you come have dinner with Marie and me? We'll celebrate your promotion."

"Thanks, but the chief's waiting for a report on my meeting with A.J.," Michael said as he pulled on his coat. "I'll take a rain check."

Scowling, he flipped off the lights and walked with Tony through the dark outer office. A.J. Duncan attracted him in a way that no woman had drawn him in years—it was as if some primal need had suddenly ignited inside him.

Michael lent silent acknowledgment to the fact that his feelings were a complication he hadn't anticipated. Didn't welcome. *Lose your objectivity, Ryan, and you'll make mistakes.*

With so many unanswered questions, he couldn't afford to slip up. Couldn't afford to get distracted.

Couldn't afford to get involved.

Chapter 2

"If you'll tell me what you're looking for, maybe I can help."

A.J. looked up from the fearsome stacks of file folders and computer printouts spread across her desk. "I wish I knew," she said, pulling off her tortoiseshell reading glasses.

Tim Ford, a short, thin man in his twenties with roughly cropped red hair and a freckled face, gave her a wild-eyed look from the chair in front of her desk. "And they called *me* mad at the home."

A.J. chuckled and leaned back, her chair thudding into the credenza behind her. Her boxlike office had barely enough room for her desk and chair, two visitor chairs and a credenza. The walls were a dim city-issue white; ancient varicose-veined linoleum covered the floor.

"I know you're in the dark on this, Tim. Trouble is, all I have is a hunch."

She'd had nothing to go on when she gave the crime analyst the assignment, just Michael Ryan's vague reference to a burglary ring. She'd gone over the information

Tim had compiled until she was cross-eyed, but found nothing to connect to Ken.

"You're the boss, A.J. I'm here eight to five. No matter what work I do, pay's the same." Tim waved a freckle-spattered hand at the desk. "That's the breakdown on all burglaries—residential, business and auto for the past six months. I can't get a handle on a pattern, but I'll keep plugging away if that's what you want."

A.J. took a thoughtful sip from the steaming mug of coffee Tim had carried in for her. Already it was the first week of December; Ken had been dead over two weeks. When she thought about his funeral, her foremost memory was the sun's unseasonable warmth, its afternoon rays a stunning reflection off the lid of the polished coffin. Last night, winter had tightened its hold on the city with two inches of paralyzing sleet. Time had trickled away, and despite her obsession with Tim's printouts, A.J. knew nothing more than the little she'd gleaned from Michael Ryan.

Like an unwanted intruder, the memory of the man's touch flashed through her thoughts. She tightened her jaw in acknowledgment of the sexual tug that came with the thought, then forced it away. Setting down the mug with decision, she said, "Go back to just doing the breakdown for Patrol like always." With a sense of failure, she folded Tim's printouts and stuffed them into the credenza.

He remained silent for a long moment. "A.J., does this have something to do with Ken?"

She felt her heart sink as she stared across the desk. Was it general knowledge around the department that Ken had involved himself with a burglary ring? She met Tim's questioning gaze, forced her own expression to remain neutral. "Why do you ask?"

"That last call Greg and Ken answered was a burglary in progress. The scuzz who killed Ken is still out there." Tim lifted a shoulder. "I thought you might be trying to help the boys in Homicide."

A.J. expelled a slow breath. "Something like that."

"I'm sorry I couldn't find anything," Tim said and rose.

"I liked Ken. It's a damn shame what happened." He gave her a sympathetic smile before he walked out, leaving the door open behind him.

A.J. watched through the single glass panel that faced the analysts' office as Tim settled behind his desk. He promptly grabbed his telephone and began punching in numbers.

Familiar sounds from the outer office filtered in as the other two analysts, Joan Allison and Katie Morton, went about their duties. Computer keys clicked, phones buzzed; two detectives laughed at a joke while they waited for Katie to finish a run on white males stopped in red pickup trucks.

A.J. gave a contented smile over her desk's clutter, proud of the unit she'd supervised for the past five years. Work got done, brisk and thorough, thanks to the analysts' friendly competence. Day after day, a soothingly repetitious operation.

She closed her eyes. Hiring on at OCPD and immersing herself in her job had proved the needed antidote for the empty space Casey's death had left in her life. Empty space, which over time had transformed from all-consuming grief into small snags of sadness when she thought of the man she'd loved and all that might have been. Acceptance had come slowly, as had contentment with the pattern in which her life had settled.

A.J.'s brows slid together as an uneasy realization played at the edge of her thoughts, then crystallized. The satisfaction she'd once derived from her work had disappeared, and she knew it was Michael Ryan's doing.

Damn him, she thought, shoving up the sleeves of her navy wool dress. She'd received no more of his expertly timed summonses, but the memory of Ryan loomed over her, his warning of her vulnerability dangling in her thoughts like grapes on a vine.

She wouldn't let him do this to her, she absolutely would not. With the heat of determination burning inside her, she opened a file folder, stared at its contents…then moments later tossed it aside, unread. Her ability to concentrate had gone down the tubes the instant she heard about the promotion. *Lieutenant Ryan.* She'd been relieved at first. Promotion meant Ryan's transfer; Internal Affairs would pass to another commander. Without Ryan pushing buttons, the Duncan investigation might fall by the wayside.

And then it had hit her. Chief McMillan had announced Ryan's promotion the day *after* Ryan called her to Internal Affairs. Ryan would have already known he was getting promoted. Why, then, hadn't he turned the investigation over to IAD's new commander? Why had *he* called her in when he knew he'd be off the case?

The strange disquiet those thoughts had instilled in her was nothing compared to the sinking feeling she experienced when she received the chief's memo announcing Ryan's new assignment. *Homicide.* She had almost daily contact with that unit. In the four days since Ryan took over Homicide, she'd managed to avoid him. But she harbored no great hope that her luck would continue.

She stared without interest at the stacks of reports and file folders cluttering her desk. An ungodly amount of work awaited her attention, yet her thoughts centered maddeningly on Michael Ryan. The man's reputation included a reference to ice water in the veins, yet when she almost fainted in his office she'd seen genuine concern in his eyes. And his expression wasn't the only thing she remembered. The feel of his hands, supporting her, guiding her onto the chair with an incongruous mix of strength and gentleness, plagued her thoughts.

A surge of latent warmth rose inside her and she muttered a self-recriminating oath. Michael Ryan had accused both her and Ken of wrongdoing, and here she was allowing thoughts of arctic blue eyes and a rock-solid grip to cloud her brain. What was the matter with her?

She dragged in a controlling deep breath and forced her thoughts to the course of action she'd decided. The first item was to prove her innocence. *She* had done nothing wrong. But what if Ryan was right? What if whatever Ken had alluded to in his message to Ryan was still ongoing?

If more classified data from her office wound up in the wrong hands, there would be no way to defend herself—and, possibly, her staff—if she remained in the dark.

She had no intention of spending the rest of her life knowing that a black cloud hung over Ken's memory. Despite the anonymous call she'd received and Ken's murderous reaction, no matter the evidence found in his locker, the part of her that loved her brother couldn't accept he'd gone bad. Like Ryan said, every story had two sides. Somehow, someway she had to find the evidence to clear Ken.

Shoulders squared, she retrieved her mug and took a swallow. The coffee had grown tepid; she choked it down with a grimace.

"That bad, huh?"

Startled, she looked toward the door. Greg Lawson, turned out neat in a gray uniform shirt and dark trousers, lounged in the doorway, a weary grin on his handsome face.

A.J. smiled. "Welcome back. How was Colorado?"

"Cold. And a long drive," he added, pushing off the door frame. "I got home last night in just enough time to throw on my uniform and make it to lineup."

He was tall and lanky, with friendly gray eyes and blond hair that would bleach pale when the summer came. As he neared her desk, A.J.'s gaze lifted and she felt a stab in her heart at the sight of the jagged cut that started in the center of Greg's forehead and veered into the hairline at his right temple.

Although healing, the wound still showed traces of inflammation. For the rest of his life, Greg would wear an eternal reminder of the night his partner died.

Swallowing against the thought and the accompanying pain, A.J. glanced at her watch. "It's almost nine. You should be home in bed by now."

"There've been a ton of accidents because of the ice. We got orders to stay on the street to help handle traffic." He pushed a stack of files aside and slid a thigh onto the edge of the desk, just as Ken had done on his last visit.

"Sorry I didn't call while I was gone. My parents live halfway up a mountain. The day I got there, a blizzard hit and played havoc with the phone." He expelled a weary breath. "Anything go on while I was away?"

A.J. shook her head. "You didn't miss much."

Greg reached across the desk, his hand tightening around hers. "You're wrong," he said softly. "I missed you."

She smiled. "I missed you, too."

"Don't forget, you promised to have dinner with me my first night back."

"I haven't forgotten."

"We still on for the Christmas dance?"

"Sure."

She dropped her gaze, waiting for Greg's touch to spark the same searing awareness she'd felt when Michael Ryan's fingers stroked her cheek.

But her pulse remained steady; no twist of dark desire warmed her flesh. With silent self-recrimination, she reminded herself she would never have gotten through the past weeks without Greg's support.

She hadn't known him before he and Ken paired up, and only slightly after that. On the night Ken died, Greg stayed at the hospital long enough to have his forehead stitched, then left against doctor's orders. He'd arrived at her house on the police chaplain's heels. Stunned with grief, she'd gratefully accepted Greg's support. He'd been at her side when she told Aunt Emily about Ken, and he'd handled all the awful details after that.

Although he hadn't spoken about it, A.J. sensed the guilt Greg felt over Ken's death. Guilt at having allowed a burglar to render him unconscious in an alley while Ken circled the warehouse and crept through the front door into the sights of a second burglar's automatic.

This man who now smiled down at her had taken care of her when she'd been beyond comfort, and A.J. wanted to repay his kindness. Needed to. But since her summons to Internal Affairs, she'd allowed caution to temper her feelings, had built an emotional barrier around herself.

Slipping her hand from his, she made a pretense of straightening the clutter on her desk. "I need to ask you about Ken's belongings," she began, her nervous fingers clumsily shuffling a stack of file folders.

"What about them?"

A.J. glanced up. "I was in a haze when you closed Ken's apartment. I don't know what happened to his things."

"I took his clothes and dishes to a charity like your aunt asked." Greg shifted his weight, his Sam Browne belt and holster groaning a leathery protest. "I hope she hasn't changed her mind about wanting that stuff."

"No. What I'm interested in are receipts...Ken's car title, bank statements. Things like that." A.J. shrugged. "I'm executor of Ken's estate, and I have to file a final tax form. I'd like to get it done before Aunt Emily comes home from the hospital."

"How's she doing?"

"She's weak. Sick from the chemo most of the time. I talked to her doctor last night. Depending on her response, the treatments may last about three weeks. She might get to come home for a day or two in between, but that depends on how her immune system holds up. If the numbers go too low, he'll keep her there until her resistance levels build up."

Greg nodded. "Think I'll drop by and see her on my way home."

"She'll like that." A.J. took a deep breath. "About Ken's things?"

"I packed everything in boxes and stacked them in my garage. I didn't want to bother you or your aunt about where to store them." Greg shrugged. "If you want, I'll load everything in my car and bring it over tonight when I pick you up."

"Thanks."

"It hasn't been that long, A.J.," he added quietly. "If you're not up to this, I can go through the boxes, pull out what you need."

"I appreciate it, but no. It's something I need to do."

"All right."

A.J. dropped her contrite gaze. Greg's unconcerned demeanor had no effort behind it; nothing flashed in his eyes to indicate that he knew about the unexplained deposits she'd find in at least one of Ken's bank statements. *Paranoia at its fullest. Thank you, Michael Ryan.*

Greg idly fingered the cut along his forehead, wincing at one point. "Have you heard about the Westfall woman?"

"Westfall?" A.J. frowned. "Why do I know that name?"

"She's the widow of that famous heart specialist."

A.J. nodded. "Right. Her picture's on the society page about once a week. What about her?"

"Somebody sliced her up last night. She lives…lived in the biggest mansion in Quail Creek. Homicide's there now."

"Any idea who did it?"

Greg eased off the desk. "Don't know. And luckily, that isn't my problem."

After plucking a file folder off her credenza, A.J. rose. "That reminds me, I finished reviewing this case. I need to drop the file off at Homicide. I'll walk you out."

Greg arched a brow. "I doubt anyone's there. Every last one of them is probably at the Westfall crime scene."

"I imagine so," A.J. murmured as she walked out the door.

Cradling the case file on a murdered female jogger in the crook of her arm, A.J. wound her way through Homicide's rows of battered desks and dreary grayness. A flash of red from the assignment board caught her attention. Someone had scribbled the greeting: *Welcome to OCPD Homicide. When your days end, our day begins.*

Her mouth curved. Nothing in the world like cop humor.

Det. Richard Warren was the only person in sight. He had a dry-looking doughnut in one hand, a phone in the other and a harried look on his face. A.J. raised the file and pointed to a door at the back of the office. Warren waved her on with the doughnut.

She let the door to the small file room swing shut behind her. The smell of stale, aging paper hung in the uncirculated air. A small table stood in the middle of the room; side-by-side cabinets full of nightmarish hell lined the dingy walls.

With the ease of familiarity, she walked to a dented file cabinet at the far end of the room and pulled open a drawer labelled *Unsolved* in vivid red slashes. Shifting through a maze of yellowing folders, she nudged the jogger's thick case file into place in the crowded drawer.

After prodding the dented drawer closed, she turned and froze in her tracks. The sight of Michael Ryan leaning against the closed door, every athletic inch of him blocking her retreat sent a jolt of wariness up her spine.

He looked like pure efficiency in his white starched shirt and charcoal slacks, his dark hair smooth and neat. His crimson tie displayed a perfect knot; a blue steel automatic nestled in the shoulder holster molded against his ribs.

"Good to see you, A.J.," he said, his voice casual and warm.

Running into Ryan had been inevitable, she'd known that. In her mind she had formulated a script that told her how to act, what to say. But it didn't tell her what to do about a stomach clenched so tight she could hardly breathe.

"I returned a file," she said and took an expectant step forward.

Ryan didn't budge, just nodded toward the drawer she'd closed. "Giving us a hand with a case?"

"Yes. Trying, anyway," she amended.

"Which case?"

She took a deep breath. "The jogger homicide."

"I'm not familiar with that one." He glanced around the room, his mouth kicking up at one corner. "Afraid I'm not familiar with any of these cases. Yet."

A.J. checked her watch. "I have to go—"

"What's happening with the jogger case?"

The distinct, unsettling feeling of Michael Ryan having her trapped in this small, airless room made her knees weak.

"Jim Cook's the lead detective on the case. He should brief you."

Ryan crossed his arms over his chest. "Detective Cook is on leave. Why don't you give me an overview?"

She moistened her lips, determined not to let her disquiet show. Ryan might have the ability to stretch her nerves to tautness, but she wasn't about to let him know. "A female jogger was stabbed to death in August. There're no witnesses, little evidence. No suspects. Before his transfer, Lieutenant Barber asked me to look at the file. He thought a suspect profile might help turn some new leads."

Ryan cocked his head. "That's right. You're the resident expert on suspect profiling. I remember a story in the paper a couple of years ago when the department got the grant for your training at Quantico."

More of Ryan's homework, A.J. thought and shifted her weight.

When she made no comment, he raised his palm. "So?"

"So...what?"

"Do you think a profile will help?"

"You'll have my report on your desk by five."

"Good. I'll read it tonight."

"You might have your hands full reviewing reports on the Westfall murder."

"Word travels fast," he said, and shrugged. "And you might be right about the paperwork. I'm waiting for Sam Rogers to call from the scene to let me know what we've got."

"Then I won't keep you."

Ryan continued leaning against the door, his cool blue eyes taking on a sudden awareness. "That's why you brought the jogger file back now, isn't it? You thought I'd be at the Westfall crime scene."

"This was a convenient time—"

"A.J." His voice softened. "Don't be afraid of me."

Everything inside her went still. "I'm not."

"I told you, I'm inclined to give you the benefit of the doubt—"

"But not Ken," she blurted, then immediately wished she could pull the words back. She didn't want to discuss her brother with Ryan. Didn't want to discuss anything with this man.

"A lot of things point to his guilt," he said simply.

She clenched her jaw. "That's what happens when someone is set up, Lieutenant. The evidence points to them."

"A.J.—"

"Then again, it doesn't matter what you think, does it?" she asked, feeling the slow heat of anger starting to build. "You're out of Internal Affairs. What Ken did or didn't do is no longer your concern."

"But it is," Ryan said, keeping his eyes steady on hers. "I'm seeing this case through to the end."

She felt the blood drain from her face. "Why? It belongs in Internal Affairs."

"I have my reasons." He moved away from the door and walked toward her. "Have you found out what Greg Lawson did with Ken's things?"

"I...yes. Greg just got back into town."

Ryan halted inches from her. His wide shoulders and formidable height gave her the impression that the small room had suddenly gotten smaller. And hotter. He was standing so close that she could feel the warmth of his body, felt her own flesh heat.

"And?" he persisted.

She took a step back, wanting, *needing* to put distance between herself and this man who evoked such disturbing responses within her. "Everything's in boxes in Greg's garage."

Ryan nodded imperceptively. "Do I need to get a search warrant?"

"No. Greg's bringing everything over tonight."

"Were you planning on telling me about this?"

"Yes."

His blue eyes rested on her face with an unreadable intensity. "When?"

She raised her chin. "I'm telling you now."

"So you are," he said, his lips forming a sardonic curve. "I'd like to take a look through the boxes. Tonight."

"Tonight's not convenient. I'm going out. I won't be home until after nine—"

"I'll come by then."

Her fingers curled in, fisted. She'd wanted to go through Ken's things before Ryan. Wanted the chance to find out on her own if Ken's evidence was something that would exonerate him or have merely allowed her brother to plea-bargain.

"Ken is dead," she said, her voice trembling. "Can't you just forget about whatever went on?"

"Whoever murdered him is still out there. I have no intention of forgetting that." Ryan reached out, closed his hand on her wrist. "I'll find out, A.J.," he said, his eyes steady on hers. "I'll find out who killed Ken. You have my word."

Ryan's touch made her nerves sizzle. The room was suddenly devoid of air. She couldn't breathe. Couldn't think.

"I'll...hold you to that," she managed.

Ryan nodded, then loosened his grip on her wrist. "I'll see you tonight...after nine." He turned and walked away, the door whooshing closed behind him.

A.J. stood motionless, her palms damp, her legs feeling like glass, ready to shatter. She let out a pent-up breath and shifted her gaze to the wall-to-wall cabinets, knowing full well their grisly contents had nothing to do with the trembling in her bones.

Chapter 3

"I want A.J."

That said, Michael slid a hand into the pocket of his trousers and shifted his gaze out the floor-to-ceiling window of the chief's office. Outside, a solid bank of gray clouds obscured the noonday sun, giving the city's granite skyscrapers the look of tombstones jutting from the depths of a fog-laden cemetery.

"Any progress on the Duncan investigation since last time we talked?"

Michael glanced across the spacious office at the man sitting behind the polished mahogany desk. "I'm going to A.J.'s tonight to look through the things from Ken's apartment. It's a long shot, but maybe the evidence he mentioned in his phone message will turn up."

"So, A.J. is continuing to cooperate?"

Michael looked back out the window. His brow furrowed with the memory of the wariness he'd seen in A.J.'s face barely two hours ago in Homicide's dim, musty file room. He wouldn't exactly call her behavior cooperative. More like forced. More like it would take a crowbar to get anything about Ken out of her. Michael narrowed his eyes. If he hadn't asked, how long would she have waited to let him know she'd gotten her hands on Ken's belongings? A day? A week? Never?

He had meant what he'd said to her—his cop's instinct told him she was telling the truth. She just wasn't telling him everything, he was sure of it. Still, he acknowledged a grudging understanding of the loyalty that drove her to protect a brother far past protecting. But that didn't mean he'd back off. Loyalty be damned, he'd find out what the hell it was A.J. Duncan knew.

Turning from the window, Michael walked across an expanse of footstep-muffling sand-colored carpet and settled into a leather chair in front of the desk.

"Yes, Chief. A.J.'s cooperating."

Brian McMillan leaned back in his chair, peering at Michael through wire-rimmed glasses. "Is it still your opinion she's clean?"

Sleet covered the sidewalks, yet the chief's skin hinted at a tan. During the past week, McMillan's thick, iron gray hair had taken on a stylist's touch. Michael kept his expression impassive as confirmation clicked in his mind that McMillan was planning a run for the mayor's job in the spring.

"Yes, A.J.'s clean."

"But you still don't have proof of that?"

"Just what my gut tells me."

"Your gut's the only reason I haven't put her on administrative suspension. Don't forget, Lieutenant, there'll be hell to pay around here if it turns out she was in on something with her brother."

"I got that message loud and clear the first time you sent it, Chief," Michael answered mildly. Now that McMillan was jumping into the mayor's race, he couldn't afford any ripples in the department. If word got out that a cop and his civilian sister had possibly sold sensitive information on the street, a major tidal wave would hit the department. McMillan's political career would end before it started.

And guilty or not, A.J. would be the one who paid. Michael almost regretted now that he'd brought the matter of Ken Duncan to McMillan's attention when he did.

Department policy dictated that the chief be informed of any evidence of wrongdoing by commissioned or civilian employees. After opening Ken Duncan's locker, the first thing Michael had done was report what he'd found to McMillan. The chief had been ready to suspend A.J. on the spot. Michael had talked him into waiting, at least until he'd called her to Internal Affairs and given her a chance to have her say.

That meeting, Michael thought. Dammit, since then he hadn't been able to get her out of his mind. He could still feel her slight, trembling body beneath his hands. The warm softness of her skin. He'd left his office that evening, gone straight to McMillan and convinced him to hold off instituting disciplinary action against her. He'd even put his neck on the block and assured the chief that he would be personally responsible if his hunch about her innocence was wrong.

Michael shoved a hand through his hair. He'd always gone by the book. He respected the laws he'd sworn to uphold, had never found it necessary to test the boundaries of the rules. A person was either right or wrong; he either screwed up or he didn't. Where the job was concerned, gray areas didn't exist.

All it had taken was fire sparking in a pair of eyes the color of moist earth for him to want to bend what he'd always considered unbendable.

"Has the DEA come up with anything on Snowman?" McMillan asked.

"They've drawn a blank so far."

McMillan reached for a pen, the gold cuff links that secured his French cuffs sparking beneath the fluorescent lights. He glanced down at the pad in front of him. "All right, Lieutenant, you want A.J. on the task force, you've got her." McMillan read off the list of names they'd compiled when Michael first got to the office, then set the paper aside.

"Mike, we've got a lot of pressure coming down to get this one solved fast. Dianna Westfall was fixed politically. She was a major contributor to the governor's campaign chest. He's already called to check on the status of the investigation." McMillan shook his head. "Dianna was my wife's best friend. She didn't deserve what happened to her. You want anyone else working on this task force, say the word. You need more equipment, ask. Just make sure you catch the bastard who did this."

"We'll find him, Chief."

McMillan scanned the list another time. "Half these people work in the investigations division. John Harris sure as hell isn't going to like this drain on his manpower." McMillan punched a button on his intercom.

"Yes, Chief?" The secretary's southern accent twanged like a banjo across the line.

"Get Captain Harris in here. If he's out to lunch, have him paged."

"Consider it done."

McMillan met Michael's gaze across the vast desk. "With you still investigating Ken Duncan, how's his sister going to take it when she hears she's working for you?"

Although that was a question he'd had trouble with himself, Michael raised a shoulder and said, "A.J.'s a pro. She'll do fine."

"I can't do it, Captain Harris," A.J. said, forcing a calmness into her voice that she was far from feeling. "You'll have to get someone else."

A large, well-molded hand hit the desk in front of her with a sharp slap. Beneath his gray military-issue crew cut, John Harris gave her a blistering stare. "This isn't a democracy, A.J. You'll work where you're assigned. What the hell's gotten into you?"

She tightened her grip on the arms of her chair. "Nothing. I got behind on my work when I was on emergency leave—I can't even see the top of my desk," she improvised. "The deadline on my divisional budget is a week away. I've got two homicides from other departments to review for suspect profiles."

Harris rubbed his chin. "E-mail me ballpark figures on your budget, and I'll take it from there. Tell those other departments if they need their cases reviewed any time soon to find another profiler. That'll ease your workload."

A.J. took a deep breath. After that morning's encounter with Michael Ryan in Homicide's file room, she'd taken an early lunch in a futile attempt to calm her nerves. She'd barely gotten back to her office when Captain Harris's secretary called, saying the boss wanted to see her, pronto. She'd come to his office with an unexplainable sense of trepidation hanging over her, and she'd been dead right to feel that way.

Why was it the harder she tried to distance herself from Michael Ryan, the closer he got?

"My aunt's in the hospital," she continued. "She'll be there a couple of weeks. I'm the only family she has now. I need to be with her in the evenings. Captain, you know what the hours are like when a task force is up and running. It's not a question of *when* you'll get home at night, it's *if*."

Harris nodded. "I'll see that your schedule's flexible enough for you to spend a few hours with her every evening. How does that suit you?"

"It doesn't," A.J. blurted. "I just think…" She shoved a hand through her hair. "Dammit, why did the Westfall woman have to get herself murdered?"

"I doubt that was the evening she planned for herself," Harris commented dryly, inspecting her with narrowed-eyed intensity. "We're wasting time here, A.J. Cut the bull and tell me what the hell's your problem."

"All right," she said, straightening in her chair. "I doubt there'd be a positive aspect of your assigning me to the Westfall task force."

Harris rose slowly, two hundred pounds of sculpted bulk

clad in a uniform so sharply creased it looked like granite. He planted both palms on his desk and leaned toward her. "You suddenly develop a talent for speaking in tongues? You got something to say, say it."

She diverted her gaze to the shadowbox of military medals and ribbons displayed on the wall behind the desk. In the five years she'd worked for the fire-and-brimstone commander she had completed every assignment wholeheartedly and on the double. She'd never balked. Until now.

"I'm not sure I can work with Lieutenant Ryan." She set her jaw. She'd always prided herself on her professionalism, on her completion of any project, any assignment. Now, she sounded like a spoiled child. But she couldn't help it.

The furrows in Harris's weathered face deepened into a scowl. "There something personal going on between you and Mike?"

"No."

"He make a pass and you turn him down? Is that what this is about?"

"No. Nothing like that."

Harris leaned further across the desk. "The department didn't spend all that money having you trained by the FBI just so you can get stubborn when someone steps on your toes."

"I know that—"

"Doesn't sound like it. Pay attention, A.J., while I make things clear. One," he said, jabbing a hole in the air with a thick index finger. "Dianna Westfall was the widow of a world-famous cardiologist. Two, she ran this city's social circles. Three, she was good friends with the chief's wife."

A.J. pressed back into the chair's hard upholstery. If Harris's face got any redder, he might explode.

"Four! I just spent half an hour with the chief. He was tossing orders like rice at a wedding. McMillan wants a task force headed by Mike Ryan. Until further notice, you work for Mike—at Mike's request."

"Joan Allison can work in my place. I've trained her. She's got the makings of a good profiler—"

"*You*, A.J. Mike asked for *you*." Mouth set into a tight line, Harris resettled into his chair. "Chief's orders, A.J. You refuse the assignment, consider yourself suspended."

"*Suspended?*" she squeaked.

"Glad to know whatever's affected your brain hasn't done the same to your hearing." Harris pulled a sheet of paper toward him and grabbed a pen. "The task force meets in the chief's conference room at two o'clock. You going to be there?"

A.J. sat in silence, her stomach roiling. She'd spent years clawing her way to the top, prided herself on her hard-earned reputation as an expert in suspect profiling. Now, thanks to Michael Ryan, she might have to kiss it all good-bye.

"Well?"

Harris had her up against a wall, and he knew it. "I'll be there."

He gave a grunt of satisfaction and jotted a note. "I'll write up authorization for you to park in the underground garage for the duration." He sent a placating smile across the precisely ordered desk. "That'll save you from having to walk to the employee lot after dark."

"Fine," she said tightly and rose.

Harris's scowl returned. "Dammit, A.J., I know things haven't been easy for you lately—first Ken's suspension, then his death...your aunt's health. I don't like getting tough with you, but when you see how the Westfall woman died, you'll understand. The guy *butchered* her. We haven't officially released the victim's name because not all her family's been notified, but the media's heard enough over their scanners to know somebody got murdered in that mansion last night. They're hovering like flies over roadkill, demanding to know who it was and when we'll make an arrest. The governor called McMillan and asked the same questions. Homicide's got zero suspects. This case'll be a nightmare, even with our top people on it."

"I'll do my best," A.J. said stiffly. "You know I'll do my best."

"Yeah, I know," Harris said, his voice quiet. "You always do." Cocking his head, he tapped his pen against the desk's polished surface. "You can't be on the outs with Mike Ryan and expect to accomplish much. Whatever's the problem, talk with him and reach some kind of understanding."

A.J. understood all right. She hadn't convinced Ryan of her innocence. Where better to have her, but assigned to his task force, under his thumb? She sat in silence, feeling her anger build. Ryan might have her in his icy blue sights, but that didn't mean she would sit around, waiting for him to toss another piece of incriminating evidence in her face. Somehow, someway, she had to find out what Ken had gotten involved in.

And she would. By God, she would.

A.J. walked into the chief's conference room at two o'clock sharp. The noise level was deafening. A mix of uniformed officers, lab techs and suited detectives filled the room, some standing in small groups, a few already seated around the long conference table.

Michael Ryan was nowhere in sight.

A.J. slid into a chair at the far end of the table and opened the leather folder she'd brought with her to jot down notes.

"You're A.J., aren't you?"

She glanced up at a tall, slim female police officer with a delicately contoured face and thick platinum-frosted hair caught into a loose braid. A glance at the brass name tag over the left pocket of her form-fitting uniform shirt displayed the name *St. John*.

"That's right."

"I'm Helene St. John," she said as she slid into the chair beside A.J.'s. She inclined her head toward a thin, lanky officer who took a seat beside her. "This is my partner, Kevin Stoner."

"I know Kevin," A.J. said as she leaned forward to look past Helene. As always, the patrol officer had one cheek stuffed with a wad of tobacco that made him look as though he was storing nuts for the winter. A.J. smiled. "How are you, Kevin?"

"Fine, except I can't figure out why Helene and I wound up on this task force."

Helene rolled her dark kohl-lined eyes. "We were the first uniforms on the scene. Remember?"

"We've arrived before anyone else on a hell of a lot of scenes," Kevin observed, then spit a blob of tobacco into the disposable cup he'd brought with him. "This is the only time we've wound up with our butts assigned to a task force. If I wanted a desk job, I'd have been an accountant."

Helene shrugged. "If you must know, I called the chief's office and volunteered us."

Kevin blanched. "Why the hell did you do an idiot thing like that?"

"Figure it out, Sherlock. You saw those pictures at the mansion. Dianna Westfall getting a kiss on the cheek from the governor. Schmoozing with the mayor. This is the type of assignment that'll get us noticed. And promoted."

"And working overtime every damn night," Kevin grumbled. "Hell, if it doesn't get solved fast, we'll be here Christmas."

Helene jerked on the collar of her uniform shirt. "Maybe you're content to drive around the rest of your life wearing one of these damn monkey suits, but not me." She shrugged, then looked back at A.J. "Besides, I've been wanting to work with you for a long time."

A.J. blinked. "With me?"

"Sure. You're one of the best suspect profilers around. That's an area I'd like to get into. I figure I can learn a lot from you."

A.J. nodded, wondering vaguely why the officer hadn't bothered coming by her office to discuss the subject.

Helene leaned in. "This might not be the right time to bring this up, but I want to say how sorry I am about Ken."

"Thanks," A.J. said, feeling the familiar tug at her heart that came with the mention of her brother. "Did you work with him?"

"I was on his shift before I transferred to days." Helene dropped her voice a fraction. "It's hard to believe the chief busted Ken from detective back to patrol. He had a reputation as a ladies' man, I'll grant you that, but even a first-day rookie could figure out that girl lied about Ken raping her."

"I know she did," A.J. said quietly. "Problem was, it was his word against hers."

"Yeah," Helene agreed. "If I'd been Ken, that would have cured me of ever talking to another suspect—or victim for that matter—without some sort of witness to back me up."

Unless you had something to hide, A.J. thought miserably, and dropped her gaze. What had Ken been hiding?

"Something wrong?" Helene asked.

"No."

"I shouldn't have brought it up. I just wanted you to know."

"Thanks," A.J. said, forcing a smile. "It's just hard to talk about Ken."

The officer regarded her for a thoughtful moment, then glanced toward the far end of the table. "My, my, McMillan sure has called in some big guns on this."

A.J. followed Helene's gaze to the petite lab-coated woman who'd just taken a seat near the head of the table. Sky Milano headed forensic services. Her assignment to the task force confirmed that the chief had pulled out all the stops for the Westfall case.

A.J. expelled a resigned breath. It was time to get down to business. She looked back at Helene and Kevin. "So, what kind of crime scene do we have?"

"A hell of a bloody one," Kevin responded. "The maid freaked when she discovered the body. Went running up and down the sidewalk, screaming Spanish at the top of her lungs. A neighbor called 911."

Helene shifted onto one hip and slid a notepad from the back pocket of her uniform trousers. "Definitely a bizarre scene. The house wasn't trashed—nothing out of place. Same for the master bedroom, except the bed. *It* was a war zone. The body looked like something you'd find in a butcher shop—"

"And that finger," Kevin chimed in. "There it was, propped against this lacy-looking pillow." He crooked his index finger in the air and wiggled it in A.J.'s direction. "I can see Dianna Westfall now, pointing toward the champagne bottles on the bedside table, saying, 'Darling, pour me another.'"

"He cut it off?" A.J. felt her interest rising, like a hound snuffling a trail. "The killer cut off her finger?"

"Hacked is more like it," Kevin answered.

"Was it a defense wound?" A.J. asked. "Had she tried to protect herself from the knife and her hands got the brunt of it?"

Helene frowned and looked at Kevin. "I didn't notice other damage to her hands. Did you?"

"Don't think so," Kevin replied. "Of course, once we saw the victim was past help, we backed out of the room so we wouldn't contaminate the scene. It wasn't like we got a real close look." He inclined his head toward a group of detectives standing at the opposite side of the table. "It's Sam Rogers and Grant Pierce's case. After they showed up, all Helene and I did was stand guard at the front door." He tapped his finger against the rim of the disposable cup. "One thing, though. While we were checking the place, I noticed beads of water in a downstairs shower. You got to figure the creep knows the drill. Looks like he cleaned himself up before he left," Kevin added before spitting a plop of tobacco into the cup.

Helene's eyes narrowed. "Get that disgusting thing the hell away from me, Stoner."

Kevin gave A.J. a lopsided grin. "Dead bodies are okay, but let me have a chew and St. John here acts like Carry Nation in a barroom."

A.J. scrunched her nose. "I don't blame…" Her voice trailed off as the door swung open, admitting Chief McMillan and Captain Harris. Michael Ryan, looking somber—and broodingly handsome in his gray suit and crimson tie—followed them in.

"Everybody find a chair," Harris rumbled. He stood at stiff attention near the head of the long table, scowling beneath his crew cut as if addressing boot-camp inductees. After everyone found a seat, he continued. "Chief McMillan has something to say before we get to work."

A.J. arched a cynical brow, wondering how hard Harris had to fight the urge to salute when the chief stepped to his side.

"Until you hear different, each of you is assigned to the Westfall task force."

A short, compact man with a voice that matched his crisp manner, Brian McMillan had backslapped his way to the chief's office by avoiding politically nasty fights. Now, it was common knowledge he had his eye on the mayor's job. Few doubted he'd make it.

McMillan's neat silver hair glinted under the conference room's recessed lights as he spoke. "Dianna Westfall was a fine, upstanding woman. She did not deserve to die, much less this way. I want you to find the person—or persons—who did this, and I want an arrest fast."

If anyone doubted the chief's seriousness, all he had to do was look around, A.J. thought. The elegant conference room was normally reserved for gatherings of high-level brass, visiting officials and press conferences. Its walls were papered; the plush sand-colored carpet could muffle the sound of a jackhammer. The expansive oak conference table was a glaring contrast to the scarred metal desks and battleship gray file cabinets that crowded the investigative offices. The previous task forces A.J. had been assigned to were shuffled into whatever cramped space was available at the time. That Chief McMillan had allowed them into his domain was a sure indication he planned to keep a close eye on their progress.

"Lieutenant Ryan is in charge," McMillan continued. "He gives the orders. You take them."

A.J.'s gaze tracked the chief's to the spot by the door where Ryan stood. His face was unreadable, his expression somber. With his wide, erect shoulders and tall, trim athletic build, he looked capable of commanding an army.

At that instant he glanced down the length of the table, his blue eyes holding A.J.'s steadily. Her pulse scrambled.

She tore her gaze from his, her fingers curving into fists against the sudden escalation of her heart rate. How could one man stir such conflicting emotions in her? The part of her that was desperate to protect Ken told her to avoid Ryan at all costs. Yet her body's unchecked reaction to his very presence had a dark, primitive appeal.

Helene leaned over. "Ryan's one hell of a good-looking man," she murmured. "This assignment is getting more interesting by the minute."

"Any questions?" McMillan asked. The chief waited all of three seconds, then headed for the door, Captain Harris on his heels.

Ryan set his briefcase at the head of the table, his gaze slowly taking in the room's occupants. "I imagine some of you aren't happy with this assignment."

Understatement, A.J. thought. On the opposite side of Helene, Kevin Stoner spit tobacco into his cup.

"Suffice it to say," Ryan continued, "the quicker we get started, the sooner we'll nail whoever did this. Then we can all go back to our regular jobs." He looked at Sam Rogers, who'd squeezed into the vacant chair beside A.J. "Sam, have you and Pierce made your initial report?"

The overweight homicide detective with age spots peeking through his thin hair nodded as he pulled a stubby cigar from between his teeth. "Dictated it to a report clerk before we came up."

"Still no witnesses?" Ryan asked.

"Not a blessed one," Sam confirmed. "After I called you from the scene, Pierce and I had the uniforms do a door-to-door of the neighborhood. Nobody saw nothing."

Sam paused to roll ashes around a thick crystal ashtray. "The couple who live directly across the street are out of town. Won't be back until late tonight."

"Talk to them in the morning," Ryan stated, then turned to Sky Milano. "Where do we stand on forensics?"

"I've got the bed linen from the scene in the lab," the chemist answered, her expression as severe as the brown bun coiled at the nape of her neck. Sky pushed her horn-rimmed glasses higher on her nose and checked her notes. "So far I've got a few long auburn hairs. Probably the victim's. I'll be sure when I compare them with known samples. The ME has agreed to collect them while he has her on the table."

"Anything else?" Ryan asked.

"I've got other hairs—could be the suspect's, but it's too early to tell." Sky leaned and looked down the length of the table at Sam Rogers. "Did the victim have a pet?"

"A dog," Grant Pierce interjected from his chair beside his partner. "The maid held it in her lap while I interviewed her. It's one of those hyper mutts with wiry hair. Looks like a toilet brush with legs."

Grant's description evoked a round of hearty laughter, but A.J. saw that the flashing smile the handsome, blond detective sent Sky's way was lost on the chemist's impenetrable facade. "I need samples from the dog," Sky said impatiently. "There's bound to be fur in the vacuumings the techs collected. I have to eliminate the animal hair so we won't go around thinking the Wolf Man's our guy."

"We'll get it taken care of, Sky," Ryan said, then glanced at his watch. "The ME won't have the autopsy done for a few hours, but his prelim report says Dianna had sex with her murderer. At this point, we have no idea if it was forced or consensual."

Ryan checked some facts with the fingerprint tech sitting across from Sky, then assigned a team of detectives to interview the Westfall family. He instructed another team to check the suspect's MO against the known-sex-offender file.

"Those of you who worked the scene," Ryan began, "get your reports to me ASAP. Be back here at eight in the morning. There'll be computers and phones up and running in here by then. Put whatever else you've got going on hold. Until we get this guy, days off don't exist."

"Talk to you later, A.J.," Helene said before she and Kevin joined the stream of people heading for the door.

Sam Rogers leaned back in his chair, thumbs hooked under the suspenders that outlined his paunch like train tracks skirting a mountain. "Here we go again, sweetheart," he said and gave A.J. a puffy-eyed wink.

She smiled. "How many of these have we worked, Sam?"

"Too many," he said with a scowl. "Used to be, no one bothered with all this task force rigmarole. We just wore out shoe leather until we made our case. Then you college kids showed up with your computers, and us old guys got the feeling we were lucky to clear a jaywalking, much less a murder."

A.J. tweaked his beefy arm. "Admit it, Sam. You don't like it because in the old days you didn't have to put anything in writing."

"Still don't," Sam said, sticking a hitchhikerlike thumb in his partner's direction. "Pretty boy makes all our reports."

Grant Pierce flashed her a dazzling smile. "Looking good, A.J.," he commented as his gaze swept down the length of her navy wool dress. "When are you going to say yes to my offer to take you out?"

"About the same time Sky does," A.J. said dryly. She glanced at the chemist, huddled now at the door with Ryan and a fingerprint tech.

"Sky?" The detective's smile melted into a frown. "She's as stiff as a wooden maiden on the prow of a ship."

Sam guffawed and stood. "Sky and A.J. are the only females around this place with sense enough to keep you at arm's length, pretty boy," he said around his cigar. "If you'd stop behaving like you wear animal skins, maybe they'd give you a chance.''

Grant rose, a blank look on his handsome face. "What fun would anybody have if I did that?" he asked as he trailed Sam toward the door.

Shaking her head, A.J. closed her folder and pushed away from the table.

"Stay for a minute, A.J.," Ryan said across his shoulder, then returned his attention to the notes in Sky Milano's hand.

Ryan's firm command jump-started her pulse. Still seated, A.J. stared at his strong, clear-cut profile. She had no choice but to endure this assignment. Endure Ryan's piercing gaze, his unsettling presence. Her own body's unwelcome reaction.

With quiet apprehension she watched Sky and the fingerprint tech close the door behind them, leaving her and Ryan alone.

He turned, his purposeful steps bringing him along the length of the table. He halted inches from her chair. "Captain Harris said you're not happy with this assignment.''

She gave him a cool look. "I doubt that surprised you.''

"It didn't," Ryan said as he slid a hip onto the edge of the table. "A.J., the killer didn't just end Dianna Westfall's life. He slaughtered her and may not stop with this one.''

"I understand that—''

"I've commanded Homicide exactly four days. *Four days.* I don't pretend to know the ins and outs of a homicide task force. All I know is that I want the best people I can get working with me. We need a feel for the guy who did this, and you happen to be the top profiler around. It's as simple as that.''

"It's not simple," she countered. "You *ordered* me to Internal Affairs and accused my brother and me of illegal activity. Now, you expect me to forget that and work for you.''

"Point taken," Ryan acknowledged with a dip of his head. "There's nothing simple about this. And as for your forgetting about our previous conversations, I doubt you could do it. So that means you should also remember I'm giving you the benefit of the doubt where Ken's concerned.''

"But you don't believe me." She wasn't about to admit how much that bothered her. "Not one hundred percent."

He narrowed his eyes. "More like ninety-nine."

"If the situation were reversed, how thrilled would you be to know that someone even remotely suspected you of committing a crime?"

"Not very," he answered. "A.J., we got off to a bad start. You have no idea how much I regret that. We've got unfinished business concerning Ken—"

"Ken and myself, you mean."

"For the sake of this task force," he continued, his eyes locked with hers, "feelings have to be put aside. You don't have to like working for me. Hell, you don't even have to like *me*. All you have to do is your job."

She shifted her gaze toward the wall of expansive windows. A flag on the building across the way snapped back and forth in the gray dusk. Ryan was right. The Westfall investigation had nothing to do with the accusations he'd made against Ken and herself. She needed to separate the two. *Had to.*

Problem was, she wasn't sure she could.

"I'll do my job," she said, keeping her gaze on the wind-whipped flag. "Don't worry about that."

Ryan placed his palm on the table and leaned in, forcing her gaze back to his. "I'm not," he said softly.

His nearness put knots of tension in her stomach. Her lungs filled with what she now recognized as the warm, musky scent of his aftershave.

Nerves humming, she pushed out of her chair and walked to the phone at the head of the conference table. "We need the cabinets brought up."

"Cabinets?"

She turned to face him. "Two locked cabinets full of supplies are ready for our use. They're restocked after each task force ends and stored in the property room." She raised a shoulder. "We'll be busy enough without having to scramble for pencils and paper clips."

Ryan smiled. "Already I'm learning from you." He rose from the edge of the table, pulling off his suit coat as he walked toward her.

A.J. dialed the phone. While she spoke to a property room clerk, she was aware of Ryan draping his jacket across the back of his chair, his long, capable fingers brushing across the gray fabric. It was the same light, sweeping motion they'd made across her cheek in his office at Internal Affairs. The same soft sweep she'd relived time and again during the past week.

Heat crept up her neck. Snap out of it, she commanded herself and forced her attention to the voice at the other end of the phone. No way was she spending the duration of the task force having hot flashes each time Ryan came near.

He settled into his chair, one dark eyebrow arching when she hung up the receiver with a thud. "Something wrong?"

"No. They'll bring the cabinets up before five." She expelled a slow breath. "If there's nothing else, I'll go back to my office. I need to clear some work off my desk."

"One thing before you go." Ryan leaned back in his chair and gave her a thoughtful look. "What do you need to start your profile on the killer?"

"A copy of all reports that come in. I need to know as much background on the victim as possible—her habits, the places she frequented. That might help pinpoint the location where she encountered the suspect. If we know that, it'll tell us a lot about the type of person he is." A.J. paused, pursing her lips in thought. "I also need a set of crime scene photos for my own use, if that's possible."

"It is. What else?"

"It's not essential, but I'd like to visit the scene. I can sometimes get a better feel for a crime if I do."

"I want to get over there, too," Ryan said, and checked his watch. "Can't now. I have to meet with the chief in half an hour. We'll go there together...sometime tomorrow.''

A.J. bit down on an automatic protest. She'd lost count of the number of crime scenes she'd visited with various officers. It was a part of her job to go to the Westfall mansion. It shouldn't make a difference whom she went with.

But it did.

"Do you have a problem with our going together?" Ryan asked.

"No." She retrieved her leather folder off the table, then walked to the door, reaching for the knob with an unsteady hand.

"See you tonight," Ryan said.

She turned. "Tonight?"

He glanced up from the notes he'd begun jotting on a legal pad. "To go through Ken's things. After nine."

Her hand curled against her thigh. "I thought..."

"You thought what?"

"In a few hours you'll be up to your knees in reports on the Westfall homicide."

"And you thought I'd put off investigating Ken until the task force ends?"

"Yes."

"I won't do that." He dropped his gaze and resumed writing. "I want to finish this business about Ken. There's only one way to do it. Get the facts. Uncover the truth."

Dread pounded like a sledgehammer at the base of A.J.'s skull. God, she wanted the truth, too. Wanted it, but feared it.

Saying nothing, she pulled open the door and walked out.

Chapter 4

Through the dim glow of streetlights that pierced the cold December night, Michael studied the muted outline of the Victorian brownstone. The house looked to be three stories, but it was hard to tell with no light shining through its windows. The only illumination came from the porch lamp, its beams forming a puddle of eerie amber light that bled over onto A.J.'s red Miata parked in the driveway.

Settling back into his Bronco's firm upholstery, Michael shifted his gaze. The neighborhood was one of Oklahoma City's older ones, the houses built in the '30s with porches wide enough to roller-skate on and attics accessible by narrow indoor staircases that creaked predictably beneath one's weight.

He nudged down the top of his leather glove and checked his watch; its luminous dial glowed nine-fifteen. A.J. wasn't late—she'd told him she would be home after nine. Michael arched a cynical brow, thinking he should have tied her to a specific time. After all, *midnight* was after nine. Considering how she felt about him going through her brother's belongings, he might be looking at a few hours of staring at her dark house like a voyeur waiting for the show to start.

He hunched his shoulders inside the leather bomber jacket he'd worn since his college days and again glanced at his watch. Why the hell did he care about the time? he wondered after he realized that less than two minutes had passed since he'd last looked. It wasn't as if he had to be somewhere. Other than the mountain of unread reports on Dianna Westfall's murder that he'd crammed into his brief-case, there was nothing awaiting him at home as there once had been. No wife keeping dinner warm, no giggling, spar-kling-eyed daughter begging a piggyback ride.

The thought of how much his life had changed in the five years since his divorce sent an ominous silence through him. If it hadn't been for the large family he called "the crowd" and his friend Tony DiMaiti, Michael knew he'd have never made it after Lauren walked out. She'd spent the first few years of their marriage in total support of his job, then over time began to resent the hours the department demanded, until finally the last thing she wanted to be was a cop's wife. So she'd left, taking their daughter, Megan, with her. It wasn't until weeks later that he learned of Lau-ren's affair with the neurosurgeon to whom she was now married and in whose southern California estate she was happily ensconced. And now, Megan was far past the age for piggyback rides. She was fifteen. In another year she'd be begging for the keys to the car. And except the few weeks during the summer when she came to visit, Mi-chael's contact with her consisted of phone calls and E-mail messages.

His gloved fingers curved against his thighs. It was there, he acknowledged, the dull ache that always settled in his heart at the thought of Megan. Of how he missed her. Of how bitter regret could taste.

Biting down on a short, pungent oath, he blocked out thoughts that did nothing but put a hollowness inside him and diverted his attention back to the Victorian brownstone. The house looked something akin to a dark mammoth crouching on the frozen lawn. He pictured his parents' expansive house on the north side of town. If he went there this minute, he knew he'd find every light in the place glowing and at least one of his brothers or sisters, their respective spouses and children settled in front of the TV in the comfortable den. There would be an obstacle course of toys strewn across the polished wood floor and the chaos wouldn't raise an eyebrow. With the holidays, the place would shimmer with Christmas inside and out, as did many houses on the street where he now sat. In contrast, A.J.'s aunt's house exhibited nothing but darkness-backed panes of glass. Michael shrugged. He doubted A.J. felt much like decorating; her brother was dead, her aunt in the hospital. From his check into her and Ken's background, he knew there was no other family.

Just as he'd decided to turn on the engine and let the heater run, the headlights of a car sliced around the corner and headed his way.

Narrowing his eyes, Michael watched a sleek white Corvette pull into the driveway behind A.J.'s Miata. After a moment the driver's door opened. In the porch light's glow, Michael made out the form of a tall black-coated man. The figure walked to the passenger door and pulled it open. Lawson, Michael decided. Greg Lawson.

Michael leaned forward in his seat, eyes narrowed. He could barely distinguish A.J.'s shadowy outline as Lawson tucked her beneath his arm and walked her to the porch. There, she turned, looked up and said a few words, her breath a gray cloud on the cold, still air. Lawson nodded, dipped his head and kissed her. A long, slow kiss that twisted Michael's stomach muscles into a nasty, clenching knot.

"Damn," he muttered. If he didn't know better, he'd say he was jealous. And of what? he asked with derision. Another man's attention to a woman he barely knew. His fingers curved on the steering wheel. That was the problem, wasn't it? He barely knew A.J. Duncan, and in this silent introspective pause he admitted the thing that had been plaguing him since the moment he'd met her. He wanted to get to know A.J. better. A hell of a lot better.

He sat unmoving, weighing that thought. Even if there could be something between them, it wasn't going to happen now. *Couldn't* happen. He was investigating her brother. Hell, officially, he was still investigating *her.* If that wasn't enough, she now worked on a task force under his command. A whole mountain of complications to dig through.

Michael's lips settled into a sardonic curve. It took two to make a relationship, he reminded himself, and A.J. Duncan wanted nothing to do with him. Matter of fact, she'd probably prefer he disappeared from her life.

On the porch, A.J. took a jerky step backward, ending the kiss. Michael dragged air into his lungs, and realized he'd been holding his breath since Lawson first locked onto her. With her hand settled on Lawson's forearm, she shook her head and said something, turned, twisted her key in the lock, then disappeared through the front door.

Throughout a slow sweep of seconds, Lawson stood motionless on the porch, staring at the door. Finally, he shoved his hands into his coat pockets, left the porch and climbed into his car. When he backed the Corvette out of the driveway and sped, wheels squealing, in the Bronco's direction, Michael slunk down in his seat.

Watching through the side mirror, he tracked the Corvette's taillights until they disappeared around a corner. He waited a few moments in darkness, then climbed out. Slamming the door behind him, he headed across the shadowy street, then up the walk, rolling his shoulders against the knots that had settled there. He'd come here to go through Ken Duncan's things and that was what he'd do. That was *all* he'd do. He was close to letting the Duncan investigation get personal, and that was one hell of a big mistake. He was a cop with a job to do, he reminded himself as he jabbed the doorbell with a gloved finger. He had to stay focused. Had to concentrate on the Duncan investigation, not the Duncan woman.

When the door swung open, Michael's first thought was that A.J. seemed to have shrunk by three inches. His gaze dropped. She was barefoot, her hose a dark web over red-polished toenails. He let his gaze slide slowly up her stock-inged legs, upward to the slim-fitting black dress that began midthigh, curved at her waist and ended in a throat-caressing neckline. She wore her dark hair swept off her face and neck, enhancing her high, sculptured cheeks.

His fingers itched to touch those cheeks. He stifled the thought and kept his hands at his sides.

"Lieutenant."

"A.J."

When he came through the door, she took an automatic step backward. Then another. Her eyes flicked across his well-worn bomber jacket and jeans before she turned away.

"Greg put everything in Aunt Emily's study," she said, walking toward an arched doorway. As she moved, light from the vaulted ceiling glinted off the silver clip that held her hair off her neck.

From the rigid set of her shoulders, Michael knew she was as tense as steel.

He expelled a slow breath and took a minute to examine his surroundings. From outside, the house had seemed de-ceptively small. Now, he stood on polished wood sur-rounded by soaring paneled walls. A thick-legged table holding a carved rock on a brass stand with a light in its base stood against one wall. Before him was a carpeted staircase, to its left a dark hallway that led toward the back of the house. The only lights on were those in the entryway and the room into which A.J. had disappeared.

Michael headed that way, the heels of his shoes sounding hollow echoes across the wood floor.

The study smelled of aging leather, with a hint of lemon polish mixed in. A.J. stood in the center of the room beside several chest-high stacks of liquor boxes. One was open; a pile of books, a worn baseball mitt and a set of weights lay on the rug beside a pair of strappy black high heels.

"You started without me," he said levelly.

She met his gaze. "You going to write me up for not waiting?"

Jaw set, Michael stopped inches from her. He found himself thinking how much he disliked the wariness that darkened her eyes whenever he came near. "Mind if I take off my jacket?"

"I mind that you're here," she said, then shifted her gaze in the direction of a pair of French doors that led to a dimly lit terrace. Her face was set, tension radiated out of her like a physical force. Clearly, she had no intention of covering the fact that she didn't want him there, didn't appreciate his intrusion into a painful examination of her brother's belongings. The irony was that if the situation were reversed, Michael knew he'd be just as determined on behalf of one of his siblings.

"I understand," he said in a quiet voice.

She looked back at him. "You aren't going to find the identity of Ken's killer in these boxes."

"You may be right."

She pinched the bridge of her nose between her thumb and forefinger. "I went by the hospital earlier to see my aunt. She's putting up a brave front, but she doesn't fool me. She feels crummy and it scares me to think what might happen." A.J.'s voice reverberated with emotion as she stared into the open box. "She asked me if we'd found Ken's killer. Every day, she asks."

The misery in her eyes put a rock in Michael's chest that had no business being there. He had to remain objective, keep his distance. Doing that was getting harder by the minute.

"I'm sorry about your aunt," he said. "A.J., if you don't feel up to going through Ken's things, you could go into another room and relax. Have a cup of coffee. I'll do it on my own. I'll let you know if I find anything. I give you my word."

She curled her bottom lip between her teeth and stared at the boxes as if considering his suggestion. "No," she said finally. "I have to be here. I *need* to be here." Beneath the black silk of her dress her shoulders straightened. "But the coffee sounds good. Want some?"

"Sure."

"It's instant."

His mouth kicked up on one side. "You stole my recipe."

Giving him a faint smile, she stepped around him and disappeared out the arched doorway.

Exhaling slowly, Michael pulled off his jacket, his gaze moving around the room. His mind registered the massive desk piled high with papers, the wall-to-wall shelves crammed with leather books and various Egyptian artifacts. An alabaster pyramid jutted from the mantel over the fireplace. Beside the pyramid sat a regal-looking cat carved from ivory, its oval eyes lined in black kohl.

It was the photograph in a silver frame angled in the bookcase beside the terrace doors that snagged his gaze and held it.

He tossed his jacket onto the arm of a leather wing chair and walked across the room. Inside the silver frame, A.J. stood in the stern of a sailboat, returning the smile of a tall, blond-haired man who had a possessive arm wrapped around her waist. Clad in shorts and T-shirt, her skin was tanned to the color of honey, her sunlit face a study in happiness.

What would it be like, Michael wondered, to have A.J. Duncan smile at him that way? To look up at him without strain in her face? To stand at his side with no wariness behind her eyes?

"I forgot to ask how you take your coffee."

He turned. The subject of his wonderings stood before him, a steaming mug in each hand, her dark, upswept hair shining like polished ebony beneath the room's lights. He had the sudden image of that dark hair loosened, spread out beneath him across a soft white pillow.

"Black." He forced the word around the knot in his throat and accepted the mug she offered. "Who's into Egypt?"

"Aunt Emily." A.J. blew across her mug, then sipped. "She teaches anthropology at the University of Oklahoma. If she hadn't gotten sick, she and ten students would be leaving for Cairo the day after Christmas."

Michael nodded. And because he couldn't stand not knowing, he inclined his head toward the bookcase at his side. "I was wondering who the man in the picture is."

Her eyes shifted, then returned to his face. "My fiancé."

In what Michael realized was an unconscious move, her hand slid to her right thigh, her long, slender fingers conducting a slow massage.

"He died in an accident," she added softly.

Michael's breath became shallow. A.J. had suffered the loss of the man she loved and a brother she clearly adored. As she stood before him, looking as though she might break if he touched her, Michael felt the need to protect. To shield her from further hurt.

Yet, that was exactly what his search through Ken's belongings might do. Hurt her further.

Michael watched her turn and walk to the box she'd opened before he arrived and realized his objectivity was in trouble. Big trouble.

With a hand that wasn't quite steady, she lifted one flap on the box. "Let's get this over with."

Two hours later, disorganized piles of receipts, junk mail and well-worn paperbacks littered the study's floor.

They'd found nothing meaningful. Nothing on a drug dealer named Snowman. Nothing to motivate Ken to leave Michael a cryptic phone message about having unnamed evidence. Nothing that condemned—or cleared—the dead cop.

With a frustrated breath, Michael lifted Ken's answering machine from the bottom of the box he'd angled onto the couch. He sat the machine on the only clear spot available—a space on the coffee table beside a stack of bank statements that documented Ken Duncan's decided lack of fiscal responsibility.

Rubbing the tight muscles in his neck, Michael glanced across the couch to where A.J. sat. Her eyes were closed, her head leaned back against the leather upholstery. Her right hand moved against her thigh, her fingers kneading softly as if to quell a deep-seated ache. Michael was keenly aware the strain in her face had deepened with each box they'd searched.

"A.J., are you all right?"

"Fine."

"I want to check for messages on Ken's machine. I'll get out of your hair after that."

She opened her eyes and stared bleakly across the top of the now-empty box. Her lips were pale; her skin seemed almost luminous against the soft fabric of her black dress.

"We found nothing. *Nothing.*" Emotion broke through her voice as she pushed off the couch and stared down at him. "You should be out looking for the burglars who killed Ken. Greg supplied a composite of the one he caught a glimpse of. Your detectives should plaster the streets with it. Instead, you're more interested in finding out what brand of boxer shorts my brother wore."

Michael remained silent as temper whipped color into her face, hardened her eyes.

"A word of advice, Lieutenant. Take off your Internal Affairs hat and start acting like a homicide cop. That is what you are, after all."

"You're right," Michael agreed in an even voice. "I'm a homicide cop and I'm doing my job. I'm investigating the line-of-duty death of a cop. A cop who had a black cloud over his head. I need to find the source of that cloud and just how far it stretches. To do that, I need to find out everything there is to know about your brother."

A tear slid down her cheek and she wiped it away with an angry dash of her hand. "You saw his bank statements. Ken didn't care about money. He didn't care about *things.*"

"So it seems. But things—and people—aren't always as they seem."

"Ken was," A.J. shot back. "He was forever giving his

last dollar to someone down on his luck.'' She wrapped her arms around her waist and walked across the room to the wall of bookshelves. As she moved, Michael saw the slight limp in her walk.

She lifted a wooden frame that held a picture of a young Ken getting a hug from a tall, dark-haired woman holding a plaster-of-paris mold of a child's handprint. ''Our parents died in a plane crash when I was a baby. Ken was only five years older than me, but in a lot of ways he was the father I never had.''

She turned to face him, but Michael could tell she wasn't seeing him. She was remembering. ''He'd beat up any kid who gave me a bad time. The night I had my first date, Ken insisted on meeting the guy. He shook the guy's hand and told him there'd be hell to pay if he got out of line with me. Ken scared him so bad I never saw him after that night.'' Tears welled in her eyes. ''Ken was always there for me,'' she said, her voice barely above a whisper. ''He was good. No matter what he said, he would never have…''

Michael rose slowly off the couch, watching the realization of what she'd said dawn in her eyes. ''What did he say, A.J.?''

Her mouth thinned and she replaced the frame on the bookshelf. ''Nothing.''

''Nothing, hell,'' Michael ground out as he advanced on her. ''You just admitted it. You have information related to an investigation, and you're concealing it. Not smart, lady.''

''I don't…'' She dragged the heel of her palm across her forehead as her tear-filled eyes took in the pitiful remnants of her brother's life. ''God, why? Why Ken?''

Michael's throat tightened. It was as if he saw the pain surge through her and clench at her heart.

She blinked, spilling more tears down her cheeks. A strangled sound welled up in her throat as she whirled away and limped toward the door.

Logic told him she needed time alone, to let her go, but instinct sent him after her. His hand wrapped around her wrist before she reached the entry hall. Tightening his grip, he forced her around to face him.

"A.J., listen to me—"

"I don't want to do this," she said through her teeth.

"Do what?"

"Cry."

"Ken was your brother, for God's sake. You have a right to grieve."

"Not in front of you." She stared up at Michael, her bloodless lips quivering. "Not you." Tears streaked down her face, her whole body shook. *"Not you!"*

"Sweet Jesus," Michael breathed as he pulled her to him, his arms circling her slight form. He held her while she wept as though she'd lost everything that mattered, and he wasn't sure she hadn't come close to just that.

"I don't want to hurt you," he said, his voice a whisper against her hair.

She smelled like roses warmed beneath the sun. As Michael drew in her scent, he acknowledged how incredibly good she felt in his arms. *How right.* His mind rushed forward, imagining how she'd feel beneath him, her naked belly and breasts sealed against his flesh. He tightened his jaw and ruthlessly pushed away the thought. He couldn't get involved, dammit. Couldn't let himself care.

So he held her. Just held her. And with monumental effort he concentrated his thoughts on Ken Duncan's scattered possessions, not on the woman in his arms.

Gradually, her crying lessened. She drew in shuddering breaths while the heat of her tears burned through his starched shirt. Leaning back, she looked up at him, her dark eyes rimmed with wet, spiked lashes. "I don't cry... I..." Her unsteady fingers trembled on his forearms. "Seeing Ken's things. The finality of it all hit me. I just..."

"You've just kept all that grief bottled up." His brows knitted as he thumbed a tear off her cheek. "That's not good. If my mother were here, she'd tell you tears are the medicine the soul needs to heal."

A.J. nodded numbly and gave him a fragile smile. "Then I should be well on the way to recovery."

Even as he told himself he had no right to want her, no right to her, Michael lowered his head and pressed his lips to the soft tendrils of dark hair that shadowed her temple. Her skin was a soft haven of warmth against his lips as they moved in a slow, irresistible journey to her cheek, then her mouth.

Beneath his hands, her spine tightened for a split second, then she softened against him like wax beneath a candle's flame. He teased her lips open with his tongue and tasted the need on her shuddering breath. A soft, yielding sound rose in her throat as her mouth accepted his.

She tasted faintly of rich coffee, tears and heaven.

His hand slid lazily up her back to the nape of her neck, then forward to the hollow of her throat. He felt the quick, faint tremor of her pulse. A primitive, masculine satisfaction swept through him as his lips took hers in a dreamy kind of possession. He wasn't the first man to kiss her tonight, but by God he wanted *his* to be the kiss she remembered.

Yet he didn't push, didn't pressure. He tasted. Savored.

Her hands rose, and he half expected her to push him away. Instead, her palms settled featherlike against his chest.

Need whipped through him quietly, painfully.

His hand rose, his fingers plunged upward through her thick hair; the silver clip loosened, then clattered against the wood floor. Long, dark curls tumbled across the delicate slope of her shoulders.

Her hair felt like silk. Dark, airy silk that a man could drown in. He wove his fingers through that silk and deepened his kiss. He had never felt such raw need, need so powerful it overrode his better judgment, his self-control.

At first he thought he imagined her spine tensing against his palm, the hard press of her hand against his chest.

"We can't." She pulled from his touch and stood before him, her hair tousled, her face flushed. "I...can't handle this," she said, her voice a raw rasp around shallow, ragged breaths.

"A.J.—"

"That shouldn't have happened. It was a mistake."

"No," he countered. "I meant to kiss you."

His hands were far from steady, so he raked his fingers through his hair and took a step back. A thin line existed between maintaining objectivity and losing it, and he'd just screwed up big time. Even as the knowledge settled into his brain, he knew he wanted more. Knew he'd never be satisfied without finishing what he'd started.

But not now, he acknowledged with churning regret. She was shouldering a heavy burden over Ken's death and the unsettling question of his guilt. On top of that, she had her aunt's illness to contend with. A.J.'s defenses were down; she was vulnerable. And gorgeous. And so damn desirable, Michael thought as she stood before him, looking disheveled and wide-eyed.

"But you're right about one thing," he added. "It shouldn't have happened. Not now, anyway."

The flush in her cheeks deepened. "I want..." Her voice quavered and trailed off.

As she turned and half limped to the terrace doors, Michael felt the patterns of his world moving, altering, realigning themselves. And for the first time since his marriage fell apart, he found he wanted more than just his job to immerse himself in. He wanted A.J. Wanted her naked beneath him, her flesh hot, her eyes wild with the same gut-twisting desire that had him entertaining thoughts of dragging her back into his arms and sating the ache in his loins.

Instead, he clenched his jaw and said in a quiet voice, "Tell me what you want."

"I want you to leave me alone."

Michael dragged air into his tight lungs. While he waited for his pulse to steady, he studied her profile as she stared out the door into the frozen darkness. Her face was all shadowed hollows and smooth planes.

"You and Ken, you mean."

"Yes."

"I can't do that." The damnable cold, hard remoteness now in her voice stirred his frustration. "And it's time you leveled with me."

"I have," she said dully as she stared out into darkness. "I don't know how that printout got from my desk to Ken's locker. I have no idea why someone deposited ten thousand dollars in his checking account or who that someone was. All I know is that my brother didn't do either of those things. He wouldn't do those things."

"You don't know that. Dammit, A.J., you're operating on fantasy, when what you need is fact. And the fact is, your brother may have stolen information from your unit, sold it and left you to answer for his actions."

She whirled to face him, fire leaping in her dark eyes. "The fact is Ken's dead. You should be looking for his killer, not rummaging through his things like a scavenger."

"Maybe the way to find out who killed him," Michael said through his teeth as he walked toward her, "is to investigate him."

A.J. blinked. "A burglar killed Ken. He and Greg surprised two burglars. Ken died in a botched burglary—"

"That sure as hell is how things look."

She took a step toward him. "Are you saying that's not what happened?"

"No. I'm saying the more time that passes since Ken's death, the more things don't add up."

Her eyes narrowed. "What things?"

"Supposedly, the burglary wasn't a pro job. Supposedly, a pair of street thieves got caught in the act, panicked and left one cop injured and another dead. The day after Ken died, the media plastered the city with the composite Greg Lawson came up with of the suspect who assaulted him. The Crime Stoppers program posted a sizeable reward for information on the crime. So far there's not a whisper on the street about who these guys are. No talk at all. I may be new to Homicide, but I rode patrol long enough to know things don't add up. Anytime you've got a reward involved, every two-bit junkie comes out of the woodwork to squeal and collect the cash.''

As Michael spoke, A.J.'s face had gone from flushed to pale. She stood motionless, one hand fisted at her throat, her other arm wrapped around her waist. ''What about Greg? Do you think he lied about what happened?''

''I have no idea. His injuries were real, I do know that. The patrol officers who found him in the alley behind the warehouse confirm he was out cold. So does the doctor in the emergency room who stitched the gash in his forehead. Lawson could be as much a victim as Ken.'' Michael lifted a shoulder. ''I'm not pointing a finger at anyone. I'm just saying some things that have to do with Ken's death aren't playing the way they should. It makes me wonder.''

Keeping his eyes steady on hers, he slowly closed the distance between them. ''You're holding something back about Ken, thinking you're protecting him. Maybe you are,'' he added. ''Then again, your silence may be protecting his killer.''

''My, God.''

The anguished despair in her eyes had him fighting the need to touch her, to comfort. He balled his hands against his thighs and forced himself to concentrate on the case. She was close to telling what she'd concealed from him. He could feel it.

''At some point, you've got to trust me,'' he said. ''I'm not on a witch-hunt. There's no burning need inside me to dig up dirt on your brother. All I want is the truth.''

She opened her mouth to speak. Her lips trembled and she said nothing.

''You knew the kind of man Ken was,'' Michael continued. ''You're convinced someone framed him. If that's true, what you know could help prove that.''

''And if it proves otherwise?'' she asked, her voice quavering.

''What's done is done, A.J. No amount of loyalty or silence on your part can change the past. Could be, all that'll come out of this is that someday you'll answer 'yes' when your aunt asks if Ken's murderer is behind bars.''

She nodded, took a few limping steps to the nearest chair and sank onto its cushions. She stared down at her lap, where her hands lay gripped in a white-knuckle clench.

Michael stood silent, watching her shadowed face. It was almost as if he could see the struggle going on inside her.

Finally, she lifted her gaze to his and said, ''I got an anonymous phone call the night before Ken died. The caller claimed Ken had gone bad. That I should tell him to co-operate with his new partners or else.''

''Or else, what?''

''He didn't say. He just hung up.''

Michael settled onto the chair's matching ottoman, his knees inches from hers. ''Did you recognize the caller's voice?''

''No. His voice sounded muffled. There was some kind of background noise that I couldn't ID. I've racked my brain trying to put a face with the voice, but I can't.''

Michael nodded. ''What did you do after he hung up?''

''I tried to find Ken.'' She lifted an unsteady hand, shoved a tumble of dark hair behind one shoulder. ''It was late. The call came in around two in the morning. I phoned dispatch, and found out Ken had called in sick and wasn't working. I phoned his apartment.'' Her gaze flicked across the coffee table where Ken's answering machine sat. ''His machine wasn't on and he didn't answer.''

''Then what?''

''I threw on some clothes and drove to his apartment.'' She shook her head. ''I had no idea who he was dating, where he might be spending the night. I just knew I had to talk to him about that damn call. I figured he'd show up eventually. And he did.''

''When did he get there?''

''Around five that morning. He didn't say where he'd been.''

''What happened when you told him about the call?''

''The look on his face...'' A.J. dropped her gaze. ''He

was furious. He paced his living room like a caged animal. He kept repeating that he'd kill the bastard for involving me in this—those were his words. I demanded, pleaded, eventually begged him to tell me what the hell was going on. He refused to say anything more. After a while he stormed out. It was…the last time I saw him alive.''

Michael leaned in. ''And you think he might have made good on his threat to kill the man who called you. That's why you didn't tell me about the call when I ordered you to Internal Affairs.''

With slow precision she raised her gaze to meet his. ''Yes. Ken was laid-back, easygoing. If I hadn't seen it for myself that morning, I'd have sworn he was incapable of such rage. But I did see. And I half believed he'd make good on his threat. I was so upset, so scared that after he walked out I went into his bathroom and threw up.''

Even now, Michael could see the agonizing uncertainty in her eyes. ''For what it's worth, we don't have any unsolved homicides that occurred in that period.''

''Except Ken's.''

''Except Ken's.'' He leaned back on the ottoman, studying her. ''Is that it? That's all you've held back?''

''Yes,'' she said without hesitation.

Again, he had no facts to back up his instincts. He just knew. She was telling the truth.

Her lips thinned. ''I withheld information about an active investigation. You can suspend me for that. Maybe fire me.''

''True.'' He gave her a ghost of a smile. ''But then, where would I find another experienced profiler to work on the task force on such short notice?''

She moistened her lips with the tip of her tongue. Her eyes were huge and dark against the pallor of her skin. ''Do you think whoever called me had something to do with Ken's death?''

''I don't know,'' Michael said quietly. ''If you get another call, I want your word you'll tell me.''

"I can't see that the man would have reason to call again."

"Maybe not. But he's got to know that his call put questions in your mind. Questions that haven't gone away with Ken's death."

Michael was suddenly aware of a deep-seated anger stirring inside him and he tore his gaze from her dark one.

Sweet Jesus. Instead of maintaining his distance from the Duncan investigation, he'd let his emotions dump him into the middle of it. At this instant, all he wanted was to catch the anonymous caller just so he could throttle the scum for threatening A.J.

"Whoever called you is still out there," he stated, his voice sharper than he'd intended. "You need to be careful. If anyone even looks at you funny, I want to know."

"Yes. All right."

He glanced again at his watch. It was near midnight. "I'll check Ken's machine for messages, then go." He rose, gathered up the answering machine and carried it to the desk. There, he plugged it in and hit the Play button.

As a message about a special offer from a portrait studio filled the study, he kept his eyes on A.J. She sat unmoving, her gaze fixed on the machine. Her face was a picture of exhaustion; the strain she felt showed in the shadows beneath her eyes, in the small lines etched at the corners of her mouth.

The next message began, and she winced when a bill collector promised dour consequences if Officer Duncan didn't pay up. Another beep sounded, and a woman's soft voice drifted on the study's warm air.

"I'm sorry I missed your call...and I'm sorry we argued. Ken, you've got to tell me what's going on. We lost each other once. We can't let it happen again. Come here when you finish your shift. We can talk. Whatever it is, I'll stand by you. I love you."

A.J.'s eyes widened. "My, God."

Michael waited for the machine to click off, then pushed the Rewind button. "I take it you know the voice?"

She nodded. "Mary."

Michael arched his eyebrows when she didn't continue. "Mary who?"

"Duncan. Ken's ex-wife." A.J. rose and walked to the desk. "I had no idea they were seeing each other."

"How long have she and Ken been divorced?"

"About a year," A.J. answered, her voice still ripe with bewilderment. "I don't know why they split up, Ken never would say, and Mary didn't come around after that." A.J.'s forehead furrowed. "I saw her at Ken's funeral. I remember hoping she'd come here afterward, but she didn't."

"If she got Ken to talk about what was going on, then she might have some answers to our questions. She might even know something about the evidence he said he had." Michael ejected the tape from the machine and slid it into the back pocket of his jeans. "How do I get in touch with her?"

"I'll try her at home," A.J. said as she reached for the phone. "As far as I know, she's still in the house where she and Ken lived." A.J. punched in a number, then waited. When someone picked up and she asked to speak to Mary, he could tell that A.J. had gotten an answering service.

"Mary's out of town," she said after hanging up. "She'll be back tomorrow afternoon."

"What does she do?"

"She's a lawyer."

"What firm?"

"Ames, Martin and Radner."

Michael arched a brow. "High-dollar criminal attorneys."

A.J. nodded. "That's how Ken met Mary. He'd busted a client of hers and she gave him hell on the witness stand. He used to say it was love at first insult." A.J.'s eyes sharpened and locked with his. "I want to be there when you talk to her."

"You may find out things about Ken that are hard to accept."

"I don't think anything could be worse than not knowing."

He studied her for a moment, saw the anguish in her eyes.

"All right. We'll talk to her together." He looked at the scattered possessions around him, at the empty boxes. "I'll help you pack—"

"I can do it."

"You're sure?"

"Yes."

Michael walked to the chair and retrieved his leather jacket. "Then I'll get out of here. I've got a briefcase full of reports on the Westfall homicide to go over."

She nodded and said nothing.

He wanted to say something to banish the pain from her dark eyes, but there weren't any words. Turning, he walked into the entry hall and out the door, locking it securely behind him.

Chapter 5

"Dianna Westfall died no more than six hours before the maid found her body."

From her place at the conference table, A.J. listened to Michael brief the task force on the medical examiner's findings. As he spoke, she shuffled through the packet of crime scene photos she'd found on her chair when she arrived moments before.

"Cause of death is multiple stab wounds," Michael continued in a deep, even voice. "The ME cataloged twenty-one during the autopsy. Seventeen incised wounds to the left lung, one to the right lung, two to the liver and one to the left lateral neck, which almost severed the spine."

A.J. winced. No wonder the woman was nothing more than a mutilated heap, bent like a gruesome fortune cookie on a mattress so saturated with blood that it looked black.

"The murder weapon has a double-edged blade, sharpened on both sides, about eight inches long. It wasn't found at the scene."

Seconds lengthened into minutes while A.J. studied the close-ups of the severed red-lacquered index finger posed amid a bank of lacy pillows. Frowning, she attempted to fit together the pieces of the puzzle swirling in her mind. Something about the finger didn't add up.

"Ought to be a law against men as good-looking as the lieutenant."

Helene St. John's whispered words jerked A.J. out of her intense concentration. She gave the patrol officer a sideways glance to acknowledge she'd heard, and said nothing.

Helene leaned in. "I wonder if Ryan knows how delectable he looks in that navy suit."

You should see him in a leather bomber jacket and faded jeans that hug his thighs, A.J. thought.

She pulled off her reading glasses and pinched the bridge of her nose. The first rays of winter sun had barely crept through the conference room windows, and already she felt the fatigue in her legs and back. She hadn't slept a wink last night. The rich, drugging memory of Michael's kiss had tied her in knots, kept her mind spinning.

Michael…

God, when had she started thinking of the man on a first-name basis?

When his lips took hers in that kiss, that was when. The kiss that had erased every rational thought from her mind and swirled her blood with quick, urgent need.

From across the table, Sam Rogers blew out a puff of gray cigar smoke and leaned forward in his chair. "Lieutenant, do we know yet if there's property missing from the scene?"

"No," Michael answered. "We'll find out later today, after the housekeeper and insurance agent finish their inventory."

A.J. barely heard the exchange. Her fingers stilled against the stack of crime scene photos, and she stared unseeingly at Dianna Westfall's antique bureau, topped with a silver tray holding crystal atomizers filled with pale, golden scents. Now that she'd let the disconcerting memory of the previous night interrupt her thoughts, A.J. found it impossible to focus on the job at hand. Couldn't concentrate on anything, except that kiss.

That kiss.

She caught her bottom lip between her teeth, savoring the tenderness lingering there.

She'd wanted that kiss. Needed it. Welcomed it. Even now, the remembered feel of Michael's hard, muscled body against hers sent a twist of desire through her belly. Beneath her jade bolero jacket and black wool skirt, her skin heated.

Was that kiss the reason she told Michael about the anonymous phone call? Had those few delicious moments in his arms lowered her defenses to such an extent that when he voiced his theory—and that was all it was, a theory—that someone other than burglars killed Ken, she'd revealed information that could further implicate her brother in wrongdoing?

In the following introspective moment, A.J. knew the answer. Knew her hormones had nothing to do with it.

She wanted to trust Michael Ryan. God help her, she had no idea why. Nor did she know if she should.

Michael had a duty to see the investigation of her and Ken through to the end, she knew that. Right now, Michael believed she was an innocent pawn, but would his thinking change if additional incriminating evidence against her and Ken emerged? And what steps would Michael take if that happened?

Where the job was concerned, he had a reputation for toughness. He went by the book, did what it took to clear a case. Michael Ryan was not the type of man who'd let a kiss influence his thinking.

A.J. let her gaze drift down the length of the table. Head cocked, Michael listened with intense concentration while Sky Milano gave an update on forensic evidence found at the scene.

"From seminal fluid found on the victim's body, we know the suspect's blood type is AB," Sky said, poking her oversize glasses up the bridge of her thin nose. "Common to only four percent of the population. Find a white male suspect with type AB, and chances are it's our guy."

Michael nodded, then glanced up, his eyes snagging A.J.'s for a brief instant before moving on. The knot in her belly tightened.

How could she work with him, see him every day, and not think about that kiss? About the need his touch had awakened in her?

She set her jaw and told herself to stop acting like a starry-eyed schoolgirl. It had only been one kiss, after all. And he hadn't even been the first man to kiss her last night.

Lifting her hand, she began a slow massage of her right temple. Who was she fooling? With Greg, she'd felt no genuine passion when his mouth descended on hers. His lips had been tender, caressing, yet she'd felt no fizz in her blood, no jump of her pulse.

It was Michael's kiss that had sent her body temperature spiraling, kicked her heartbeat into overdrive. Michael's touch that had robbed her of sleep, causing her to lie awake the entire night, tangling the bed sheets as if in a fever.

From where she sat, A.J. studied his strong, clear-cut profile. If he'd lost any sleep, he didn't show it. His thick, dark hair was neatly combed, his face freshly shaved, his navy suit pressed with sharp creases. What would it feel like to lie beneath him, flesh to flesh? To be held in his arms, her body smoldering beneath his touch as his wide, sensuous mouth—

At that instant, Michael finished making assignments and ended the meeting. A general murmur of voices and a rustling of paper brought A.J. plummeting back to earth. Most of the people around the table pushed back in their chairs and rose. Some headed for the door; others made a beeline for the newly installed computers and banks of phones that lent a war-room atmosphere to task force headquarters.

As Helene stood, A.J. noted the officer had taken advantage of the plainclothes aspect of the assignment. Her black suit fit her sleek body like sausage casing; her platinum hair hung loose and wild, framing her striking, high-cheek-boned face.

"Oh, I almost forgot," Helene said and handed A.J. a piece of paper. "I took a call for you before you got here. The woman said she's Mary Duncan's secretary. Said to tell you Ms. Duncan's in Dallas taking a deposition and should be back in the office around four today. You can come by then."

"Thanks," A.J. said, and tucked the message into her folder.

"Mary Duncan." Helene pursed her lips. "She's Ken's ex, isn't she?"

A.J. nodded. "Do you know her?"

"No. By the time I came on the night shift, she'd already filed for divorce. As I recall, Ken wasn't at all happy about the split."

"He wasn't."

"Speaking of Ken, a bunch of us who worked his shift are getting together tomorrow night at Buck Newton's house. Sort of a bring-your-own-booze-and-food type deal. Starts at eight, ends when the last person passes out. Greg has the address. Why don't you ask him to bring you?"

A.J. took a deep breath. Last night when she'd ended Greg's kiss and pulled from his embrace, her gaze had fixed on the angry cut on his forehead. Guilt pressed in around her. Greg had been there for her when Ken died, and she owed him. She *wanted* to give back to him. But the emotion he seemed to want from her simply wasn't there. In the glow of the porch light, his expression told her that he had seen the truth in her eyes.

Even then, Michael Ryan had been on the periphery of her mind, knowing he would arrive soon to go through Ken's things. Feeling a dark, primitive desire to be near him, yet frightened of what his search might find.

"You *are* seeing Greg, aren't you?" Helene asked, a faint line of impatience sounding in her voice.

"We're good friends."

"Word on the grapevine is that you're more than that."

A.J. shrugged. "If that's all people have to talk about, things must be slow around this place."

Helene's lips curved. "You're like me, A.J. You don't appreciate people sticking their noses in your business." She glanced across the room, her gaze settling on the doorway where her tobacco-cheek-stuffed partner waited.

"Well, Kevin and I are off to investigate. I just need to check something with the lieutenant first."

Helene turned and walked to the head of the conference table, her hips swaying like a flag in a soft breeze. She exchanged a few words with Michael, then smiled at something he said.

A.J. attempted to block out the sound of Helene's soft, smoky laughter by forcing her concentration back to the picture of Dianna Westfall's bureau. Beside the tray of crystal atomizers lay a necklace of pearls interspersed with colored jewels; the matching pearl earrings sat a few inches away. A black haze of fingerprint powder covered everything, even the bottle of fingernail polish on the corner of the bureau. She shoved on her glasses and checked the label: *Reentry Red.* Despite her wealth, Dianna Westfall had scrimped when it came to polish—A.J. owned a bottle of the same discount brand.

"I need you to do something."

She jerked up her chin, surprised to find Michael standing beside her chair.

"This came from the desk in Dianna Westfall's study," he said, indicating the contents of the plastic evidence bag in his hand. The bag held a mauve leather address book, its cover smudged with fingerprint powder.

"She carried the smaller twin to this in her purse," Michael continued. "Since you need to know Dianna's habits and the places she frequented for your profile, I'd like you to go through the books, build a database of individuals and businesses listed."

"I'll start now."

Michael's fingers brushed hers as she accepted the bag. A.J. tensed against the low-grade buzz that swept through her. God, she needed this attraction to Michael Ryan like a giraffe needed a sore throat.

"Where's Dianna's other book?" she asked, forcing a businesslike tone into her voice. She might be attracted to the man, but she could control it. Control her emotions; concentrate on the job.

"In the lab. They'll send it up after it's checked for prints."

Despite her firm intent to keep her mind on business, A.J.'s gaze drifted to Michael's lips as he spoke. She knew what it was like to kiss that wide, sensuous mouth. Knew the need one kiss could ignite.

"Anything else?" he asked.

She forced her attention back to the stack of crime scene photos. "Something's bothering me."

Michael slid a hip onto the edge of the table. "Something about last night?"

The sudden softness in his voice brought A.J.'s eyes slowly back to his. He watched her with quiet purpose, waiting.

"Something about the Westfall case," she answered evenly.

"What?" he asked, arching a dark brow.

How many times had she sat inches away from a cop while they discussed a case one-on-one? Too many to count, she told herself. That Michael Ryan had slid his hip onto the table and had leaned in so close she could smell the spicy scent of his cologne shouldn't matter.

But it mattered, dammit. It mattered too much. It was that kiss that had done it.

"The suspect wasn't interested in anything except Dianna," A.J. blurted, then dragged in a deep, controlling breath. "That's where his rage centered. On her. On what was on that bed. I'm wondering about the finger."

"What about it?"

"Did he cut it off before or after she died?"

"The autopsy report says after."

"So, he didn't do it as a means of torture."

"No."

"Why'd he go to the trouble after she was dead and not take the finger with him?"

"You think he should have?"

"Maybe." A.J. fanned the photographs out onto the table. "Look at the silver, the jewelry lying around in just the bedroom. He could have gotten a bundle fencing it. But he left it alone. He didn't go to the mansion to steal, he went there because of Dianna."

Michael stared down at the pictures. "Since we found no signs of forced entry, we're going with the assumption she knew him on some level. Trusted him enough to let him into her home."

"I think that's on target," A.J. said as she shuffled through the pictures until she unearthed the one she wanted.

"Her clothes came off without a struggle. You can see her skirt and blouse folded over the arm of the love seat. We know she had sex with her killer, and from what the ME said, it wasn't forced. He had some sort of relationship with Dianna, and I think he'd have wanted a souvenir of their time together." A.J. shook her head. "It's just a feeling."

Michael lifted his eyes from the photos. "I make it a habit to go with my instincts. They're usually on the mark."

A.J. stared at the photographs spread before her. She could help catch the monster who'd wreaked this horrific devastation. That, after all, was the reason for the task force. Irritated at Captain Harris, angry with Michael Ryan, she hadn't brought her usual intensity to the case.

Now, she felt her determination to track the killer settle around her like a warm, familiar cloak.

"Tell me what you're thinking," Michael prodded.

"We have a scene where hardly anything is disturbed," she said. "He brought the weapon with him—nothing was spontaneous. He knew what was going to happen ahead of time."

"The guy came prepared, all right," Michael agreed as

he pointed to a photograph of Dianna's bedside table, where a pair of champagne bottles sat—one empty, one with its cork still wrapped in gold foil. Two stemmed glasses accompanied the bottles, one glass sat upright, the other had toppled onto its side, a small pool of champagne still in its bowl. Some of the pale liquid had spilled onto the snowy silk tablecloth that swooped to the floor.

"The lab found nonporous glove prints on a bottle of nail polish and on the unopened champagne bottle," Michael continued. "Everything else was wiped clean of prints."

A.J. frowned. "We're sure he handled the polish?"

"That's what the lab says. Do you think that's significant?"

"I'm not sure." She gathered the photos back into a stack, thumping their edges into alignment against the table.

Michael leaned back and crossed his arms over his chest. "Heard from your ex-sister-in-law yet?"

A.J. blinked at his change of subject, then nodded. "Helene took a message from her secretary. Mary's in Dallas until this afternoon. We can catch her at her office after four."

"Good. Plan on our going to the crime scene around two," Michael said quietly.

"All right."

"Then we'll go have a chat with Mary Duncan."

"You were right," Michael said as he slid his cellular phone into the inside pocket of his suit coat. "The bastard took..."

His voice drifted off as he scanned the law firm's reception area. Decorated in a heavy English motif, with polished brasses and pewters displayed with a curator's care, the room held an air of quiet refinement. Except for the blond receptionist ensconced behind the marble-topped rosewood counter, he and A.J. had the waiting area to themselves.

They'd been cooling their heels since a stiff-spined secretary appeared out of nowhere to inform them that Mary

Duncan was on an overseas conference call. After he and A.J. declined the offer of coffee, the woman walked purposefully away, their coats folded over her gray-suited arm.

The subtle trill of a telephone drifted on the leather-scented air. The receptionist answered before the second ring. Assured that no one could overhear their conversation, Michael shifted his gaze back to the opposite end of the tufted leather couch where A.J. sat.

"You were right," he repeated. "There's something missing from the Westfall mansion. The bastard got himself a souvenir."

"What did he take?"

A.J.'s voice held all the tension that Michael had sensed settling over her the instant they walked through the law firm's towering mahogany doors. Tension that had her long, graceful fingers absently kneading her right thigh. Tension that emanated from her like a physical force. It was as if he could see her very thoughts skitter in the dark richness of her eyes. Anticipation over what they might find out about Ken had her anxious. Uptight.

In truth, so was he. But he doubted their tension came from the same source. A.J. wanted to protect her dead brother. Michael wanted the truth. He wondered if she'd let her thinking take her far enough to realize that ultimately the only way to clear herself might be to help prove Ken a criminal.

The sleepless night he'd spent shuffling through crime scene reports while his thoughts centered maddeningly on a curvaceous body in a black silk dress had heightened his determination to find the anonymous caller. Whoever he was, he was out there, watching A.J. Wondering if she'd told anyone about the call. Wondering if someone was on his trail.

Someone was.

A.J. gave an impatient tilt to her head. "What's missing from the crime scene?"

Michael arched a brow and realized he'd been staring. For the past two days he'd done a lot of that. Staring at

A.J. down the length of the task force's conference table. Watching. Studying. Already, he was familiar with the slight wrinkle that formed between her eyebrows when she concentrated on her work.

He shoved a hand through his hair, reminding himself again that with the Duncan investigation active and A.J. assigned to his command, she was basically forbidden to him.

Yet, he watched her because he wanted her. And he wanted her to want him.

His gaze moved to the high neckline of her jade jacket, to the dark tumble of hair that drifted past her shoulders, then on to her mouth, her eyes. He felt the heat rise inside him.

Michael expelled a resigned breath. He couldn't have her, he accepted that. Not now. Maybe not for a long time. Still, he knew without question that where A.J. Duncan was concerned, there would be no calming of the storm brewing inside him.

He wrenched his thoughts back to business. "A ring is gone from Dianna's jewelry box," he answered. "A six-carat oval diamond on a platinum band. The insurance adjuster faxed its picture and description to the task force room. I've assigned Helene St. John and Kevin Stoner to check every jewelry store in town to see if Dianna left the ring somewhere for repair. A team of detectives is hitting the pawn shops in case the suspect unloaded it."

"You have to go through the motions," A.J. agreed. "But if he took the ring, he won't part with it. Through it he'll relive his time with her. He'll hoard the ring in some velvet-lined box as if it were his grandmother's best sterling."

"Here's something else to think about," Michael said. "The housekeeper says the bottle of fingernail polish on the bedroom bureau didn't belong to her employer. Dianna never wore red polish."

A.J.'s chin snapped up. "She did the night she died."

Michael watched A.J.'s eyes sharpen and he knew she

was picturing the same thing he was—Dianna Westfall's severed red-lacquered finger propped against a bank of lace-covered pillows.

"He brought the polish with him," A.J. stated quietly.

"I guess he's got a thing for red."

"The ME found no ligature marks on Dianna's wrists, so we know he didn't tie her up. He must have painted her nails after she died, otherwise her struggling would have messed up the polish."

"It looks that way," Michael said. "I've sent an evidence tech to the mansion to pick up the polish and submit it to the lab. Sky says she can compare what's in the bottle to the polish on Dianna's nails and determine if it's the same."

Michael glanced across the room to where the prim receptionist was now engrossed in straightening two dozen red roses in a crystal vase positioned on the rosewood counter. On the wall behind her hung a grouping of oil portraits of prosperous-looking gray-haired men. Michael scrubbed a hand across his face. The place was so proper and dignified, one could feel at ease popping in wearing a tux. He wondered if Mary Duncan was as staid as the atmosphere in which she worked.

Looking back at A.J., he said, "By the way, we're sure now that none of the knives from Dianna's kitchen is the murder weapon. The suspect brought it with him."

"He went there to kill her," A.J. said. "He knew her enough to want to kill her."

"And maybe we'll find his name in one of her address books."

"Maybe."

At that instant, the same stiff-spined secretary who'd seated them approached.

"Ms. Duncan can see you now."

Michael rose, then walked by A.J.'s side as the woman led them along a mahogany-paneled corridor flanked with closed doors. He was aware of his shoes sinking into the pearl gray wall-to-wall carpet, of the discreet gleaming brass sconces that dotted the walls at precise intervals like neat ellipses.

They passed an empty secretarial desk, which Michael surmised belonged to their officious guide. Just then the woman stopped, swept open a paneled door and stepped back, allowing them to enter.

Aware of Ken Duncan's reputation with women, Michael had expected a knockout. Instead, the first thing that hit him about Mary Duncan was her distinct plainness. Big boned and tall, she almost matched his six-foot-two height. Her black suit appeared expensive, but it was clear from the way the jacket hung that she'd recently dropped maybe twenty pounds. The brown hair that curved just above her shoulders was styled, but the sides seemed to close in on her round face. If she wore makeup, he couldn't tell.

"A.J."

Mary Duncan's smile was her saving grace. It transformed her face from plain to expressive, put life in her dark wide-set eyes and gave a subtle hint of well-sculpted cheekbones. When she walked from her desk and gripped A.J.'s hands, Michael saw the sincere pleasure in the attorney's eyes.

And in A.J.'s. In these first few seconds it became evident that a fondness existed between the two women, yet A.J. had told him she hadn't had any contact with Mary since her divorce from Ken. Nor had Mary dropped by the house to visit with the family after Ken's funeral.

"I'm so glad to see you," Mary said. "I think about you often, you and Emily." Her gaze flicked sideways to acknowledge Michael's presence, then went back to A.J. "How are you?"

"Fine. Mary, this is Lieutenant Ryan. We need to talk to you about Ken."

She pulled her hands from A.J.'s. Turning slowly, the attorney gave Michael a cool narrow-eyed look. He could have sworn the air around him plummeted ten degrees.

"You're Michael Ryan?" she asked without inflection.

He nodded, wondering if he'd met the woman somewhere, and forgotten. "That's right."

"I'm familiar with your name. With you. You're the Internal Affairs bastard who demoted Ken."

Chapter 6

Her muscles as stiff as cardboard, A.J. stared at Michael, waiting for him to react to Mary's remark.

He didn't—not outwardly, anyway. His shoulders stayed relaxed, his expression remained implacable as he matched the attorney's defiant stare.

"Actually, I'm no longer with Internal Affairs," he said after a moment. "I command Homicide now. As to my being a bastard, I assure you my mother and father were married at the time of my birth."

"Too bad they didn't transfer you out of IAD sooner," Mary stated, refusing to back down. "Then maybe Ken wouldn't have gotten demoted for something he didn't do. Maybe he wouldn't have wound up in a patrol car on the graveyard shift. If that hadn't happened, Lieutenant, don't you agree he'd still be alive?"

"That's a question no one can answer."

A.J. let out a slow breath as she diverted her gaze to a built-in bookcase filled with leather-bound legal volumes. With her senses on alert, she was aware of the soft purr of the building's central heat. Of faint wisps of sweet dried herbs emanating from a brass bowl on a table across the room. Of Mary's hostility. An unbridled hostility toward Michael that made A.J.'s throat thick with nerves.

"I know the answer, Lieutenant," Mary persisted. "It's your fault he's dead."

"You're wrong," A.J. countered, surprised at her sudden, insistent need to defend Michael. Squaring her shoulders, she looked back at Mary, whose cold stare gave her eyes the look of hard copper. "Ken was like every other cop who signs on the department. He knew the risks. He worked where he was assigned. Period. If you need to blame someone, look to the person who pulled the trigger, not the one who put Ken in the patrol car."

"I blame them both."

Her ex-sister-in-law's hard-edged demeanor didn't exactly surprise A.J. She'd seen Mary in court making legal mincemeat of witnesses. What astonished A.J. was that where Ken was concerned, Mary's defenses had gone up like a drawbridge. For whatever reasons, she'd filed for divorce and had said no to Ken's attempts at reconciliation.

But at some point they'd begun seeing each other. That was evident by the message Mary left on Ken's answering machine. The knowledge that Ken hadn't seen fit to reveal he'd reconciled with Mary intensified the now-familiar feeling of disquiet that hung over A.J. But then, she acknowledged, Mary wasn't the only secret her brother had kept.

"Detective Duncan was demoted because he violated department policy." Michael nudged back the flap of his suit coat and slid a hand into the pocket of his slacks. "He conducted several interviews with a female juvenile without her parent or guardian present. Without anyone present. As a criminal attorney, I'm sure you're aware that's a definite no-no for a cop."

"She was a snitch," Mary countered. "Snitches wouldn't have much to say if cops insisted on having a witness lurking about."

"True. Still, Ken should have arranged to have a third party present. Then he could have proved the girl lied when she claimed he conducted their interviews while they shared a bed.''

Mouth set in a tight line, Mary turned back to A.J. "I'm sorry. I'm not sure why you're here, but I imagine it isn't to hear a debate on the merits of Ken's demotion."

"No, but he's the reason we're here. We need to ask you some questions."

Mary's gaze slanted to Michael for a moment before going back to A.J. "I've missed you," she said, her voice softening. "And I do want us to spend time together. But my schedule's tight—I only have a few minutes right now. I can call you tomorrow. Maybe we can have dinner."

"Ms. Duncan, I'm conducting an official police investigation into your ex-husband's activities," Michael stated. "I need to ask you some questions."

Mary whirled on him. "Ken is dead!" Her hands fisted against her thighs. "Wasn't getting him demoted enough? Can't you let him rest in peace?"

"I have a job to do," Michael answered, his voice level, controlled. "I heard a message you left on his answering machine, so I know you were seeing him. Eventually you will talk to me about Officer Duncan. Now, you can invite A.J. and me to have a seat on that couch over there and get this over with. Or by this time tomorrow you'll have a subpoena that says you have to talk to me." He shrugged. "Either way, it'll happen."

Mary's lips curled into a sneer that mirrored the derision in her eyes. "I love a challenge, Lieutenant. Send your subpoena."

"Mary." A.J. placed a light hand on the woman's arm, then looked to Michael for consent. She couldn't discuss details of an active case—even this one—without permission from the lead investigator.

As if reading her thoughts, Michael nodded. "Go ahead."

She met Mary's gaze. "There's evidence that implicates Ken in illegal activity—"

"That's absurd!"

"Of course, it is," A.J. agreed. "But someone set things up to make him look guilty. Something was going on with Ken and we need to find out what it was."

Mary gave her a wary look. "What sort of thing?"

"I don't know," A.J. answered. "The night before Ken died, a man called me. I have no idea who. He warned me to tell Ken to cooperate or else."

"To cooperate with what?"

"I have no idea. I confronted Ken about it, but he refused to tell me anything. All I know is that he was angry. Furious. Maybe even afraid. It's possible someone other than a burglar killed Ken."

"My, God..." Mary's face paled to the color of cotton.

"He wasn't himself the week before he died," A.J. continued. "Something was going on. I...we need to find out what it was to clear him. If you know something, please tell us."

"It wasn't a burglar who shot him?"

"At this point, we don't know," Michael said. "And A.J. left something out. The evidence that implicates Ken in illegal activity points to her, as well. Right now there's no way to prove or disprove anything. Frankly, she could use your help."

Dismay settled into Mary's eyes. "It's clear, Lieutenant, that you don't know A.J. at all. If you did, there'd be no way you'd believe she'd do anything wrong."

"I didn't say I believe it," Michael countered levelly. "What I said is, there's no way to prove her innocent." He cocked his head toward the tufted leather couch. "Feel like having that chat?"

Mary stared at him long and hard, then nodded. Walking stiffly across the expanse of thick gray carpet, she settled into a straight-backed chair upholstered in a burgundy flame-stitch pattern. A.J. slid onto one end of the leather couch; Michael positioned himself a few inches from her and leaned forward.

"When did you and Ken start seeing each other again?"

Mary blinked. "Why do you want to know?"

"Like A.J. said, something had your ex-husband strung tight. I need to find out not only what it was, but when it began affecting him."

"Two months," Mary stated. "We started seeing each other almost two months before he died."

A.J. shook her head. "I had no idea."

"It was something that just happened," Mary explained. "My car got a flat near his apartment. It was raining like there'd be no tomorrow. Ken drove by, saw my car and stopped. There was a little bar across the street. He suggested we go in and wait out the storm, then he'd change the tire. I almost refused—A.J., you remember how it was when Ken and I were married."

"Something akin to World War II," A.J. said with frankness.

"Right. I figured Ken and I would be at each other's throats before we finished our drinks. I know sometimes it must have seemed like we hated each other. We didn't, of course. We were just on opposite sides of any issue that came up. Some relationships thrive on that. Ours didn't." She shook her head. "Seeing Ken that day made me realize how much I'd missed him."

In the silent moment that followed, A.J. saw memories and more in Mary's eyes. She saw love. And loss. Misery.

"So, you went to the bar for a drink?" Michael prompted.

"Yes." Mary took a deep breath. "For the first time since we separated, we talked. Really talked. Before we left we'd both admitted how stupid we'd been not to figure out the only thing that should have mattered was our marriage."

"And you continued to see each other after that?" A.J. asked softly.

"We spent all our free time together until…he walked into that warehouse."

The wrenching sadness in Mary's voice cut A.J. to the heart. She reached for Mary's hand, and as their fingers linked she felt a connection that had not existed before.

Mary was hurting over Ken's death, hurting perhaps even more than she was, A.J. realized, feeling a tug of guilt. She'd lost a brother; Mary had lost a lover, a man to whom she'd once pledged her life.

"Why," A.J. began softly, "didn't Ken tell me or Aunt Emily that you'd gotten back together?"

"It wasn't that we had some deep, dark secret. We just weren't sure we could get past the hurt, and we didn't want to have to deal with people asking if the relationship was going to work until we knew the answer ourselves." A faint smile curved her lips. "I know we'd have made it. It was like we were kids again, crazy in love, determined not to let anything stand in our way. Now I wish we'd told you and Emily. It seems so senseless not to have shared our happiness."

Michael shifted on the couch. "Do you have any idea what it was that had Ken so uptight?"

"Two things." Mary continued to cling to A.J.'s hand as if desperate for comfort. "One was Emily's illness. He felt helpless that he couldn't do anything for her."

A.J. nodded, remembering the deep concern for their aunt that had shown in Ken's eyes the day he sat on the edge of her desk holding the printout in his hands. *That damn printout.*

"And the other?" Michael prompted.

"He refused to talk about it."

"Something to do with the job?" Michael asked.

"I think so. Whatever it was started a couple of weeks before Ken died. He showed up here one morning after his shift ended. He wasn't just upset. He was mad. Royally hacked. He asked to borrow my microcassette recorder."

"Did he say why?"

Mary slowly lifted her chin and gave Michael a level look. "He said he needed it to prove something, because he wasn't going to give you a chance to take him down a second time."

"Me?" Michael asked, his eyebrows arching.

"You, Lieutenant. He mentioned you specifically."

"Do you know for sure he carried the recorder with him?"

"Once when he was going out to run errands, I saw him slip it into the pocket of his coat."

"What about while he was on duty?"

"I don't know. Except for the day he borrowed it, I only saw him with it that one other time."

"Did you ever ask him why he needed the recorder?"

"Once. He told me to butt out, so I dropped it. I didn't want to start arguing. Whatever it was, it wasn't worth losing him a second time. I didn't ask again."

"Do you have the recorder?"

"No." Mary shifted her gaze to A.J. "I assumed the department sent you the things he had with him...that night. My name's engraved on the back of the recorder."

A.J. knew the exact contents of the cardboard box she'd shoved into the dusty attic over her room: one Sam Browne belt with holster and handcuff case attached, Ken's service revolver, his hat, commission card, the brass name tag, buttons and badge removed from his bloody uniform. But no tape recorder. And no tapes.

"It isn't among the things the department returned," A.J. said, meeting Michael's gaze. "If Ken had the recorder with him that night, it must have been booked into evidence."

"I've seen the list from the property room," Michael said quietly. "It's not on it." He looked back at Mary. "I need any tapes Ken made."

"I don't know that he made any. If he did, I don't have them."

"There has to be a place he considered safe. Maybe at your home, with your things."

"No." Mary's brows knitted. "I went on a cleaning spree a week or so ago. If Ken had left any tapes at my place, I'd have found them."

Michael pursed his lips. "Did Ken ever mention the name Snowman to you?"

"No." Mary rubbed at her forehead as if a pain had settled there. "Who is he?"

"Just a name Ken mentioned in a message he left on my machine."

Mary's eyes rounded. "He called you?"

"Yes. He said he had evidence to turn over to me. I didn't get the message until after his death."

"If he called you, he must have gotten something on tape. After all, that's the reason he borrowed the recorder."

"That's safe to assume," Michael agreed.

Mary shook her head, her dark blunt-cut hair dashing against her cheeks. "I'm sorry, A.J. Maybe if I'd pressed the matter, Ken would have told me what was going on. But he was already upset that he couldn't come up with the money for Emily's treatment. I just didn't want to add to it."

"Her treatment?" For no reason she could name, A.J. felt a slight tightening in her stomach. "Aunt Emily has medical coverage through the university. The insurance company's paying for her treatment."

"No, I mean the experimental treatment."

At A.J.'s blank look, Mary continued. "A couple of years ago, the mother of one of Ken's friend's died of leukemia. Ken remembered all the horror stories. He was determined not to let the same thing happen to Emily. He checked around, found out about some treatment under development at a Houston cancer center. Things sounded good at first, then Ken ran into a brick wall when he talked to your aunt's doctor. He told Ken he didn't put much stock in the program since the drugs they use are waiting FDA approval. That means they're considered experimental. Insurance companies won't foot the bill for anything like that. Just to get on the waiting list for the Houston program, the patient has to come up with over fifty thousand dollars."

A.J. felt, rather than saw Michael stiffen. "How did Ken plan to come up with the money?"

Michael asked the question so effortlessly. Casually. Yet his query sent tremors along her nerves.

The hardness returned to Mary's face. "You ought to start doing your homework before you jump into a case, Lieutenant. It's clear you didn't know Ken any better than you do A.J. He didn't *plan* to get the money. He had no way to get it. It's no secret his credit record was a nightmare. Ken never could manage to save a dime."

"I'm familiar with Officer Duncan's spending habits." Michael's toneless voice wrapped A.J.'s tension tighter, until she could barely breathe.

"Then you understand why he gave up the idea of getting Emily into the program," Mary continued. "I'm sure all that money's the reason he didn't mention it to you, A.J. That, and the fact that the doctor had such strong reservations about the treatment."

"What about you?" Michael asked, his gaze flicking around the expansive, polished office.

"What about me?"

"I presume you make a decent salary. Did Ken ask you to loan him the money?"

"My parents are both in a nursing home and I'm footing the bill. Ken knew there was no way I could help." Mary's gaze went to A.J. "Ken told me that Emily was strapped for cash a year or so ago, and you used most of your savings to help refinance the house."

A.J. nodded and said nothing.

"That's why Ken didn't come to you about a loan. He knew what a hardship that would have put on you."

A.J. sat motionless, her pulse pounding in her throat. She felt simultaneously hot and cold. The last thing she wanted to do was look at Michael, but she couldn't help it. Couldn't keep her gaze from meeting his.

He didn't say a word. He didn't have to, not when his eyes could go that flat. That hard.

Not when Mary had just presented a solid motive for Ken to have crossed the line.

"We need to talk to Aunt Emily's doctor," A.J. stated. Michael slanted a look across the Bronco as he twisted the key in the ignition. She sounded calm. Controlled. Almost too calm, he thought as he shifted in his seat to face her.

"My thoughts exactly," he said. "He'll know how serious Ken was about getting your aunt into the Houston clinic."

"Yes."

With the engine idling, static from the police radio installed in the dash crackled on the cold air. Michael leaned forward and turned down the volume, then rested a wrist on the steering wheel. "I'm surprised you made the suggestion. At this point, I think your aunt's doctor would be the last person you'd want me talking to."

"We agreed the only way to get a lead on who killed Ken is to find out what went on the last couple months of his life."

"A.J., my theory that someone other than a burglar killed Ken is just that—a theory."

"A sound one."

"Maybe. Maybe not."

"You think the doctor will confirm Ken's determination to get Aunt Emily into the clinic, no matter the cost."

He hated to say it, but he couldn't lie to her. "That's right."

"And I think he'll tell us Ken gave up the idea because of the money."

A.J. had said little during the remainder of the time they spent in Mary Duncan's office. She hadn't spoken at all while she walked at his side, head bent forward, hands deep in her coat pockets, through the law building's parking garage. Now she sat beside him as stiff as a blade, her gloved hands clenched in her lap.

He ached for her, knowing the doubt over Ken she must be suffering. *Had* to be suffering. He pulled off his leather gloves, reached out and laid a light hand over hers. "I'm sorry, but you've got to face the facts—"

She jerked away as if he'd stung her. "You think the

facts are that Ken stole the printout from my office so he could sell information and get money to help Aunt Emily.''

"You told me once he didn't care about material things. That he didn't have a use for a lot of cash.'' Michael's shoulders rose beneath his coat. "Your ex-sister-in-law just proved you wrong.''

"I'm not blind, I know how it looks. But Ken wouldn't have done those things." Her voice wavered. "He just wouldn't.''

Expelling a heavy breath, Michael glanced at his watch. It was just after five. For the next hour or so, the downtown streets would be a gridlock of cars, trucks and buses battling their way toward the highway on-ramps.

"The hospital's two blocks from here," he said. "We might as well stop there and let the traffic die down before we head for the station. Maybe we'll catch your aunt's doctor making rounds.''

Saying nothing, A.J. stared out the windshield as if mesmerized by the Visitor Parking sign on the wall directly in front of the Bronco.

Michael watched her hands curl, then uncurl. "I not only have to question your aunt's doctor, but her as well.''

A.J. whipped her face toward him, her eyes sparking. "She doesn't know anything.''

He cocked his head. "You've questioned her about Ken, have you?''

Damn, Michael thought. He had a high regard for loyalty, but A.J. Duncan had taken the concept to new heights. Why couldn't she at least admit he had a job to do? And why did he care what she thought?

He shoved a hand through his hair. The hell of it was that he *did* care. He cared a lot. So much that he no longer had the ability to jostle thoughts of her into a corner of his mind and get on with his work. Soon, he'd have to deal with the emotions that accompanied that realization.

"You may not carry a commission card and a badge," he began, "but you know how an investigation works. You question everyone who might have knowledge of the crime. And of the suspect.''

"Aunt Emily's ill. She...isn't supposed to get upset.'' A.J.'s voice broke. "If you start asking questions about Ken the minute I introduce you, she'll know something's wrong.''

The anguish in her eyes hit Michael like a punch in the gut. People routinely got upset when questioned by the police. That was the nature of the business. When it happened, he handled it, and got on with his investigation. But this wasn't just any investigation, he conceded, and was mildly surprised to find himself make a conscious decision to soften his approach to Emily Duncan. Still, certain questions had to be asked of her. If he put it off, the woman might become too ill to respond. He didn't want to put it off, he thought, letting his gaze glide along the smooth, enticing curve of A.J.'s jaw. It was more than just a sense of justice that deepened his resolve to get the Duncan investigation over with.

"You talk to your aunt," he said quietly. "Ask the questions about Ken that we need answered. For the time being, I won't ask her a thing. Except maybe how she's feeling.''

"She feels crummy." A.J. swallowed hard before she went on. "Awful. And she doesn't know anything that has bearing on this.''

"You can't be sure of that until you ask.''

From somewhere behind them, a driver blasted rudely on his horn. The sound boomed a strident echo through the parking garage's low-roofed confines.

Michael checked his rearview mirror and watched the red glow of twin taillights disappear around a corner. "We had no idea your ex-sister-in-law knew anything. As it turns out, Mary had quite a lot to tell us.''

He paused, a frown tightening his brow. "At this point, we need to find out if Ken carried the recorder on duty, as well as off. Think back, A.J. Did Greg Lawson ever mention Ken having a recorder? Maybe even just seeing him with a tape?''

"I don't remember Greg saying anything." She lifted her hand, pinched the bridge of her nose between her finger and thumb. "Ken wouldn't have made a tape that implicated him in illegal activity and then offer to give it to you."

"He didn't offer a tape. He offered evidence. We don't know for sure what he had."

When she remained silent, Michael gave voice to the issue that hung between them like a dark physical presence. "What we know for sure is that Ken had a motive to get his hands on a large amount of cash—"

Her hand shot out to ward off his words. "No matter how sick Aunt Emily was, he wouldn't have crossed the line to get money for her treatment."

Michael saw the glint of determination in the dark eyes that stared at him and he conceded the inevitability of the confrontation that was about to take place. Dammit, he didn't want to argue with her, didn't want to debate the issue of Ken Duncan's morals. He wanted to protect her. Shield her. Find out who called her anonymously, then beat the son of a bitch into the pavement. Problem was, the only way to get a line on the bastard was to find out what the hell her brother had been up to.

Keeping his eyes locked with hers, Michael stretched his arm across the top of the seat, his fingers brushing the shoulder of her wool coat. The dim lights of the parking garage shadowed her cheeks, darkened her eyes to the color of rich, dark coffee. He pictured the need that had flared in those eyes when he lowered his mouth to hers, remembered the heat that spiked through him when her body molded, hot and willing, against his.

Now, he wanted to touch her so badly it hurt.

His hand fisted around the steering wheel. The ache that was never far from him since the moment she first walked into his life deepened.

"Look," he said through his teeth, aware that the churning frustration inside him lent a sharp edge to his voice. "We can sit here all night debating the issue of your brother's innocence or guilt. But we won't resolve anything until we get some answers. So let's start with the doctor. If he knows for sure Ken dropped the idea of getting your aunt into the Houston program, that's one point in his favor.''

"Mary said he gave up the idea."

"Yeah, I heard."

"That's what he did."

"Dammit, A.J.!" Michael's voice lashed out like a whip. "You can't be sure of that."

"I knew Ken. Granted, he was always willing to push the rules, but not break them.''

"Wrong. He broke them—that's why he got demoted."

Her eyes turned cold. "Because of one mistake, you've branded him a criminal. You decided that before you ever ordered me to Internal Affairs for questioning."

"I don't have any preconceived agenda where your brother's concerned," Michael ground out, his voice clipped with anger. He fought the urge to clamp his hands on those slender shoulders of hers and shake her until she admitted her pigheaded defense of her brother had rendered her incapable of seeing what was plain to him—what would be plain when he reported their conversation with Mary Duncan to the chief. That Officer Duncan had sold information to get money to give their ailing aunt an edge on survival. Granted, such a motive put Ken Duncan in a better light than if he'd dumped on his badge for no reason other than basic greed. But odds were he'd crossed the line, just the same.

That near certainty wasn't the thing that put the burning knot in Michael's chest. It was the realization that, to Chief McMillan's way of thinking, it would be a short mental step to assume A.J. had conspired with her brother to save their aunt.

Had she? The intruding voice in Michael's head belonged to the cop long trained to investigate. To suspect. To question a person's motives. He slowly raised his gaze to hers, wondering if he'd been a fool to give her the benefit of the doubt.

As if reading his thoughts, her chin went up.

"And now, Lieutenant, you're no longer ninety-nine per-cent sure of my innocence," she said coolly. "Are you thinking your belief in me should have only registered fifty percent? Maybe a lowly ten?"

In those silent seconds that followed, reason warred with instinct. Against all logic, all evidence, he wanted to be-lieve her. When she didn't flinch under his scrutiny, he went with his instinct. She couldn't be guilty. Just couldn't be.

His hand moved from the top of the upholstered seat onto her shoulder. As his fingers slid into a shadowy nest of thick, silky hair, he battled the urge to inch his hand even further toward the remembered soft flesh of her throat.

Tightening his jaw, he banked down on every emotion. "The only thing I'd accuse you of is holding on beyond all good sense to an unbending, blind loyalty to your brother."

"Ken didn't do anything wrong. He couldn't. Wouldn't."

"Couldn't and wouldn't don't prove a thing," he coun-tered. "A stolen printout is proof. So is ten grand in a bank account. Then there's the ex-wife who supplies one hell of a solid motive. Admit it, A.J., if it were anyone but Ken, you'd have hollered 'guilty' before we left Mary's office."

"Maybe so," she agreed, her voice quiet. "But it isn't just anyone. It's my brother."

"I don't need a reminder of that." The warm air spewing out of the Bronco's vents, combined with the arc in Mi-chael's blood pressure, had his flesh heating. He switched off the heater, then jerked open his coat.

"You're letting your heart do your thinking, instead of your head. You won't consider any other scenario but the one where Ken stumbled onto something illegal and taped evidence to that effect."

"It could be true—"

"Then explain your anonymous caller. He said Ken had gone bad. He said to tell him to cooperate with his new partners or else. Just because Ken planned to turn evidence over to me, doesn't make him innocent. Maybe he got into something illegal, then got scared. So he made the tape, hoping to work a deal for himself by implicating someone else. Maybe that person sensed Ken was getting nervous. A sure way to jerk your brother back into line was to involve you."

"No—"

"Remember Ken's reaction when you confronted him about the call? He had the opportunity to explain everything. Instead, he threatened to kill the bastard for involving you. You believed he might do it, so much so that you went into his bathroom and lost your breakfast."

"I...was upset," she said, her voice trembling. "I hadn't slept...wasn't thinking right."

"You were thinking fine."

She gave a furious shake of her head. "Ken wouldn't have committed murder. Wouldn't have gone against everything he believed in—"

"Not even to save your aunt's life?"

She clenched her teeth. "Not even that."

Michael expelled a muffled oath. He didn't know if he should drag her out of her seat and throttle her, or hold her in his arms while she fought the battle that surely waged inside her.

Thumping his fist against the steering wheel, he sucked in a deep breath that pulled the scent of warm Chanel into his lungs and tried to pinpoint the exact moment his objectivity had gone down the sewer. He didn't know. All he knew was that by turning a blind eye to the prospect of her brother's guilt, A.J. had rendered herself vulnerable to whoever it was whose secrets Ken Duncan had known.

A surge of frustrated anger had him snagging her wrist and jerking her across the seat.

"Don't—!"

"I watched you in Mary's office," he said, the harshness in his voice quelling her sputtering protests. "I saw your expression when she told us about Ken needing money for your aunt's treatment. It was there, A.J., all over your face. It was brief. You covered it fast, I'll give you that. But I watched and I saw."

She tore her gaze from his. "I…don't know…what you're talking about."

Heat pulsed off her skin, sending another wave of the soft scent of her through his senses. Even as need arrowed through him, Michael checked it ruthlessly.

"Doubt." He tightened his hand on her wrist and yanked her back to face him. "Doubt about Ken," he continued. "For an instant, maybe less than a heartbeat, you believed him capable of doing whatever it took to save your aunt."

"Let go." She pulled against his touch, but his hand held fast.

"Ken *was* capable," he added, then softened his voice. "If it were either of my parents in that hospital, I'm not sure I wouldn't be capable."

Her dark eyes bore into his. "You're wrong about Ken."

"Am I?"

"Yes! And somehow, someway, I'll prove that to you."

Michael set his jaw. He could almost feel the ghost of Ken Duncan haunting the very air around him.

"I don't care if you admit your doubts about Ken to me," he ground out. "But the sooner you admit them to yourself, the better off you'll be."

Without waiting for her to comment, Michael released her wrist. When she scooted away from him, a fist clenched in his chest.

His intent had been to disconcert her, he thought as he turned and gripped the steering wheel. He'd done it many times—to suspects, witnesses, even victims—to get the information needed to move a case off high center. He was good at it, sometimes even enjoyed it, he acknowledged, and glanced across at A.J.'s shadowed, angry face.

This was the first time his hands had gone unsteady doing it. The first time a sense of guilt had crept in, making his mouth go dry. The first time he'd tossed silent recriminations at himself for doing his damn job.

Chapter 7

"Your brother was insistent," Dr. Luther Newell advised as he shrugged into his tan camel coat. "Determined to get your aunt on the clinic's waiting list."

"How determined?" A.J. asked.

"Extremely."

With a sinking feeling, she watched the tall gray-haired man glance at the digital clock over the hospital's information desk. It was his third check of the time since she and Michael had caught him rushing through the lobby, in a hurry to leave for Tulsa to dine with colleagues.

"I voiced my reservations about the drugs used in the program and the fifty-thousand-dollar initial sign-up fee," the doctor added. "That didn't dissuade him. Ken had his mind made up. He said he'd already arranged the financing."

Michael's brows drew together. "Is there some kind of insurance that would cover the cost? A grant, maybe?"

"None that I'm aware of."

The doctor went on to explain about the experimental

nature of the drugs used at the Houston clinic, but A.J. barely heard. Inside her, despair rose like floodwater.

Seconds later, Michael offered his hand. "Thanks for your time, Doctor. Sorry to hold you up."

A.J. closed her eyes as the man retreated. Her stomach roiled; she fought desperately to control the trembling that seized her shoulders. Motive. The doctor had supplied motive for Ken to have crossed the line.

"Do you want to sit down?"

"No," she said, opening her eyes.

Michael's fingers grazed her hand in a subtle, almost imperceptible motion. "You're sure?"

She tensed against his touch. "I'm fine."

He took a step toward her, his eyes locked with hers. "I can see you're not."

"I...we need to go upstairs to Aunt Emily's room. Visiting hours..."

He reached out and caught her shoulders as she turned. "There's time yet."

She lifted a hand and rubbed hard at her temple. Time was what she needed. Time to deal with what Mary had told them, time to sort out the damning implications of Dr. Newell's words. Time to get her churning emotions under control. Time to think. But she couldn't think, not with Michael's all-seeing eyes piercing through her, not while his hands rested on her shoulders with such gentleness.

"A.J., I'm sorry."

If the look in Michael's eyes had been one of triumph, instead of concern, maybe she could view him as a foe. If only it were victory in his voice, not grim reality, she could erect an emotional wall to keep him out. If his touch had been harsh, not the soft caress now against her shoulders, then she wouldn't feel such heart-wrenching desire to lay her head against his chest and seek the comfort she desperately needed.

Her fingers curled into the soft folds of her coat, which was draped across her arm. She knew if she succumbed to temptation and stepped into his arms, the last thing she'd be able to do was think. And thinking was what she needed to do. *Had* to do. She had to find a way to fight the doubt over Ken that had feathered up her spine while in Mary's office. Doubt that had grown fangs and now raged inside her, tearing her to shreds.

"A.J.?"

"I'm fine." She swiveled, forcing him to drop his hands as she reached for the elevator's call button. "Aunt Emily's on the seventh floor."

A profusion of white pressed in on A.J. as she stepped into the oncology ward's central corridor. Medical personnel in lab coats and uniforms scurried about; laundered sheets draped an abandoned gurney; the clean, faint scent of soap and disinfectant rose from the pale, polished floor.

Michael exited the elevator behind her, his footsteps sounding time with hers. She slanted him a glance, taking in the shadowed lines at the corners of his eyes.

Was he thinking about Ken? Was his mind assessing the evidence, which with every passing interview stacked higher against her brother?

She gritted her teeth against the ache that had settled in her right thigh. She understood how helpless Ken must have felt, knowing their aunt was ill. Knowing that other than prayer, he had no means to help her. God, she agonized against those feelings every day.

But she hadn't committed a crime because of them. Now, she wasn't sure about Ken.

With pain ripping into her heart, A.J. sidestepped around a scrubs-clad orderly shoving a cart of aromatic dinner trays along the corridor.

Damn you, Ken, for not having faith in me. He had to have known that no matter the reason for his silence when she confronted him about the anonymous call that she would have stood by him. Had to have known, once the caller pulled her in, she'd persist until she found the truth. So why hadn't he just told her?

Her steps wavered as the half-open door to her aunt's

room came into view. She paused, struggling to get a firm grip on her emotions.

Following her lead, Michael halted at her side.

"A.J., I need to know if you're all right," he said in a quiet voice.

From inside the room, the faint sounds of "Have Yourself a Merry Little Christmas" drifted on the sterile air.

"I'm fine." She turned toward the door but Michael's hand caught her arm, staying her steps. The fluorescent lights from above glinted against the dark sheen of his hair, transformed his eyes into chips of blue marble.

"I'm sorry I got rough with you in the car. I don't want to hurt you. Or your aunt." He reached toward her and took her coat, folding it over his own, which he held in the crook of his arm. "But I have a job to do. I have to see this investigation through, until I find out what Ken was involved in. You understand that, don't you?"

His words brought a sudden, unexpected wave of instinctive protectiveness surging to the surface. "Ken could have planned to take out a loan," she blurted, hating the desperate intensity she heard in her voice. "There are companies—legitimate ones—that'll loan anyone money. They charge interest rates that are in the clouds, but it's legal."

Michael took a step closer, his lean, broad-shouldered body blocking out everything else from her senses. For the space of a heartbeat, he was the only person who existed in her world.

"At times," he began, giving her a long, steady look, "that obstinate loyalty of yours frustrates the hell out of me. But it's also one thing I admire about you. One of many things." He nodded toward the door. "How about introducing me to your aunt?"

With her pulse unsteady, A.J. attempted a smile, then pushed the door open a few inches and started in.

"Which tape do you want me to hear next?"

Tape. Her aunt's words had A.J. halting in midstride.

Michael bumped into her back, forcing an unladylike *oof* up her throat.

"Sorry," he said under his breath.

Propped up in bed against an array of overstuffed pillows, Emily Duncan turned her head toward the door, nose wrinkled and eyes narrowed. At age fifty-five she was distinctly nearsighted but detested admitting it; the only time she wore her glasses was when she drove. After a few seconds of squinting, her face lit up. "A.J., we were just talking about you. Weren't we?"

"Bet her ears are burning."

Greg Lawson smiled as he pushed his muscular frame from a chair beside the bed. "Hi. Did you ever get my message?"

"Message?" A.J. asked blankly. Her eyes slid to the cassette recorder positioned next to the dinner tray on the roll-away table by the bed. A stack of plastic tape cases sat beside the recorder. She took a deep breath to ease the knot of paranoia that had settled in her chest at her aunt's mention of tapes. The recorder and tapes on the table weren't the microsize ones Mary had loaned Ken.

"I called the task force room about two o'clock," Greg continued, his expression turning thoughtful when her gaze met his. "Helene St. John said you and Ryan were out. Said she'd give you a message to call my pager when you got back."

A.J. nodded. "We...went to the Westfall scene."

He raised his chin. "I know." The raw, jagged cut he'd received the night Ken died looked thin and pink beneath the blond hair lapping across one side of his forehead. "I called again around four and you weren't back yet. Where else did you go?"

At that instant, Michael stepped around the door into view. "We had a few leads to check."

A.J. caught an almost imperceptible tightening at the corners of Greg's mouth. "Lieutenant," he said quietly.

"Lawson."

"A.J., you brought a friend," Emily said pleasantly, reaching out a hand that sported slashes of tape securing an IV needle and tubing.

Her aunt's hand looked small and sickly pale, almost as pale as her cheeks, A.J. thought as she walked to the bed and wrapped her fingers around flesh that was cold to the touch.

"This is Lieutenant Ryan," she said, glancing across her shoulder at Michael, who'd opted to remain just inside the door. "You remember I told you I'm working for him on the Westfall task force?"

"Lord, child, why wouldn't I remember?" Emily asked with a scowl. "It's my body that's gone haywire, not my brain."

"So it is." Smiling, A.J. dropped a kiss against the colorful scarf that was wrapped turban-style around her aunt's head. The few remaining salt-and-pepper curls that peeked out at the nape of her neck had a dry, brittle look. A.J. supposed the chemotherapy treatments would render her completely bald by Christmas.

Emily turned the full power of her squinted gaze on Michael. "Lieutenant, is it?"

"Around the station," he said, dropping their coats onto an empty chair. "Michael everywhere else."

"Well, Michael, I don't feel like digging for my glasses, so you'll have to come close if I'm to get a look at you."

"Yes, ma'am."

A.J. caught a glint of amusement in his eyes as he stepped to her side.

"Michael Ryan," Emily mused, arching an almost invisible eyebrow while giving him a not-so-subtle once-over. "That's a fine Irish name for a police officer."

"Third-generation cop," Michael affirmed. "Both my grandfather and father wore an OCPD badge."

"I see."

A.J. sent a bland look toward the bed. A professor of anthropology, her aunt habitually dug to the roots of a new acquaintance's family tree the minute introductions were made.

"That must be a matter of pride. Do you have a son who will carry on the family tradition?"

"A daughter. Megan's fifteen and says she can't wait for the day she can apply to the academy." He leaned to study the gold pin holding the graceful sweep of the turban in place. "That's an interesting piece of jewelry."

"Queen Nefertiti," Emily said, a pleased look settling into her eyes. "Are you interested in Egyptology?"

He lifted a shoulder. "Sorry. I wouldn't know a scarab from a salamander."

To A.J.'s amazement, a girlish, carefree laugh rose up her aunt's throat. "You enroll in one of my classes, Michael Ryan, and I'll straighten you out."

A grin tugged at the corners of his mouth. "I bet you would."

Emily gave a satisfied nod, then turned her attention to Greg. "Which tape is next?"

The furrows in Greg's forehead relaxed. "Give me a minute." He popped a tape out of the player, then plucked a plastic case off the top of the stack.

"A.J., wasn't it thoughtful of Greg to bring me Christmas music?"

"Yes," she agreed. "Thanks."

He glanced up from the recorder and gave her a wink. "My pleasure."

Guilt tightened A.J.'s chest. Although she'd visited the hospital every evening, she realized now how totally her concern over Ken had dominated her thoughts. Christmas was just a little over a week away. She should have brought her aunt music. She should have already brought a wreath, candles, any number of things to help ease the endless hours Aunt Emily spent in bed while mixtures of chemicals dripped into her veins.

"Aunt Emily, I can buy a small tree. I'll get some ornaments, tinsel..." A.J.'s voice drifted off at the narrow look her suggestion received, and she tightened her grip on her aunt's hand. "Are you in pain? Shall I get the nurse?"

"Don't you dare call that harpoon-school dropout. She marched in here not ten minutes ago and stabbed me with my nightly dose. And no, I'm not in pain—I've got enough drugs in me to make an addict happy for a year. I want to know if you offered to decorate this room because Dr. Newell told you he's keeping me prisoner here over Christmas?''

"No. I keep asking, but he won't say."

"The man's maddening," Emily explained to Michael. "Has an annoying aversion to giving straight answers."

Michael crossed his arms over his chest. "Something tells me you aren't about to let him get away with that."

"Correct." Emily paused, pursing her pale lips. "You know, I didn't think I was up to celebrating the holidays until Greg brought his tapes. Christmas music has a way of lifting the spirit."

Greg wiggled his eyebrows. "I know what's best for the women in my life," he said, then punched the recorder's Play button. "I keep telling A.J. that, but I'm not sure I've got her convinced. Yet."

"My niece likes to make her mind up for herself," Emily said with a chuckle. "I imagine she's let you know that."

Greg shrugged as the strains of "Little Drummer Boy" flowed over the air. "She has."

Although she didn't look directly at him, A.J. sensed Michael's intent observation of Greg's interaction with her aunt…and herself.

Emily pressed her head back against the pillows, her shadowed eyes meeting A.J.'s. "If Dr. Newell insists on keeping me here over Christmas, then I'd like a tree. But don't buy new ornaments. I'll want the family ones."

A.J. blinked. "You're sure?"

In her mind's eye she pictured the dog-eared storage box that had held an assortment of her mother's handmade needlepoint ornaments for as long as she could remember. Ornaments that Emily Duncan, a single woman dedicated to her career and knowing little about raising children, had made certain her niece and nephew hung on the family tree the first Christmas after their parents' death, then each successive Christmas Eve. Even after A.J. and Ken were grown, they'd all observed the tradition.

"I'm sure. Bring our ornaments," Emily said. "Kenneth would expect us to…" Her voice caught. "Goodness," she said, blinking back tears. "Here I go getting weepy again."

Michael looked at Greg. "I could use some coffee. How about you?"

Greg waited a beat before agreeing. "Sure."

A.J. caught the softening in Michael's expression as he turned toward her. His hand rose, his fingers grazed her elbow for a fleeting second. "What can I bring you?"

"Coffee sounds good."

Greg leaned over the bed. "How about I smuggle you something from the dessert line tonight?"

"Wait until Tuesday," Emily said, giving him a watery smile. "That's when they serve that yummy carrot cake."

"You've got it." He walked around the bed, pausing at A.J.'s side to kiss her cheek. His hand curved onto the slope of her waist. "We need to talk," he murmured. "Later."

She nodded. His touch swept her back twenty-four hours to the moment she'd stood on the front porch, enfolded in his arms. At that moment she'd known with unwavering certainty that she could never give Greg more than just friendship. Now, she felt so removed from him. So detached.

He strode past Michael, pulled open the door, then looked across his shoulder. "I'll be back."

Michael flicked an idle glance toward the door where Greg waited, then captured A.J.'s gaze in a web of intense blue. "So will I."

The softness of his voice seemed to pulse across her flesh. With her heart doing a slow roll in her chest, she watched him disappear out the door.

"Men," Emily said, eyeing A.J. with interest. "The minute they think there's danger a woman might break into tears, they disappear."

"I suppose," A.J. muttered as she slid a hip onto the edge of the bed. "What's this about carrot cake?" she asked, her voice mixing with a symphonic rendition of "Silent Night" coming from the cassette player.

"Greg stops by nearly every day to talk. Mostly about Kenneth. He's never actually said so, but I think he feels guilty his partner died and he didn't."

"I've sensed that, too. He shouldn't, but he does." A.J. took a deep breath. "Aunt Emily, did you know that Ken and Mary had started dating again?"

"Lord, no." Emily cocked her head. "For how long?"

"A couple of months before he died."

"Kenneth never said a word about it. Did he tell you?"

"No."

"How'd you find out?"

"I...ran into Mary. She told me."

"Those two, I never heard such arguing. I suppose it was a battle royal all over again."

"Mary says it wasn't. Apparently they learned not to sweat the small stuff." A.J. used her fingertips to massage the icy palm cradled in her hand. "Did Ken ever mention a tape recorder to you? Maybe some tapes he made?"

She followed her aunt's gaze to the recorder on the table over the bed. "A microcassette recorder," A.J. amended. "One that would fit in your pocket."

"No. Why do you ask?"

A.J. shrugged. "Ken borrowed the recorder from Mary. I checked the boxes Greg packed from his apartment, but it wasn't there."

"This is the night for recorders. First, Greg showing up with his, then you asking about Kenneth's." Frown lines peeked from beneath Emily's turban. "Since you've checked through his things, I wouldn't know where else to look."

A.J. waited a beat, then went on. "Mary said Ken was considering signing you up for a treatment program."

"What kind of program?"

"At a Houston clinic. They treat leukemia patients with experimental drugs."

"Experimental?" Emily scoffed. "I've got enough holes in me now to rent myself out as a lawn sprinkler. Why would I go to Houston just to be somebody's guinea pig?"

"Ken wanted you to have the option of going, is all."

"Well, if he'd mentioned it, I'd have told him it was a bad idea." She flicked a blue-veined hand at the fluid-filled bag and plastic tubing that dangled from the IV pole at the head of the bed. "I've got my own special brew right here. Kenneth may have forgotten that I'm tough as nails, but I haven't. I plan to beat this damn disease and get on with my life."

A.J. wanted to throw her arms around her aunt and hold her tight. But she looked so fragile, so bony beneath the flannel robe she wore to ward off chills that A.J. settled for squeezing the older woman's hand. "I doubt Ken ever forgot how tough you are. After all, he was on the receiving end of a few of your paddlings."

"That's because he was ornery," Emily stated and tilted her head against the pillow. "Now, let's talk about you."

"What about me?"

"I want to know if you're all right."

"I'm fine."

"You're sure?"

"Yes, why?"

"Greg doesn't just talk about Kenneth. He talks about you, too. He said he's sensed a change in you. That you're closing yourself off from him. He thinks it may be because a part of you blames him for Kenneth's death."

A.J. frowned. "He said that?"

"Yes. I told him it was ridiculous to think that, but he's dealing with so much guilt."

"I had no idea..." She shook her head, remembering the regret that had filled her the previous night when she stood in Greg's arms while thoughts of Michael stirred her blood. "Greg's been so good to us since..." A.J. closed her eyes. "I'll talk to him. I'll make sure he knows I don't blame him."

"He told me he's crazy about you."

"Did he?"

Aware of the weariness that had crept into her aunt's voice, A.J. slid off the side of the bed. With deft hands she smoothed the sheet, then refilled the plastic glass on the nightstand while Emily yawned.

"Something tells me you don't share Greg's feelings."

"He's a good friend."

"A good friend," Emily repeated. "Is that what you call Michael Ryan?"

A.J.'s hand faltered as she reached for the control to lower the head of the bed. "No. I call him my boss as long as the Westfall task force is up and rolling."

"What about when it's over?"

"Then he'll be my former boss," A.J. said firmly. "I love you, Aunt Emily. Go to sleep."

"Is he married?"

"Is who married?"

"Don't be coy, dear."

"Divorced." A.J. used the control panel to flick off the overhead light. The single bulb that glowed above the door threw weak shadows in every direction.

"Wonderful."

"No matchmaking," A.J. cautioned with forced sternness as she adjusted the pillows, careful not to disturb her aunt's turban.

"Won't be necessary. I saw the way you look at Michael. Your feelings are as clear as print."

"Is that the same print you can't see without your glasses?"

"Didn't need glasses to see the look in *his* eyes when Greg gave you that peck on the cheek," Emily persisted. "Your boss didn't like it one little bit."

"Good night, Aunt Em," A.J. said, dropping a kiss on her forehead.

"Night, dear."

Michael stepped into the hallway, one side of his suit coat shoved back by the hand he'd slipped into the pocket of his slacks. He'd been looking for an excuse to have a chat with Greg Lawson at a time and place that wouldn't alert him to the fact that unanswered questions existed concerning his former partner. Michael figured this was as good a chance as he was going to get.

Arms crossed over his chest, Lawson leaned against the wall beside a wheeled cart holding an instrument laden with an array of cords, dials and switches. As Michael approached, Lawson flashed him a quick, annoyed look.

"In case you're wondering, Lieutenant, A.J. and I are more than friends."

"I wasn't wondering," Michael answered. He had, after all, seen her wrapped in the man's arms the previous evening.

Lawson shrugged. "Just wanted to make it clear she's taken."

"You have. Now, how about that coffee?"

"Sure."

They walked to the elevators, where a man and woman dressed in green scrubs waited. Michael punched the call button. "I like Emily Duncan."

"She's easy to like. She's almost a second mother to me."

A pager's sharp chirp sounded. The scrubs-clad man and woman checked their beepers, then shared a relieved smile.

"Mine," Greg said.

As he checked the pager's display, Michael saw the instant squaring of his shoulders. "I need to make a call."

"Go ahead. I'll wait."

Michael walked to the nurses' station, propping an elbow against the counter. Twice, he shook his head when someone asked if he needed help. "Waiting for someone," he explained, while keeping the banks of pay phones in sight. The longer Lawson talked, the stiffer his spine got.

A few minutes later, the patrolman turned abruptly and walked toward him. Michael noted the tense set of his shoulders, the small vein that pulsed in his neck.

"I have to leave," Lawson said. Jaw muscles flexing, he glanced across his shoulder in the direction of Emily Duncan's room. "Do me a favor. Tell A.J. I'll call her."

Michael couldn't pinpoint an exact reason, but at that

instant he felt the distinctive clutch in his gut that put his senses on full alert. Greg Lawson bore watching…to a certain extent. Michael had no desire to again witness the man standing on Emily Duncan's front porch while he kissed her niece.

"Sure," Michael said. "I'll tell her."

Indulging in a low sigh, A.J. depressed the Stop button on the recorder. She stood by the bed in silence, listening for the delicate change in her aunt's breathing as she drifted into sleep.

With her heart in her throat, she stared down into the wan face of the woman who had been her substitute mother. The woman who could deliver severe tongue-lashings or gentle lectures, depending on the circumstances. The woman who had always had the ability to see through her, zero in on her true feelings.

As she'd done tonight, A.J. acknowledged. Aunt Emily had seen the attraction for Michael that she'd battled since the moment she'd walked into his office in Internal Affairs. Now, anytime he was near, her knees weakened and her nerves fizzed.

She should be thinking about Ken, not her out-of-kilter hormones. Searching for evidence that would clear him…and herself. Making sure no hint of wrongdoing on either of their parts would ever reach her aunt's ears.

Her hands curled against her thighs. Ken had made a tape, she knew it. She could *feel* it. Made it, then hid it. Just because he hadn't mentioned anything to her or their aunt didn't mean he hadn't hidden the tape somewhere in their house. She'd start searching tonight, go through every box, bookshelf and cabinet.

If it wasn't there, she'd figure out somewhere else to look.

Starting now, she'd take a long step back mentally from Michael Ryan. If there were ever to be anything between them, it wouldn't—couldn't—happen with this cloud of doubt over Ken. Not just Ken, she thought, pulling her bottom lip between her teeth. In the Bronco, she had seen the question of her own innocence flash in Michael's eyes. Without proof to clear herself he would never be sure, never completely know.

And she could never give herself to him, knowing that someday she might look up unexpectedly and see again that thread of suspicion in his eyes.

She had to keep her distance. Had to throw herself into the search for Ken's evidence. That, combined with her work on the task force, was more than enough to keep her mind occupied...and her hormones suppressed.

A faint, almost imperceptible noise caught her attention. She turned and saw the silhouette of Michael's tall, broad-shouldered frame as he stepped through the doorway.

"I got a call from the station," he said in a hushed voice, advancing toward her with brisk, efficient steps.

In the faint wash of light she saw the intense glint of his eyes, spied the stiff set of his shoulders. The very air around him seemed to hum with urgency.

Her senses went on alert. "What's going on?"

"We'll talk in the hall." He looked toward Emily's sleeping form. "Is she set for the night? Can you leave?"

"Yes." A.J.'s gaze skittered to the door. "Where's Greg?"

Michael's mouth tightened as he jostled her coat into her arms, then grabbed his own off the chair. "Lawson's pager went off after we walked out of here. He made a call, said he had some business to take care of, said he'd..."

She frowned when his voice trailed off. "He said what?"

"Nothing important." Michael clamped his hand on her wrist and headed for the door.

"What's happened?" A.J. demanded as he propelled her along the hallway. Her heart pounded as she double-timed her steps to keep up with his long strides.

He glanced down at her, his expression sharp and intense. "We've got a possible suspect in the Westfall murder."

Chapter 8

"Billy Hollis is a nickel-bag hustler with a rap sheet thicker than a heifer's butt," Sam Rogers observed as he leaned his elbows on the conference table and dumped a second packet of sugar into a disposable coffee cup. "A real scum wad."

"He's Dianna Westfall's nephew?" A.J. asked the detective, confirming the information Michael had given her on their drive from the hospital. She pulled off her coat, smoothing the jade bolero jacket where it curved at her waist. Seconds earlier, she and Michael had walked into the brightly lit task force room to find officers and civilians bustling about, the very air humming with anticipation. They had a name. A possible suspect.

As she dropped into the chair beside Sam, A.J. glanced toward the far end of the conference table. Sky Milano and two lab techs already had Michael involved in an intense discussion. A.J. noted that Sam's partner, Grant Pierce, stood at the edge of the group, his gaze locked on the forensic chemist's sculpted profile.

"Actually, Billy's not blood kin." Sam used his stubby

cigar to gesture at Dianna Westfall's photograph on the bulletin board that spanned one wall. "She has a sister who lives back east. He's the sister's adopted kid."

"What does Hollis's record look like?"

"He did lots of juvie time for petty stuff, been popped for assault, burglary. Got a couple of drug busts mixed in with everything else." Sam blew on his coffee. "Two years ago, Billy celebrated his eighteenth birthday by pulling a convenience-store hijacking. Cut a couple of brand-new openings in the clerk."

"Cut?"

"Cut." Sam leaned back in his chair and hooked a thumb under one suspender strap. "That got him a year in slam. In every assault he's gone down on, he's used a knife as his weapon. Makes you think the kid has an affinity for blades."

A.J. pursed her lips in thought. "Enough to stab his aunt twenty-one times?"

"Could be. Either way, we'll find out soon. There's three good arrest warrants out on him for unpaid traffic tickets. We issued a radiogram to have Hollis picked up. Won't take the uniforms long to round up a maggot like him."

"Do we have a picture?"

"You bet." Sam stabbed his cigar into an ashtray overflowing with cigarette butts and wadded yellow sticky notes, then reached into his shirt pocket. "I stopped by Records and picked up his latest mug shot. Get a load of him—garden-variety ugly with a fish-belly-white complexion. A cop'll arrest a guy who looks like that purely on reflex."

Ignoring the smoky stench of cigar that hung in the air, A.J. looked into the acne-plagued face with eyes that stared out with dark hostility. A dirty, torn T-shirt emphasized the aggressive squareness of Hollis's shoulders; a tattoo of the Grim Reaper glared from his right bicep.

She returned the mug shot with a skeptical look. "You really think Dianna Westfall took her clothes off for this guy without a struggle?"

"Hold a big enough knife to someone's throat and he'll sing the national anthem, if that's your pleasure."

"She drank champagne with her killer, Sam. They had sex."

"Ever hear the term 'rape?' And who says *he* didn't do most of the drinking after she was dead? Maybe Hollis just made it look like they partied before he did her. That way, we wouldn't think she'd been forced."

Shrugging her acquiescence, A.J. glanced up as Helene St. John and Kevin Stoner came through the door. Helene's face was red from the cold; her platinum hair hung in a windblown tumble down the back of her white wool coat. From where she sat, A.J. could see the strained set of Helene's mouth as she headed in Michael's direction. Kevin strolled slowly in his partner's wake, his eyebrows rising as she stepped around Sky, seemingly interrupting the chemist in midsentence.

A.J. met Sam's gaze. "Wonder what's with Helene."

"Mike's had St. John and Stoner checking jewelry stores to see if Dianna left her missing diamond ring somewhere for repair," Sam commented. "Maybe they came up with something."

"Maybe."

A.J. watched as Michael shook his head at something Helene said. With that, Helene jerked off her coat, settled at a computer terminal and began pounding on the keyboard.

"A.J., the lab sent this up."

She jolted at the nearness of Michael's voice. Looking up, she saw that he now stood beside her chair, a plastic evidence envelope in his hand. "I'm sorry, what?"

"I've got the address book Dianna carried in her purse," he stated. "The names need to be fed into the computer."

"Fine."

"We'll need to do a cross-check to see if any names in this match the ones in the address book from Dianna's desk."

"Right."

She accepted the bag, then shoved her dark hair behind her shoulders as she leaned to dig in her purse for her reading glasses. Michael's nearness made her nerves shimmer, made her pulse pound. She curled her bottom lip between her teeth, not at all enjoying the emotional effect he had on her. She'd made a decision at the hospital to concentrate on finding Ken's tape, which in her heart she believed was the key to finding the truth about what he'd been involved in. Right now, there was no room in her thoughts—or her life—for Michael Ryan. He was her boss, she his employee. Period. Problem was, her hormones hadn't yet gotten that message.

Snapping her glasses open with a resolute flick of her wrist, she shoved them on her nose. Glancing down, she noted that the small book encased in plastic matched the larger one whose contents—over 150 names of individuals and businesses—she'd entered in the computer's database that morning. As with the large book, a coat of black fingerprint powder covered its smaller twin's mauve leather cover.

She looked up. "Did the lab get any prints?"

"Just the victim's," Michael commented, then turned to Sam.

"Who came up with the lead on Hollis?"

"Gianos and Smith," the detective said, inclining his head in the direction of the team of detectives Michael had assigned to interview the Westfall family. Sam paused, giving A.J. an assessing look over the rim of his cup. "You got something other than this case on your mind, sweetheart?"

"No," she answered as heat crept up her neck.

A smile crinkled Sam's puffy eyes. "I've been a detective nearly thirty years. Not much gets by me. Want to tell old Sam what's got you preoccupied?"

"What I want is for 'old Sam' to tell me how we got the lead on Billy Hollis."

"One of the people that Gianos and Smith interviewed was Dianna's brother-in-law, William Westfall. He's CEO of Westco Industries. Westfall called Gianos this afternoon, saying he all of a sudden remembered Dianna saying something last summer about Hollis calling her. He was hassling her for money, wanting her to put him up at the mansion, things like that. Guess he kept it up because she got an unlisted number a couple of months ago."

Michael dropped into the chair beside A.J.'s. "Any idea how long Hollis has been in town?"

"About a year, as close as we can figure," Sam said. "Except for the traffic tickets, the only record he has with OCPD is a possession charge that got dropped on a technicality. You ever hear of Benito Penn?"

"No," Michael answered.

"He's a dealer who's gone from street hustler to major player. According to the Narcotics boys, one of Benito's men put up Billy's bail money on the possession arrest. It's a sure bet he figures somewhere in Benito's network."

A.J. cocked her head. "Any idea where Hollis stays?"

"His mama talked to him last week. He mentioned some hotel over on Stiles. Pierce checked to see if anybody'd run across Hollis and filled out a field-interview card that'd give us a firm address. When that came up empty, we issued the radiogram."

"If it turns out his blood type is AB, maybe we can pack up and go home," A.J. said almost to herself. If that happened, the task force would end. She would no longer work under Michael's command. No longer face the prospect of seeing him every day. No longer sit beside him as she did now, her nerves sending flashpoints of heat across her skin.

"Can't happen too soon for me," Sam said. He put his palms on the table, then rose, his stomach lapping over the gold badge clipped to his belt.

"Or me," A.J. added as she ripped the red evidence tape off the plastic bag.

"Meanwhile, we have to follow up leads," Sam continued. "That means pretty boy and I have a plane to meet."

"Who's coming in?" A.J. asked while sliding the address book from the bag.

"The Rawlings couple—Dianna's across-the-street neighbors. Their house has the best view of her place. They've been in London for two weeks so there's no chance they saw anything the night she died." Sam shrugged. "But most of the neighbors say nothing happens around there that Pamela Rawlings doesn't know about. Sounds like she's the equivalent of the neighborhood snoop. Maybe she can add something about Dianna that nobody else was privy to."

As she reached to flip on the computer terminal in front of her, A.J.'s palm grazed the folder containing close-ups of Dianna Westfall's severed, polished finger.

Reentry Red.

She sat as still as stone while something edged its way forward from the back of her mind. In less than a heartbeat, the thought faded into a gray haze. She blew out a breath.

Michael leaned in. "Something wrong?"

She met his gaze. "Let's suppose Billy Hollis killed his aunt."

"Okay."

"What reason would he have had to paint her fingernails after he killed her?"

Sam gave her a sardonic smile as he pulled on his suit coat. "Why the hell do these sons of bitches do anything?" he asked, then strolled away.

"Why, indeed," A.J. mumbled as she opened the address book and began thumbing through the pages.

Around her, the rapid clicking of keys from a computer terminal across the room drifted on the air. Someone's pager sounded a dim beep. Outside the floor-to-ceiling windows, the frigid wind howled as the evening gloom set in.

Staring at what she now recognized as Dianna Westfall's spidery handwriting, A.J.'s eyes grew wider with each page she scanned.

"Dear, Lord." Without conscious thought, she reached for Michael's arm as he rose from the chair. "I don't believe this."

His gaze dropped to the hand she'd draped across his

sleeve. "Neither do I," he said softly, capturing her gaze with his.

The realization that she'd reached for him put a tightness in her belly. She pulled her hand back, the quickening in her stomach spreading into a slow burn.

Her fingers faltered against the address book. "I...there must be a hundred names in here."

"I imagine Dianna had lots of friends." Michael settled back into the chair, watching across A.J.'s shoulder as she continued flipping through the pages.

"There aren't any full names in here—just first initials followed by a last name. No addresses or telephone numbers..." Her hands stilled. "Look at what Dianna wrote here. 'W. Kennedy—a double-duty 10. Dining room table.'"

She glanced across at Michael. "Do you think that means what I think it means?"

"I don't imagine Kennedy is a furniture salesman," he commented dryly.

"Dianna's made notes covering every room in the mansion," A.J. said. "Here's 'P. Cowan...major gorgeous—on the washing machine.'"

An embarrassed heat settled in A.J.'s cheeks. She was used to discussing every intimate detail of a sex crime with cops. Male cops. But to her, the man sitting only inches away wasn't just a cop. He was a man whom she'd lately spent a good deal of time fantasizing about. A man whose kiss had left an indelible mark on her soul. The sudden image of Michael and her...and a dining room table flashed into her mind with shocking clarity.

"Mind if I have a look?" he asked.

"No, I..." She handed him the book, then pulled off her glasses. "I guess this won't surprise Sam."

"Why's that?" Michael asked as he thumbed through the pages.

"It's a theory of his. He says if you get a good-looking woman for a stiff, just turn her life upside down and shake hard. A bushel of men'll fall out. Sam says it happens every time."

"Looks like this case won't prove him wrong," Michael said. He closed the book, his mouth grim. "Now, I get to tell Chief McMillan that his wife's best friend kept records that'd put a prostitute's trick book to shame."

Two hours later, the telephone's persistent ringing pulled A.J. from her intense study of Dianna Westfall's address book. Sliding off her glasses, she looked around and realized she had the room to herself.

"Task force," she said into the receiver.

"Hi!" a bright voice said across the line. "Is Lieutenant Michael Ryan there? This is his daughter."

"Megan…" A.J.'s thoughts immediately went to Michael's office in Internal Affairs, where the photograph of the preteen girl with the impish, lopsided smile had leaned on the credenza.

"Yeah, who's this?"

"A.J. Duncan."

"Do I know you?"

A.J. shook her head, as if the girl were in the room to see her. "No. But your dad's mentioned you." A.J.'s forehead furrowed. Now that she thought about it, she wasn't sure she could picture Michael as a father.

"Are you a policewoman?"

"No, a civilian crime analyst."

"What's that?"

"I link crimes, do suspect profiles. I try to help the officers get a line on the bad guys."

"Cool. I'm going to sign up for the OCPD academy the minute I'm old enough."

"We'll be glad to have you—"

"My mom doesn't want me to."

"It can be a dangerous job."

"Yeah. I think it's mainly because she doesn't want me to follow in my dad's footsteps."

A.J. arched a brow at Megan's candor. "Well..." She let her voice drift off, having no idea how to respond.

"Do you know where my dad is?"

A.J. glanced down the length of the conference table at Michael's vacant chair. She had no idea how long he'd been gone, where he'd gone or when he'd be back. "Sorry, no. I can have him call you."

Across the phone line, a muffled voice sounded in the background, then Megan responded in a similar muffled tone. "That's okay," she finally said into the receiver. "Mom's changed her mind. She says we have to leave for the airport now. I just wanted to tell Dad Merry Christmas. I was supposed to spend my break with him, but I'm going with my mom and stepdad to Cancún instead."

Regret. A.J. pictured the regret she'd seen in Michael's eyes as he stared at Megan's photograph. Dark, raw regret.

"Megan, please call again when you get to Mexico. I know your dad will want to talk to you."

Again, the girl's voice became muffled as she spoke to someone in the background. "Mom says she's not sure how good the telephone service is in Cancún."

"I hear it's excellent," A.J. ad-libbed, having no idea why she should feel irritation over a situation that in no way involved her.

Megan related the information. The voice in the background sharpened instantly.

"Got to go," Megan said. "Tell Dad I love him. Bye."

"Goodbye—"

A.J.'s throat tightened as she sat with the receiver humming in her ear. She had no idea what the telephone service was like in Cancún, so why had she said that?

Regret. The answer drifted back on the room's still air. It was an emotion A.J. knew well and understood. An emotion she'd lived with since that rainy night in college when she slid into the driver's seat beside Casey and half an hour later their car skidded head-on into a massive oak.

She rose, walked to stand before the wall of floor-to-ceiling windows and stared out unseeingly into the frozen darkness.

Granted, a dog had dashed onto the road and she'd swerved to miss it. And yes, both the police and insurance company had cleared her of all responsibility. But she'd been so involved with getting her happily inebriated fiancé, who'd aced his final exams, into the car without getting soaked that she'd neglected to check if he'd fastened his seatbelt. Just one little detail. One detail that, if done, might have saved his life when their car crashed into the oak.

Regret, she thought again as the familiar ache stirred in her right thigh. Dark, raw regret.

The sound of the door sweeping open had A.J. turning. Michael strode in, his concentration centered on the report in his hand. Sometime in the past two hours he'd shed his suit coat and rolled his starched sleeves up on his forearms. His shirt collar was unbuttoned and his tie loose. His thick, dark hair gleamed beneath the room's lights.

A.J. expelled a slow breath. If just his entering a room had the effect of a roller coaster dip on her stomach, how the hell was she going to maintain the distance she'd resolved to keep?

"Lieutenant?"

He looked up from the report and glanced around the room. "Anything come in on Hollis yet?"

She shoved her hair behind her shoulders. "To tell you the truth, I wouldn't know if it had. I was concentrating on Dianna Westfall's address book and had no idea I was alone in the room until the phone rang."

He nodded as he pulled his chair out from the conference table. "I've got everyone checking leads on Hollis and passing out flyers to the patrol units. The sooner we find him, the better."

"I...the phone call was for you. I took a message."

The tightness that she heard in her own voice had his eyes narrowing. "Who called?"

"Your daughter."

Michael's expression transformed immediately to one of

pleasure as he settled into his chair and grabbed the phone. "I'll call her back."

"You can't."

"Why not?" he asked, then began stabbing in the number without waiting for her answer.

A.J. wrapped her arms around her waist. "I mean, you can try, but they... She was leaving for the airport. I asked her to try to call you from Cancún."

Michael sat with the receiver pressed to his ear, listening. Moments later he hung up, muttering a ragged oath. "Answering machine. It seems the only time I ever hear my daughter's voice is on that damn answering machine."

A.J. had no idea what force it was that drew her across the room to stand beside his chair. All she knew was that to try to resist its pull would have been like standing still in a tornado—impossible to do.

"I'm sorry you missed her."

"Yeah." He raked his fingers through his hair, which only heightened his rugged look. "Missing my daughter is the story of my life. When her mother and I were still married, I missed a lot about Megan. Her first word. Her first step. I missed them all, because I let my job take precedence." He shook his head. "Now, Megan lives two thousand miles away, and I just miss her."

The stark loneliness of his statement clenched at A.J.'s heart as she slowly lowered herself into the chair beside him. Here was the father she could not picture before. The father whose very voice ached for the daughter he loved.

"She said she can't wait until she's old enough to enroll in the academy. She wants to follow in your footsteps." Her lips curved. "It sounds as if she's very proud of you."

Michael swiveled his chair slightly, leaned and rested his elbows on his knees. His firm, capable hands dangled inches from her own knees. "And when she graduates from the academy, I'll worry every minute she's on the street."

"Maybe you can talk her into becoming a crime analyst. She thinks my job is cool." A.J. paused, then added, "She said to tell you she loves you."

Michael reached for her hand in a gesture so swift and smooth that A.J. didn't have time to feel shock. All she felt was the warmth of his flesh against hers, the firmness in his touch, the jolt of desire deep inside her.

"Thank you." His palm cradled her fingers while his thumb grazed her knuckles in a swift, light caress.

"I..." A.J. couldn't speak, not while he touched her. Not while he sat inches from her, absorbing her with his eyes.

"You what?"

"I just answered the phone, is all—"

It was as if they both sensed another presence at the same time, their heads swiveling in unison toward the door.

Helene stood half in, half out of the doorway, her dark, sleek suit and hose giving her the look of a leggy black spider. Her gaze was assessing, measuring, her red-glossed mouth set in a thin line.

"Officer St. John," Michael said as his hand casually slid from A.J.'s and he turned in his chair. "Did you get anything on Hollis?"

Helene cocked her head, sending a cascade of platinum hair down one shoulder. The tension already present in A.J.'s stomach turned into knots under the woman's cool, scrutinizing gaze.

"Lieutenant, if I'm interrupting—"

"You're not," Michael said evenly. "What have you got on Hollis?"

From the nightstand, the clock's digital display glowed an eerie red 2:00 a.m. Outside, winter blustered, pinging pellets of sleet against the second-story windows. A burglar alarm, triggered by the storm, wailed somewhere in the distance. As he had for three consecutive nights, Michael lay staring at the ceiling's shifting patterns of black-and-gray shadows while trying to figure out what the hell he was going to do about A.J. Duncan.

Three days, he thought. In the time since he and A.J. visited her ex-sister-in-law's office and Emily Duncan's hospital room, A.J. had performed her task force work with cool, controlled efficiency. Now, she spoke to him only about the Westfall case, and only when a memo or E-mail message wouldn't suffice.

A.J. had accomplished what Michael hadn't managed. Couldn't begin to manage. She'd put emotion aside and relegated their relationship to one of business. Which was what he should have done the night she walked into his office in Internal Affairs. But he hadn't. He'd broken the first law of being a cop—he'd replaced discipline with emotion and gotten involved.

Good, God, had he gotten involved!

Each day he watched her down the length of the report-laden conference table while the subtle nuance of her every movement branded itself in his brain. He had a picture frozen in his mind—A.J. with her head bent over her work, dark, thick hair draping her breasts, molding her curves with intimate detail.

He watched her. And he wanted her.

"Damn!" Michael scrubbed a hand across his face while the thought of those curves sent heat arrowing straight to his loins.

"Get your head on straight, Ryan."

A.J. wanted distance between them, which was exactly how their relationship had to stay until they resolved the unfinished business of Ken. So why couldn't he leave it at that? Michael wondered. Why couldn't he relegate her to some dark part of his subconscious and get on with business? And why the hell did her obvious desire to avoid all but essential interaction with him only fuel his need to demolish the wall she'd built?

The wall intended to keep him out.

"Because you're crazy about her," he muttered.

Giving up on any chance of sleep, he sat up and flicked on the lamp beside the clock, illuminating the room in a dim wash of light. The rumpled sheets and pillows around him added to his discontent. There had never been such a cold emptiness to his bed, not even in the weeks after Lauren walked out, ending their marriage.

It sure as hell wasn't his ex-wife whom he wanted naked beside him now. He wanted A.J. Wanted her hot, silken flesh sealed against his. Wanted to see desire for him glistening in her dark eyes as he lowered himself onto her and sated an urgent, primitive hunger to make her his.

Damn. It was insane, unbelievable, this need he felt for her. He'd held her in his arms *once*. Tasted her lips *once*. Yet, in his mind, she was his.

As if sensing his restlessness, the wind picked up, hammering sleet against the windows with an unearthly wail.

Tossing back blankets, he rose and walked across the room, his pajama bottoms riding low on his hips. He paused to push aside the curtains that covered the window over the antique rolltop desk, the one piece of furniture he'd salvaged from his marriage. In the overlapping puddles of security lights, his backyard resembled a dazzling world of glass. He thought of a long-ago winter night when he'd stood at this window holding his daughter in his arms while promising to take her on a sled ride the following day. But when morning dawned the phone rang and he'd been called in to work. Another opportunity missed, just as he'd missed Megan's phone call three days ago.

Expelling a slow breath, he popped open the locks on his briefcase and pulled out Billy Hollis's mug shot.

The persistent drone of the storm faded from his hearing as he concentrated on Hollis's face. They'd issued a radiogram three days ago, and Hollis still wasn't in custody. The special projects unit had staked out the church parking lot during Dianna Westfall's funeral, but her nephew hadn't shown up to pay his last respects. Not that Hollis's absence had surprised anyone. But the guy was a hand-to-hand dealer, selling nickel bags on street corners—a profession that didn't require a vast amount of intelligence in its workers. Unless Hollis had been tipped off that he was hot property and told to lie low, some patrolman should have run across him by now.

Michael stared into the hopeless eyes that glared from the depths of the mug shot. Hollis might be worth questioning, but at this point Michael wasn't sure he'd had anything to do with his aunt's death.

And after what Dianna Westfall's neighbor Pamela Rawlings said when interviewed, Michael wondered if they'd ever clear the case. According to Mrs. Rawlings, it was a wonder Dianna had time for volunteer endeavors, what with all the men she'd brought home over the past year. The neighbor's assumption that Dianna had invited the men to her mansion for something other than philanthropic endeavors was supported by the dozens of male names listed in Dianna's address book.

Rolling his shoulders to ease his tight muscles, Michael flicked the mug shot idly back into his briefcase. If the investigation dragged on, if they never made an arrest, he might spend an eternity sitting at one end of a table, wanting the woman at the other. "Hell of a life," he muttered.

The phone's sudden ring jarred his senses. He had the receiver against his ear before the second ring could sound. "Ryan."

"Lieutenant, this is Morales at dispatch. Unit 433 asked me to call. He just picked up the subject of your radiogram."

"Hollis?"

"Yes."

Michael grabbed his holstered 9mm Sig Sauer out of the briefcase, then slammed the lid shut. "I'll be downtown in twenty minutes."

"You need me to contact anyone else?"

"Sam Rogers and Grant Pierce. Have them meet me there."

"That it?"

"Call Sky Milano. Tell her we'll need her to take a blood sample."

"Got it. Anyone else?"

For a fleeting instant, Michael thought of A.J. But no, there was no reason to call her in. No reason, save for his personal one.

"That's it. Morales, before you make those calls, get Unit 433 back on the air. Tell him to make sure he reads Hollis his rights."

Chapter 9

A.J. stood over the bathroom sink, finishing off her makeup with a stroke of blush to her cheeks. It was Saturday. In deference to the department's relaxed weekend dress code, she'd pulled on a snow white cable-knit sweater and a pair of jeans that clung snugly to her legs. Her dark hair fell in soft waves across her shoulders.

In the mirror's reflection she could see one side of the door behind her, then a wedge of her bedroom beyond that. The place looked like a burglar had tossed it. Drawers gaped from the bureau, their contents littering the area rug and wood floor. The closet door stood open, every purse, piece of clothing and pair of shoes stripped from its interior. The mattress, void of bedding, lay at an odd angle atop the box springs.

She had searched every pocket, nook and crevice large enough to hold a microcassette tape.

The bedroom had been the last of the rooms she'd explored on her nightly forays through the rambling Victorian brownstone. Other than a dust-laden box of Egyptian bric-a-brac shoved behind the attic staircase that her aunt had thought long lost, A.J. had found nothing out of the ordinary. Nothing to suggest Ken had hidden a tape...or anything else for that matter.

Propping her wrist against her ribs, A.J. squinted at the clasp of her watch, which stubbornly refused to snap closed. She blinked, struggling to get the gold band into focus. Her eyes burned, her head felt light. She'd gotten little sleep over the past few nights and she was punchy with fatigue. Her reflection in the bathroom mirror confirmed as much. All the makeup in the world couldn't conceal the dark smudges beneath her eyes, couldn't hide the small lines that had settled at the corners of her mouth.

"Duncan, you look like warmed over poop," she muttered.

It was barely 6:00 a.m. She needed about eight hours of oblivion in her future. Instead, she faced a full day of intense work on the profile of Dianna Westfall's killer.

And truth was, a full day of forcing her mind to ignore Michael Ryan's unsettling presence while her body went as tense as strung wire each time she looked at him.

Which was getting harder and harder to avoid.

She'd never realized how appealing a man could look shuffling through a stack of police reports with smooth, economic movements. Or leaning back in a chair, phone caught between his shoulder and cheek, while he thoughtfully shifted a roll of red evidence tape from hand to hand. Or standing before a ceiling-high window, his tall, athletic build silhouetted by the fading light of a December day.

And those eyes. Deep, fathomless blue eyes that, if she didn't know better, followed her every move.

Scowling into the mirror, she shoved her hands through her hair. "Get a grip!"

She walked out of the bathroom, making a concerted effort to ignore the quickening in her stomach and concentrate instead on the chaos around her. When she got home—however late that was—she'd clean up the mess. And while she straightened out the jumble, she'd figure out where to look next.

"Ken, I *know* you made a tape," she said, gesturing her arms in frustration. "Where did you hide it?"

As if an eerie sign from above, her watchband loosened and slithered down her hand.

"Dammit!" Kicking a discarded blouse aside, A.J. moved past the bed while fumbling with the clasp. Her attempt at using her thumbnail to bend the tiny metal hinge left a chip in her crimson fingernail polish.

Reentry Red.

A series of images clicked in her brain, halting her steps.

"My, God!" She blinked, inhaling a shuddering breath. The hazy, unformed image that had plagued her from the moment she first saw the photos of Dianna Westfall's severed finger settled into sharp focus.

In that time-stopping instant, A.J. knew that Dianna Westfall wasn't her killer's first victim. There was another.

The previous night's sleet storm had left the roads as slick as a toboggan run. It took A.J. nearly an hour to make the drive downtown. She didn't waste time checking in with the task force, but went directly to Homicide's small, dimly lit file room.

Glasses perched on her nose, she carried the file on the murdered jogger to the small wooden table centered in the room and flipped open the cover. Ignoring the reports, she went straight for the crime scene photos.

The top one showed the victim, Laura Sawyer, lying facedown, her long auburn braid tangled in the thick underbrush of the vacant lot where she died. She was naked, except for blood-spattered socks and running shoes. In the distance, a For Sale sign leaned in front of a house under construction.

The crime scene techs had taken numerous photos, but wildflowers and weeds partially obscured the body. A.J. sifted through half the stack before she found close-ups of Sawyer's hands. Nerves humming, she shuffled to the morgue shots of Sawyer, sans bloody socks and shoes, and found the photo she wanted. "You did her, too," she said, her voice quavering on the stale air. Her fingers tightened on the photos. "You did her, and I've got you. I've got you—"

"A.J.?"

She jolted and whirled, slamming her knee against the table leg. "Lord!"

Michael raised a hand. "Sorry. Didn't mean to startle you."

"It's okay." She leaned to rub her knee through her jeans, sending a slither of dark hair down her arm. "I didn't hear you come in."

He walked toward her, pausing at the edge of the table. "I stopped by my office and saw the light on under the door in here." His mouth hitched up on one side. "Thought I'd better check to see what crazed detective was working at this hour of the morning."

He was wearing khaki slacks and a smoky blue sweater that matched his eyes. The shadow of stubble that darkened his chin told her he hadn't taken time to shave. He looked rugged, with a hint of wildness mixed in. The effect of his presence went straight to A.J.'s stomach like a hot lance.

He glanced at the open file. "What's going on?"

"Do you remember the jogger homicide?" she asked as his eyes came back to hers. The fiery coil in her belly had left her voice a rasp. She cleared her throat and forced her muscles to relax. She was a professional, she had a job to do. She refused to let her emotions rule her, refused to allow Michael Ryan's proximity to tie her in knots. "We talked about the case once."

He slid one hip onto the table. "As I recall, we talked *around* the case," he countered easily. "When I asked you about the particulars, you referred me to Detective Cook." Michael folded his arms across his chest. "He's still on leave, and because of the task force I haven't had a chance to read the report you compiled. If you've got something, you'll need to bring me up to date."

She glanced at the file, wishing she'd had time to go through the reports before she presented her theory to Michael. But if she was right, spare time wasn't in the formula.

Anticipation had her turning to pace the length of the small room. The heels of her leather flats clicked on the tile floor as she pulled details of the case from her memory. "The jogger, Laura Sawyer, died sometime after dawn the last day of August," A.J. began, her hands gesturing as she spoke. "A boy playing with his dog found her body in a field that same morning."

"What area of town?"

A.J. gave a location in the far northwest part of the city. "Out in the sticks, basically. Sawyer was a marathon runner who jogged up to twenty miles at a time. The place she died was about the halfway point on her regular workout route." A.J.'s brows drew together in concentration as she paced. "If I remember right, her husband said she could do a mile in something around eight minutes."

Michael gave a soft whistle, his eyes following A.J.'s progress from one end of the small room to the other. "Not world-class, but a time like that would leave most people eating dust."

"That tells you what kind of physical shape she was in."

"How did she die?"

"Multiple stab wounds." Whirling, A.J. walked to the table where she turned the file folder in Michael's direction. She flipped to the autopsy report which showed a frenzied assault directed toward the woman's left chest. Beneath her hands, A.J. could almost feel the suspect's rage rise off the page. "Sawyer put up a big fight. Her legs, arms and hands were covered with defense wounds. But her fingers were left intact."

Michael's eyes whipped up to meet hers. "Go on."

"The polish on Sawyer's fingers is a deep red," A.J. continued. "Her toenails are painted a frosted pink color."

"Is that significant?"

"I think so," A.J. said as she fanned the photographs across the table. "You can see the different polish colors in the morgue shots. I noticed it when I first reviewed the file, but I figured Sawyer had polished her fingernails with a different color and hadn't bothered with her toenails.'' Leaning across the table, she pointed at a picture of the victim's hands, then searched until she found one of the feet and placed the photos side by side. "It's something a man probably wouldn't notice. But a woman would. I've done the same thing myself when I was in a hurry. If I'm not wearing sandals, nobody knows my polish doesn't match.''

"You think the guy took the time to paint her fingernails after he killed her?''

"The man who murdered Dianna Westfall did.''

"Was Sawyer raped?''

"Yes,'' A.J. answered. "Prior to death.''

Michael remained silent for a moment, then said, "Dianna Westfall and Laura Sawyer both died of stab wounds. By the look of these photos, both women were similar in build. Both had auburn hair—''

"And the polish on their fingernails was the same shade of red. *Reentry Red,*'' A.J. said, the mounting comparisons quickening her pulse.

"Fingernail polish. I'll be damned.'' Michael smiled as he said it, an unmistakable undertone of admiration in his voice. "Let's put your theory to the test, A.J. What about forensics?''

She tossed back her hair and shoved up the sleeves of her sweater. "I didn't have a chance to check the lab report on Sawyer before you came in.'' With quick efficiency, she flipped through the thick sheaf of reports. When she got to the last one, she lifted a palm. "Not here. Damn.''

"You'll have to get Sky to pull up the report on the lab computer. Have her compare their findings on Sawyer with what she's got on Westfall. Tell her this takes priority.''

A.J. looked at her watch. "I'm not sure Sky will be here yet.''

"She's here. We pulled Billy Hollis in about three this morning. I called Sky in to take blood and hair samples.''

"Oh.''

Michael raised a hand to rub his unshaven chin. It wasn't his usual casual gesture, A.J. realized. It was one of fatigue. Instinctively she searched his face. The inadequate wash of light from above had helped mask the shadows she now saw beneath his eyes.

"You've been up most of the night?" she asked.

"All night." His lips curved. "Comes with the job. I'll catch up when all this is over."

A.J. nodded, looking back at the file. "What about Hollis? Do we know yet if his samples matched those from his aunt's crime scene?"

"They didn't. His blood type is O. Dianna's killer has AB." Michael glanced away for a moment. "We had to cut Hollis loose a couple of hours ago."

"So, we're back to square one."

"If you're right and the same guy killed Sawyer and Westfall, we're back to a whole different square one," Michael commented.

Leaning alongside him, A.J. began gathering up the photographs. "Do you want me to wait at the lab while Sky checks things out?"

Michael's hand settled lightly over hers, stilling her movements. "A.J., we need to talk. Something came up during Hollis's interview."

"What?" She turned her head, and found herself eye to eye and mouth to mouth with Michael. His fingers curled around hers, sending heat creeping into her cheeks. One touch and the wall she'd built to keep him out began to shake.

For an insane, unthinking moment, she wanted him to kiss her as he'd done before. No, she corrected, as her lashes fluttered against her cheeks. Not like before, when his lips had been gentle, savoring. Now she ached to feel the passion, the same fierce, urgent need in him that threatened to engulf her.

She opened her mouth but couldn't speak. Not while she couldn't breathe. Not while her heart refused to beat.

"We need to get together later," Michael said.

"I...I'll be here all day."

"Away from here, someplace where we can talk. We need to talk about Hollis."

If either of them leaned in, their lips would touch. The thought made her heart stick in her throat. With a tug of longing, she realized all she had to do was close the space between them....

She jerked her hand from beneath his. God, what was she thinking? What the hell was she thinking? She took a step backward. Her stomach did a slow roll when Michael rose off the table and moved with her.

"We've got one hell of a problem here, A.J."

She pulled off her glasses. "I know. If Sky links these cases—"

His hand came up, his fingers feathered against her chin, forcing her gaze to his. "I'm talking about what's going on between us." In the dim light, Michael's eyes shone like lightly tarnished silver.

"There...can't be anything between us." She turned and began shuffling the photos into a clumsy stack. Her face was on fire, her heart pounded in her ears.

Michael stood motionless at her side, the silence between them lengthening until it seemed to A.J. that an eon had passed.

"You're right," he agreed softly. "There can't be anything between us. But you and I know there damn well is. And I think it'd be incredibly naive on both our parts to pretend that things will stay the way they are now after Ken's case is resolved."

"Ken's and my case, you mean," she said, then slowly turned, giving him a long, level look. "And what if it's never resolved? What if you never find proof one way or another, to clear the Duncan case?"

"Then it continues—"

"And so do your doubts. About Ken. And me."

At the far end of the room the door swung open, admitting a wedge of bright light and a sleepy-faced detective.

"Lieutenant, there's a DEA agent—Demenchi, Delmonte—something like that, looking for you. I told him to wait in your office.''

"DiMaiti," Michael said, giving the detective a glance across his shoulder. "I'm on my way." He looked back at A.J., his eyes somber. "Let me know what Sky finds on the jogger case."

"I will."

When he was gone, she sagged against the table. It was a long time before the hard, thick throbbing of her pulse slowed.

"They cut his tongue out by the roots, Mike," Tony DiMaiti said over the rim of his coffee mug. "Left the damn thing in Hollis's pocket. That'll make the other street slime think twice about squealing on the big boys."

Michael's thoughts went back to the early morning hours when Billy Hollis sat in the grimy interview room, his fear of being charged with his aunt's murder so intense you could smell him sweat. Shaken to the bone from having pictures of his mutilated aunt shoved under his nose, the man had offered to work a deal. Hell, he'd *begged* for the chance to tell all he knew about Benito Penn and Benito's boss, Snowman.

Snowman. As he'd stood watching the interrogation through two-way glass, Michael had felt his spine go rigid as Ken Duncan's words played in his mind. *I'm into something...need help getting out. Has to do with a dealer named Snowman. I've got evidence to turn over.*

Michael had stared into Hollis's face, his cop's instincts telling him that Dianna Westfall's streetwise drug-dealing nephew held the key to the Duncan investigation.

The man had been busting a gut to talk, yet in the space of ten minutes he'd clammed up and screamed for a lawyer. Ten minutes. That had been just long enough for Sky Milano—accompanied by Helene St. John—to draw a vial of Hollis's blood. What had happened in those ten minutes to change the man's mind?

"You still with me, Mike?"

"Yeah." Michael propped his elbows on his desk and gave Tony a bleak look. "We had him. Hollis was ready to tell everything he knew about Benito Penn and Snowman, then all of a sudden he clammed up." Michael's hands clenched into fists. "Dammit, how long have we been looking for a lead on that bastard, Snowman?"

"Since someone blew Ken Duncan away."

Michael stared across the desk. Tony DiMaiti was another of the growing list of law enforcement personnel whom Billy Hollis's arrest had dragged out of bed. The DEA agent's brown hair showed signs of a wind combing; his jeans and flannel shirt looked suspiciously as if they'd been pulled from the bottom of the laundry hamper. His eyes were bloodshot; he needed a shave. Michael figured he didn't look much better.

Tony cocked his head. "Speaking of Duncan, is there anything new on him?"

"Plenty. I've got a mountain of circumstantial evidence that says he dumped on his badge. And a motive."

"Greedy bastard."

"Wrong. The guy didn't want the money for himself. He needed to get his very likable aunt on a high-dollar cancer clinic's waiting list."

"And," Tony began, his eyes narrowing in thought, "one might ask, did the niece also take part in this so-called honorable attempt to save her aunt?"

"One might ask that."

Tony leaned forward, his coffee mug cradled between his thick fingers. "Bet that was the first question out of your chief's mouth when you told him."

"McMillan didn't ask," Michael said evenly. "Because I haven't had a chance to bring him up to date."

"Okay, Mike. How about you? Have you asked yourself if A.J. was in on it?"

Michael nodded slowly. "Only about a hundred times. Dammit, I just don't think she had a clue what her brother was doing."

"You don't think," Tony echoed. "But you don't know."

"That's right. I don't know."

Michael closed his eyes as the vision of A.J. leaning over the small table in the file room formed in his mind. He'd been intrigued, not just by the way her slender jeans had shown off her legs better than any miniskirt could. Her tense roaming of the room, the excited spark in her eyes as she performed the mental exercises that linked the homicides had entranced him. It was an aspect of A.J. Duncan he'd not seen before. An aspect that had attracted him as surely as if she'd stepped into his arms.

"You're unsure of her innocence, but you're protecting her," Tony said carefully. "Want to tell me what's going on here?"

Michael expelled a breath. "She's gotten to me."

A slow smile formed beneath the agent's scraggly mustache. "Excuse me, Lieutenant, could you repeat that? I thought you just admitted that a woman has gotten to you."

"You heard me, DiMaiti."

"I'll be damned."

Michael leaned in. "You enjoying yourself?"

"Matter of fact, I am. I've got a right to. After all, I'm the guy who hauled you around for weeks after your divorce, listening to how you'd had it with the entire female population. 'To hell with them all' is how you put it right before you swore you'd never get involved again."

"Put a lid on it."

Chuckling, Tony rose and settled his mug on the corner of the desk. "I've got to check in at the office. I'll let you know if we get anybody wanting to squeal about who offed Hollis. But don't count on it. I don't imagine anybody'll be talking to the cops for a long time. Don't blame 'em. I'm kind of partial to my own tongue, myself."

He paused, his eyes glinting as he hooked his thumbs into the front pockets of his jeans. "Pop's under the weather, so I'm subbing for him at the restaurant tonight. Why don't you and A.J. drop by?"

"Don't push it, DiMaiti."

* * *

"In comparing hairs, we look for matches between pigment granules and their distribution."

A.J. peered through the lens of a comparison microscope at a lit field, divided in half. In the left field lay a hair from the suspect in the Westfall murder; the right field held a suspect hair found on one of Laura Sawyer's bloody socks.

Sky Milano sat on a stool opposite A.J., continuing her commentary while staring through a separate eyepiece. "Most of the time we can tell a person's race but not sex by their hair."

Except for the two women bent over the microscope, the forensic lab with its U-shaped counters lined with beakers and test tubes was deserted this Saturday morning. A boxy instrument with dials and blinking red lights made a soft whirring noise. The evidence refrigerator beside the emergency shower clicked on and hummed.

"With this scope we can do side-by-side comparisons of two objects at the same magnification." Sky twisted a knob. "Now, I'll scan the hairs and we'll see how they compare."

A.J. nodded vaguely. To her untrained eye the hairs looked like long transparent worms with dark, fragmented spines.

"You can easily distinguish variations in each hair's microscopic characteristics," Sky stated.

"Uh-huh."

"The structural features of the cortex of both hairs are similar. Ditto the medulla."

A.J. looked up, blinking to get her eyes into focus. "Are they from the same person?"

Sky clicked off the scope and smiled. She'd taken off her thick glasses and for the first time A.J. was aware of the intense aquamarine color of the eyes that stared back at her.

"Relax," Sky said, patting her dark hair, lashed into its usual tight bun. "We've already checked the report on the jogger. Suspect had AB blood—same as the Westfall case. Probably the same guy.''

"And the hairs?" A.J. persisted.

"They exhibit similar morphological characteristics."

A.J. linked her fingers prayerlike. "In English."

Smiling, Sky pulled her glasses out of her lab coat pocket. "I guess this means I should skip my standard dissertation on the amazing aspects of a hair's cuticle."

"Only if you want me to stay awake."

"My money's on one guy, with medium-length straight brown hair," Sky said, sliding on her glasses. "He washes it regularly. Whoever cuts it uses a razor."

"Okay. You're saying the same guy killed both Westfall and Sawyer?"

"To know for sure we'll have to do DNA tests on both samples and that'll take time. All I can say right now is it's probably the same guy."

"What guy?" Grant Pierce's inquiring voice came from behind A.J. In the instant before she turned, she saw the chemist's eyes spark behind her glasses.

"What guy?" the detective repeated as he leaned his tall, muscled frame against a counter.

A.J. slid off the stool. "No guy," she said. Her next step was to report Sky's findings to Michael. He would then advise the chief of the high probability that the same man killed Laura Sawyer and Dianna Westfall. If the press got wind of it before McMillan, there would be hell to pay.

Grant looked unconvinced. "Sure, keep me in the dark. And here I was, ready to tell you what just came in from dispatch."

Sky swept him a look behind her dark lashes. "Tell us, detective," she coaxed softly.

Grant flashed a careless smile. "Remember Dianna Westfall's nephew?"

"Billy Hollis. Type O blood."

"Yeah. Patrol found him in an alley. Someone caught him center shot to the chest with a .44."

A.J. frowned. "Didn't he just get cut loose a couple of hours ago?"

"Right," Grant said with a shrug. "Too bad the scum wad decided to zip his lip about the drug stuff. He'd be in a cell right now, instead of headed for a morgue slab."

"That was the oddest thing," Sky said to A.J. as she slipped the slides with the hairs off the microscope's viewing surface. "Sam and Grant interviewed Hollis, had him singing like a church choir. Then Helene and I go in to take samples—"

"Helene?" A.J. asked. "Why did Ryan call her in?"

"I'm not sure he did," the chemist said. "I think she heard on her scanner that patrol had picked Hollis up, so she just came on in. Anyway, she showed up, so Ryan sent her in with me. No doubt he hoped she'd keep Hollis's mind off the matter of his rights—one being that he didn't have to give us body samples. I got his blood okay, but all of a sudden he went ballistic." Sky sighed. "Never did get any hairs."

"First time I've seen anyone lawyer-up like that," Grant said. "One minute Hollis is ready to squeal like a kid on Christmas about Benito Penn and some dude called Snowman. The next thing I know—"

"Snowman?" A.J. asked faintly. She placed a hand against the counter, unsure her legs would continue to support her.

"Snowman," Grant verified, then picked up where he'd left off. "Hollis starts screaming that he had rights and he wanted a lawyer."

"The guys in narcotics tried to get him to talk, but by then he wasn't having any of that," Sky added. "And once I checked his blood and eliminated him as a suspect in the Westfall case, they had to cut him loose."

A.J. swallowed past the tightness in her throat and turned to face Grant. "Did Hollis give you any idea who Snowman is?"

"No, but he made it sound like the guy controls most of

the drug traffic on the street," Grant answered. "Benito Penn is big-time, and he supposedly reports to Snowman."

"That's all you know?" A.J. asked as she wiped a clammy palm against her jeans-clad hip.

"Well, if Snowman offed Hollis, I know the guy's bad news. He not only shot the kid, he cut out his tongue."

Grant crossed his arms and turned a high-voltage smile in Sky's direction. "We on for the dance, sweet thing? It's Monday night, you know."

The chemist flicked him a cool look. "I haven't decided."

Grant shook his head. "A.J., this woman won't cut me any slack. I bet when Lawson asked you to go, you said a polite 'yes.'"

"Dance?" A.J. used the tip of her tongue to wet her dry lips. *Snowman.* Ken told Michael he had information about Snowman, and Ken was dead. Hollis had information about Snowman. And now, Hollis was dead.

"The Christmas dance," Grant said, giving her a curious look. "You know, the chief's pet social event of the season? The one he insists all off-duty personnel attend?"

"I…we talked about it." Weeks ago, Greg had asked her to go, and she'd said yes, A.J. remembered. But right now, going to a dance was the furthest thing from her mind.

All she could think about was Snowman.

Without another word, A.J. grabbed the lab report Sky had printed off the computer, then headed out the door.

Tony had been gone less than five minutes when A.J. walked into Michael's office, her face dead white. The glittering look in her dark eyes brought him out of his chair.

"I know about Hollis," she said as he rounded the desk. "I know he talked about Snowman. And I know he's dead. Just like Ken, he's dead."

Michael grabbed her shoulders and lowered her onto a chair. He settled into the one beside hers. "A.J., Hollis didn't *talk* about Snowman. He mentioned him, said he had information about him if we'd cut him a deal. That's as far as Hollis got before he started yelling for a lawyer.''

"You were going to tell me this later?"

"Yes."

"Why later?"

"I just thought it'd be easier..." Michael glanced away, then looked back at her. "Hell, nothing about this will ever be easy. I was hoping by the time I told you about Hollis, we'd have something on Snowman. The minute we cut Hollis loose, a DEA agent picked up his tail. It turns out Hollis was on foot. He climbed a fire escape and went over a couple of warehouse roofs. The agent lost him in an alley. Next thing we know, he's dead."

"With his tongue cut out."

Michael grimaced. "You didn't miss any details."

"Word spreads fast." She turned her head to meet his gaze, and he saw the torment in her eyes. "That's why Ken died, isn't it? Because he knew something about Snowman?"

Instinctively, Michael skimmed a hand over her hair. He could have sworn he'd just touched silk. "I don't know why he died. I wish to God I did, but I don't."

"If we could find Ken's tape, we would know."

"Maybe." At this point, Michael was close to believing Ken Duncan had used his ex-wife's recorder for the sole purpose of blackmail. Getting people to incriminate themselves on tape, then blackmailing them for money wasn't a new angle on crime, but it was one that worked.

A.J. dropped her gaze. "The lab report," she said, staring at the paper clenched in her hand as if she'd forgotten why she'd come to his office.

"What did Sky say?"

A.J. handed him the crinkled paper.

"She's almost sure the same man killed Sawyer and Westfall."

Michael stared at the report. "So, we have a serial killer."

A.J. nodded. "And if Sky's right, he's been in town at least six months."

"Great," Michael said and wrapped his hand around A.J.'s unsteady one. "Just great."

Chapter 10

"**I** damn well don't believe this!"

Michael turned and met Brian McMillan's hard-edged stare. As always, the chief presented an imposing figure, with his tall, athletic build and erect posture. Dressed in a tailored tuxedo, his thick mane of silver hair brushed with a stylist's touch, the man stood at one end of the conference table looking sleek and vigorous...and a touch rabid, considering the fury that emanated from him.

"Dammit, I don't believe this!" McMillan's face reddened as he swept a hand over the mix of crime scene photos and mug shots spread before him.

The chief had detoured by the department on his way to a party after getting Michael's phone call. His wife, Zelda, had opted to wait in the car. Considering the man's mood, that was one smart move on her part, Michael decided.

"Believe it, Chief," he said in a matter-of-fact voice. "You've got the proof in front of you."

McMillan's fist crashed against the table. "I don't know what the people around here think they're doing, but it sure as hell isn't their jobs! You call me, saying you think *one* man has killed three women since June and your detectives haven't caught on until now? Seven months later? Jesus, the media will be down my throat!''

Michael flicked a look toward the bank of windows where A.J. stood. After Sky Milano verified a match of the hairs from the Westfall and jogger homicides, he and A.J. had started digging through Homicide's other unsolved files. Now, hours later, the carnage they'd waded through in the form of autopsy reports and nightmarish photos of violated flesh had taken their toll. Shadows darkened the skin beneath A.J.'s eyes; her mouth was set in a solemn line. In a gesture that Michael associated with fatigue and stress, her fingers performed a slow up-and-down massage of her right thigh.

"Mistakes were made, Chief," he acknowledged. "No one's denying that.''

"That's why I put you in charge of Homicide. To make sure things like this don't happen.''

"They won't, once I have time to establish controls—''

"Meanwhile it falls to me to clean up the mess left by your predecessor. Do you know how inept this makes my department look?''

And you, Michael thought. He doubted it was the media attention McMillan dreaded, but the ammunition this would give his opponent in the upcoming mayoral race. A serial killer operating undetected under the police chief's nose didn't exactly inspire voter confidence.

"We'll look worse if this gets out before you announce it to the press," Michael pointed out. "That's why I had the rest of the task force clear out an hour ago. We can't afford leaks.''

McMillan's lips thinned. "I can hear the first question the press'll put to me tomorrow. 'Chief, Dianna Westfall died Wednesday. This is Sunday. Why didn't the forensic lab, on which the voters have spent half a million dollars, spot the connection between the cases?'''

"I asked that same question of Sky Milano," Michael said. "She told me Quint Williams, the chemist who worked the jogger case, is attending DNA recertification classes at Quantico." Michael kept his voice level and controlled. He understood the chief's anger—he'd almost come unglued himself when Sky told him about the clerical mistake that had kept the connection between the two cases from being made. But getting mad wasn't going to solve their problems. And they had big ones.

"It's a fluke," Michael continued, "but the clerk who entered the data on the jogger homicide typed the wrong suspect blood type. When Sky ran a cross-check, nothing came up. And Quint wasn't around to hear the other chemists talk about a suspect with AB blood—"

"I will not abide screwups in my department! You tell Captain Harris I want the clerk who typed that information fired."

"You'll have fewer headaches if you change that to a reprimand. Other than this one mistake, the clerk has a spotless record." Michael lifted his shoulders beneath his blue sweater. "Fire her, and you'll have the union down your throat."

"All right, she stays," McMillan said with a disgusted sweep of his manicured hand. "But you inform the rest of the people who had anything to do with this incompetent mess to watch it, or they'll be looking for a job."

"Consider it done," Michael said.

McMillan's jaw tightened as if he were trying to gain some control over his anger. He stared down at the table for a long moment, then said through his teeth, "I want a detailed report on every aspect of these crimes."

"I'll have it at your house by noon tomorrow."

"Make that 0800 hours."

"Yes, sir."

"You'd better give me a rundown on the first victim now, just in case the media get wind of this before I see your report."

"I'll let A.J. brief you. She spotted the connection between the crimes and she's familiar with the suspect's MO from the jogger homicide."

McMillan's hard eyes flicked across the room to where A.J. stood. It was the first time he'd acknowledged her presence since he'd stormed into the room. "Whatever."

Michael met her gaze. "Go ahead, A.J."

She nodded and walked to the conference table, a slight limp evident as she moved. When she leaned to pick up a mug shot, her dark, glossy hair slithered across her shoulders. The sensuous effect of the movement went straight to Michael's brain. He tightened his jaw against his body's reaction and forced his thoughts to what A.J. was saying.

"Melissa Thomas." She handed the mug shot to McMillan before continuing. "Stabbed to death at a charge-by-the-hour motel last June. Her fingernails were painted bright red, which was her usual color. In this mug shot her hair is blond. In the crime scene photos, you'll see that it's auburn. She dyed her hair a week before the murder."

"Same weapon?" the chief asked, tossing the mug shot back onto the table.

A.J. deferred the question to Michael, who'd been on the phone with the ME when McMillan arrived. "A knife with a double-edged blade killed all three women."

"What about forensics?"

"We've got a few hairs in evidence from the Thomas scene," Michael explained. "Sky Milano is comparing them to see if they match those from the other cases. We know the same man killed Westfall and Sawyer. Our guess is he got the prostitute, too."

McMillan's gaze sliced back to A.J. "The press will ask about the suspect. Tell me what you know."

Michael stood in silence, tracking A.J.'s quick, efficient movements as she retrieved a file folder from beneath a stack of reports and flipped it open. At one point that afternoon she had taken time to review the notes she'd made a month ago and placed in the jogger's file. After that, she compared her findings with the suspect's MO from the Westfall case. In the hours that followed, A.J. had gone about her work with meditative precision, her eyes glittering as if a composite of the suspect's personality were churning and bubbling like a witch's brew in her mind.

"I don't have a full profile yet," A.J. began. "But I can give you a general idea of the type of person we're looking for."

McMillan glanced at his watch. "Zelda and I are due at the governor's mansion at seven. You've got five minutes."

Michael felt a stirring of anger at the man's contentious attitude but fought it down. It would do no one any good if he lost his temper. Nor would it be smart to point out to the chief what a Class A bastard he was to worry about arriving late for a Christmas party while his constituents were being murdered.

A.J. looked up slowly from her notes, her eyes flat. "Five minutes? You'll want the condensed version, then."

"The clock is running."

Her hands clenched into a tight white grip, but her voice was cool and even when she spoke. "Even if we didn't have forensics on the suspect, we can assume he's white. In these type murders, the killer usually selects victims the same race as his. I put his age in the twenties or early thirties. He has good hygiene. He's right-handed, nice looking, has an above average IQ. The man is cunning, self-confident and methodical. These murders occurred miles from each other, so that means he's not territorial. He moves around. That tells us he either owns or has easy access to a car."

She paused to scan her notes.

"You've got four minutes," McMillan said.

Lightning bolts of temper flashed beneath Michael's skin. "Chief, A.J. has a lot to cover here. You might want to ease up."

McMillan sliced him a sharp look. "And you might want to take a step back, Lieutenant." He looked at A.J. "Go on."

She turned toward the window, staring out at the lights that outlined the blackening downtown skyline, her forehead knit in thought. Outside, the wind wailed, gnashing against the glass as though it was a monster wanting in.

"Dianna Westfall was rich, beautiful, self-confident," A.J. began. "Her killer couldn't have just gone up to her and said, 'Hi, doll, how about a date?' and expect her to say yes. For that reason, he needed a plan on how to approach her. We know from what her neighbor said and from the names in her second address book, that she spent a lot of evenings out and she brought numerous men home with her. Once we find out where she spent her evenings—"

"Mrs. Westfall's habits are confidential," the chief broke in. "She was a lovely woman, my wife's best friend. I better not hear one word from the press about how she needed...companionship."

A.J. turned. "That need is the reason she's dead. That, and the fact she was slim, petite and had auburn hair— which obviously carries great meaning to the killer. Wherever Dianna went on her nighttime forays is probably the place where he gained access to her. It's possible he watched her before confronting her. And not just her—the mansion, too."

Michael kept his eyes on A.J. Against the stark whiteness of her sweater, her skin seemed almost translucent, her eyes pools of inky darkness. She began pacing, talking as she moved along the length of the windowed wall.

"I don't think it was coincidence the guy picked the servant's night off to go home with her. I think he knew ahead of time they'd have the mansion to themselves. Therefore, he'd have total control."

"It could have just been a lucky guess on his part," McMillan observed.

A.J. lifted her chin. "He showered after he killed her. He wouldn't have done that unless he knew for sure he had plenty of time."

McMillan pursed his lips in thought. "Any hope of him having an attack of conscience and turning himself in?"

"No. He knows what he does is wrong. That's why he's careful not to leave evidence. But he doesn't feel remorse.

He thinks only of satisfying his needs and he isn't sorry for what he does. He's probably as casual about murder as you are about scratching your ear."

Michael turned to McMillan. "Which means there's no chance in hell he's going to stop killing."

McMillan spat a crude curse. "This is all I need!"

A.J. headed back to the table and closed the file folder over her notes. "You need to remember one thing about this profile."

McMillan arched a silver brow. "What's that?"

"I could be wrong. Our suspect might be short, fat and fifty."

The chief gave her a thin smile as he gathered his black cashmere coat off the chair where he'd draped it. "If so, I doubt Dianna would have allowed him into her home." He looked down at the photos on the table. "There's another aspect of this mess I have to deal with. The fact that we've linked Dianna's homicide with that of a hooker could cause her family considerable embarrassment."

Michael caught the flash of anger in A.J.'s eyes. "Whose family do you mean?" she asked levelly. "The hooker's?"

The question earned her a frigid stare. "You know exactly whose family. And I advise you to hold your tongue. In my mood, it won't take much to make me sorry I listened to Lieutenant Ryan and kept you on active status when everything about your brother came out."

Michael heard the buzz in his head seconds before his temper snapped, and then the dam broke. "You're out of line," he said, rounding on the man. "You didn't suspend A.J. because there wasn't evidence that warranted your doing so. There still isn't."

"That's enough—"

"People have made mistakes around here, but A.J. isn't one of them," Michael continued, his voice ringing like surgical steel on the room's cool air. "In fact, you ought to thank her for linking these cases. You'd have a damn bigger problem if it'd been some reporter who first picked up on the fact we have a serial killer operating in this city."

McMillan's eyes turned to stone. "I don't thank my employees for doing their jobs. They get paychecks every other Friday that take care of that." He turned his head slowly and gave A.J. an assessing look that she steadily returned with a barely perceptible lift of her chin.

After a moment, his gaze swung back to Michael. "I assumed work on the task force made you unable to supply me with timely updates on the Duncan investigation. Now I realize it's because you're unwilling."

Michael set his jaw. "There's nothing to update you about."

"Remember, you're accountable if you're wrong—"

"I'm not."

"You'd better hope so, Lieutenant." McMillan walked to the door, reached for the knob, then paused. "I have my pager. Call me when you get confirmation on forensics."

"The minute I hear," Michael said, fighting the urge to slam his fist into the arrogant SOB's surgically perfect nose.

"If the same man killed all three women, I'll have the PIO arrange a press conference for noon tomorrow." Michael felt a flash of sympathy for the department's public information officer who was about to have his evening ruined. "That will give the impression we're on top of things, even if it's a lie," McMillan added, then pulled open the door. "I want you there, Lieutenant. As commander of the task force, you'll give a summary of the type of suspect we're looking for."

"Yes, sir."

"Get me an arrest fast. If you need more people on this, fine, you've got them. Just make sure you have a suspect in custody. Preferably before Christmas Day."

The door clicked shut, and Michael expelled a ripe curse.

Fingers digging into the top of an upholstered chair, he stood motionless while he stared at the photos on the table through a haze of anger. After a moment, he shoved a hand through his hair and turned his head toward A.J.

She stood staring at the door, her cheeks pale, her dark hair enfolding her face like a shadow. "I hadn't..." She took a deep breath. "I hadn't even thought that other people know you're investigating Ken and me."

"A.J.—"

"It's logical." She dragged the heel of her palm across her forehead. "It's an active IAD investigation. You'd have had to go to the chief." She leaned over the table, her unsteady hands shoving the photos into a disorganized heap.

"A.J.—"

"I shouldn't have mouthed off to him," she said, with a derisive shake of her head. "He just made me so angry. We've got a cold-blooded killer on the loose, and all the man's worried about is how he'll come across on the six o'clock news—"

Michael caught her wrists. "I'm sorry," he said quietly. "You didn't deserve his belligerence. You didn't need to hear what he said."

She looked up, her eyes softening. "What I heard was that you've gone out on a limb for me."

"I don't see it that way. It's like I told you, I listen to my instincts."

"Instincts that have you ninety-nine percent convinced that I didn't conspire with Ken to…do everything you believe he did. There's a one percent chance you're wrong about me. That could cost you your badge."

He released one of her wrists, reached out and slicked his knuckles down her cheek. "Where you're concerned, I'm leaning toward one hundred percent."

She kept her eyes locked with his. "What about Ken?"

"The evidence points to his guilt."

"It's circumstantial, every bit of it."

"True, but there's a lot."

She closed her eyes. "I know." Her voice shook. "God, I know."

Michael's throat tightened. He knew how much it must have cost her to concede that. Cupping a finger beneath her chin, he nudged upward until her dark-lashed lids fluttered open. "You think I haven't worked this from every angle a hundred times in my mind? You think I haven't tried to come up with a reasonable, logical explanation for what I found in Ken's locker? Any way I work it, the result's the same.''

''That he's guilty.''

''I'm a cop, A.J., I can't overlook the obvious.''

''You could trust what I say. You could trust me.''

Michael tightened his fingers on her wrist and drew her a step closer. ''I do trust you. And I respect your feelings for your brother. But those feelings are based on emotion.'' He eased her to him, degree by degree, until a mere inch separated their bodies. He felt the heat of her flesh; the soft, fresh scent of her swirled in his brain. ''I have to look at the facts.''

''Only when it suits you,'' she countered, temper flashing in her eyes. ''You have the same facts about me that you have about Ken, yet you're trusting your instincts where I'm concerned.''

''There's a lot more stacked up against Ken—the printout in his locker, the cash in the bank, his insistence in putting your aunt in a clinic he couldn't dream of affording on a cop's salary.'' Michael shook his head. ''Ken broke the rules once and got himself demoted—''

''That doesn't make him a thief. Or a murderer. I'm not saying that because he was my brother. I'm saying it because I know the kind of man he was. Why can't you trust my instincts about him?''

''It's not that simple.''

She nodded slowly, her fisted hand coming up to press against his chest, forming a barrier between them. ''Nothing about this is simple.''

''That's where we agree.''

She flicked a look at the conference table, piled high with file folders and computer printouts, then looked back, refusing to meet his eyes. ''If you'll let go of me, I'll start on McMillan's report.''

Michael sensed the battle waging through her, the conflict between her love for her brother and her feelings for him—whatever the hell those feelings were. In the next silent span of seconds, her eyes darkened with something indefinable. Just as quickly, he had a name for the emotion: withdrawal. The wall had come back up. The wall meant to keep him out, to keep them apart.

Her wrist stiffened beneath his hand and she increased the pressure of her fist against his chest. "Let go, Lieutenant."

The coolness in her voice sent frustrated anger surging through Michael's brain, summoning reaction before thought.

"Like hell," he muttered.

His hands shot up, cupping her cheeks, lifting her face to give him access to her mouth. He dipped his head, settled his lips on hers and kissed her, a long, hard kiss that shot lightning bolts through every nerve in his body.

For a long moment she didn't move, barely breathed as his lips devoured hers. Then an almost imperceptible moan sounded in her throat, and her lips parted beneath his. Her body shuddered, then seemed to melt against his in a surrender he knew hadn't come easy.

He fed on her mouth as if he were a starving man, all the while wondering how it was possible that her flesh felt even softer than he remembered. And how, dammit, *how* could the taste of her be more potent, more addictive than before? His arms captured her waist, his hands molding over the snug denim that curved her hips. Sweeping her against him, he pressed their bodies center to center and deepened the kiss.

A tiny purr of passion sounded in her throat, sending greed, quick and urgent, spiraling to his groin.

"Michael…" Her hands slid up his arms.

Reason, faint and glimmering, resurfaced from the dark recesses of his brain, pushing away the unthinking insanity that had overtaken him. However much satisfaction it gave him to hear her breathe his name in a hoarse whisper, to feel her curvy body pressed to his, he knew this was wrong.

All wrong.

Even as a fresh swell of need arrowed through him, he checked it. As much as he wanted to devour her, wanted to tumble her to the carpet and claim her, a far greater hunger stirred inside him. He wanted her, not just physically but emotionally. Wanted more than just the fast, molten ride of urgent sex in a room filled with pictures of murdered women. He wanted A.J. Duncan in his bed, her body slicked with passion, the prospect of long, unending hours stretching before them.

And when he took her, there wouldn't be any residual regret on her part. Wouldn't be a reason for her to look back and wonder how she could give herself to a man who, only moments before, had refused when she asked him to trust her.

Michael forced his hands to surrender their hold on her waist and slide unsteadily upward to her shoulders. He softened his kiss, then lifted his head and stepped back. "A.J...."

Her eyes flickered open, wide and glittering. Her face was no longer pale but flushed. Her body shuddered beneath his hands as she met his gaze and saw the look in his eyes. His hands tightened, holding her in place when she attempted retreat.

The flush deepened on her skin as her breasts rose and fell in an uneven rhythm. "I don't know...what happened..."

"I do," he said softly. "I lost my head, and I'm sorry for that."

"You're sorry," she repeated dully.

"Make no mistake about it, lady, I want you," Michael continued softly. "I want us to be together. But not here. And not with unresolved issues between us."

She pulled her bottom lip between her teeth. "God, nothing's simple." Her voice was hoarse, raw.

"Far from it," he agreed. "All I know is that I couldn't stand looking into your face and seeing regret. Regret for having been with me."

She met his gaze, her hands clenching, then unclenching

against her thighs. "We may never resolve our... differences over Ken."

Michael's hands went up, his fingers feathering her cheeks as he lifted her dark hair back over her shoulders. "Your being with me won't negate your loyalty to your brother. I'm certain of that. And if you ever are, too, I'll be waiting."

A.J. fastened the hook on the black dress shimmering with sequins that she'd retrieved from the back of her closet. She twisted her dark hair into a loose chignon, then secured the clasp of her mother's diamond choker, which lay like a jeweled ribbon around her neck.

Her fingers faltered against her throat, and she slowly raised her eyes to the mirror over the bureau. Two days had passed, yet her flesh still burned with the feel of Michael's touch. Two days, during which the emotional wall she'd once managed to maintain between them had crumbled and vanished.

Two days, and the need for him simmered in her blood like an incurable fever.

"And what," she asked her reflection, "are you going to do about it?"

No answer was forthcoming, just as none had been the previous hundred times she'd put the question to herself.

"Damn!" Frustration had her jerking the pins out of her hair. Dark waves tumbled over her shoulders and across her face.

"Damn, damn, damn!"

She took a deep breath, then another. Less than a week ago she'd vowed to put everything else aside while she searched for the truth about Ken. She'd put up a wall to keep Michael out, had been determined to do what she had to do. Yet now, the path that had seemed so logical and essentially uncomplicated had turned torturous.

She had no idea how to resolve her loyalty to Ken with what she felt for Michael.

Shoving her hair out of her eyes, she stared dazedly back

at her reflection. She was falling in love with Michael Ryan—she was far past denying that. And the knowledge made a strange disquiet surface inside her. He had taken her at her word, gone out on a limb to keep her off the chief's suspension list. Yet, he'd refused to trust her feelings about Ken, refused to trust *her*.

She tightened her jaw. She wasn't a fool. She knew there was a mountain of evidence that implicated Ken; knew exactly how guilty her brother's actions looked. Yet she couldn't bring herself to believe the accusations, couldn't stop believing in him.

And that left things at an impasse to which there seemed no resolution, she thought, dragging a brush through her disheveled hair. Or was there? She tossed the brush aside in frustration at another unanswerable question. At this point, the only thing she was certain of was that if Michael hadn't ended their kiss, hadn't pulled back when he did, she would have been powerless to stop the inevitable outcome of their passion.

"A quickie on the chief's conference room floor," she muttered, wincing at the thought.

And tonight at the Christmas dance, she'd have to face seeing Helene St. John draped over Michael's arm. A.J.'s thoughts skittered back to that morning when she'd passed him a copy of a follow-up report just as Helene put a hand on his shoulder, gave him a smile that reeked of seduction and asked if he'd be at the dance. He said yes, then gave a vague nod when she suggested he save her a dance. The memory of that exchange had become a splinter beneath A.J.'s skin, annoying and festering.

The ring of the doorbell jerked her chin around. "Damn," she said softly. Squaring her shoulders, she grabbed her evening bag and headed down the stairs.

"God, I've missed you," Greg Lawson said as he stepped through the door, a blast of frozen air gushing in behind him. He shrugged out of his coat while his gaze did an appreciative sweep across black sequins. "You look gorgeous."

She smiled. "So do you." The entry-hall lights put sandy streaks in his blond hair, made the satin lapels of his tuxedo glint like black oil.

He glanced at his watch. "I'm early. How about a drink before we leave?"

She nodded, thinking it would take a barrel of alcohol to unknot her stomach. "Sure."

Greg draped his coat across the staircase's oak banister, then trailed her into the study. "I saw the chief's press conference yesterday. McMillan sure didn't look happy about having three dead women and no suspects."

"Believe me, he's not." A.J. paused at the credenza, where a carafe and matching glasses sat on a brass tray. "Is Scotch all right?"

"Fine." Greg walked over, his fingers brushing hers as he accepted the drink she'd poured. "Has the task force come up with any leads?"

"Actually, we got a break," A.J. answered across her shoulder while she poured a drink for herself. "We found the nightclub where Dianna Westfall hung out."

"Which one?"

"Encounters."

Greg emitted a low whistle between his teeth. "Pretty high class of clientele."

"There's a good chance one of them killed her," A.J. said. She leaned a hip against the edge of her aunt's desk and lifted her glass. The Scotch slid down her throat like liquid gold, pooling warm in her stomach. Maybe it wouldn't take a barrel of the stuff after all, she thought before continuing. "We did a run of field-interview cards that patrol filled out on all white males stopped over the past six months within a square mile of Encounters."

"That's a high-traffic area. Bet you've got one hell of a long list."

"Thousands of names," A.J. confirmed. "But one bartender gave us a vague description of a man he saw Dianna Westfall talking to the night she died. Using that, we pared the list of men who've been FI'ed to less than three hundred who match the description. This afternoon we started running a cross-check of those names with ones from Dianna's address books. The computer went down about ten minutes into the run.'' She sighed. ''When I left, the city's MIS people were still trying to get us back on line.''

Greg sipped his drink, watching her over the rim of his glass. ''Wasn't the Westfall woman's nephew a suspect?''

A.J. tilted her head. The chief had taken great pains to keep that information under wraps. ''Where did you hear that?''

''I don't remember,'' Greg replied as he turned and inspected a shelf of leather-bound volumes. ''You know how word gets around the department.''

She set her glass aside, suddenly losing her desire for alcohol. ''He's not a suspect anymore.''

''He's not anything anymore,'' Greg said. ''Got shot and had his tongue cut out.''

''You know a lot about him.''

''I talked to the day-shift officers who found Hollis.''

''Hollis? You knew him?''

Greg moved to the fireplace and idly examined the alabaster cat with kohl-lined eyes that stared from the mantel. ''I ran across him a couple of times on the street. Hollis was a two-bit piece of scum.''

''Is that what Ken thought?'' she asked quietly.

Greg turned, looking at her with cool scrutiny. ''Is that what Ken thought about what?''

''About Hollis. Did he think he was a two-bit piece of scum?''

''I don't know that he ever ran across him. Does it matter?''

A.J. shrugged. ''Hollis tried to work a deal by squealing on Snowman.''

''Who?''

''Snowman. Benito Penn's boss.''

For a fleeting instant, A.J. thought she could hear Greg's breathing change.

''I know all about Penn. What street cop doesn't?'' he

commented easily. "Never heard of Snowman." His mouth curved into a smile. "We were supposed to have a drink and relax. How'd we wind up talking about lowlife drug scum?"

A.J. lifted a hand and rubbed her temple. "I'm not sure. You mentioned the task force—"

"So I did. Let's hope you nail your guy soon. Then maybe things can get back to normal."

A.J. dropped her hand and stroked her index finger along the sheath of a brass letter opener that lay atop the desk blotter. She was far past getting back to what Greg perceived as normal. To him, normal was her walking around in shock as the days spooled before her in a ribbon of grief. Normal for Greg was her depending on his strength when she'd been too hurt to be strong.

The sound of his footsteps against the wood floor brought her gaze up. She watched in silence, tracking his progress as he crossed to her.

He reached out, his fingers curving at the side of her throat over the diamond choker. He stared down, his eyes boring into hers. "Let's forget the dance."

She gave him a puzzled look. "Why?"

"Because I don't want to share you with all those other cops. Because I want to be with you." His fingers tightened. "I want us to be together."

She took a step back, forcing him to drop his hand. "The other night at the hospital you said we needed to talk. You were right."

He raised his hand again, then let it drop. "Look, I'm sorry I haven't been around. I've been on duty every night since then. I have to work tonight, too. I tried to get someone to trade days off with me so we wouldn't have to leave the dance early, but everyone had already made plans—"

"That's not what I mean," she said quietly. "You don't have to apologize for having to work. Lord knows that's all I've done lately. The only reason I'm not at the station right now is that the chief sent out a memo reminding all division heads that attendance at the Christmas dance is a *good* idea—''

''Meaning mandatory.''

''Right.'' She took a deep breath. ''What I'm saying is, now that we have time, we need to talk about our friendship.''

''Friendship?'' A muscle twitched in his jaw. ''Not relationship but friendship?''

''That's what I feel for you, Greg. Friendship.'' She took a step toward him, softening her voice. ''I think you already know that.''

''Maybe.'' His eyes narrowed. ''What brought this on?''

''Nothing.''

''Something must have.''

Her gaze rose to trace the scar that jagged from the center of his forehead into his hairline. The familiar knot of guilt tightened her chest. ''You took care of me through the worst time of my life,'' she said quietly. ''I don't think I'd have made it without you.''

He turned and walked to the French doors at the far end of the room. ''Ken was my partner,'' he said, staring out into the winter darkness. ''My friend. The least I could do was lend his sister a shoulder to cry on.''

''That was exactly what I needed then.''

''But not now. You're over the worst of it, and it's time to tie up loose ends.''

She walked to his side, her heels clicking against the floor, then going silent when she stepped onto the braided rug. ''You're not a loose end.'' A flash of emotion in his eyes made her feel like a jerk. ''I'm sorry, Greg. I can't make myself feel what isn't inside me.''

''Hell, I know that.''

Her fingers curved around his. ''You're not to blame for what happened to Ken. I wish you could believe that.''

He expelled a slow breath. Beneath the room's recessed lights she saw pain in his eyes…and acceptance. ''Do you have any idea how much I'm going to miss you?''

''There's no need. You're welcome here any time.''

He gave her a resigned nod and slid an arm around her shoulders. "Well, friend, how about let's go to the dance and have a good time?"

A.J. allowed herself a moment to feel the spring release of tension that came with relief. Then she looked up and smiled. "My pleasure."

Chapter 11

Michael's first thought when A.J. stepped through the ballroom's mistletoe-draped doorway was that she was quite deliberately trying to drive him out of his mind.

Shimmery black sequins hugged sensuous curves, revealing nearly as much flesh as fabric. Diamonds circled her throat. The overhead lights turned her skin luminous, ivory touched by gold. Her hair was a tumble of dark waves, shot with streaks that brought warm, rich brandy to mind.

The need that rose inside him was so total he could hardly breathe. Hardly stop himself from walking the few steps it would take to reach her and forcibly remove Greg Lawson's arm from its possessive hold around her waist.

Clenching his fingers on his tumbler of Scotch, Michael turned toward the sea of round tables covered with red cloths and centerpieces of foil packages. He dragged in a ragged breath. Then another. He wished the party goers would all disappear. All except a gorgeous dark-haired woman in black sequins.

He cursed the moronic reasoning of two days ago that

had prompted him to break off their kiss and take a step back. It had been an idiotic attempt on his part to spare her from later regret. A deep-seated masculine need to claim her rose in him, and he thought with a sudden start how truly he regretted not having tossed her to the carpet and plundered her.

The volume of voices rose as people packed the ballroom, becoming swirls of color in a sea of holiday gaiety. Michael barely noticed. He was too busy labeling himself a fool for expecting A.J. to give herself to a man who put conditions on his trust in her. Without trust, no relationship stood a chance. He *knew* that, so why the hell had he thought theirs different?

He downed the contents of his glass, letting the hard bite of the Scotch course through him. He was falling in love with her. Hell, maybe he was already there. And with love, came trust. She was innocent of everything he'd once suspected her guilty of. He knew that. In his heart he knew.

And what about her brother?

Michael bit down on a frustrated curse. The evidence against Ken Duncan was overwhelming. Still, as A.J. was quick to point out, it was circumstantial, every bit of it. She loved her brother, believed him innocent—she knew he was; in her heart she knew.

"Dammit!" Michael muttered, shoving his empty glass onto the tray of a scurrying waiter. In the back of his mind he'd always acknowledged the possibility that Duncan had been set up. But the evidence against the man was so compelling....

Go back to the beginning, he told himself. Turn Ken Duncan's life inside out *again*. Instead of looking for the black and white of things, focus on the gray.

For the first time since he became a cop, Michael hoped the instincts that guided him like radar had somehow erred. For A.J.'s sake, he wanted Ken Duncan cleared of wrongdoing. Wanted it, but doubted it would ever happen.

Expelling a resigned sigh, Michael turned in the direction where he'd last seen A.J. His eyes instantly narrowed against the wall of platinum and silver that blocked his view.

"I've looked all over for you," Helene St. John said, her red-glossed lips curving into a sensuous smile.

"You found me." He lifted an eyebrow, wondering how many of their fellow officers had experienced heart failure at the sight of Helene's strapless slit-to-the-thigh dress of silver beads with a plunging neckline. Platinum hair pulled back in loose curls accented sculpted cheekbones, making her eyes seem enormous. She looked coolly regal, like a snowy ice princess who'd come in from the cold.

Helene tilted her head, sweeping cascading silver earrings across her bare shoulders. "You look like a man with some heavy thoughts."

"It's the tux," Michael said easily, wondering how long he'd been under her scrutiny. And why.

She sipped champagne from the crystal flute she'd brought with her. "How so?"

"I get morose when I put on one of these things. Makes me feel like I'm going to a funeral. My own."

Helene's soft, smoky laughter drifted on the air. "Most men ought to avoid wearing a tux, that's for sure. Just the thought of all the cummerbunds strapped around potbellies in this very room makes me shudder." Closing the gap between them, she tucked her hand into the curve of his elbow while her eyes performed a slow, intimate slide down his body. "You make me shudder, Lieutenant, but for far different reasons."

"I'll take that as a compliment."

"It's more than that." Her eyes came up to meet his. "It's an invitation."

"One I have to turn down," Michael said quietly. "I'm involved with someone."

"Oh." For a split second her nails curled into his sleeve, then just as quickly she dropped her hand. "Sorry."

"Nothing to be sorry about." He flicked a look across her shoulder. A.J. and Lawson had found chairs at a table on the far side of the dance floor. Grant Pierce and Sky

Milano, sans horn-rimmed glasses and lab coat, had joined them.

Helene's gaze followed his. After a moment she lifted her chin and gave him a narrow smile. "Doesn't A.J. look...nice?"

"Yes." Try gorgeous, he thought.

"She and Greg Lawson make an attractive couple, don't you think?"

"Can't say I've thought about it."

"You know, when I started on the task force I had my doubts whether you and A.J. could work together."

Helene's tone was matter-of-fact, her expression guileless. But Michael knew when someone was digging for information, and the woman standing at his side had a shovel.

"A.J. and I work together just fine."

"Mmm."

He cocked his head. "Make your point, Helene."

"Oh, there's really no point. It's just that you busted her brother from detective to patrolman. There's bound to be some resentment on A.J.'s part."

"If there is, she hasn't let it interfere with her work."

"Well, I'd never tell her this, but between you and me, Ken deserved that demotion. He wasn't a man to let little things like rules and procedures get in his way."

Michael's eyes narrowed. Helene had his full attention. "Meaning?"

"Maybe I shouldn't tell you." She pursed her lips while tracing a frosted fingernail around the rim of her glass. "Oh, hell, it hardly matters now that he's dead."

"I wouldn't think so."

"I went to a shift party about a week after Ken died. You know how it is at those things—you drink, tell jokes. Pretty soon the conversation centers on what's gone down on the street."

Michael nodded and waited.

"The subject turned to Ken, and we all made a pact to nail the bastard who shot him. Then somebody mentioned how Ken was the kind of officer you wanted next to you any time there was trouble. How, in a pinch, he was absolutely fearless, always right out in front when you faced the bad guys.''

"I've heard that about him," Michael commented.

"The talk went on like that for a while. After a couple more rounds of drinks, the mood changed. Somebody spoke up about how he'd seen Ken palming cash more than once.''

Michael felt the hairs on the back of his neck rise and just as quickly he forced back his hound-on-a-scent reaction. Focus on the gray, he reminded himself.

Helene snagged the attention of a roving waiter, pausing until he refilled her glass with a gush of champagne before continuing. "Don't get me wrong. It wasn't like Ken cheated little old ladies out of their social-security checks or anything like that.''

"How was it?"

"You did your time on the street, Lieutenant. You know what goes on.''

"Remind me."

Her lips curved. "You bust in on a drug dealer and there's a mountain of illegal money piled on the kitchen counter. The doper is the last one who'll holler if some evidence against him disappears.''

"True."

"Anyway, that night at the party, there were about three or four cops who wound up agreeing that anytime Ken Duncan ran onto a situation like that, there'd be a couple thousand less booked into evidence.''

"You want to give me those officers' names?''

A pale plucked brow arched as she regarded him. "Why does it matter who they are?" she asked quietly. "Ken's dead, after all.''

Michael kept his expression even, his gaze locked with hers. His senses sounded the message that a subtle, undefinable shift in the Duncan investigation had just taken place. He had no idea what that shift was, but hell if he wouldn't give it a push in the new direction.

"When I took over Homicide, I reviewed the file on Duncan's death," he said, crossing his arms over his chest. "There's one thing bothering me."

Helene blinked. "What's that?"

"The handcuff case on his belt was empty."

"Maybe whoever shot him took his cuffs for a souvenir."

"No. He carried his cuffs on a leather strap on his belt."

Helene lifted a shoulder. "He probably kept a backup gun in his handcuff case, then. Lots of cops do."

"Maybe a gun," Michael agreed thoughtfully. "Maybe a recorder."

He caught the instant tightening of Helene's fingers on her glass. "A recorder? Why would you think that?"

"Something came up about Ken making tapes."

"Really? What?"

"Nothing specific." Michael shook his head and gave her an easy smile. "Like you said, it doesn't matter now that he's dead."

The high-pitched squeal of a microphone split the air. Chief McMillan's cultured voice boomed from the dais, asking everyone to take a seat.

Helene kept her eyes on Michael, saying nothing.

"Is something wrong?" he asked.

"No." She inhaled a deep breath and took a step closer, brushing a breast discreetly against his arm. "I'm sitting with Kevin Stoner and his wife. Come join us. I promise I'll make him keep his disgusting cup of tobacco spit out of sight."

"Thanks, but I can't," Michael said, amazed by how quickly the wariness had disappeared from her eyes. "McMillan has the division heads sitting at a table by the dais." He inclined his head in the direction of an enormous Christmas tree, twinkling with multicolored lights. "I figure the chief wants to keep an eye on us."

"Someone should," she said quietly, then raised on tiptoes and pressed her lips against his cheek. "I definitely think someone should." She swept off, leaving a cloud of rich floral scent in her wake.

Michael watched her go. Why, he wondered, had she felt the need to hammer a few nails into Ken Duncan's coffin?

Two undercover cops ventured by, snaring his attention. They visited a moment, then Michael started toward the front of the ballroom. Halfway there, he stopped in his tracks. He didn't analyze why he turned, didn't question what fine-honed instinct prompted him to look in the direction of the table where A.J. sat. He just did it.

In the split second that followed, he saw that Helene had circled back toward the table. Saw her give Greg Lawson a cold, narrowed-eyed look, then turn and stalk away.

Ten seconds later, Lawson followed her out the door.

A.J. used her fork to nudge the untouched roast beef on her plate. Around her, sounds of clinking china and the murmur of voices raised in festivity filled the ballroom. The clamor made her head pound. She couldn't think. She couldn't eat, not with the vicious ache that had settled inside her when she watched Helene rise on tiptoes and plant a kiss on Michael's cheek.

Envy, white hot and fang infested, had stormed through her system, ripped through her heart. Now, she sat as stiff as a nail at the gaily decorated table, trying valiantly to appear normal with every muscle in her body clenched in agonizing knots.

"A.J., is something wrong?" Sky Milano asked from the chair beside hers.

"What?" She laid her fork aside. "No."

"I was saying that Colorado got a foot of snow today," the chemist offered. "Greg's probably having trouble getting his call through. I'm sure he'll be back in a minute."

A.J. turned her head and stared at the empty chair beside her. She had no idea how long Greg had been gone. All her senses had focused on the pulse-stopping memory of a silver-clad body pressed against a black tux.

Setting her jaw, A.J. dropped her gaze and realized she had the hem of the tablecloth wadded in her fist. She forced her hand to unclench, then reached for her wineglass. She drained its contents in two quick gulps.

Grant Pierce wrapped an arm around Sky's shoulders and leaned in. "A.J., it's your fault your date's having to spend his time on the phone, you know that, don't you?"

She blinked. The wine had gone straight to her empty stomach, then shot to her brain. "What?"

"You look so fine tonight, Lawson couldn't think straight. That's why he forgot until now to call and check on his sick mother."

Sky gave a decidedly unladylike snort. "Why is it men always blame their screwups on the nearest woman?"

"Reflex." Grant gave Sky an unrepenting grin while his eyes did a slow examination of her slim red dress dotted with tiny seed pearls. "I almost fell off your front porch tonight when you opened the door. If I'd been injured, it would have been your fault."

Sky plucked an olive off his plate and popped it into her mouth. "Is that right?"

"You bet. I was expecting Madame Curie and got Miss America. The shock nearly did me in."

Sky rolled her eyes. "You're full of it, Detective."

On the dais, Chief McMillan rose and made his usual polished, politically refined remarks. He introduced the mayor and members of the city council while a flurry of white-jacketed waiters discreetly traded empty dinner plates for slices of chocolate cheesecake.

Greg reappeared at the table just as the lights dimmed and the band's first steady, sensuous notes filled the air.

"How's your mom?" A.J. asked over the soft strains of "Completely."

He stared down at her for a long moment, then shoved his empty chair under the table with silverware-rattling force. "I have to go."

The sharpness in his voice had her straining to see his

expression in the wash of dim light. His mouth was set, his eyes hard. "What's wrong?"

Ignoring her question, he turned to Grant Pierce. "Do me a favor. Give A.J. a lift home."

"Be happy to," Grant said after exchanging a puzzled glance with Sky.

"I'll talk to you later, A.J." Without further explanation, Greg turned and walked away, disappearing into the maze of moving bodies on the dance floor.

"Wait!" A.J. tossed her napkin onto her cheesecake and was out of her chair in one smooth move. "Greg, wait."

She plunged through the swirl of dancers, nearly losing her footing on the floor's waxed surface before she snagged his sleeve.

He swung around, his eyes narrowing. "I don't have time to talk—"

"Why? What's wrong?"

"Nothing."

"But—"

His hands shot out, grabbing her by the shoulders in a hard grip that made her wince. "Dammit, leave it alone," he hissed. "Leave everything the hell alone!"

The sudden ferocity in his tone had her pulling back in a futile attempt to free herself from his grasp. "Leave what—"

"Forget it!" He spat a crude curse. "I should have known. I damn well should have known." He released his grip, turned and shouldered his way toward the door.

She stood in shocked stillness, staring at his retreating form, wondering through an incredulous haze if she should go after him. In the next instant when her brain resumed functioning, she dismissed the idea. She was riding an emotional roller coaster herself; she was in no state to deal with someone taking a crazy ride of his own.

She set her jaw, fighting for control. She needed to think. Needed to get away from everything and everybody.

Her hands curled in frustration when she realized all she'd stuffed into her evening bag was a tube of lipstick and a couple of dollars—nowhere near enough for cab fare. She either had to bum money off someone or hang around until Grant and Sky decided to leave.

"Dammit to hell!" She whirled, and collided with an immovable wall of muscled iron.

"Is there a problem?" Michael asked, reaching out a steadying hand to cup her elbow.

"No. Yes."

His brows drew together, smoothed again. "Which is it?"

"Both."

"That clears things up," he murmured.

"I'm fine." She dragged a palm across her forehead, trying to think past the effects of the wine and her swirling emotions. "Oh, hell, will you loan me twenty dollars?"

"Yes," he said, but made no move to reach for his wallet. "Mind telling me what for?"

"Cab fare."

"For you?"

"Yes."

His gaze flicked to the arched door. "Usually on a date, one gets picked up and taken home."

"Greg...had to leave."

"Pity." In one smooth movement, Michael's arm slid around her waist, pulling her against his body.

She stiffened in surprise. "What are you doing?"

"Dancing with you." He shifted his grip into dance position, his fingers threading through hers.

"Oh." She glanced around, suddenly aware that she and Greg had argued in the center of the packed dance floor. So much for keeping your personal business to yourself, she thought.

"Why didn't you leave with Lawson?"

A.J. tilted her head back to meet his gaze. "He didn't want me to."

"Strange dating pattern." Michael tucked their entwined fingers against his chest. "One I intend to reap the benefits of. How is it you wound up stranded?"

"I don't know. I don't," she repeated when he continued to stare. "Greg called to check on his sick mother and when he got back to the table he was...hostile."

Michael's grip tightened. "Hostile?"

She could see the line of concern between his strong black brows, the firm set of his mouth. His reaction made her smile. She felt safe. Protected. Why had she ever wanted walls between them?

"I'm not sure why Greg reacted the way he did," she said after a moment. "Maybe he didn't take what I said earlier as well as I thought."

"What did you say?"

"That I wanted to be his friend."

"And he got upset? Imagine that."

A.J. sighed, letting her hips move gently against Michael's body to the music's beat. He smelled wonderful, she realized, all musky cologne and masculine soap.

"Just friends?" he asked. His hand rose from her waist, settling against her spine where sequins gave way to bare flesh.

"Just," she breathed. The subtle, almost imperceptible feel of his palm on her skin put an unsteady bump in her pulse rate.

"You can't have enough friends," he said, his voice a soft whisper against her temple.

"Guess not."

The song ended and she shifted to step from his embrace. His hand tightened on hers; his arm remained an unrelenting bond around her waist, keeping her firmly against him. They stood unmoving, their bodies locked together in the soft glow of twinkling Christmas lights.

Out of the corner of her eye, A.J. saw curious heads turning their way. "People are staring."

"Let them." The beginning silky strains of "Unchained Melody" drifted on the air. Michael pulled her closer, again moving gracefully to the soft music.

She gazed up. "Didn't you promise to dance with Officer St. John?"

"Helene's not happy with me right now."

"Why?"

"I told her I want to be friends."

A.J. felt the agonizing jealousy of a few moments before slip away, replaced by something else—something softer and warmer and altogether soothing. Suddenly, the night felt right. Michael's arms felt right, more right than anything she'd ever felt before.

She took a long, languorous breath and leaned into him, savoring the relaxed light-headedness that had settled over her. "You can't have enough friends."

"Guess not."

Michael's hand moved against her bare back, sending flashes of desire skittering along her nerve endings.

"I..." Her voice faltered and her body quavered against a rush of need. Good Lord, how was she supposed to dance when her legs had gone wobbly? "You shouldn't...do that. Not if you want me to keep standing."

"I want you standing—or otherwise," he murmured as his fingers cruised up her spine.

Her heart did a slow whirl at the quiet intensity of his words. He wasn't the only one who wanted. She couldn't deny it any longer. Didn't even try.

"A.J., I was wrong the other night."

"Other night?" She dipped her head, rested her cheek against his chest while her heart hammered in her ears. Or was it *his* heart?

"Look at me." His hand slid up to cup the nape of her neck. "Look at me," he repeated quietly, nudging her head up. "One hundred percent."

She tried to read his expression but his cool touch against her hot flesh had sent her eyes out of focus. In the space of a few seconds her body had gone from relaxed to taut with nerves, and now she was molten wax, warm and pliable, conforming to every sinewy, masculine inch of him. "I don't—"

"I believe you. I believe in you, one hundred percent. No matter what."

A small burning knot of desire began to flame down low, stealing her breath as his lips skimmed along her temple.

"What...changed?"

His fingers roamed up into her hair. "I came to my senses." His voice was soft and silky, like water gliding over a smooth stone. "You don't have it in you to do anything illegal. I know that."

Her steps faltered and she stood motionless in his arms while the music continued. "Are those your instincts talking?"

"My heart. I know in my heart."

"Oh." He believed in her, but only her. Not Ken. She saw the truth in his eyes.

But did it matter? Did it really matter that Michael thought her brother guilty?

Lowering her gaze, A.J. stared at the shadowy bodies gliding around them, while need for Michael rose like floodwater in her brain. Need that obliterated any lingering uncertainty. Need that peeled resistance away one thin strip at a time. It didn't matter what Michael thought about Ken, what he believed. Not tonight. Maybe tomorrow it would, but not tonight.

Until this moment, she had never known such searing want. Never had desire for a man set off fireworks in her blood. This was the man she loved. The abrupt sureness of her feelings left her shaken. As did the realization that Michael had become more important to her than Ken.

Her eyes came up to meet his. It was difficult to talk with her heart in her throat. "Will you...do something for me?"

"Anything."

"Take me home."

He stared into her face. "I plan on it. You didn't have to ask."

He hadn't understood her meaning. "Not take me home," she amended, her voice a throaty whisper. "Come home with me."

His eyes narrowed, then darkened in comprehension. "If

I come home with you, A.J., I won't leave. Not until morning.''

The raw hunger in his voice transformed the pulse between her legs into a slow, hard throb. ''That's what I want.''

''I can't make you promises about Ken. I don't know that I could keep them.''

''I'm not asking for promises.''

His arm tightened around her. ''Dammit, I don't want you to regret this. I don't ever want you to regret being with me.''

''I won't.'' Her hand slid up, curving at the side of his neck. She reveled at the heat of his skin beneath her palm. ''This is right. I know it.''

''You're sure?''

Her mouth curved into a soft smile. ''One hundred percent.''

His lips brushed hers, soft, caressing, full of promise. ''Then let's go home.''

Chapter 12

The night was clear, cold and moonlit. Headlights licked across a brick wall as Michael steered the Bronco around a corner. When they left the convention center, he'd turned the volume down on the police radio and slid a CD into the player. Now, the bluesy ache of a tenor sax hung on the warm air.

A.J. sat beside him in silence, one gloved hand entwined with his, the other turning her evening bag over and over in her lap. The sultry, arousing scent of her perfume inundated his brain.

He could feel her nervousness. In truth, the humming of his own nerves had him wound tight.

"Are you all right?" he asked quietly, glancing across at her.

"Yes." Her face was a mixture of shadowy, creamy contours. She gave a shaky laugh. "I feel like a teenager on a first date."

Michael smiled. "So do I."

"Really?"

"Really."

Her fingers tightened on his when he turned into the driveway of the Victorian brownstone where a single light glowed in an upstairs window.

With his breath a gray cloud on the frozen air, he walked around the Bronco and opened the door. Already his blood was racing close to the surface. He knew the minute he touched her the world would tilt off its axis.

Her skin looked almost translucent beneath the wash of the porch light. Silently, he took the keys from her fingers and opened the lock.

She walked to the table at the base of the staircase and flicked on a small lamp, filling the entryway with muted, dusty shadows. She left her gloves and purse beside the lamp, then turned to face him. "Would you like a drink?"

"No."

Her gaze went to the door of the dark study. "I...can light a fire."

"You already have."

He crossed the wooden floor and cupped her face in his hands. Her breath shuddered out when he touched his lips to hers. "If you've changed your mind, A.J., you have about two seconds to tell me."

Her hands reached for him, her fingers curling into his coat sleeves. The light and heat playing in her face stirred everything male inside him. "I want this, Michael. I want you."

His hands went to her shoulders, and in one smooth movement her coat slid to the floor.

Unmoving, he stared down, taking in the sensuous curves of black sequins, letting the lust build inside him until it bubbled molten lava.

"And I want you, lady." He shifted his hand, cupped it at the front of her throat against the diamond choker. "When you walked into the ballroom with Lawson tonight, I wanted to take you out of there right then. Take you and claim you."

He felt the skitter of her pulse beneath his palm, felt the heat rise in her skin.

"You took me out of there," she said, her voice an almost tangible caress that stroked along his flesh. "The only question left is who's to do the claiming?"

"I..."

She snaked up on tiptoes, used her teeth to nip at his lips, sending blood sizzling through his veins. Her impatient hands shoved his coat and jacket off his shoulders, down his arms then onto the floor. "You thought you'd be the one, did you?" she murmured while her busy mouth raced from his cheek to his jaw to his ear.

"Mother of..." Words temporarily failed him. So he tightened his hold on her throat, arched her chin back and captured that wonderful, maddening mouth with his. He feasted on her lips, savoring the dark, erotic pleasure that came with her fevered jerking at his bow tie, his cummerbund, fumbling with the buttons on his shirt. Her fingers faltered against the leather straps of his shoulder holster.

He tore his mouth from hers. "Let me." He pulled away long enough to strip off the holster and shirt and drop them onto the growing pile of clothing. Reaching out, he dragged her against him, his hands going to the slope of her waist, his fingers yanking down the zipper of her dress. Black sequins slithered down her hips, her legs, puddling intimately over leather and blue steel.

"Oh, A.J.," he murmured, absorbing her with his eyes as his heart did a quick, hard lurch.

Skin-caressing wisps of black lace molded her curves; dark hose held by a garter belt encased her long, slinky legs. "If I had known..." His voice hitched as his hand closed possessively over one firm breast. His thumb brushed across a nipple that budded hard and tight beneath lace. "If I'd known what was under that dress when we were dancing..." Michael buried his face in her hair, drowning in its intoxicating scent as need slammed into him.

"You know now," she breathed. Her fingers splayed against his chest, making erotic patterns in the crisp black hairs. "It's all yours, Michael." Hot, moist lips circled one of his nipples, licking, suckling until he had to concentrate just to breathe.

It took every ounce of control, every degree of will to keep from ripping away those insanely indecent pieces of lace, shoving her onto the heap of clothing and taking her there. His hands clenched when her mouth skimmed across his chest and settled on his other nipple.

He wanted more.

Wanted his hands exploring every silken inch of her while his mouth took a languorous journey across smooth curves and soft hollows. Wanted her lying beneath him, trembling from the inside out while he slowly took her from cool ice to molten fire.

Teeth nipped his flesh. He groaned at the almost unbearable combination of pleasure and pain. His hands shot down, clasping her half-naked bottom, lifting her off the floor until she was eye level with him. Her warm, lush body felt like velvet against his skin.

"This isn't going to be fast," he said, his eyes blazing into hers.

Slowly, his hand slid down between her legs; his palm pressed firmly on the damp mound between her thighs. He watched her eyes glaze as his fingers moved, massaged. She went limp against him, her head heavy on his shoulder as she moaned indecipherable words against his throat.

In one deft move he cradled her in his arms and was halfway to the polished oak staircase when the persistent ring of the phone seeped through the haze of his arousal. Her body tensed against his.

"Let the damn thing ring," he growled, while twisting his hand into her hair, his fingers curling tight.

"Can't..."

For a mindless instant he arched her head back and ravaged her mouth with his until all he wanted was to consume her, swallow her whole.

Something between a whimper and a sigh rose in her throat. She dragged her lips from his, her hands tightening on his shoulders as though she'd fall if she let go.

"Might...be hospital," she panted. She looked toward the study, her face flushed, her breath coming in small, ragged gasps. "Aunt Emily..."

A low, gravelly groan lodged in Michael's throat as he lowered her to the floor. Easing his grip, he slid his hands up her arms, then down again before letting go. He set his jaw, watching her hurried, unsteady steps take her into the dark room while half-crazed desire and frustrated need knotted in his gut.

The ringing stopped. He heard her husky answer at the same time she reached and clicked on the desk lamp. The sight of her went straight to his brain, a sight he would remember for the rest of his life. A.J. Duncan standing beside that desk, diamonds glittering at her throat, her hair a wild tumble of dark gypsy waves, her flushed skin glowing in the lamplight. And that body, clad in raven black lace, dark hose and strappy heels that made her legs look outrageously long and slender.

Michael fought the urge to march across the room, jerk the receiver out of her hand and...

"He's here," she said, shoving her hair back off her face. "How did you know to call—? Oh. Yes, we'll leave now." She shifted the receiver from one ear to the other and grabbed a pen. "Go ahead." Her voice sounded remarkably calm, yet he saw the unsteadiness of her hand as she wrote.

"Holy hell!" Michael muttered. He stepped back into the entry hall and dug through the clothing heaped on the floor. Jerking his tux jacket from beneath his wool coat, he instantly heard his pager's insistent beep. The display flashed OCPD dispatch's private number.

He snatched up his hopelessly wrinkled shirt and shrugged it on while he headed into the study. A.J. had replaced the receiver by the time he reached the desk.

"That was dispatch." She took a deep breath and handed him a piece of paper. "We've got a homicide."

He glanced down, saw that the address she'd scrawled

in bold, uneven numbers was less than a mile away. Saw, too, the unsteadiness of his own hands.

"A stabbing," she continued. "The detectives on call took one look at the victim, then told dispatch to notify you."

"Auburn hair?" Michael asked as he crammed his shirt-tail into his slacks.

"Yes."

"We'll go by the scene on our way downtown."

"I...should take my own car."

He paused. He wasn't ready to let her go, he realized, to let distance come between them. But she was right. They'd only fuel the fires of the department's grapevine by arriving at a crime scene together. He shoved a hand through his hair, waited for his heart to stop hammering. Waited for his mind to switch gears and the detached, objective cop to take over. "How did dispatch know to call me here?"

She managed a small smile that only reminded him how seductive her mouth could be. "McMillan. He left orders to contact him on any homicide with an MO matching our suspect's. The chief saw us leave the dance together—"

"And told dispatch to call here when I didn't answer my page."

"Right." Her eyes lowered; the flush deepened across her cheeks as if she were suddenly aware of her near na-kedness. Her lipstick was smeared at one corner of her soft, luscious mouth, her breathing still rapid. She looked all mussed and fragile...and so damn gorgeous. "I need to...change."

Michael reached out, stroked the smear away, kissed the corner of her mouth. "Every person has one thing in his life he can pinpoint as his biggest regret. That phone call is mine."

She raised her hand, skimmed her fingers unsteadily along the line of his jaw. "Mine, too."

The air in the apartment building's foyer held the Christ-massy scent of cedar and bayberry...and a frosty chill that made A.J. shudder. She shifted in an attempt to find a more comfortable position on the bottom step of the staircase and tightened her coat over her slacks and oversize sweater. It was not lost on her that a few hours ago she'd been in another foyer, wearing wisps of black lace over flesh that radiated heat....

Shaking her head, she forced away the thought. She didn't want to think about what might have happened if Linda Ann Edwards hadn't gotten killed. Didn't want to imagine the hours she and Michael might have spent in each other's arms. Couldn't do her job if she opened that intriguing door and breathed new life into the needy throb of her unsated body.

Her fingers tensed against her notepad. Her own needs were something she had no business thinking about, not when a woman lay dead fifteen yards away. Not with a sadistic killer on the loose. A killer who had seemingly sprung from some dark hole in hell.

She glanced at the rookie guarding the front door. He didn't look old enough to vote, she decided. He just looked scared, standing there with his hand clenched on the grips of his holstered Glock as if he expected the killer to walk out of the open door of apartment 1A.

As if sensing her gaze on him, he looked her way and forced a halfhearted smile. "I guess the lab'll be done pretty soon, ma'am."

"I imagine so. Officer..." She squinted at the brass name plate on his right coat pocket. "Gilchrist. Are you okay?"

"Fine, ma'am."

"Call me A.J."

"Yes, ma'am."

Across the foyer, the four uniforms who'd conducted a door-to-door of the neighborhood stood in a tight knot, sipping steaming coffee from disposable cups. One officer made a comment, which evoked laughter from the others. A.J. suspected they were enjoying the rookie's greenish complexion. The poor kid had been the first on the scene, she'd learned. The pure horror in his eyes verified the grisly devastation the killer had left in his wake.

She leaned forward on the step and gazed into the open door of apartment 1A. Inside, cameras flashed; a lab tech clad in a blue jumpsuit swished a brush loaded with black fingerprint powder across a fiberboard coffee table. The tech hunched down to examine the surface, shook his head, then snapped the lid on his container of fingerprint powder.

No prints, A.J. thought. Just like all the other scenes, the killer had wiped down every surface. All they could hope was that Sky Milano and her forensic team had better luck ferreting out minute bits of almost invisible evidence.

"Hairs, you bastard. I hope you left some hairs."

The rookie jerked his head around. "What, ma'am?"

A.J. blinked. "Nothing."

"Yes, ma'am."

She inhaled a slow breath meant to calm, but it did nothing to ease the edginess that gripped her. It wasn't the first time she'd found herself talking to the killer. In her mind he'd evolved from a shadow lurking on the pages of police reports into a flesh-and-blood entity, driven by some twisted motive. A motive that eluded her. A motive shrouded in some perverse logic that made sense only in his sick brain.

Pulling off her reading glasses, she rubbed a latex-gloved fingertip up and down the bridge of her nose. The only thing she knew for sure was that he'd killed two women in as many weeks. The clock was ticking. If they didn't find him in the next few days, they'd be posting another picture of an auburn-haired woman on a bulletin board that was filling with frightening speed.

"No prints, A.J.," the lab tech said when he toted his equipment case out of the apartment.

She nodded. "No surprise, Tom."

He stopped, spoke to the four officers. As if by mutual consent, they simultaneously tossed their coffee cups into a trash can below the bank of mailboxes, then followed the tech across the foyer.

When the rookie swung the door open to let them out, A.J. glimpsed the crush of gawkers that the urgent screech of sirens had drawn into the frozen night. Emergency lights strobed in rhythm, washing the crowd with an eerie tinge of blood red and blue. The door whooshed shut, admitting a gust of frigid air into the foyer.

Shivering, A.J. rose off the step just as Michael walked out of the victim's apartment. His black wool coat hung open, revealing the bow tie that dangled loose beneath the open collar of his pleated shirt. The image of her hands yanking frantically at that tie sent a bolt of sensation straight to her center. She felt her knees go weak. Reaching out, she curled her hand around the banister and concentrated her gaze on the gold badge clipped to the breast pocket of his coat.

"The lab's done, A.J." The grimness in his voice put her thoughts squarely back on business.

From inside the apartment, a police radio squawked. Michael stripped off his latex gloves while he waited for the dispatcher to sign off. "I asked the ME to hold off moving the body until you had a look. I think it's important that you see how he positioned her. What he did to her hand." Michael paused, his eyes steady on hers. "I hate the thought of you going in there, seeing it."

"I'll handle it."

"What he did to this one makes his other killings look like a walk in the park."

"I understand," she said, and squared her shoulders. She'd been to numerous crime scenes, had seen enough dead bodies that she no longer feared losing her latest meal. But her detached approach to viewing the ravages of homicide didn't stop her stomach from clenching at the prospect of getting near a mutilated corpse.

"She was only eighteen," Michael said quietly. "A nursing student. She moved here two months ago from Arnette, Oklahoma. Eighteen."

The bleakness in his eyes closed around A.J. She reached out, touched her hand to his sleeve in an attempt to comfort.

"I sat in when Sam interviewed the landlord," she said quietly. "He doesn't think Linda Ann had any friends here. She'd gotten into the habit of going out most nights by herself—to clubs. A lot of mornings he'd see some guy leave her apartment. It was never the same one twice."

"Shades of Dianna Westfall."

"Sounds like it."

"Might as well start at the most obvious place," Michael commented. "I'll send a team of detectives to Encounters to show Linda Ann's picture around."

The cell phone protruding from his coat pocket rang. He answered, listened for a few moments, his eyes narrowing. "Fax a copy of the field-interview card to the crime scene van. I'll look at it, then get back to you. Meanwhile, run him through records, then for wants locally and nationwide. Check the car for registration and run it stolen."

Michael clicked off the phone, then cradled it in his palm for a long, silent moment.

"What is it?" A.J. asked.

He met her gaze, his blue eyes intense. "They finally got the computer back on-line and finished our run."

"How many?" She could feel the anticipation humming in Michael's nerves, felt her own jump. "How many names in Dianna's address book matched the FI cards on men stopped near Encounters?"

"One," Michael answered. "R. Thornton. Patrol stopped a guy named Robert Thornton in November, two blocks from Encounters. His car had a taillight out. The officer noted Thornton was overly polite."

A.J. stuffed her notepad under her arm and began to pace. "In her book, Dianna wrote the location she had sex with her dates. What did she put after Thornton's name?"

"She didn't," Michael said, his gaze tracking her movement across the foyer. "All she wrote was his name."

"Maybe..." A.J. began, her brows knitting with thought as she sidestepped around the stiff-spined rookie.

Michael rested an elbow against the banister. "Maybe what?"

"What if Dianna had some sort of ritual she went through?"

"Go on," he encouraged.

"She'd meet a guy at Encounters who looked like a promising companion for the night. After things heated up between them, she'd excuse herself to the ladies' room where she wrote his name in her book…"

"Then she took him home," Michael finished. "The next morning she'd jot the location of where they had their fun."

"Right," A.J. said, crossing back to stand beside him. "Only with Thornton, Dianna wasn't alive to do that."

"Works for me." Michael's eyes played over her face. "I've said it before, A.J. We work well together."

She smiled up at him. "I think so."

In a moment of silent intimacy he reached out, touched her arm. She felt the strength of his hand when his fingers tightened on her sleeve for a brief instant.

He glanced over at the rookie. "Gilchrist, go out to the crime scene van. Pick up a fax for me."

"Yes, sir, Lieutenant."

"And don't let any reporters see what you've got."

The door swung closed behind the rookie. Michael looked down at her, his eyes solemn. "You ready to take a look?"

A.J. took a deep breath. "Ready," she said, then followed as Michael escorted her into the crime scene's bloody depths.

Chapter 13

The noise level in the conference room was the lowest it had been since the computer spit out Robert Thornton's name. Michael tossed down his pen, leaned back in his chair and surveyed the tired faces of the people grouped around the long table. The collective surge of adrenaline that had electrified the air throughout the past two days and nights had ebbed. Now, the members of the task force seemed something akin to lethargic stuffed animals.

He felt physically depleted himself. His body ached from a combination of fatigue and the few hours of fitful sleep he'd managed on a lumpy couch in the officers' locker room. Except for a quick run home that morning to shower and change clothes, he'd spent the past forty-eight hours on duty. He didn't remember when he'd last gotten a full night's sleep. Couldn't say how long it had been since he'd eaten a meal off a plate.

He rubbed his eyes, then glanced out the bank of windows at the sleek skyscrapers huddled together in the frigid air. The late afternoon sky looked thin, gray and drab.

"Everyone take off," he said, and pushed out of his chair. "Go home. Spend an evening with your family."

Michael stood at the head of the table, waiting for his words to register. The blank stares he received didn't surprise him—they'd all worked like demons since Robert Thornton became their prime suspect.

"Go home," he repeated.

Sam Rogers was the first to react. The homicide detective pulled the glowing stub of a cigar from between his teeth and said, "You just say that to get our attention, Mike?"

Michael smiled. "No, Sam. We've issued flyers on Thornton nationwide. California authorities are on the lookout in case he returns there. The wanted notice is posted on NCIC and the Internet. Local media's airing his description every half hour. We've done all we can at this point. The thing that's left to do is find him. We don't have to be here for that to happen."

"Yeah," Sam agreed as several people rose, grabbed their coats and headed toward the door. "I'd feel a hell of a lot better if we had a recent picture of the bastard."

"No kidding," Helene said from the chair beside Sam's. She plucked up the fax sent from the California State Bureau of Investigation. "A ten-year-old picture of a pimply-faced teenager hardly makes for a good ID." Her pale eyes met Michael's. "I guarantee you, Lieutenant, if this guy's the one Dianna Westfall invited home, he's undergone a major overhaul in the looks department."

"It's him." Sky Milano flipped her leather portfolio closed with a confident snap. "Thornton's blood type is AB."

Helene let the fax sheet flutter onto a stack of file folders. "I wonder if the ACLU lawyer who sprang Thornton from that mental hospital is having second thoughts."

"Yeah, and I'm Prince Charming," Sam guffawed. "Thornton machetes his grandparents to death and winds up in a juvie facility where some of his scuzzball peers force a few up-close-and-personal encounters on him. Who does poor Robbie blame all this on? The auburn-haired judge who shook a red-polished fingernail in his face when she sentenced him to the place.''

Sam pushed out of his chair and pulled on his coat before continuing. ''Then here comes a bleeding-heart lawyer who frees Thornton on a technicality. The bastard's out two days when the judge winds up stabbed to death, with that very finger hacked off. As we all know, ole Rob was just getting started.''

Sam checked his watch, then glanced across the table at his partner. ''You ready to leave, pretty boy?''

Grant Pierce looked at Sky, who gave him a demure smile. The detective grinned, shook his head. ''Nah, Sam, you go on.''

''Ain't love grand?'' Sam grumbled, then headed for the door.

''Night, Sam,'' Michael said as he loaded file folders into his briefcase. Around him, people shut off computers, straightened papers. Someone turned off the coffeepot.

Out of the corner of his eye, Michael glimpsed Helene making her way to the far end of the table where A.J. sat, conversing with a crime scene tech. Giving the tech a weary smile, A.J. propped her glasses on top of her head and accepted a thick ream of paper.

Helene halted inches away, her narrowed gaze on A.J., her mouth set in a thin line. Michael slowly lowered the lid of his briefcase. More than once over the past two days, he'd caught Helene's pale eyes inspecting A.J. with catlike intensity, watching, waiting.

For what, dammit?

He shoved a hand through his hair. He had no idea, no hint of what was going on in Helene's sharp brain. All he knew was that when she looked at A.J. like that, his nerves went on full alert.

The tech moved off. Michael walked the length of the table, his footsteps silent on the thick carpet. He halted behind Helene and heard her ask, ''Did you return Greg's call?''

"No." A.J. stuck the papers the tech had left into a file folder, then glanced up. "Why do you ask?"

"No reason," Helene said as she shrugged on her coat. She slid a manicured hand against the nape of her neck and pulled a waterfall of platinum hair from beneath the coat's collar. "I took the call. I don't want Greg to think I forgot to give you the message."

"I doubt he thinks that."

Michael stepped forward, put a hand on the back of A.J.'s chair. "I can't lock up until everyone's gone," he said pleasantly. "How long are you two going to make me wait?"

Helene gave him a cool smile. "I'm on my way, Lieutenant. See you tomorrow."

Her feathery brows knit in thought, A.J.'s eyes tracked Helene out the door. "She keeps asking me about Greg."

Michael slid a hip onto the table. "What about him?"

"How involved are Greg and I? Have I talked to him in the past five minutes? Are we spending Christmas together?"

Michael had wondered those things himself. The thought of Lawson—or any other man—holding her lush body in his arms as he'd done two nights ago had his hands curving into fists.

"I don't get the connection," A.J. continued while straightening a stack of papers, her slow, deliberate movements betraying her weariness. "Greg and Helene aren't close, not that I know of. I never heard him mention her. Yet, every time I see Helene, she brings up his name."

"Makes one wonder," Michael said thoughtfully.

"It does."

When A.J. reached for an unorganized stack of file folders, he caught her hand in his. "What I said still goes. I can't leave until everyone's gone. You're holding me up."

She raised her chin and blinked. "Oh, you have plans—"

"*We* have plans, I hope." Using his free hand, he plucked her glasses off the top of her head. "That is, if you're up to having dinner with about twenty adults. Then, there're the nieces and nephews—I lost count of the exact number a few years ago.''

"Your family," she said, a startled look in her eyes. "You want me to meet your family?"

"I want you to brave stepping into their midst." He smiled, and tightened his grip on her fingers when she tried to pull her hand away. "We're Irish, you know."

The deep, rolling brogue he'd added to his voice had her returning his smile. "I know."

"It'll be loud. There'll be enough whiskey to get this whole department feeling good. People will ask you nosy questions and you'll get kissed on the cheek by men you've never met."

"But this is your family's Christmas dinner—"

"That's two days away. Mother's just getting warmed up. The night before Christmas Eve, she and Dad always invite everyone over—family, neighbors, friends. They put on big pots of stew, bake mountains of breads and desserts. After we eat, we sing carols."

A.J. leaned back and gave him a considering stare. "You sing?"

Michael grinned. "Like a saint."

She sighed. "I'd love to hear that, but I can't. I need to go to the hospital and spend time with Aunt Emily."

"We'll stop there on the way, stay as long as you want. There's no set time to be at my parents'."

She glanced down at her slim tailored slacks and black sweater, then shook her head. "I'm not dressed right."

His knuckles stroked the side of her throat as he toyed with her gold hoop earring. "You could wear rags and still look good."

Seeing he still hadn't convinced her to go, he leaned forward, put his hands on the arms of her chair, caging her in. "It's been hell these past two days trying to keep my mind on work and off you." Her warm scent stirred his senses. "I keep thinking of us together. Of what would have happened between us if dispatch hadn't called."

She swept him a look through dark lashes. "Me, too."

"I want to take you to bed, A.J. I want to make love with you until we both know every inch of each other's bodies."

"I...thought you wanted to go to your parents'."

"That first." He took her hand, brought her fingers to his lips. "We have all night, don't we?"

In the space of two hours, A.J. had an enormous bowl of Irish stew, a mountain of fudge, uncountable hugs from sticky-fingered children and three proposals of marriage thrust upon her. Two good-natured offers of eternal bliss had come from Michael's youngest brothers, Patrick and Sean. The other from an unnamed gray-haired gentleman who had to be pushing ninety.

"Is it always this crazy around here?" A.J. asked as she swabbed a dish towel across a damp plate.

"No," Michael said. "This is sedate compared to St. Patrick's Day. Pop has a recipe for green beer that glows in the dark." He held up a glass, checked it through the light over the sink. "Kerrie, it's the dishwasher's job to get the lipstick off, not the person drying."

Kerrie Ryan Jones glanced up from the pot she was scrubbing. "Step right up and wash it yourself, smart guy. There's plenty of suds for both of us."

"My little sister gets a law degree, and all of a sudden she forgets how to wash a glass," Michael said, giving A.J. a wink.

"So sue me," Kerrie countered, and elbowed him in the ribs without missing a stroke with her scouring pad.

Laughing, A.J. placed the plate on a stack of already dried ones, leaned a hip against the kitchen's massive center island and lifted her wineglass. Around her, the delicious aroma of baked bread commingled with that of simmering apples and cinnamon. The mind-numbing fatigue of the past forty-eight hours had disappeared, as had the case of nerves she'd battled when Michael first escorted her across the threshold of the huge rambling house filled with a sea of cheerful celebrants. Now she felt warm and content, as if she were floating. How could she not feel relaxed, when the entire Ryan clan had drawn her instantly into its lively circle?

"Who needs a refill?" Ian Ryan asked, as he strode through the door. Tall and lean as a whippet, Michael's father was a striking man, with a head of thick, dark hair just going gray at the temples. With a bottle of whiskey secured in his large hand, he walked jauntily across the kitchen, eyeing A.J.'s glass with suspicion.

"Wine," he said and shook his head. "Who in the world forced that vile liquid on you, girl?"

She smiled. "It wasn't forced, Mr. Ryan—"

"Call me Ian."

She hesitated, saw Michael send her a smile across his shoulder as he scrubbed a skillet. "Might as well do what he says, A.J. He'll wear you down until you do."

"All right, Ian," she said, meeting the man's expressive blue gaze. "Mrs. Ryan kindly offered—"

"Colleen."

Michael laughed. "The same goes for Mother."

A.J. exhaled a resigned breath. "Colleen offered the wine. It's very good."

Ian threw a companionable arm across her shoulders and gazed down. "I love my wife, truly I do, A.J., but when it comes to spirits, her taste is questionable." He wiggled his dark eyebrows and winked. "Her other fine attributes make up for that one flaw."

"I'm sure," A.J. said. She had the image of Ian Ryan lounging in a turf-heated Irish pub, spinning yarns and sharing rounds of rich whiskey with the locals.

He dropped a kiss on the top of her head, gave her shoulders a numbing squeeze, then sauntered out the door, his voice booming a hearty, "Ho, ho, ho! Who needs a refill?"

Kerrie poked a suds-covered finger in Michael's ribs. "You've made a big mistake."

"How so?" he asked, almost dropping the skillet.

"You shouldn't have brought A.J. here. Now she knows insanity runs in the family."

He flashed a careless smile. "That's okay, Sis. I wanted her to meet you anyway."

"Fun-ny."

Chuckling, A.J. watched brother and sister work side by side at the sink. Any stranger off the street could have picked out Ian and Colleen Ryan's children, she decided. They'd all inherited their parents' lanky height and their leanness. All had thick, dark hair and blue eyes that ranged from dark and simmering to cool ice, like Michael's. The daughters were stunning, the sons broodingly handsome. Not one wallflower in the horde—A.J. could swear to it, she'd been hugged by them all.

"So, A.J.," Kerrie said, craning her neck to meet A.J.'s gaze. "Is my brother a tyrant at the office, like he always was at home?"

"I wouldn't use the word 'tyrant,'" A.J. commented.

"See," Michael said as he rinsed the skillet. "I'm a pussycat."

"Slave driver fits him better," A.J. added. "This is the first night off I've had in a week."

Michael gave her a scowl, which softened into a slow, alluring smile that turned her suddenly shaky. How could a man look so perfectly at home, so sensual with his sleeves crammed up and his arms submerged in dishwater? she wondered.

"A week?" Kerrie sent her brother a derisive look. "She gets a night off, and you force her to wash dishes?"

"Hey, whose hands are wet here?"

"A.J.'s right, you're a slave driver." Kerrie whooped when Michael flicked water in her face.

A.J.'s smile faded as an incomprehensible feeling of unease crept through her. She set her glass aside while brother and sister discussed the trip to Ireland they and their siblings had chipped in to buy for their parents' Christmas present. Kerrie laughed and rubbed her cheek, leaving a trail of suds. In a gesture of easy affection, Michael reached up and flicked the bubbles away with a finger.

A.J.'s heart shuddered against a surge of painful emotion. Envy, she realized, her fingers tensing on the edge of the counter.

She and Ken had shared that same simple sense of companionship. They'd been close, shared their thoughts... except at the end. All that was gone, she thought bleakly. Forever.

Envy gave way to sorrow...then to an overwhelming flood of emotion she had no idea was brewing inside her. Gnawing on her bottom lip to keep from sobbing, she turned and walked out of the kitchen.

By the time Michael escorted A.J. to the front door of the Victorian brownstone, he was biting back nerves. Something had happened, driven her from his parents' kitchen. While at the sink, he'd glanced over his shoulder in time to see her eyes go blank and her face pale. She had walked out without a word, as if something dark and haunting had taken her in its grip.

He'd finally found her nudged into the shadows of a third-floor window seat. His twin four-year-old nieces were ensconced on her lap, sleepily oblivious to the boisterous Christmas carols blasting up the staircase. A.J., too, had been oblivious, he'd thought as he studied her profile while she stared into the icy December night. He'd settled his hand on her arm and felt his chest tighten when she looked up with wounded eyes. "Please take me home, Michael," was all she'd said.

Now, he stood watching her turn the key in the lock of her front door and push it open. She didn't look at him, issued no invitation, but he followed her in anyway.

"My family's crazy about you," he said, closing the door behind him on a blast of frigid wind. He made no move to take off his coat, made no move toward her.

"I liked them, too. A lot."

"Tell me what's wrong."

She shook her head. "It's…" She pulled off her gloves, scrubbed the heel of her palm across her forehead. "I'm tired—"

"We were in the kitchen," he said, taking a step toward her. "All of a sudden you were gone. When I found you upstairs, I could see it was all you could do not to cry."

"I shouldn't have gone with you tonight," she said dully.

His eyes narrowed. "Did someone say something to upset you?"

"Of course not—"

"Tell me what's wrong."

"Seeing you and Kerrie together, seeing how close you are, made me think about Ken."

Michael bit back a groan. "God, I'm sorry. The holidays. This has to be hard—"

"It's not just the holidays, Michael. Seeing all the love, the closeness, started me thinking about other things. Things I'm not necessarily proud of myself for thinking."

"Such as?"

She dragged in a breath. "Like what you would do if someone presented evidence that implicated Kerrie in illegal activity. Activity you knew her incapable of."

Michael had no idea what he'd expected her to say, but not words that hit him like a fist in the gut. There was hurt beneath her even tone, and he knew he had caused it. Without comment, he took off his coat and laid it across the small chair by the door. When he turned back, her eyes were on him as if waiting for him to think through what she'd said. He didn't need to think it through—he knew his exact reaction to that scenario. Just as he knew the question A.J. was about to put to him.

"What would you do, Michael? What would you do if someone accused Kerrie?"

"Defend her," he said quietly. "No matter what."

"Why is it so wrong for me to do the same for Ken?"

"It's not." He spoke carefully, studying her. There was

no anger in her eyes, just a resolve that turned his blood cold.

"From the first of this, even now, you've made me feel as if it is."

He looked away, his jaw clenching. "God, A.J."

"You haven't meant to," she added hastily. "It's just..." She shook her head, pulled off her coat, tossed it negligently across the banister. "The other night at the dance and...here...I had myself convinced it doesn't matter that you think Ken is guilty. He's dead, after all. It shouldn't matter, I know that. But it does, Michael. It would matter to you if our situations were reversed and I had no faith—"

"I hadn't thought..." He walked to her, laid a hand on her shoulder. "I hadn't equated things that way."

"Neither had I. Not until tonight. Not until I saw you with your family." She shrugged from his touch and began pacing, her low heels sounding hollow echoes across the wood floor.

"You're a cop, Michael. Cops don't deal in faith—they can't. They deal in cold facts and piles of evidence. You have to look at things without emotion, I understand that."

Unsteadiness seeped into his hands and he clenched them against his thighs. "I can't look at you without emotion."

"You've been nothing but fair," she continued as if he hadn't spoken. She reached the entrance to the study, turned. A slight limp evidenced itself when she retraced her steps. "You believe in my innocence, when all the proof you have is my word. You risked your badge by going to bat for me with McMillan. I'm grateful for that."

"Grateful?" He wasn't sure if it was her words or the resignation in her voice that sent him after her. "Dammit," he said, when he snagged her arm and whirled her around to face him. "I don't want your gratitude!" he grated, locking his hands on her shoulders.

"I believe in Ken," she said quietly as she stood passive beneath his touch. "You don't. I thought because I..." She closed her eyes for a heartbeat, then opened them and met his gaze. "Because of how I feel about you, I thought it didn't matter that you can't accept on faith what I know is true about Ken. Tonight showed me it matters a great deal."

His fingers bit into her flesh. "Stop sounding like you're saying goodbye!"

"I can't change what I believe about Ken. What I know is true. And you can't change how you feel, can't change the fact that you have a mountain of damning evidence against him..." Her body trembled beneath his hands. "You said you want me to be sure I can accept your feelings about Ken, that you don't want me to regret our being together—"

"A.J.—"

"Right now, I think I'd regret it a great deal."

When she started to step back, he tightened his hold. It stunned him that, for the first time in his life, he felt capable of begging.

"I don't want to feel this way, Michael." Her voice cracked. "But I do, and I have to be honest. I owe you that."

"Owe me?" he asked with derision, before dropping his hands.

He turned, went to stand in front of the narrow window beside the door. Jaw tight, breathing unsteady, he watched the wind sweep a handful of brown leaves across the dimly lit porch as he thought of what A.J. had endured the past month. The agony of her brother's murder, the pain of burying him, the numbing grief she'd had to deal with while he, himself, came full steam at her with evidence and accusations. Through it all, her faith in Ken had held firm. And now tonight she had so simply made him see that had they traded places, his actions would have mirrored hers.

It humbled him to realize that, after nearly fifteen years of doing his job in a cool, emotional void, he'd suddenly come face to face with the fact that he was just as human as the next man. Just as human and just as full of faults.

How the hell could having your eyes opened so thoroughly rip your guts apart? he wondered, as the leaves formed a swirling whirlpool beneath the porch light.

With a resigned shake of his head, he turned to face her. "What I said about Kerrie goes for every member of my family. No matter what anyone claimed, no matter how damning the evidence against them, I'd defend them all to my last breath."

"Because you believe in them."

"Yes."

"Trust, belief—those aren't bad things, Michael."

"You're right, they're not. And I'll regret for the rest of my life that for even a moment I made you feel like they were. I did what I've always done, A.J.—gone by the book, not let the emotional side of things interfere with my handling of a case." Even from where he stood he could smell her perfume, the beguiling scent of her hair and skin. "You hit the mark on something else," he said quietly. "I can't change how I feel. Wouldn't want to."

Her face was pale as ice. "I'm not asking—"

"You want my faith and my trust where Ken's concerned? You've got them."

She opened her mouth, shut it. Her lips trembled before she pressed them together.

He walked back to her, cursing himself for not realizing how much his refusal to trust had hurt her. "You're not asking anything of me that you haven't asked since that night I ordered you to Internal Affairs. You're asking me to trust you, have some faith."

His hand went up, brushed her dark hair behind her shoulder. "You say Ken was incapable of doing the things to which the evidence points. I know you well enough to know you wouldn't say that if you absolutely didn't believe it. All right, A.J., I accept what you know in your heart. Someone planted that evidence. Ken is innocent. One hundred percent."

Seconds passed in silence as she stared up at him, her eyes unreadable.

"Dammit," he said quietly, terrified that his understanding had come too late, that she was about to walk out of his life. "Say something."

"Michael, I..." She reached up, traced an unsteady fingertip along his jaw, triggering a wave of warmth through his body. "Will you do something for me?" she asked, her voice nothing more than a whisper.

He grasped her hand, pressed it hard to his lips. He'd tear the walls down if she asked him to leave. "Anything."

"Take me to bed."

The pain-filled understanding she'd witnessed in Michael's eyes only moments before had made A.J. weak...as did the desire that now burned in them. Never in her life had she been so afraid of losing something. Never in her life had she felt such elation as in the instant when Michael's fingers wound through hers and she turned to lead him up the oak staircase.

As they walked, the house engulfed them in a cocoon of warm silence; the lamp from the entry hall sent a mixture of dim light and charcoal shadows drifting up the stairs.

As if an unspoken agreement had passed between them, she knew this time would be far different from the frantic near coupling that had ended with the telephone's ring two nights earlier. Now, there was no annihilating heat throbbing beneath her skin, no fatal voltage zinging in her nerves. It was Michael's simple linking of his fingers with hers that stunned her, as if an inescapable possession had taken place.

He now accepted her faith in Ken, trusted what she believed in her heart. In all her life she would never forget the solemn intensity in his eyes that had accompanied the words.

In her bedroom she switched on the lamp on the nightstand, then turned. Michael's clear blue gaze moved over her entire body, then came back to her face as he drew her to him.

These were not the same impatient hands of two nights ago that undid the small buttons at the neck of her sweater but hands that moved with slow ease, as if endless hours stretched before them. As he worked, his fingertips grazed her flesh, sending little ripples of sensation down her spine.

When he eased the garment over her head, his eyes flashed and darkened, as if her simple cotton camisole were as tantalizing as the black lace she'd worn before. He touched his lips to hers, her breath shuddering at the tenderness of his kiss. His hands came up, caressing nipples that swelled beneath cotton while his mouth played with hers until time spun away.

She had the heady sense of him easing off her slacks and panties in one smooth movement, confirmed by the cool rush of air against her bare flesh. Heat curled deep inside her, sparked by the dark, intoxicating appeal of standing before him in the ivory camisole with her lower half exposed.

His eyes blazed as his palm journeyed across the flat range of her belly, making her nerves quiver. "You're so beautiful."

Her hands went to his sides, gripping his sweater, pulling it over his head. Seconds later, his shirt followed. When she reached for his belt, he caught her wrists. "There's time for that," he said in a low voice and placed a kiss on her temple. "I want you in my arms, first."

Suddenly he was behind her, drawing her back against his chest, his thighs. The heat of his flesh burned through cotton. She felt the roughness of his slacks, the hardness of his arousal against her bare bottom. His arms slid around her; his hands cupped her breasts while his lips nuzzled the nape of her neck. Her nipples burned against his palms as his mouth journeyed to her shoulder, using the thin strap as a guide to trail paralyzing kisses across her flesh.

Her heart pounded in her throat, her ears, her head. She lifted an impossibly heavy arm, hooked her hand around the back of his neck, turned her head and found his mouth.

"I want to hold you, feel you," he murmured. His hand took a slow, intoxicating slide downward to the juncture of her thighs, cupping her. He deepened his kiss while his fingers kneaded her sensitized flesh with caressing slowness. Every pulse point in her body stirred to life, heating her skin until all sensations melded together, sparking into flame deep inside her belly.

"I love the smell of your skin," he whispered against her mouth. "You smell of flowers. Soft, silky flowers."

His lips nipped the back of her neck with dizzying tenderness as his fingers continued stroking between her thighs.

Heat shimmered inside her. She moaned his name as her head toppled back against his shoulder. She clung to him, feeling as though she were floating.

She closed her eyes and melted against the rock-hard press of his body while he took her to the summit of a cliff with erotic slowness, then sent her plummeting into a silver abyss that was too rich, too exquisite to be anything but heaven.

Her body convulsed; she cried out weakly when her legs gave out. She'd have folded to the floor if he hadn't swept her into his arms.

He lowered her sweat-glazed body onto the cool white comforter that covered the bed like a field of gleaming snow. His eyes never left her as he fought off his shoes, stripped off his slacks.

She lay limp and spent, gazing up at him through the dreamy, dim light that shone against his flesh like gold. He was magnificent, his body stunningly male; muscles hardened by exercise rippled and tightened as he moved. Dark hair covered the planes of his chest, veed down to the thick, erect flesh of his loins.

He came to her, heat flaring in his eyes as he slid onto the bed beside her. Murmuring her name, he kissed her eyelids, her cheeks, her chin. His mouth lowered, settled over the cotton camisole where one taut nipple budded, then moved to the other. He suckled slowly, his hot mouth moistening the fabric that swaddled her sensitized flesh.

"Michael..." His name ended on a moan. She couldn't move, couldn't breathe. Couldn't think of anything but the dark appeal of having been made completely his by his tender, incredible hands and mouth.

He raised his head from her swollen flesh, pulled the camisole slowly upward, then tossed it aside. Need sparked in his eyes as his gaze ravaged her naked body. "You're mine," he said, his voice low and thick. "Every stunning inch of you is mine."

"Yes." Panting, she reached for him greedily, felt his hot, tight muscles under her unsteady palms as she pulled him to her, her nails digging heedlessly into the damp flesh of his back. "I want you, Michael. Inside me."

His hungry lips met hers, his tongue invading her mouth, exploring, taking what he wanted. His hands fisted into her hair, tightened, and she understood he was done with gentleness. He was all raw need and hunger now, his skin hot, his body demanding as he mounted her, his weight crushing her breathlessly.

He entered her with possessive force, summoning desperate, needy sounds up her throat. She reveled in the feel of his sweat-slick flesh plundering hers. He was all she had ever wanted, all she wanted for the rest of her life.

He moved in her with increasing urgency, flooding her with a swelling pleasure that grew and spread. Her body weightless, she felt the clenching spasm begin again, deeper than before, more powerful. Pleasure shattered inside her in a whirling haze. She cried his name, wrapped her legs around him and they went over the edge together.

Eyes closed, Michael lay unmoving, feeling as though he'd fallen out of a plane without a parachute and landed in cottony-soft clouds. Slowly, he became aware of the howl of the wind against the windows, of the settling groans of the old house, of A.J.'s soft breathing against his shoulder.

He opened his eyes, turned his head on the pillow and stared down at her. She lay curled on her side, her knees bent, one arm thrown across his midsection. Dark lashes feathered her cheek; her hair flowed softly over her shoulder, pooling like an ink spot against the white pillowcase. The dim light coming from the nightstand transformed her body into intriguing ivory curves and shadowed valleys.

He thought of the small, needy sounds that had welled up in her throat, of the quivering softness of her glorious body surrendering in his very hands. She was his in every way, and he silently acknowledged he would kill to keep her safe.

He levered up on one elbow, placed a soft kiss at the corner of her swollen mouth. Her lips curved.

"I thought you were asleep," he said.

"I can't move," she murmured, keeping her eyes closed. "Someone snuck in here and ripped out my spine."

He smiled. "They got mine, too."

"We should report it. Who handles that type of thing? Larceny? Burglary?"

"Sex Crimes."

"Hmm," she breathed in agreement and slid a silky leg across his.

For the first time Michael saw the pale scar that ran the length of her right thigh. With a fingertip, he traced the scar as if his touch could eliminate the pain the injury sometimes caused.

Her lashes fluttered open at his touch. "I was in an accident—"

"I know. I investigated you. Your aunt told me the doctors said you'd never walk again. You proved them wrong."

She lifted her head. "You talked to Aunt Emily?"

"Yes."

"When?"

"A couple of days ago."

"You went to see her?"

Casually, he brushed his fingertips down the length of her throat. "I had some free time."

"You're running a task force and you had free time?" she asked, her voice ripe with disbelief.

"I made time. I know how lonely hospitals can get around the holidays."

"Oh, my gosh!" Eyes wide, she sprang up as if an electrical current had switched on inside her. "Tomorrow's Christmas Eve!"

"All day." Arching a brow, Michael watched her snag his shirt off the end of the bed and pull it on.

"I have to take the tree I bought to the hospital tomorrow. And my mother's ornaments." She shoved her hair off her face, her gaze rising to the ceiling. "They're in a box somewhere in the attic. It's a mess up there. It'll take me forever to find them."

He sat up slowly, taking in the outrageously arousing sight of her kneeling amid rumpled sheets and pillows, her hair an alluring mess, his shirt hanging open to reveal the soft swell of her breasts, the black triangle of tight curls at the cleft of her thighs. Heat poured into him. He'd had a taste of her, which only made him want more. Where she was concerned, he would always want more.

He gave her a bland smile. "In the attic?" he asked as his hand snaked forward and curved on her wrist.

"Right—"

In one smooth move he jerked her forward, snagged off the shirt and rolled her onto her back.

"How did you do that?" she sputtered.

"Training." He levered his chest over hers, effectively pinning her writhing body to the mattress before indulging himself in a long, lingering kiss.

"What sort of training?" she breathed, then gasped when he pulled the lobe of her ear between his teeth.

"Strip searches. Patting bodies down for weapons." He clamped her wrists in one hand and levered them above her head. "Effective uses of handcuffs." He gave her a wicked grin. "Tell me, Miss Duncan, do my diverse talents make your heart pound?"

"Considering half of you is sprawled on my chest, I should think you could answer that for yourself."

Lying motionless, he felt the unsteady hammering of her heart against his.

He expelled a soft laugh. "We've worked nearly forty-eight hours straight. We should have both passed out by now."

She squirmed beneath him. "From my perspective, Lieutenant, I'd wager sleep is not first on your list of priorities."

He released her wrists, plunged his hands into her hair and kissed her. She was right. He was as hard as stone.

"I want you, A.J."

"Have me, Michael."

Chapter 14

Morning sunlight streamed through the blinds, glinting off the brass headboard. Dressed only in slacks and socks, Michael stood at the edge of the rumpled bed and took a moment to check the room for the first time since he'd entered the night before.

He took in the wall of bookcases, jammed with dog-eared true-crime paperbacks and criminology textbooks, the watercolor of an ocean sunset, the curtains that matched a plaid comforter that was heaped somewhere on the wood floor. The chest and dresser were made of sturdy, dark oak, the lamps brass. He could find nothing feminine about the room...except its owner. She stood on the opposite side of the bed, dressed only in his gaping shirt, looking gloriously decadent with an array of Christmas ornaments suspended on gold cords from her fingertips.

"Snowflakes, candy canes, a snowman, several angels, one Santa Claus with elves and eight tiny reindeer," A.J. inventoried. She wiggled her fingers, sending the ornaments dancing like puppets.

Even to Michael's inexperienced eye, the elegant hand-crafting of each needlepoint ornament was obvious. The sunlight highlighted the yarns' rich colors, the minute stitches, the painstaking detail. Little wonder the ornaments dangling from A.J.'s fingers were considered family heir-looms.

She lifted her gaze, her large brown eyes sparkling from across the chaos they'd made of the bed. "Beautiful, aren't they?"

"Yes," he said as he conducted a slow survey of the lush body beneath his gaping shirt. "Gorgeous." The sight of her had his blood stirring…again.

He shoved a hand through his hair, still damp from the shower they'd shared…shower and more. He shook his head, forcing his thoughts away from the lovemaking that had consumed them throughout the night and well into the morning. If they kept up the pace, he'd be dead by nightfall.

He retrieved his sweater from beneath a heap of pillows. "When are you going to the hospital?" he asked, keeping his eyes on her face and off her silken cleavage.

"This afternoon, if I can sneak away from the task force."

"You can."

Her lips curved. "It's nice to have an 'in' with the boss."

"Well, you've got one, lady, so enjoy it."

"I intend to." Her gaze lowered to the sweater in his hand and she swept him a look beneath dark lashes. "I suppose you want your shirt so you can finish getting dressed."

"The thought crossed my mind."

"Well, come and get it, Lieutenant." She wiggled her fingers, letting the ornaments drop into a box overflowing with tissue paper.

"My pleasure." He walked around the bed, sidestepping a heap of pillows. She smiled up at him, her eyes glittering. He smelled her sweet, clean scent mingled with her perfume. The thought of all she meant to him put an unsteadiness in his pulse.

"Do something for me?" he asked quietly, cupping his palm against her cheek.

"Anything."

"Be careful."

Her brows knitted. "What's wrong?"

"Nothing specific. Just remember, whoever planted the printout and bank statements in Ken's locker is still out there. Whoever called you anonymously might still be watching."

He felt her body's slight shiver beneath his palm. "I haven't forgotten. I'll never forget."

"I want you to watch yourself around Lawson."

Her eyes flickered. "Why? What do you know?"

"Nothing." His hands went to her shoulders, stroked her flesh through the shirtsleeves. "It's just a feeling. I think he knows something about Ken—what, I have no idea. And I'll be the first to admit I might be wrong. Just…watch yourself when he's around."

"I don't think that'll be a problem. I haven't talked to him or seen him since he stormed out of the dance."

"He's called, left messages. Depending on what he has to say to you, he may show up on your doorstep any time."

"If he does, I'll handle it." She raised her hands, spread her fingers out flat against his bare chest and smiled up at him. "You don't need to worry about me. But it's nice that you do."

He pulled her to him, placed a soft kiss on her temple. "Get used to it, lady," he said as he peeled the shirt down her arms.

A.J.'s high heels clicked along the hospital's antiseptic-smelling corridor. Her purse hung off her shoulder, thumping against her hip as she walked. She had the box containing the needlepoint ornaments and a set of twinkle lights crammed under one arm. An artificial tree sprouted out of the top of the carton hooked beneath her other arm.

The clock at the nurse's station glowed a red 6:00 p.m. A.J. groaned over the realization that she was three hours behind schedule—and it was Robert Thornton's fault. At this moment, the serial killer was holed up in a Phoenix hotel room, surrounded by police. She'd left for the hospital only after Michael had shoved his cellular phone into her hands and swore he'd call the minute the situation with Thornton changed.

Nudging her shoulder against the door of her aunt's room, A.J. pushed away all thoughts of murder and mayhem. It was Christmas Eve and she intended to make the most of it.

"Goodness," Emily Duncan said, squinting from the depths of an overstuffed recliner. "I thought I might have to call the police and report you missing."

"Sorry I'm late, Aunt Emily." A.J. dropped the boxes onto the bed and stripped off her coat. She walked over, placed a kiss on her aunt's cheek. "Merry Christmas, a day early."

"Same to you, dear."

A.J. slid onto the arm of the recliner, careful not to bump the nearby IV stand with its inverted bags and tubes. "New pin?" she asked, examining the golden scarab that secured the colorful scarf around her aunt's head.

Emily nodded. "An early Christmas present."

"It's beautiful."

"Be sure and tell that lieutenant of yours what you think of it."

A.J. cocked her head. "It's from Michael?"

"Got delivered today," Emily said. "The card said he now knows the difference between a scarab and a salamander." She smiled. "From seeing the two of you together last night, I get the distinct feeling he's now more than just a friend."

"You're right," A.J. said softly as a calming feeling of

rightness swept over her. She realized she was far beyond just desiring him. "Aunt Emily, I'm in love with Michael."

"I know, dear. I thought you might be the first time you brought him here."

A.J. arched a brow. "I didn't think that."

"I've been around longer than you have, dear." Emily turned her gaze toward the bed, squinted at the boxes. "You brought the tree? The ornaments?"

"At your service," A.J. said.

"Well let's get started before Nurse Evil shows up with her needles and knocks me out for the night."

With the cellular phone propped between her cheek and shoulder, A.J. fastened the last twinkle light into place and listened to Michael detail the facts of Thornton's arrest.

"He took a bullet in the abdomen," Michael said, his voice sounding crisp and clean over the phone line, full of relief that the nightmare had ended. "He's in surgery."

"Any question that he's our killer?"

"None. Phoenix PD found Dianna Westfall's diamond ring in his pocket." Fierce satisfaction laced Michael's deep voice. "We nailed him, A.J., or rather you did with your nail polish theory."

"Hey," she said softly, "it was a team effort. We make a pretty good team."

"Yeah, we do."

"Can you get here before visiting hours are over?" she asked, taking a step back to check the placement of the glowing lights.

"I'll try. McMillan's on his way in for a briefing on Thornton."

"That could take forever."

"I'll make sure it doesn't."

Smiling, A.J. clicked off the phone. She felt an edge of anticipation deep in her belly. She couldn't wait to feel Michael's arms around her, couldn't wait to tell him she loved him.

Emily grinned from the recliner, the open box of needlepoint ornaments set securely in her lap. "You don't know what a relief it is to see you so happy."

"More than happy," A.J. amended. "I can't wait for you to meet Michael's family. They're...unique."

Emily tapped an index finger against her colorful scarf. "You have a bald aunt. That's pretty unique."

A.J. laughed. "You'll fit right in." When she leaned and slid the phone into her purse, a movement in the doorway snagged her attention.

She straightened, turned. "Hello, Greg."

There was a stillness about him as he stood watching her, a shadowy wariness in his eyes. Michael's warning rang in her mind, put a slight buzz in her nerves.

"Mind if I crash the party?" He walked toward her, his mouth lifting at the edges.

She blinked. No, there was nothing different about him, she corrected, searching his face. The familiar, calm awareness was there; his muscular body moved with the same fluid ease. Her eyes rose to the pale scar visible beneath the blond hair that lapped across one side of his forehead.

Nothing about him had changed, she told herself as his arm slid around her shoulders and he placed a kiss on her cheek. Nothing, she thought as her spine stiffened against his touch, except her own sudden doubts.

"There's no excuse for my walking out on you at the dance," he said softly. "But I'd like a chance to explain why."

"Later." She stepped back, forcing him to drop his arm.

Greg's gray stare took her in for a long, considering moment. "Everything all right?" he asked.

"Fine."

His gaze flicked to the artificial tree sitting on the rollaway table. "Mind if I stay a while?"

"Of course not."

He grinned at Emily. "How's my girl tonight?" he

asked, settling into the plastic chair he pulled beside the recliner.

"I'd be better if that damn doctor hadn't insisted I stay here over Christmas."

"He probably wants to keep a charmer like you all to himself," Greg answered, giving her a wink.

Emily chuckled as she dug through tissue paper. "Every year I'm struck by how beautiful these are," she observed, plucking a star-shaped needlepoint ornament from the box.

Greg arched an idle brow. "Nice."

"A.J. and Kenneth's mother owned a needlepoint shop. She designed these, sewed every stitch." Emily handed the star to A.J., then selected another from the box. She smiled at Greg, dangling an angel on a golden cord from her fingertips. "Want to do the honors?"

"Thanks, but A.J. looks like she's got things under control."

Her hands were shaking, A.J. realized as she hung the angel on a branch. There was no reason for her nervousness, she told herself. No justification for the tight feeling in her stomach. She accepted a cloud white snowflake ornament from her aunt, keenly aware of Greg's watchful gaze.

She hung three more snowflakes, rolling her shoulders in an attempt to ease the tension that had settled there. Nothing's wrong, she told herself. Nothing.

Greg leaned forward in his chair, resting his elbows on his knees. "Tired?" he asked.

A.J. met his inquiring gaze as she took the reindeer ornament her aunt offered. "The task force. We've been working round the clock."

"I dropped by the station last night to see you before my shift started. The conference room was locked up tight."

"Lieutenant Ryan thought we needed a break—"

"So I came by your house after I answered a call in your neighborhood. I didn't stop, figured my timing was off."

Her fingers faltered against the tree's soft branches. He'd just told her he had seen Michael's Bronco parked in her driveway, maybe was aware it had been there all night. She turned, saw her aunt stifling a knowing smile as she dug earnestly through tissue paper.

"It probably wouldn't have been a good time," A.J. agreed, meeting Greg's intense gaze while the knots in her muscles eased. So this was the reason for the edge she'd sensed in Greg—his knowledge that she and Michael were lovers.

"What in the world..?" Emily squinted down at the snowman in her hands. "Oh, dear, poor Frosty is about to fall apart."

Greg gave the ornament a cursory glance. "Can't you just sew it?"

"Me?" Emily asked, giving him a mock look of horror. "You should see what happened to the sock I tried to darn once. I'm afraid my niece takes after me in that department." Emily shook her head. "A.J., we'll have to find someone to repair this."

"I will—"

"Goodness, there's something hard..." Emily looked up as the door swung open, her narrowed gaze going past A.J. "Oh, Lord, not you."

"Afraid so." The nurse's starched uniform rustled as she headed across the room, her crepe soles squeaking against the floor. "Sorry, folks. Visiting hours are over." She left the small tray she'd carried in on the roll-away table beside the tree. "Time for your nightly dose, Ms. Duncan."

Emily flipped a blue-veined hand the woman's way. "Can't you see we're having a party?"

"That I can," the nurse said as she leaned and gathered the box of ornaments off her patient's lap. "It's about to end."

Emily harrumphed. "This is Christmas Eve—"

"*This* is a hospital." The woman's stern expression softened. "I'm sorry."

"Sure you are," Emily said, scowling as the nurse closed the lid of the box and handed it to A.J.

A.J.'s fingers felt stiff as knife blades against the cardboard. *Snowman*. Why hadn't she thought of the ornament?

Even with its stuffing, there was room inside for a small microcassette tape. It made sense Ken would hide the tape so ingeniously, yet in an ornament he knew she'd handle.

She pulled her bottom lip between her teeth and bit down, trying to keep herself from trembling. Last week, she'd conducted a hasty search of the barrels and trunks that overflowed across the attic floor, but the thick layer of dust that covered the boxes containing the Christmas decorations had convinced her they hadn't been handled in the past year. But Ken had done that purposely, she now realized, had made sure no searcher's eye would be drawn to the boxes....

"You can finish the tree tomorrow," Greg said, pulling the box of ornaments from her hands. He settled it on the chair he'd just risen from, then snagged the IV pole as the nurse helped Emily out of the recliner.

"Right. Tomorrow." A.J. stood motionless, watching the nurse smooth the sheet over her aunt's fragile, bony body. Her gaze slid sideways to the cardboard box. God, why hadn't she noticed the snowman this morning when she was with Michael? Why hadn't she realized?

She jumped when Greg slid her coat onto her shoulders. "You're as tense as strung wire," he said quietly. "Why don't we go somewhere, have a drink?"

"I...have to get back to the task force."

He stepped around her, blocking her view of the box. "Some other time?"

She searched his face, looking for some reaction. His eyes stared back at her, unreadable. She forced a smile. "Sure, some other time."

The nurse picked up a syringe from her tray, went to the IV stand.

A.J. gripped her aunt's pale hand, dropped a kiss on her forehead. "I'll be back in the morning. Sleep tight."

Emily glanced at the syringe then patted her hand. "I doubt that'll be a problem."

Spine stiff, A.J. preceded Greg into the hallway, the usual hospital mix of disinfectant and soap hardly registering in her brain. Her mind was back in that room, on that box.

"What level did you park on?" she asked as they entered the elevator, packed with visitors who'd been shooed away when visiting hours ended.

"Five."

She nodded, pushed the button for that floor. "I'm on three. You don't need to walk me to my car."

Greg leaned and pushed the button for her level. "I may not need to, but I'm going to."

"Dammit," Michael muttered as he hung up the phone. He'd tried to call A.J. for the past fifteen minutes, ever since McMillan walked out the door. "Must have turned the power off on the cell phone."

None of the task force members crowded into the conference room paid him any attention. They were too busy celebrating Robert Thornton's capture.

Elbows propped on the table, Michael rubbed his eyes with the heels of his palms. He couldn't remember ever having been this mentally exhausted, so physically tired. His mouth curved into a sardonic arch. He couldn't exactly blame his lack of sleep the previous night on the task force. On a gorgeous dark-eyed member of the task force, yes, but not on the job itself.

He got up from the conference table, then walked around the room to stretch his cramped leg muscles. Several detectives shook his hand; one thumped him on the back. They were wrapping things up, faxing last-minute information on Thornton to the Phoenix PD before shutting down.

Michael stopped at the wall of windows. As he stared out into the darkness, his mind conjured up the vision of A.J. lying in his arms, her face flushed with desire, her eyes glittering with need for him. It hit him then. He wasn't just falling in love with her. He *had* fallen. Hard. He wanted her in his life tonight, tomorrow. Forever.

He continued to stare out into the cold December night. The edges of his mouth lifted as he pictured A.J. standing before him in only his shirt, which barely covered her delectable body, her eyes sparkling with laughter, while stars, Santa Clauses, a snowman, and numerous snowflakes dangled from her fingertips. Desire for her heated his blood as he entertained the prospect of hanging a few ornaments himself, and not on any tree...

His mind hesitated, took a step back. His smile slowly faded as the image of the ornament in the shape of a snowman leapt into his mind. *Snowman!* If Ken had hidden an incriminating cassette tape anywhere, what better spot than that innocuous ornament that he knew beyond a doubt A.J. would handle?

Michael rushed back to the table, shoved aside a stack of computer printouts and file folders before he finally unearthed a phone book. He stabbed in the hospital's main number and asked for Emily Duncan's room. Because visiting hours had ended, the call went to the nurse's station.

"Miss Duncan and her companion left about five minutes ago," a woman's voice explained.

"Her companion?" Michael asked.

"The blond-haired police officer who visits often—I'm not sure of his name."

Michael hung up. *Lawson.* Nothing's wrong, he told himself. Lawson made a habit of visiting Emily Duncan. There was nothing out of the ordinary about that.

Michael clenched his jaw. If things were so ordinary, why the hell was every nerve in his body screaming for him to find A.J.?

Pulse thrumming, he grabbed his coat and headed to his car.

A.J. walked by Greg's side, their footsteps hollow echoes against the concrete floor of the parking garage. They traversed rows lit by bright overhead lights, finally stopping when her red Miata came into view. Her keys jiggled as he took them from her gloved hand, then opened the driver-side door.

"Thanks." She held out her hand for the keys.

He hesitated, looking down at her in silence until she bit back the urge to grab the keys, shove him away and run back into the hospital, into her aunt's room. "Greg, I have to go."

He put a finger beneath her chin, raised her gaze to his. "I guess there's no sense in asking if you know what you're doing where Ryan's concerned?"

"No sense."

"Didn't think so." He turned his head, looked back at the elevator. "I might drop by here tomorrow and see your aunt."

"She'll be happy to see you."

He leaned, placed a kiss on her cheek. "If you need anything…"

"I'll call."

"Right." He shrugged, handed her the keys, watched her slide into the seat.

A.J. turned on the engine, the headlights, and sat motionless, watching him retrace his steps toward the elevator. The instant he was out of sight, she switched off the engine, shoved open the door and took off at a mad run.

Bypassing the elevator, she pulled open a door, her footsteps clanging down the metal staircase. Only when she reached the hospital's now dim hallway did she slow her steps. Holding her breath, she passed the seemingly deserted nurse's station, praying her luck would hold and she'd avoid detection by her aunt's starch-spined nurse. The idea of using the cell phone to call Michael flashed through her mind. She frowned when she realized that in her haste to get back in the building, she'd left her purse in her car.

It didn't matter, she told herself. It would only take a few seconds—a minute at tops—to walk in her aunt's room and snatch the snowman ornament out of the box. She'd be back in her car in less than five minutes. If Ken's tape was inside that ornament, she'd call Michael from the car.

The tape had to be there, she thought. It made such perfect sense now.

Inside her aunt's room, the light that glowed above the door threw weak shadows in every direction. A.J. paused, heard the heavy sound of her aunt's sedative-induced sleep.

The lid on the box lifted noiselessly beneath her hands. The yarn that formed the snowman's plump form looked stark white beneath the wash of dim light. A.J. reached in, grabbed the ornament and squeezed. Her pulse pounded as her fingers pressed down on the outline of the small cassette tape.

She felt a rush of blood to her head, a sudden disorientation. A door she thought sealed had opened, an answer to a puzzle had suddenly emerged. Ken's tape! God, she couldn't breathe.

"You and I had the same thought."

Her breath sucked in on a gasp as she whirled. Her leg knocked against the chair; the box of ornaments teetered over, sending snowflakes and reindeer pooling at her feet.

"Hand it over, A.J." The dim light shadowed Greg's features, added an almost unearthly sheen to his blond hair.

She clenched the ornament in her fist. "Hand what over?"

"The tape."

"Tape?"

A hardness settled in his eyes as he reached into his jacket, pulled out a blue steel automatic.

The room seemed to shift. She stared into the dark barrel while Michael's warning echoed in her mind.

"If I don't have that tape in my hand in the next five seconds, your aunt gets a 9mm slug through her brain."

"God, no…" A.J. tore her gaze from the gun, looked at the bed. Her aunt's narrow hand, looking as fragile as porcelain, extended from the sleeve of a felt nightgown.

"Give me the tape."

"Don't hurt her." A.J.'s eyes searched his face wildly for a moment. "Please…"

"The tape!"

She felt faint and weak, on the verge of hysteria. She clenched her jaw, calling upon her reserve of inner strength and fought down the panic that had her body trembling.

"Don't hurt her." She held out the ornament, her hand shaking so badly that Greg's mouth curved upward.

He jerked the snowman from her grasp, held it against the muscled planes of his stomach as he burrowed his fingers through the seams. Cotton stuffing fell to the floor, followed by the needlepoint casing. The cassette tape looked small and insignificant in his palm.

"Now, you and I are going to walk out of here, slow and nice, like we're best friends." He shoved the cassette into the pocket of his coat. "You even blink to draw attention, I'll come back here and blow a hole through your aunt."

Fear made the back of A.J.'s throat burn. Standing before him, staring into the automatic's dark barrel, she felt cold and desperately helpless. Her mind whirled, her thought processes skittering to a sickening conclusion. He would kill her. There was no way out of this for him unless he killed her.

"How..?" Her trembling whisper hung on the air.

"How did I know you were on to me? The night of the dance you asked me about Snowman."

She squeezed her eyes tight for a brief moment. "I asked because his name…came up in the Westfall investigation."

"You asked because Ken told you about him."

"No—"

"Satisfy my curiosity. What did Ken tell you?"

She didn't answer, just sliced her gaze past his shoulder to the door while her body continued its quiet trembling. If only a nurse would come in, give the few seconds of diversion she'd need to grab the chair behind her and smash it into Greg's gun hand.

His gaze followed hers. "Don't try it, sweetheart," he said, keeping his voice at whisper level. "You won't get far."

He was right. Without something to distract him, A.J. knew a run for the door would be suicide. Maybe if she played for time, someone would come, someone would help....

"Ken didn't tell you much," Greg mused. "Otherwise, you'd never have allowed me around you and your aunt." His eyes sharpened. "But Ryan knows."

"He doesn't—"

"Maybe no one ever told you, A.J., but you can't lie worth a damn. You took Ryan with you to visit Ken's ex. Mary's name was on the tape recorder Ken used to make this tape," he said, patting his coat pocket. "You hadn't spoken to Mary in a year, and suddenly you and Ryan go see her. I doubt you chatted about the weather."

A.J. struggled through a haze of fear for the explanation of how Greg had found out about her and Michael's meeting with Mary. Nothing came.

"Mary doesn't know anything," she blurted. "Michael doesn't know—"

"*Michael* knows plenty," Greg countered. "He found the printout and bank statements in Ken's locker. That was enough for him to haul your ass into Internal Affairs—"

"You stole that printout from my office, planted it in Ken's locker."

Greg took a step forward, touched the automatic's barrel to the soft cartilage at the base of her throat. "Prove it."

"You bastard, you murdered my brother—"

Her words died out when he shoved the barrel against

her windpipe. "I wasn't the shooter. I figured we could control Ken by involving you. That was the reason for the anonymous call. It worked—you went running to Ken."

"If it worked, why did you kill—" She winced when the barrel jabbed into her throat.

"I told you, I didn't kill him." The Beretta looked black against his white knuckles. "My partner did."

"Ken was your partner," A.J. hissed through her teeth.

Greg gave her a cold, flat stare. "Ken was a fool. We started riding together right after he got demoted. He was bitter—had a hell of a lot of animosity toward the department. When your aunt got sick, he went nuts trying to figure out how to get enough money to help her." Greg shrugged. "I offered to deal him in on an operation that'd supply all the money he needed."

"He turned you down," A.J. said, her heart hammering against her ribs. A measure of satisfaction crept through her fear at the acknowledgment she saw in Greg's eyes. "And because he was honest, your partner killed him."

"Now you've got it. My partner set up the fake burglary at the warehouse." Greg lifted his free hand, fingered the scar on his forehead. "I didn't like getting clubbed with a pipe, but it was convincing. I was out cold in that alley when the black-and-white found me." He gave the door a quick, assessing glance, then looked back at her. "My partner searched Ken, found the recorder in his handcuff case. I had no idea how long Ken had been carrying it. All I knew was that I had to find out if he'd gotten me on tape when I tried to deal him in on the operation."

"Snowman's operation. Drugs," A.J. added, giving him a look as cold as steel.

"The streets are thick with the stuff," Greg said with derision. "Why the hell should the scum be the only ones making money off it?"

"I'm sure you fit in."

His mouth curved in an arrogant smile as his hand

whipped out, seized her wrist. "Okay, sweetheart, you got your dig in. Now it's time you and I take a ride."

His touch had her flesh crawling with ice-edged terror. "Leave," she said, her voice quavering. "Walk away. I won't say a thing."

"I'll say you won't. Because dead people don't talk."

The primitive instinct to survive clamored over fear and disgust. Using all the strength she could muster, she rammed her knee upward toward his groin.

Finely honed reflexes had him twisting in time to deflect a direct hit. In less than a second, he'd yanked her back against his hard body, had her neck locked in a choke hold.

"Not smart," he said. The automatic gleamed dully in the dim light as he waved it in front of her face. "Say bye-bye to Auntie," he whispered, then aimed the barrel at the bed where Emily lay drugged with sedatives.

"Don't kill her." Terror transformed A.J.'s voice into a frantic sob. "I'll go with you. God, please don't kill her."

Chapter 15

Michael had his hand on the doorknob of Emily Duncan's room when he heard A.J.'s terrified plea. He jerked his hand back, reached beneath his coat and slid his 9mm Sig Sauer from the shoulder holster. He'd done a cursory drive through the hospital's parking garage, had seen A.J.'s Miata parked there, then Lawson's Corvette. Michael knew exactly who was in the room with A.J.

He clenched his jaw, then lowered his shoulder and shoved through the door. Going in low, he kept the Sig close, chest high in a two-handed grip, as his eyes scanned the dim recesses of the room. In the space of a heartbeat, he registered the terror in A.J.'s eyes as she struggled against the arm locked around her throat.

"Let her go, Lawson!"

Instantly, Greg crammed the barrel of a 9mm Beretta against her ear and dragged her backward with him.

"I'll kill her!" he snarled. "You understand me, Ryan?"

"Yeah," Michael said, a mix of barely controlled rage

and dread tearing his insides apart. All he could hear was A.J.'s tormented struggling for breath against the pressure of the bastard's arm.

"Ease up, she can't breathe." Michael's voice was calm. Viciously calm.

"You're taking orders, Ryan, not giving them. Leave the gun on the counter behind you, then walk to that corner." He jerked his head toward the shadowy part of the room farthest from the door.

Michael's index finger remained firm on the cool steel of the trigger while his brain quickly analyzed the prospects of taking a shot. There were none. Lawson had A.J.'s body firmly shielding his. Michael knew he couldn't chance it.

"Move!" Lawson shoved the barrel hard against A.J.'s ear, eliciting a strangled moan.

"All right." Full of impotent fury, Michael placed the Sig on the edge of the counter. He walked across the room, never breaking eye contact with Lawson as the man backed slowly around to keep him in his sights.

"Sit in the recliner," Lawson ordered. "Put your hands behind your neck. Link your fingers."

Michael complied.

"Your lady's leaving with me." Keeping the barrel of the automatic pressed securely against her ear, Greg began a quick backward retreat toward the door. A.J.'s high heels nearly went out from under her on the waxed tiles as he dragged her with him.

Michael felt a moment's pure fear as he stared into her ashen face. She had worth to Lawson only as long as it took him to get out of the hospital and away. After that, he'd consider her a liability and kill her. Michael clamped down on a curse. He had to stop the bastard before he got her out of the room.

"She'll slow you down," Michael said, his voice lowering to a tone of forced calmness. "Leave her."

"Not a chance," Lawson said with snarling fury. Beads

of sweat lined his hairline. His index finger moved up and down the trigger as he glanced behind him to check the door.

"Leave her," Michael repeated. "I'll give you an hour's head start before I call it in."

"You're not going to call at all," Greg hissed. "You bring in the troops, I'll know. Anybody tries to pull me over, she's dead. You got that?"

"Got it."

Michael shifted his gaze back to A.J.'s. Her eyes locked with his steady gaze, then sharpened, narrowed. He saw she'd come to the same conclusion about her chance of survival as he had. Saw, too, something akin to control surface through her fright. He nodded minutely, leaned forward and waited.

Raspy, guttural sounds rose in her throat. "Can't breathe," she gasped. Her hands went up, her white-knuckled fingers locking on the forearm that pressed against her windpipe.

"Let go of my arm, goddammit!" Lawson spat.

"Can't...breathe." Instantly, she buckled her knees and sagged. The sudden weight of her body dangling from his forearm had Lawson half bent toward the floor.

Michael lunged. One hand clamped on Lawson's right wrist and jerked. The other hand grabbed the Beretta's barrel, twisting up and out. A shot blasted through the window.

Michael registered the stab of pain as the sight on the Beretta sliced his palm.

"He's got Ken's tape!" A.J. shouted, her body still suspended from Lawson's arm.

"Let go, A.J.!" Michael shouted as he grappled with the Beretta, still entangled in Lawson's fingers. "Get the hell out of here!"

Michael increased the pressure of his hand, twisting the barrel savagely to keep it pointing upward.

Instead of scrambling to safety, A.J. clamped her teeth on Lawson's wrist and bit.

He roared with pain and slung her away. Michael registered her yelp when she crashed into the roll-away cart, sending the Christmas tree flying.

Free of her weight, Lawson righted himself, swinging his fist as he came up. Michael twisted his body, caught a knuckle on the jaw. He tasted rusty iron blood as he lodged a leg behind Lawson's and shoved, using the momentum of the man's own body to send him flailing backward.

Before Lawson could regain his equilibrium, Michael slammed a hard fist into his stomach, then followed with one to his chin.

Spouting a crude oath, Lawson crashed to the floor. Michael was on him instantly, shoving the Beretta's barrel into his ear. He screwed it in for good measure.

"How does that feel, you bastard?"

Two hours later, A.J.'s body had yet to cease its slow tremble. She sat in Michael's office, staring down into the steaming cup of coffee a detective had coaxed into her hands.

It's over, she assured herself, and for good measure glanced out the open door. At nearly ten o'clock on Christmas Eve, the Homicide squad room was filled with cops milling about, waiting. Greg at this moment sat in an interrogation room down the hall.

It's over.

A deep-seated coldness seeped into her bones, and she shivered. For a brief instant she was back in her aunt's hospital room, staring down the barrel of an automatic. The thought of what would have happened if Michael hadn't shoved through the door when he did put a new wave of sickness rising in her throat.

She closed her eyes and concentrated on the soothing hum of conversation coming from the squad room.

Her hands continued to shake.

Get a grip, Duncan, she told herself. You're alive and well.

She managed to slide the cup onto the corner of the desk without sloshing the steaming brew over the rim. Lifting her chin, she met Michael's gaze as he sat spine straight in his chair, phone against his ear while he conversed with the homicide detective who'd called from the interrogation area. The grimness that settled in his eyes tightened her stomach.

She dragged in a deep breath, keeping her eyes on Michael's face even after he dropped his gaze and began jotting notes. The garish fluorescent lights lent a purple hue to the bruise that had formed on his jaw; the small, swollen cut at the corner of his mouth was a painful red. The hand he used to cradle the phone to his ear sported the bandage a nurse had wrapped around the gash left by the Beretta's sight. He looked tired, battered, bruised...and all around like a knight in shining armor.

He hung up the phone, rose and walked around the desk, his eyes solemn. "Lawson just gave up his partner," he said quietly, placing his unbandaged palm on her shoulder.

His partner. A.J. closed her eyes. If Greg was to be believed, it was his partner who killed Ken.

She took a deep breath, then met Michael's gaze. "Who?"

"Helene St. John."

A.J. blinked. For a moment, the words didn't register. "She...killed Ken?"

"That's what Lawson contends. A patrol unit just picked her up."

"Oh, God."

"I'm sorry, A.J."

She rubbed her forehead, forcing her mind to work, forcing herself to think. "It was Helene," she said quietly.

"What?"

"When Greg...had me in the hospital room, he said he

knew you and I went to see Mary. I couldn't think, couldn't figure out how he knew that. It was Helene. She took the message from Mary's secretary.''

"There's so much I saw that I didn't *see*," Michael said. "Helene showing up when we arrested Billy Hollis, then Hollis yelling for a lawyer the minute Helene and Sky stepped into the room to take blood samples."

Brows knit, he studied his bandaged palm. "Still, Lawson had no reason to think you knew anything. You treated him the same, let him come around you and your aunt."

"Until the night of the dance when he picked me up," A.J. said, everything making sense now.

Michael's eyes sharpened. "What happened?"

"I mentioned Snowman."

Michael's hand tightened on her shoulder. "You didn't tell me that."

"Greg knew so much about Hollis and Hollis knew about Snowman...."

"So it was natural for you to ask Lawson about Snowman."

"Yes. He said he'd never heard of him." She gave Michael a look of self-derision. "I believed him."

"You're not the only one who tested the waters that night," he said. "At the dance, Helene filled me in on how dishonest Ken was. Something didn't sit right, so I let it drop that I knew Ken carried a recorder, made some tapes. In less than five minutes she had your date out the door."

"And when Greg came back to the table, he was furious."

Michael brushed his hand down her hair. "Your asking about Snowman and me confirming I knew Ken had made tapes was too much to put off as coincidence. Still, they weren't sure what we knew. So Greg kept calling, leaving you messages."

"That I never returned. Which made him and Helene

more nervous..." A.J.'s hands clenched into fists. "All because of greed," she said, her voice shaking. "They got involved with the drug operation and killed Ken because of money." Her eyes blazed. "I want them to pay. I want them both to pay for what they did."

"They will, I promise you that."

She tightened her jaw. "What else is Greg saying?"

"Not much...yet. He's holding out on what he knows about Snowman. He's hoping to work a deal."

"If he deals, things will go easy for him," she said as she rose stiffly off her chair. "He won't pay—"

"He will. We've got him cold, thanks to the tape Ken made."

The fierce satisfaction in Michael's eyes helped ease the pain in her heart.

"Ken got Lawson on tape," Michael continued, "trying to recruit him to work in Snowman's operation. Lawson talked about how the drugs are distributed and by whom. There's no doubt about how deep into the organization he was."

"But if Greg turns over Snowman—"

"If he does, it's possible he'll get less time on the drug charges, but not on Ken's murder. You've got cops killing a cop. The DA won't deal on that."

"I hope you're right."

"I am." Michael's palm rose, cupped her cheek. "Just like you were right from the very start about Ken. And I was wrong."

"But you came around." She gave him a soft smile and leaned into his arms. "You believed in me and in Ken. That's what matters."

A quick cessation of noise from the outer office sent the signal that every cop within range of vision was looking their way.

A.J. lifted her head from Michael's chest, glanced out the door. "We have an audience."

"Show's over, folks," Michael said as he reached out and swung the door closed on the roomful of curious gazes.

He looked down at her, his blue eyes taking her in. "Are you okay?"

"Yes."

"Really okay?"

"Really okay."

His hands tightened on her arms and he leaned her slightly back. "Then tell me what the hell you were doing, hanging onto Lawson's arm while you took a bite out of his wrist."

She arched a brow. "Helping you?"

"That was crazy, A.J. He could have killed you."

"He could have killed you. I wasn't about to let that happen."

She raised on tiptoes, placed a soft kiss against his bruised jaw. She wanted to climb into bed with him, make love to him, then watch him sleep until the shadows of fatigue disappeared from beneath his eyes.

His hand came up, cupped her cheek. "Promise you'll never pull a stunt like that again."

She gazed up at him, taking in the fierce protectiveness in his glittering eyes, the battered mouth so utterly kissable. Heat ran beneath her skin, bringing with it the desperate need to lose herself in his arms. "Only if it's necessary."

He gave her a stern look. "If you won't promise, I'll have to keep you within arm's reach to make sure you stay safe."

She tilted her head. "And how long do you intend to do that?"

"For the rest of my life," he said, pulling her back into his warm embrace. "I love you, A.J."

Her heart did a slow roll in her chest. "And I love you." She pulled in a trembling breath. "Your keeping me within arm's reach sounds like an awesome undertaking, Lieutenant. Are you sure you're up for it?''

"I'm sure." He gave her a slow, intimate smile. "One hundred percent."

*   *   *   *   *

Watch for Maggie Price's next romantic suspense in early 1998!

Daniel MacGregor is at it again...

New York Times bestselling author

NORA ROBERTS

introduces us to a new generation of MacGregors
as the lovable patriarch of the illustrious MacGregor
clan plays matchmaker again, this time to his three
gorgeous granddaughters in

THE MACGREGOR BRIDES

From Silhouette Books

Don't miss this brand-new continuation of Nora Roberts's
enormously popular *MacGregor* miniseries.

Available November 1997 at your favorite retail outlet.

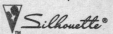

Welcome to the Towers!

In January
New York Times bestselling author

NORA ROBERTS

takes us to the fabulous Maine coast mansion
haunted by a generations-old secret and introduces
us to the fascinating family that lives there.

Mechanic Catherine "C.C." Calhoun and hotel magnate
Trenton St. James mix like axle grease and mineral
water—until they kiss. Efficient Amanda Calhoun finds
easygoing Sloan O'Riley insufferable—and irresistible.
And they all must race to solve the mystery
surrounding a priceless hidden emerald necklace.

Catherine and Amanda

THE Calhoun Women

**A special 2-in-1 edition containing
COURTING CATHERINE and A MAN FOR AMANDA.**

Look for the next installment of
THE CALHOUN WOMEN with Lilah and Suzanna's
stories, coming in March 1998.

Available at your favorite retail outlet.

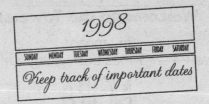

1998

| SUNDAY | MONDAY | TUESDAY | WEDNESDAY | THURSDAY | FRIDAY | SATURDAY |

Keep track of important dates

Three beautiful and colorful calendars that celebrate some of the most popular trends in America today.

Look for:

Just Babies—a 16 month calendar that features a full year of absolutely adorable babies!

1998 CALENDAR
Just Babies
16 months of adorable bundles of joy!

Hometown Quilts
1998 Calendar
A 16 month quilting extravaganza!

Hometown Quilts—a 16 month calendar featuring quilted art squares, plus a short history on twelve different quilt patterns.

Inspirations—a 16 month calendar with inspiring pictures and quotations.

Inspirations

A 16 month calendar that will lift your spirits and gladden your heart

Steeple Hill™

◆ HARLEQUIN®

Value priced at $9.99 U.S./$11.99 CAN., these calendars make a perfect gift!

Available in retail outlets in August 1997. CAL98

SHARON SALA

Continues the twelve-book series—36 HOURS— in October 1997 with Book Four

FOR HER EYES ONLY

The storm was over. The mayor was dead. Jessica Hanson had an aching head...and sinister visions of murder. And only one man was willing to take her seriously— Detective Stone Richardson. He knew that unlocking Jessica's secrets would put him in danger, but the rugged cop had never expected to fall for her, too. Danger he could handle. But love...?

For Stone and Jessica and *all* the residents of Grand Springs, Colorado, the storm-induced blackout was just the beginning of 36 Hours that changed *everything!* You won't want to miss a single book.

36HRS4

Share in the joy of yuletide romance with brand-new stories by two of the genre's most beloved writers

DIANA PALMER

and

JOAN JOHNSTON

in

LONE STAR CHRISTMAS

Diana Palmer and Joan Johnston share their favorite
Christmas anecdotes and personal stories in this
special hardbound edition.

Diana Palmer delivers an irresistible spin-off of her
LONG, TALL TEXANS series and Joan Johnston crafts an
unforgettable new chapter to **HAWK'S WAY** in this wonderful
keepsake edition celebrating the holiday season. So
perfect for gift giving, you'll want one for yourself...and
one to give to a special friend!

Available in November at your favorite retail outlet!

Only from

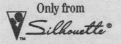

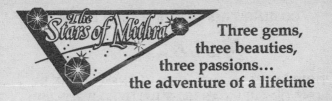

The Stars of Mithra

**Three gems,
three beauties,
three passions...
the adventure of a lifetime**

SILHOUETTE·INTIMATE·MOMENTS®
brings you a thrilling new series by
New York Times bestselling author

Nora Roberts

**Three mystical blue diamonds place three close
friends in jeopardy...and lead them to romance.**

In October
HIDDEN STAR (IM#811)
Bailey James can't remember a thing, but she knows
she's in big trouble. And she desperately needs private
investigator Cade Parris to help her live long enough to
find out just what kind.

In December
CAPTIVE STAR (IM#823)
Cynical bounty hunter Jack Dakota and spitfire
M. J. O'Leary are handcuffed together and on the run
from a pair of hired killers. And Jack wants to know
why—but M.J.'s not talking.

In February
SECRET STAR (IM#835)
Lieutenant Seth Buchanan's murder investigation takes
a strange turn when Grace Fontaine turns up alive. But
as the mystery unfolds, he soon discovers the notorious
heiress is the biggest mystery of all.

Available at your favorite retail outlet.